SelectEditions

SELECTED AND EDITED

Select Editions

BY READER'S DIGEST

VOLUME 4 1998
THE READER'S DIGEST ASSOCIATION, INC.
PLEASANTVILLE, NEW YORK

READER'S DIGEST SELECT EDITIONS

The condensations in this volume have been created by The Reader's Digest Association, Inc., by special arrangement with the publishers, authors, or holders of copyrights.

FIRST EDITION: Volume 238

Library of Congress Catalog Card Number: 50-12721
Printed in the United States of America

CONTENTS

The STREET LAWYER

John Grisham

Is Michael Brock cracking up?

He thought he knew what he wanted: the elegant suits, the luxury car, the beautiful wife, the million-dollar partnership.

But now it seems Michael's priorities have changed. He no longer wants to practice law for the money.

He wants to do it for his soul.

CHAPTER ONE

THE man with the rubber boots stepped into the elevator behind me, but I didn't see him at first. I smelled him, though—the pungent odor of smoke and cheap wine and life on the street without soap. We were alone as we moved upward, and when I finally glanced over, I saw the boots, black and dirty and much too large. A tattered trench coat fell to his knees. Under it, layers of foul clothing bunched around his midsection, so that he appeared stocky. He was black and aging—his beard and hair were half gray and hadn't been washed or cut in years. He looked straight ahead through thick sunglasses, ignoring me.

He didn't belong. It was not his building, not his elevator, not a place he could afford. The lawyers on all eight floors worked for my firm at hourly rates that still seemed obscene to me, even after seven years. He was just another street bum in from the cold. Happened all the time in downtown Washington, D.C. But we had security guards to deal with the riffraff.

We stopped at six, and I noticed for the first time that he had not pushed a button, had not selected a floor. He was following me. I made a quick exit, and as I stepped into the splendid marble foyer of Drake & Sweeney, I glanced over my shoulder and saw him standing in the elevator, still looking at nothing.

Madame Devier, one of our very resilient receptionists, greeted me with her typical look of disdain. "Watch the elevator," I said.

"Why?"

"Street bum. You may want to call security."

"Those people," she said in her affected French accent.

I walked away, wrestling my overcoat off my shoulders, forgetting the man with the rubber boots. I had nonstop meetings throughout the afternoon, important conferences with important people. I turned the corner and was about to say something to Polly, my secretary, when I heard the first shot.

Madame Devier was standing behind her desk, petrified, staring into the barrel of an awfully long handgun held by our pal the street bum. Since I was the first one to come to her aid, he politely aimed it at me, and I too became rigid.

"Don't shoot," I said, hands in the air.

"Shut up," he mumbled with a great deal of composure.

There were voices in the hallway. Someone yelled, "He's got a gun!" And then the voices grew fainter as my colleagues hit the back door. I could almost see them jumping out the windows.

To my immediate left was a heavy wooden door that led to a large conference room, which at that moment happened to be filled with eight hard-nosed lawyers from our litigation section. The toughest was a scrappy little torpedo named Donald Rafter, and as he yanked open the door, saying, "What the hell?" the barrel swung from me to him.

"Put that gun down," Rafter ordered, and a split second later another shot rang through the reception area, a shot that went into the ceiling somewhere above Rafter's head and reduced him to a mere mortal. Turning the gun back to me, the street bum nodded, and I complied, entering the conference room behind Rafter.

The man with the rubber boots slammed the door behind me and slowly waved the gun through the air so that all eight litigators could admire it.

The room was dominated by a long table, covered with documents and papers that only seconds ago had seemed terribly important. A row of windows overlooked a parking lot. Two doors led to the hallway.

"Up against the wall," he said, using the gun as a very effective prop. Then he placed it near my head and said, "Lock the doors." Which I did. Not a word from the eight litigators as they scrambled backward.

Using a series of grunts and gun thrusts, he lined the eight up against the wall. When their positions suited him, he turned his attention to me. What did he want? I couldn't see his eyes, because of the sunglasses, but he could see mine. The gun was pointed at them.

He removed his filthy trench coat, folded it as if it were new, and placed it in the center of the table. Then he slowly removed the next layer—a bulky gray cardigan.

Bulky for a reason. Under it, strapped to his waist, was a row of red sticks, which appeared to my untrained eye to be dynamite. Wires ran like colored spaghetti from the tops and bottoms of the sticks, and silver duct tape kept things attached.

My first instinct was to bolt, to lunge with arms and legs flapping and flailing for the door. But my knees shook, and my blood ran cold. There were gasps and moans from the eight against the wall. "Please be quiet," our captor said in the tone of a patient professor. His calmness unnerved me. From a pocket in his large trousers he produced a neat bundle of yellow nylon rope.

For good measure he waved the gun at the horrified faces in front of him and said, "I don't want to hurt anybody."

That was hard to take seriously. I counted twelve red sticks.

Then the gun was back on me. "You," he said, "tie them up."

Rafter had had enough. He took one very small step forward and said, "Look, pal, just exactly what do you want?"

The third shot sailed over his head into the ceiling. It sounded like a cannon, and Madame Devier shrieked in the foyer. Rafter ducked, and as he attempted to stand upright, the beefy elbow of fellow litigator Wayne Umstead caught him squarely in the chest and returned him to his position against the wall.

"Do not call me pal," the man said.

"What would you like us to call you?" I asked very delicately.

"Mister," he said. Mister was perfectly fine with everyone.

The phone rang, and he waved it over. I placed it squarely before him on the table. He lifted the receiver with his left hand; his right still held the gun, still pointed at Rafter. If the nine of us had a vote, Rafter would be the first sacrificial lamb. Eight to one.

"Hello," Mister said. He listened briefly, then hung up. He carefully backed himself into the seat at the end of the table and sat down. "Take the rope," he said to me.

He wanted all eight of them attached at the wrists. I tied knots and tried my best not to look at the faces of my colleagues as I hastened their deaths. I could feel the gun at my back.

Rafter mumbled something under his breath, and I wanted to slap him. Umstead was able to flex his wrists so that the ropes almost fell loose when I finished with him. Nate Malamud was sweating and breathing rapidly. He was the oldest, the only partner in the room, and two years past his first heart attack.

I couldn't help but look at Barry Nuzzo, my one friend in the bunch. We were the same age, thirty-two, and had joined the firm the same year. He went to Princeton; I went to Yale. Both of our wives were from Providence. His marriage was working—three kids in four years. Mine was deteriorating. Our eyes met. Thinking about his kids, I felt lucky to be childless.

The first of many sirens came into range of hearing, and Mister instructed me to close the blinds over the five large windows. I went about this methodically, scanning the parking lot below as if being seen might somehow save me. A lone police car sat empty with its lights on; the cops were already in the building.

Mister then instructed me to call "the boss" and inform him that he was armed and wired with twelve sticks of dynamite. I called Rudolph Mayes, managing partner of my division, antitrust, on the speakerphone and relayed the message.

"You okay, Mike?" he asked.

"Wonderful," I said. "Please do whatever he wants."

"What does he want?"

"I don't know yet."

Mister waved the gun, and the conversation was over.

He glanced down and gave a slight tug at a red wire. "This red one here—I give it a yank, and it's all over." The sunglasses were looking at me when he finished this little warning.

I felt compelled to say something. "Why would you do that?"

"I don't want to, but why not?"

I could not believe that we were going to die. There appeared to be no motive, no reason to kill us. He was just a nut in search of hostages, which unfortunately would make the killings seem almost normal by today's standards.

It was precisely the kind of senseless slaughter that would grab the headlines for twenty-four hours and make people shake their heads. Then the dead-lawyer jokes would start.

But I refused to believe it would happen. I heard voices in the foyer and a police radio squawk somewhere down the hallway.

Mister's voice broke the silence. "What did you eat for lunch?"

Too surprised to lie, I said, "A grilled chicken Caesar salad."

"Alone?"

"No. I met a friend." A law school buddy from Philly.

"How much did it cost, for both of you?"

"Thirty bucks."

He didn't like this. "Thirty bucks," he said. "For two people." He shook his head. "You know what I had?" he asked me.

"No."

"I had soup at a shelter. And I was glad to get it. You could feed a hundred of my friends for thirty bucks, you know that?"

I nodded gravely, as if I suddenly realized the weight of my sin.

"Collect all the wallets," he said, waving the gun again.

"May I ask why?" I asked, and began rummaging through the pockets of my fellow hostages.

"It's for the next of kin," Mister said, and we all exhaled.

He instructed me to place the loot in a briefcase, lock it, and toss it into the hallway. I did not see a person anywhere when I cracked open the door.

THE MINUTES DRAGGED ON. MY buddies had been standing for almost two hours, backs to the wall, still joined together, barely able to move. I caught myself picturing the other four hundred lawyers in the office, out there in the parking lot, most of them sitting in their cars to keep warm, chatting away on cell phones, billing somebody. The firm wouldn't miss a beat. Some of the cutthroats down there didn't care *how* it ended. Just hurry up and get it over with.

Mister seemed to doze for a second. His chin dipped, and his breathing was heavier. Rafter grunted to get my attention, then jerked his head as if to suggest I make a move. Rafter wanted me to be the hero. But we weren't in the army. I didn't take orders.

"How much money did you make last year?" Mister, very much awake, asked me, his voice clear.

Again I was startled. "I, uh, gosh, let me see—"

"Don't lie."

"A hundred and twenty thousand."

He didn't like this either. "How much did you give away?"

"Give away?"

"Yes. To charities."

"Oh. Well, I don't remember. My wife takes care of that."

All eight litigators seemed to shift at once.

Mister didn't like my answer. "What's your name?"

"Michael Brock," I answered politely. Nice to meet you.

"How much did you give to the hungry last year?" He continually toyed with the red wire, and that kept my heart rate racing.

"I paid around fifty thousand in taxes, and a nice chunk of it went for welfare, Medicaid, stuff like that."

"And you did this voluntarily, with a giving spirit?"

"I didn't complain," I said, lying like most of my countrymen.

"Have you ever been hungry?"

"No," I said, "I have not."

"Have you ever slept in the snow?"

"No."

"You make a lot of money, yet you're too greedy to hand me some change on the sidewalk." He waved the gun at the rest of them. "All of you. You walk right by me as I sit and beg. You spend more on fancy coffee than I do on meals. Why can't you help the poor, the sick, the homeless? You have so much."

I caught myself looking at those greedy bastards along with Mister. It was not a pretty sight. Most were staring at their feet.

Silence again. A helicopter hovered nearby, and I could only imagine what the police were planning in the parking lot.

"Which of these guys makes the most money?" he asked me.

Malamud was the only partner. "That would be me," he offered.

"How much?" Mister asked.

Malamud's salary from the firm was fifty thousand dollars a month, and his annual bonus, the one we all dreamed about, was five hundred and ten thousand.

"One point one million," he said.

Mister contemplated this for a moment. "You made a million dollars," he said to Malamud, who wasn't the least bit ashamed.

"Yes, I did."

"How much did you give to the hungry and the homeless?"

"I don't recall exactly. My wife and I give to a lot of charities. I know there was a donation, I think for five thousand, to the Greater D.C. Fund. We give a lot. And we're happy to do it."

"I'm sure you're very happy," Mister replied with the first hint of sarcasm. He instructed me to list on paper all nine names and, beside each, write last year's income, then gifts to charities.

I didn't know whether to hurry or be deliberate. Would he slaughter us if he didn't like the math? Perhaps I shouldn't hurry. He hadn't mentioned executing a hostage every hour. He didn't want his buddies freed from jail. He didn't seem to want anything, really. I took my time. Malamud set the pace. The rear was brought up by Colburn, a third-year associate who grossed a mere eighty-six thousand. I was dismayed to learn my pal Barry Nuzzo earned eleven thousand more than I did. We would discuss it later.

"If you round it off, it comes to three million dollars," I reported to Mister, whose fingers were still on the red wire.

He slowly shook his head. "And how much for the poor?"

"Total contributions of one hundred eighty thousand."

"I don't want total contributions. Don't put me and my people in the same class with the symphony and the Boy Scouts. I'm talking about food. Food for hungry people who live here in the same city you live in. Food for little babies. Right in this city, with all you people making millions, we got little babies starving at night, crying 'cause they're hungry. How much for food?"

He was looking at me. I just looked at the list in front of me.

He waved the damned gun again. "How about homeless shelters—places we sleep when it's ten degrees outside?"

Invention failed me. "None," I said softly.

He jumped to his feet, startling us, the red sticks fully visible under the silver duct tape. He kicked his chair back. "How 'bout clinics? We got these little clinics where doctors—good decent people who used to make lots of money—come and donate their time to help the sick. They don't charge nothing. Government used to help pay the rent, help buy the medicine and supplies. Now all the money's gone. How much do you give to the clinics?"

Rafter was looking at me again as if I should do something, when Mister walked to the windows and peeked around the miniblinds. "Cops everywhere," he said, just loud enough for us to hear.

He then forgot about the scene below and shuffled along the edge of the table until he stopped near his hostages. They watched every move, with particular attention paid to the explosives. He slowly raised the gun and aimed it directly at Colburn's nose, less than three feet away.

"How much did you give to the clinics?"

"None," Colburn said, closing his eyes tightly, ready to cry. My heart froze, and I held my breath.

"How much to the soup kitchens?"

"None."

"How much to the homeless shelters?"

"None."

Instead of shooting Colburn, he aimed at Barry Nuzzo and repeated the three questions. Barry had identical responses, and Mister moved down the line, pointing, asking, getting the same answers. He didn't shoot Rafter, much to our dismay.

"Three million dollars," he said in disgust, "and not a dime for the sick and hungry. You are miserable people."

We felt miserable.

AT DUSK he said he was hungry, and he told me to call the boss and order soup from the Methodist Mission at L Street and Seventeenth, N.W. They put more vegetables in the broth, Mister said. And the bread was not as stale as in most kitchens.

"The soup kitchen does carryout?" Rudolph asked, his voice incredulous. It echoed around the room from the speakerphone.

"Just do it, Rudolph!" I barked back at him. "And get enough for ten people." Mister told me to hang up.

He made another trip to the windows when we heard the helicopter again. He peeked out, stepped back, and tugged at his beard.

Finally he told me to untie Umstead, and he had the two of us move the conference table next to the windows. It was twenty feet long, solid walnut. We managed to inch it over about six feet until Mister said stop. Next he forced the bound hostages to sit on the table with their backs to the wall. No one dared ask why, but I figured he wanted a shield from sharpshooters.

After standing for five hours, Rafter and company were relieved to be off their feet. Umstead and I were told to sit in chairs, and Mister took a seat at the end of the table. We waited.

Life in the streets must teach one patience. He seemed content to sit in silence for long periods of time, perfectly still.

"Who are the evictors?" he mumbled to no one in particular, and he waited a couple of minutes before saying it again.

We looked at each other, confused. He appeared to be staring at a spot on the table, not far from Colburn's right foot.

"Not only do you ignore the homeless, you help put them in the streets."

We, of course, nodded along. If he wanted to heap verbal abuse on us, we were perfectly willing to accept it.

There was a sharp knock on the door. Our carryout had arrived. Mister told me to call Rudolph and stress that no rescue should be attempted, that we were negotiating. Rudolph said he understood.

Umstead then walked to the door, unlocked it, and looked at Mister for instructions. Mister was behind him, with the gun less than a foot from Umstead's head.

"Open the door very slowly," Mister said.

I was standing a few feet behind Mister when the door opened. The food was on a small cart. I could see four large plastic containers of soup and a brown paper bag filled with bread. I don't know if there was anything to drink. We never found out.

Umstead took one step into the hallway and was about to pull the cart back into the conference room when the shot cracked through the air. A lone police sniper was hiding behind a credenza next to Madame Devier's desk, forty feet away, and when Umstead bent over to grab the cart, the sniper got the clear look he needed.

Mister lurched backward without uttering a sound, and my face was instantly covered with blood. I thought I'd been hit too, and I remember screaming in pain. Umstead was yelling somewhere in the hall. The other seven scrambled off the table like scalded dogs, all yelling and digging toward the door, half of them dragging the other half. I was on my knees, clutching my eyes, waiting for the dynamite to explode; then I bolted for the other door. I unlocked it, yanked it open, and the last time I saw Mister, he was twitching on one of our expensive Oriental rugs. His hands were loose at his sides, nowhere near the red wire.

The hallway was suddenly filled with SWAT guys, all clad in fierce-looking helmets and thick vests, dozens of them crouching and reaching. They were a blur. They grabbed us and carried us through the reception area to the elevators.

"Are you hurt?" they asked me.

I didn't know. There was blood on my face and shirt.

OUTSIDE, families, friends, and dozens of our colleagues were waiting for our rescue. A loud cheer went up when they saw us.

Because I was covered with blood, they took me to an ambulance. I was instantly surrounded by doctors, none of whom happened to be my wife. Once I convinced them the blood was not mine, they relaxed and conducted a routine exam. Blood pressure was up; pulse was crazy. They gave me a pill.

What I really wanted was a shower. They made me lie on a gurney for ten minutes while they watched my blood pressure. "Am I in shock?" I asked.

"Probably not."

I certainly felt like it. Where was Claire? For six hours I was held at gunpoint, life hanging by a thread, and she couldn't be bothered to come wait with the rest of the families.

My secretary, Polly, appeared and gave me a long hug. I needed it desperately. She had tears in her eyes.

"Where's Claire?" I asked her.

"On call. I've tried calling the hospital."

Polly knew there wasn't much left of the marriage.

"Are you okay?" she asked.

"I think so."

I thanked the doctors and left. Rudolph came over and gave me a clumsy embrace. He used the word "congratulations," as if I had accomplished something.

"No one expects you to work tomorrow," he said. Did he think a day off would cure all my problems?

"I haven't thought about tomorrow," I said.

"You need some rest," he added.

I wanted to speak to Barry Nuzzo, but my fellow hostages had already left. No one was injured, just a few rope burns.

Polly had my overcoat. "I'll drive you home," she said. "Follow me." I was very thankful someone was telling me what to do.

Polly ran to get her car, and I watched the circus out front. There were police cars, ambulances, television vans, even a fire truck.

"I'm alive! I am alive!" I said this over and over, smiling for the first time. "I'm alive!" I closed my eyes tightly and offered a short prayer of thanks.

AS POLLY SAT BEHIND THE wheel, driving slowly and waiting for me to say something, I heard again the clap of the sniper's rifle, then the stampede as the other hostages scrambled through the door.

"He was not going to kill us," I said quietly.

"What was he doing, then?" Polly asked.

"I don't know. He never said what he wanted. We sat for hours just looking at each other."

"Are you working tomorrow?"

"What else would I do tomorrow?"

"Just thought you might need a day off."

"I need a year off. One day won't help."

My apartment was the third floor of a row house on P Street in Georgetown. Polly stopped, and I thanked her and got out. I could tell from the dark windows that Claire was not home.

I HAD met Claire the week after I moved to D.C. I was just out of Yale, with a great job in a rich firm, a brilliant future like the other fifty rookies in my class. She was finishing her degree in political science at American University. Her grandfather was once the governor of Rhode Island; her family was well connected.

Drake & Sweeney, like most large firms, treats the first year as a boot camp. I worked fifteen hours a day, six days a week, and on Sundays, Claire and I would have our weekly date. We thought that if we got married, we would have more time together.

The wedding was large, the honeymoon brief, and when the luster wore off, I was back at the office ninety hours a week. She was a sport for the first few months, but she grew weary of being neglected. I did not blame her, but young associates don't complain in the hallowed offices of Drake & Sweeney. Less than ten percent of each class will make partner, so the competition is ruthless. The rewards are great—at least a million bucks a year. Billing lots of hours is more important than a happy wife. Divorce is common. I didn't dream of asking for a lighter load.

By the end of our first year together Claire was very unhappy and we started to quarrel. Tired of sitting at home watching TV, she figured she could become as self-absorbed as I was. She decided to go to med school. I thought it was a wonderful idea. It took away most of my guilt.

After four years with the firm they started dropping hints about our chances of making partner. The hints were compared among the associates. It was generally felt that I was on the fast track to a partnership. But I had to work even harder.

Claire became determined to spend more time away from the apartment than I did, and so both of us slid into the silliness of workaholism. We stopped fighting and simply drifted apart.

I wish I had done things differently. We were in love once, and we let it get away.

As I entered the dark apartment, I needed Claire for the first time in years. You come face to face with death, and you need to talk about it. You need to be told that someone cares.

The shower I took was long and hot. I washed my hair three times with heavy shampoo; then I stood and dripped for an eternity. Time was frozen. Nothing mattered. I was alive.

I fixed a vodka with ice and sat on the sofa in the den. I fumed and pouted because I was alone; then my thoughts switched to the six hours I'd spent with Mister.

TWO vodkas later I heard her at the door. She unlocked it and called, "Michael."

I didn't say a word, because I was still pouting and fuming. She walked into the den and stopped when she saw me. "Are you all right?" she asked with genuine concern.

"I'm fine," I said softly.

She dropped her bag and overcoat, and walked to the sofa.

"Where have you been?" I asked.

"At the hospital." She hovered over me.

"Of course." I took a long drink. "Look, I've had a bad day."

"I know all about it, Michael."

"You do?"

"Of course I do."

"Then where were you? Nine of us held hostage for six hours by a crazy man. Eight families show up because they're somewhat concerned. And I have to catch a ride home with my secretary."

She sat down in a chair next to the sofa. "They made us stay at the hospital," she began, very icy. "We knew about the hostage situation, and there was a chance there could've been casualties. It's standard procedure in that situation—they notify the hospitals, and everyone's placed on standby. I couldn't help you at your office. I was waiting at the hospital."

"Did you call?"

"I tried. The phone lines were jammed."

"It was over two hours ago. Where have you been?"

"In OR. We lost a little boy in surgery; he was hit by a car."

"I'm sorry," I said. I could never comprehend how doctors faced so much death and pain. Mister was only the second corpse I had ever laid eyes on.

"I'm sorry too," she said, and with that, she went to the kitchen and returned with a glass of wine. We sat in the semidarkness. Because we did not practice communication, it did not come easy.

"Do you want to talk about it?" she asked.

"No. Not now." And I really didn't. The alcohol was making my breathing heavy. Silence was what I wanted. Tomorrow I would talk.

CHAPTER TWO

AT FOUR the next morning I awoke to the harsh smell of Mister's blood weaving through my nostrils. I was frantic for a moment in the darkness. I rubbed my nose and eyes, and thrashed around the sofa until I heard someone move. Claire had been sleeping in a chair next to me. "It's okay," she said softly, touching my shoulder. "Just a bad dream."

We talked for an hour. I told her everything I could remember about the event. She sat close to me, rubbing my knee, listening carefully. We had talked so little in the past few years.

She had to make her rounds at seven, so we cooked breakfast together, waffles and bacon. We ate at the kitchen counter, with a small television in front of us. The six-o'clock news began with the hostage drama. There were shots of the building during the crisis, the mob outside. A news camera had zoomed in for a tight shot of a window. Through it Mister could be seen for a few seconds as he peeked out.

His name was DeVon Hardy, age forty-five, a Vietnam vet with a short criminal record. A mug shot from an arrest for burglary was put on the screen behind the early morning newsperson. It looked nothing like Mister—no beard, no glasses, much younger. He was described as homeless, with a history of drug use. No motive was known. No family had come forward.

There were no comments from the firm, and the story fizzled.

The weather was next. Heavy snow was expected to hit by late afternoon. It was the twelfth day of February, and already a record had been set for snowfall.

Claire drove me to the office, where at six forty I was not surprised to see my Lexus parked among several other imports. The lot was never empty. We had people who slept at the office.

I promised to call her later in the morning, and we would try to have lunch at the hospital. She wanted me to take it easy, at least for a day or two.

What was I supposed to do? Lie on the sofa and take pills? I said good morning to the two very alert security guards in the lobby. Three of the four elevators were open, waiting, and I had a choice. I stepped onto the one Mister and I had taken, and things slowed to a crawl.

A hundred questions at once: Why had he picked our building? Our firm? Why the sixth floor? Why me?

And what was he after? I did not believe DeVon Hardy went to the trouble of wrapping himself with explosives and risking his life to chastise a bunch of wealthy lawyers over their lack of generosity.

His question, "Who are the evictors?" was never answered. But it wouldn't take long to find the answer.

The elevator stopped, and I stepped off, this time without anyone behind me. Madame Devier was still asleep at that hour, somewhere, and the sixth floor was quiet. In front of her desk I paused and stared at the doors to the conference room, then moved on to my office.

On my desk every morning, in precisely the same spot, were *The Wall Street Journal* and the Washington *Post.* I used to know the name of the person who put them there, but it was long forgotten. On the front page of the *Post*'s Metro section was the same mug shot of DeVon Hardy and a large story about yesterday's little crisis. I figured I knew more details than any reporter. But I learned a few things. The red sticks were not dynamite. Mister had taken a couple of broom handles, sawed them into pieces, wrapped the ominous silver tape around them, and scared the living daylights out of us. The gun was a .44 automatic, stolen.

According to one Mordecai Green, director of the 14th Street Legal Clinic, DeVon Hardy had worked for many years as a janitor at the National Arboretum. He'd lost his job as a result of budget cutting, then landed in the streets. He'd struggled with alcohol and drugs, and was routinely picked up for shoplifting. Green's legal clinic had represented him several times.

As to motive Green had little to offer. He did say that DeVon Hardy had been evicted recently from an old warehouse in which he had been squatting. An eviction is a legal procedure, carried out by lawyers. I had a pretty good idea which one of the thousands of D.C. firms had tossed Mister into the streets.

Polly arrived a few minutes before eight with a big smile and a plate of homemade cookies. She was not surprised to see me at work. In fact, all nine of the hostages punched in, most ahead of schedule. It would've been a glaring sign of weakness to stay home with the wife and get pampered.

"Arthur's on the phone," Polly announced. Our firm had at least ten Arthurs, but only one needed no last name. Arthur Jacobs was the senior partner, the CEO, the driving force, a man we admired and respected greatly, the firm's heart and soul. In seven years I had spoken to him three times.

I told him I was fine. He complimented me on my courage and grace under pressure, and I almost felt like a hero. He had probably talked to Malamud first and was working his way down the ladder. He wanted to meet with the ex-hostages at ten, in the conference room, to record our statements on video.

"Why?" I asked.

"The boys in litigation think it's a good idea," he said, his voice razor-sharp in spite of his eighty years. "His family will probably sue the cops. And they'll probably name us as defendants. People will sue for anything, you know."

Thank goodness, I almost said. Where would we be without lawsuits? I thanked him for his concern, and he was gone, off to call the next hostage.

The parade started before nine, a steady stream of well-wishers deeply concerned about me but also desperate for the details. I had a pile of work to do, but I couldn't get to it.

It didn't matter. I was numb. The work was not important. My desk was not life and death. I had seen death, and I couldn't simply shrug it off as if nothing had happened.

I thought about DeVon Hardy and his red sticks with the multicolored wires. He'd spent hours building his toys and planning his assault. He'd stolen a gun, found our firm, made a crucial mistake that cost him his life, and no one, not one single person I worked with, gave a damn about him.

I finally left. I told Polly I had errands to run, and she reminded me of the meeting with Arthur Jacobs. I went to my car, started it, and sat debating whether to participate in the video. If I missed it, Arthur would be upset. No one misses a meeting with Arthur.

I drove away. It was a rare opportunity to do something stupid. I'd been traumatized. I had to leave. Arthur and the rest of the firm would just have to give me a break.

I drove in the general direction of Georgetown but to no place in particular. The clouds were dark; people scurried along the sidewalks; snow crews were getting ready. I passed a beggar on M Street and wondered if he knew DeVon Hardy. Where do the street people go in a snowstorm?

I called the hospital and was informed that my wife would be in emergency surgery for several hours. So much for our romantic lunch in the hospital cafeteria.

I turned and went northeast, past Logan Circle, into the rougher sections of the city, until I found the 14th Street Legal Clinic. I parked at the curb, certain I would never again see my Lexus.

The clinic occupied half of a three-story red brick Victorian mansion that had seen better days. The entrance was covered by a bright yellow canopy, and I didn't know whether to knock or to just barge in. The door wasn't locked, and I slowly turned the knob and stepped into another world.

It was a law office of sorts, but one very different from the marble and mahogany of Drake & Sweeney. In the large room before me there were four metal desks, each covered with a suffocating collection of files stacked a foot high. The wastebaskets were filled with wadded sheets of legal paper. The word processors and phones were ten years old. The wooden bookshelves were sagging. Several smaller offices branched off the front room.

It was busy and dusty, and I was fascinated with the place.

A fierce Hispanic woman stopped typing after watching me for a moment. "You looking for somebody?" she asked. It was more of a challenge than a request. A receptionist at Drake & Sweeney would be fired on the spot for such a greeting.

She was Sofia Mendoza, according to a nameplate tacked to the side of her desk. A loud roar came from one of the side rooms and startled me without fazing Sofia.

"I'm looking for Mordecai Green," I said politely, and at that moment he stomped out of his side office and into the main room, yelling for someone named Abraham.

Sofia nodded at him, then dismissed me and returned to her typing. Green was a huge black man, at least six five, with a wide frame that carried a lot of weight. He was in his early fifties, with a gray beard and round eyeglasses that were framed in red. He took a look at me and said, "Can I help you?"

I walked forward and introduced myself.

"Nice to meet you," he said. "What's on your mind?"

"DeVon Hardy," I said.

He looked at me for a few seconds, then nodded toward his office. I followed him into a twelve-by-twelve room with no windows and every square inch of available floor space covered with manila files and battered lawbooks.

I handed him my gold-embossed Drake & Sweeney card, which he studied with a deep frown. Then he gave it back to me and said, "Slumming, are you? What do you want?"

"I come in peace. Mr. Hardy's bullet almost got me."

"You were in the room with him?"

"Yep."

He took a deep breath and lost the frown. He pointed to the only chair on my side. "Have a seat. But you might get dirty."

We both sat, my knees touching his desk, my hands thrust deep into the pockets of my overcoat.

"Guess you had a bad day, huh?" he said, his raspy voice lower and almost compassionate.

"Not as bad as Hardy's. I went back to my desk this morning like nothing happened, but I couldn't think straight. I saw your name in the paper and took a drive. Here I am."

He shook his head slowly, as if he was trying to understand this. "You want some coffee?"

"No thanks. You knew Mr. Hardy pretty well."

"Yeah. DeVon was a regular."

"Where is he now?"

"Probably in the city morgue at D.C. General."

"If there's no family, what happens to him?"

"The city buries the unclaimed. On the books it's called a pauper's funeral. There's a cemetery near RFK Stadium where they pack 'em in. You'd be amazed at the number of unclaimed."

"I'm sure I would." I was not in the mood to chat. "Do you know if he had AIDS?"

He cocked his head back and rattled that around. "Why?"

"I was standing behind him. I got a face full of blood."

With that, I crossed the line from bad guy to average guy.

"I don't think he had AIDS."

"Can you find out?"

He shrugged and thawed some more. "Sure," he said reluctantly. "Is that why you're here? Worried about AIDS?"

"I guess it's one reason. Wouldn't you be?"

"Sure."

Abraham stepped in then, a small hyper man of about forty, with a dark beard and glasses. He had public-interest lawyer stamped all over him. He did not acknowledge me, and Green was not one for social graces. "They're predicting a ton of snow," Green said to him. "We need to make sure every shelter is open."

"I'm working on it," Abraham snapped, then abruptly left.

"I know you're busy," I said.

"Is that all you wanted? A blood check?"

"Yeah, I guess." I paused, then asked, "Any idea why he did it?"

Green removed his red glasses, then rubbed his eyes. "He was mentally ill, like a lot of these people. You spend years on the streets, it makes you crazy. Plus he had a bone to pick."

"The eviction."

"Yep. A few months ago he moved into an abandoned warehouse at the corner of New York and Florida. Somebody threw up some plywood, chopped up the place, and made little apartments. Wasn't a bad place as far as homeless folk go—a roof, some toilets, water. A hundred bucks a month, payable to an ex-pimp who fixed it up and claimed he owned it."

"Did he?"

"I think so." He pulled a thin file from one of the stacks on his desk and studied its contents for a moment. "This is where it gets complicated. The property was purchased last month by a company called RiverOaks—some big real estate outfit."

"And RiverOaks evicted everyone?"

"Yep."

"Odds are, then, that RiverOaks was represented by my firm."

"Good odds, yes."

"Why is it complicated?"

"I've heard that they got no notice before the eviction. The people claim they were paying rent, and if so, they were more than squatters. They were tenants, thus entitled to due process."

"Squatters get no notice?"

"None. And it happens all the time. Street folk will move into an abandoned building. The owner, if he's inclined to show up, can toss 'em without notice. They have no rights at all."

"How did DeVon Hardy track down our firm?"

"Who knows? He was crazy, but not stupid."

"Do you know the pimp?"

"Yeah. Completely unreliable."

"Where did you say the warehouse was?"

"It's gone now. They leveled it last week."

I had taken enough of his time. He glanced at his watch; I glanced at mine. We swapped phone numbers and said we'd keep in touch.

On my way out, I ignored Sofia, because she certainly ignored me. My Lexus was still at the curb, already covered with an inch of snow.

I DRIFTED through the city as the snow fell. I couldn't recall the last time I had driven the streets of D.C. without being late for a meeting. I was warm and dry in my luxury car, and I simply moved with the traffic. There was no place to go. The office would be off-limits for a while, what with Arthur Jacobs mad at me.

My car phone rang. It was Polly, panicky. "Where are you?"

"Who wants to know?"

"A lot of people. Arthur for one. Rudolph. A reporter. Clients need advice. And Claire called from the hospital."

"What does she want?"

"She's worried, like everybody else."

"I'm fine, Polly. Tell everybody I'm at the doctor's office."

"Are you?"

"No, but I could be. What did Arthur say?"

"He didn't call. Rudolph did. They were waiting for you."

"Let 'em wait."

A pause, then, "Okay. When might you be dropping by?"

"Don't know. I guess whenever the doctor releases me. Why don't you go home? We're in the middle of a storm. I'll call you tomorrow." I hung up on her.

The apartment was a place I had rarely seen in the light of day, and I couldn't stand the thought of sitting by the fire and watching it snow. If I went to a bar, I'd probably never leave.

So I drove. I flowed with the traffic as the commuters began a hasty retreat into the suburbs, and I found the cemetery near RFK where they buried the unclaimed, and I passed the Methodist Mission on Seventeenth where last night's uneaten dinner originated. I drove through sections of the city I had never been near.

By four the city was empty. The skies were darkening; the snow was quite heavy. Several inches already covered the ground, and they were predicting a lot more.

I headed over to Drake & Sweeney. I was informed by a security guard in the lobby that most of the staff had been sent home at three. I took Mister's elevator again.

In a neat row in the center of my desk were a dozen pink phone messages, none of which interested me. I went to my computer and began searching our client index.

RiverOaks was a Delaware corporation, organized in 1977, headquartered in Hagerstown, Maryland. The attorney was Braden Chance, a name unknown to me.

I looked him up in our vast database. Braden Chance was a partner in our real estate division, somewhere on the fourth floor. Age forty-four, married, law school at Duke.

With eight hundred lawyers worldwide threatening and suing daily, our firm had over thirty-six thousand active files. To make sure our office in New York didn't sue one of our clients in Chicago, each new file was entered immediately into our data system. There were forty-two files for RiverOaks, almost all of them real estate transactions in which the company had purchased property. Chance was the attorney of record on every file. Four were eviction actions, three of which took place last year.

On January 31 RiverOaks purchased property on Florida Avenue. The seller was TAG, Inc. On February 4 our client evicted a number of squatters from an abandoned warehouse on the property, one of whom, I now knew, was Mister DeVon Hardy.

I copied the file number and strolled down to the fourth floor.

AT DRAKE & Sweeney each lawyer kept his current files in his office, often under lock and key. No lawyer could be compelled to show a file to another lawyer, unless requested by a senior partner or a member of the firm's executive committee. The eviction file I wanted was still listed as current, and after the Mister episode I was certain it was well protected.

I saw a paralegal scanning blueprints at a desk next to a secretarial pool, and I asked him where I might find the office of Braden Chance. He nodded to an open door across the hall.

To my surprise Chance was at his desk, projecting the appearance of a very busy lawyer. He was perturbed by my intrusion and rightfully so. Proper protocol would have been for me to call ahead and set up a meeting. I didn't care about protocol.

He didn't ask me to sit. I did so anyway.

"You were one of the hostages," he said irritably when he made the connection. "Must've been awful."

"It's over. The guy with the gun, the late Mr. Hardy, was evicted from a warehouse on February fourth. Was it our eviction?"

"It was," he snapped. "What about it?"

"Was he a squatter?"

"Damned sure was. They're all squatters. Our client is trying to clean up some of that mess."

"Are you sure he was a squatter?"

His chin dropped, and his eyes turned hard. Then he took a breath. "What are you after?"

"Could I see the file?"

"No. It's none of your business."

"Maybe it is."

"Who is your supervising partner?" He yanked out his pen.

"Rudolph Mayes."

He wrote in large strokes. "I'm very busy," he said. "Would you please leave?" He stood, his hand shaking as he pointed to the door. I smiled at him and left.

The paralegal had heard everything, and we exchanged puzzled looks as I passed his desk. "What an ass," he said very quietly, almost mouthing the words.

I smiled again and nodded my agreement. And a fool. If Chance had been pleasant and explained that the file had been ordered sealed, then I wouldn't have been as suspicious. But it was obvious there was something in the file.

Getting it would be the challenge.

WITH all the cell phones and pagers Claire and I owned, communication should've been a simple matter. But nothing was simple with our marriage. We didn't hook up until around nine. She was exhausted from another one of her days, which were inevitably more fatiguing than anything I could possibly have done. It was a game we shamelessly played—my job is more important because I'm a doctor/lawyer. I was tiring of the games.

She drove a Miata sports car, no four-wheel drive, and I was worried about her in the bad weather. She would be through in an hour, and I said I'd pick her up at the hospital, and we would try to find a restaurant. If not, it would be Chinese carryout, our standard fare.

I began arranging papers and objects on my desk. I was expected to bill twenty-five hundred hours a year. That's fifty hours a week, fifty weeks a year. My average billing rate was three hundred dollars an hour, so I would gross for my beloved firm a total of seven hundred and fifty thousand dollars. They paid me a hundred and twenty thousand of this, plus another thirty for benefits, and assigned two hundred thousand to overhead. The partners kept the rest, divided annually by some horrendously complex formula that usually caused fistfights.

It was rare for one of our partners to earn less than a million a year, and some earned over two. That was the dream that kept us at our desks at all hours of the day and night.

The phone rang. It was Mordecai Green.

"Mr. Brock," he said politely, his voice clearly audible but competing with a din in the background.

"Yes. Please call me Michael."

"Very well. Look, I made some calls, and you have nothing to worry about. The blood test was negative."

"Thanks," I said as the racket rose behind him. "Where are you?"

"At a homeless shelter. A big snow brings 'em in faster than we can feed them, so it takes all of us to keep up. Gotta run." He hung up.

I studied my finely appointed office. My desk was old mahogany; the rug was Persian; the chairs were a rich crimson leather; the technology was state-of-the-art. I thought of Mordecai Green, who at that moment was volunteering his time in a shelter, serving food to the cold and hungry, no doubt with a warm smile.

Both of us had law degrees; both of us had passed the same bar exam; both of us were fluent in legalese. We were kindred to a degree. I helped my clients swallow up competitors so they could add more zeros to the bottom line, and for this I would become rich. He helped his clients eat and find a warm bed.

Lost in thought, I was startled by the phone when it rang again.

"Why are you at the office?" Claire asked, each word spoken slowly because each word was covered with ice.

I looked in disbelief at my watch. "I, uh, well, a client called from the West Coast. It's not snowing out there."

I think it was a lie I'd used before. It didn't matter.

"I am waiting, Michael. Should I walk?"

"No. I'll be there as fast as I can."

I ran from the building, into the storm, not really too concerned that another night had been ruined.

CHAPTER THREE

THE snow had finally stopped. Claire and I sipped our coffee by the kitchen window. I was reading the paper by the light of a brilliant morning sun. They had managed to keep National Airport open.

"Let's go to Florida," I said. "Now."

She gave me a withering look. "Florida?"

"Okay, the Bahamas. We can be there by early afternoon."

"There's no way."

"Sure there is. I'm not going to work for a few days, and—"

"Why not?"

"Because I'm cracking up, and around the firm if you crack up, then you get a few days off."

"You are cracking up."

"I know. It's kinda fun, really. People treat you with velvet gloves. Might as well make the most of it."

The tight face returned, and she said, "I can't."

And that was the end of that.

Suddenly she was in a hurry—appointments, classes, rounds, the life of an ambitious young surgical resident. She showered, changed, and was ready to go. I drove her to the hospital.

We didn't talk as we inched through the snow-filled streets.

"I'm going to Memphis for a couple of days," I said matter-of-factly when we arrived at the hospital entrance.

"Oh, really," she said with no discernible reaction.

"I need to see my parents. It's been almost a year. I figure this is a good time. Cracking up, you know."

"Well, call me," she said, opening her door. Then she shut it—no kiss, no good-bye, no concern.

It was over. And I hated to tell my mother.

MY PARENTS WERE IN THEIR early sixties, both healthy and trying gamely to enjoy forced retirement. Dad had been an airline pilot for thirty years. Mom had been a bank manager. They were solid people, conservative, patriotic, fiercely devoted to each other. They went to church on Sundays, Rotary Club once a week.

They were still grieving over my brother Warner's divorce three years earlier. He was an attorney in Atlanta who had married his college sweetheart, a Memphis girl from a family we knew. After two kids the marriage went south. His wife got custody and moved to Portland. My parents got to see the grandkids once a year if all went well. It was a subject I never brought up.

I rented a car at the Memphis airport and drove east into the sprawling suburbs. My parents lived on a golf course, in a new glass house designed so that every window overlooked a fairway. I hated the house because the fairway was always busy.

I had called from the airport, so my mother was waiting when I arrived. Dad was somewhere on the back nine.

"You look tired," she said after the hug and kiss.

"Thanks, Mom. You look great." And she did. Slender and bronze from her daily tennis at the country club.

She fixed iced tea, and we drank it on the patio, where we watched other retirees fly down the fairway in their golf carts.

"What's wrong?" she said before I took the first sip.

"Nothing. I'm fine."

"Where's Claire? You guys never call us, you know. I haven't heard her voice in two months."

"Claire's fine, Mom. We're both working very hard."

"Are you spending enough time together?"

"No."

She frowned with motherly concern. "Are you having trouble?"

"Yes."

"I knew it. I knew it. I could tell. Surely you're not headed for a divorce too. Have you tried counseling?"

"No. Slow down."

"Is it affairs? Drugs? Alcohol? Any of the bad things?"

"No. Just two people going their separate ways. I work eighty hours a week. She works the other eighty."

"Then slow down. Money isn't everything." Her voice broke just a little, and I saw tears in her eyes.

"I'm sorry, Mom. At least we don't have kids."

She bit her lip and tried to be strong, but she was dying inside. And I knew exactly what she was thinking. She would take my divorce as a personal failure, the same as my brother's. She would find some way to blame herself.

To move things along, I told her the story of Mister and, for her benefit, downplayed the danger I'd been in. If the story had made the Memphis paper, my parents had missed it.

"Are you all right?" she asked, horrified.

"Of course. The bullet missed me. I'm here."

"Is Claire safe?"

"As safe as anybody in Washington. She lives at the hospital."

"I worry about you so much. I see the crime statistics."

We watched a ball land near the patio and waited for its owner to appear. A stout lady rolled out of a golf cart, hovered over the ball for a second, then shanked it badly.

My mother left to get more tea and to wipe her eyes.

Later that afternoon my dad and I did nine holes. I repeated the Mister tale to him.

"I'm getting kind of sick of the big firm, Dad," I said as we sat by the third tee, waiting for the foursome ahead to clear.

"What's that supposed to mean?"

"Means I'm tired of what I'm doing."

"Welcome to the real world. You think the guy working in a factory doesn't get tired? At least you're getting rich."

So he took round one, almost by a knockout. Two holes later, as we stomped through the rough looking for his ball, he said, "Are you changing jobs?"

"Thinking about it."

"Where are you going?"

"I don't know. It's too early. I haven't been looking."

"Then how do you know the grass is greener if you haven't been looking?" He picked up his ball and walked off.

I wondered why that gray-haired man scared me so much. He had pushed his sons to set goals, work hard, strive to be Big Men, with everything aimed at making lots of money and living the American dream. Like my brother, I was not born with a social conscience. We gave offerings to the church because the Bible strongly suggests it. We paid taxes to the government because the law requires it. Surely, somewhere in the midst of all this giving, some good would be done, and we would have a hand in it.

My father double-bogeyed the fifth hole and was blaming it on his putter when he climbed into the cart.

"Maybe I'm not looking for greener pastures," I said.

"Why don't you just say what you're trying to say?" he said.

"I'm thinking about public-interest law."

"What the devil is that?"

"It's when you work for the good of society without making a lot of money."

"What are you, a Democrat now? You've been in Washington too long."

We rode to the next tee in silence. He was a good golfer, but his shots were getting worse. I'd broken his concentration.

Stomping through the rough again, he said, "So some wino gets his head blown off, and you gotta change society. Is that it?"

"He wasn't a wino. He fought in Vietnam."

Dad flew B-52s in the early years of Vietnam, and this stopped him cold. But only for a second. He wasn't about to yield an inch. "One of those, huh?"

I didn't respond.

"I hate to see you blow a good career, son," he said. "You need some time off, that's all." That seemed to be everybody's remedy.

That night I took my parents to dinner at a nice restaurant. We worked hard to avoid the topics of Claire and my career. We talked about old friends and old neighborhoods. I caught up on the gossip, none of which interested me in the least.

I left them at noon on Friday, four hours before my flight, and I headed back to my muddled life in D.C.

OF COURSE, the apartment was empty when I returned that night, but with a new twist. There was a note on the kitchen counter. Following my cue, Claire had gone home to Providence for a couple of days. No reason was given. She asked me to phone when I got home. I called her parents' house and interrupted dinner. We labored through a five-minute chat in which it was determined that both of us were indeed fine, Memphis was fine and so was Providence, and she would return Sunday afternoon.

I hung up, fixed coffee, and drank a cup staring out the bedroom window, watching the traffic crawl along P Street.

I suspected Claire was telling her parents the same dismal story I had burdened mine with. It was sad and odd and yet somehow not surprising that we were being honest with our families before we faced the truth ourselves. I was tired of it.

I practiced the words I would say to her out loud until they sounded convincing; then I went for a long walk. It was ten degrees with a sharp wind, and the chill cut through my trench coat. I passed cozy row houses, where I saw real families eating and laughing and enjoying the warmth, and moved onto M Street, where throngs of those suffering from cabin fever filled the sidewalks. I stood at the window of a music club, listening to the blues with snow packed around my ankles, watching the young couples drink and dance. For the first time in my life I felt like something other than a young person. I was thirty-two, but in the last seven years I had worked more than most people do in twenty. I was tired—not old, but bearing down hard on middle age. Those pretty girls in there would never look twice at me now.

I was frozen, and it was snowing again. I bought a sandwich, stuffed it into a pocket, and slogged my way back to the apartment. I fixed a strong drink and a small fire, and I ate in the semidarkness, very much alone.

In the old days Claire's absence for the weekend would have

given me guilt-free grounds to live at the office. Sitting by the fire, I was repulsed by that thought. Drake & Sweeney would be standing proudly long after I was gone. My departure would be a slight bump in the road for the firm, scarcely noticeable. My office would be taken minutes after I walked out.

At some time after nine the phone rang, jolting me from a long, somber daydream. It was Mordecai Green, speaking loudly into a cell phone. "Are you busy?" he asked.

"Uh, not exactly. What's going on?"

"It's cold as hell, snowing again, and we're short on manpower. Do you have a few hours to spare?"

"To do what?"

"To work. We need able bodies down here."

"I'm not sure I'm qualified."

"Can you spread peanut butter on bread?"

"I think so."

"Then you're qualified."

"Okay, where do I go?"

I scribbled down the directions, each word getting shakier because Mordecai was calling me into a combat zone. I wanted to ask if I should pack a gun. I wondered if he carried one. But he was black, and I wasn't.

"Got that?" he growled. "Yellow church on your right. Ebenezer Christian Fellowship. We're in the basement."

"Yeah. Be there in twenty minutes," I said bravely.

I changed into jeans, a sweatshirt, and designer hiking boots. I took the credit cards and most of the cash out of my wallet. In the top of a closet I found an old wool-lined denim jacket, stained with coffee and paint, a relic from law school, and I hoped it would make me look nonaffluent. I desperately wanted a bulletproof vest. I was scared, but as I locked the door and stepped into the snow, I was also strangely excited.

THE drive-by shootings and gang attacks I had expected did not materialize. The weather kept the streets empty. I found the church and parked in a lot across the street. Some men were huddled together, waiting by the door. I brushed past them as if I knew where I was going, and I entered the world of the homeless.

As badly as I wanted to barge ahead, to pretend I had seen this before and had work to do, I couldn't move. I gawked in amazement at the sheer number of poor people stuffed into the basement. Some were lying on the floor, trying to sleep. Some were eating at long tables. Every inch along the walls was covered with people sitting with their backs to the cinder blocks. Small children cried and played as their mothers tried to keep them close. Volunteers passed out blankets and walked among the throng, handing out apples.

The kitchen was at one end, bustling with action as food was prepared and served. I could see Mordecai in the background, pouring fruit juice into paper cups. A line waited patiently.

I went straight to Mordecai, who was delighted to see me. We shook hands like old friends. "It's crazy," he said. "A big snow, and we work all night. Grab that bread over there." He pointed to a tray of sliced white bread. I took it and followed him to a table.

"It's real complicated. You got bologna here, mustard and mayo there. Half the sandwiches get mustard; half get mayo. One slice of bologna, two slices of bread. Do a dozen with peanut butter every now and then. Got it?"

"Yeah."

"You catch on quick." He slapped me on the shoulder and left.

I hurriedly made ten sandwiches and declared myself to be proficient. Then I slowed and began to watch the people as they waited in line, their eyes downcast but always glancing at the food ahead. They were handed a paper plate, a plastic bowl and spoon, and a napkin. As they shuffled along, the bowl was filled with soup, half a sandwich was placed on the plate, then an apple and a small cookie were added. A cup of apple juice was waiting at the end.

Most of them said a quiet "Thanks" to the volunteer handing out the juice; then they moved away, gingerly holding the plate and bowl. Even the children were careful with their food.

"We need more peanut butter sandwiches," Mordecai announced

as he returned. He grabbed a two-gallon jug of peanut butter. "Can you handle it?"

"I'm an expert," I said.

The line was momentarily short, and he watched me work.

"I thought you were a lawyer," I said, spreading peanut butter.

"I'm a human first, then a lawyer—it's possible to be both. Not quite so much on the spread there. We have to be efficient."

"Where does the food come from?"

"Food bank. It's all donated. Tonight we're lucky because we have chicken for the soup. Usually it's just vegetables."

"This bread is not too fresh."

"No, but it's free. Comes from a bakery, their day-old stuff." He sat on the edge of the table. "Is this your first trip to a shelter?"

"Yep."

"What's the first word that comes to mind?"

"Hopeless."

"That's predictable. But you'll get over it."

"How many people live here?"

"None. This is just an emergency shelter. The kitchen is open every day for lunch and dinner, but it's not technically a shelter. The church is kind enough to open up when the weather is bad."

I tried to understand this. "Then where do these people live?"

"In abandoned buildings, on the streets, in parks, in bus stations, under bridges. They can survive there as long as the weather is tolerable. Tonight they would freeze."

"Then where are the shelters?"

"Scattered about. There are about twenty."

"How many beds?"

"Five thousand, give or take."

"How many homeless?"

"Ten thousand is a good guess, and that's just the people on the street. There are probably another twenty thousand living with families and friends, a month or two away from homelessness."

A volunteer asked for sandwiches. Mordecai helped me, and we made another dozen. The door opened, and a young mother entered slowly, holding a baby and followed by three small children, one of whom wore a pair of shorts and mismatched socks, no shoes. The baby appeared to be asleep.

The mother seemed dazed and, once inside the basement, was uncertain where to go next. She led her family toward the food, and two smiling volunteers stepped forward. One parked them in a corner and began serving them food, while the other covered them with blankets. Mordecai and I watched.

"What happens to her when the storm is over?" I asked.

"Who knows? Why don't you ask her?"

That put me on the spot. I was not ready to get my hands dirty. We kept watching. The two toddlers ate their cookies first while the soup was cooling. The mother was either stoned or in shock.

"Is there a place she can go to right now and live?" I asked.

"Probably not," Mordecai answered. "As of yesterday the waiting list for emergency shelter had five hundred names on it."

The soup chef had to leave, and since I was the nearest volunteer, I was pressed into duty. While Mordecai made sandwiches, I chopped celery, carrots, and onions for an hour, under the careful eye of Miss Dolly, a founding member of the church, who'd been in charge of feeding the homeless for eleven years. It was her kitchen.

"Do you ever get used to seeing these people?" I asked her.

"Never, honey," she said, wiping her hands on a towel. "It still breaks my heart. But in Proverbs it says, *Happy is the man who feeds the poor.* That keeps me going."

She turned and gently stirred the soup. "Chicken's ready," she said in my direction.

"What does that mean?"

"Means you take the chicken off the stove, pour the broth into that pot, let the chicken cool, then bone it."

There was an art to boning, using Miss Dolly's method. My fingers were hot and practically blistered when I finished.

MISS Dolly made coffee for the volunteers after she had turned off her stove. The homeless were bedding down for the night.

Mordecai and I sat on the edge of a table in the darkened kitchen, sipping coffee and looking through the serving window at the huddled masses. "How late will you stay?" I asked.

He shrugged. "Depends. You get a coupla hundred people like this in one room, something usually happens. The Reverend would feel better if I stay."

"All night?"

"I've done it many times."

I hadn't planned on sleeping with these people. Nor had I planned on leaving the building without Mordecai to guard me.

"Feel free to leave whenever you want," he said.

"You have a family?" I asked.

"Yes. My wife is a secretary in the Department of Labor. Three sons. One's in college; one's in the army. . . ." His voice trailed away as he got to son number three. "And one we lost on the streets ten years ago. Gangs."

"I'm sorry."

"What about you?"

"Married, no kids." I thought about Claire. How would she react if she knew where I was? I didn't care.

"What does your wife do?" he asked.

"She's a surgical resident at Georgetown."

"You guys'll have it made, won't you? You'll be a partner in a big firm; she'll be a surgeon. Another American dream."

"I guess."

Miss Dolly appeared from nowhere and pulled Mordecai deep into the kitchen for a hushed conversation. I took four cookies from a bowl and walked to the corner where the young mother sat sleeping with her head propped on a pillow and the baby tucked under her arm. The toddlers were motionless under the blankets. But the oldest child was awake.

I squatted close to him and held out a cookie. His eyes glowed, and he grabbed it. I watched him eat every bite; then he wanted another. He was small and bony, no more than four years old.

"What's your name?" I whispered.

"Ontario," he said, and extended his hand for another cookie, which I gladly gave him. I would have given him anything.

"Where do you stay?" I whispered.

"In a car," he whispered back.

It took a second for this to sink in. They lived in a car.

I wanted to run and ask Mordecai what you do when you find people who live in a car, but I kept smiling at Ontario. He smiled back. He finally said, "You got more apple juice?"

"Sure," I said, and walked to the kitchen, where I filled two cups.

Ontario gulped one down, and I handed him the second cup.

"Say thanks," I said.

"Thanks," he said, and stuck out his hand for another cookie.

I found a folding chair and took a position next to Ontario, with my back to the wall. The basement was quiet at times, but never still. Occasionally Mordecai would pick his way around the bodies to settle some flare-up. He was so large and intimidating that no one dared challenge his authority.

With his stomach filled again, Ontario dozed off, his little head resting on his mother's feet.

Then the baby erupted. Its pitiful voice wailed forth with amazing volume, and the entire room seemed to ripple with the noise. The mother was dazed, tired, frustrated at having been aroused from sleep. She told it to shut up, then placed it on her shoulder and rocked back and forth. It cried louder.

With a complete lack of thought I reached over and took the child, smiling at the mother as I did so in an attempt to win her confidence. She didn't care. She was relieved to get rid of it.

The child weighed nothing and was soaking wet. I realized this as I gently placed its head on my shoulder and began patting its rear. I moved to the kitchen, desperately searching for Mordecai to rescue me. To my relief and surprise the child grew quiet as I walked around the stove, looking for a towel or something. My hand was soaked.

What would my friends think if they could see me in this dark kitchen, humming to a little street baby?

Mordecai appeared and turned on a switch. "How cute."

"Do we have any diapers?" I hissed at him.

"Big job or little job?" he asked happily, walking toward the cabinets.

"I don't know. Just hurry."

He pulled out a pack of Pampers, and I thrust the child at him. My denim jacket had a large wet spot on the left shoulder. With incredible deftness he placed the baby on the cutting board, removed the wet diaper, revealing a baby girl, cleaned her with a wipe of some sort, rediapered her with a fresh Pamper, then thrust her back at me. "There," he said proudly. "Good as new."

"The things they don't teach you in law school," I said, taking the child. I paced the floor with her until she fell asleep. Then I wrapped her in my old denim jacket and gently placed her between her mother and Ontario.

It was almost three a.m. Saturday, and I had to go. My freshly pricked conscience could take only so much. Mordecai walked me to the street, thanked me, and sent me away coatless into the night. My car was sitting where I left it, covered with new snow.

He stood in front of the church, watching me as I drove away.

CHAPTER FOUR

SINCE my run-in with Mister on Tuesday I had not billed a single hour for dear old Drake & Sweeney. I'd been averaging eight per day, six days a week, with a couple left over for Sunday. No wonder Claire went to med school.

As I stared at the bedroom ceiling late Saturday morning, I was almost paralyzed with inaction. I did not want to go to the office. I dreaded the rows of pink phone messages Polly had on my desk, the memos from higher-ups, the nosy chitchat from the gossipers. What I dreaded most, though, was the work. Antitrust cases are long and arduous, with files so thick they require boxes, and what was the point anyway? One billion-dollar corporation fighting another. A hundred lawyers cranking out paper.

I admitted to myself that I'd never loved the work. It was a means to an end. By sheer will I forced myself out of bed and into the shower.

Breakfast was a croissant from a bakery on M, with strong coffee, all taken with one hand on the wheel. I wondered what Ontario was having for breakfast, then told myself to stop the torture. I had the right to eat without feeling guilty.

The radio said the day's high would be twenty degrees, the low near zero, with no more snow for a week.

I made it as far as the elevator before being accosted by one of my brethren. Bruce somebody from communications said gravely, "How you doin', pal?"

"Fine. You?" I shot back.

"Okay. Look, we're pulling for you. Hang in there."

I nodded as if his support was crucial. Mercifully, he left on the second floor, but not before favoring me with a locker-room pat on the shoulder. Give 'em hell, Bruce.

I was damaged goods. My steps were slower as I passed Madame Devier's desk and the conference room. I found my office and slumped into the leather swivel, exhausted.

In the center of my desk was a sea of pink phone messages, all perfectly arranged in chronological order. I counted thirty-nine, several urgent. Rudolph especially seemed to be irritated. I was determined to finish my coffee in peace and without pressure, and so I was sitting at my desk, holding the cup with both hands, staring into the unknown, looking very much like someone teetering on the edge of a cliff, when Rudolph walked in.

"Hello, Mike," he said crisply, taking a seat.

"Hi, Rudy," I said. I had never called him Rudy. It was always Rudolph. Only his current wife and the partners called him Rudy.

"Where have you been?" he asked.

"Memphis."

"Memphis?"

"Yeah. I needed to see my parents. Plus the family shrink."

"A shrink?"

"Yes. He observed me in one of those swanky little units with Persian rugs and salmon for dinner. A thousand bucks a day." If I could thaw him, life would be easier.

After a long pause he said, "Are you okay?"

"The shrink said I'm fine."

"One hundred percent?"

"A hundred and ten. No problems, Rudolph. I needed a little break, that's all. I'm fine. Back at full throttle."

That was all he wanted. He smiled. "We have lots of work to do."

"I know. I can't wait."

He practically ran from my office. He would go straight to the phone and report that one of the firm's many producers was back in the saddle.

I locked the door and turned off the lights, then spent a painful hour covering my desk with papers and scribblings. Nothing was accomplished, but at least I was on the clock.

When I couldn't stand it any longer, I stuffed the phone messages into my pocket and walked out without getting caught.

I STOPPED at a large discount pharmacy on Massachusetts Avenue and had a delightful shopping spree. Candy and small toys for the kids, soap and toiletries for them all, socks and sweatpants in a variety of children's sizes. A large carton of Pampers. I had never had so much fun spending two hundred dollars.

And I would spend whatever was necessary to get them into a warm place. If it was a motel for a month, no problem. They would become my clients, and I would litigate with a vengeance until they had adequate housing. I couldn't wait to sue somebody.

I parked across from the church, much less afraid than I had been the night before, but still sufficiently scared. Wisely, I left the care packages in the car. If I walked in like Santa Claus, it would start a riot.

Miss Dolly was pleased to see me. She said hello and pointed to a pile of vegetables in need of chopping. First, though, I checked for Ontario and family, and couldn't find them.

"Where would they go?" I asked Miss Dolly as I chopped.

"Honey, these people move. They go from kitchen to kitchen, shelter to shelter. You never know."

Mordecai arrived as the line was forming for lunch. When our eyes made contact, his entire face smiled.

A new volunteer had sandwich duty; Mordecai and I worked the serving tables, ladling soup into plastic bowls. There was an art to it. Too much broth, and the recipient might glare at you. Too many vegetables, and there would be nothing left but broth. Mordecai had perfected his technique years ago; I suffered a number of glaring looks before I caught on.

As noon approached, the doors grew busier and the lines longer. I kept looking for Ontario. Santa Claus was waiting, and the little fella didn't have a clue.

Eventually the lines were gone, and Mordecai and I both got a sandwich.

"You remember that diaper you changed last night?" I asked between bites.

"As if I could forget."

"I haven't seen that family today."

He chewed and thought about it for a second. "They were here when I left this morning."

"What time was that?"

"Six. They were in the corner over there, sound asleep."

"Where would they go?"

"You never know."

"The little boy told me they stayed in a car."

"And now you want to find him, don't you?"

"Yeah."

"Don't count on it. The homeless like to roam around," Mordecai explained. "They have rituals and routines, favorite places, friends on the streets, things to do. They'll go back to their parks and alleys and dig out from the snow."

"It's twenty degrees outside. Near zero tonight," I said.

"They'll be back. Wait till dark, and this place will be hopping again. It's quiet now. Let's take a ride."

We checked with Miss Dolly, who excused us for a while.

We got into Mordecai's well-used Ford Taurus and slid out of the parking lot. Within seconds I realized Mordecai Green was a horrible driver, and I attempted to fasten my seat belt. It was broken. He seemed not to notice.

We drove the well-plowed streets of Northwest Washington, past blocks of boarded-up row houses, projects so tough ambulance drivers refused to enter, schools with razor wire glistening on top of the chain link, neighborhoods permanently scarred by riots. He was an amazing tour guide. Every inch was his turf; every corner had a story; every street had a history. We passed other shelters and kitchens. He knew the cooks. Churches were good or bad, with no blurring of the lines. They either opened their doors to the homeless or kept them locked. He pointed out the law school at Howard, a place of immense pride for him. His legal education had taken five years, at night, while he worked two jobs. He showed me a burned-out row house where crack dealers once operated. His son Cassius had died on the sidewalk in front of it.

When we were near his office, he asked if it would be all right to stop in for a minute. He wanted to check his mail. I certainly didn't mind. I was just along for the ride.

It was dim, cold, and empty. He flipped on light switches and began talking. "There are three of us. Me, Sofia Mendoza, and Abraham Lebow. Sofia's a social worker, but she knows more street law than me and Abraham combined." I followed him around the cluttered desks. "Used to have seven lawyers crammed in here. Can you believe it? That was when we got federal money for legal services. Now we don't get a dime, thanks to Congress."

"Who owns the building?" I asked.

"The Cohen Trust. Leonard Cohen was the founder of a big New York law firm. He died in '86; must've been a hundred years old. He made a ton of money, and one of his many creations was a trust to help poverty lawyers assist the homeless. That's how this place came to be. I was hired in '83, became the director in '84."

"All your funding comes from one source?"

"Practically all. Last year the trust gave us a hundred and ten thousand dollars. Year before, it was a hundred fifty, so we lost a lawyer. It gets smaller every year. The trust has not been well managed, and it's now eating the principal. I doubt if we'll be here in five years. Maybe three."

"Can't you raise money?"

"Oh, sure. Last year we raised nine thousand bucks. But it takes time. We can practice law, or we can raise funds. Sofia is not good with people. Abraham is abrasive. That leaves just me and my magnetic personality."

We made our way into his office, and I sat across from him.

"Did you forget to pay your heating bill?" I asked, shivering.

"Probably. The climate doesn't bother us. We figure our clients are cold and hungry, so why should we worry about a little heat. Did you feel guilty when you ate breakfast this morning?"

"Yes."

He gave me the smile of a wise old man who'd seen it all. "That's very common. We used to work with a lot of young lawyers from the big firms, pro bono rookies I call them, and they would tell me all the time that they lost interest in food at first." He patted his ample midsection. "But you'll get over it."

"What did the pro bono rookies do?" I asked. I knew I was moving toward the bait, and Mordecai knew I knew.

"We sent them into the shelters. They met the clients, and we supervised. Most of the work is easy. It just takes a lawyer on the phone barking at some bureaucrat. Food stamps, veterans' pensions, housing subsidies, Medicaid, aid to children—about twenty-five percent of our work deals with benefits."

I listened intently, and Mordecai began to reel me in.

"You see, Michael, the homeless have no voice. No one listens, no one cares, and they expect no one to help them. So when they try to use the phone to get benefits due them, they get nowhere.

They are put on hold, permanently. Their calls are never returned. But you get a lawyer on the phone, barking and raising hell, and things happen. Bureaucrats get motivated. Papers get processed."

His voice was rising, both hands waving through the air. On top of everything else, Mordecai was the consummate storyteller. I suspected he was very effective in front of a jury.

The stories rolled out, one after the other, all ending with the street lawyers as the good guys, the homeless as the victors. I knew he had tucked away in his repertoire just as many heartbreaking tales, probably more, but he was laying the groundwork.

I lost track of time. He never mentioned his mail. We finally left and drove back to the shelter.

Miss Dolly had somehow procured a pile of whole chickens, and she was lying in wait for me. She boiled the birds; I picked their steaming flesh.

Mordecai's wife, JoAnne, joined us for the rush hour. She was as pleasant as her husband and almost as tall. Both sons were six six. Cassius had been six nine, a heavily recruited basketball star when he was shot at the age of seventeen.

I left at midnight. No sign of Ontario and his family.

SUNDAY began with a late morning call from Claire, another stilted chat she initiated only to tell me what time she would be home. I suggested we have dinner at our favorite restaurant, but she was not in the mood. I didn't ask her if anything was wrong. We were beyond that.

The TV weatherman predicted a high of twenty-five, and I dressed in layers to go get a Sunday *Post.* As I was getting ready to leave, the newsperson rattled off the morning's top story. It stopped me cold. I heard the words, but they didn't register immediately. I walked closer to the TV on the kitchen counter, my feet heavy, my heart frozen, my mouth open in shock and disbelief.

Sometime around eleven p.m., D.C. police had found a small car near Fort Totten Park, in Northeast, in a war zone. It was parked on the street, its bald tires stuck in the frozen slush. Inside were a young mother and her four children, all dead from asphyxiation. The police suspected the family lived in the car and was trying to stay warm. The automobile's tailpipe was buried in a pile of snow plowed from the street. A few details, but no names.

I raced to the sidewalk, sliding in the snow but staying on my feet, then down P Street to Wisconsin, over to Thirty-fourth to a newsstand. Out of breath and horrified, I grabbed a paper and yanked open section A, dropping the rest of the paper onto the wet sidewalk. The story continued on page 14 with a few standard comments from the police. Then the heartbreaking details: The mother was twenty-two. Her name was Lontae Burton. The baby was Temeko. The toddlers, Alonzo and Dante, were twins, age two. The big brother was Ontario, age four.

I must have made a strange sound, because a jogger gave me an odd look, as if I might be dangerous. I began walking away, holding the paper open, stepping on the other twenty sections.

"Excuse me!" a nasty voice called from behind. "Would you like to pay for that?" I kept walking. "Hey, pal!"

I stopped long enough to pull a five-dollar bill from my pocket and throw it at the newsstand guy's feet, hardly looking at him.

On P, near the apartment, I leaned on a brick retaining wall in front of someone's splendid row house. I read the story again, hoping that somehow the ending would be different. Thoughts and questions came in torrents. Why didn't they return to the shelter? And did the baby die wrapped in my denim jacket?

Walking was almost impossible. After the shock the guilt hit hard. Why didn't I do something Friday night when I first saw them? I could have taken them to a warm motel and fed them.

The phone was ringing when I entered my apartment. It was Mordecai. He asked if I'd seen the story. "I'm very sorry, Michael," he said.

"So am I." I couldn't say much more; the words wouldn't form. We agreed to meet at noon.

Then I went to my car and removed the bags of food and toys and clothing I'd bought for them.

MORDECAI PICKED ME UP IN his car. He'd been busy on the phone.

"I found Lontae Burton's grandmother in a housing project," he informed me. "Lontae's mother is thirty-eight, serving a ten-year sentence for selling crack. Lontae had a history of prostitution and drugs. No idea of who the father, or fathers, of the children might be."

"Who buries them?"

"Same people who buried DeVon Hardy."

"How much would a decent funeral cost?"

"It's negotiable. Are you interested?"

"I'd like to see them taken care of."

We were on Pennsylvania Avenue, moving past the mammoth office buildings of Congress, the Capitol in the background, and I couldn't help but offer a silent curse or two at the fools who wasted billions each month while people were homeless. How could four innocent children die in the streets, practically in the shadow of the Capitol, because they had no place to live?

The bodies had been taken to the Office of the Chief Medical Examiner, which also housed the morgue. They would be held there until claimed. If no one came forward within forty-eight hours, they would be quickly buried in the cemetery near RFK.

Mordecai parked, paused for a second, and said, "Are you sure you want to go in?"

"I think so."

Mordecai led the way to the morgue. "I'm Mordecai Green, attorney for the Burton family," he said to the young man behind the morgue's front desk.

The young man looked up. "Just a minute," he said, and went to his computer. Soon a pale gentleman with badly dyed black hair and a clammy handshake appeared and introduced himself as Bill.

We followed him through a door, down a sterile hallway where the temperature began dropping, and, finally, to the main holding room. Bill pushed the metal door, and we stepped in. The air was frigid, the smell antiseptic, the lighting blue fluorescent. I followed Mordecai, my head down, trying not to look around at all the bodies covered from head to ankle with white sheets.

We turned and stopped in a corner, a gurney to the left, a table to the right.

Bill said, "Lontae Burton," and dramatically pulled the sheet down to her waist. It was Ontario's mother all right, in a plain white gown. Death had left no marks on her face. She could've been sleeping. I couldn't stop staring at her.

"That's her," Mordecai said, as if he'd known her for years. He looked at me, and I managed a nod. Bill wheeled around, and I held my breath. Only one sheet covered the children.

They were lying in a perfect row, tucked closely together, hands folded over their matching gowns, cherubs sleeping, little street soldiers finally at peace.

I wanted to pat Ontario on the arm and tell him I was sorry. I wanted to wake him up, take him home, and give him everything he could ever want. I took a step forward for a closer look.

"Don't touch," Bill said.

When I nodded, Mordecai said, "That's them."

I closed my eyes and said a short prayer, one of mercy and forgiveness. Don't let it happen again, the Lord said to me.

THE funeral parlor was owned by a minister Mordecai knew. He didn't like him, because the Reverend's church was not friendly enough to the homeless, but he could deal with him.

We parked in front of the church, on Georgia Avenue near Howard University, a cleaner part of town. "It's best if you stay here," he said. "I can talk to him a lot plainer if we're alone."

Mordecai left, and I locked the doors. The sidewalk was busy. I watched the people scurry by, the wind cutting them sharply. Where were they last night when Ontario and family were huddled in the frigid car, breathing the odorless carbon monoxide until they floated away? Where were the rest of us?

The world was shutting down. Nothing made sense. In less than a week I had seen six dead street people, and I was ill equipped to handle the shock. I was an educated white lawyer, well fed and affluent, on the fast track to serious wealth and all the wonderful things it would buy. Sure the marriage was over, but I would bounce back. There were plenty of fine women out there. I had no serious worries.

I cursed Mister for derailing my life. I cursed Mordecai for making me feel guilty. And Ontario for breaking my heart.

A knock on the window jolted me. It was Mordecai, standing in the snow next to the curb. I cracked the window.

"He says he'll do it for two thousand bucks, all five."

"Whatever," I said, and he disappeared.

Moments later he was back, behind the wheel and speeding away. "The funeral will be Tuesday, here at the church. Wooden caskets, but nice ones. He'll get some flowers too. He wanted three thousand, but I convinced him that there would be some press, so he might get himself on television. He liked that."

"Thanks, Mordecai."

"Are you okay?"

"No."

We said little as he drove me back to my apartment.

That night I learned that Claire's younger brother, James, had been diagnosed with Hodgkin's disease—thus the family summit in Providence. It had had nothing to do with me. I listened to her talk about the shock of the news. Hers is a family of huggers and criers, and I was thrilled she had not called me to come up. The treatment would start immediately; the prognosis was good.

She was happy to be home and relieved to have someone to unload on. We sipped wine in the den, by the fire, a quilt over our feet. It was almost romantic, though I was too scarred to even think of being sentimental.

I listened hard until she finished; then the conversation slowly drifted to me and my weekend. I told her everything—my new life as a volunteer in the shelters, then Ontario and his family. I showed her the story in the paper.

She was genuinely moved but also puzzled. I was not the same person I'd been a week earlier, and she was not sure she liked the latest version any better than the old. I was not sure either.

AS YOUNG WORKAHOLICS, Claire and I did not need alarm clocks, especially for Monday mornings, when we faced an entire week of challenges. We were up at five, eating cereal at five thirty, practically racing to see who could leave first.

Because of the wine, I had managed to sleep without being haunted by the nightmare of the weekend. And as I drove to the office, I was determined to place some distance between me and the street people. I would endure the funeral. I would drop in occasionally on Miss Dolly and help her feed the hungry. I would give money to the poor and help raise more of it for Mordecai. Certainly I could be more valuable as a source of funds than as another poverty lawyer.

Driving in the dark, I decided that I needed a string of eighteen-hour days to readjust my priorities. My career had suffered a minor derailment; an orgy of work would straighten things out. Only a fool would jump away from the gravy train I was riding.

I chose a different elevator from Mister's. He was history; I shut him out of my mind. I did not look at the conference room. Bouncing down the hallway to my office before six in the morning, removing my jacket, rolling up my sleeves—it was great to be back.

I scanned the *Post.* On the front page of the Metro section there was a small story about Lontae Burton's family, with a photo of her grandmother weeping. I read it, then put it aside.

Under the *Post* was a plain manila legal-sized file, the kind our firm used by the millions. It was unmarked, and that made it suspicious. I opened it slowly.

There were only two sheets of paper inside. The first was a copy of yesterday's story in the *Post.* Under it was a copy of something lifted from an official Drake & Sweeney file. The heading read EVICTEES—RIVEROAKS/TAG, INC. The left-hand column contained the numbers one through seventeen. Number four was DeVon Hardy. Number fifteen read: Lontae Burton and three or four children. Under the second sheet of paper, on the inside of the file itself, my anonymous informant had printed in block letters: "The eviction was legally and ethically wrong."

THE MORNING WAS PACKED with meetings and conferences, two of them with Rudolph and clients. I performed adequately, though I couldn't remember anything we said or did. Rudolph was so proud to have his star back at full throttle.

I was almost rude to those who wanted to chat about the hostage crisis and its aftershocks. I appeared to be the same, and I was my usual hard-charging self, so the concerns about my stability vanished. Late in the morning my brother, Warner, called from his office high above downtown Atlanta. He was six years older than I, a partner in another megafirm. Because of the age difference Warner and I had never been close as kids, but we enjoyed each other's company. During his divorce three years earlier he had confided in me weekly.

"Talked to Dad," he said to me now. "I understand how you feel. You work hard, make the big money, never stop to help the little people. Then something happens, and you think back to the first year of law school, when we wanted to use our law degrees to save humanity. I don't know what happened."

"Law school makes you greedy."

"I suppose. Our firm has a program where you can take a year off and do public-interest law. After twelve months you return as if you never left. You guys do anything like that?"

Vintage Warner. I had a problem; he already had the solution.

"Not for associates," I said.

"But you've been traumatized, nearly killed, simply because you were a member of the firm. I'd throw my weight around some, tell 'em you need time off."

"It might work," I said, trying to placate him. He was a type A personality, always one word away from an argument, especially with the family. "I gotta run," I said. We promised to talk more later.

The afternoon was nonstop calls and conferences. Through sheer willpower I kept my game face and got through it, billing heavily as I went. Antitrust law had never seemed so hopelessly boring.

It was almost five before I found a few minutes alone. I locked the door and opened the mysterious file. My principal suspect for who had left the file on my desk was Braden Chance's paralegal, the young man who had heard our sharp words and had referred to Chance as an ass. He would know the details of the eviction, and he would have access to the file. I needed to get his name.

Using a pocket phone to avoid any D&S records, I called a paralegal in antitrust. He referred me to another, and with little effort I learned that the paralegal I wanted was Hector Palma. He'd been with the firm about three years, all in real estate. I planned to track him down, but outside the office.

Mordecai called. He inquired about my dinner plans for the evening. "I'll treat," he said.

"Soup?"

He laughed. "Of course not. I know an excellent place."

We agreed to meet at seven. Claire was back in her surgeon's mode, oblivious to time, meals, or husband. She had checked in midafternoon, just a quick word on the run. Had no idea when she might be home, but very late.

I MET Mordecai at a restaurant near Dupont Circle. The bar at the front was packed with well-paid government types. We had a drink in the back, in a tight booth.

"The Burton story is big and getting bigger," he said.

"I'm sorry. I've been in a cave all day. What's happened?"

"Lots of press. Four dead kids and their momma living in a car. They find them a mile from Capitol Hill, where they're in the process of reforming welfare to send more mothers into the streets." He sipped his draft beer. "It's beautiful."

"So the funeral should be quite a show."

"No doubt. I've talked to a dozen homeless activists today. They'll be there with their people. The place will be packed. We're having a rally before and a march afterward."

"Maybe something good will come from their deaths."

"Maybe."

As a seasoned big-city lawyer, I knew there was a purpose behind every lunch and dinner invitation. Mordecai had something on his mind. I could tell by the way his eyes followed mine.

"Any idea why they were homeless?" I asked, fishing.

"No. Probably the usual. I haven't had time to ask questions."

Driving over, I had decided that I could not tell him about the mysterious file and its contents. It was confidential, known to me only because of my position at Drake & Sweeney. To reveal what I had learned about the activities of a client would be an egregious breach of professional responsibility.

The waiter brought salads, and we began eating. "We had a firm meeting this afternoon," Mordecai said between bites. "Me, Abraham, Sofia. We need some help."

I was not surprised to hear that. "What kind of help?"

"Another lawyer."

"I thought you were broke."

"We keep a reserve. And we have a new marketing strategy."

We both smiled at the idea of a marketing strategy.

"If we could get the new lawyer to spend ten hours a week raising money, then he could afford himself."

Another series of smiles.

"What's the rest of the job?" I asked.

"Street law. You've had a good dose. You've seen our place. It's a dump. The clients smell bad, and the money is a joke."

"How much money?"

"We can offer you thirty thousand a year."

"Abraham and Sofia agreed to this?"

"Yep. After a little speech by me. We figure you have good contacts. You should be a natural at raising money."

"What if I don't want to raise money?"

"Then we could lower our salaries even more, and when the trust dries up, we could hit the streets, just like our clients. Homeless lawyers. You're the future of the clinic, Michael. We'll take you in as a full partner. Let's see Drake and Sweeney top that."

"I'm touched," I said. I was also a bit frightened. The job offer was not unexpected, but it opened a door I was hesitant to walk through.

Black bean soup arrived, and we ordered more beer.

"The money is certainly appealing," I said, a weak effort at humor.

He grinned anyway. "You don't do it for the money. You do it for your soul."

MY SOUL kept me awake most of the night. Did I have the guts to walk away? I was literally saying good-bye to millions. The possessions I longed for would become fading memories.

The timing wasn't bad. With the marriage over, it somehow seemed fitting that I make drastic changes on all fronts.

CHAPTER FIVE

I CALLED in sick Tuesday. "Probably the flu," I told Polly, who, as she was trained to do, wanted specifics. Fever, sore throat, headaches? Any and all of the above. One had better be completely sick to miss work. She would do a form and send it to Rudolph. Anticipating his call, I left the apartment and wandered around Georgetown during the early morning.

At ten I got my car and headed for the funeral.

The sidewalk in front of the church was barricaded. Cops were standing around, their motorcycles parked on the street. Farther down were the television vans.

A large crowd was listening to a speaker yell into a microphone as I drove by. There were a few hastily painted placards held above heads for the benefit of the cameras. I parked on a side street three blocks away and hurried toward the church. I avoided the front by heading for a side door, then went up a flight of shaky stairs until I emerged on a balcony overlooking a beautiful sanctuary below. The carpet was burgundy, the pews dark wood, the windows stained glass and clean.

The doors opened, and the stampede began. The balcony floor

shook as the mourners poured into the sanctuary. The choir took its place behind the pulpit. The Reverend directed traffic—the TV crews in one corner, the activists and their homeless down the center section. Mordecai ambled in with two people I didn't know. A door to one side opened, and the prisoner marched out—Lontae's mother, clad in blue prison garb, escorted by an armed guard. She was placed in the second pew, center aisle, behind the grandmother.

When things were still, the organ began, low and sad. There was a racket at the front door, and all heads turned around. The Reverend assumed the pulpit and instructed us to stand.

Ushers with white gloves rolled the wooden coffins down the aisle and lined them end to end across the front of the church, with Lontae's in the center. The ushers arranged flowers around the caskets. The baby's was tiny, less than three feet long. Ontario's, Alonzo's, and Dante's were midsized. It was an appalling sight, and the wailing began. The choir started to hum and sway.

I had never been to a black funeral before, and I had no idea what to expect. We sat down, and the Reverend served up a lengthy prayer, then read Scripture and preached for a bit. He was followed by a homeless activist who delivered a scathing attack on a society that allowed such a thing to happen. She blamed Congress and the city and the courts and the bureaucracy. But she saved her harshest diatribe for the rich, who didn't care for the poor and the sick. She was very articulate. People clapped when she finished.

Then the choir launched into a soulful hymn that made me want to cry. A procession formed to lay hands upon the dead, but it quickly broke down when the mourners began wailing and rubbing the caskets as the choir cranked it up several notches. The grandmother was the loudest, and she was stroked and soothed by the others.

I couldn't believe it. Where were these people during the last months of Lontae's life? Those little bodies lying up there in boxes had never known this much love.

The cameras inched closer as more and more mourners broke down. The service lasted an hour and a half. For two thousand bucks it wasn't a bad production. I was proud of it.

They rallied outside and began a march in the direction of Capitol Hill. Mordecai was in the middle of it, and as they disappeared around a corner, I wondered how many marches he had been in. Not enough, he would probably say.

RUDOLPH Mayes had become a partner at Drake & Sweeney at the age of thirty, still a record. And if life continued as he planned, he would one day be the oldest working partner. The law was his life, as his three former wives could attest. Rudolph was the consummate big-firm team player.

At six p.m. I found him in his office behind a pile of work. I closed the door, sat down. "Thought you were sick," he said.

"I'm leaving, Rudolph," I said as boldly as I could, but my stomach was in knots.

He put the cap on his expensive pen. "I'm listening."

"I have an offer to work for a public-interest firm."

"Don't be stupid, Michael."

"I'm not being stupid. I've made up my mind. And I want out of here with as little trouble as possible."

"You'll be a partner in three years."

"I've found a better deal."

He couldn't think of a response, so he rolled his eyes in frustration. "Come on, Mike. You can't crack up over one incident."

"I'm not cracking up, Rudolph. I'm simply changing fields."

"Where are you going?"

"A legal clinic near Logan Circle specializing in homeless law."

"Homeless law? How much are they paying you?"

"A bloody fortune. Wanna make a donation?"

"You're losing your mind. Take a month off. Go work with the homeless, get it out of your system, then come back. This is a terrible time to leave, Mike. You know how far behind we are."

"Won't work, Rudolph. It's no fun if there's a safety net."

"Fun? You're doing this for fun?"

"Absolutely. Think how much fun it would be to work without looking at a time clock."

"What about Claire?" he asked, revealing the depths of his desperation. He hardly knew her.

"She's okay," I said. "I'd like to leave Friday."

He closed his eyes in defeat. "I don't believe this."

"I'm sorry, Rudolph."

We shook hands and promised to meet for an early breakfast to discuss my unfinished work.

I didn't want Polly to hear it secondhand, so I went to my office and called her. She was at home in Arlington, cooking dinner. It ruined her week.

I picked up Thai food and took it home. I chilled some wine, fixed the table, and began rehearsing my lines.

IF CLAIRE suspected an ambush, it wasn't evident. It was almost ten; she had eaten on the run hours earlier, so we went straight to the den with glasses of wine. I stoked the fire, and we settled into our favorite chairs. After a few minutes I said, "We need to talk."

"What is it?" she asked, completely unworried.

"I'm thinking of leaving Drake and Sweeney."

"Oh, really." She took a sip. I admired her coolness.

"Yes. I'm ready for a change. The corporate work is boring and unimportant, and I want to do something to help people."

"That's nice. In fact, that's very admirable, Michael."

"I told you about Mordecai Green. His clinic has offered me a job. I'm starting Monday."

"Monday? So I have no say in the matter?"

"I can't go back to the firm, Claire. I told Rudolph today."

Another sip, a slight grinding of the teeth, a flash of anger, but she let it pass. Her self-control was amazing.

We watched the fire, hypnotized by the orange flames. She spoke next. "Can I ask what this does for us financially?"

"It changes things."

"How much is the new salary?"

"Thirty thousand a year."

"Thirty thousand a year. That's less than what I make."

Her salary was thirty-one thousand, a figure that would increase dramatically in the years to come—serious money was not far away. I had no sympathy for any whining about money.

"You don't do public-interest law for the money," I said. "As I recall, you didn't go to med school for the money."

Like every med student in the country, she had begun her studies vowing that money was not the attraction. She wanted to help humanity. Same for law students. We all lied.

She watched the fire and did the math. I guessed she was probably thinking about the rent. It was a very nice apartment; at twenty-four hundred a month it should've been even nicer. Moving would be an adjustment, but we could endure it.

We had always been open about our finances; nothing was hidden. She knew we had around fifty-one thousand dollars in mutual funds and twelve thousand in the checking account.

"I guess we'll have to make adjustments, won't we?" she said, coldly. The word "adjustments" was dripping with connotations.

"I suppose so."

"I'm tired." She drained her glass and went to the bedroom.

How pathetic, I thought. We couldn't even muster enough rancor to have a decent fight. I put a log on the fire and slept on the sofa.

THE partners had a private dining room on the eighth floor, and it was supposed to be an honor for an associate to eat there. Rudolph was the sort of klutz who would think that a bowl of Irish oatmeal at seven a.m. in their special room would help return me to my senses. How could I turn my back on a future filled with power breakfasts?

Rudolph was desperate for me to stay, and it had little to do with friendship. Our antitrust division was logjammed with work. It was a terrible time for me to leave, but I didn't care. The firm had eight hundred lawyers. They'd find the bodies they needed.

We proceeded to review the most pressing matters in my files. We were listing things to do when Braden Chance sat at a table not far from ours. He didn't see me at first. There were a dozen or so partners eating, most deep in the morning papers. I tried to ignore him, but I finally looked over and caught him glaring at me.

"Good morning, Braden," I said loudly, startling him and causing Rudolph to turn around to see who it was.

Chance nodded and said nothing.

"You know him?" Rudolph asked under his breath.

"We've met," I said. Though during our brief encounter in his office Chance had demanded the name of my supervising partner, it was obvious he had not lodged any complaints.

"An ass," Rudolph said, barely audible. It was unanimous. He flipped a page, immediately forgot about Chance, and plowed ahead. There was a lot of unfinished work in my office.

I found myself thinking of Chance and the eviction file. He had a soft look, with delicate features, a fragile manner. I could not imagine him examining abandoned warehouses filled with squatters, actually getting his hands dirty to make sure his work was thorough. Of course, he never did that; he had paralegals. Chance sat at his desk while the Hector Palmas of the firm took care of the nasty details. Chance had lunch and played golf with the executives of RiverOaks; that was his role as a partner.

He probably didn't know the names of the people evicted from the RiverOaks warehouse, and why should he? They were just squatters, nameless, faceless. He wasn't there with the cops when they were dragged from their dwellings and thrown into the streets. But Hector Palma probably saw it happen. And if Chance didn't know the names of Lontae Burton and family, then he couldn't make the connection between the eviction and their deaths. Or maybe he did know now.

These questions would have to be answered by Hector Palma, and soon. It was Wednesday. I was leaving on Friday.

Rudolph wrapped up our breakfast at eight, just in time for another meeting in his office with some very important people. I went to my desk and read the *Post.* There was a gut-wrenching photo of the five closed caskets in the sanctuary.

There was also an editorial, a well-written challenge to all of us with food and roofs to stop and think about the Lontae Burtons of our city. They were not going away. They could not be swept from the streets and deposited in some hidden place so we didn't have to see them. We shared the same city; they were part of our society. If we didn't help them, they would continue to die in our streets.

I cut out the editorial, folded it, and placed it in my wallet.

THROUGH the paralegal network, I made contact with Hector Palma. It would not be wise to approach him directly; Chance was probably lurking nearby. We met in the main library, on the third floor, between stacks of books, away from security cameras. He was extremely nervous.

"Did you put that file on my desk?" I asked him point-blank.

"What file?" he asked, cutting his eyes around as if gunmen were tracking us.

"The RiverOaks eviction. You handled it, right?"

He didn't know how much I knew or how little. "Yeah."

"Where's the main file?"

He pulled a book off the shelf and opened it. "Chance keeps all the files locked in his office." We were practically whispering. I caught myself glancing around.

"What's in the file?" I asked.

"Bad stuff."

"Tell me."

"I have a wife and four kids. I'm not about to get fired."

"You have my word."

"You're leaving. What do you care?" Word traveled fast.

"Why did you put that file on my desk?" I asked.

He reached for another book, his right hand literally shaking. "I don't know what you're talking about."

He flipped a few pages, then walked to the end of the row. I followed along, certain no one was anywhere near us. He stopped and found another book; he still wanted to talk.

"I need that main file," I said.

"You'd have to steal it."

"Fine. Where do I get a key?"

He studied my face for a moment, trying to decide how serious I was. "You're crazy, man," he said, and walked out of the library.

I HAD no intention of breaking my back my last three days at the firm. Instead, I covered my desk with antitrust litter, shut the door, stared at the walls, and smiled at all the things I was leaving behind. The pressure was lifting with every breath. No more eighty-hour weeks. No more brownnosing. No more nightmares about not getting the partnership.

I called Mordecai and formally accepted the job. He laughed, and joked about finding a way to pay me. I would start Monday, but he wanted me to stop by earlier for a brief orientation.

By late afternoon I was accepting grave farewells from colleagues who were convinced I had truly lost my mind.

MEANWHILE, my wife was visiting a divorce lawyer, a female one with the reputation of being a merciless man-eater.

Claire was waiting for me when I arrived home at six. The kitchen table was covered with notes and computer spreadsheets. A calculator sat ready. She was icy and well prepared.

"I suggest we get a divorce on the grounds of irreconcilable differences," she began pleasantly. "We don't fight. We don't point fingers. We just admit that the marriage is over."

She stopped and waited for me to say something. Her mind was made up; what good would it do to object? "Sure," I said.

To keep the upper hand, she then mentioned her meeting with Jacqueline Hume, her lawyer, dropping the name as if it were a mortar round.

"Why did you hire a lawyer?" I asked.

"You're a lawyer. I want a lawyer. It's that simple."

She handed me exhibit A, a worksheet of our assets and liabilities. Exhibit B was a proposed split of these. Not surprisingly she intended to get the majority. We had cash of twelve thousand dollars, and she wanted to use half of it to pay off the bank lien on her car. I would get twenty-five hundred of the remainder. No mention of paying off the sixteen thousand owed on my Lexus. She wanted forty thousand of the fifty-one thousand dollars we had in mutual funds.

"Not exactly an even split," I said.

"It's not going to be equal," she said with all the confidence of one who had just hired a pit bull.

"Why not?"

"Because for reasons known only to you, you've decided to take a cut in pay of ninety thousand dollars a year. Why should I suffer the consequences? My lawyer is confident she can convince a judge that your actions have wrecked us financially. You want to go crazy, fine. But don't expect me to starve."

"Small chance of that."

She ignored me and continued down her list of notes. "The apartment lease is up June thirtieth, and I'll stay here until then. That's ten thousand in rent."

"When would you like me to leave?"

"As soon as you'd like."

"Fine." If she wanted me out, I wasn't about to beg to stay. Instead, I kept my cool. "I'll be gone by the weekend," I said. She had no response, but she didn't frown.

Exhibit C was a thorough list of the personal property, beginning with the den and ending in the bedroom. "Take what you want," I said several times, especially when addressing items such as towels and bed linens. I wanted a television and some dishes. Bachelorhood had been sprung suddenly upon me, and I had trouble contemplating the furnishing of a new place. She, on the other hand, had already spent hours living in the future.

We finished the drudgery of exhibit C and declared ourselves to be equitably divided. We would sign a separation agreement, wait six months, then go to court and legally dissolve our union.

Neither of us wanted any postgame chat. I found my overcoat and went for a long walk through the streets of Georgetown, wondering how life had changed so dramatically. Things were moving much too fast, but I was unable to stop them.

CHAPTER SIX

ANOTHER file awaited me upon my return from lunch the next day. Same spot on my desk. Inside, two keys were taped to the left side, a typed note was stapled to the right. It read:

> Top key is to Chance's door. Bottom key is to file drawer under window. Copy and return. Careful—Chance is very suspicious. Lose the keys.

Polly appeared suddenly, with no knock, and I quickly closed the file, not knowing if she had seen it. I waited for a moment as she busied herself with my storage boxes. She didn't mention it—strong evidence that she was unaware of it.

Barry Nuzzo, fellow hostage and friend, dropped by to have a serious talk. He shut the door and stepped around the boxes. I didn't want to discuss my leaving, so I told him about Claire.

He was surprised, then saddened, then seemed to shake it off quite well. "You're having a bad month," he said. "I'm sorry."

"It's been a long slide," I said.

We had not bothered to replay the Mister affair over a beer, and that now struck me as strange. Two friends face death together, then get too busy to help each other with the aftermath.

We eventually got around to it; it was difficult to avoid with the storage boxes in the middle of the floor.

"I'm sorry I let you down," he said. "I should've been here."

"Why?"

"Because it's obvious you've lost your mind," he said with a laugh.

I tried to enjoy his humor. "Yeah, I'm a little crazy now, I guess, but I'll get over it."

"No, seriously, I heard you were having trouble. I tried to find you last week, but you were gone. I was worried about you, Mike, but I've been in trial. You know—the usual."

"I know. Forget it."

"When did you realize you were leaving?"

I had to think about this for a moment. The truthful answer was at the point Sunday when Bill yanked the sheets back and I saw my little pal Ontario finally at peace. It was then and there, at that moment in the city morgue, that I became someone else.

"Over the weekend," I said. "You couldn't have stopped me, Barry. No one could."

He nodded, because he understood somehow. A gun in your face, the clock stops, priorities emerge at once—God, family, friends. Money falls to the bottom. The firm and the career vanish as each awful second ticks by.

"How about you?" I asked. "How are you doing?"

The firm and the career stay on the bottom for a few hours.

"We started a trial on Thursday. We couldn't ask the judge for a continuance, because the client had been waiting four years for a trial date. So we kicked into high gear. The trial saved us."

Of course it did. Work is therapy, even salvation, at Drake & Sweeney. I wanted to scream at him, because two weeks ago I would have said the same thing.

"Good," I said. How nice. "So you're okay?"

"Sure." He was a litigator, a macho player with Teflon skin. He also had three kids, so the luxury of a thirtysomething detour was out of the question.

The clock suddenly called him. We shook hands, embraced, and made all the usual promises to keep in touch.

After he left, I kept the door closed so I could stare at the file and decide what to do. If the keys worked and it was possible to get the main file without being caught, it could be copied in a short period of time, then be returned as if nothing had happened. I was assuming it actually contained damning evidence.

Taking the file would be grounds for instant dismissal, but I didn't care about that. Copying it would be the challenge. Since no file at the firm was less than an inch thick, there would probably be a hundred pages to Xerox. I would have to stand in front of a machine for several minutes, exposed. That would be too dangerous. Secretaries did the copying, not lawyers.

I would have to leave the building with the file, and that would border on being a criminal act. I wouldn't steal it, though, just borrow it after everyone had gone for the day.

AT FIVE I left and bought sandwiches at a deli and drove to my new office.

My partners were still there, waiting for me. Sofia actually smiled as we shook hands, but only for an instant.

"Welcome aboard," Abraham said gravely, as if I were climbing onto a sinking ship. Mordecai waved at a room next to his.

"How about this?" he said. "Suite E."

"Beautiful," I said, stepping into my new office. It was about half the size of the one I'd just left. My desk at the firm wouldn't fit in it. There were four file cabinets, each a different color. The light was a bare bulb hanging from the ceiling.

"I like it," I said, and I wasn't lying.

Mordecai and I ate dinner at his desk—the sandwiches I'd brought, with the bad coffee he'd brewed.

The copier was a bulky one of '80s vintage. It sat in a corner of the main room, near one of the desks covered with files.

"What time are you leaving tonight?" I asked Mordecai.

"I don't know. In an hour, I guess. Why?"

"Just curious. I'm going back to Drake and Sweeney for a couple of hours, last-minute stuff. Then I'd like to bring a load of my office junk here tonight. Would that be possible?"

He was chewing his food. He reached into a drawer, pulled out a ring with three keys on it, and tossed it to me. "Come and go as you please," he said.

THE drive back to Drake & Sweeney took eleven minutes. If it took thirty minutes to copy Chance's file, then it would be out of his office for about an hour. Assuming all went well. I waited until eight, then walked casually down to real estate, my sleeves rolled up as if I were hard at work.

The hallways were deserted. I checked for security cameras, then knocked on Chance's door—no answer. It was locked. The key worked perfectly, and I was suddenly inside. I locked the door, turned on the lights, went straight to the file drawer under the window, and unlocked it with the second key. On my knees I quietly pulled the drawer out.

There were dozens of files, all relating to RiverOaks, all arranged neatly. Chance was well organized, a trait our firm cherished. A thick one was labeled RIVEROAKS/TAG, INC. I gently removed it and made sure it was the right file.

I took the file, locked the drawer, and turned off the lights. Then I quietly opened the door and slowly looked up and down the hall. No one. I scooted out, passed Hector's desk, and headed for the reception area, walking briskly while trying to appear casual.

"Hey!" someone yelled from behind. I turned a corner and glanced back just quickly enough to see a guy coming after me. The nearest door was to a small library. I ducked inside; luckily it was dark. I moved between tiers of books until I found another door on the other side. I opened it, and at the end of a short hallway I saw an EXIT sign above a door. I ran through it. Figuring I could run faster down the stairs than up them, I bounded down, even though my office was two floors above. If by chance he recognized me, he might go there looking for me.

I emerged on the ground floor, out of breath, without a coat, not wanting to be seen by anyone, especially the security person guarding the elevators. I used a side exit. It was freezing, and a light rain was falling as I ran to my car.

THE thoughts of a bungling first-time thief. It was a very stupid thing to do. I shouldn't have run. No one saw me leave Chance's office. When the guy yelled, I should've stopped, chatted him up, acted as if everything were fine, and if he wanted to see the file, I'd rebuke him and send him away. He was probably just a lowly clerk.

But why had he yelled like that? If he didn't know me, why was he trying to stop me from the other end of the hallway? I drove onto Massachusetts, in a hurry to get the copying done and somehow get the file back where it belonged.

I relaxed a little. The heater was blowing at full blast.

There was no way to know that a drug bust had gone bad, a cop had been shot, a Jaguar owned by a drug dealer was speeding down Eighteenth Street. I had the green light, but the boys who shot the cop weren't concerned with the rules of the road. The Jaguar was a blur to my left; then the air bag exploded in my face.

When I came to, the driver's door was pinching my left shoulder. Black faces were staring in at me through the shattered window. I heard sirens, then drifted away again.

I awoke briefly sometime in the night. I was in a private room in a hospital. Claire was sleeping in a chair next to my bed.

SHE left before dawn. A sweet note on the table told me that she had to make her rounds and that she would return midmorning. She had talked to my doctors, and it was likely that I would not die. We seemed perfectly normal and happy, a cute couple devoted to each other. I drifted off, wondering why, exactly, we were going through a divorce.

A nurse woke me at seven and took my blood pressure. I asked her for a newspaper. She brought it thirty minutes later with my cereal. The story was front page, Metro section. The narc was shot several times in a gun battle; his condition was critical. He'd killed one dealer. The second dealer was the Jaguar driver, who died at the scene of the crash. I was not mentioned, which was fine.

My left upper arm was swollen and already turning blue, the left shoulder and collarbone stiff and tender to the touch. My ribs hurt only when I breathed. I made it to the bathroom, where I relieved myself and looked at my face. An air bag is a small bomb, but the damage was minimal: slightly swollen nose and eyes and upper lip. Nothing that wouldn't disappear over the weekend.

The doc popped in at seven thirty for a quick going-over. With nothing broken or ripped, my hours as a patient were numbered. He suggested another round of X rays, to be safe. I tried to say no, but he'd already discussed it with my wife. So I limped around my room for an eternity, testing my wounded body parts, watching the morning newsbabble, wondering how I was going to find my wrecked car and the file.

I started by calling Mordecai, my new source for all information related to the street. I assured him I was in great shape in spite of being in a hospital and asked him if he knew how to find the car. He had some ideas.

I called Polly with the same story.

"You're not coming in?" she asked, her voice faltering.

"I'm in the hospital, Polly. Are you listening to me?"

There was hesitation on her end. I envisioned a cake with a punch bowl next to it in a crowded conference room. I had been to a couple of those parties myself. They were awful.

"When are you getting out?" she asked.

"Don't know. Maybe tomorrow." It was a lie; I was leaving before noon, with or without my medical team's approval.

"I'm sorry," she said.

"Me too. Gotta go now. They want more tests."

And so my once promising career at Drake & Sweeney sputtered to an end. I was going to skip my own retirement party.

Claire arrived after eleven. She huddled with my doctor in the hall. I could hear them out there, speaking their language. They stepped into my room, jointly announced my release, and I changed into clothes she had brought from home. She drove me there, a short trip during which little was said. There was no chance at reconciliation. Why should a simple car wreck change anything? She was there as a friend and a doctor, not a wife.

She fixed tomato soup and tucked me into the sofa. She lined up my pills, gave me my instructions, and left.

I was still for ten minutes, long enough to eat half the soup, then I was on the phone. Mordecai had found nothing.

Working from the classifieds, I began calling apartment-locating services. Then I called for a sedan from a car service. I took a long, hot shower to loosen my bruised body.

My driver was Leon. I sat in the front with him, trying not to grimace and groan with each pothole he hit.

I couldn't afford a nice apartment, but at the least I wanted one that was safe. In Leon's opinion a good place to live right now was Adams Morgan, north of Dupont Circle. The streets were lined with turn-of-the-century row houses. The bars and clubs were hot at the moment, according to Leon, and the best new restaurants were there. There were seedy sections just around the corner, so of course one had to be careful.

Driving toward Adams Morgan, Leon was suddenly confronted with a pothole larger than his car. We bounced through it, went airborne, then landed very hard. I couldn't help but scream as the entire left side of my torso collapsed in pain.

Leon was horrified. I had to tell him where I'd slept last night. He slowed down considerably and became my Realtor, helping me up and down the stairs of one run-down flat after another.

The last was a loft four floors up, but with a nice clean elevator, in a row house on Wyoming, a pretty street just off Connecticut. The rent was five hundred and fifty a month for three tiny rooms in an attic with sloping ceilings and a bathroom with plumbing that seemed to be working. I was sinking fast and ready to rent anything.

"We'll take it," Leon said to the landlord. In a small office in the basement I hurriedly signed the lease and wrote a check.

I'd told Claire I'd be out by the weekend. I was determined to make it happen.

If Leon was curious about my move from the swankiness of Georgetown to a three-room pigeonhole in Adams Morgan, he didn't ask. He was too much of a professional. He returned me to our apartment, and he waited in the car while I went upstairs to swallow my pain pills.

The phone rang, and it was Rudolph. "Thought you were in the hospital," he said.

"I was," I said. "Now I'm not. What do you want?"

"We missed you this afternoon."

Ah, yes. The punch-and-cake show. "I didn't plan to be in a car wreck, Rudolph. Please forgive me."

"You feel lousy, don't you?"

"Yes, Rudolph. I feel like I've just been hit by a car."

"Sorry. Look, Braden Chance was in my office an hour ago. He's quite anxious to see you. Odd, don't you think?"

"See me about what?"

"He wouldn't say. But he's looking for you."

"Tell him I've left."

"I did. Sorry to bother you. Stop by if you get a minute. You still have friends here."

"Thanks, Rudolph."

I stuffed more pills into my pockets, then went back out to the car. As Leon sped away, I called Mordecai. He'd found the accident report; the police had the car impounded in a lot up on Georgia Avenue, north of Howard University.

It was getting dark by the time we found the lot, half a city block lined with chain link and razor wire. Inside were hundreds of wrecked cars, arranged haphazardly.

Leon stood with me on the sidewalk, peering through the chain link. "Over there," I said, pointing. The Lexus was parked near a shed, facing us. The impact had demolished the left front. The fender was gone, the engine exposed and crushed.

"You're a very lucky man," Leon said.

There was an office of some type in the shed, but it was closed and dark. The gates were locked with heavy chains. The razor wire glistened in a light rain. There were tough guys hanging around a corner, not far away. I could feel them watching us.

"Let's get out of here," I said.

Leon drove me to National Airport, where I could rent a car.

When I got back to the Georgetown apartment, the table was set; carryout Chinese was on the stove. Claire was waiting, and worried to some degree, though it was impossible to tell how much. I told her

I'd had to go rent a car. She examined me like a good doctor and made me take a pill. "I thought you were going to rest," she said.

"I tried. It didn't work. I'm starving."

It would be our last meal together as husband and wife, ending the way we'd begun, with something fast, prepared elsewhere.

"Do you know someone named Hector Palma?" she asked halfway through dinner.

I swallowed hard. "Yes."

"He called an hour ago. Said it was important that he talk to you. He wants to meet you at nine tonight, at Nathan's on M."

My appetite vanished, but I kept eating to appear unmoved. Not that it was necessary. She couldn't have cared less.

IN SIGNIFICANT pain I walked to M Street in a rain that was turning to sleet. Parking would've been impossible on Friday night. And I hoped to stretch my muscles some and clear my head. The meeting could be nothing but trouble, and I prepped for it as I walked. I thought of lies to cover my trail and more lies to cover the first set. Hector might be working for the firm; he could be wired.

Nathan's was only half full. I was ten minutes early, but he was there, waiting in a small booth. As I approached, he suddenly jumped up and thrust a hand at me. "You must be Michael. I'm Hector Palma, from real estate. Nice to meet you."

It was an assault, a burst of personality that put me on my heels. I shook hands, reeling, and said, "Nice to meet you."

"Here, have a seat," he said, all warmth and smiles. I delicately bent and squeezed my way into the booth.

"What happened to your face?" he asked.

"I kissed an air bag."

"Yeah, I heard about the accident," he said as the waiter appeared. "What'll you have?"

"Black coffee," I said. At that moment, as he pondered his choice of drinks, one of his feet began tapping me on the leg.

"What kind of beer do you have?" he asked the waiter, who looked straight ahead and began rattling off brands.

The tapping brought our eyes together. His hands were together on the table. Using the waiter as a shield, he barely curled his right index finger and pointed to his chest.

"Molson," he announced suddenly, and the waiter left.

He was wired, and they were watching. Wherever they were, they couldn't see through the waiter. Instinctively I wanted to turn and examine the other people in the bar. But I withstood the temptation, thanks in part to a neck as pliable as a board.

"I'm a paralegal in real estate," he explained. "You've met Braden Chance, one of our partners."

"Yes." Since my words were being recorded, I'd offer few.

"I work primarily for him. You and I spoke briefly one day last week when you visited his office."

"If you say so. I don't remember seeing you."

I caught a very faint smile, a relaxing around the eyes, nothing a surveillance camera could catch. Under the table I tapped his leg with my foot. Hopefully, we were dancing to the same tune.

"Look, the reason I asked you to meet me is because a file is missing from Braden's office. It was the file you asked for when you sort of barged into his office last week."

"Am I being accused of taking it?" I said.

"Well, no. The firm is doing an investigation, and we're simply talking to everyone we can think of."

"I know nothing about the file."

"Would you take a polygraph?"

"Certainly," I said firmly, even indignantly. There was no way in hell I would take a polygraph.

"Good. They're asking everybody near the file to do it."

The beer and coffee arrived, giving us a brief pause to evaluate and reposition. Hector had just told me he was in deep trouble. A polygraph would kill him. He could never lie and survive the test.

"They're fingerprinting too," he said. He said this in a lower voice, not to avoid the hidden mike, but rather to soften the blow.

It didn't work. The thought of leaving prints had never occurred to me. "Good for them," I said. "Hope they find their man."

"In fact, they lifted prints all afternoon—from the door, the light switch, the file cabinet. Lots of prints." He took a long drink. "Did someone give you a set of keys to Braden's office?"

"Of course not."

"Well, they found an empty file on your desk, with a note about two keys—one to the door, the other to a file cabinet."

"I know nothing about it," I said as arrogantly as possible.

Another long drink by Hector, another sip of coffee by me.

Enough had been said. The messages had been delivered—one by the firm, the other by Hector himself. The firm wanted the file back with its contents uncompromised. Hector wanted me to know that his involvement could cost him his job. It was up to me to save him.

"Anything else?" I asked, suddenly ready to leave.

"Nothing. When can you do the polygraph?"

"I'll give you a call." I picked up my coat and left.

CHAPTER SEVEN

MORDECAI had contacts and could pull enough strings to get me to my car. Shortly after nine Saturday morning, with Mordecai doing the driving, we rode through the rain-slick streets into Northeast. Traffic was light. It was another raw February morning.

We parked at the curb near the padlocked gates to the city lot just off Georgia Avenue. Mordecai said, "Wait here." I could see the remains of my Lexus.

He walked to the gates, pushed a button on a pole, and the door to the office shed opened. A small, thin uniformed policeman with an umbrella came over, and they exchanged a few words.

Mordecai returned to the car, slamming the door and shaking the water off his shoulders. "He's waiting for you," he said.

I stepped into the rain, raised my umbrella, and walked quickly to the gates, where the officer was waiting without the slightest trace of humor or goodwill. He produced keys by the dozens, somehow found the three that fit the heavy padlocks, and said to me, "Over here," as he opened the gates. I followed him through the gravel lot to my car. My entire body ached with every move.

I went right to the front seat. No file. After a moment of panic I found it behind the driver's seat, on the floor, intact. I grabbed it and was ready to go.

"Is that it?" the officer asked.

"Yes," I said, ready to bolt.

"Follow me."

We entered the shed, where a butane heater roared in a corner, blasting us with hot air. He selected one of ten clipboards from the wall and began staring at the file I was holding. "Brown manila file," he said as he wrote. "Is there a name on it?"

"Why do you need it?" I asked.

"Put it on the table," he said.

On the table it went. "RiverOaks slash TAG, Inc.," he said, still writing. "File number TBC3381." My trail widened even more.

"Do you own this?" he asked, pointing at the file.

"Yes."

"Okay. You can go now."

I thanked him, and got no response.

Mordecai looked down at the file once I was inside the car. He didn't have a clue. I had told him only that the file was very important. I needed to retrieve it before it was destroyed. I was tempted to flip through it as we drove back to the clinic. But I didn't.

Once back at the clinic I thanked Mordecai, then drove my rental car, cautiously, to my new loft.

THE source of the money was the federal government, I read in the file. The U.S. Postal Service planned to construct a twenty-million-dollar bulk-mail facility in the city, and RiverOaks was one of several aggressive real estate companies hoping to build, lease, and manage it. Several sites had been considered, all in rough and decaying sections of the city. RiverOaks had begun snapping up all the cheap real estate it might need.

TAG was a registered corporation whose sole stockholder was Tillman Gantry, described in a file memo as a former pimp, small-time hustler, and twice-convicted felon. One of many such characters in the city. After crime Gantry had discovered real estate. He purchased abandoned buildings, sometimes doing quickie renovations and reselling, sometimes offering space for rent. Gantry's path crossed that of RiverOaks when the Postal Service needed more space.

On January 6 the Postal Service informed RiverOaks by registered mail that the company had been chosen to be the contractor/owner/landlord of the new bulk facility. A memorandum of agreement provided for annual rental payments of $1.5 million for twenty years. The letter also said, with nongovernmental-like haste, that a final agreement would have to be signed no later than March 1, or the deal was off. The March 1 deadline was now only seven days away. Small wonder Chance missed the file so quickly.

RiverOaks and its lawyers had gone to work. In January the company purchased four properties on Florida Avenue near the warehouse where the eviction took place.

The warehouse on Florida had been purchased by TAG the previous July for a sum not revealed. RiverOaks bought it for two hundred thousand dollars on January 31, four days before the eviction that sent DeVon Hardy and the Burton family into the streets. It was a cash deal; no bank was involved.

On the bare floor of my living room I removed each sheet of paper from the file, examined it, then described it in detail on a legal pad so that I could put the file back together in perfect order.

On the left inside flap of the manila folder was the journal, a preprinted form used to log each entry by date and brief description. Chance's file was meticulous. But there had been tampering.

On January 22 Hector Palma went to the warehouse, alone, for a routine inspection. As he was entering a designated door, he was mugged by two street punks, who hit him over the head with a stick of some sort and took his wallet and cash at knifepoint. He stayed at home on January 23 and prepared a memo to the file describing the assault. The last sentence of that memo read, "Will return on Monday, January 27, with guard, to inspect."

But there was no memo from his second visit. A January 27 entry into the journal said, "HP memo—site visit." Hector had gone to the warehouse on the twenty-seventh, with a guard, inspected the place, no doubt found that serious squatting was under way, and prepared a memo, which, judging by his other paperwork, was probably quite thorough.

The memo had been removed from the file.

The closing took place on January 31, a Friday. The following Tuesday, Hector returned to the warehouse to remove the squatters. He was assisted by a private security guard, a District cop, and four roughnecks from an eviction company. It took three hours, according to his two-page memo. Though he tried to mask his emotions, Hector didn't have the stomach for evictions.

My heart stopped when I read the following:

> One woman had four children, including an infant. She lived in a two-room apartment with no plumbing. They slept on two mattresses on the floor. She fought with the policeman while her children watched. She was eventually removed.

So Ontario watched while his mother fought.

There was a list of those evicted, seventeen in all, the same list someone had placed on my desk Monday morning. In the back of the file were eviction notices for the seventeen. They had not been used. Squatters have no rights, including the right to be notified. The notices had been prepared as an afterthought, probably stuck in after the Mister episode in an effort to cover the trail.

The tampering was obvious and foolish. But then, Chance was a partner, and it was virtually unheard of for a partner to have to surrender a file. It hadn't been surrendered, though; it had been stolen. An act of larceny, a crime for which evidence was now being gathered. The thief was an idiot.

As part of my preemployment ritual seven years earlier, I had been fingerprinted by private investigators. It would be a simple matter to match those prints with the ones lifted from Chance's file cabinet. I was certain it had already been done. Could there be a warrant for my arrest? It was inevitable.

Most of my living-room floor was covered when I finished, three hours after I started. I carefully reassembled the file, then drove to the clinic and copied it.

SHE was shopping, Claire's note said. We had nice luggage, an item we failed to mention when we split the assets, but I took the cheap stuff—duffel and gym bags. I hurriedly cleaned out my drawers and my side of the medicine cabinet. Wounded and aching, physically and otherwise, I hauled the bags down two flights of stairs to my rental car, then went back up for a load of suits and dress clothes. I found my old sleeping bag, unused for at least the last five years, and carried it down, along with a pillow. I was entitled to my alarm clock, radio, portable CD player with a few CDs, thirteen-inch color TV on the kitchen counter, one coffeepot, and the set of blue towels.

When the car was full, I left a note telling her I was gone. I placed it next to the one she'd left. My emotions were mixed and just under the skin, and I was not equipped to deal with them. I'd never moved out before; I wasn't sure how it was done.

I locked the door and walked down the stairs. I knew I would be back in a couple of days to get the rest of my things, but the trip down felt like the last time.

THE clinic was cold on Sunday morning. I wore a heavy sweater, corduroy pants, thermal socks. After I locked myself inside the office, I read the paper at my desk with two steaming cups of coffee in front of me.

I missed my chair, my leather executive swivel that rocked and reclined and rolled at my command. My new one was a small step above a folding job you'd rent for a wedding. The desk was a battered hand-me-down, probably from an abandoned school. The two clients' chairs on the other side were indeed folding types—one black, the other a greenish color I'd never seen before.

Oh, how the mighty had fallen! If my dear brother, Warner, could've seen me sitting there on Sunday, shivering at my sad little desk, staring at the cracks in the plaster, locked in so that my potential clients couldn't mug me, he would've hurled insults so rich and colorful that I would've been compelled to write them down.

A loud bang at the door scared the wits out of me. I bolted upright, unsure of what to do. Were street punks coming after me? Another knock as I moved toward the front, and I could see a figure trying to look through the thick glass of the door.

It was Barry Nuzzo, shivering and anxious to get to safety. I got things unlocked and let him in.

"What a slum hole!" he began pleasantly, looking around the front room as I relocked the door.

"Quaint, isn't it?" I said, reeling from his presence and trying to figure out what it meant. "We keep the overhead low so we can take all the money home."

"So you're here for the money?" he asked, grinning.

"Of course."

"You've lost your mind."

"I've found a calling."

"Yeah, you're hearing voices."

"Is that why you're here? To tell me I'm crazy?"

He shrugged. "What's wrong with your face?"

"Air bag."

"Oh, yeah. I forgot. I heard it was just a fender bender."

"It was. The fenders got bent."

He walked around, peeking into the small offices to the side. "How'd you find this operation?" he asked.

"Mister hung out here. These were his lawyers."

"Good old Mister," he said. He stopped for a moment and stared at a wall. "Do you think he would've killed us?"

"No. Nobody was listening to him. He was just another homeless guy. He wanted to be heard."

"Did you ever consider jumping him?"

"No. But I thought about grabbing his gun and shooting Rafter."

"I wish you had."

"Maybe next time."

"Got any coffee?"

"Sure." I found a cup, washed it quickly, and filled it with coffee. I invited Barry into my office.

"Nice," he said, looking around.

"This is where all the long balls are hit," I said proudly. We took positions across the desk, both chairs squeaking.

"Is this what you dreamed about in law school?" he asked.

"I don't remember. I've billed too many hours since then."

He finally looked at me, without a smirk or a smile, and the kidding was set aside. As bad as the thought was, I couldn't help but wonder if Barry was wired.

"So you came here searching for Mister?" he said.

"I guess."

"What did you find?"

"Are you playing dumb, Barry? What's happening at the firm? Are you guys coming after me?"

He weighed this carefully while taking quick sips from his mug. "This coffee is awful," he said, ready to spit.

"At least it's hot."

"There's a file missing, Michael. Everyone's pointing at you."

"Why are they pointing at me?"

"The file has something to do with Mister. You went to Braden Chance and demanded to see it. There is evidence someone gave you some keys."

"Is that all?"

"That, and the fingerprints."

"Fingerprints?" I asked, trying to appear surprised.

"All over the place. Perfect matches. You were there, Michael. You took the file. Now what will you do with it?"

"How much do you know about the file?"

"Mister got evicted by one of our real estate clients."

"Is that all?"

"That's all they've told us. We got memos Friday—the entire firm, everybody—informing us that a file had been taken, you were the suspect, and that no member of the firm should have any contact with you. I am forbidden to be here right now."

"I won't tell."

"Thanks."

"Then why are you here?"

"I'm your friend. Things are crazy right now. My God, we had cops in the office on Friday. Can you believe that? Last week it was the SWAT team, and we were hostages. Now you've jumped off a cliff. Why don't we take a break? Let's go somewhere for a couple of weeks. You bring back the file; the firm forgives and forgets; you and I go play tennis for two weeks on Maui; then you go back to your plush office where you belong."

"They sent you, didn't they? It won't work, Barry."

"Give me a good reason. Please."

"There's more to being a lawyer than billing hours and making money. I'm tired of it, Barry. I want to make a difference."

"You sound like a first-year law student."

"Exactly. We got into this business because we thought the law was a higher calling. We could fight injustice and social ills, and do all sorts of great things because we were lawyers. We were idealistic once. Why can't we do it again?"

"Mortgages."

"I'm not trying to recruit. You have three kids; luckily Claire and I have none. I can afford to go a little nuts."

A radiator in a corner, one I had not yet noticed, began to rattle and hiss. We watched it and waited hopefully for a little heat.

"They're gonna come after you, Michael," he said, still looking at the radiator, but not seeing.

"They? You mean we?"

"Right. The firm. You can't steal a file."

"Criminal charges? A warrant for my arrest?"

"Probably. They're mad as hell, Michael."

"The firm has more to lose than I do."

He studied me. "There's more than Mister?" he asked.

"A lot more. The firm has tremendous exposure. If they come after me, I go after the firm. Tell them to back off."

"They were just a bunch of squatters, Michael."

"It's much more complicated. Believe me, Barry, this is front-page stuff. You guys will be afraid to leave your homes."

"So you're proposing you keep the file, we leave you alone."

"For now. I don't know about next week or the week after."

"Why can't you talk to Arthur Jacobs? I'll referee. The three of us will get in a room, work this thing out. What do you say?"

"It's too late. People are dead."

"Mister got himself killed."

"There are others." And with that, I had said enough. Though he was my friend, he would repeat our conversation to his bosses.

"Would you like to explain?" he said.

"I can't. It's confidential."

The radiator gurgled and burped, and it was easier to watch it than to talk for a while. Neither of us wanted to say things we would later regret. He asked about the clinic, and I gave him a quick tour. "Unbelievable," he mumbled more than once.

"Can we keep in touch?" he asked as I walked him to the door.

"Sure," I said, and he left.

MY ORIENTATION on Monday morning lasted the time it took Mordecai and me to drive from the clinic to the Samaritan House in Petworth, in Northeast. Mordecai handled the driving and the talking; I sat quietly, holding my briefcase, as nervous as any rookie about to be fed to the wolves. I wore jeans, a white shirt and a tie, an old navy blazer, and on my feet I had well-worn Nike tennis shoes. I had stopped shaving. I was a street lawyer, and I could dress any way I wanted.

"Your clientele will be a mixture of thirds," Mordecai said, driving badly with one hand, holding coffee with the other, oblivious to any of the other vehicles crowded around us. "About a third are employed; a third are families with children; a third are mentally disabled; a third are veterans. And about a third of those eligible for low-income housing receive it." The statistics flowed forth with no effort whatsoever. This was his life and his profession. I just listened.

"These people have minimum-wage jobs, so they don't even dream about private housing. And their earned income has not kept pace with housing costs. So they fall farther and farther behind. About half of all poor people spend seventy percent of their income trying to keep the housing they have. HUD says they should spend a third. There are tens of thousands of people in this city who are clinging to their roofs; one missed paycheck, one unexpected hospital visit, one unseen emergency, and they lose their housing." We squealed to a stop at a red light.

"Where do they go?"

"They rarely go straight to the shelters. At first they'll go to their families, then friends. The strain is enormous. They move around; sometimes they leave a kid with this sister and a kid with that friend. Things go from bad to worse. A lot of homeless people are afraid of the shelters and desperate to avoid them."

He paused to drink his coffee. "Why?" I asked.

"Not all shelters are good. There have been assaults, robberies, even rapes."

And this was where I was expected to spend the rest of my legal career. "What will my first cases be?"

"Anxious, aren't you?"

"Yeah. And I don't have a clue."

The light changed, and Mordecai hit the gas. "Relax. The work's not complicated; it takes patience. You'll see a person who's not getting benefits, probably food stamps. A divorce. A complaint against a landlord. You're guaranteed a criminal case."

"What type of criminal case?"

"Small stuff. The trend in urban America is to criminalize homelessness. Cities have passed all sorts of laws designed to persecute those who live on the streets. Sweeps are common."

"Sweeps?"

"Yes. They'll target one area of the city, shovel up all the homeless, dump them somewhere else like manure." A quick sip of coffee as he adjusted the heater—no hands on the wheel for five seconds. "Remember, Michael, everybody has to be somewhere. These people have no alternatives. If you're hungry, you beg for food. If you're tired, then you sleep wherever you can find a spot. If you're homeless, you have to live somewhere."

And with that, orientation ended.

AHEAD on the right was a group of heavily clad men huddled over a portable butane burner on a street corner. We turned beside them and parked at the curb. The building was once a department store. A hand-painted sign read SAMARITAN HOUSE.

"It's a private shelter," Mordecai said. "Ninety beds, decent food, funded by a coalition of churches in Arlington."

Mordecai spoke to an elderly gentleman who worked the door, and we were allowed inside.

"I'll give you a quick tour," Mordecai said. I stayed close to him as we walked through the main floor. It was a maze of short hallways, each lined with small square rooms made of unpainted Sheetrock. Each room had a door with a lock. One was open. Mordecai looked inside and said, "Good morning."

A tiny man with wild eyes sat on the edge of a cot, looking at us. "This is a good room," Mordecai said to me. "It has privacy, a nice bed, room to store things, and electricity."

"Have a nice day," he said to the resident, who nodded.

Radios were on. People were moving about. It was Monday morning; they had jobs and places to be.

"Is it hard to get a room here?" I asked, certain of the answer.

"Nearly impossible. There's a waiting list a mile long."

Clients awaited us. Our office was in a corner of the dining hall. Our desk was a folding table we borrowed from the cook. Mordecai unlocked a file cabinet in the corner, and we were in business. Six people sat in chairs along the wall.

"Who's first?" he asked, and a woman came forward. She sat across from her lawyers, both ready with pen and legal pad—one a seasoned veteran of street law, the other clueless.

Her name was Waylene, age twenty-seven, two children, no husband. Her problem was not complicated. She had worked in a fast-food taco restaurant before quitting for some reason Mordecai deemed irrelevant, and she was owed her last two paychecks. Because she had no permanent address, the employer had sent the checks to the wrong place. The checks had disappeared; the employer was unconcerned.

"Where will you be staying next week?" Mordecai asked her.

She wasn't sure. Maybe here, maybe there.

"I'll have the checks sent to my office." He handed her a business card. "Phone me at this number in a week."

She took the card, thanked us, and hurried away. Mordecai said to me, "Call the taco place, identify yourself as her attorney, be nice at first, then raise hell if they don't cooperate."

I wrote down these instructions as if they were complicated. Waylene was owed two hundred and ten dollars. The last case I worked on at Drake & Sweeney was an antitrust dispute with nine hundred million dollars at stake.

The line grew as we efficiently worked the clients. Mordecai had seen it all before: food stamps disrupted for lack of a permanent address, a landlord's refusal to refund a security deposit, unpaid child support. After two hours and ten clients, I moved to the end of the table and began interviewing them myself. During my first full day as a poverty lawyer I was on my own, taking notes and acting just as important as my co-counsel.

The morning passed quickly; my nervousness vanished. I was reaching out to help real people with real problems, people with no other place to go for legal representation. I learned to smile and make them feel welcome. Some apologized for not being able to pay me. The money was not important, I told them.

At twelve we surrendered our table so lunch could be served. The dining area was crowded; the soup was ready.

Back at the clinic that afternoon, I retreated to the privacy of my office. Mordecai had suggested that I spend the rest of the day working on the cases we had taken in at Samaritan. There was a total of nineteen. If I thought the pace would be slower on the street, I was wrong. I was suddenly up to my ears with other people's problems.

My first phone call, however, went to Drake & Sweeney. I asked for Hector Palma in real estate and was put on hold. After five minutes the abrasive voice of Braden Chance was suddenly barking in my ear, "Can I help you?"

I swallowed and said, "Yes. I'm holding for Hector Palma."

"Who is this?" he demanded.

"Rick Hamilton, an old friend from school."

"He doesn't work here anymore. Sorry." He hung up, and I stared at the phone. I thought about calling Polly—or maybe Rudolph or Barry. Then I realized that they were no longer my friends. I was gone. I was off-limits. I was the enemy.

I was in no hurry to leave the clinic at the end of my first day. Home was an empty attic, a bedroom with no bed, a living room with cableless TV, a kitchen with a card table and no fridge.

Sofia left promptly at five, her standard hour. Her neighborhood was rough, and she preferred to be home with the doors locked at dark. Mordecai left around six, after spending thirty minutes with me discussing the day. Don't stay too late, he warned, and try to leave in pairs. He had checked with Abraham, who planned to work until nine, and suggested we leave together. Park close. Walk fast. Watch everything.

I called the three Hector Palmas I found in the phone book. The first was not the Hector I wanted. The second number was not answered. The third was voice mail. The message was brusque: "We're not home. Leave message. We'll return your call." It was his voice.

I wrote down his address from the phone book. With my newly acquired street savvy I was sure I could track him down tomorrow.

CHAPTER EIGHT

THE District police waited until almost one a.m., then struck like commandos.

The cell phone rang next to my head, on the floor at the opening of my sleeping bag. It was the third night I'd slept on the floor, part of my effort to identify with my new clients. I was eating little, sleeping even less, trying to acquire an appreciation for park benches and sidewalks. The left side of my body was purple down to the knee, extremely sore and painful, and so I slept on my right side.

I found the cell phone and said, "Hello."

"Michael!" Claire hissed in a low voice. "The cops are searching the apartment."

"What?"

"They're here now. Four of them, with a search warrant."

"What do they want?"

"They're looking for a file."

"I'll be there in ten minutes."

"Please hurry."

I ROARED into the apartment like a man possessed. I confronted the first cop I encountered. "I'm Michael Brock. Who are you?"

"Lieutenant Gasko," the man said with a sneer.

"Let me see some identification." I turned to Claire, who was leaning on the refrigerator holding a cup of coffee. "Get me a piece of paper," I said.

Gasko pulled his badge from his coat pocket and held it high.

"Larry Gasko," I said. "You'll be the first person I sue, at nine o'clock this morning. Now, who's with you?"

"There are three others," Claire said, handing me a sheet of paper. "I think they're in the bedrooms."

I walked to the rear of the apartment, Gasko behind me, Claire somewhere behind him. I saw a plainclothes cop in the guest bedroom on all fours, peeking under the bed. "Let me see some identification," I yelled at him. He scrambled to his feet, ready to fight. I took a step closer, gritted my teeth, and said, "ID, turkey."

"Who are you?" he asked, looking at Gasko.

"Michael Brock. Who are you?"

He flipped out a badge. "Darrell Clark," I announced loudly as I scribbled it down. "Defendant number two."

"You can't sue me," he said.

"Watch me, big boy. In eight hours, in federal court, I will sue you for a million bucks for an illegal search. And I'll win, and then I'll hound you until you file for bankruptcy."

The other two cops appeared from my old bedroom, and I was surrounded by them.

"Claire," I said. "Get the video camera please. I want this recorded." She disappeared into the living room.

"We have a warrant signed by a judge," Gasko said. The other three took a step forward to tighten the circle.

"The search is illegal," I said bitterly. "The people who signed the warrant will be sued. Each of you will be sued. You will be placed on leave, probably without pay, and you will face a civil lawsuit."

"We have immunity," Gasko said, glancing at his buddies.

"Like hell you do."

Claire was back with the camera. "Did you tell them I didn't live here?" I asked her.

"I did," she said, and raised the camera to her eye.

"Yet you boys continued the search. At that point it became illegal. You should've known to stop. You had a chance, boys, and you blew it. Now you'll have to pay the consequences."

"You're nuts," Gasko said. They tried not to show fear—but they knew I was a lawyer, so maybe I knew what I was talking about. I did not. But at that moment it sounded good.

"Now, why don't you leave," I said.

"Where's the file?" Gasko asked.

"The file is not here, because I don't live here. That's why you're going to get sued, Officer Gasko."

"Get sued all the time, no big deal."

"Great. Who's your attorney?"

He couldn't pull forth the name of one in the crucial split second that followed.

"Leave," I said. "The file is not here."

Claire was nailing them with the video, and that kept their grumbling to a minimum. Clark mumbled something about lawyers as they shuffled toward the door.

I read the warrant after they were gone. Claire watched me, sipping coffee at the kitchen table. The shock of the search had worn off; she was once again subdued, even icy.

"What's in the file?" she asked. She didn't really care.

"It's a long story." In other words, don't ask. She understood.

"Are you really going to sue them?"

"No. I just wanted to get rid of them."

"It worked."

I folded the search warrant and stuck it into a pocket. It covered only one item—the RiverOaks/TAG file, which at the moment was well hidden in the walls of my new apartment.

"Did you tell them where I live?" I asked.

"I don't know where you live," she answered. Then there was a space of time during which it would have been appropriate for her to ask where, in fact, I did live. She did not.

"I'm very sorry this happened, Claire."

"It's okay. Just promise it won't happen again."

"I promise."

I left without a hug, a kiss. I simply said good night and walked through the door. That was precisely what she wanted.

TUESDAY was an intake day at the Community for Creative Non-Violence, or CCNV, by far the largest shelter in the District. Once again Mordecai handled the driving.

My threat to Barry Nuzzo that I'd go after the law firm if they came after me had fallen on deaf ears. Drake & Sweeney would play hardball, and I wasn't surprised. The predawn raid of my former apartment was a rude warning of what was to come. I had to tell Mordecai the truth about what I'd done.

As soon as we were in the car and moving, I said, "My wife and I have separated. I've moved out."

The poor guy was not prepared for such dour news at eight in the morning. "I'm sorry," he said, looking at me and almost hitting a jaywalker.

"Don't be. Early this morning the cops raided the apartment where I used to live, looking for me and a file I took when I left the firm."

"What kind of file?"

"The DeVon Hardy and Lontae Burton file."

"I'm listening."

"Drake and Sweeney evicted DeVon Hardy and sixteen others from their homes. Lontae and her little family were in the group. The abandoned warehouse happened to be on land RiverOaks planned to use for a twenty-million-dollar postal facility."

"I know the building. It's always been used by squatters."

"Except they weren't squatters. At least I don't think so."

"Are you guessing? Or do you know for sure?"

"For now I'm guessing. The file has been tampered with: papers taken, papers added. A paralegal named Hector Palma handled the dirty work—the site visits and the actual eviction. He's become my deep throat. He sent an anonymous note informing me that the evictions were wrongful. He provided me with a set of keys to get the file. As of yesterday he no longer works at the office here in D.C."

"Where is he?"

"I'd love to know."

"You used the keys he gave you to steal the file?"

"I didn't plan to steal it. I was on my way to the clinic to copy it when some fool ran a red light and sent me to the hospital."

"That's the file we retrieved from your car?"

"That's it. I was going to copy it, take it back to its little spot at Drake and Sweeney, and no one would have ever known."

"What's missing from it?" he asked.

I summarized the history of RiverOaks and its race to build the mail facility and told him about the missing memo.

"So what's in the memo?"

"Don't know. But I have a hunch that Hector inspected the warehouse, found the squatters in their makeshift apartments, talked to them, and learned that they were, in fact, paying rent to Tillman Gantry. They were not squatters, but tenants, entitled to all the protections under landlord-tenant law. By then the wrecking ball was on its way, so the memo was ignored and the eviction took place."

"There were seventeen people. Do you know all their names?"

"Yes. Someone—Palma, I suspect—gave me a list. Placed it on my desk. If we can find those people, then we have witnesses."

"How much did Gantry get for the building?" he asked.

"Two hundred thousand. He'd bought it six months earlier from the city; there's no record in the file indicating how much he paid for it."

"He probably paid five thousand for it. Ten at the most."

"Not a bad return."

"Not bad. I know Gantry. It's a step up for him. He's been a nickel-and-dimer—buying duplexes and car washes and quick-shop groceries, small ventures."

"Why would he buy the warehouse?"

"Cash. Let's say he pays five thousand for it, then spends another thousand throwing up a few walls and installing a couple of toilets. He gets the lights turned on, and he's in business. Unregulated housing. It happens all the time around here."

It was almost eight thirty when we arrived at the CCNV—a long, three-story building, home to thirteen hundred people. It was time for the residents to leave for their jobs. A hundred men loitered around the front entrance, smoking cigarettes and talking.

Inside the door on the first level Mordecai spoke to a supervisor. He then signed his name, and we walked across the lobby, weaving around a swarm of young, tough street men leaving in a hurry. I avoided eye contact.

"Weapons and drugs are automatic lifetime bans," Mordecai said as we came to the intake room. I felt somewhat safer.

"Do you ever get nervous in here?" I asked.

"You get used to it." Easy for him to say.

On a clipboard next to the door was a sign-up sheet for the legal clinic. Mordecai took it, and we studied the names of our clients. Thirteen so far.

We set up our clinic and were ready to dispense advice. I rapidly learned that one of the challenges of being a street lawyer was to be able to listen. Many of my clients just wanted to talk to someone. All had been beaten down in some manner, and since free legal advice was available, why not unload on the lawyers? Mordecai was a master at gently poking through the narratives and determining if there was an issue for him to pursue.

I also learned that the best case was one that could be handled on the spot, with no follow-up. Twenty-six clients passed through our session before noon. We left exhausted.

"Let's take a walk," Mordecai said when we were outside the building. The sky was clear, the air cold and refreshing after three hours in a stuffy room with no windows.

I mustered the courage to explain to Mordecai that I needed the afternoon off to settle some personal matters, and he very brusquely informed me that no one monitored my hours and that if I needed time off, then I should take it.

I spent an hour with the claims adjuster. The Lexus was a total wreck; my company was offering $21,480, with a release so it could then go after the insurer of the Jaguar. I owed the bank $16,000, so I left with a check for $5,000 and change, certainly enough to buy a vehicle appropriate to my new position as a poverty lawyer, one that wouldn't tempt car thieves.

Another hour was wasted in the reception area of my doctor. Then a nurse made me strip to my boxers, and I sat for another twenty minutes on a cold table. The bruises were turning dark brown. The doctor poked and made things worse, then pronounced me good for another two weeks.

I arrived at Claire's lawyer's office promptly at four. Jacqueline Hume had first made a ton of money cleaning out wayward doctors, then had created a fierce reputation by destroying a couple of philandering Senators. Her name struck fear into every unhappily married D.C. male with a nice income. I read the separation agreement carefully, signed it, and quickly left.

My fourth stop of the afternoon was Hector Palma's address. According to the phone book, it was an apartment building in Bethesda. Since I was in no hurry and needed to think, I circled the city on the beltway, bumper to bumper with a million others.

I gave myself fifty-fifty odds of being arrested within the week. The firm had no choice but to come after me, and there was enough circumstantial evidence of my theft to convince a magistrate to issue an arrest warrant.

The Mister episode had rattled the firm. Chance must have been called on the carpet, grilled at length by the brass, and it was inconceivable that he admitted any deliberate wrongdoing. He lied, and he did so hoping that he could doctor the file and somehow survive.

Chance needed Hector to keep the truth hidden. Hector needed Chance to protect his job. At some point the partner must have blocked any notion of a polygraph if, in fact, it had ever been seriously considered. If I were Chance, I would have offered cash to Hector and arranged for his quick transfer to one of our other offices at a higher salary.

The apartment complex was long and rambling, new sections added as the sprawl moved northward, away from the city. I parked next to some tennis courts and began a tour of the various units. I took my time; there was no place to go after this adventure. District cops could be lurking anywhere with a warrant and handcuffs. I tried not to think of the horror stories I'd heard about the city jail.

The phone address had not listed an apartment number. I trudged along a sidewalk in search of an office. A security guard stopped me. Once he determined that I posed no threat, he pointed toward the main office, at least a quarter of a mile away.

The night manager was a student eating a sandwich, a physics textbook opened before him. But he was watching the Bullets-Knicks game on a small TV. I asked about Hector Palma, and he pecked away on a keyboard. G-134 was the number.

"But they've moved," he said with a mouthful of food.

"Yeah, I know," I said, ready for this response. "I worked with Hector. Friday was his last day. I'm looking for an apartment, and I was wondering if I could see his."

He was shaking his head no before I finished. "Only on Saturdays, man. There's a waiting list."

"I'm gone on Saturday."

"Sorry," he said, glancing at the game.

I removed my wallet. "How much a month?" I asked.

"Seven-fifty."

I took out a one-hundred-dollar bill, which he immediately saw. "Here's the deal. Give me the key. I'll take a look at the place and be back in ten minutes. No one will ever know."

Dropping the sandwich onto a paper plate, he found the key in a locked drawer and grabbed the money. "Ten minutes," he said.

The apartment was nearby, on the ground floor. The smell of fresh paint escaped through the door before I went inside.

A team of fingerprinters could not have found a trace of the Palma clan. All drawers, cabinets, and closets were bare. Every room had a fresh coat of dull white. The place was sterile.

I returned to the office and tossed the key on the counter.

"How about it?" he asked.

"Too small," I said. "But thanks anyway."

"You want your money back?"

"Are you in school?"

"Yes."

"Then keep it."

"Thanks."

I stopped at the door and asked, "Did Palma leave a forwarding address?"

"I thought you worked with him," he said.

"Right," I said, and quickly closed the door behind me.

CHAPTER NINE

THE little woman was sitting against our door when I arrived for work Wednesday morning. It was almost eight; the office was locked; the temperature was below freezing. When she saw me approach, she jumped to her feet and said, "Good morning."

I smiled, said hello, and started fumbling keys.

"Are you a lawyer?" she asked.

"Yes, I am."

"For people like me?"

I assumed she was homeless, and that was all we asked of our clients. "Sure. Be my guest," I said as I opened the door. It was colder inside than out. I adjusted a thermostat—one that, as far as I had been able to determine, was connected to nothing. I made coffee and found some stale doughnuts in the kitchen. I offered them to her, and she quickly ate one.

"What's your name?" I asked. We sat in the front, next to Sofia's desk, waiting for the coffee and praying for heat.

"Ruby Simon."

"I'm Michael Brock. Where do you live, Ruby?"

"I sleep in the back of a car." She was dressed in a gray Georgetown Hoya sweat suit, thick brown socks, dirty white sneakers. She was between thirty and forty, rail thin, and slightly cockeyed.

I poured two large paper cups of coffee, and we retreated to my office, where, mercifully, the radiator was alive and gurgling. Ruby sat on the edge of my brown folding client's chair, her shoulders slumped, her entire upper body wrapped around the cup of coffee, as if it might be the last warm thing in life.

"What can I do for you?" I asked, armed with a legal pad.

"It's my son, Terrence. He's sixteen. They've taken him away."

"Who took him?"

"The city, the foster people."

"Where is he now?"

"They got him." Her answers were short, nervous bursts.

"Why don't you relax and tell me about Terrence?" I said.

And she did. With no effort at eye contact, she zipped through her narrative. Several years earlier, when Terrence was around ten, they were living alone in a small apartment. She was arrested for selling drugs and went to jail for four months. Terrence went to live with her sister. Upon her release she collected Terrence, and they began a nightmare existence living on the streets. They slept in cars, squatted in empty buildings, and retreated to the shelters when it was cold. She begged on the sidewalks; she did whatever it took to keep Terrence fed, in decent clothes, and in school.

But she was an addict and couldn't kick the crack. The city began asking questions about him, and mother and child slid deeper into the shadows of the homeless. Out of desperation she went to a family she had once worked for as a maid, the Rowlands, a couple whose children were grown and away from home. They had a warm little house near Howard University. She offered to pay them fifty dollars a month if Terrence could live with them. There was a small bedroom above the back porch, one she'd cleaned many times, and it would be perfect for Terrence. The Rowlands hesitated at first but finally agreed. They were good people back then. Ruby was allowed to visit Terrence for an hour each night. His grades improved. He was clean and safe, and Ruby was pleased with herself.

She rearranged her life around his: new soup kitchens and dinner programs closer to the Rowlands, different shelters. She scraped together the money each month and never missed a nightly visit with her son. Yet she was unable to stop using crack.

Ruby began crying at that point in her story. As I made some notes, I heard Mordecai and Sofia arrive in the front room.

It had been three years now, continued Ruby. Terrence was an A student, excellent in math and Spanish, a trombone player, and an actor in school dramas. He was dreaming of the Naval Academy.

She had arrived one night recently for a visit in bad shape. A fight started when Mrs. Rowland confronted her. Harsh words were exchanged, ultimatums thrown down. Either she would get help or she would be banned from the house. Ruby declared that she would simply take her boy and leave. Terrence said he wasn't going anywhere.

The next night a social worker from the city was waiting for her with paperwork. Someone had already been to court. Terrence was being taken into foster care. The Rowlands would be his new parents. Visitation would be terminated until she underwent rehab and was clean for a period of sixty days.

Three weeks had passed.

"I want to see my son," she said. "I miss him so bad."

"Are you in rehab?" I asked.

She shook her head quickly and closed her eyes.

"Why not?" I asked.

"Can't get in."

I had no idea how a crack addict off the street got admitted to a recovery unit, but it was time to find out. In a city where five hundred families waited for a small space in an emergency shelter, there couldn't be many beds available for drug addicts.

"This will take some time, Ruby. You won't see Terrence until you're drug free," I said, trying not to sound pious.

Her eyes watered, and she said nothing.

She had no paperwork, no address, no identification, nothing but a heartbreaking story. She seemed perfectly content sitting in my chair, and I began to wonder how I might ask her to leave.

Sofia's shrill voice brought back reality. There were sharp voices around her. I raced for the door and saw that Lieutenant Gasko was back, again with plenty of help. Three uniformed cops were approaching Sofia, who was protesting loudly but to no avail. As I walked out of my office, Mordecai walked out of his.

"Hello, Mikey," Gasko said to me.

"What the hell is this!" Mordecai growled, and the walls shook. One of the cops actually reached for his revolver.

"It's a search," Gasko said, pulling out the required papers and flinging them at Mordecai.

"The file's not here," I yelled at Gasko.

"Haven't seen your lawsuit," Gasko said. "Lotta big talk."

"It's not here," I said. "You're wasting your time."

"Then we'll just have to waste it, won't we?"

I tried to say something lawyerly and bright, some piercing legal nugget that would stop the search cold and send the cops running. But words failed me. Instead, I was embarrassed at having brought the police to nose through the clinic. I asked Ruby to leave, then locked the front door so our clients wouldn't see the search.

"Here's the way we'll do it," Mordecai announced. The cops glared, but they were anxious for some direction. Searching a law office was quite unlike raiding a bar filled with minors. "The file isn't here, okay. We'll start with that premise. You can look at all the files you want, but you can't open them. That would violate client confidentiality. Agreed?"

The other cops looked at Gasko, who shrugged.

We started in my office—all crammed into the tiny room, working hard at avoiding contact. I removed each file from my cabinets, waved them under Gasko's nose, and returned them to their places. I'd only been there since Monday, so there wasn't much to search.

Mordecai slipped from the room and went to Sofia's desk, where he used the phone. When Gasko declared my office to be officially searched, we left it, just in time to hear Mordecai say into the receiver, "Yes, Judge, thank you. He's right here."

His smile showed every tooth as he thrust the phone at Gasko. "This is Judge Kisner, the gentleman who signed the search warrant. He would like to speak to you."

Gasko took the phone as if it were owned by a leper. "This is Gasko," he said, holding it inches from his head.

Mordecai turned to the other cops. "Gentlemen, you may search this room, and that's it. Judge's orders."

Gasko mumbled, "Yes sir," and hung up.

We monitored their movements as they went from desk to desk.

After a few minutes they realized the search was futile, and so they left without saying good-bye. I apologized to Sofia and Mordecai for the intrusion and retreated to my office.

NUMBER five on the list of evictees was Kelvin Lam, a name vaguely familiar to Mordecai, who worked the phones, calling around the shelters. After dark we drove downtown to a church wedged between high-priced office buildings and ritzy hotels. In the large basement the Five Loaves dinner program was in full swing.

"I haven't been here in years," Mordecai said as we stood by the entrance, looking down at the crowded dining area. "Isn't it wonderful? They collect excess food from local restaurants—not leftovers, but uncooked food that will simply go bad if not used immediately. They have a fleet of refrigerated trucks, and they run all over the city collecting food, which they take to the kitchen and prepare."

A young lady named Liza came up to us. She was new at Five Loaves. Mordecai had known her predecessor, whom they talked about briefly. Liza did not know Kelvin Lam, but she would ask around. We watched her as she moved through the crowd, speaking to the people at one table, then another.

Soon she was back. "Kelvin Lam is in the rear," she said, nodding. "Second table from the back. Wearing a Redskins cap."

"Is there a small room we can use?"

"Sure."

"Tell Lam a homeless lawyer needs to talk to him."

When Lam showed up, he didn't say hello. Mordecai sat at a table. I stood in a corner. Lam took the other chair.

"Nothing's wrong," Mordecai said in his best soothing tone. "We need to ask you a few questions, that's all."

Not a peep out of Lam.

"Do you know a woman named Lontae Burton or a man named DeVon Hardy?" Mordecai asked.

Lam shook his head no.

"Last month were you living in an abandoned warehouse at the corner of New York and Florida?"

"Uh-huh."

"Were you paying rent?"

"Yep. A hundred dollars a month. Cash."

"To Tillman Gantry?"

Lam closed his eyes. "I paid rent to some dude named Johnny."

"Who did Johnny work for?"

"Don't know. Don't care. Didn't ask."

"How long did you live there?"

" 'Bout four months. Got evicted."

"Who evicted you?"

"I don't know. The cops showed up one day with some other dudes. They yanked us and threw us on the sidewalk."

"Did you explain to the cops that you were paying rent?"

"A lot of people were saying that. This one woman with little kids tried to fight with the police. It was a bad scene, man."

"Were you given any written notice before the eviction?"

"No. Nothing. They just showed up. Cops said we were just squatters, had to get out right then."

"Did you know the other people in the warehouse?"

"I knew a couple. Herman Harris and Shine somebody."

"Where are they now?"

"I haven't seen them."

"Where are you staying?"

"CCNV."

Mordecai pulled a business card from his pocket and handed it to Lam. "Can you keep in touch with me?" he asked.

"Why?"

"You might need a lawyer. Just call me if you change shelters or find a place of your own."

Lam took the card without a word. We thanked Liza and returned to the office.

AS WITH any lawsuit there were a number of ways to proceed with our action against the three defendants—RiverOaks, Drake & Sweeney, and TAG.

The first method was the ambush. The other was the serve and volley.

With the ambush, we would prepare the skeletal framework of our allegations, run to the courthouse, file the suit, leak it to the press, and hope we could prove what we thought we knew. The advantage was surprise and embarrassment for the defendants. The downside was the legal equivalent of jumping off a cliff with the strong but unconfirmed belief that there was a net down there somewhere.

The serve and volley would begin with a letter to the defendants in which we would make the same allegations, but rather than sue, we would invite them to discuss the matter. The letters would go back and forth, and if liability could be proved, a quiet settlement would probably occur. Litigation could be avoided.

The ambush appealed to Mordecai and me for two reasons. Arthur on the top floor of the firm and Rafter and his band of litigators had shown no interest in leaving me alone; the two searches were clear proof of that. My arrest would make a nice news story, one they would undoubtedly leak to humiliate me and build pressure.

The second reason went to the heart of our case. Hector and the other witnesses could not be compelled to testify until we filed suit and forced them to give their depositions. We would be able to depose anybody we wanted—Hector Palma, other evictees. If we could find them.

In theory our case was really quite simple: The warehouse squatters had been paying rent, in cash with no records, to Tillman Gantry or someone working on his behalf. Gantry had an opportunity to sell the property to RiverOaks, but it had to be done quickly. Gantry lied to RiverOaks and its lawyers about the squatters. Drake & Sweeney, exercising diligence, had sent Hector Palma to inspect the property prior to closing. Hector was mugged on the first visit, took a guard with him on the second, and upon inspecting the premises, learned that the residents were, in fact, not squatters, but tenants. He reported this in a memo to Braden Chance, who made the ill-fated decision to disregard it and proceed with the closing. The tenants were summarily evicted as squatters, without due process.

A formal eviction would have taken at least thirty more days, time none of the participants wanted to waste. Thirty days, though, and the worst of winter would have been gone.

It was not a complicated case, in theory. But the hurdles were enormous. Hector Palma had to be found. Then we somehow had to convince him either to produce the hidden memo or to tell us what was in it. Finding him would be the easy part; getting him to talk might be impossible. He quite likely wouldn't want to, since he needed to keep his job. He had a wife and four kids.

Mordecai and I had settled ourselves at the desk next to Sofia's, where the aging computer worked most of the time. I was typing, Mordecai pacing and dictating. We plotted until midnight, drafting and redrafting the lawsuit, arguing theories, discussing procedure, dreaming of ways to haul RiverOaks and my old firm into court for a noisy trial. Mordecai saw it as a watershed, a pivotal moment to reverse the decline in public sympathy for the homeless. I saw it simply as a way to correct a wrong.

COFFEE again with Ruby the next morning. She was waiting by the front door when I arrived at seven forty-five, happy to see me. How could anyone be so cheerful after spending eight hours trying to sleep in the back seat of an abandoned car?

"Got any doughnuts?" she asked as I was flipping on the lights.

"I'll see. You have a seat, and I'll make us some coffee." I rattled around the kitchen, cleaning the coffeepot, looking for something to eat. Yesterday's stale doughnuts were even firmer, but there was nothing else. She ate one doughnut, nibbling around the hard edges, trying to be polite.

"Where do you eat lunch and dinner?" I asked.

"Lunch is at Naomi's. I stay there during the day. For dinner I go to Calvary Mission over on Fifteenth Street."

"Is that Naomi's Women's Center on Tenth Street? That's only for homeless women, right?"

"Yeah, that's right. They want me to go to meetings for drunks and people on dope."

She was curled around her paper cup again, trying to keep her frail body warm.

"Did you get high last night?" I asked. The words echoed in my ears. I found it hard to believe I was asking such questions.

Her chin fell to her chest; her eyes closed.

"Tell me the truth," I said.

"I had to. I do it every night."

I wasn't about to scold her. I had done nothing since the day before to help her find treatment. It suddenly became a priority.

She asked for another doughnut. I wrapped the last one in foil. She was late for something at Naomi's, and off she went.

DINNER that night was a taco and a beer in a chain restaurant. The crowd was dominated by young government workers, all talking policy and politics while drinking draft beer and yelling at a game.

Loneliness was an adjustment. My wife and friends had been left behind. At the age of thirty-two I was ill prepared for the single life. As I watched the game and the women, I asked myself if I was expected to return to the bar scene to find companionship. Surely there was some other way. I got dejected and left.

I drove slowly home, not anxious to arrive at my apartment. My name was on a lease, in a computer somewhere, and I figured the police could find my loft without too much trouble. If they were planning an arrest, I was certain it would happen at night. They would enjoy terrifying me with a midnight knock on the door, a little roughing up as they frisked me and slapped on the cuffs, throwing me into a holding cell with the usual assortment of thugs, and leaving me there to fend for myself.

I carried with me two things, regardless of what I was doing. One was a cell phone with which to call Mordecai as soon as I was arrested. The other was a folded stack of bills—twenty hundred-dollar bills—to use to make bail and hopefully spring myself before I got near the holding cell.

I parked two blocks away from my building and watched every

empty car for suspicious characters. I made it to the loft, untouched, unapprehended.

My living room was now furnished with two lawn chairs and a plastic storage box used as a coffee table and footstool. The television was on a matching storage box. I was amused at the sparse furnishings and determined no one would see how I was living.

I punched Claire's number on the phone. We had not talked in several days, and I thought I'd show some civility and break the ice.

After the third ring a male voice reluctantly said, "Hello."

For a second I was too stunned to speak. It was eleven thirty on a Thursday night. Claire had a man over. I almost hung up but then collected myself and said, "Claire, please."

"Who's calling?" he asked gruffly.

"Michael, her husband."

"She's in the shower," he said with a trace of satisfaction.

"Tell her I called," I said, and hung up as quickly as possible. The marriage was over, plain and simple.

THE next morning I bought a box of a dozen assorted at a Krispy Kreme, with two tall coffees and a newspaper. Ruby was waiting faithfully at the office door, shivering from the cold. Her eyes were redder than usual; her smile was not as quick.

I cleared the top of a desk in the front and served the coffee and doughnuts. She didn't like chocolate, but instead preferred the ones with the fruit filling.

"Do you stay in the car when it gets real cold?" I asked.

"Yes."

"How do you keep from freezing?"

"I got plenty of blankets. I just bury down in them."

"You never go to a shelter?"

"Never."

"Would you go to a shelter if it would help you see Terrence?"

She rolled her head to one side and gave me a strange look. "Say it again," she said.

"If you want to see Terrence, you have to get clean. To get clean, you'll have to live in a detox center for a while. Is that something you're willing to do?"

"Maybe," she said. "Just maybe."

It was a small step, but not an insignificant one.

"I can help you see Terrence again, and you can be a part of his life. But you have to get clean and stay clean."

"How do I do it?" she asked, her eyes unable to meet mine. She cradled her coffee, the steam rising to her face.

"Are you going to Naomi's for lunch today?"

"Yes."

"I talked to the director over there. They have two meetings today, alcoholics and drug addicts together, called AA/NA. I want you to attend both of them. The director will call me."

She nodded like a scolded child. I would push no further, not at that moment. She nibbled her doughnuts, sipped her coffee.

A soft freezing rain began falling, so I drove Ruby to Naomi's, a four-level row house on Tenth Street, N.W. The center provided food, showers, and counseling for any homeless woman who could find the place. Ruby was a regular and received a warm greeting from her friends when we entered.

I spoke quietly with the director, a young woman named Megan. We conspired to push Ruby toward sobriety. Half the women there were mentally ill; half were substance abusers. When I left, they were all crowded into the main room, singing songs.

I WAS hard at work at my desk when Sofia knocked on my door.

"Mordecai says you're looking for someone," she said. She held a legal pad, ready to take notes.

I thought, then remembered Hector. "Oh yes, I am."

"I can help. Tell me everything you know about the person." She sat down and began writing as I rattled off his name, last known address and place of employment, physical description, and the fact that he had a wife and four kids.

I couldn't think of anything else about him. She left and returned to her desk. I kept my door open so I could listen. The first call went to someone with the Postal Service. The conversation changed to Spanish, and I was lost. One call followed another.

An hour later she walked to my door and announced, "They moved to Chicago."

"How did you . . . ?" I stared at her in disbelief.

"Don't ask."

Drake & Sweeney had more than a hundred lawyers in its Chicago branch. I had been there twice on antitrust cases. The offices were in a skyscraper near the lakefront. The building's foyer was several stories tall, with fountains and shops around the perimeter, escalators zigzagging upward. When the time came, it would be the perfect place to hide and watch for Hector Palma.

CHAPTER TEN

"THE police are out there," one of our clients said to Sofia on Friday afternoon. She walked to the front door, looked down Q, and there she saw what appeared to be an unmarked police car. She waited half an hour, checked it again, then went to Mordecai.

I was oblivious because I was fighting with the food stamp office. Mordecai and Sofia delivered the news together.

"The cops might be waiting," Mordecai announced solemnly.

My first reaction was to duck under the desk, but of course, I did not. I tried to appear calm. "Where?" I asked.

"At the corner. They've been watching the building."

"I've called," Sofia said. "And there's a warrant for your arrest. Grand larceny."

A felony! Prison! Thrown into the pit. I shifted weight from one side to another, and I tried my best to show no fear.

"That's no surprise," I said. "Let's get it over with."

A quick game plan was devised. Sofia would call a bail bondsman, who would meet us at the jail. Mordecai would try to find a friendly judge. What was not said was the obvious—it was Friday afternoon. I might not survive a weekend in the city jail.

They left to make their calls, and I sat at my desk, petrified, unable to think or do anything but listen for the squeaking of the front door. I didn't have to wait long. At precisely four p.m. Lieutenant Gasko entered with a couple of his men behind him.

He was swaggering like an aging jock, somehow sneering and smiling at the same time, holding yet more papers, folded and just waiting to be slapped against my chest.

"I need to see Mr. Brock," he said to Sofia, and about that time I walked into the front room, smiling.

"Hello, Gasko," I said. "Still looking for that file?"

"Nope. Not today."

Mordecai appeared from his office. Sofia was standing at her desk. "You got a warrant?" Mordecai asked.

"Yep. For Mr. Brock here," Gasko said.

I shrugged and said, "Let's go." I moved toward Gasko. One of the goons unsnapped a pair of handcuffs from his waist.

"I'm his lawyer," Mordecai said. "Let me see that." He took the arrest warrant from Gasko and examined it as I was getting cuffed, hands behind my back, wrists pinched by cold steel.

"Where will he go?" Mordecai asked.

"Central."

"I'll follow you there," Mordecai said to me. Sofia was on the phone, and that was even more comforting than knowing that Mordecai would be somewhere behind me.

One of the goons yanked me through the front door toward a dirty unmarked white car. Gasko got into the rear with me. I stayed low in the seat, eyes watching nothing, the shock settling in.

There was an element of relief because it was finally happening. I could stop running and hiding and looking to see if anyone was behind me. And it was not a midnight raid, one that would certainly keep me in jail until morning. With luck I could get processed and bailed out before the weekend rush hit.

But there was also an element of horror, a fear I had never felt in my life. I closed my eyes and tried to get comfortable, which I found impossible to do while sitting on my hands.

THE processing was a blur—surreal movements from one point to the next, with Gasko leading me like a lost puppy. Eyes on the floor, I kept telling myself. Don't look at these people. Inventory first, everything from the pockets, sign a form. Down the dirty hall to photos, shoes off, up against the measuring tape. Look at the camera. Then a profile. Then to fingerprinting.

No phone calls were needed. My lawyer was somewhere close by. The doors got heavier as we descended into the jail. We were going in the wrong direction; the street was back behind us.

"Can't I make bail?" I finally asked. I saw bars ahead.

"I think your lawyer's working on it," Gasko said.

He gave me to a Sergeant Coffey, who pushed me against a wall, kicked my legs apart, and frisked me as if searching for a dime. Finding none, he pointed and grunted at a metal detector, which I walked through without offense. A buzzer, a door slid open, a hallway appeared, one with rows of bars on both sides. A door clanged behind me, and my prayer for an easy release vanished.

Hands and arms protruded through the bars into the narrow hall. The men watched us as we moved past. Coffey looked into each cell. We stopped at the third one on the right.

My cellmates were black, all much younger than I was. I counted four at first, then saw a fifth lying on the top bunk. There were two beds, for six people. The cell was a small square with three walls of nothing but bars, so I could see the prisoners next door and across the hall. The rear wall was cinder block, with a small toilet in one corner.

Coffey slammed the door behind me. The guy on the top bunk sat up and swung his legs over the side, so that they dangled near the face of a guy sitting on the bottom bunk. All five glared at me as I stood by the door, trying to appear calm and unafraid, trying desperately to find a place to sit on the floor. The front of the cell would be safer than the rear. I ignored their eyes and took my spot on the floor, my back resting on the door. Down the hall someone was yelling for a guard.

A fight broke out two cells away. Other voices encouraged them, and the entire wing grew rowdy. A shrill whistle, a door opened, and Coffey was back, nightstick in hand. The fight ended abruptly. Coffey went to the cell and inquired as to what happened. No one knew; no one had seen a thing.

"Keep it quiet!" he demanded, then left.

Minutes passed. One of my cellmates got to his feet and walked to where I was sitting. His bare feet touched my leg. I glanced up, then away. He glared down, and I knew this was the end.

"Nice jacket," he said.

"Thanks," I mumbled. The jacket was an old navy blazer. It certainly wasn't worth being slaughtered over.

"Nice jacket," he said again, and he added a slight nudge with his foot. The guy on the top bunk jumped down and stepped closer for a better look.

"Thanks," I said again.

The first punk was eighteen or nineteen, lean and tall, and anxious to impress the others with his bravado.

"I don't have a jacket that nice," he said. A firmer nudge.

I pulled my feet in so that my knees were close to my chin. It was a defensive position. When he kicked or swung, I was not going to fight back. Resistance would bring in the other four.

"Dude says you got a nice jacket," said his friend.

A third one stepped forward and closed the semicircle around me. The first one kicked my foot, and all inched closer. I quickly removed my blazer and thrust it forward.

"Is this a gift?" the first one asked, taking it.

"It's whatever you want it to be," I said. I was looking down, still avoiding eye contact; thus I didn't see his foot. It was a vicious kick that slapped my left temple and jerked my head backward, where it cracked against the bars. "All right! All right!" I yelled as I felt the back of my head. "You can have it."

"Is it a gift?"

"Yes."

"Thanks, man."

"Don't mention it," I said. My entire head was numb.

They backed away, leaving me curled in a tight ball.

Minutes passed, though I had no concept of time. My face throbbed, but there was no blood. If I received no further injuries as an inmate, I would consider myself lucky. I began to ponder what the night might bring. Six inmates, two very narrow beds. Were we expected to sleep on the floor, with no blanket and pillow? The floor was getting cold.

"Nice shoes," a voice said, startling me. I looked up to see another one of them standing above me. He wore dirty white socks, no shoes. The shoes in question were my old Nike tennis shoes.

"Would you like to have them?" I said. I immediately began unlacing them. "Here, I would like to present you with a gift of my shoes." I quickly kicked them off, and he took them.

MORDECAI finally broke through around seven p.m. Coffey fetched me from the cell, and as we made our way toward the front, he asked, "Where are your shoes?"

"In the cell," I said. "They were taken. A navy blazer too."

"I'll get them." He looked at the left side of my face where the corner of my eye was beginning to swell. "Are you okay?"

"Wonderful. I'm free."

My bail was ten thousand dollars. I paid the bondsman a thousand in cash and signed the paperwork. Coffey brought my shoes and blazer, and my incarceration was over. Sofia waited outside with her car, and she whisked me away.

STRICTLY in physical terms I was paying a price for my journey from the tower to the street. The bruises from the car wreck were almost gone, but the soreness in the joints would take weeks. My back ached from sleeping on the floor. And then a street punk almost cracked my skull with his foot. Every time I awoke during the night, my head seemed to be expanding. But I felt lucky to be in one piece after descending into hell for a few hours. The fear of the unknown had been removed, at least for the present. There were no cops lurking in the shadows.

Grand larceny was nothing to laugh at, especially since I was guilty. The maximum was ten years in prison. I would worry about it later.

I left my apartment just before sunrise Saturday, in a rush to find the nearest newspaper. My new neighborhood coffee shop was a tiny all-night bakery run by a rowdy family of Pakistanis. I sidled up to the counter and ordered a large latte. Then I opened the newspaper and found the one little story I'd lost sleep over.

My friends at Drake & Sweeney had planned it well. On page 2 of Metro, there was my face, in a photo taken a year earlier for a recruiting brochure the firm had developed. LOCAL ATTORNEY ARRESTED FOR GRAND LARCENY read the headline.

The story was four paragraphs, to the point, and filled primarily with information fed to the reporter by the firm. I had worked there for seven years, in antitrust, no prior criminal record. No one got quoted, because no quotes were necessary. The sole purpose of the story was to humiliate me, and to that end it worked well.

The Pakistanis didn't bake fruit-filled doughnuts. I bought oatmeal cookies instead and drove to the office.

Ruby was asleep in the doorway, and as I approached, I wondered how long she had been there. She was covered with two or three old quilts and sprang to her feet after I coughed.

I unlocked the door, turned on lights, and went to make coffee. She, according to our ritual, went straight to what had become her desk and waited.

Ruby had walked out of the AA/NA meeting the afternoon before. Megan, the director, had called me.

"How do you feel this morning?" I asked Ruby after I brought the coffee and cookies.

"Fine. And you?"

"Fine. I'm clean. Are you?"

Her chin dropped an inch; her eyes cut to one side. "Yes," she said. "I'm clean."

"No, you're not. Don't lie to me, Ruby. I'm your friend and your lawyer, and I'm going to help you see Terrence. But I can't help you if you lie to me. Now, look me in the eyes and tell me why you walked out of the AA/NA meeting yesterday."

"I thought they was through."

I was not going to be sucked into an argument I couldn't win. "Are you going to Naomi's today?"

"Yes."

"Good. I'll take you, but promise me you'll go to the meetings. You'll be the first one in and the last one to leave, okay?"

"Okay." She nodded and took another cookie, her fourth.

As we drove to Naomi's, Ruby suddenly said, "You got arrested, didn't you?"

I almost ran a red light. How could she have heard?

"Yes, I did. How did you know?"

"You hear stuff on the street."

Ah, yes. Forget papers. The homeless carry their own news.

"It's a misunderstanding," I said, as if she cared.

They'd started singing without her; we could hear them as we walked up the steps to Naomi's. Megan unlocked the front door and invited me into her office for coffee. As soon as I sat down, she tossed a copy of the *Post* into my lap.

"Rough night, huh?" she said with a smile.

I looked at my photo again. "It wasn't too bad."

"What's this?" she asked, pointing to her temple.

"My cell partner wanted my shoes. He took them."

"How long were you in jail?"

"Couple of hours. Made it through rehab. Now I'm a new man."

She smiled again, a perfect smile, and our eyes lingered for a second, and I thought, Oh, boy! No wedding ring on her finger. She was tall and a little too thin. Her hair was dark red and cut short and smart, above the ears like a preppy. Her eyes were light brown, very big and round and quite pleasant to gaze into for a second or two. It struck me that she was very attractive, and it seemed odd that I hadn't noticed it sooner.

We swapped bios. Her father was an Episcopal priest in Maryland and a Redskins fan who loved D.C. As a teenager, she had decided to work with the poor. There was no higher calling.

I had to confess I had never thought about the poor until two weeks earlier. She was captivated by the story of Mister and its purifying effects on me.

She invited me to return for lunch to check on Ruby. If the sun was out, we could eat in the garden.

Poverty lawyers are no different from other people. They can find romance in odd places, like a shelter for homeless women.

AFTER a week of driving through D.C.'s roughest sections and spending hours in shelters, I no longer felt the need to hide behind Mordecai. To survive on the streets, I had to jump into the lake and learn to swim.

I had a list of almost thirty shelters where the homeless came and went. And I had a list of the names of the seventeen people evicted, including DeVon Hardy and Lontae Burton. I had many stops to make and little time. I talked to a doctor at the Capitol Clinic, a privately funded walk-in facility for the homeless. The clinic kept a record of every patient. It was Saturday, and on Monday he would have the secretary check the computer files against my list. If there was a match, the secretary would call.

I drank tea with a Catholic priest at the Redeemer Mission off Rhode Island. He studied the names with great intensity, but no bells went off. "There are so many," he said.

I called Megan and begged off lunch. My excuse was that I was across town, with a long list of people yet to see. The truth was that I couldn't tell if she was flirting. She was pretty and smart and thoroughly likable, and she was the last thing I needed.

But Megan had great news. At the morning session of AA/NA, Ruby had vowed to stay clean for twenty-four hours. It had been an emotional scene.

"She needs to stay off the streets tonight," Megan said. "She hasn't had a clean day in twelve years."

I, of course, was of little help. Megan had several ideas.

THE afternoon was as fruitless as the morning, though I did make contacts, swapping cards with folks I'd probably see again.

Kelvin Lam remained the sole evictee we'd been able to locate. DeVon Hardy and Lontae Burton were dead. I was left with fourteen people who had fallen through the cracks.

At four p.m. Ruby met me at the door of Naomi's with a gleaming smile and a fierce hug. She had completed both sessions. Megan had already laid the groundwork for the next twelve hours—Ruby would not be allowed to stay on the streets.

Ruby and I left the city and drove north into Maryland. In a suburban shopping center we bought a toothbrush and toothpaste, soap, shampoo, and enough candy to get through Halloween. We drove a little farther, and on the northern fringe of Bethesda I found a motel advertising single rooms for forty-two dollars a night. I paid with a credit card and left her there with strict instructions to stay in the room with the door locked until I came for her Sunday morning.

SATURDAY night, the first day of March, I had beer and pizza and watched college basketball, alone in my loft and not unhappy.

I decided to check on Ruby. The phone rang eight times before she answered, and I was about to panic. She was enjoying herself immensely, having taken a long shower, eaten a pound of candy, and watched TV nonstop. She had not left the room.

During halftime of the Duke-Carolina game, the cell phone squawked and startled me. A pleasant female voice said, "Hello, jailbird." It was Claire, without the edge.

"Hello," I said, muting the television.

"You okay?"

"Just doing great. How about you?"

"Fine. I saw your smiling face in the paper this morning, and I was worried about you."

"It was an experience," I said, then told her the entire story, beginning with Gasko and ending with my release.

"How serious are the charges?" she asked.

"Grand larceny carries up to ten years," I said gravely. I liked the prospect of her being concerned. "But I'm not worried."

"Could you lose your license to practice?"

"Yes. If I'm convicted of a felony, it would be automatic."

"That's awful, Michael. What would you do then?"

"Truthfully, I haven't thought about it."

We politely inquired about each other's family, and I remembered to ask about her brother, James, and his Hodgkin's disease. His treatment was under way; the family was optimistic.

I thanked her for calling, and we promised to keep in touch. When I laid the cell phone down, I stared at the muted game and grudgingly admitted to myself that I missed her.

SUNDAY morning Ruby was showered and wearing fresh clothing Megan had given her yesterday. Her motel room was on the ground floor. She was waiting for me. She stepped into the sunlight and hugged me tightly. "I'm clean!" she said with a huge smile. "For twenty-four hours I'm clean!"

A couple in their sixties stepped from the room two doors down and stared at us. Who knows what they were thinking.

We returned to the city and went to Naomi's, where Megan and her staff were waiting for the news. A small celebration erupted when Ruby made her announcement.

Megan and I drank coffee in the garden and worked out the next twenty-four hours. In addition to prayer and worship Ruby would get two heavy sessions of AA/NA. But our optimism was guarded. Megan was convinced Ruby would slide as soon as she returned to the streets. She saw it every day.

I was leaving for Chicago at four that afternoon to begin my search for Hector, and I wasn't sure how long I would be away. We decided to take things one day at a time. Megan would drive Ruby to the motel, which I would pay for, and deposit her there for Sunday night. She would retrieve her Monday morning, and we would then worry about what to do next.

"Twenty-four hours is a big step," Megan said. "But there is still a mountain to climb."

She invited me for lunch again. We could eat in her office, just the two of us, and discuss important matters. Her eyes were dancing and daring me to say yes. So I did.

DRAKE & Sweeney lawyers always flew first class; they felt as if they deserved it. My seat on the flight to Chicago was in coach, booked at the last minute and therefore in the dreaded middle. The window seat was occupied by a hefty gentleman whose knees were the size of basketballs, and on the aisle was a smelly youngster of eighteen or so with a jet-black Mohawk. I closed my eyes for two hours and tried not to think about the pompous fools sitting up there in first class, where I once rode.

The trip was in direct violation of my bail agreement—I was not to leave the District without permission of the judge. But Mordecai and I agreed that it was a minor violation, one that would be of no consequence as long as I returned to D.C.

The Chicago branch of Drake & Sweeney had one hundred and six lawyers, third highest after Washington and New York. I made my way from my inexpensive hotel to their building shortly after seven Monday morning. The day was gloomy, with a vicious wind whipping across Lake Michigan. I bought a newspaper to hide behind and found a vantage point at a table in a corner of the ground floor's vast atrium. The escalators crisscrossed to the second level, where a dozen elevators stood waiting.

By seven thirty the ground floor was crawling with people. At eight the escalators were packed with hundreds of lawyers and secretaries, all bundled in heavy coats and looking remarkably similar.

At eight twenty Hector Palma entered the atrium from the south side of the building, stepping hurriedly inside with a swarm of other commuters. He raked his fingers through his wind-tossed hair and went straight for an escalator.

It was definitely Hector. I knew where he was now, and I knew he wouldn't be leaving for the next eight to ten hours. From the second level of the atrium I phoned Megan. Ruby had survived the night; we were now at forty-eight hours and counting. I then called Mordecai to report my finding Hector.

According to last year's Drake & Sweeney handbook, there were three partners in the real estate section of the Chicago office. The building directory in the atrium listed all three on floor number 51. I picked one of them at random: Dick Heile.

I rode the nine-o'clock surge upward to the fifty-first floor and stepped off the elevator into a familiar setting—marble, brass, walnut, recessed lighting, fine rugs.

As I walked toward the busy receptionist, I frowned and tried to look as pained as possible.

"Yes sir," she said with a bright smile between calls.

I gritted my teeth, sucked in air, said, "Yes. I have a nine-o'clock appointment with Dick Heile, but I'm afraid I'm about to be sick. It must've been something I ate. Can I use your rest room?" I clutched my stomach.

The smile vanished as she jumped to her feet and began pointing. "Down there, around the corner, to your right."

I was already moving, bent at the waist as if I might blow up at any second. "Thanks," I managed to say. Around the corner I ducked into the men's rest room and waited.

At the rate her phone was ringing, she would be too busy to worry about me. I was dressed like a big-firm lawyer, so I did not appear to be suspicious. After ten minutes I walked out of the men's room and started down the hall, away from the receptionist. At the first empty desk I grabbed some papers and scribbled as I walked, as if I had important business. My eyes darted in every direction—names on doors, names on desks.

Hector had his own office. I saw him through his half-open door, and I immediately burst in and slammed it behind me.

He jerked back in his chair with both palms up, as if he were facing a gun. "What the . . . !" he said in disbelief.

"Hello, Hector."

His palms fell to his desk, and he actually smiled. "What are you doing here?" he asked.

"I could ask you the same question."

"I'm working," he said. "How'd you find me?"

"It was very easy, Hector. I'm a street lawyer now, savvy and smart. You run again, I'll find you again."

"I'm not running anymore," he said, looking away.

"We're filing suit tomorrow," I said. "The defendants will be RiverOaks, TAG, and Drake and Sweeney. There's no place for you to hide."

"Who are the plaintiffs?"

"Lontae Burton and family. We'll add the other evictees when we find them. You remember Lontae, don't you, Hector? She was the young mother who fought with the cops when you were evicting everyone. You saw it all, and you felt guilty because you knew she was paying rent to Gantry. You put it all in your memo, the one dated January twenty-seventh, and you made sure the memo was properly indexed into the file because you knew Chance would remove it at some point. And he did. And that's why I'm here, Hector. I want a copy of the memo."

"What makes you think I have a copy?"

"Because you're too smart not to copy it. You knew Chance would remove the original to cover himself. But now he is about to be exposed. Don't go down with him."

He was shaking his head.

"If you give me the memo," I said, "I will not tell where it came from."

"I could lie, you know," he said.

"Sure you could. But you won't, because you'll get nailed. It's easy to prove your memo was logged into the file, then removed. You can't deny writing it. Then we have the testimony of the people you evicted. They'll make great witnesses before an all-black jury in D.C."

Every punch landed flush on the jaw, and Hector was on the ropes. He was too honest to lie. He was, after all, the person who had slipped me the list of the evictees and the keys. He had a conscience, and he couldn't be happy hiding in Chicago.

"They'll fire me, you know."

"Maybe, but you'll have a beautiful lawsuit against them. I'll handle it for you, and I won't charge you a dime."

There was a knock on his door. It scared both of us.

"Yes," Hector said, and a secretary put her head in.

"Mr. Peck is waiting," she said.

"One minute," he said, and she closed the door. He then turned to me. "I have to go."

"I'm not leaving without a copy of the memo."

"Meet me at noon by the fountain in front of the building."

"I'll be there."

I winked at the receptionist as I passed through the foyer. "Thanks," I said. "I'm much better."

"You're welcome," she said.

WE MET, and from the fountain we went west on Grand Avenue to a crowded Jewish deli. As we waited in line to order a sandwich, Hector handed me an envelope. "I have four children," he said. "Please protect me."

I took the envelope and was about to say something, when he stepped backward and got lost in the crowd. I saw him squeeze through the door and go past the deli, his overcoat flapping as he almost ran to get away from me.

I forgot about lunch. I walked four blocks to the hotel, checked out, and threw my things into a cab. Sitting low in the back seat, doors locked, cabbie half asleep, no one in the world knowing where I was at that moment, I opened the envelope.

The memo was in the typical Drake & Sweeney format, dated January 27, sent to Braden Chance from Hector Palma, regarding the RiverOaks/TAG eviction. On that day Hector had gone to the warehouse with an armed guard, arriving at nine fifteen a.m. and leaving at twelve thirty.

On the west end of the ground level Hector found eleven temporary apartments, all assembled from plywood and Sheetrock. Each place was the same size and had a door with a dead bolt.

On the east end of the building ten units of similar design and construction were found. A crying child drew Hector to one of the doors, and he asked the guard to stand back. A young mother answered his knock. She held a baby; three other children swarmed around her legs. Hector informed her that he was with a law firm, that the building had been sold, and that she would be asked to leave in a few days. She quickly went on the attack. It was her apartment. She rented it from a man named Johnny, who came around on the fifteenth of each month to collect a hundred dollars.

Hector asked if she had any proof that she was paying rent. She found her purse and handed him a scrap of paper, a tape from a grocery-store cash register. On the back someone had scrawled, "Recd frm Lontae Burton, Jan 15, $100 rent."

The memo was two pages long. But there was a third page attached to it, a copy of the scarcely readable receipt. The writing was hurried, the spelling flawed, but it was stunning. I must have made some ecstatic noise, because the cabdriver jerked his head and examined me in the mirror.

At O'Hare I faxed the memo to Mordecai. If my plane crashed, or if I got mugged and someone stole it, I wanted a copy tucked away deep in the files of the 14th Street Legal Clinic.

CHAPTER ELEVEN

AFTER three nights I couldn't afford any more lockdown therapy for Ruby Simon. During a Monday night phone call Megan said it was time for Ruby to return home. If she was going to stay sober, the real test would come on the streets.

At seven thirty Tuesday morning I knocked on Ruby's motel door. There was no answer. I knocked again and again, and tried the knob. It was locked. I ran to the lobby and asked the receptionist to call the room. Again, no answer. No one had checked out. Nothing unusual had been reported.

An assistant manager was summoned, and I convinced her that there was an emergency. The room was empty. The bed was meticulous—no sign of use during the night. Not a single item was out of place, and nothing of Ruby's had been left behind.

I thanked the manager and left. I called Megan to alert her, then fought my way into the city with a million other commuters. At eight fifteen, sitting in stalled traffic, I called the office and asked Sofia if Ruby had been seen. She had not.

THE lawsuit was brief and to the point. The estates of Lontae Burton and her children were suing RiverOaks, Drake & Sweeney, and TAG, Inc., for ten million dollars for the wrongful deaths of the Burtons. The causal connection was obvious. Our clients would not have been living in their car had they not been wrongfully evicted. And they wouldn't have died had they not been living in their car. It was a lovely theory of liability because of its simplicity. Any jury could follow the rationale.

Drake & Sweeney would immediately ask the judge to require me to hand over the file. The judge might very well make me do it, and that would be an admission of guilt. It could also cost me my license to practice law. Further, any evidence derived from anything in the stolen file could be excluded.

Mordecai and I reviewed the final draft Tuesday, and he asked me if I wanted to proceed. To protect me, he was willing to drop the lawsuit entirely. I shook my head.

He signed the pleadings, and we left for the courthouse. He drove, and I read the lawsuit again, the pages growing heavier the farther we went.

Negotiation would be the key. Drake & Sweeney was wrong, though I suspected the firm had no idea how very wrong it was. I imagined Braden Chance was cowering behind his locked door, praying fervently.

But I was wrong too. Perhaps we could meet in the middle somewhere and cut a deal. If not, then Mordecai Green would have the pleasure of presenting the case to a friendly jury one day soon and asking them for big bucks. And the firm would have the pleasure of pushing my grand larceny case to the limit.

Tim Claussen, a pal of Abraham's and a reporter for the *Post,* was waiting outside the clerk's office. We gave him a copy of the lawsuit. He read it while Mordecai filed the original, then asked us questions, which we were more than happy to answer, but off the record.

The Burton tragedy was fast becoming a political hot potato in the District. Blame was being passed around with dizzying speed. The city council blamed the mayor, who blamed Congress. The idea of pinning the whole thing on a bunch of rich white lawyers would make for an astonishing story. Claussen—callous and jaded by years in journalism—couldn't suppress his enthusiasm.

I DID intake at the CCNV shelter, alone. I was amazed at how far I'd come in a week. I had walked into the building a few minutes earlier without the fear of being shot, without thinking of being white. I listened to my clients patiently but efficiently, because I knew what to do. They basically wanted someone to listen to them, and that was my job. I spent four hours counseling. I forgot about the coming battle with Drake & Sweeney. I forgot about Claire, though, sadly, I was finding that easier to do. I even forgot about Hector Palma.

But I couldn't forget about Ruby. Why would she leave a clean motel room with a television and strike out through the city?

She was an addict, and that was the plain and unavoidable answer. Crack was a magnet, pulling her back to the streets. If I couldn't keep her locked away in a suburban motel for three nights, then how was I supposed to help her get clean?

THE routine of late afternoon at the office was shattered by a phone call from my brother, Warner. He was in town, on business, unexpectedly. Could we meet for dinner? He was paying. He'd heard about a great new place called Danny O's—fantastic food!

Danny O's was fine with me. Trendy, loud, overpriced, typical.

I stared at the phone long after our conversation was over. Warner was not in town on business. I was pretty sure my parents had sent him. They were grieving down in Memphis, heartbroken over my sudden fall from the ladder.

We met in the crowded bar at Danny O's. Before we could shake hands or embrace, he took a step backward to inspect the new image: week-old beard, shaggy hair, khakis, everything.

"A real radical," he said with humor and sarcasm.

"It's good to see you," I said, trying to ignore his theatrics.

"You look thin," he said.

"You look great," I said. And he did. Tailored suit and shirt. Expensive tie. I had a closet full of the stuff.

We ordered Heinekens and sipped them in the crowd.

"How's Claire?" he asked.

"I suppose she's fine. We filed for divorce. I've moved out."

"Is she happy?"

"I think she was relieved to get rid of me."

"Has she found someone else?"

"I don't think so," I said. I had to be careful because most, if not all, of our conversation would be repeated to my parents.

"Have you?" he asked.

"Nope."

"So why the divorce?"

"You've been through it, Warner. It's not simple."

The maître d' led us deep into the restaurant. We passed a table where Wayne Umstead was sitting with two men I did not recognize. Umstead had been a fellow hostage, the one Mister had sent to the door to fetch the food. He didn't see me.

A copy of the lawsuit had been served on Arthur Jacobs, chairman of the firm's executive committee, at eleven a.m., while I was at the CCNV. I wondered if Umstead knew.

Fortunately, our table could not be seen from his. I glanced around to make sure no other bad guys were in the restaurant.

Warner ordered martinis for both of us, but I quickly begged off. Just water for me.

With Warner everything was at full throttle—work, play, food, drink, women, travel. As a partner in a large Atlanta firm, he made plenty of money. And he spent a lot.

"Water?" he said in disgust. "Come on. Have a drink."

"No," I protested.

"Wimp," he mumbled. I browsed the menu. He examined every skirt.

His drink arrived, and we ordered. "Tell me about your work," he said, trying desperately to seem interested.

"Why?"

"Because it must be fascinating. You walked away from a fortune. There must be a damned good reason."

"There are reasons, and they're good enough for me." I wasn't sure where Warner was headed with this meeting. To divert him, I said, "I was arrested last week." It worked.

"You what?"

As we ate, I told him the story, stretching it out with every detail because I was in control of the conversation. He was critical of my thievery, but I didn't try to defend it.

"So the Drake and Sweeney bridge has been burned?" he asked.

"Permanently."

"How long can you work for nothing?"

"As long as I can survive."

"So survival is the standard?"

"For now. What's your standard?" It was a ridiculous question.

"Money—how much I make, how much I spend, how much I can stash away so that one day I'll not have to worry."

I had heard this before. Unabashed greed was to be admired. Work hard and make plenty, and somehow society would benefit.

"How much do you have?" I asked.

"When I'm forty, I'll have a million bucks buried in mutual funds. When I'm forty-five, it'll be three million. When I'm fifty, it'll be ten. And that's when I'm walking out. What about you?"

"Well, let's see. I'm thirty-two, got a net worth of five thousand bucks, give or take. When I'm thirty-five, if I work hard and save money, it should be around ten thousand. By the time I'm fifty, I should have about twenty thousand buried in mutual funds."

"That's something to look forward to. Eighteen years of living in poverty."

"You know nothing about poverty. What would you do if someone forced you to work for thirty thousand bucks a year?"

"Kill myself. There's no way I could work that cheap."

"Oh, you could work that cheap, but you couldn't live that cheap."

"Same thing."

"That's where you and I are different," I said.

"Damned right we're different. But how did we become different, Michael? A month ago you were like me. Now look at you—silly whiskers and faded clothes, trying to save humanity. Where'd you go wrong?"

I took a deep breath and enjoyed the humor of his question. He relaxed too. We were too civilized to fight in public.

We became interested in our food, and the conversation waned. Warner had been arrogant enough to think that a blunt confrontation would snap me back to my senses. "I'll talk to him," I could hear him say to my parents.

We said good-bye on the sidewalk in front of the restaurant. I assured him I knew what I was doing, that I would be fine, and that his report to our parents should be optimistic. "Don't worry them, Warner. Tell them everything is wonderful here."

"Call me if you get hungry," he said in an effort at humor.

I waved him off and walked away.

THE Pylon Grill was an all-night coffee shop in Foggy Bottom, near George Washington University. It was known as a hangout for insomniacs and news addicts. The earliest edition of the *Post* arrived each night just before twelve, and the place was as busy as a good deli during lunch. I bought a paper and sat at the bar. I was struck by how quiet the Pylon was. Every person there was buried in the news.

Tim Claussen's story was a natural for the *Post.* It began on page 1, under a bold headline, and was continued on page 10, where the photos were—a photo of Lontae, one of Mordecai, and a set of three others that no doubt would humiliate the blue bloods at Drake & Sweeney. White-haired Arthur Jacobs was in the center, a mug shot of DeVon Hardy was on the left, and on the right was a mug shot of a menacing-looking Tillman Gantry.

I could see the lawyers at my old firm huddled in their conference rooms, doors locked, phones unplugged. They would devise a hundred different strategies, call in public relations people. It would be their darkest hour.

The story was long and thorough. And the reporter was true to his word—Mordecai and I were never referred to by name, only as informed sources. I couldn't have written it better myself.

Not a word from any of the defendants. It appeared as if the reporter made little or no effort to contact them.

Warner called me at five a.m. "Are you awake?" he asked. He'd seen the paper and was in his hotel suite, hyper, bouncing off the walls with a hundred questions about the lawsuit.

Trying to stay warm in my sleeping bag, I listened as he told me exactly how to proceed with the case. Warner was a litigator, a very good one, and the jury appeal of the Burton case was more than he could stand. We hadn't asked for enough in damages—ten million wouldn't cut it. The right jury, and the sky was the limit. Oh, how he'd love to try it himself.

Warner howled with laughter at the sight of old man Jacobs sitting there in the paper with a convict on each side. His flight to Atlanta left in two hours, and he'd be at his desk by nine; he couldn't wait to pass around the photos.

He hung up in the middle of a sentence.

I'd slept for three hours. There had been too many changes in my life to rest comfortably. I showered and left, drank coffee with the Pakistanis until sunrise, then bought cookies for Ruby.

There were two strange cars parked next to our office. I drove by slowly at seven thirty, and my instincts told me to keep going. Ruby was not sitting on the front steps.

If Tillman Gantry thought violence would somehow help his defense of the lawsuit, he wouldn't hesitate to use it, Mordecai had cautioned me. I called him at home and told him what I had seen. He'd arrive at eight thirty, and we agreed to meet then.

Gantry didn't kill us the day after we sued him and his two co-defendants. The office was quite normal. The phones were no busier than usual. The foot traffic was the same. With the lawsuit temporarily set aside, my other cases were easier to concentrate on. I could only imagine the panic in the marbled halls of Drake & Sweeney. There would be no smiles, no gossip by the coffeepot, no jokes or sports talk in the hallways.

The only sad aspect of slandering four hundred lawyers was the inescapable reality that almost all of them were not only innocent of wrongdoing but completely ignorant of the facts. I felt sorry for them—the old-timers who'd built a great firm and trained us well, the guys in my class who would carry on the tradition of excellence, the rookies who had awakened to the news that their employer was somehow responsible for wrongful deaths.

But I felt no sympathy for Braden Chance and Arthur Jacobs and Donald Rafter and his little band of litigators. They had gone for my jugular. Let them sweat.

MEGAN took a break from the rigors of keeping order in a house filled with eighty homeless women, and we went for a short drive through Northwest. She had no idea where Ruby lived, and we didn't really expect to find her. It was, however, a good reason to spend a few minutes together.

"This is not unusual," she said, trying to reassure me. "As a rule, homeless people are unpredictable."

"You've seen it before?"

"I've seen everything. There are more valleys than mountains."

"How do you keep from being depressed?"

"You draw strength from the clients. They are remarkable people. Most were born without a prayer or a chance, yet they survive. They trip and fall, but they get up and keep trying."

We observed the street people. Every beggar came under our scrutiny as we drove slowly by. We walked through parks, looking at the homeless, dropping coins in their cups, hoping we would see someone we knew. No luck.

I left Megan at Naomi's and promised to call later in the day. Ruby had become a wonderful excuse to keep in touch.

THE Congressman was a five-termer from Indiana, a Republican named Burkholder who had an apartment in Virginia but liked to jog in the early evenings around Capitol Hill. He was mildly ambitious, squeaky-clean, a health nut, forty-one years old. He chaired a subcommittee of Ways and Means.

Burkholder was shot early Wednesday evening near Union Station as he jogged alone. He was wearing a sweat suit—no wallet, no cash. There appeared to be no motive. He encountered a street person in some manner, perhaps a collision or a bump, and two shots were fired. One missed the Congressman; the other traveled through his shoulder and stopped very near his neck.

The shooting occurred not long after dark, on a sidewalk next to a street filled with late commuters. It was witnessed by four people, all of whom described the assailant as a male black homeless-looking type, who vanished into the night. The Congressman had been rushed to the hospital, where the bullet was removed during a two-hour surgery and he was pronounced stable.

I saw the story at eleven. I'd been napping in my chair. It was a slow news day in the District, slow until Burkholder got shot. The reporter stood shivering in the cold in a live report from the scene of the shooting, four hours after it happened. In the background there were flashing lights of police cars, which the reporter did not notice, but I did.

A sweep was under way. The D.C. police were out in force, cleaning the streets, shoveling the street people into cars and vans and taking them away. Throughout the night they swept Capitol Hill, arresting anyone caught sleeping on a bench, sitting in a park, begging on a sidewalk, anyone who obviously appeared to be without a home.

EARLY the next morning the Pylon Grill was warm and stuffy, a layer of cigarette smoke not far above the tables, the aroma of coffee beans from around the world waiting just inside the door. As usual it was filled with news junkies.

Burkholder was the man of the hour. His face was on the front page of the *Post,* and there were several stories about the man, the shooting, the police investigation. Nothing about the sweep.

A pleasant surprise was waiting in the Metro section. Tim Claussen was evidently a man on a mission. Our lawsuit had inspired him. In a lengthy article he examined each of the three defendants, beginning with RiverOaks. The company was twenty years old, privately held by a group of investors. The value of its holdings was estimated at three hundred and fifty million.

Then on to Drake & Sweeney. Not surprisingly, there was no source of information from within the firm. Phone calls had not been returned. Claussen gave the basics—size, history, a few famous alumni. Partners averaged $910,500 in compensation.

Had I really walked away from that much money?

The last member of the unlikely trio was Tillman Gantry, and his colorful life made for easy investigative journalism. Cops talked about him. A former cellmate from prison sang his praises. A former prostitute remembered the beatings. He operated behind two corporations—TAG and Gantry Group—and through them he owned three used-car lots, an apartment building where two people had been shot to death, a video store, and numerous vacant lots he'd purchased from the city for almost nothing.

Of the three defendants Gantry was the only one willing to talk. He admitted paying eleven thousand dollars for the Florida Avenue warehouse in July of the previous year and selling it for two hundred thousand to RiverOaks on January 31. He got lucky, he said.

The warehouse had always attracted squatters, he said. In fact, he had been forced to run them off. He had never charged rent and had no idea where that rumor originated. His lawyers would mount a vigorous defense.

For the second day in a row the venerable old firm of Drake & Sweeney was maligned as a conspirator with a former pimp.

Tomorrow, the story promised, there would be another installment—a look at the sad life of Lontae Burton. The *Post* reporter was obviously working around the clock. How long would Arthur Jacobs allow his beloved firm to be dragged through the mud?

IT WAS twenty minutes past nine when I arrived with my lawyer downtown at the Carl Moultrie Building. Mordecai knew where we were going. I had never been near the Moultrie Building, home of civil and criminal cases in the District. Inside, the place was a zoo—a lobby packed with anxious people, and four levels of hallways lined with courtrooms.

The Honorable Norman Kisner held court on the first floor, room number 114. A daily docket by the door listed my name with eleven other criminals. Mordecai disappeared into the back, and I took a seat in the second row. I read a magazine and tried to appear utterly bored.

"Good morning, Michael," someone said from the aisle. It was Donald Rafter, clutching his briefcase.

I nodded and managed to say, "Hello."

Rafter was the smartest and meanest of all litigators. I was supposed to shake with fear at the sight of him. He scooted away and found a seat on the other side of the courtroom. He represented the victims and as such had the right to be present at each stage of my proceedings.

At nine thirty Mordecai emerged from behind the bench and motioned for me. The judge was waiting in his chambers. Mordecai introduced me to him, and the three of us settled casually around a small table.

Judge Kisner was at least seventy, with bushy gray hair, a scraggly gray beard, and brown eyes that burned holes as he talked. He and my lawyer had been acquaintances for years.

"I was just telling Mordecai," he said, "that this is a very unusual case."

I nodded in agreement. It certainly felt unusual to me.

"I've known Arthur Jacobs for thirty years. In fact, I know a lot of those lawyers over there. They're good lawyers."

They were indeed. They hired the best and trained them well. I felt uncomfortable with the fact that my trial judge had such admiration for the victims.

"A working file stolen from a lawyer's office might be hard to evaluate from a monetary point of view. It's just a bunch of papers. I'm not accusing you of stealing the file, you understand."

"Yes. I understand." I wasn't sure if I did or not, but I wanted him to continue.

"Let's assume you have the file. If you returned it now, I would be inclined to place a value on it of something less than a hundred dollars. That, of course, would be a misdemeanor, and we could sweep it under the rug. Of course, you would have to agree to disregard any information taken from the file."

"And what if I don't return it? Still assuming, of course."

"Then it becomes much more valuable. The grand larceny sticks, and we go to trial. If the prosecutor proves his case and the jury finds you guilty, I will have to sentence you." The creases in his forehead and the hardening of his eyes left little doubt that sentencing would be something I would rather avoid.

"In addition," he continued, "if the jury finds you guilty of grand larceny, you will lose your license to practice law."

"Yes sir," I said, very much chastised.

Mordecai was holding back, listening, absorbing everything.

"Unlike most of my docket, time is crucial here," Kisner continued. "I'd like to have the criminal matter resolved before your civil case progresses too far. Again, assuming you have the file."

"How soon?" Mordecai asked.

"I think two weeks is sufficient time to make your decision."

We agreed. Mordecai and I returned to the courtroom, where we waited another hour while nothing happened.

Tim Claussen from the *Post* arrived. He saw us sitting in the courtroom but did not venture over. Mordecai moved away from me and eventually cornered him. He explained that there was a lawyer in the courtroom from Drake & Sweeney, Donald Rafter, and perhaps he might have a word for the paper.

Claussen went right after him. Voices could be heard from the back bench where Rafter had been killing time. They left the courtroom and continued their argument outside.

My appearance before Kisner was as brief as expected. I entered a plea of not guilty, signed some forms, and left in a hurry. Rafter was nowhere in sight.

THERE were two stories in the morning *Post,* both prominently displayed and accompanied by photos.

The first was the one promised in yesterday's edition—a long history of the tragic life of Lontae Burton. With its typical aggressiveness and unlimited budget, the paper was doing a splendid job of gathering the facts we would need for our case.

Lontae's mother was sixteen when she was born, the second of three children, all out of wedlock. Lontae grew up in the rough neighborhoods in Northeast, moving from place to place with her troubled mother, who was in and out of jail, and Lontae quit school after the sixth grade. Then her life became predictably dismal. Drugs, boys, gangs, petty crime, the dangerous life on the street. She worked at various minimum-wage jobs and proved to be completely unreliable. Her four children were born by the time she was twenty-one.

In the midst of this sad obituary a glimmer of hope sprang forth. After the last baby arrived, Lontae stumbled into the House of Mary, a women's day center similar to Naomi's, where she met a social worker named Nell Cather.

According to Ms. Cather, in Lontae's last months she was determined to get off the streets and clean up her life. She attended AA/NA meetings at the center and fought her addictions with great courage, though sobriety eluded her. She quickly improved her reading skills and dreamed of getting a job with a steady paycheck to provide for her little family. Ms. Cather eventually found her a job unpacking produce at a large grocery store—twenty hours a week at four dollars and seventy-five cents an hour. She never missed work.

One day last fall she whispered to Nell Cather that she had found a place to live, though it must be kept a secret. As part of her job Nell wanted to inspect the place, but Lontae refused. It wasn't legal, she explained. It was a small two-room squatter's apartment, and she paid a hundred dollars a month in cash.

I wrote down the name of Nell Cather, at the House of Mary, and smiled to myself at the thought of her on the witness stand.

Most homeless women had lost their children, and the more Lontae heard their horror stories, the more determined she became to keep her family together. She studied harder, even learned the basics of a computer.

Then she was evicted, her meager belongings tossed into the street along with her children. Ms. Cather saw her the next day, and she was a mess. The kids were hungry and dirty; Lontae was drunk. The House of Mary had a policy forbidding the entry of any person obviously intoxicated. The director was forced to ask her to leave. Ms. Cather never saw her again; not a word until she read about the deaths in the paper.

As I read the story, I thought of Braden Chance. I hoped he was reading it too, in the early morning warmth of his fine home in the Virginia suburbs. I wanted him to suffer, to realize that his callous disregard for the rights and dignities of others had caused so much misery. I wanted to call him at home, jolt him from his morning coffee, and say, "How do you feel now, Braden?"

The second story was a pleasant surprise, at least from a legal point of view. An old boyfriend of Lontae's had been found, a nineteen-year-old street tough named Kito Spires. His photo would frighten any law-abiding citizen. Kito was an unemployed high school dropout with a criminal record. His credibility would be questioned. But Kito had a lot to say. He claimed to be the father of Lontae's last three children—the twins and the baby. He had been with her off and on over the last three years. He had lived in the warehouse with Lontae and the children. He had helped her pay the rent whenever he could. A dude named Johnny collected rent on the fifteenth of each month. A hundred bucks. Sometime after Christmas, Lontae and Kito had fought and he had left. He knew nothing about the eviction, but he felt it was wrong.

Mordecai and I would find Kito soon. Our witness list was growing, and Mr. Spires might well be our star.

Our lawsuit was getting more press than we could have dreamed of. Meanwhile, with four hundred aggressive lawyers unwilling to keep their opinions to themselves, Drake & Sweeney had to be on the verge of an insurrection. Had I still been there and been faced with a similar scandal in another division of the firm, I would have been raising hell to get the matter settled and out of the press. The option of battening down the hatches and riding out the storm did not exist. The exposé by the *Post* was only a sample of what a full-blown trial would entail. And a trial was a year away.

Drake & Sweeney marketed its image, its public perception. All big firms did. And no firm could take the hammering being inflicted upon my alma mater.

CHAPTER TWELVE

RUBY reappeared on Monday morning with a ferocious appetite for cookies. She was waiting on the doorstep with a smile and a warm hello when I arrived at eight, a bit later than usual. With Gantry out there, I wanted the extra daylight and the increased activity when I got to the office.

She looked the same. I thought perhaps I could study her face and see the evidence of a drug binge, but there was nothing unusual.

Her eyes were hard and sad, but she was in a fine mood. We entered the office together and fixed our spots at the desk.

"How have you been?" I asked.

"Good," she said, reaching into a bag for a cookie. There were three bags, all bought the week before, just for her, though Mordecai had left a trail of crumbs.

"Where are you staying?"

"In a car." Where else? "I sure am glad winter is leaving."

"Me too. Have you been to Naomi's?" I asked.

"No. But I'm going today. I ain't been feeling too good."

"I'll give you a ride."

"Thanks."

The conversation was stiff. She expected me to ask about her last motel visit. I certainly wanted to but thought better of it.

When the coffee was ready, I poured two cups and set them on the desk. She was on her third cookie.

"How about I read you some of the newspaper?" I asked.

"That would be nice."

There was a picture of the mayor on the front page. He was asking for a Justice Department investigation into the deaths of Lontae Burton and family. Had there been civil rights violations? The mayor strongly implied that he thought so, but bring in Justice!

Ruby was fascinated with the Burton story.

On the bottom corner of the front page was a brief story about the Postal Service's decision to halt the bulk-mail project in Northeast Washington. The controversy surrounding the purchase of the warehouse and the litigation were factors in the decision.

RiverOaks had lost its twenty-million-dollar project. RiverOaks would react like any other real estate developer who'd spent almost a million dollars in cash purchasing useless inner-city property. RiverOaks would go after the lawyers who botched the job.

The pressure on the firm swelled some more.

We scanned world events. An earthquake in Peru caught Ruby's attention, and we read about it. On to Metro, where the first words I saw made my heart stop. Under a large photo of Kito Spires was the headline KITO SPIRES FOUND SHOT TO DEATH. The story recounted Friday's introduction of Mr. Spires as a player in the Burton drama, then gave the scant details of his death. No witnesses, no clues, nothing. Just another street punk shot in the District.

"You okay?" Ruby asked, waking me from my trance.

"Uh, sure," I said, trying to breathe again.

"Why ain't you reading?"

Because I was too stunned to read aloud. Tillman Gantry had spoken. Other witnesses from the streets would either remain quiet or disappear after we found them. Killing witnesses was bad enough. What if Gantry came after the lawyers?

"Keep going," Ruby said, again waking me.

We raced through Metro, where there was a story about the street sweeps being conducted by the police in response to the Burkholder shooting. An advocate for the homeless was bitterly criticizing the operation and threatening litigation. Ruby loved the story. She thought it wonderful that so much was being written about the homeless.

I drove her to Naomi's, where she was greeted like an old friend. The women hugged her and passed her around the room, squeezing her and even crying. I spent a few minutes flirting with Megan in the kitchen, but my mind was not on romance.

SOFIA had a full house when I returned to the office. The foot traffic was heavy; five clients were sitting against the wall by nine o'clock. She was on the phone, terrorizing someone in Spanish. I closed my office door and began pulling files. In two weeks I had opened ninety-one of them and closed thirty-eight. I was falling behind, and I needed a morning to catch up. It would not happen.

Sofia knocked, and opened the door. No hello. No excuse me.

"Where is that list of people evicted from the warehouse?" she asked. She had reading glasses perched on the end of her nose.

The list was always nearby. I handed it to her, and she took a quick look. "Bingo," she said.

"What?" I asked, rising to my feet.

"Number eight, Marquis Deese," she said. "I thought that name was familiar."

"Familiar?"

"Yes. He's sitting at my desk. Picked up the other night in Lafayette Square. Got caught in a sweep. It's your lucky day."

I followed her into the front room, where Mr. Deese sat next to her desk. He looked remarkably similar to DeVon Hardy—late forties, grayish hair and beard, thick sunshades, bundled heavily like most homeless in early March. I examined him from a distance as I walked to Mordecai's office to give him the news.

We approached him carefully, with Mordecai in charge of the interrogation. "Excuse me," he said very politely. "I'm one of the lawyers here. Can I ask you some questions?"

Mr. Deese raised his head and said, "I guess so."

"We're working on a case involving some people who used to live in an old warehouse at the corner of Florida and New York," Mordecai explained slowly.

"I lived there," he said. I took a deep breath.

"You did?"

"Yep. Got kicked out."

"Yes, well, that's why we're involved. We think the eviction was wrongful."

"You got that right."

"Did you pay rent?"

"Sure did. To a guy named Johnny. Hundred bucks a month."

Mordecai pulled up a chair and got serious with Mr. Deese. "We'd like to have you as a client," he said.

"Do what?"

"We're suing some people over the eviction. We'd like to represent you and sue on your behalf. We can get you some money."

"How much?"

"I don't know yet. What have you got to lose?"

"Nothing, I guess."

I tapped Mordecai on the shoulder. We excused ourselves and withdrew into his office. "What is it?" he asked.

"In light of what happened to Kito Spires, I think we should record his testimony. Now."

Mordecai scratched his beard. "Not a bad idea. Let's do an affidavit. He can sign it; Sofia can notarize it; then if something happens to him, we can fight to get it admitted."

We finished questioning Marquis Deese in thirty minutes. He thought he knew where two of the other evictees were staying, and he promised to find them.

As Deese was leaving, Mordecai warned him against talking about the lawsuit. I sat at a desk near Sofia and typed a three-page complaint on behalf of our new client, Marquis Deese.

The phone rang a few minutes before noon. Sofia was on the other line, so I grabbed it. "Legal clinic," I said, as usual.

A dignified old voice on the other end said, "This is Arthur Jacobs, attorney, with Drake and Sweeney. I would like to speak to Mr. Mordecai Green."

I could only say, "Sure," before punching the HOLD button. I slowly rose and walked to Mordecai's door.

"What is it?" he said. His nose was buried in a lawbook.

"Arthur Jacobs is on the phone."

We stared at each other for a few seconds; then he smiled. "This could be the call," he said. I just nodded.

He reached for the phone, and I sat down.

It was a brief conversation, with Arthur doing most of the talking. I gathered that he wanted to meet, the sooner the better.

After it was over, Mordecai told me, "They would like to sit down tomorrow and have a little chat about settling the lawsuit."

"Where?"

"At their place. Ten in the morning, without your presence."

I hadn't expected to be invited. "Are they worried?" I asked.

"Of course they're worried. They are very worried."

AFTER another sleepless night, I spent the morning at the Redeemer Mission, counseling clients with all the finesse of one who'd spent years tending to the legal problems of the homeless. Temptation overcame me, and at eleven fifteen I called Sofia to see if she had heard from Mordecai. She had not.

It was difficult to concentrate on food stamps and delinquent fathers when my life was hanging in the balance. I left the shelter when lunch was ready; my presence was far less important than the daily bread.

When I returned to the clinic, Mordecai's car was parked there. He was in his office, waiting for me. I went in and closed the door.

THE meeting had taken place in Arthur Jacobs's personal conference room on the eighth floor, in a hallowed corner of the building I'd never been near. Mordecai was treated like a visiting dignitary by the receptionist and staff. He sat on one side of the table, facing Arthur, Donald Rafter, an attorney for the firm's malpractice insurance carrier, and an attorney for RiverOaks. Tillman Gantry's lawyers had not been invited. If there was a settlement, no one expected Gantry to contribute a dime.

Arthur handled most of the talking from his side of the table, and Mordecai had trouble believing the man was eighty. The facts were not only memorized but instantly recalled.

Arthur began by saying they had been blindsided by the lawsuit—they were rattled and reeling, unaccustomed to the battering they were taking in the press. He spoke very frankly about the distress his beloved firm was suffering. Mordecai just listened.

Arthur pointed out that there were a number of issues involved. He started with Braden Chance and revealed that Chance had been expelled by the firm. He did not withdraw; he was kicked out. Arthur spoke candidly about Chance's misdeeds. He was solely in charge of all RiverOaks matters. He'd probably committed malpractice by allowing the eviction to proceed.

"Probably?" Mordecai said.

Well, okay then, beyond probably. Chance had doctored the file and attempted to cover up his actions. He lied to them, plain and simple, and he was history.

"How did he doctor the file?" Mordecai asked.

Arthur explained that certain papers had been removed.

"Have you seen Hector Palma's memo of January twenty-seventh?" Mordecai asked, and they went rigid.

"No," came the response, delivered by Arthur.

So Chance had, in fact, removed the memo, along with Lontae's receipt, and fed them to the shredder. With great ceremony and relishing every second of it, Mordecai removed from his briefcase several copies of the memo and receipt. He slid them across the table, where they were snatched up by hardened lawyers too terrified to breathe.

There was a long silence as the memo was read.

"May I ask where you got this?" asked Arthur politely.

"That's not important, at least for now."

The lawyers held the copies in disbelief. But they rallied nicely, laying the memo aside as if they could handle it at a later date.

"I guess that brings us to the missing file," Arthur said, anxious to find more solid footing. They had fingerprints. They had the mysterious note that mentioned the keys. I had gone to Chance demanding to see the RiverOaks/TAG file. There was motive.

"But it's all circumstantial," Mordecai said.

"Do you know where the file is?" Arthur asked.

"No."

"We have no interest in seeing Michael Brock go to jail."

"Then why are you pressing criminal charges?"

"Everything's on the table, Mr. Green. If we can resolve the lawsuit, we can also dispose of the criminal matter."

"That's wonderful news. How do we settle the lawsuit?"

Rafter slid over a ten-page summary filled with multicolored graphs and charts, all designed to convey the argument that children and young, uneducated mothers are not worth much in wrongful-death litigation.

With typical big-firm thoroughness the minions at Drake & Sweeney had spent untold hours spanning the nation to survey the latest trends in tort compensation. State by state. City by city. How much were juries awarding for the deaths of preschoolers? Not very much. The national average was forty-five thousand dollars, lower in the South and Midwest, slightly higher in California and big cities.

The estimate of Lontae's lost earnings was quite liberal; Rafter had arrived at the sum of five hundred and seventy thousand dollars. To settle the case, and admitting no wrongdoing whatsoever, the firm generously offered to pay fifty thousand dollars per child, plus the full sum of Lontae's earnings, for a total of seven hundred and seventy thousand dollars.

"That's not even close," Mordecai said. "I can get that much out of a jury for one dead kid." They sank in their seats.

He went on to discredit almost everything in Rafter's pretty little report. He didn't care what juries were doing in Dallas or Seattle and failed to see the relevance. He knew what he could do with a jury here in the District, and that was all that mattered.

"Here in the District" meant only one thing: a black jury.

"We can negotiate," Arthur said. "What figure do you have in mind?"

We had debated what number to first place on the table. We had sued for ten million dollars, but we had pulled the number out of the air. It could've been forty or fifty or a hundred.

"A million for each of them," Mordecai said. The words fell heavily on the mahogany table.

"Five million?" Rafter asked.

"Five million," boomed Mordecai. "One for each victim."

After a silence Arthur reentered the fray by moving to their strongest hand—me. Specifically, my actions in taking the file from Chance's office after being told I couldn't have it. Their position was not negotiable. They were willing to drop the criminal charges if a settlement could be reached in the civil suit, but I had to face disciplinary action on their ethics complaint.

"What do they want?" I asked Mordecai.

"A two-year suspension," he said gravely.

I couldn't respond. Two years, nonnegotiable.

"I told them they were nuts," he said, but not as emphatically as I would have liked.

I kept repeating to myself the words, Two years, two years.

They had actually agreed on nothing, except for a plan to meet again as soon as possible. The last thing Mordecai did was hand them a copy of the Marquis Deese lawsuit. It listed the same three defendants and demanded the paltry sum of fifty thousand dollars for his wrongful eviction. More would follow, Mordecai promised them, until all evictees had been accounted for.

"You plan to provide this to the newspapers?" Rafter asked.

"Why not?" Mordecai said. "It's public record."

"It's just that, well, we've had enough of the press."

"You started it. You leaked the story of Michael's arrest."

"We did not."

"Then how did the *Post* get his photograph?"

Arthur told Rafter to shut up.

LONG after Sofia and Abraham had left, I was sitting in the semi-darkness of my office when Mordecai walked through the door and settled into one of the folding chairs. He had been on the phone all afternoon, so I had stayed away from his office.

"Things are moving faster than we ever thought," he said.

I was listening, with nothing to say.

"Back and forth with Arthur, back and forth with Judge DeOrio. DeOrio's a tough guy, but he's good, fair."

"I think I've heard his name."

"I would hope so. You've practiced law in this city for seven years. Anyway, here's the upshot. We've agreed to meet at one tomorrow in DeOrio's courtroom. Everybody will be there—the three defendants with counsel, me, you."

"Me?"

"Yep. The judge wants you present. He said you could sit in the jury box and watch. And he wants the missing file."

"Gladly."

"He is notorious, in some circles I guess, for hating the press. He's already irritated with the notoriety this case has generated. He's determined to stop the leaks."

"So he wants it settled?"

"Of course he does. He's a judge, isn't he? Every judge wants every case settled. More time for golf."

"What does he think about my end of the case?"

There was a long pause from my friend as he struggled to find words both truthful yet soothing. "He'll take a hard line."

Nothing soothing about that. "What's fair, Mordecai? It's my neck on the line. I've lost perspective."

"It's not a question of fairness. You took the file to right a wrong. It was an honorable act but still a theft."

"Did DeOrio refer to it as a theft?"

"He did. Once."

So the judge thought I was a thief. It was becoming unanimous. I didn't have the guts to ask Mordecai his opinion. He might tell me the truth, and I didn't want to hear it.

He shifted his considerable weight. "I want you to know something," he said soberly. "You say the word, and we'll walk away from this case. We don't need the settlement; no one does really. The victims are dead. Their heirs are either unknown or in jail. I could call Arthur right now and tell him we would drop everything if they would drop everything. He would jump at it."

"The press would eat us alive."

"So? You think our clients care what the *Post* says about us?"

"All right, we walk away," I said. "And what have we accomplished? They get away with murder."

"It's the only way to protect your license to practice law."

"Nothing like a little pressure, Mordecai," I said a bit too harshly. But he was right. It was my mess and only fitting that I make the crucial decisions. Two years was a long time.

Mordecai would be devastated if I suddenly got cold feet. His entire world was helping poor folks pick themselves up. The money meant nothing to him. He wanted a trial, an enormous, noisy production with lights and cameras and printed words focused not on him, but on the declining plight of his people.

"I'm not jumping ship, Mordecai," I said.

"I didn't expect you to."

CHAPTER THIRTEEN

DeORIO'S courtroom was on the second floor of the Carl Moultrie Building, and getting there took us close to Judge Kisner's, where my grand larceny case was awaiting the next step in a cumbersome process. The halls were busy with low-end criminal lawyers, the ones who advertise on TV and bus stop benches. They huddled with their clients, almost all of whom looked guilty of something, and I refused to believe that my name was on the same docket with those thugs.

The timing of our entry was important. We didn't dare flirt with tardiness. DeOrio was a fanatic for punctuality. But I couldn't stomach the thought of arriving early and being subjected to stares and whispers. I also had no desire to be in the room with Tillman Gantry unless His Honor was present. We entered at two minutes before one.

DeOrio's law clerk was passing out copies of the agenda. She directed us to our seats—me to the jury box, where I sat alone and content, and Mordecai to the plaintiff's table next to the jury box.

The defense table was a study in strategic positioning. Drake & Sweeney was clustered at one end, Tillman Gantry and his two lawyers at the other. Acting as a buffer in the center were two corporate types from RiverOaks and three lawyers. The agenda listed thirteen names for the defense.

I expected Gantry, being an ex-pimp, to be adorned with rings on his fingers and bright gaudy clothing. Not so. He wore a handsome navy suit and was dressed better than his lawyers. He was reading documents and ignoring everyone.

I saw Arthur. And Rafter and Nathan Malamud and Barry Nuzzo—three of my fellow ex-hostages. The firm was delivering a subtle message: Every other lawyer terrorized by Mister survived without cracking up. What happened to me? Why was I the weak sister?

The fifth person in their pack was an attorney for an insurance company. Drake & Sweeney was heavily insured against malpractice. Negligence by a firm lawyer would be covered. Willful wrongdoing would not. There would be a nasty fight on the side, out of our view, between Drake & Sweeney and its malpractice carrier. Let 'em fight.

At precisely one Judge DeOrio appeared from behind the bench and took his seat. "Good afternoon," he said gruffly as he settled into place. He adjusted his microphone. "I am informed by my clerk that all parties are now present," he said, glancing at me as if I were just another thief. "The purpose of this meeting is to attempt to settle this case. After numerous conversations yesterday with the principal attorneys, it became apparent to me that a conference such as this, held at this time, might be beneficial. We'll work from the agenda. Mr. Green, you filed the lawsuit. You may proceed. You have five minutes."

Mordecai stood, without notes, hands stuck deep in pockets, completely at ease. In two minutes he stated our case clearly, then sat down. DeOrio appreciated brevity.

Arthur spoke for the defendants. He conceded the factual basis for the case but took issue on the question of liability. He laid much of the blame on the "freak" snowstorm that covered the city and made life difficult for everyone.

He also questioned the actions of Lontae Burton.

"There were places for her to go," Arthur said. "There were emergency shelters open. The night before, she had stayed in the basement of a church, along with many other people. Why did she leave? I don't know, but no one forced her. Shouldn't some of the responsibility rest with the mother? Shouldn't she have done more to protect her little family?"

"Why was she in the street to begin with?" DeOrio asked sharply, and I almost smiled.

Arthur was unfazed. "For purposes of this meeting, Your Honor, we are willing to concede that the eviction was wrongful."

"Thank you."

"You're welcome. Our point is that some of the responsibility should rest with the mother. We may have put her in the street, but she was there for more than a week before the tragedy."

"Mr. Green?"

Mordecai stood, shaking his head as if Arthur were a first-year law student grappling with elementary theories. "These are not people with immediate access to housing, Mr. Jacobs. That's why they're called homeless. You admit you put them in the street, and that's where they died. I would love to discuss it with a jury."

Arthur's shoulders slumped. Rafter, Malamud, and Barry listened to every word, their faces stricken with the notion of Mordecai Green loose in a courtroom with a jury of his peers.

"Liability is clear, Mr. Jacobs," DeOrio said. "You can argue the mother's negligence to the jury if you want, though I wouldn't advise it." Mordecai and Arthur sat down.

The issue of damages was next on the agenda. Rafter went through the motions of submitting the same report on current trends in jury awards and arrived at the same amount, seven hundred and seventy thousand dollars, that they had offered the day before.

"That's not your final offer, is it, Mr. Rafter?" DeOrio asked.

"No sir," Rafter said.

"Mr. Green."

Mordecai stood again. "We reject their offer, Your Honor. The trends mean nothing to me. The only trend I care about is how much I can convince a jury to award, and, with all due respect to Mr. Rafter, it'll be a helluva lot more than what they're offering."

No one in the courtroom doubted him.

He disputed their view that a dead child was worth only fifty thousand dollars. He implied rather strongly that such a low estimation was the result of a prejudice against homeless street children who happened to be black. "You have a son at St. Alban's, Mr. Rafter. Would you take fifty thousand for him?"

Rafter's nose was three inches away from his legal pad.

"I can convince a jury in this courtroom that these little children were worth at least a million dollars each, same as any child in the prep schools of Virginia and Maryland."

It was a nasty shot, one they took in the groin.

Rafter's summary made no provision for the pain and suffering of the victims. The rationale was obvious: They had died peacefully, breathing odorless gas until they floated away. There were no burns, breaks, blood.

Rafter paid dearly for his omission. Mordecai launched into a detailed account of the last hours of Lontae and her children: the search for food and warmth, the snow and bitter cold, the fear of freezing to death, the desperate efforts to stay together, the horror of being stuck in a snowstorm in a rattletrap car, motor running, watching the fuel gauge.

It was a spellbinding performance, given off the cuff with the skill of a gifted storyteller. As the lone juror, I would have handed him a blank check.

Mordecai saved his best for last. He lectured on the purpose of punitive damages—to punish wrongdoers, to make examples out of them so they would sin no more. He hammered at the evils committed by the defendants, rich people with no regard for those less fortunate. Greed had made them ignore the law. A proper eviction would have taken at least thirty more days. It would have killed the deal with the Postal Service. Thirty days and the heavy snows would've been gone; the streets would've been a little safer.

It was the perfect case for the levying of punitive damages, and there was little doubt in his mind a jury would agree with him. I certainly did.

"We'll settle for five million," he said. "Not a penny less."

There was a pause when he finished. DeOrio made some notes, then returned to the agenda. The matter of the file was next. "Do you have it?" he asked.

"Yes sir." Mordecai opened his battered briefcase and removed the file. He handed it to the clerk, who passed it up to His Honor. We watched for ten long minutes as DeOrio flipped through every page. When he was finished, he said, "The file has been returned,

Mr. Jacobs. There is a criminal matter pending down the hall. I've spoken to Judge Kisner about it. What do you wish to do?"

"Your Honor, if we can settle all other issues, we will not push for an indictment."

"Is this agreeable with you, Mr. Brock?" DeOrio said.

You bet it was agreeable with me. "Yes sir."

"Moving right along. The next item is the matter of the ethics complaint filed by Drake and Sweeney against Michael Brock. Mr. Jacobs, would you care to address this?"

"Certainly, Your Honor." Arthur sprang to his feet and delivered a condemnation of my ethical shortcomings. He was not unduly harsh or long-winded. He seemed to get no pleasure from it. Arthur was a lawyer's lawyer, an old-timer who preached ethics and certainly practiced them. He and the firm would never forgive me for my screwup, but I had been, after all, one of them. I was not a criminal, and they had no difficulty in forgetting the grand larceny charge. But I was a lawyer, and as such I should be held responsible. They would not, under any circumstances, withdraw the ethics complaint.

"Mr. Brock," DeOrio said. "Do you have any response?"

I had not prepared any remarks, but I wasn't afraid to stand and say what I felt. I looked Arthur squarely in the eyes and said, "Mr. Jacobs, I have always had great respect for you, and I still do. I was wrong in taking the file, and I've wished a thousand times I had not done it. I was looking for information which I knew was being concealed, but that is no excuse. I apologize to you, the rest of the firm, and to your client RiverOaks."

I sat down and couldn't look at them. Mordecai told me later that my humility thawed the room by ten degrees.

DeOrio then did a very wise thing. He proceeded to the next item, which was the litigation yet to be commenced. We planned to file suit on behalf of Marquis Deese and Kelvin Lam and eventually for every other evictee we could find. There were fifteen potential plaintiffs out there. This had been promised by Mordecai, and he had informed the judge.

"If you're conceding liability, Mr. Jacobs," His Honor said, "then you have to talk about damages. How much will you offer to settle these other fifteen cases?"

Arthur whispered to Rafter and Malamud, then said, "Well, Your Honor, we figure these people have been without their homes for a month now. If we gave them five thousand each, they could find a new place, probably something much better."

"That's low," DeOrio said. "Mr. Green."

"Much too low," Mordecai agreed. "Again, I evaluate cases based on what juries might do. Same defendants, same wrongful conduct, same jury pool. I can get fifty thousand per case easy."

"What will you take?" the judge asked.

"Twenty-five thousand."

"I think you should pay it," DeOrio said to Arthur.

"Twenty-five thousand to each of the fifteen?" Arthur asked, his unflappable demeanor cracking under the assault.

"That's right."

A fierce huddle ensued in which each of the four Drake & Sweeney lawyers had his say. It was telling that they did not consult the attorneys for the other two defendants. It was obvious the firm alone would foot the bill for the settlement.

"We will pay twenty-five," Arthur announced quietly, and three hundred and seventy-five thousand dollars left the coffers of Drake & Sweeney.

The wisdom was in the breaking of the ice. DeOrio knew he could force them to settle the smaller claims. Once the money started flowing, it wouldn't stop until we were finished.

"Gentlemen, we are down to two issues. The first is money—how much will it take to settle this lawsuit? The second is the matter of Mr. Brock's disciplinary problems. It appears as though one hinges on the other. It's at this point in these meetings that I like to talk privately with each side. I'll start with the plaintiff. Mr. Green and Mr. Brock, would you step into my chambers?"

The clerk escorted us into the hallway behind the bench, then down to a splendid oak-paneled office where His Honor was disrobing. "We're making progress," DeOrio said. "I've got to tell you,

Mr. Brock, the ethics complaint is a problem. Do you realize how serious it is?"

"I think so. Suspended for two years."

"No way we're agreeing to a two-year suspension, Judge," Mordecai said.

"How much will you agree to?"

"Six months max. And it's not negotiable. Look, Judge, these guys are scared to death. You know that. They're scared, and we're not. Why should we settle anything? I'd rather have a jury."

"There's not going to be a jury." The judge stepped close to me and studied my eyes. "You'll agree to a six-month suspension?" he asked.

"Yes," I said. "But they have to pay the money."

"How much money?" the judge asked Mordecai.

"Five million. I could get more from a jury."

DeOrio walked to his window, deep in thought, scratching his chin. "I can see five million from a jury," he said.

"I can see twenty," Mordecai said.

"Who'll get the money?" the judge asked.

"It'll be a nightmare to figure out," Mordecai admitted.

"How much in attorneys' fees?"

"Twenty percent. Half of which goes to the Cohen Trust in New York."

The judge snapped around and began pacing again, hands clenched behind his head. "Six months is light," he said.

"That's all we're giving," Mordecai retorted.

"All right. Let me talk to the other side."

OUR private session with DeOrio lasted less than fifteen minutes. For the bad guys it took an hour.

We drank colas on a bench in the bustling lobby of the building, saying nothing as we watched a million lawyers scurry about, chasing clients and justice. Mordecai spoke to a couple of lawyers he knew. I recognized no one. Big-firm lawyers did not spend time in superior court.

The clerk found us and led us back to the courtroom, where all players were in place. Things were tense. DeOrio was agitated. Arthur and company looked exhausted. We took our seats.

"Mr. Green," the judge began, "I have met with the lawyers for the defendants. Here's their best offer: the sum of three million dollars and a one-year suspension for Mr. Brock."

Mordecai had barely settled into his seat, when he bounced forward. "Then we're wasting our time," he said, and grabbed his briefcase. I jumped up to follow him.

"Please excuse us, Your Honor," he said. "But we have better things to do." We started for the aisle between the pews.

"You're excused," the judge said, very frustrated.

We left the courtroom in a rush.

WE WERE unlocking the car when the cell phone rattled in my pocket. It was Judge DeOrio. Mordecai laughed when I said, "Yes, Judge, we'll be there in five minutes." We took ten, stopping in the rest room, walking slowly, using the stairs, giving DeOrio as much time as possible to further pummel the defendants.

The first thing I noticed when we entered the courtroom was that Jack Bolling, one of the three attorneys for RiverOaks, had removed his jacket, rolled up his sleeves, and was walking away from the Drake & Sweeney lawyers. I doubted if he had physically slapped them around, but he looked willing and able.

The huge verdict Mordecai dreamed about would be lodged against all three defendants. Evidently, RiverOaks had been sufficiently frightened by the settlement conference. Threats had been made, and perhaps the company had decided to chip in with some cash of its own. We would never know.

I avoided the jury box and sat next to Mordecai.

"We're getting close," the judge said.

"And we're thinking of withdrawing our offer," Mordecai announced with one of his more violent barks. We had not discussed such a thing, and neither the other lawyers nor His Honor had contemplated it. Their heads jerked as they looked at each other.

"Settle down," DeOrio said.

"I'm very serious, Judge. The more I sit here, the more convinced I am that this travesty needs to be revealed to a jury. We'll have us an old-fashioned spitting contest." He pointed at Arthur and said, "You run to the newspaper; we run to the newspaper."

"Are you finished?" DeOrio asked Mordecai.

"I guess."

"Good. The offer is up to four million."

"If they can pay four million, then they can certainly pay five." Mordecai pointed again, back to Drake & Sweeney. "This defendant had gross billings last year of almost seven hundred million dollars." He paused as the numbers echoed around the courtroom. "Seven hundred million dollars, last year alone." Then he pointed at RiverOaks. "And this defendant owns real estate worth three hundred and fifty million dollars. Give me a jury."

When it appeared that he was silent, DeOrio again asked, "Are you finished?"

"No sir," he said, and in an instant became remarkably calm. "We'll take two million up front—a million for our fees, a million for the heirs. The balance of three million can be spread over the next ten years—three hundred thousand a year, plus a reasonable interest rate."

A structured settlement with an extended payout made sense. Mordecai's latest onslaught was nothing short of brilliant. There was a noticeable relaxing in the Drake & Sweeney group. He had given them a way out.

Jack Bolling huddled with them. Gantry's lawyers watched and listened, but were almost as bored as their client.

"We can do that," Arthur announced. "But regarding Mr. Brock, it's a one-year suspension, or there's no settlement."

I suddenly hated Arthur again. I was their last pawn, and to save what little face they had left, they wanted all the blood they could squeeze. But poor Arthur was not negotiating from a position of power. He was desperate and looked it.

"What difference does it make?" Mordecai yelled at him. "He's agreed to suffer the indignity of surrendering his license. What does an extra six months give you? This is absurd!"

And he was right. It really made no difference, especially for a street lawyer like me—one whose status would remain wonderfully unaffected by a temporary suspension.

I stood and very politely said, "Your Honor, let's split the difference. We offered six months; they want twelve. I'll agree to nine." I looked at Barry Nuzzo, and he actually smiled at me.

If Arthur had opened his mouth at that point, he would've been mugged. Everyone relaxed, including DeOrio. "Then we have a deal," he said, not waiting for confirmation from the defendants.

His wonderfully efficient law clerk pecked away at a word processor, and within minutes she produced a one-page settlement memorandum. We quickly signed it and left.

IF ANY law office in America could absorb five hundred thousand dollars in fees without showing it, it was the 14th Street Legal Clinic. Mordecai wanted new computers and phones, and probably a new heating system. The bulk of the money would be buried in the bank, drawing interest and waiting for the lean times. It was a nice cushion, one that would guarantee our meager salaries for a few years.

If he was frustrated by the reality of sending the other five hundred thousand to the Cohen Trust, he concealed it well. Mordecai was not one to worry about the things he couldn't change. His desk was covered with the battles he could win.

It would take at least nine months of hard labor to sort out the Burton settlement, and that was where I would spend much of my time. Heirs had to be determined, then found, then dealt with when they realized there was money to be had. It would get complicated.

There were two other projects of particular interest to Mordecai. The first was the pro bono program the clinic had once organized. At its peak the program had a hundred lawyers volunteering a few hours a week to help the homeless. He asked me to consider reviving it. I liked the idea; we could make more contacts within the established bar and broaden our base for raising funds.

Fund-raising was the second project. Sofia and Abraham were incapable of effectively asking for money. Mordecai could, but he hated to beg. I was the bright Waspy star who could mingle with all the right professionals and convince them to give.

"With a good plan you could raise two hundred thousand bucks a year," he said.

"And what would we do with it?"

"Hire a couple of secretaries, a couple of paralegals, maybe another lawyer." As we sat in the front after Sofia left, watching it grow dark outside, Mordecai began dreaming. He longed for the days when there were seven lawyers bumping into each other at the clinic. Every day was chaos, but the little street firm had been a force. It helped thousands of homeless people. Politicians and bureaucrats listened to the clinic. It had been a voice that was heard.

"We've been declining for five years," he said. "And our people are suffering. This is our golden moment to turn it around."

EARLY that Friday I was sitting at my desk, happily going about my business, when Drake & Sweeney, in the person of Arthur Jacobs, suddenly appeared at my door. I greeted him pleasantly and cautiously, and he sat in one of the folding chairs. He didn't want coffee. He just wanted to talk.

Arthur was troubled, and I was mesmerized as I listened to the old man.

The last few weeks had been the most difficult of his professional career—all fifty-six years of it. The settlement had given him little comfort. The firm was back on track after the slight bump in the road, but Arthur was finding sleep difficult. One of his partners had committed a terrible wrong, and as a result innocent people had died. Drake & Sweeney would be forever at fault for the deaths of Lontae and her four children. And Arthur doubted if he would ever get over it.

I was too surprised to say much, so I just listened. I wished Mordecai was hearing this.

Arthur was suffering, and before long I felt sorry for him. He was eighty, tired of chasing money, and had been contemplating retirement. "I don't have a lot of years left," he admitted.

He was fascinated by our legal clinic and asked how it operated. He gave me the opening, and I slipped in. Because I couldn't practice law for the next nine months, I told him, the clinic had decided that I should implement a new pro bono volunteer program using attorneys from the big firms in town. The volunteers would work only a few hours a week, under my supervision, and we could reach thousands of homeless people.

Arthur was vaguely aware of such programs. He hadn't performed free work in twenty years, he admitted sadly. But he liked the idea. In fact, the longer we discussed it, the larger the program grew. After a few minutes he was talking openly of requiring all four hundred of his D.C. lawyers to spend a few hours a week helping the poor.

"Can you handle four hundred lawyers?" he asked.

"Of course," I said, without any idea as to how to even begin such a task. But my mind was racing. "I'll need some help, though," I said.

"What kind of help?" he asked.

"What if Drake and Sweeney had a full-time pro bono coordinator within the firm? This person would work closely with me on all aspects of homeless law. Frankly, with four hundred volunteers, we'll need someone on your end."

He pondered this. It sounded good. I plowed ahead.

"And I know just the right person," I said. "He doesn't have to be a lawyer. A good paralegal can do it."

"Who?" he asked.

"Does the name Hector Palma ring a bell?"

"Vaguely."

"He's in the Chicago office, but he's from D.C. He worked under Braden Chance and got pinched."

Arthur's eyes narrowed as he struggled to remember.

"He lived in Bethesda until three weeks ago, when he suddenly moved in the middle of the night. A quickie transfer to Chicago. He knew everything about the evictions, and Chance wanted to hide him. I'm sure he'd love to return to D.C."

"Does he have an interest in helping the homeless?" he asked.

"Why don't you ask him?" I said.

"I'll do that. It's an excellent idea."

The program took shape before our eyes. Every Drake & Sweeney lawyer would be required to handle one case each week. The younger associates would do the intake under my supervision, and once the cases arrived at the firm, they would be assigned by Hector to the other lawyers.

I almost felt sorry for the politicians and bureaucrats at the thought of four hundred Drake & Sweeney lawyers suddenly seized with a fervor to protect the rights of street people.

Arthur stayed almost two hours and then apologized for taking so much of my time. But he was much happier when he left. He was going straight to his office with a new purpose, a man on a mission. I walked him to his car, then ran to tell Mordecai.

MEGAN'S uncle owned a house on the Delaware shore. She described it as a quaint old house, two stories, with a large porch that almost touched the ocean, three bedrooms, a perfect spot for a weekend getaway. It was the middle of March, still cold, and we could sit by the fire and read books.

She slightly stressed the part about three bedrooms, so there would be plenty of space for each of us to have privacy, without matters getting complicated. She knew I was limping away from my first marriage, and after two weeks of cautious flirting, we had both come to realize that things would proceed slowly. But there was another reason for mentioning the three bedrooms.

We left Washington Friday afternoon. I drove. Megan navigated. And Ruby nibbled on oatmeal cookies in the back seat, wild-eyed at the prospect of spending a few days outside the city, off the streets, on the beach, clean and sober.

She had been clean Thursday night. Three nights with us in Delaware would make four. Monday afternoon we would check her into Easterwood, a small women's detox center off East Capitol. Mordecai had leaned heavily on someone there, and Ruby would have a small room with a warm bed for ninety days.

We found the house at dusk. Megan used it once or twice a year. The key was under the front doormat.

I was assigned the downstairs bedroom, which Ruby thought odd. The other two bedrooms were upstairs, and Megan wanted to be near Ruby during the night.

IT RAINED Saturday, a cold, blowing shower that came from the sea. I was alone on the front porch, rocking gently in a swing under a thick blanket, lost in a dreamworld, listening to the waves break below. The door closed, the screen slammed behind it, and Megan walked to the swing. She lifted the blanket and tucked herself next to me. I held her firmly. She was easy to hold.

"Where's our client?" I asked.

"Watching TV."

A strong gust threw mist in our faces, and we squeezed tighter. The chains holding the swing squeaked louder, then faded as we became almost still. We watched the clouds swirl above the water. Time was of no importance.

"What are you thinking?" she asked softly.

Everything and nothing. Away from the city I could look back for the first time and try to make sense of it all. Thirty-two days earlier I had been married to someone else, living in a different apartment, working in a different firm, a complete stranger to the woman I was now holding. How could life change so drastically in a month?

I didn't dare think of the future; the past was still happening.

JOHN GRISHAM

© DEBORAH FEINGOLD

"Before writing this book," says John Grisham, "I had not worried too much about the homeless. And I certainly didn't know anyone who worked with them." To research *The Street Lawyer,* his ninth novel, Grisham repeatedly made the two-hour drive north from his home in Albemarle County, Virginia, to Washington, D.C. There he explored the world of the homeless, interviewing street people, volunteers, and public-interest advocates. And there, in a homeless shelter, he was brought to tears by the sight of a frightened mother and her young children devouring the soup-kitchen meal as if there were no tomorrow. As readers will recognize, a similar family touches the heart of the novel's main character. *The Street Lawyer* marks Grisham's eighth appearance in Reader's Digest books.

Message

in a Bottle
Nicholas Sparks

The powerful currents of the Gulf Stream sweep northward up the Atlantic coast, carrying with them a message of love lost—and the promise of love to come.

"A deeply moving, beautifully written, and extremely romantic love story."

—*Booklist*

Prologue

The bottle was dropped overboard on a warm summer evening, a few hours before the rain began to fall. Like all bottles, it was fragile and would break if dropped a few feet from the ground. But when sealed properly and sent to sea as this one was, it became one of the most seaworthy objects known to man. It could float safely through hurricanes or tropical storms; it could bob atop the most dangerous of riptides. It was, in a way, the ideal home for the message it carried inside, a message that had been sent to fulfill a promise.

Like all bottles left to the whim of the oceans, its course was unpredictable. Winds and currents play large roles in any bottle's direction; storms and debris may shift its course as well. Occasionally a fishing net will snag a bottle and carry it a dozen miles in the opposite direction from the one in which it was headed. The result is that two bottles dropped simultaneously into the ocean might end up a continent apart or even on opposite sides of the globe.

This bottle contained a message that would change two people forever, two people who would otherwise never have met. For six days it slowly floated in a northeasterly direction, driven by winds from a high-pressure system hovering above the Gulf of Mexico.

Two and a half weeks after its launch the bottle began to drift toward New England. Without the Gulf Stream forcing it along, the bottle slowed again, and it zigzagged in various directions near the Massachusetts shore for five days until it was snagged in a fishing net by John Hanes. Hanes found the bottle surrounded by a thousand flopping perch and tossed it aside while he examined his catch. The bottle remained near the bow of the boat for the rest of the afternoon and early evening as the boat made its journey back to Cape Cod. At eight thirty that night—and once the boat was safely inside the confines of a bay—Hanes stumbled across the bottle again and tossed it overboard without a second glance.

The bottle drifted back and forth for a few days before it washed up along the shore on a beach near Chatham. And it was there, after twenty-six days and seven hundred and thirty-eight miles, that it finally ended its journey.

Chapter One

A COLD December wind was blowing, and Theresa Osborne crossed her arms as she stared out over the water. Earlier, when she'd arrived, there had been a few people walking along the shore, but they'd taken note of the heavy clouds and were long since gone. Now she found herself alone on the beach, and she took in her surroundings. The ocean, reflecting the color of the sky, looked like liquid iron, and a fog was beginning to thicken, making the horizon invisible. In another place, in another time, she would have felt the majesty of the beauty around her, but as she stood on the beach, she realized that she didn't feel anything at all. In a way, she felt as if she weren't really here, as if the whole thing were nothing but a dream.

She scarcely remembered the trip from Boston this morning, and watching the ocean swirl and churn made her realize that she didn't want to stay. She would drive home as soon as she was finished, no matter how late it was.

When she was ready, Theresa slowly started to walk toward the water. Beneath her arm she carried a bag that she had carefully packed that morning. Soon it would be high tide, and it was then that she would finally be ready. After finding a spot on a small dune that looked comfortable, she sat in the sand and opened her bag. Searching through it, she found the envelope she wanted. Taking a deep breath, she slowly lifted the seal.

In it were three letters, carefully folded, letters that she'd read more times than she could count.

He'd used a fountain pen when he'd written them, and there were smudges in various places where the pen had leaked. The stationery, with its picture of a sailing ship in the upper right-hand corner, was beginning to fade with the passage of time. She knew there would come a day when the words would be impossible to read, but hopefully, after today, she wouldn't feel the need to look at them so often.

When she finished reading, she slipped them back into the envelope as carefully as she'd removed them. Then, after putting the envelope back into the bag, she looked at the beach again. From where she was sitting, she could see the place where it had all started.

SHE'D been jogging at daybreak, she remembered. It was the beginning of a beautiful summer day. As she took in the world around her, she listened to the high-pitched squawking of terns and the gentle lapping of the waves as they rolled up on the sand. Even though she was on vacation, she had risen early enough to run so that she didn't have to watch where she was going. In a few hours the beach would be packed with tourists lying on their towels in the hot New England sun, soaking up the rays. Cape Cod was always crowded at that time of year, but most vacationers tended to sleep a little later, and Theresa enjoyed the sensation of jogging on the hard, smooth sand left from the outgoing tide. She considered it to be a kind of meditation, which was why she liked to do it alone.

As much as she loved her son, she was glad he wasn't with her. Every mother needs a break sometimes, and she was looking forward to taking it easy while she was here. No evening soccer games or swim meets, no MTV blaring in the background, no homework to help with. She had taken Kevin to the airport three days ago to catch a plane to visit his father—her ex—in California, and it was only after reminding him that he realized he hadn't kissed her goodbye yet. "Sorry, Mom," he said as he wrapped his arms around her. "Don't miss me too much, okay?" Then, turning around, he handed the ticket to the flight attendant and almost skipped onto the plane.

She didn't blame him for almost forgetting. At twelve he was in that awkward phase when he thought that kissing his mom in public wasn't *cool.* Besides, his mind was on other things. He and his father were going to the Grand Canyon; then they would spend a week rafting down the Colorado River and finally go on to Disneyland. Although he would be gone for several weeks, she knew it was good for Kevin to spend time with his father.

David hadn't been the greatest husband, but he was a good father to Kevin. Annette, his new wife, had her hands full with the baby, but Kevin liked her a lot, and he usually raved about his visits and how much fun he had. There were times when Theresa felt a twinge of jealousy at that, but she did her best to hide it from Kevin.

Now, on the beach, she ran at a moderate clip. Deanna would be waiting for her to finish her run before she started breakfast—Brian would already be gone, she knew—and Theresa looked forward to visiting with her. They were an older couple—both of them nearing sixty—but Deanna was the best friend she had.

The managing editor at the newspaper where Theresa worked, Deanna had been coming to the Cape with her husband, Brian, for years. They always stayed in the same place, the Fisher House, and when she found out that Kevin was leaving to visit his father in California, Deanna insisted that Theresa come along. "Brian golfs every day he's here, and I'd like the company," she'd said, "and besides, what else are you going to do?" Theresa knew she was right, and after a few days she agreed. "I'm so glad," Deanna had said with a victorious look on her face. "You're going to love it there."

Theresa had to admit it was a nice place to stay. The Fisher House was a beautifully restored captain's house that sat on the edge of a rocky cliff overlooking a bay, and when she saw it in the distance, she slowed to a jog. Unlike the younger runners who sped up toward the end of their runs, she preferred to slow down and take it easy. At thirty-six she didn't recover as fast as she once did.

As her breathing eased, she thought about how she would spend the rest of her day. She had brought five books with her for the vacation, books she had been wanting to read for the last year but had never gotten around to. As a syndicated columnist for the Boston *Times,* she was under deadline pressure to put out three articles a week. To constantly come up with something original wasn't easy. Already her column, "Modern Parenting," went out in sixty newspapers across the country, and if she wanted to syndicate further, she couldn't afford even a few "off" days.

Theresa slowed to a walk and finally stopped as a Caspian tern circled overhead. After a moment she took off her shoes and socks, then walked to the water's edge to let the tiny waves lap over her feet. The water was refreshing, and she spent a few minutes wading back and forth. She was glad she had taken the time to write extra columns over the last few months so that she would be able to forget work this week. It almost felt as if she were in control of her own destiny again, as if she were just starting out in the world.

But when she closed her eyes, the only thing she could think about was Kevin. Lord knew she wanted to spend more time with him. She wanted to be able to sit and talk with him, play Monopoly, or simply watch TV without feeling the urge to get up from the couch to do something more important.

The problem was that there was always something to do—dishes to be washed, bathrooms to be cleaned, the cat box to be emptied. Cars needed tune-ups, laundry needed to be done, and bills had to be paid. Even though Kevin helped a lot with his chores, he was almost as busy as she was, with school and friends and all his other activities. Sometimes she worried that her life was slipping past her.

But how to change all that? "Take life one day at a time," her mother always said, but her mother didn't have to work outside the home or raise a son without benefit of a father. She didn't understand the pressures that Theresa faced on a daily basis. Neither did her younger sister, Janet, who had followed in the footsteps of their mother. She and her husband had been happily married for almost eleven years, with three wonderful girls to show for it. Edward provided for his family well enough that Janet didn't have to work. There were times when Theresa thought she might like a life like that even if it meant giving up her career.

But that wasn't possible. Not since David and she divorced. Three years now—four if you counted the year they were separated. She didn't hate David for what he had done, but her respect for him had been shattered. Adultery wasn't something she could live with. The breach of trust was irreparable.

Since the divorce there had been only a handful of dates. It wasn't that she was not attractive. She was, or so she was often told. Her hair was dark brown, cut just above her shoulders, and straight as spider silk. Her eyes, the feature she was most often complimented on, were brown with flecks of hazel that caught the light when she was outside. Since she ran daily, she was fit and didn't look as old as she was. But when she glanced in the mirror lately, she seemed to see her age catching up with her.

Her friends thought she was crazy. "You look better now than you did years ago," they insisted, and she still noticed a few men eyeing her across the aisle in the supermarket. But she wasn't, nor would she ever be, twenty-two again.

When the divorce papers finally arrived, she felt as if a little part of her had died. Her initial anger had turned to sadness, and now it had become something else, almost a dullness of sorts. Even though she was constantly in motion, it seemed as if nothing special ever happened to her anymore. Each day seemed exactly like the last, and she had trouble differentiating among them. One time, about a year ago, she sat at her desk for fifteen minutes trying to remember the last spontaneous thing she'd done. She couldn't think of anything.

She still missed David sometimes, or rather the good parts about him. Most of all she missed the intimacy that came from holding and whispering to another behind closed doors.

Though she loved Kevin deeply, it wasn't the same kind of love that she wanted right now. Her feeling for Kevin was a mother's love, probably the deepest, most holy love there is. Even now she liked to go into his room after he was asleep and sit on his bed just to look at him. He always looked so peaceful, so beautiful, with his head on the pillow and the covers piled up around him. Yet even those wonderful feelings didn't change the fact that once she left his room, she would go into the living room and have a glass of wine with only Harvey the cat to keep her company.

She dreamed about falling in love, having someone take her in his arms and make her feel she was the only one who mattered. But it was hard to meet someone decent these days. Most men in their thirties were already married, and the ones who were divorced seemed to be looking for someone younger. She also had Kevin to worry about. She wanted a man who would treat him the way he should be treated, not simply as the unwanted by-product of someone he desired.

She hadn't been with a man since she and David divorced. There had been opportunities, of course—finding someone to sleep with was never difficult for an attractive woman—but that simply wasn't her style. She hadn't been raised that way and didn't intend to change now. Sex was too important, too special, to be shared with just anyone.

So now, vacationing at Cape Cod, she wanted to do some things for herself alone—read some books, write letters to friends she hadn't heard from in a while, sleep late, eat too much, and jog in the mornings. She wanted to experience freedom again, if only for a short time.

She also wanted to shop. She wanted to try on some new dresses and buy a couple that flattered her figure and made her feel she was still alive and vibrant. And if a nice guy happened to ask her out, maybe she'd go, just to have an excuse to wear the new things she bought.

With a somewhat renewed sense of optimism, she started toward the house. She walked close to the water's edge and saw a large rock half buried in the sand, a few inches from a spot where the early morning tide had reached its highest point. Strange, she thought, it seemed out of place here.

As she approached, she noticed something different about the way it looked. It was smooth and long, for one thing, and as she drew nearer, she realized it wasn't a rock at all. It was a bottle, probably discarded by a careless tourist or one of the local teens who liked to come here at night. When she reached it, however, she was surprised to see that it was corked. She picked it up, holding it in better light, and saw a note inside.

She began to pull at the cork, and her fingers slipped as she tried to open it. She couldn't get a very good grip. She dug her short fingernails into the exposed cork and twisted the bottle slowly. Nothing. She switched hands and tried again. Tightening her grip, she put the bottle between her legs for more leverage, and just as she was about to give up, the cork moved a little. She changed back to her original hands . . . squeezed . . . twisting the bottle slowly. More cork. Suddenly it loosened, and the remaining portion slipped out easily.

She tipped the bottle upside down, and the note dropped to the sand by her feet almost immediately. When she leaned over to pick it up, she noticed it was tightly bound with yarn.

She untied the yarn carefully, and the first thing that struck her as she unrolled the message was the paper. It was expensive, thick and sturdy, with a silhouette of a sailing ship embossed in the upper right-hand corner. There was a date in the upper left corner.

June 22, 1997. A little more than three weeks ago.

She felt a twinge of curiosity as she held the message in front of her, and it was then, in the rising sunlight of a hot New England day, that she first read the letter that would change her life forever.

My Dearest Catherine,

I miss you, my darling, as I always do, but today is especially hard because the ocean has been singing to me, and the song is that of our life together. I can almost feel you beside me as I write this letter, and I can smell the scent of wildflowers that always reminds me of you. But at this moment these things give me no pleasure. Your visits have been coming less often, and I feel sometimes as if the greatest part of who I am is slowly slipping away.

I am trying, though. At night when I am alone, I call for you, and whenever my ache seems to be the greatest, you still find a way to return to me. Last night, in my dreams, I saw you on the pier near Wrightsville Beach. The wind was blowing through your hair, and your eyes held the fading sunlight. You are beautiful, I think as I see you. I slowly begin to walk toward you, and when you finally turn to me, I notice that others have been watching you as well. "Do you know her?" they ask me in jealous whispers, and as you smile at me, I simply answer with the truth, "Better than my own heart."

I stop when I reach you and gently touch your cheek, and you tilt your head and close your eyes. Then, as always, a mist slowly creeps in, enveloping the world around us, fencing us in as if to prevent escape. Like a rolling cloud, it blankets everything, closing, until there is nothing left but the two of us. The look you give me at that moment haunts me. I feel your sadness and my own loneliness. And then you spread your arms and step back into the mist because it is your place and not mine. I long to go with you, but your only response is to shake your head because we both know that is impossible.

And I watch with breaking heart as you slowly fade away. I find myself straining to remember everything about this moment, everything about you. But soon, always too soon, your image vanishes and I am alone on the pier and I do not care what others think as I bow my head and cry and cry and cry.

Garrett

Chapter Two

HAVE you been crying?" Deanna asked as Theresa stepped onto the back deck, carrying the bottle and the message.

Theresa felt embarrassed and wiped her eyes as Deanna put down the newspaper and rose from her seat. Though she was overweight—and had been since Theresa had known her—she moved quickly around the table, her face registering concern.

"Are you okay? What happened out there? Are you hurt?" She bumped into one of the chairs as she reached out and took Theresa's hand.

Theresa shook her head. "No, nothing like that. I'm fine really. I just found this letter. It was in a bottle washed up on the beach. When I opened it and read it . . ." She brushed away a strand of hair that had blown onto her face. "It just really hit me. It's silly, I know." She wiped her eyes, handed the letter to Deanna, and walked over to the wrought-iron table where Deanna had been sitting.

Deanna read the letter slowly, and when she finished, she looked up at Theresa. Her eyes too were watering. "It's . . . it's beautiful," she finally said. "It's one of the most touching things I've ever read."

"That's what I thought."

Deanna ran her finger over the writing and paused for a moment. "I wonder who they are. And why was it sealed in a bottle?"

"I don't know."

"Aren't you curious?"

The fact was that Theresa was indeed curious. Immediately after reading it, she had read it again, then a third time. What would it be like, she mused, to have someone love her that way?

"A little. But so what? There's no way we'll ever know."

"What are you going to do with it?"

"Keep it, I guess. I haven't really thought about it that much." Theresa sipped a glass of juice she had poured. "So what's on the agenda today?"

"I thought we'd do a little shopping and have lunch in Provincetown. Are you up for something like that?"

"That's what I was hoping you'd say."

The two women talked about the places they might go. Then Deanna got up and went inside for another cup of coffee, and Theresa watched her as she left.

Deanna was fifty-eight and round-faced, with hair that was slowly turning to gray. She kept it cut short, dressed without an excess of vanity, and was, Theresa decided, easily the best person she knew. She was knowledgeable about music and art and lived in a world of optimism and humor.

When Deanna came back to the table, she sat down and picked up the letter again. As she perused it, her eyebrows raised. "I just wonder . . ." she said quietly.

"Wonder what?"

"Well, when I was inside, I got to thinking we should run this letter in your column this week."

"What are you talking about?"

Deanna leaned across the table. "Just what I said. I think we should run this letter. It really is so touching. I can picture a hundred women cutting it out and taping it to their refrigerators so their husbands can see it when they get home from work."

"We don't even know who they are. Don't you think we should get their permission first?"

"We won't use their real names, and as long as we don't take credit for writing it or divulge where it might be from, I'm sure there wouldn't be a problem."

"I know it's probably legal, but I'm not sure if it's right. I mean, this is a very personal letter."

"Theresa, it's a human-interest story. People love those sorts of things. And remember, this Garrett person sent it in a *bottle* in the *ocean.* He had to know it would wash up somewhere."

Theresa shook her head. "I don't know, Deanna. . . ."

"Well, think about it. Sleep on it if you have to. I think it's a great idea."

THERESA did think about the letter as she undressed and got into the shower. She found herself wondering about the man who wrote it—Garrett, if that was his real name. And who was Catherine? His lover or his wife, obviously. Was she dead, she wondered, or did something else happen that forced them apart? In all her years she had never received a letter even close to that. David had never been much of a writer, nor had anyone else she had dated. What would such a man be like? she wondered. Would he be as caring in person as the letter seemed to imply?

She lathered and rinsed her hair, the questions slipping from her mind as the cool water rolled down her body. She washed the rest of her body with a washcloth and moisturizing soap, spent longer in the shower than she had to, and finally stepped out of the stall.

She looked at herself in the mirror as she toweled off. Not too bad for a thirty-six-year-old with an adolescent son, she thought. Her breasts had always been smallish, and they hadn't started to sag or droop like those of other women her age. Her stomach was flat, and her legs were long and lean from exercise. All in all she was pleased with how she looked this morning, and she attributed her unusually easy acceptance of herself to being on vacation.

After putting on a little makeup, she dressed in beige shorts, a sleeveless white blouse, and brown sandals. It would be hot and humid in another hour, and she wanted to be comfortable.

SHOPPING with Deanna was an experience.

Once they got to Provincetown, they spent the rest of the morning and early afternoon in a variety of shops. Theresa bought three new outfits and a new swimsuit before Deanna dragged her into a place called Nightingales, a lingerie shop.

Deanna went absolutely wild in there. Not for herself, of course, but for Theresa. She would pick up lacy underwear off the racks and hold them up for Theresa to evaluate. "This looks pretty steamy," she'd say, or "You don't have any this color, do you?" Naturally, there would be others around as she blurted these things out, and Theresa couldn't help but laugh whenever she did it. Deanna's lack of inhibition was one of the things that Theresa loved most about her. She really didn't care what other people thought, and Theresa often wished she could be more like her.

When they returned to the house, Brian was reading the paper in the living room.

"Hey there. How was your day?"

"It was good," Deanna answered. "We had lunch in Provincetown, then did a little shopping. How did your game go today?"

"Pretty well. If I hadn't bogeyed the last two holes, I would have shot an eighty."

"Well, you're just going to have to play a little more until you get it right."

Brian laughed. "You won't mind?"

"Of course not."

Brian smiled as he rustled the paper, content with the fact that he could spend a lot of time on the course this week. Recognizing his signal that he wanted to get back to reading, Deanna turned her attention to Theresa. "Are you up for some gin rummy?"

Deanna loved card games of any kind. She was in two bridge clubs, played hearts like a champion, and kept a record of every time she won a game of solitaire. But gin rummy had always been the game that she and Theresa played, because it was the only game that Theresa actually stood a chance of winning.

"Sure."

"I hoped you'd say that. The cards are on the table outside."

Theresa went outside to the table where they had eaten breakfast. Deanna followed shortly with two cans of Diet Coke and sat across from her as she picked up the deck. Theresa shuffled the cards and dealt them.

Deanna looked up from her hand. "I'm kind of hoping you'll meet someone special this week."

"You're special."

"You know what I mean—a man. One who takes your breath away."

Theresa looked up in surprise. "I haven't really been looking, Deanna."

She put down the six of diamonds, and Deanna picked it up before discarding the three of clubs. Deanna spoke in the same tone Theresa's mother used when they talked about the same thing.

"It's been almost three years since the divorce. Have you been dating at all?"

"Not really. Not since Matt What's-his-name told me he didn't want a woman with children."

Deanna scowled for a moment. "Sometimes men can be real jerks, and he was a perfect example. But they aren't all like that. There are lots of real men out there—men who could fall in love with you at the drop of a hat."

Theresa picked up the three of clubs and discarded the four of diamonds. "That's why I like you, Deanna. You say the sweetest things."

Deanna picked from the stack. "It's true, though. Believe me. I could find a dozen men who would love to go out with you."

"But that doesn't mean that I would like them."

Deanna threw down the two of spades. "I think you're scared."

"Why do you say that?"

"Because I know how much David hurt you. It's human nature. Once burned, twice shy. There's a lot of truth in old sayings."

"There probably is. But I'm sure if the right man comes along, I'll know it. I have faith."

"What kind of man are you looking for?"

"I don't know."

"Sure you do. Everyone knows a little bit about what they want. Start with the obvious, or if you can't do that, start with what you don't want. Like . . . is it all right if he's in a motorcycle gang?"

Theresa smiled and picked from the stack. Her hand was coming together. Another card and she'd be done. She threw down the jack of hearts.

"No motorcycle gang, that's for sure," she said with a shake of her head. She thought for a moment. "Um . . . I guess most of all he'd have to be the kind of man who would be faithful. And I think I'd like someone my own age or close to it." Theresa stopped and frowned a little.

"And?"

"Give me a second. This isn't as easy as it sounds. I guess I'd go with the standard clichés—handsome, kind, intelligent, and charming—you know, all those good things that women want in a man." Again she paused.

Deanna picked up the jack. Her expression showed her pleasure at putting Theresa on the spot. "And?"

"He would have to spend time with Kevin as if he were his own son. That's really important to me. Oh, and he'd have to be romantic, too. And athletic. I can't respect a man if I could beat him in arm wrestling."

"That's it?"

"Yep, that's all."

"So let me see if I've got this right. You want a faithful, charming, handsome, thirtysomething-year-old-man, who's also intelligent, romantic, and athletic. And he has to be good with Kevin, right?"

"You got it."

She took a deep breath as she laid her hand on the table. "Well, at least you're not picky. Gin."

AT SIX that evening Brian and Deanna went for a walk along the beach. Theresa stayed behind and watched from a window as they strolled hand in hand along the water's edge. They had an ideal relationship, she thought as she watched them. They had completely different interests, yet that seemed to keep them together instead of driving them apart.

After the sun went down, the three of them drove to Hyannis

and had dinner at Sam's Crabhouse. It was crowded, and they had to wait an hour for seats, but the steamed crabs and drawn butter were worth it. The butter had been flavored with garlic, and between the three of them they went through six beers in two hours.

Toward the end of dinner Brian asked about the letter that had washed up. "I read it when I got back from golfing. Deanna had pinned it to the refrigerator."

Deanna shrugged and turned to Theresa with an I-told-you-someone-would-do-that look in her eyes but said nothing.

Brian went on. "It was quite a letter. It seemed so sad."

"I know," Theresa said. "That's how I felt when I read it."

"Do you know where Wrightsville Beach is?"

"No. I've never heard of it."

"It's in North Carolina," Brian said as he reached into a pocket for a cigarette. "I had a golf trip down there once. Great courses. A little flat, but playable."

Deanna chimed in, "With Brian everything is connected to golf."

He lit his cigarette and inhaled. As he exhaled, he spoke. "Wrightsville Beach is an island right off the coast, near Wilmington. Very developed, but the beaches are beautiful—white sand, warm water. It's a great place to spend a week if you ever get the chance."

Theresa didn't respond, and Deanna spoke with a hint of mischief in her tone. "So now we know where our mystery writer is from."

Theresa shrugged. "I suppose so, but there's still no way to tell for sure. It could have been a place where they vacationed or visited. It doesn't mean he lives there."

Deanna shook her head. "I don't think so. The way the letter was written—it just seemed like his dream was too real to include a place he had only been to once or twice. I'd be willing to bet that Wrightsville Beach or Wilmington is his home."

"So what?"

Deanna leaned forward. "Have you given any more thought to having the letter published?"

"Not really. Is it so important to you?"

"Theresa, I know a good story when I see one. Nowadays people are so busy that romance seems to be slowly dying out. This letter shows that it's still possible."

Theresa absently reached for a strand of hair and began to twist it. A habit since childhood, it was what she did whenever she was thinking about something. After a long moment she finally responded. "All right."

"You'll do it?"

"Yes, but we'll use only their initials and we'll omit the part about Wrightsville Beach. I'll write a couple of sentences to introduce it."

"I'm so glad," Deanna cried with girlish enthusiasm. "I knew you would. We'll fax it in tomorrow."

Later that night Theresa wrote out the beginning of the column in longhand on some stationery she found in a desk drawer. When she was finished, she set the two pages on the bedstand behind her, then crawled into bed. That night she slept fitfully.

THE following day Theresa and Deanna went into Chatham and had the column faxed to Boston. It would run in the next day's paper.

The rest of the morning and afternoon were spent like the day before—shopping, relaxing at the beach, easy conversation, and a delicious dinner. When the paper arrived at breakfast the next morning, Deanna was the first to read it.

> Four days ago, while I was on vacation, I found a bottle on the beach with a deeply moving message inside. I haven't been able to get it off my mind, and although it isn't something I'd normally write about, in a time when everlasting love and commitment seem to be in such short supply, I was hoping you would find it as meaningful as I did.

The rest of the column was devoted to the letter. "Marvelous," she said when she finished. "It looks even better in print than I thought it would. You're going to get a lot of mail from this column."

"We'll see," Theresa said as she ate a bagel, not really sure whether to believe Deanna or not, but curious nonetheless.

Chapter Three

On Saturday, eight days after she'd arrived on the Cape, Theresa returned to Boston.

She entered her stuffy apartment and slid open the glass doors that led to the back patio to air the place out. After unpacking her bags, she poured herself a glass of wine, went to the stereo, and popped in a John Coltrane CD. As the sound of jazz filtered through the room, she sorted through her mail. As usual, it was mainly bills, and she put them aside for another time.

There were no calls from Kevin on her recorder when she checked it. By now he was rafting and camping with his father somewhere in Arizona. Without Kevin the house seemed strangely silent.

She thought about the two weeks of vacation she still had left this year. She and Kevin would spend some time at the beach because she had promised him they would. But that left another week. She could use it around Christmas, but this year Kevin would be at his father's, so there didn't seem to be much point in that. Perhaps she could use the week to do the things around the house she had been meaning to do, but who wanted to spend their vacation painting and hanging wallpaper?

She finally gave up and decided that if nothing exciting came to mind, she would just save it for the following year. Maybe she and Kevin would go to Hawaii.

She got into bed and picked up one of the novels she had started at Cape Cod. She read quickly and without distraction and finished almost a hundred pages before she was tired. At midnight she turned off the light. And for the second time in six days she dreamed she was walking along a deserted beach.

THE MAIL ON HER DESK Monday morning was overwhelming. There were almost two hundred letters when she arrived, and another fifty came later that day with the postman. As soon as she walked into the office, Deanna pointed proudly at the stack. "See, I told you so," she said with a smile.

Theresa asked that no calls be put through to her, and she started opening the mail right away. Without exception they were responses to the letter she had published in her column. Most were from women, though a few men wrote in as well, and their uniformity of opinion surprised her. One by one she read how much they had been touched by the anonymous letter.

By the end of the day she had worked through most of the stack, and she was tired. At five thirty she started working on a column about Kevin being away and what that was like for her. It was going better than she expected, and she was almost finished when her phone rang.

It was the newspaper's receptionist. "Hey, Theresa, I know you asked me to hold your calls, and I have been," she started. "But this woman keeps calling. This is the fifth time today, and she called twice last week. She keeps asking to be put on hold until you have a minute. She says she's calling long-distance but that she has to talk to you."

"Okay, what line is she on?"

"Five."

"Thanks." Theresa picked up the receiver and pressed line 5. "Hello."

The line was silent for a moment. Then in a soft, melodic voice the caller asked, "Is this Theresa Osborne?"

"Yes, it is." Theresa leaned back in her chair and started twirling her hair.

"Are you the one that wrote the column about the message in a bottle?"

"Yes. How can I help you?"

The caller paused. "Can you tell me the names that were in the letter?"

Theresa closed her eyes and stopped twirling. "No, I'm sorry, I can't. I don't want that information made public."

"Please," the caller said, "can you answer a question? Was the letter addressed to Catherine and signed by a man named Garrett?"

Theresa sat up higher in her seat. "Who is this?" she asked with sudden urgency, and by the time the words were out, she knew the caller would know the truth.

"It is, isn't it?"

"Who is this?" Theresa asked again, this time more gently. She heard the caller take a deep breath before she answered.

"My name is Michelle Turner and I live in Norfolk, Virginia. Three years ago I was walking along the beach here, and I found a letter like the one you found. After reading your column, I knew the same person wrote it."

Theresa stopped for a moment. It couldn't be, she thought. Three years ago?

"What kind of paper was it written on?" she asked.

"The paper was beige, and it had a picture of a sailing ship in the upper right-hand corner. Your letter had a picture of a ship, too, didn't it?"

"Yes, it did," Theresa whispered.

"I knew it. I knew it as soon as I read your column." Michelle sounded as if a load had been lifted from her shoulders.

"Do you still have the letter?" Theresa asked.

"Yes. It's a little different from the letter you copied in your column, but the feelings are the same."

"Could you fax me a copy?"

"Sure," she said before pausing. "It's amazing, isn't it?"

"Yes," Theresa whispered, "it is."

After giving the fax number to Michelle, Theresa could barely proofread her column. Michelle had to go to a copy store to fax the letter, and Theresa found herself pacing from her desk to the fax machine every five minutes as she waited for the letter to arrive. Forty-six minutes later she heard the machine come to life. It took only ten seconds to copy the page, but even that wait seemed too long.

She reached for the copy as the fax machine beeped, signaling an end to the transmission. She took it to her desk without reading it.

Taking a deep breath, she lifted the page. A quick glance at the ship's logo proved to her that it was indeed the same writer. She put the page into better light and began to read.

March 6, 1994
My Darling Catherine,

Where are you? And why have we been forced apart?

I don't know the answer to these questions, no matter how hard I try to understand. The reason is plain, but my mind forces me to dismiss it and I am torn by anxiety in all my waking hours. I am lost without you. I am soulless, a drifter without a home, a solitary bird in a flight to nowhere.

I try to remember the way we once were, on the breezy deck of *Happenstance.* Do you recall how we worked on her together? We became a part of the ocean as we rebuilt her, for we both knew it was the ocean that brought us together. At night we sailed on blackened water, and I watched as the moonlight reflected your beauty. I would watch you with awe and know in my heart that we'd be together forever. We were destined to be together.

But now, alone in my house, I have come to realize that destiny can hurt a person as much as it can bless him, and I find myself wondering why—out of all the people in all the world I could ever have loved—I had to fall in love with someone who was taken away from me.

Garrett

After reading the letter, Theresa leaned back in her chair and brought her fingers to her lips. The sounds from the newsroom seemed far away. She reached for her purse, found the initial letter, and laid the two next to each other on her desk.

Were there more? she wondered. And what type of man would send them in bottles? She knew it shouldn't really matter much to her, but all at once it did.

As a girl, she had come to believe in the ideal man—the prince or knight of her childhood stories. In the real world, however, men like that simply didn't exist. Real people had real agendas, real demands, real expectations about how other people should behave. But here and now she knew such a man did exist—a man who was now alone—and knowing that made something inside her tighten.

It seemed obvious that Catherine—whoever she was—was probably dead, or at least missing. Yet Garrett still loved her enough to send letters to her for at least three years. If nothing else, he had proved that he was capable of loving someone deeply and, more important, remaining fully committed even long after his loved one was gone.

The opening line of the second letter rolled through her head. *Where are you?*

She didn't know exactly, but he did exist, and one of the things she had learned early in her life was that if you discovered something that made you tighten inside, you had better try to learn more about it.

Deep down she knew the fascination with Garrett would lead to nothing at all. She would go on with her life, writing her column, spending time with Kevin, doing all the things a single parent had to do.

And she was almost right. Her life would have proceeded exactly as she imagined. But something happened three days later that caused her to charge into the unknown with only a suitcase full of clothes and a stack of papers that may or may not have meant anything.

She discovered a third letter from Garrett.

THE day she discovered the third letter, she had, of course, expected nothing unusual. It was a typical midsummer day in Boston—hot and humid. Theresa was in the newsroom, researching a column on autistic children. Through her computer she could access the library at Harvard University, and in a couple of hours she had been able to find almost thirty articles written in the last three years. Six of the titles looked interesting enough to possibly use. Since she would be passing by Harvard on the way home, she decided to pick them up then.

As she was about to turn her computer off, a thought suddenly crossed her mind and she stopped. Why not? she asked herself. It's a long shot, but what can I lose? She accessed the database at Harvard again and typed in the words "Message in a bottle."

After hitting the RETURN key, she leaned back and waited for the computer to retrieve the information she requested.

The response surprised her. A dozen different articles had been written on the subject in the last few years. Most were published by scientific journals, and their titles seemed to suggest that bottles were being used in various endeavors to learn about ocean currents, but three seemed interesting. She jotted down the titles, deciding to pick those up as well.

Traffic was heavy and slow, and it took longer than she thought it would to get to the library and copy the nine articles she was looking for. She got home late, and after ordering in from the local Chinese restaurant, she sat on the couch with the three articles in front of her.

The first, published in *Yankee* magazine in March of the previous year, chronicled stories about bottles that had washed up in New England over the past few years. Toward the end of the article she came across two paragraphs that told of a message that had washed up on Long Island.

> Most messages sent by bottle ask the finder to respond. Sometimes, however, the senders do not want a response. One such letter, a moving tribute to a lost love, was discovered washed up on Long Island last year. In part it read:
>
> "Without you in my arms I feel an emptiness in my soul. I find myself searching the crowds for your face—I know it is an impossibility, but I cannot help myself. You and I had talked about what would happen if we were forced apart by circumstance, but I cannot keep the promise I made to you that night.

> I am sorry, my darling, but there will never be another to replace you. You—and you alone—have always been the only thing I wanted, and now that you are gone, I have no desire to find another."

She stopped eating and abruptly put down her fork.

It can't be! She found herself staring at the words. It's simply not possible.

She wiped her brow, aware that her hands were suddenly shaking. Another letter? She flipped to the front of the article and looked at the author's name. It had been written by Arthur Shendakin, Ph.D., a professor of history at Boston College.

She jumped up and retrieved the phone book on the stand near the dining-room table. There were fewer than a dozen Shendakins listed, but only two had A listed as the first initial. She checked her watch before dialing. Nine thirty. Late, but not too late. She punched in the numbers and waited as the phone started to ring.

Once.

Twice.

Three times.

On the fourth ring she began to lose hope, but on the fifth ring she heard the other party pick up.

"Hello," a man said.

She cleared her throat. "Hello. This is Theresa Osborne of the Boston *Times*. Is this Arthur Shendakin?"

"Yes, it is," he answered, sounding surprised.

"Oh, hi. I was just calling to find out if this is the same Arthur Shendakin who had an article published last year in *Yankee* magazine about messages in bottles."

"Yes, I wrote that. How can I help you?"

Her hands felt sweaty on the receiver. "I was curious about the message you said had washed up on Long Island. I know this is an unusual request, Mr. Shendakin, but I am interested in obtaining a copy of it. It would mean a lot to me."

"Just a copy?"

"Yes, of course. I can give you a fax number, or you can send it."

He paused before answering. "I . . . I suppose so."

"Thanks, Mr. Shendakin." Before he could change his mind, Theresa gave him the fax number.

THE next day she went to work with her head spinning. The possible existence of a third letter made it difficult to think of anything else, but when she got to her desk, she purposely waited before going to the fax machine. She turned on her computer, called two physicians she needed to speak with about the column on autism, and jotted a few notes on possible other topics.

She finally went to the fax machine when she couldn't think of anything else to do and began to look through the stack. It hadn't been sorted yet, and there were a few dozen pages addressed to various people. In the middle she found a cover letter addressed to her. With it were two more pages, and when she looked more closely at them, the first thing she noticed was the sailing ship embossed in the upper right corner.

September 25, 1995

Dear Catherine,

A month has passed since I've written, but so slowly. Life passes by now like the scenery outside a car window. I do not know where I am going or when I will get there.

Even work does not take the pain away. I may be diving for my own pleasure or showing others how to do so, but when I return to the shop, it seems empty without you. I stock and order as I always did, but even now I sometimes glance over my shoulder without thinking and call for you.

Without you in my arms I feel an emptiness in my soul. I find myself searching the crowds for your face—I know it is an impossibility, but I cannot help myself. You and I had talked about what would happen if we were forced apart by circumstance, but I cannot keep the promise I made to you that night. I am sorry, my darling, but there will never be another to replace you. You—and you alone—have always been the only thing I wanted, and now that you are gone, I have no desire to find another. Till death do us part, we whispered in the church, and I've come to believe that the words will ring true until the day finally comes when I, too, am taken from this world.

Garrett

"DEANNA, do you have a minute? I need to talk to you."

Deanna looked up from her computer and took off her reading glasses. "Of course I do. What's up?"

Theresa laid the three letters on Deanna's desk and explained how she'd come across them. When she finished her story, Deanna read the letters in silence. Theresa sat in the chair opposite her.

"Well," she said, putting the last letter down, "you've certainly been keeping a secret, haven't you?"

Theresa shrugged, and Deanna went on. "But there's more to this than just finding the letters, isn't there? You're interested in this Garrett fellow."

Theresa thought for a moment.

"It's been really strange these last few days. I mean, I can't stop thinking about him, and I don't know why. We've never spoken, I've never even seen him. For all I know, he could be a seventy-year-old man."

Deanna leaned back in her chair and nodded thoughtfully. "That's true . . . but you don't think that's the case, do you?"

Theresa slowly shook her head.

"Neither do I," Deanna said as she picked up the letters again. "He talks about how they fell in love when they were young. He teaches diving and writes about Catherine as if he had only been married a few years. I doubt if he's that old."

"That's what I thought, too."

"Do you want to know what I think?"

"Absolutely."

Deanna spoke the words carefully. "I think you should go to Wilmington to try to find Garrett."

"But it seems so . . . so ridiculous. I don't know anything about him. What if . . ." She paused, and Deanna finished her statement.

"What if he's not what you imagine? Theresa, I can guarantee he's not. No one ever is. But to my mind, that shouldn't make any difference in your decision. If you want to find out more, just go."

"You don't think this whole thing is crazy?"

Deanna shook her head thoughtfully. "I'm older than you, and I've gone through a lot. One of the things I've learned in my life is that sometimes you've got to take a chance. Besides, Kevin isn't around, and you have plenty of vacation left this year."

Theresa began twisting a strand of hair around her finger. "You make this sound so easy."

"It is easy. The hard part is going to be finding him. But I think these letters have some information we can use to help you. What do you say we make a few phone calls?"

Theresa pulled her chair around to the other side of Deanna's desk. "Where do we start?"

"First off," Deanna began, "I think it's fair to say that his name actually is Garrett. That's how he signed all the letters, and I don't think he would have bothered using a name other than his own."

"And," Theresa added, "he's probably in Wilmington or Wrightsville Beach, or another community close by."

"Okay, good," Deanna said, nodding. "There was a boat that was mentioned . . ."

"*Happenstance,*" Theresa said. "The letter said that they used to sail together. So it's probably a sailboat. And also it looks like he owns a scuba-diving shop where he and Catherine used to work."

"Well, it's a beginning. This might be easier than we think."

The first place Deanna called was the Wilmington *Journal,* the newspaper that served the area. She asked to talk to someone who was familiar with boating and found herself speaking with Zack Norton, who covered ocean sports. After explaining that she wanted to know if there was a place that kept a registry of boat names, she was told that there wasn't.

"Boats are registered with an identification number, almost like cars," he said in a slow drawl, "but if you have the name of the person, you might be able to find out the name of the boat if it's listed on the form. It's not a required piece of information, but a lot of people put it down anyway."

After thanking Zack Norton for his time and hanging up, Deanna looked over the list of clues again. She thought for a moment, then decided to call information for the phone numbers of scuba-diving shops in the Wilmington area. Theresa watched as Deanna wrote down the numbers of the eleven shops that were listed.

She hung up the phone, and Theresa looked at her curiously. "What are you going to ask them when you call?"

"I'm going to ask for Garrett."

Theresa's heart skipped a beat. "Just like that?"

"Just like that," Deanna said, smiling as she dialed. She motioned for Theresa to pick up the other extension, "just in case it's him," and they both waited quietly for someone to answer at Atlantic Adventures, the first name they were given.

When the phone finally picked up, Deanna took a deep breath and asked pleasantly if Garrett was available to teach any classes.

"I'm sorry, I think you have the wrong number," the voice said quickly.

Deanna apologized and hung up. Unswayed, she went down the list to the next name and dialed again. Expecting the same answer, she was surprised when the person on the line hesitated.

"Are you talking about Garrett Blake?"

Theresa nearly fell from the chair at the sound of his name. Deanna said yes, and the man who answered went on.

"He's with Island Diving. Are you sure we can't help you? We've got some classes starting soon."

Deanna quickly excused herself. "No, I'm sorry. I really need to work with Garrett. I promised him I would." When she put the phone back in the cradle, she was smiling broadly. "So we're getting close now."

"I can't believe it was that easy. Do you really think it's the same Garrett?"

Deanna cocked her head and raised an eyebrow. "Well, we'll find out soon enough."

She then called information again and got the number for the ship registry of Wilmington. After dialing, she asked for someone who could verify some information. "My husband and I were vacationing down there," she explained, "when our boat broke down. This nice gentleman found us and helped us get back to shore. His name was Garrett Blake, and I think the name of his boat was *Happenstance.*"

The woman who answered was more than willing to help. Deanna heard tapping on a keyboard, then a strange beep. After a moment the woman said the words that both Deanna and Theresa hoped she would.

"Yes, here it is. Garrett Blake. Um . . . you got the name right, at least according to the information we have. It says here that the boat is named *Happenstance.*"

Deanna thanked her profusely and hung up the phone, beaming.

"Garrett Blake," she said with a victorious smile. "Our mysterious writer is named Garrett Blake."

Deanna handed her a slip of paper with the name. Theresa hesitated. Deanna looked at her for a moment; then she picked up the phone one more time.

"Now who're you calling?"

"My travel agency. You'll need a flight and a place to stay."

"I haven't even said I was going yet."

"Oh, you're going."

"But—"

"But nothing." She paused for a moment, and her words came softer. "Theresa, remember, you've got nothing to lose. The worst that could possibly happen is that you fly home in a couple of days. That's all."

They were both silent as they stared at each other. Deanna had a slight smirk on her face, and Theresa felt her pulse quicken as the finality of the decision hit her. I'm actually going to do this. I can't believe I'm going along with this.

Her mind was awhirl. Garrett Blake. Wilmington. Island Diving.

Happenstance. The words kept rolling through her head as if she were rehearsing for a part in a play.

Deanna told her to take off the rest of that day and the next, and on her way out of the office Theresa felt as if she had been cornered into something in the same way she had cornered Mr. Shendakin. But deep down she was pleased about it, and when the plane touched down in Wilmington the following day, Theresa Osborne was still wondering where all this would lead.

Chapter Four

THERESA woke early and rose from the bed to look out the hotel-room window. The North Carolina sun was casting golden prisms through an early morning haze, and she slid open the balcony door to freshen the room.

She thought about how easy it had been to get here. A little less than forty-eight hours ago she had been sitting with Deanna, studying the letters, making phone calls, and searching for Garrett. The plan she finally came up with was simple. She would go to Island Diving and browse around the store, with the hope of getting a look at Garrett Blake. If he seemed to be approximately her age, she would try to speak with him.

She showered and dressed in a short-sleeved white blouse, denim shorts, and a pair of white sandals. She wanted to look casual. When she was finally ready to leave, she found the phone book, thumbed through it, and scribbled the address of Island Diving on a piece of paper. Two deep breaths later she was walking down the hall.

Her first stop was at a convenience store, where she bought a map of Wilmington. Kure Beach, Carolina Beach, and Wrightsville Beach were reached by bridges that crossed from the city, and that was where most of the traffic seemed to be headed. After reaching the road she needed, Theresa slowed her rental car and looked for the shop.

Island Diving was an older wooden building, faded from the salt air and sea breezes, with one side of the store facing the Intracoastal Waterway. The hand-painted sign hung on two rusty metal chains, and the windows had the dusty look of a thousand rainstorms.

Theresa stepped out of the car, brushed the hair from her face, and started toward the entrance. She paused before opening the door to take a deep breath and collect her thoughts, then stepped inside.

She browsed through the store, walking among the aisles, watching assorted customers pull and replace items from the racks. She worked her way to the back wall and found herself staring at a series of framed newspaper and magazine articles hanging above the racks. After a quick glance she leaned forward for a closer look and suddenly realized she had stumbled across the answer to the first question she had about the mysterious Garrett Blake.

She finally knew what he looked like.

The first article was about scuba diving, and the caption beneath the photo read simply, "Garrett Blake of Island Diving, readying his class for its first ocean dive."

In it he was adjusting the straps that held the tank to a student's back. Garrett looked to be in his thirties, with a lean face and short brown hair that seemed to have bleached a little from hours spent in the sun. He was taller than the student by a couple of inches, and the sleeveless shirt he was wearing showed well-defined muscles in his arms. The picture was a little grainy, so she couldn't make out the color of his eyes.

The second article was about *Happenstance.* Eight pictures of the boat had been taken from various angles, inside and out, all detailing the restoration. The boat, she learned, was made entirely of wood and had been manufactured in Lisbon, Portugal, in 1927. It had a long and adventurous history, including being used in the Second World War to study the German garrisons that lined the shores of France. Eventually the boat made its way to Nantucket, where it was bought by a local businessman. By the time Garrett Blake purchased it four years ago, it had fallen into disrepair, and the article said that he and his wife, Catherine, had restored it.

Catherine . . .

Theresa looked at the article's date. April 1992. The article didn't mention that Catherine had died, and because one of the letters Theresa had was found three years ago in Norfolk, it meant that Catherine must have died sometime in 1993.

"Can I help you?"

Theresa turned instinctively toward the voice behind her. A young man was smiling at her, and she was suddenly glad she had seen the picture moments before. This person obviously wasn't Garrett.

"She's something, isn't she?" he asked.

"Who?"

"*Happenstance.* Garrett—the guy that owns the shop—rebuilt her. She's a wonderful boat, now that she's done."

"Is he here? Garrett, I mean."

"No, he's down at the docks. He won't be in until later this morning. Can I help you find something?"

"No, I was just browsing, actually."

"Okay, but if I can help you find something, let me know."

"I will," she said, and the young man started toward the counter at the front of the store. Theresa spent the next three minutes pretending to look at different items on the racks, then walked out after waving good-bye to the young man.

But instead of going to her car, she headed toward the marina.

THERESA found *Happenstance* easily because the vast majority of boats were white and *Happenstance* was natural wood. As she approached, however, she noticed that no one seemed to be around. After looking for any sign of Garrett, she checked the name on the back of the boat. It was indeed *Happenstance.* She brushed aside some hair that had blown onto her face and took a moment to admire the boat. It was beautiful—rich and textured. It had much more character than the sailboats docked on either side of it, and she knew why the paper had done an article on it. In a way it reminded her of a much smaller version of pirate ships she had seen in the movies. She paced back and forth for a few minutes, studying it from different angles.

She finally decided to try Island Diving a little later. It was obvious the man at the store was mistaken. After one last glance at the boat she turned to leave.

A man stood a few feet from her.

Garrett . . .

He was sweating in the morning heat, and his shirt was soaked through in a couple of places. The sleeves had been torn off, revealing tight muscles in his arms and forearms. He wore tan shorts and Top-Siders without socks and looked like someone who spent most, if not all, of his time near the ocean.

He watched her as she took an involuntary step backward. "Can I help you with something?" he asked.

For a moment all she could do was stare at him. Despite the fact she had seen a picture of him, he looked better than she expected, though she wasn't sure why. He was tall and broad-shouldered, not strikingly handsome, but there was something compelling about him, something masculine in the way he stood before her.

She motioned toward *Happenstance.* "I was just admiring your boat. It's really beautiful."

"Thank you," he said politely. "Have we met before?"

Theresa shook her head slowly. "I don't think so."

"Then how did you know the boat was mine?"

Relieved, she answered, "Oh, I saw your picture at your shop, in the articles on the wall. The young man said you would be here, and I thought that as long as you were, I'd come down to see for myself."

"He said I was here?"

She was silent as she remembered the exact words. "Actually, he told me you were at the docks. I just assumed that meant here."

He nodded. "I was at the other boat, the one we use for diving."

A small fishing boat blared its horn, and Garrett turned and waved to the man standing on the deck. After it had gone by, Garrett faced her again and was struck by how pretty she was. On impulse he lowered his eyes and reached for the red bandanna he had in his back pocket. He wiped the sweat from his forehead.

"You did a wonderful job restoring it," Theresa said.

He smiled faintly as he put the bandanna away. "Thanks. That's kind of you to say."

Theresa glanced toward *Happenstance* as he spoke, then back to him. "I know it's not any of my business," she said casually, "but would you mind if I asked you a little bit about it?"

She could tell by his expression that it wasn't the first time he'd been asked to talk about the boat.

"What would you like to know?"

She did her best to sound conversational. "Well, was it in as bad a condition when you first got it as the article implied?"

"Actually, it was worse." He stepped forward and pointed to the various spots on the boat as he mentioned them. "A lot of the wood had rotted near the bow, there were leaks along the side—it was a wonder she was still afloat at all. We ended up replacing a good portion of the hull, and what was left had to be sanded completely and then sealed and varnished again. And that was just the outside. The inside took a great deal longer."

Though she noticed the word "we" in his answer, she decided not to comment on it.

"It must have been a lot of work."

She smiled as she said it, and Garrett felt something tighten inside. She *was* pretty.

"It was, but it was worth it," he said. "She's more fun to sail than other boats."

"Why?"

"Because she was built by people who used her to make their living. They put a lot of care into designing her, and that makes sailing a lot easier."

"I take it you've been sailing a long time."

"Ever since I was a kid."

She nodded. After a short pause she took a small step toward the boat. "Do you mind?"

He shook his head. "No. Go ahead."

Theresa stepped forward and ran her hands along the side of the hull. Garrett couldn't help but notice her figure and how her straight, dark hair grazed her shoulders. But it wasn't only the way she looked that caught his eye. There was a confidence in the way she moved. It was as if she knew exactly what men were thinking as she stood near them, he realized suddenly. He shook his head.

"How long did it take you to restore it?" she asked, turning to face him.

"It was almost a year before we got her out on the water."

Again she heard the word "we."

After admiring the boat for another few seconds, she returned to his side. For a moment neither one of them spoke.

"Well," she finally said as she crossed her arms, "I've probably taken enough of your time."

"It's okay," he said. "I love to talk about sailing."

"I would too. It always looked like fun to me."

"You sound like you've never gone sailing before."

She shrugged. "I haven't. I've never had the chance."

She looked at him when she spoke, and when their eyes met, Garrett heard the words coming out of his mouth before he could stop them. "Well, if you'd like to go, I usually take her out after work. You're welcome to come along this evening."

Why he said that, he wasn't exactly sure. Maybe, he thought, it was a desire for female companionship after all these years, if only for a short time. Or maybe it had something to do with the way her eyes lit up whenever she talked.

Theresa, too, was a little surprised, but she quickly decided to accept. "I'd love to," she said. "What time?"

"How about seven o'clock? The sun begins to drop then, and it's the ideal time to go out."

"Seven o'clock is great for me. I'll bring along something to eat."

She shifted her weight from one foot to the other, waiting to see if he'd say anything else. When he didn't, she absently adjusted the purse on her shoulder. "I guess I'll see you tonight. Here at the boat, right?"

"Right here," he said. "It will be fun. You'll enjoy it."

"I'm sure I will. See you later."

She turned and started down the docks, her hair blowing in the breeze. As she was walking away, Garrett realized he'd forgotten something.

"Hey!" he shouted.

She stopped and turned to face him. "Yes?"

He took a couple of steps in her direction. "I forgot to ask. What's your name?"

"I'm Theresa. Theresa Osborne."

"My name's Garrett Blake."

"Okay, Garrett, I'll see you at seven."

With that she turned and walked briskly away. Garrett watched her retreating figure, trying to make sense of his conflicting emotions. Though part of him was excited about what had just happened, another part of him felt that there was something wrong with the whole thing. He knew there wasn't any reason to feel guilty, but the feeling was definitely there, and he wished there was something he could do about it.

But there wasn't, of course. There never was.

THE clock rolled past the dinner hour and onward toward seven, but for Garrett Blake time had stopped three years ago, when Catherine stepped off the curb and was killed by an elderly man who lost control of his car. In the ensuing weeks his anger at the driver eventually gave way to a sorrow that rendered him incapable of any action whatsoever. He couldn't sleep more than three hours a night, cried whenever he saw Catherine's clothes in the closet, and lost almost twenty pounds on a diet that consisted of coffee and Ritz crackers. His father temporarily took over the business, while Garrett sat in silence on the back porch of his home, trying to imagine a world without her. Sometimes as he sat there, he hoped that the salty, humid air would swallow him up completely so he wouldn't have to face the future alone.

What made it so hard was that it seemed as though he couldn't remember a time when she wasn't around. They had known each other most of their lives. In third grade they were best friends, and he gave her two cards on Valentine's Day, but after that they drifted apart and simply coexisted as they progressed from one grade to the next. Catherine was gangly and thin, always the smallest in her class, and though Garrett always held a special place in his heart for her, he never noticed that she was slowly becoming an attractive young woman. After four years at Chapel Hill, where he majored in marine biology, he bumped into her at Wrightsville Beach and suddenly realized how foolish he had been. She was no longer the gangly girl he remembered. In a word she was beautiful. Her hair was blond, and her eyes held infinite mystery; and when he finally closed his gaping mouth and asked her what she was doing later, they started a relationship that eventually led to marriage and six wonderful years together.

On their wedding night, alone in a hotel room lit only by candles, she handed him the two Valentines he'd once given her, and she laughed aloud at the expression on his face when he realized what they were. "Of course I kept them," she whispered as she wrapped her arms around him. "It was the first time I ever loved someone, and I knew that if I gave you enough time, you'd come back to me."

Whenever Garrett found himself thinking of Catherine, he remembered either the way she looked that night or how she looked the very last time they went sailing. Even now he remembered that evening clearly, her blond hair blowing wildly in the breeze, her face rapturous as she laughed aloud.

"Feel the spray!" she cried exultantly as she stood at the bow of the boat. Holding on to a rope, she leaned out into the wind, her profile outlined against the glittering sky.

"Be careful!" Garrett shouted back, holding the wheel steady.

She leaned out even farther, glancing back with a mischievous smile.

"I'm serious!" he shouted again. For a moment it looked as if her grip were weakening. Garrett quickly stepped away from the wheel, only to hear her laugh again as she pulled herself upright. Ever light on her feet, she made her way back easily to the wheel and put her arms around him.

Kissing his ear, she whispered playfully, "Did l make you nervous?"

"You always make me nervous when you do things like that."

"Don't sound so gruff," she said as she kissed him again. "Why don't we lower the sails and drop the anchor?"

"Now?"

She nodded. "Unless of course you'd rather sail all night." With a subtle look she opened the door to the cabin and vanished from sight. Four minutes later the boat was stabilized, and he opened the door to join her.

Garrett exhaled sharply, dispelling the memory like smoke. Though he could remember the events of that evening, he found that as time was rolling on, it was becoming difficult to visualize exactly the way she looked. Now he saw her clearly only at night, when he dreamed of her. Yet upon waking, he always felt exhausted and depressed.

His father tried to help as best he could. He, too, had lost a wife and so knew what his son was going through. "It isn't right that you're always alone," he'd said. "It's almost like you've given up." Garrett knew there was a measure of truth to that. But the simple fact was that he had no desire to find anyone else.

In time he returned to the shop and started working again, doing his best to go on with his life. He got used to living alone—cooking, cleaning, and doing his own laundry.

He thought he was getting better, but when the time came to pack up Catherine's things, he didn't have the heart to do it. His father eventually took matters into his own hands. After a weekend spent diving, Garrett came home to a house stripped of her belongings. Without her things the house was empty; he no longer saw any reason to stay. He sold it within a month and moved to a smaller house on Carolina Beach.

His father sometimes commented that Garrett seemed to be doing better, but to him nothing would ever be the same again.

GARRETT Blake went to the marina with a few minutes to spare so he could get *Happenstance* ready.

His father had phoned just as he was stepping out the door on the way to the docks, and Garrett found himself remembering the conversation.

"Would you like to come for supper?" his father had asked.

Garrett had replied that he couldn't. "I'm going sailing with someone tonight."

His father had stayed quiet for a moment. Then, "With a woman?"

Garrett explained briefly how he and Theresa had met.

"You sound like you're a little nervous about your date," his father remarked.

"It's not a date. We're just going sailing."

"Is she pretty?"

"What does that matter?"

"It doesn't. But it still sounds like a date to me."

"It's not a date."

"If you say so."

GARRETT saw her walking up the dock a little after seven, dressed in shorts and a red sleeveless shirt, carrying a small picnic basket in one hand and a sweatshirt and light jacket in the other.

"Hi," she said when she reached the boat. "I hope you haven't been waiting long."

"Oh, hi. And no, I haven't been waiting long at all. Can I help you up?" He extended his arm.

Theresa handed him her things, and he set them on one of the seats that ran along the deck. When he took her hands to pull her up, she felt the calluses on his palms. After she was safely aboard, he motioned toward the wheel, taking a small step backward. "Are you ready to head out?"

"Whenever you are."

"Then go ahead and take a seat. I'm going to get us out onto the water."

She looked around the boat before finding a seat in the corner. He turned a key, and an engine hummed to life. Slowly *Happenstance* began to back out of its slip. A little surprised, Theresa said, "I didn't know there was an engine."

He turned and answered over his shoulder. "It's a small one—just enough power to get us in and out of the slip."

Once *Happenstance* was safely in the open water of the Intracoastal Waterway, Garrett turned into the wind and cut the engine. After putting on gloves, he raised the sail quickly. *Happenstance* heeled to the breeze, and in one quick motion Garrett was back at the wheel. Theresa felt the boat gradually picking up speed.

"All right, I think we've got it," he said. "We should be able to make it without having to tack."

They moved toward the inlet. Because she knew he was concentrating on what he was doing, she kept quiet and looked around. Like most sailboats, this one had two levels—the lower, outside deck, where they were standing, and the forward deck, about four feet higher, which stretched to the front of the boat. That was where the cabin was located.

The sails rumbled loudly as they moved with the wind. Water rushed along the side of the boat, and terns circled directly overhead, gliding on updrafts. Everything seemed to be in motion.

Theresa slipped on the sweatshirt she had brought along. Already the air seemed a lot cooler than it had when they'd left. The sun was dropping, and the fading light reflected off the sails, casting shadows across most of the deck.

Waves from a larger boat passing in the distance made them bob, and Theresa stood and made her way toward Garrett. He turned the wheel again, more sharply this time. Theresa watched him until the boat was safely clear of the inlet.

Once there was enough distance between *Happenstance* and the other boats, Garrett tied a small loop in the jib line and looped it around the wheel.

"Okay, that should do it," he said. "We can take a seat if you want."

"You don't have to hold it?"

"That's what the loop is for. Sometimes, when the wind is really shifty, you have to hold the wheel the whole time. But we got lucky with the weather tonight. We could sail in this direction for hours."

With the sun descending slowly in the evening sky behind them, Garrett led the way back to where Theresa had been sitting earlier. They sat in the corner—she on the side, he against the back. Feeling the wind in her face, Theresa pulled her hair back, looking out over the water.

"It's really beautiful out here," she said as she turned toward him. "Thanks for inviting me along."

"You're welcome. It's nice to have some company once in a while."

She smiled at his answer. "Do you usually sail alone?"

He leaned back as he spoke, stretching his legs out in front of him. "Usually. It's a good way to unwind after work. No matter how stressful the day is, once I get out here, the wind seems to blow it all away."

"But you like your work, don't you?"

"Yeah, I do. I wouldn't trade what I do for anything." He paused and adjusted the watch on his wrist. "So, Theresa, what do you do?"

She paused only slightly before answering. "I'm a columnist for the Boston *Times.* I write about parenting."

She saw the surprised look in his eyes, the same look she saw whenever she dated someone new. You may as well get this over with right away, she thought to herself. "I have a son," she went on. "Kevin's twelve. He's with his father in California right now. We divorced a few years ago."

Garrett nodded without judgment, then asked, "Would you like to see the rest of the boat?"

She nodded. "I'd love to."

Garrett rose and checked the sails again before leading the way inside the cabin. On the left, a seat ran along one side of the boat. Directly opposite was a small table with room enough for two people to sit. Near the door were a sink and a stove burner, with a small refrigerator underneath, and straight ahead was a door that led to the sleeping cabin.

Garrett stood off to one side with his hands on his hips as Theresa explored the interior. After a moment she said, "From the outside you wouldn't think it's as large as it is."

"I know." He cleared his throat awkwardly. "Surprising, isn't it?"

He stepped around her and bent over to pull a can of Coca-Cola from the refrigerator. "Are you up for something to drink?"

"Sure," she said. She ran her hands along the walls, feeling the texture of the wood.

He stood and handed her a can. Their fingers touched briefly as she took it.

She opened it and took a swallow before setting it on the table.

As he opened his own can of soda, she turned her attention to a framed photograph that hung on the wall. In it Garrett Blake was standing on a pier with a marlin he'd caught, looking much younger than he was now.

"I see you like to fish," she said. He stepped toward her, and once he was close, she felt the warmth radiating from him. He smelled like salt and wind.

"Yeah, I do," he said quietly. "My father was a shrimper, and I pretty much grew up on the water."

"How long ago was this taken?"

"That one's about ten years old. It was taken right before I went back to college for my senior year."

She looked at the picture again. "Is that your father standing next to you?"

"Yeah, that's him."

"He looks like you," she said.

Garrett smiled a little, wondering whether or not it was a compliment. He motioned to the table, and Theresa sat down opposite him.

Once she was comfortable, she asked, "You said you went to college?"

He met her eyes. "Yeah. I went to U.N.C. and majored in marine biology. After graduating, I worked for the Duke Maritime Institute as a dive specialist, but there wasn't much money in that. So I got a teaching certificate and started taking in students on weekends. The shop came later." He cocked an eyebrow. "How about you?"

"I grew up in Omaha, Nebraska, and went to school at Brown. I've been with the *Times* for nine years now."

"How do you like being a columnist?"

She thought about it for a moment. "It's a good job," she finally said. "I can pick Kevin up after school, and I have the freedom to write what I want. It pays fairly well, too, but . . ." She paused. "I guess that right now I'm your typical overworked single mother, if you know what I mean."

He nodded and spoke softly. "Life doesn't often turn out the way we think it will, does it?"

"No, I guess it doesn't," she said, and again she caught his gaze. His expression made her wonder if he'd said something he rarely said to anyone else. She smiled and leaned toward him.

"Are you ready to eat? I brought some things in the basket."

"Whenever you are. Would you like to eat down here or outside?"

"Outside, definitely."

They picked up their cans of soda and left the cabin. On their way out Garrett motioned for her to go on without him. "Give me a minute to drop the anchor," he said, "so we can eat without having to check the boat every few minutes." Theresa reached her seat and opened the basket she had brought with her. On the horizon the sun was sinking into a bank of cumulus clouds. She pulled out a couple of sandwiches wrapped in cellophane, as well as some Styrofoam containers of coleslaw and potato salad.

She watched as Garrett lowered the sails. With his back to her, she again noticed how strong he looked. His shoulder muscles appeared larger than she had first realized, amplified by his small waist. She couldn't believe she was actually sailing with this man when only two days ago she had been in Boston. The whole thing seemed unreal.

Once the boat had stopped completely, Garrett lowered the anchor. Then he took his seat next to Theresa.

"Is everything okay?" she asked.

He nodded. "But I was just thinking that if the wind keeps picking up, we'll have to tack a bit more often on our way back."

She put some potato salad and coleslaw along with his sandwich on his plate and handed it to him, conscious of the fact that he was sitting closer than he had before.

"Will it take longer to get back, then?"

"A little, but it won't be a problem unless the wind stops completely. On the ocean it usually doesn't."

"How come?"

He smiled in amusement. "Well, winds are driven by differences in temperature—when warm air rushes to cooler air. For the wind to stop blowing, you'd need the air temperature to exactly equal the water temperature for miles around. Down here the air is usually hot during the day, but as soon as the sun starts to set, the temperature drops quickly. That's why the best time to go out is at dusk, when the temperature is changing constantly."

"What happens if the wind does stop?"

"The sails empty and the boat comes to a halt. You're powerless."

"What do you do?"

"Nothing, really. Just sit back and wait it out."

"Sounds enjoyable."

"It is." He looked away from her intent gaze, suddenly uncomfortable. "Anyway, tell me something about yourself. You said you were married once?"

She nodded. "For eight years. But David—that's his name—seemed to lose heart in the relationship. He ended up having an affair. I just couldn't live with that."

"I couldn't either," Garrett said softly, "but it still doesn't make it any easier."

"No, it didn't." She paused and took a drink of her soda. "But he's a good father to Kevin, and that's all I want from him now."

A large swell passed beneath the hull, and Garrett turned his head to make sure the anchor would hold. When he turned back, Theresa said, "Okay, your turn. Tell me about you."

Garrett talked about growing up in Wilmington as an only child. He told her that his mother had died when he was twelve. He spoke about what it had been like to start the shop and what his typical days were like now. Strangely, he said nothing at all about Catherine.

As they talked on, the sky turned to black and fog began to settle in around them. With the boat rocking slightly in the waves, a kind of intimacy descended upon them.

When they reached a quiet point in the conversation, Garrett leaned back and ran his hands through his hair. He closed his eyes and seemed to be savoring a silent moment for himself.

On their last sail together Catherine surprised Garrett with a candlelight dinner and wine, and they talked quietly for hours. The sea was calm, and the gentle rise and fall of the swells were comforting in their familiarity.

Later that night, after making love, Catherine lay by Garrett's side, skimming her fingers across his chest, saying nothing.

"What are you thinking?" he asked finally.

"Just that I didn't think it was possible to love someone as much as I love you," she whispered.

"I didn't think it was possible either," he answered softly. "I don't know what I'd ever do without you."

"Will you make me a promise?"

"Anything."

"If anything ever does happen to me, promise me that you'll find someone else."

"I don't think I could love anyone except you."

"Just promise me, okay?"

It took a moment to answer. "All right. If it makes you happy, I promise."

Catherine snuggled into him. "I'm happy, Garrett."

When the memory finally faded, Garrett cleared his throat. "I think it's about time we start back," he said.

A few minutes later the boat was under way again. Garrett stood at the wheel, keeping *Happenstance* on course. Theresa stood next to him with her hand on the railing. Neither of them spoke for a long while, and Garrett Blake found himself wondering why he felt so off-balance.

The lights from the buildings along the shore flickered in the slowly thickening fog. As *Happenstance* moved closer to shore, Theresa suddenly doubted that they would see each other again. In a few minutes they'd be back at the docks and they would say good-bye.

They made their way through the inlet, turning toward the marina. Garrett kept the sails up until approximately the same spot where he'd first raised them, then lowered them with the same intensity he had used to guide the boat all evening. The engine kicked to life, and within a few minutes they had made their way past the boats that had been moored all evening. When they reached his dock, Theresa stood on the deck while Garrett jumped off and secured *Happenstance* with the ropes.

Theresa walked to the stern to get the basket and her jacket, then stopped. Thinking for a moment, she picked up the basket, but instead of grabbing her jacket, she pushed it partway under the seat cushion. She walked to the side of the boat, and Garrett offered his hand. Again she felt the strength in it as she took it, and she stepped down onto the dock.

They stared at each other for just a moment, as if wondering what would come next, before Garrett finally motioned toward the boat. "I've got to close her up for the night, and it's going to take a little while. Can I walk you to your car first?"

"Sure," she said, and he started down the dock with Theresa beside him. When they reached her car, Garrett watched as she unlocked the door and opened it.

"I had a wonderful time tonight," she said.

"So did I."

For a moment their eyes met.

"I'd better get back," he said quickly. "I've got an early morning tomorrow." She nodded, and not knowing what else to do, Garrett held out his hand. "It was nice to have met you, Theresa. I hope you enjoy the rest of your vacation."

"Thanks for everything, Garrett. It was nice meeting you, too."

She took her seat behind the steering wheel and turned the ignition. Garrett shut the door for her and listened as she put the car into gear. Smiling at him one last time, she glanced in the rearview mirror and slowly backed the car out. When she was safely on her way, Garrett turned and walked back up the docks, wondering why he felt so unsettled.

Within twenty minutes Theresa was back in her hotel room. Later, lying in bed, she thought about Garrett. She turned off the bedside lamp, and once her eyes adjusted to the darkness, she looked toward the space between the loosely drawn curtains. The crescent moon had risen, and a little moonlight spilled onto the bed. Staring at it, she found herself unable to turn away until her body finally relaxed and her eyes closed for the night.

Chapter Five

"AND then what happened?"

Jeb Blake leaned over his cup of coffee, speaking in a raspy voice. Nearly seventy, he was lean and tall, with a deeply wrinkled face. The thinning hair on his head was white, and his Adam's apple protruded from his neck like a small prune. His arms were tattooed and scarred, the knuckles on his hands permanently swollen from years of wear and tear as a shrimper.

"Nothing happened. She got into her car and drove away."

Rolling the first of the dozen cigarettes he would smoke a day,

Jeb Blake stared at his son. "Well, that's kind of a waste, isn't it?"

Garrett was surprised by his bluntness. "No, Dad, it wasn't a waste. I had a good time last night. I enjoyed her company."

"But you're not going to see her again."

Garrett took a drink of coffee and shook his head. "I doubt it. Like I said, she's here on vacation."

"For how long?"

"I don't know. I didn't ask. Why are you so interested anyway? I went out sailing with someone and had a good time. There's not much more I can say about it."

Jeb leaned over his coffee again. "You liked her, didn't you?"

"Yeah, Dad, I did. But like I said, I probably won't see her again. I don't know where she's staying, and for all I know, she could be leaving town today."

His father watched him in silence for a moment before asking the next question carefully. "But if she were still here and you knew where she was, do you think you would?"

Garrett looked away without answering, and Jeb reached across the table, taking his son's arm.

"Son, it's been three years. I know you loved her, but it's okay to let it go now."

A few minutes later they finished their coffee. Garrett tossed a couple of dollars onto the table and followed his father out of the diner, toward his truck in the parking lot.

When he finally got to the shop, a dozen different things were going through his head. Unable to concentrate on the paperwork he needed to do, he decided to go back to the docks to finish working on the engine he had started repairing the day before. He definitely had to spend some time in the shop today, but at the moment he needed to be alone.

As he removed the engine casing, he thought about the conversation he'd had with his father. He'd been right, of course, but Garrett didn't know how to stop feeling the way he did. Catherine had meant everything to him. All she'd had to do was look at him, and he'd feel as if everything were suddenly right in the world. To have something like that taken away . . . it just seemed *wrong.* Why her of all people? For months he lay awake at night asking himself, What if? What if she'd waited an extra second before crossing the street? What if they had lingered at breakfast for another few minutes? A thousand what-ifs, and he was no closer to understanding the whole thing than he had been when it first happened.

The sun rose overhead as he worked steadily, and he found himself wiping the sweat as it formed on his forehead. Yesterday at about this time, he remembered, he'd watched as Theresa walked down the docks toward *Happenstance.* When she stopped at his boat, he'd been surprised. He'd expected her to pause for only a moment, but after watching her for a little while, he realized that she had come to see *Happenstance.*

There was something odd in the way she had first looked at him. It was almost as if she recognized something about him. It was as if she knew more about him than she was willing to admit.

She said she'd read the articles in the shop—maybe that's where the strange look came from. It was the only plausible explanation, but even now something didn't sit quite right about the whole situation.

Not that it mattered.

Just before eleven he headed back to the shop. Ian, one of his summertime employees, was on the phone, and when Garrett walked up, he handed him three messages. The first two were from distributors.

He read the third as he was walking back to his office and stopped when he realized who it was from. Making sure it wasn't a mistake, he entered his office and closed the door behind him. Picking up the phone, he dialed the number.

Theresa Osborne picked up on the second ring.

"Hey, Theresa, this is Garrett. There's a message here that you called."

"Oh, hi, Garrett. Thanks for returning my call. I left my jacket on the boat last night, and I was wondering if you found it."

"I didn't. But let me run down there and take a look."

"Is that too much trouble?"

"Not at all. I'll call you right back."

Garrett said good-bye and left the shop, walking quickly back to *Happenstance*. After stepping aboard, he spotted the jacket near the stern, partially hidden under one of the seat cushions.

Back in his office, he dialed the number written on the slip. This time Theresa picked up on the first ring.

"This is Garrett again. I found your jacket."

"Thanks. I appreciate your looking for it." She sounded relieved. "Could you hold it for me? I can be down at your shop in about twenty minutes to pick it up."

"I'd be glad to," he answered. After hanging up the phone, he leaned back in his chair, thinking about what had just happened. She hasn't left town yet, he thought, and I'm going to get to see her again.

Not, of course, that it mattered.

THERESA arrived twenty minutes later, dressed in shorts and a low-necked sleeveless blouse that did wonderful things for her figure. She smiled and called out, "Hi," and Garrett moved toward her with her jacket in hand.

"Good as new," he said, offering it to her.

"Thanks for picking it up for me," she said, and there was something in her eyes that made the initial attraction he'd felt the day before begin to rise again. Absently he scratched the side of his face.

"I was glad to do it. The wind must have forced it from view."

"I guess so," she said with a slight shrug, and Garrett watched as she adjusted the shoulder of her blouse with her hand. He said the first words that came to mind.

"I had a good time last night."

"So did I."

Her eyes caught his as she said it, and Garrett smiled softly.

"Did you come all the way down here just for your jacket, or were you going to do a little sight-seeing as well?"

"I was going to get lunch." She looked at him expectantly. "Any recommendations?"

He thought for a moment before responding. "I like Hank's, down at the pier. The view is out of this world, and they have great shrimp and oysters."

She waited to see if he would add anything else, and when he didn't, she glanced away, looking toward the windows. Finally, gathering himself, he spoke.

"I'd be happy to take you there if you want some company."

She smiled. "I'd like that, Garrett."

He looked relieved and led her through the shop and out the back door.

HANK'S had been in business since the pier was built, and was frequented by locals and tourists alike. Low in ambience but high in character, it had wooden floors scraped and scuffed by years of sandy shoes, and large windows offering a view of the ocean. The tables and chairs were wooden, sturdy-looking, and decorated by the carvings of hundreds of former visitors.

"Trust me," he said as they were walking to a table. "The food is great no matter what this place looks like."

They took their seats at a table near the corner, and Garrett pushed aside two bottles of beer that hadn't yet been cleared. Cheaply laminated menus were stacked between squeeze bottles of Tabasco, tartar sauce, and another sauce simply labeled HANK'S. Glancing around, Theresa saw that nearly every table was occupied.

"It's crowded," she said, making herself comfortable.

"It always is. We were lucky to get a table."

She glanced at the menu. "So what do you recommend?"

"Do you like seafood?"

"I love it."

"Then go with the tuna or the dolphin. They're both delicious."

"Dolphin?"

He laughed. "Not Flipper. It's dolphinfish. That's what we call it around here."

"I think I'll go with the tuna," she said with a wink, "just to make sure."

"You think I'd make up something like that?"

She spoke in a teasing voice. "We just met yesterday, remember. I don't know what you're capable of."

"I'm hurt," he said in the same voice, and she laughed. He laughed, too, and after a moment she surprised him by reaching across the table and touching his arm briefly. Catherine, he suddenly realized, used to do the same thing to get his attention.

"So do they have anyone to serve you here," she asked, "or do we have to catch and cook our own fish?"

"Damn Yankees," he mumbled while shaking his head, and she laughed again.

A few moments later the waitress arrived and took their orders. Both Theresa and Garrett ordered beers, and after putting the order into the kitchen, the waitress brought two bottles to the table.

"No glasses?" Theresa asked with a raised eyebrow after the waitress had left.

"Nope. This place is nothing if not classy."

"I can see why you like it so much."

"Is that a comment about my lack of taste?"

"Only if you're insecure about it."

"Now you sound like a psychiatrist."

"I'm not, but I am a mother, and that makes me something of an expert in human nature."

"Is that so?"

"It's what I tell Kevin."

Garrett took a sip of his beer. "Did you talk to him today?"

She nodded and took a drink as well. "Just for a few minutes. He's having a great time with his father. David's always been good with him. Whenever Kevin goes out there, he expects fun."

Garrett looked at her curiously. "You sound like you're not so sure about it."

She hesitated before continuing. "Well, I just hope it doesn't lead to disappointment later. David and his new wife have started a family, and as soon as the baby gets a little older, it's going to be harder for David and Kevin to be alone together."

Garrett leaned forward as he spoke. "It's impossible to protect your kids against disappointment in life."

"I know that, I really do. It's just that . . ."

She stopped, and Garrett gently finished her thoughts for her. "He's your son, and you don't want to see him hurt."

"Exactly." Beads of condensation had formed on the outside of her bottle of beer, and Theresa began to peel off the label. Again it was the same thing Catherine used to do. Garrett took another drink of beer and forced his mind back to the conversation at hand.

"I don't know what to say except that if Kevin's anything like you, I'm sure he'll end up all right."

"What do you mean?"

He shrugged. "No one's life is easy—yours included. By watching you overcome adversity, he'll learn how to do it as well."

"Now you're the one sounding like a psychiatrist."

"I'm just telling you what I learned growing up. I was about Kevin's age when my mom died of cancer. Watching my dad taught me that I had to go on with life, no matter what."

"Does your dad still live in town?" she asked.

"Yeah, he does. I see him a lot these days. We try to get together at least once a week. He likes to keep me on the straight and narrow."

She smiled. "Most parents do."

The food arrived, and they continued their conversation as they ate. Garrett told her about some of the adventures that had happened to him while sailing or scuba diving. She listened, fascinated. The stories that men told up in Boston usually focused on business accomplishments. He spoke about the sea creatures he had seen on his dives and what it was like to be chased by a hammerhead shark. He had loosened up, compared to the evening before. There was energy in the way he spoke to her now, and Theresa found the change appealing.

When the bill arrived, Garrett put some money on the table and motioned for them to leave. "Are you ready?"

"Whenever you are. And thanks for lunch. It was great."

As they walked out the front door, she fully expected that Garrett would want to return to the shop right away, but he surprised her by suggesting something different.

"How about a walk along the beach?" When she said yes, he led her to the side of the pier and down the steps. When they reached the compact sand at the edge of the tide, both of them stopped for a moment to remove their shoes.

They began to stroll in silence, taking in the sights.

"Is it like the beaches up north?" Garrett asked.

"Some of them, but the water's a lot warmer here. Haven't you ever been to the coast up north?"

"I've never been outside North Carolina."

She smiled at him. "A real world traveler, huh?"

He laughed under his breath. "No, but I don't feel like I'm missing that much." After a few steps he changed the subject. "So how long are you staying in Wilmington?"

"Until Sunday. I have to go back to work on Monday."

Five more days, he thought.

It was a few moments before Garrett spoke again. "Can I ask you a personal question?"

"It depends on the question."

He stopped walking and picked up a couple of small seashells and handed them to her. "Are you seeing anyone up in Boston?"

She took the shells as she answered. "No."

"Why not? A woman like you should have your pick of men."

She smiled at that, and they slowly started walking again. "Thanks. That's nice of you to say. But it's not that easy, especially when you have a son." She paused. "But what about you? Are you seeing anyone right now?"

He shook his head. "No. I guess I haven't met anyone I'd really like to see on a regular basis."

"Is that all?"

It was a moment of truth, and they both knew it. Theresa felt something tighten inside.

"I was married once," Garrett said. "She passed away."

"I'm sorry," Theresa said quietly.

"It happened three years ago. Ever since then I haven't been interested in dating or even looking." He stopped for a moment.

"It must get lonely sometimes," Theresa said.

"It does, but I try not to think about that too much. I keep busy at the shop, and it helps the days go by."

When Garrett didn't add anything else, she asked, "What was she like?"

"Catherine?" His throat went dry. "Do you really want to know?"

Part of him wanted Theresa to understand. Despite himself, he was drawn back in time once more.

"Hey, sweetheart," Catherine said as she looked up from the garden. "I didn't expect you home so soon."

"It's been pretty slow in the shop this morning, and I thought I'd pop home for lunch to see how you were doing."

"I'm feeling a lot better."

"You think it was the flu?"

"I don't know. It was probably something I ate. About an hour after you left, I felt good enough to do a little gardening." She gestured at a freshly turned patch of soil.

"That's great, but don't you think you should have left some of the dirt in the flower bed?"

She wiped her forehead with the back of her hand and stood, squinting up at him in the bright sunlight. "Do I look that bad?"

Her knees were dark from kneeling in the dirt, and a streak of mud ran across her cheek. Her hair was escaping from a messy ponytail, and her face was red and sweating from exertion.

"You look perfect."

Catherine took off her gloves and tossed them on the porch. "I'm not perfect, Garrett, but thanks. C'mon, let me get you some lunch. I know you've got to get back to the shop."

He sighed and turned to Theresa, who was staring at him, waiting. He spoke softly.

"Catherine was everything I ever wanted. She was beautiful and charming, with a quick sense of humor. She supported me in everything I did. She . . ." He paused, at a loss for words. "I don't know whether I'll ever get used to being without her."

Theresa hurt for him more than she would have imagined. It wasn't just his voice, but the look on his face before he described her—as if torn between the beauty and the pain of remembering.

"I'm sorry about that," he said. "I didn't mean to come off sounding like I did."

Theresa's reaction was almost instinctive. Stepping toward him, she reached for his hand. Taking it slowly in hers, she squeezed it gently. "Your feelings say a lot about you, Garrett. You're the kind of person who loves forever. That's nothing to be ashamed of."

"I know. It's just that it's been three years."

"Someday you'll find someone special again. People who've been in love once usually do. It's in their nature."

She squeezed his hand again, and Garrett felt her touch warm him.

"I hope you're right," he said finally.

"I am. I know these things. I'm a mother, remember?"

He laughed under his breath, trying to release the tension he felt. "I remember. And you're probably a good one."

They turned around and started back to the pier, talking quietly and still holding hands. By the time they reached his truck and headed back to the shop, Garrett was more confused than ever.

"What are you thinking?" she asked as Garrett shifted the truck into a higher gear and they made their way over the bridge toward Wilmington.

"I was thinking," he said, "that if you don't have plans, I'd like to have you over for supper tonight."

She smiled. "I was hoping you'd say that."

He was still surprised at himself for asking as he turned left onto the road that led to his shop.

"Can you come by my place about eight? I have some things I have to do at the shop, and I probably won't finish until late."

"That's fine."

They pulled into the lot, and Theresa followed Garrett into his office. He scribbled the directions to his house on a slip of paper, trying not to look as confused as he felt. "You shouldn't have any trouble finding the place," he said. "Just look for my truck out front. But if you have any problems, my number's at the bottom."

THERESA spent the rest of the afternoon exploring Wilmington's historic district, while Garrett faced one small crisis after another in the shop.

He was tired, and he breathed a sigh of relief when he closed up for the night. After work he drove first to the grocery store and picked up the items he needed for dinner. He showered and put on a pair of clean jeans and a light cotton shirt, then went out onto the back deck and sat in one of the wrought-iron chairs.

Finally he heard the sound of a slowly idling motor making its way down the block. He stepped off the deck and went around the side of the house, watching as Theresa parked on the street.

She was wearing jeans and the same blouse she had worn earlier. She looked relaxed as she walked toward him, and when she smiled warmly at him, he realized that his attraction had grown stronger since their lunch this afternoon, and it made him a little uneasy. As he got close to her, he smelled the scent of perfume.

"I brought some wine," she said, handing it to him. "I thought it might go well with dinner." Then, after a short pause, "How was your afternoon?"

"It was busy. In fact, I just got home a little while ago." He started toward the front door, Theresa right beside him. "I was thinking of grilling some steaks, but then I got to wondering if you ate things like that."

"Are you kidding? I grew up in Nebraska. I love a good steak."

"Then you're in for a pleasant surprise. I happen to make the best steaks in the world."

As they approached the front steps, Theresa looked at the house for the first time. It was relatively small—one story—with painted wooden siding that was peeling badly in more than one place. The first thing she noticed upon entering was the view. In the main room, windows extended from the floor to the ceiling along the entire back of the house, overlooking the beach.

"This view is incredible," she said, surprised.

"It is, isn't it? I've been here for a few years now, but I still don't take it for granted."

Off to one side was a fireplace, surrounded by a dozen underwater photographs. She moved toward them. "Do you mind if I look around?"

"No, go ahead. I have to get the grill out back ready."

After Garrett left through the sliding glass door to the deck, Theresa looked at the pictures for a while, then toured the rest of the house. The front portion contained a kitchen, a small dining area, and the bathroom. There was only one bedroom, reached by a door off the living room.

She stopped and glanced inside. When she looked toward his nightstand, she saw a framed picture of a woman. Making sure that Garrett was still outside cleaning the grill, she stepped in to take a closer look.

Catherine must have been in her mid-twenties when it was taken. She was attractive—a little more petite than Theresa—with blond hair that hung to mid-shoulder and deep green eyes that gave her an exotic look. They seemed to be staring back at Theresa. She put the photo down gently, making sure it was set at the same angle it was before. Turning around, she continued to feel as if Catherine were watching her every move.

She left the bedroom, walked to the sliding glass doors that led from the main room onto the deck, and opened them. Garrett smiled at her when he heard her come out. She strolled to the edge of the deck and leaned against one of the rails, one leg over the other.

"Did you take all the photos on the walls?" she asked.

He used the back of his hand to wipe the hair from his face. "Yeah. For a while there I took my camera out on most of my dives." As he spoke, he dumped some charcoal into the grill. Then he added a bit of lighter fluid. "I'm going to let this soak for a couple of minutes. Do you want anything to drink?"

Theresa asked, "What do you have?"

"Beer, soda, or the wine you brought."

"A beer sounds good."

While he was inside, Theresa turned and looked up and down the beach. Now that the sun was going down, most of the people were gone, and the few that were left were jogging or walking.

"Do you ever get tired of having all these people around?" she asked when he returned.

He handed her the beer. "Not really. Usually by the time I get home, the beach is pretty much deserted. And in the winter no one is out here at all."

For just a moment she imagined him sitting on his deck, watching the water, alone as always. Garrett reached into his pocket and took out a box of matches. He lit the charcoals, stepping back when the flames shot up.

"Now I'm going to get supper going. And if you're lucky, maybe I'll share my secret recipe with you."

She cocked her head and looked at him slyly. "You know you're setting a pretty high standard for these steaks."

"I know. But I have faith."

He winked at her, and she followed him to the kitchen. Garrett opened one of the cabinets and pulled out a couple of potatoes. He wrapped them in foil and set them in the oven.

"Can I give you a hand with something?"

"I think I've got it pretty much in control. I bought one of those prepackaged salads."

Theresa stood off to one side as Garrett got the salad out of the refrigerator. From the corner of his eye he glanced at her as he emptied it into a bowl. What was it about her that made him suddenly want to be as close to her as possible? Wondering, he opened the refrigerator and pulled out the steaks.

She shot him a challenging smile. "So what's so special about these steaks?"

He poured some brandy into a shallow bowl. "There's a few things. First you get a couple of thick filets like these. Then you season them with a little salt, pepper, and garlic powder, and you let them soak in the brandy while the coals are turning white." He did this as he spoke.

"That's your secret?"

"It's only the beginning," he promised. "The rest of it involves *how* you cook them."

Theresa was relaxing against the counter, and Garrett was suddenly aware of how beautiful she looked. Something about the way she was standing struck him as familiar—the smile playing across her lips maybe or the slant of her gaze as she watched him. He was reminded again of that lazy summer afternoon with Catherine, when he'd come home to surprise her for lunch. They had stood in the kitchen, just as he and Theresa were doing now.

"I take it you've already eaten," Garrett said as Catherine stood in front of the open refrigerator.

Catherine glanced at him. "I'm not very hungry," she said. "But I am thirsty. Do you want some iced tea?"

"Tea sounds great."

She opened the cupboard and reached for two glasses. After she set the first glass on the counter, the second slipped from her hand.

"Are you all right?" Garrett asked.

Catherine ran her hand through her hair, embarrassed, then bent to pick up the glass shards. "I just got a little woozy there for a second. I'll be okay."

Garrett moved toward her and began to help clean up. "Are you feeling sick again?"

"No, but maybe I spent too much time outside this morning."

He was quiet as he picked up the glass.

He swallowed hard, suddenly aware of the stillness in the kitchen. "I'm going to check the coals to see how they're doing," he said.

While he was outside, Theresa set the table. She put a wineglass beside each plate and sorted through a drawer for some silverware. Beside the utensils were two candles with small holders for each. After wondering whether it would be too much, she decided to put them on the table as well. Garrett came in as she was finishing up.

"Will you show me the rest of your secret recipe?"

"With pleasure," he said. He removed both filets from the brandy, then opened the refrigerator and pulled out a small plastic bag. "This is tallow, the fatty part of the steak that's usually trimmed off. I had the butcher save some when I bought the steaks."

"What's it for?"

"You'll see," he said.

Returning to the grill with the steaks and a pair of tongs, he set them on the railing. Then, taking a small handheld bellows, he began to blow the ashes off the briquettes.

"Part of cooking a great steak is making sure the coals are hot. You use the bellows to blow off the ashes. That way you don't have anything blocking the heat."

He used the tongs to put on the steaks. In the little while it took them to cook, Garrett watched Theresa out of the corner of his eye. The sky was turning orange, and the warm light darkened her brown eyes. Her hair lifted tantalizingly in the breeze.

Finally Garrett turned away and reached for the tallow. "I think we're ready for this now."

He put pieces of tallow on the briquettes, directly beneath the steaks. Then he leaned over and blew on them until they burst into flame.

"What are you doing?"

"The flames will sear in the juices and keep the steak tender. That's the same reason you use tongs instead of a fork." He threw a couple more pieces of tallow onto the briquettes and repeated the process.

Looking around, Theresa commented, "It's so peaceful out here. I can see why you bought the place." She turned toward him. "Tell me, Garrett, what do you think about when you're out here alone?"

"I think about Catherine," he wanted to say, but didn't.

He sighed. "Sometimes I think about work; sometimes I dream about sailing away and leaving everything behind."

She watched him carefully as he spoke the last words. "Garrett, you can't run away from what you're going through." She gave him a reassuring smile. "Besides, you've got so much to offer someone."

Garrett stayed silent. For the next few minutes the only sounds around them were the steaks sizzling on the grill, and waves rolling up on the shore—a soothing, continuous roar. The tension Garrett had felt earlier was almost gone now, and as they stood beside each other in the deepening twilight, he sensed that there was something more to this evening than either of them wanted to admit.

Just before the steaks were done, Theresa went back inside to get the rest of the table ready. She lit the candles and was placing the bottle of wine on the table as Garrett came inside.

After closing the sliding glass door, he saw what she had done. It was dark in the kitchen except for the small candle flames pointing upward, and the glow made Theresa look beautiful. Her eyes seemed to capture the moving flames. They watched each other from across the room, both frozen for a moment by the shadow of distant possibilities. Then Theresa glanced away.

"I couldn't find a wine opener," she said, grasping for something to say.

"I'll get it," he said quickly. "It's probably buried in one of the drawers."

He carried the plate of steaks to the table, then went to the drawer. After sorting through the utensils, he found the opener and brought it to the table. In a couple of easy moves he opened the bottle and poured just the right amount into each glass. Then, sitting down, he used the tongs to put steaks on their plates.

"It's the moment of truth," she said right before taking her first bite. Garrett smiled as he watched her try it.

"Garrett, this is delicious," she said earnestly.

"Thank you."

The candles burned lower as the evening wore on, and Garrett twice told her how glad he was that she had come this evening. Outside, the ocean slowly rose toward high tide, driven by a crescent moon that had seemingly come from nowhere.

After dinner Garrett suggested another walk along the beach.

The night was mild. They stepped off the deck and made their way over a small sand dune and onto the beach itself. Slipping off their shoes, they walked slowly, close to each other, and Garrett reached for her hand. Feeling his warmth, Theresa wondered for just a moment what it would be like to have him touch her body, lingering over her skin.

"I haven't had a night like this in a long time," Garrett said finally.

"Neither have I," she said.

The sand was cool beneath their feet. "Garrett, do you remember when you first asked me to go sailing?"

"Yes."

"Why did you ask me to go with you?"

He looked at her curiously. "What do you mean?"

"I mean that you looked like you regretted it the moment you said it."

He shrugged. "I'm not sure that regret is the word I'd use. I think I was surprised that I asked, but I didn't regret it."

She smiled. "Are you sure?"

"Yeah, I'm sure. Besides, these last couple of days have been the best days I've had in a long time."

They walked together quietly. There were a few others on the beach, though they were far enough away that Theresa couldn't make out anything but shadows.

"Do you think you'll ever come back here again? I mean, for another vacation?"

"Would you make dinner for me again if I did?"

"I'd cook you anything you want. As long as it's a steak."

She laughed under her breath. "Then I'll consider it."

"How about if I threw in a few scuba lessons as well?"

"I think Kevin would enjoy that more than me."

"Then bring him along."

She glanced over at him. "You wouldn't mind?"

"Not at all. I'd love to meet him."

They stopped for a moment and looked out over the water. He stood close to her, their shoulders barely touching.

"What are you thinking?" Garrett asked.

"I was just thinking how nice the silence is with you."

He smiled. "And I was just thinking that I've told you a lot of things I don't tell anyone."

"Is that because you know I'm going back to Boston and I won't tell anyone?"

He chuckled. "No, I guess it's because I wanted you to know who I really am. Because if you really know me and still want to spend time with me . . ."

Theresa said nothing but knew exactly what he was trying to say.

Garrett looked away. "I'm sorry about that. I didn't mean to make you feel uncomfortable."

"It didn't make me feel uncomfortable," Theresa began. "I'm glad you said it."

She paused. After a moment they slowly started walking again.

"But you don't feel the same way I do," he said.

She looked over at him. "Garrett, I . . ." She trailed off.

"No, you don't have to say anything—"

She didn't let him finish. "Yes, I do. You want an answer, and I want to tell you." She paused. Then, taking a deep breath, "It scares me a little, Garrett. Because if I tell you how much I care for you, then I guess I'm opening myself up to get hurt again."

"I'd never hurt you," he said gently.

She stopped walking and made him face her.

"I know you believe that, Garrett. But you've been dealing with your own demons for the past three years. I don't know if you're ready to go on yet, and if you're not, then I'm going to be the one who gets hurt."

The words hit hard, and it took a moment for him to respond.

"Theresa, since we met . . . I don't know . . ."

He raised his hand and softly touched the side of her face with his finger, tracing so lightly that it felt almost like a feather against her skin. The moment he touched her, she closed her eyes and, despite her uncertainty, let the tingling feeling travel through her body.

With that, she felt everything begin to slip away, and suddenly it felt right to be here. The warm summer breeze blew through her hair, heightening the sensation of his touch. The moonlight lent an ethereal sheen to the water, while the clouds cast shadows along the beach.

They gave in then to everything that had been building since the moment they met. She sank into him, feeling the warmth of his body, and he released her hand. Then, slowly wrapping both arms around her, he drew her against him and kissed her softly on the lips.

They stood with their arms around each other, kissing in the moonlight for a long time, neither of them caring if anyone could see them. They had both waited too long for this moment. Then, taking his hand again, Theresa slowly led him back to his house.

Chapter Six

"WHAT do you mean, you can't have lunch with me today? We've been doing this for years. How could you forget?"

"I didn't forget, Dad. I just can't do it today."

Jeb Blake paused on the other end of the phone. "Why do I get the feeling you're not telling me something?"

"There's nothing to tell."

Theresa called to Garrett from the shower, asking him to bring her a towel. Garrett covered the mouthpiece and told her he'd be right there. When he returned his attention to the phone, he heard his father inhale sharply.

"What was that?"

"Nothing."

Then, in a tone of sudden understanding, "That Theresa gal's there, isn't she?"

Knowing he couldn't hide the truth from him now, Garrett replied, "Yeah, she's here."

Jeb whistled, obviously pleased. "It's about time."

Garrett tried to downplay it. "Dad, don't make a big deal out of this."

"I won't, I promise. But can I ask you something?"

"Sure." Garrett sighed.

"Does she make you happy?"

It took a moment for him to answer. "Yeah, she does," he said finally.

"It's about time," Jeb said again with a laugh before hanging up.

Garrett stared at the phone as he replaced it in its cradle. "She really does," he whispered to himself with a small smile on his face. "She really does."

FOR the next four days Theresa and Garrett were inseparable. Garrett ceded control of the shop to Ian, even allowing him to teach dive classes, something he'd never done before. Twice Garrett and Theresa went sailing; the second time they stayed out all night on the ocean, rocked by the gentle swells of the Atlantic. Theresa wondered if Garrett had been as intuitive with Catherine as he seemed to be with her. It was as if he could almost read her mind whenever they were together. If she wanted him to hold her hand, he reached for it before she said anything. If she just wanted to talk for a while without interruption, he listened quietly. If she wanted to know how he was feeling about her, the way he looked at her made it all clear. No one—not even David—had ever understood her as well as Garrett seemed to, and yet how long had she known him? A few days?

Theresa spent Saturday evening at Garrett's house. As they held each other, both of them knew that she had to return to Boston the following day. It was a subject they had avoided talking about.

"Will I ever see you again?" she asked.

He was quiet, almost too quiet. "I hope so," he said finally. "I just don't want it to end. I don't want us to end."

She reached for his hand and spoke quietly. "Oh, Garrett, I don't want it to end either. We can make it work if we try. I could come down here, or you could come up to Boston. Either way, we can try, can't we?"

"How often would I see you? Once a month? Less than that?" He shook his head almost dismissively. "Theresa, it's just so hard right now. The things I've been going through . . ."

She watched him closely as he spoke, sensing the presence of something else.

"Garrett, what's wrong?"

He didn't answer, and she went on. "Is there a reason you don't want to try?"

Still he remained quiet. In the silence he turned toward Catherine's picture.

Theresa could feel tears beginning to form. "Look, Garrett, I know you lost a wife. I know you suffered terribly for it. But you've got your whole life ahead of you. Don't throw it all away by living in the past."

He paused for a long moment.

"You're right," he began, struggling with his words. "In my mind I know you're right. But my heart . . . I just don't know."

"But what about my heart, Garrett? Doesn't that matter to you?"

The way she looked at him made his throat tighten.

"Of course it does. It matters more than you think. I haven't felt like this in so long, Theresa, it's almost like I've forgotten how important another person could be to me. I don't think I could just let you go and forget you, and I don't want to." For a moment there was only the soft, even sound of his breathing. Finally he whispered, "I promise we'll try to make it work."

He opened his arms, his eyes pleading with her. She hesitated for a second, myriad conflicting feelings rushing through her. Then she lowered her face onto his chest, not wanting to see his expression. He kissed her hair, speaking softly as his lips fluttered over her.

"Theresa, I think I'm in love with you."

I think I'm in love with you, she heard again. *I think . . .*

Not wanting to respond, she simply whispered, "Just hold me, okay? Let's not talk anymore."

THE flight to Charlotte the next morning was only partly full, and the seat next to Theresa was vacant. She leaned back, thinking over the amazing events of the past week. Not only had she found Garrett but he had stirred deep feelings in her, feelings she had long thought were buried.

But did she love him?

Idly she ran through their conversation of last night—his fears of letting go of the past, his feelings about not seeing her as much as he wanted too. These things she understood completely. But . . . *I think I'm in love with you.*

She frowned. Why did he add the word think?

She shut her eyes tiredly, suddenly unwilling to confront her warring emotions. One thing was for sure, though. She wasn't ever going to tell him that she loved him until she was certain he could put Catherine behind him.

ON MONDAY morning Theresa felt the effects of her whirlwind adventure finally catching up with her. She hadn't slept much, and the first place she went once she got to work was the break room for a cup of coffee.

"Well, hello, Theresa," Deanna said happily, striding in behind her. "I never thought you'd get here. I've been dying to hear everything that happened."

"Good morning," Theresa mumbled, stirring her coffee. "I'm sorry for not calling, but I was a little worn out from my week," she said.

Deanna leaned against the counter. "Well, that's not a surprise. I've already put two and two together."

"What do you mean?"

Deanna's eyes were bright. "Come with me," she said with a conspiratorial grin as she led her back into the newsroom. When Theresa saw her desk, she gasped. Next to the mail that had accumulated while she was gone stood a dozen roses, beautifully arranged in a large, clear vase.

"They arrived first thing this morning."

Theresa reached for the card leaning against the vase and opened it immediately. It read:

To the most beautiful woman I know—
Now that I'm alone again, nothing is as it once was.
The sky is grayer, the ocean is more forbidding.
I miss you,
Garrett

Theresa smiled at the note and slipped it back inside the envelope, bending to smell the bouquet.

"You must have had a memorable week," Deanna said.

"Yeah, I did," Theresa answered simply.

"Listen, Theresa, I've got some work to do. Do you think we could have lunch today? Then we can talk."

"Sure. Where?"

"How about Mikuni's? I bet you didn't find much sushi down in Wilmington."

"That sounds great."

Deanna patted Theresa's shoulder gently and headed back to her office. Theresa leaned over and smelled the roses again before moving the vase to the corner of her desk. She began to sort through her mail for a couple of minutes, pretending not to notice the flowers until the newsroom resumed its chaotic patterns. Making sure that no one was paying attention, she picked up the phone and dialed Island Diving.

Ian answered the phone. "Hold on. I think he's in his office. Who's calling, please?"

"Tell him it's someone who wants to schedule some dive lessons in a couple of weeks." She tried to sound as distant as she could, not sure if Ian knew about them.

Ian put her on hold, and there was silence for a short moment. Then the line clicked and Garrett came on.

"Can I help you?" he asked, sounding a little frazzled.

"They're beautiful. How did you know I loved roses?"

He recognized her voice, and his tone brightened. "Hey, it's you. I didn't, but I've never heard of a woman who didn't, so I took a chance."

She smiled. "So you send lots of women roses?"

"Millions. I have a lot of fans. Dive instructors are almost like movie stars, you know."

"They are, huh?"

"Sure. Did anyone ask who the flowers were from?"

She smiled. "Of course. I told them you were sixty-eight and fat, with a horrible lisp. But since you were so pitiful, I went ahead and had lunch with you. And now you're stalking me."

"Hey, that hurts," he said. He paused. "But I *am* thinking about you."

She glanced at the roses. "Ditto," she said.

After they had hung up, Theresa sat quietly for a moment, reaching for the card again. She read it once more, then placed it in her purse for safekeeping. Knowing this crowd, someone would read it when she wasn't looking.

OVER lunch Theresa recapped the last week. She left very little out, and Deanna listened with rapt attention.

"It sounds like you had a wonderful time," she said.

"I did. It was one of the best weeks I've ever spent. It's just that . . ."

"What?"

She fidgeted, trying to collect her thoughts. "I'm not sure he'll ever get over Catherine."

Deanna laughed suddenly.

"What's so funny?" Theresa asked, startled.

"*You* are, Theresa. You knew he was still struggling with Catherine before you went down there. Remember, it was his undying love that you found so attractive in the first place. Did you think that he'd completely get over Catherine in a couple of days just because you two hit it off so well?"

Theresa looked sheepish.

Deanna's voice softened. "You've got to take this one step at a time. See how you both feel over the next couple of weeks, and when you see him the next time, you're bound to know a lot more than you know now."

"Do you think so?" Theresa eyed her friend worriedly.

"I was right about twisting your arm to get you down there in the first place, wasn't I?"

OVER the next two weeks Garrett and Theresa spoke on the phone every night, sometimes for hours.

Kevin arrived home, and that made the time pass more quickly for Theresa than for Garrett. His first night home Theresa told him about her trip to Wilmington. She mentioned Garrett, trying to convey how she felt about him without alarming Kevin. At first, when she explained how they were going to visit him the following weekend, Kevin didn't sound so sure about it. But after she told him what Garrett did for a living, Kevin began to show some signs of interest.

"You mean he might teach me how to scuba dive?" he asked.

"He said that he would if you wanted to."

"Cool," he said.

When the day finally came for Theresa and Kevin to visit, Garrett bought some groceries and washed his truck inside and out, then showered before nervously heading to the airport.

When Theresa stepped off the plane with Kevin beside her, all Garrett's nervousness suddenly faded away. She was more beautiful than he remembered. And Kevin—he looked exactly like his picture and a lot like his mother, with her dark hair and eyes. He was wearing long Bermuda shorts, Nike shoes, and a shirt from a concert by Hootie and the Blowfish.

When Theresa saw Garrett, she waved, and he moved toward

them, reaching for their carry-on bags. Theresa leaned over and gaily kissed him on the cheek.

"Garrett, I'd like you to meet my son, Kevin," she said proudly.

"Hi, Kevin. Are you up for some scuba lessons this weekend?"

"I think so. I've been reading up on it," he said, trying to sound older than he was.

"Well, good. If we're lucky, we may even be able to get you certified before you head back."

"You can do that in a few days?"

"Sure. You're required to take a written test and spend a few hours in the water with an instructor. But since you'll be my only student this weekend—unless your mother wants to learn, too—we should have more than enough time."

"Cool," Kevin said. "Are you gonna learn, too, Mom?"

"I don't know. Maybe."

"I think you should," Kevin said. "It would be fun."

"Fine," she said, rolling her eyes, "I'll go, too. But if I see any sharks, I'm quitting."

"You mean there might be sharks?" Kevin asked quickly.

"Yeah, we'll probably see some sharks. But they're little and they don't bother people."

"Are you sure?"

"Positive."

"Cool," Kevin repeated to himself.

AFTER picking up their bags and stopping for a bite to eat, Garrett drove Theresa and Kevin to a motel a mile up the beach from his house. Once their things were inside, Garrett went back to his truck, returning with a book and some papers.

"Kevin, these are for you."

"What are they?"

"It's the book and the tests you need to read for your certification. If you want to head out to the pool tomorrow, you have to have the first two sections read and complete the first test." He handed Kevin the book.

"We can do it together tomorrow morning if you're too tired to start now," Theresa said.

"I'm not too tired," he said quickly.

"Then would you mind if Garrett and I talked on the patio for a while?"

"No, go ahead," he said absently, turning to the first page.

Once outside, Garrett and Theresa sat across from each other.

"I appreciate you doing this for him."

"Hey, you forget this is what I do for a living." After making sure that Kevin was still reading, he scooted his chair a little closer. "You look wonderful," he added. "You were easily the prettiest woman who got off the plane."

Despite herself, Theresa blushed. "Thanks. You look good yourself." She leaned over and kissed him. "I wish we didn't live so far apart. You're kind of addicting."

"I'll take that as a compliment."

Three hours later, long after Kevin was asleep, Theresa led Garrett out into the hall and closed the door behind them. They kissed for a long time, both of them finding it hard to let each other go.

"I wish you could stay here tonight," she whispered.

"I do, too, but I should really be going." He didn't sound as if he meant it.

"Do me a favor?"

"Anything."

"Dream about me, okay?"

KEVIN woke early the next morning and opened the curtains, letting sunlight flood into the room. Theresa squinted and rolled over, trying to get a few more minutes' rest, but Kevin was persistent. "Mom, you've got to take the test before we go."

"It's too early," she said, closing her eyes again. "Can you give me a few more minutes, honey?"

"We don't have time," he said, sitting on her bed and nudging her shoulder gently. "You haven't even read the first section."

"Did you finish it all last night?"

"Yep," he said. "My test is over there, but don't copy, okay? You have to know this stuff."

"Okay, okay," she said. After standing and stretching her arms above her head, she made her way to the small table. She picked up the book and started in on the first chapter. Luckily, the information wasn't difficult, and she was finished by the time Kevin was showered and dressed. Finding her test, she set it in front of her. Kevin walked over and looked over her shoulder until she finally told him to go watch television.

"But there's nothing on," he said, sounding dejected.

"Then read something."

"I didn't bring anything."

"Then sit quietly. Let me take the test in peace."

"Okay. I won't say another word. I'll be as quiet as a mouse."

And he was—for two minutes. Then he started whistling.

She put her pen down and faced him. "Why are you whistling?"

"I'm bored."

"Then turn on the TV."

"There's nothing on. . . ."

And so it went until she finished. It had taken almost an hour to do something she could have done in her office in half the time.

Garrett knocked at the front door of their motel room promptly at nine, and Kevin raced to answer it.

"Are you two ready?" he asked.

"We sure are," Kevin answered quickly. "The tests are over there. Let me get them for you."

He skipped over to the table as Theresa rose from the bed and gave Garrett a quick kiss good-morning.

Garrett smiled as Kevin returned with the tests. He took them and began to look through the answers.

"My mom had some trouble with a couple, but I helped her out," Kevin went on, and Theresa rolled her eyes. "Ready to go, Mom?"

"Whenever you are," she said.

"Then c'mon," Kevin said, leading the way down the hall, toward Garrett's truck.

Throughout the morning and early afternoon Garrett taught them the basics of scuba diving. They learned how the equipment worked, how to put it on and test it, and how to breathe through the mouthpiece, first on the side of the pool, then underwater. Kevin, always the adventurer, thought that after a few minutes underwater he knew all there was to know.

"This is easy," he said to Garrett. "I think I'll be ready for the ocean this afternoon."

"I'm sure you would, but we still have to do the lessons in the proper order."

"How's Mom doing?"

"Good."

"As good as me?"

"You're both doing great."

After a few hours in the water both Kevin and Theresa were tired. They had lunch, and once again Garrett told his diving stories, this time for Kevin's benefit. Kevin asked what seemed like a hundred wide-eyed questions. Garrett answered each one patiently, and Theresa was relieved at how well they seemed to get along.

After stopping at the motel to pick up the book and the lesson for the following day, Garrett brought them both to his house. Though Kevin had planned on starting the next few chapters right away, a look at the beach changed everything. Seizing the towel Garrett handed him, he ran down to the water. Garrett and Theresa sat on the deck and watched him.

"He's quite a young man," Garrett said quietly. "You've done a good job raising him."

She reached for his hand and kissed it gently. "It means a lot to me to hear you say that. I haven't met many men who want to talk about him, let alone spend time with him."

"Then it's their loss."

She smiled. "How come you always know exactly what to say to make me feel good?"

"Maybe it's because you bring out the best in me."

"Maybe I do."

THE FOLLOWING MORNING THE lessons were a little more advanced. Theresa and Kevin practiced buddy breathing in the event that either one of them ran out of air and they had to share one tank, and Garrett warned of the dangers of panicking while diving and rushing to the surface too quickly. "If you do that, you'll get what's called the bends. It can be life-threatening."

They also spent time in the deep end of the pool, swimming underwater for extended periods and practicing how to clear their ears. Toward the end of their lesson Garrett showed them how to jump off the side of the pool without having their masks come off. Predictably, both of them were tired after a few hours and ready to call it a day.

"Will we go into the ocean tomorrow?" Kevin asked as they were walking back to the truck.

"If you'd like to. I think you're ready, but if you'd rather spend another day in the pool, we could do that instead."

"No, I'm ready."

"Are you sure? I don't want to rush you."

"I'm sure," he said quickly.

"What's up for the rest of the day?" Theresa asked.

Garrett started loading the tanks in the back of the truck. "I thought we'd go sailing. It looks like it's going to be great weather."

"Can I learn how to do that, too?" Kevin asked eagerly.

"Sure. I'll make you my first mate."

"Do I need to be certified for that?"

"No. That's up to the captain, and since I'm the captain, I can do it right now."

"Awesome." Kevin looked at Theresa with wide eyes and she could almost read his thoughts: First I learn how to dive, then I become a first mate. Wait until I tell my friends.

GARRETT was accurate in predicting ideal weather, and the three of them had a wonderful time on the water. Garrett taught Kevin the basics of sailing—from how and when to tack to anticipating the direction of the wind based on the clouds. As on their first date together, they had sandwiches and salads, but this time they were treated to a family of porpoises that frolicked around the boat as they ate.

It was late by the time they made it back to the docks, and after Garrett showed Kevin how to close up the boat to protect it from unexpected storms, Garrett brought them back to their motel. Since all three of them were exhausted, Theresa and Garrett said good-bye quickly, and both Theresa and Kevin were in bed by the time Garrett arrived back at his house.

Garrett took them out for their first ocean dive the next morning. After the initial nervousness wore off, they began to enjoy themselves and ended up going through two tanks each over the course of the afternoon. Thanks to the calm coastal weather, the water was clear, with excellent visibility. Garrett took a few photos of them as they explored one of the shallow-water wrecks off the North Carolina coast.

They spent the evening at Garrett's house again. After Kevin fell asleep in front of the television, Garrett and Theresa sat close to each other on the deck, caressed by the warm, humid air.

"I can't believe we'll be leaving tomorrow night," Theresa said. "These last couple of days have flown by."

He put his arm around her, pulling her close. She rested her head on his shoulder. In the silence they listened as the waves rolled up along the beach.

"You know, Garrett, I really feel comfortable around you."

"Comfortable? You make it sound like I'm a couch."

"I don't mean it like that. I mean I just feel good about myself when we're together."

"You should. I feel pretty good about you."

"Pretty good? That's all?"

He shook his head. "No, that's not all."

He glanced at her, then looked out over the water. After a moment he spoke quietly. "I love you."

Theresa listened as the words rolled through her head again. *I love you.* No ambivalence this time.

"Oh, Garrett—" she began uncertainly, before he interrupted her with a shake of his head.

"Theresa, I don't expect you to feel the same way. I just wanted you to know how I feel." His finger gently moved across her cheek and lips. "I love you, Theresa."

"I love you, too," she said softly, trying out the words and hoping they were true.

They held each other for a long time afterward.

THEY spent their last day in Wilmington practicing as they had before, and once they had finished their final lesson, Garrett gave them their certificates. "You can dive whenever and wherever you want now," he said to Kevin, who handled the certificate almost as if were gold. "But remember, it's never safe to dive alone. Always go with someone else."

Theresa checked them out of the hotel, and Garrett drove them to the airport. After Theresa and Kevin had safely boarded, he stayed a few minutes, watching until the plane finally began to back out of the gate.

In their seats, Theresa and Kevin thumbed through magazines. Halfway through the first leg of their trip home Kevin suddenly turned to her and asked, "Mom, are you gonna marry Garrett?"

It took her a few moments to answer. "I'm not sure. I do know that I don't want to marry him right now. We're still getting to know each other."

"But you might want to marry him in the future?"

"Maybe."

Kevin looked relieved. "I'm glad. You seemed like you were really happy when you were with him."

She reached over and touched his hand. "Well, what would you have said if I'd told you I did want to marry him now?"

He was quiet for a moment. "I guess I'd wonder where we're gonna live."

For the life of her, Theresa couldn't think of a good response. Where, indeed?

Chapter Seven

FOUR days after Theresa left Wilmington, Garrett had a dream about Catherine. In the dream they were in a grassy field bordered by a cliff overlooking the ocean. They were walking together, holding hands and talking, when all at once she broke away from him. Looking over her shoulder and laughing, she called for Garrett to chase her. He did, feeling much as he had the day they were married.

He was slowly gaining on her when he noticed that she was heading toward the cliff. Garrett called for her to stop. Instead she ran faster.

He screamed for her to turn around, but she didn't appear to hear him. He felt the adrenaline rush through his body, fed by a paralyzing fear. "Stop, Catherine," he shouted.

The cliff was only a few feet away. He was closing ground, but he was still too far behind. *I'm not going to make it,* he thought, panicking.

Then, just as suddenly as she had broken away, Catherine stopped. She turned to face him, only inches from the edge.

"Don't move," he shouted. He stopped a few feet from her and held out his hand, breathing heavily.

She smiled and glanced behind her. "Did you think you were going to lose me?"

"Yes," he said quietly, "and I promise never to let it happen again."

GARRETT woke and sat up in bed, staying awake for several hours afterward. When he finally fell back to sleep, it was fitful at best, and it was almost ten o'clock the next morning before he was able to get up. Still exhausted and feeling depressed, he called his father, who met him for breakfast in their usual place.

"I don't know whether I can see Theresa again," he told him after a few minutes of small talk.

His father cocked an eyebrow but didn't reply. Garrett went on.

"Maybe it's just not meant to be. I mean, she's a thousand miles away, she's got her own life, she's got her own interests. I don't want to move to Boston, and I'm sure she doesn't want to move here, so where would that leave us?"

Garrett stopped and waited for his father to respond.

"It sounds to me like you're making excuses," Jeb said quietly.

"No, Dad, I'm not. I'm just trying to figure out this whole thing."

"Who do you think you're talking to, Garrett?" Jeb Blake shook his head. "I know exactly what you're going through. When your mom died, I made excuses, too. Over the years I told myself all sorts of things. And you wanna know where it got me?"

He stared at his son. "I'm old and tired, and most of all I'm alone. If I could go back in time, I'd change a lot." Jeb paused, his tone softening. "I'd try to find someone. Because you know what, Garrett? I think your mom would have wanted me to find someone. She would have wanted me to be happy. And you know why?"

Garrett didn't answer.

"Because she loved me. And if you think that you're showing your love to Catherine by suffering the way you've been doing, then somewhere along the way I must have messed up in raising you."

"You didn't mess up."

"I must have. Because when I look at you, I see myself, and to be honest, I'd rather see someone different. I'd like to see someone who learned that it's okay to go on, that it's okay to find someone who can make you happy. But right now it's like I'm looking in the mirror and seeing myself twenty years ago."

GARRETT spent the afternoon alone, walking on the beach, thinking about what his father had said.

By the time he called Theresa later in the evening, the feelings of betrayal he'd felt as a result of the dream had subsided. When she answered the phone, he felt them diminish even further.

"I'm glad you called," she said cheerfully. "I thought a lot about you today."

"I thought about you, too," he said. "I wish you were here right now."

"Are you okay? You sound a little down."

"I'm fine. Just lonely, that's all. How was your day?"

"Typical. Too much to do at work, too much to do at home. But it's better now that I've heard from you. How about you?"

"I really missed you today."

"I've only been gone a few days," she said gently.

"I know. And speaking of that, when will we get to see each other again?"

"Um . . . how about in three weeks? I was thinking that maybe you could come up here this time. Kevin has a weeklong soccer camp, and we'd be able to spend some time alone."

As she spoke, he found himself staring at Catherine's picture on the nightstand. It took him a few seconds to respond. "Well, I guess I could do that."

"You don't sound too sure about it."

"I am."

"Is there something else, then?"

"No."

She paused uncertainly. "Are you really okay, Garrett?"

IT TOOK Garrett a few days and several more phone calls to Theresa to feel somewhat normal again. Eventually the image of the dream did begin to fade. The heat of late summer seemed to make time pass more slowly than usual, but Garrett kept himself as busy as he could, doing his best not to think about the complexities of his new situation.

Two weeks later he arrived in Boston.

After picking him up from the airport, Theresa showed Garrett around the city. They had lunch at Faneuil Hall, watched the scullers gliding on the Charles River, and reveled in each other's company. When the day began to cool and the sun dipped below the trees, they stopped for some Mexican food to bring back to her apartment. Sitting on her living-room floor in the glow of candle-light, Garrett looked around the room.

"You have a nice place," he said. "For some reason I thought it would be smaller than it is. It's bigger than my house."

"Only by a little, but thanks. It works for us."

Outside her apartment the sound of traffic was clearly audible. A car screeched, a horn blared, and all at once the air was filled with noise as other cars joined in the chorus.

"Is it always this quiet?" he asked.

She nodded toward the windows. "Friday and Saturday nights are the worst, but you get used to it if you live here long enough."

The sounds of city living continued. A siren blared in the distance, growing steadily louder as it approached.

"Would you like to put on some music?" Garrett asked.

"Sure. What kind do you like?"

"I like *both* kinds," he said, pausing dramatically. "Country *and* western."

She laughed. "I don't have anything like that here. How about some jazz?"

She got up and chose something she thought Garrett might like and slipped it into the CD player. In a few moments the music started just as the traffic congestion outside seemed to clear.

"So what do you think of Boston so far?" she asked, reclaiming her seat.

"I like it. For a big city it's not too bad. I guess I pictured crowds, asphalt, tall buildings, not a tree in sight, and muggers on every corner. But it's not like that at all."

She smiled. "It is nice, isn't it? I mean, it's not beachfront, but it has its own appeal. Especially if you consider what the city has to offer. You could go to the symphony or to museums or just stroll around in the Common. There's something for everyone here—they even have a sailing club."

It sounded as if she were selling the place, and Garrett decided to change the subject.

"You said Kevin's at soccer camp?"

THE next morning Garrett and Theresa toured the Italian neighborhoods of Boston's North End, wandering the narrow, twisting streets and stopping for cannoli and coffee. Garrett asked her about her job as they made their way through the city.

"Can't you write the column from your home?"

"In time I suppose I could. But right now it's not possible."

"Why not?"

"Well, it's not in my contract, for starters. Often I have to interview people, so there's time involved in that—sometimes even a little travel. Besides, there's all the research I have to do, and when I'm in the office, I have access to a lot more sources. And then there's the fact that I need a place where I can be reached. A lot of the stuff I do is human interest, and I get calls all day long. If I worked out of my home, I know a lot of people would call in the evenings, and I'm not willing to give up my time with Kevin."

Garrett stopped at a sidewalk store selling fresh fruit. He picked out a couple of apples from a bin, then handed one to Theresa. "What's the most popular thing you've ever written about in your column?" he asked.

Theresa felt her breath catch. *The most popular? Easy. I found a message in a bottle once, and I got a couple of hundred letters.*

She forced herself to think of something else. "Oh, I get a lot of mail when I write about disabled children," she said finally.

"That must be rewarding," he said, paying the shopkeeper.

"It is."

Before taking a bite of his apple, Garrett asked, "Could you still write your column even if you changed papers?"

She considered the question. "It would be hard to do, especially if I want to continue to syndicate. I'm still establishing my name, and having the Boston *Times* behind me really helps. Why?"

"Just curious," he said quietly.

THE REST OF THEIR VACATION flew by. In the mornings Theresa would go into work for a few hours, then come home and spend the afternoons and evenings with Garrett. Sometimes they rented a movie to watch after dinner, but usually they preferred to spend their time without other distractions.

OVER the next two months their long-distance relationship began to evolve in a way that neither Theresa nor Garrett expected, though both should have foreseen.

Working around their schedules, they were able to get together three more times, each time for a weekend. Once, Theresa flew down to Wilmington so they could be alone, and they spent their time holed up in Garrett's house. Garrett traveled to Boston twice, spending much of his time on the road for Kevin's soccer tournaments.

When they were together during those weekends, it was as if nothing else mattered in the world. Yet neither of them broached the subject of what was going to happen in the future.

Because they didn't see each other very often, their relationship had more ups and downs than either of them had experienced before. Everything felt right when they were together; everything felt wrong when they weren't. Garrett, especially, found himself struggling with the distance between them. As he saw it, one of them was going to have to change his or her life dramatically.

But which one?

He had his own business in Wilmington. Theresa had a blossoming career in Boston.

He didn't want to think about it. Instead he focused on the fact that he loved Theresa, clinging to the belief that if they were meant to be together, they would find a way to do it.

Deep down, however, he knew it wasn't going to be that easy, and not just because of the distance between them. After he'd returned from his second trip to Boston, he had a picture of Theresa enlarged and framed. He set it on the bedstand opposite Catherine's picture, but despite his feelings for Theresa, it seemed out of place in his bedroom. A few days later he moved the picture across the room, but it still didn't help. Wherever he put it, it seemed to him as if Catherine's eyes would follow it. He found himself finally slipping Theresa's picture into the drawer and reaching for Catherine's instead. Sighing, he sat on the bed and held it in front of him.

"We didn't have these problems," he whispered as he ran his finger over her image. "With us everything always seemed so easy, didn't it?"

When he realized the picture wouldn't answer, he cursed his foolishness and retrieved Theresa's picture.

Staring at them both, even he understood why he was having so much trouble with it all. He loved Theresa more than he ever thought he could, but he still loved Catherine.

Was it possible to love them both at once?

"I CAN'T wait to see you again," Garrett said.

It was the middle of November, a couple of weeks before Thanksgiving. Theresa and Kevin were flying home to see her parents for the holidays, and Theresa had made arrangements to come down the weekend before to spend some time with Garrett.

"I'm looking forward to it, too," she said. "And you promised that I'd finally get to meet your father, right?"

"He's planning on cooking an early Thanksgiving dinner for us at his place. He keeps asking me what you like to eat. I can tell he's nervous about it."

"Do you think he'll like me?"

"I know he will."

THE day before Theresa's arrival Garrett mowed the lawn at his father's house while Jeb unpacked the wedding china he seldom, if ever, used anymore.

"What time do you think she'll want to eat?"

"I don't know."

"You didn't ask her?"

"No."

"Then how will I know when to put the turkey in the oven?"

"Just plan on us eating sometime in the middle of the afternoon. It's not that big of a deal."

"Maybe not to you. But it's the first time I'll be meeting her, and if you two end up getting married, I don't want to be the subject of any humorous stories later on."

Garrett raised his eyebrows. "Who said we're getting married?"

"No one."

"Then why did you bring it up?"

"Because," he said quickly, "I wasn't sure if you were ever going to get around to it."

Garrett stared at his father. "So you think I should marry her?"

Jeb winked as he answered. "It doesn't matter what I think. It's what you think that's important, isn't it?"

LATER that evening Garrett opened his front door just as the phone began to ring. Rushing to the phone, he picked it up and heard the voice he expected.

"Garrett?" Theresa asked. "You sound out of breath."

He smiled. "Oh, hey, Theresa. I just walked in. My father had me over at his house all day getting the place ready. He's really looking forward to meeting you."

There was an uncomfortable pause. "About tomorrow . . ." she said finally.

He felt his throat tighten. "What about tomorrow?"

It took a moment for her to answer. "I'm really sorry, but I'm not going to be able to make it down to Wilmington after all."

"Is something wrong?"

"No, everything's fine. It's just that something came up at the last minute—a big conference that I've got to go to."

He closed his eyes. "What's it for?"

"It's for bigwig editors and media types. They're meeting in Dallas this weekend. Deanna thinks it would be a good idea if I met some of them."

"Did you just find out about it?"

"No . . . I mean, yes. I knew there was going to be a meeting, but

I wasn't supposed to go. Deanna pulled some strings." She hesitated. "I'm really sorry, Garrett, but it's an opportunity of a lifetime."

He was silent for a moment. Then he said simply, "I understand."

"You're angry with me, aren't you?"

"No."

She knew by his tone that he wasn't telling the truth, but she didn't think there was anything she could say that would make him feel any better.

"Will you tell your father that I'm sorry?"

"Yeah, I'll tell him."

"Can I call you this weekend?"

"If you want to."

THE next day he ate dinner with his father, who did his best to play down the whole affair.

"If it's like she said," his father explained, "she had a good reason. She has a son to support, and she's got to do her best to provide for him. Besides, it's just one weekend—not much in the grand scheme of things."

Garrett leaned back, pushing his half-eaten plate to the side. "I understand all that, Dad. It's just that I haven't seen her for a month now and I was really looking forward to her visit."

"Don't you think she wanted to see you, too?"

"She said she did."

Jeb leaned across the table and pushed Garrett's plate in front of him again. "Eat your dinner," he said. "I spent all day cooking, and you're not going to waste it."

Garrett looked at his plate. Though he wasn't hungry anymore, he picked up his fork and took a small bite.

"You know," his father said as he picked at his own food, "this isn't the last time this is going to happen. As long as you two continue to live a thousand miles apart, things like this are going to come up, and you won't see each other as much as either one of you wants."

"I know," Garrett said simply.

His father cocked his eyebrow, waiting. When Garrett didn't add anything else, Jeb spoke again. " 'I know'? That's all you have to say?"

He shrugged. "What else can I say?"

"You can say that the next time you see her, you two are going to figure this out. That's what you can say."

"Why are you so adamant about it?"

"Because," he said, "if you two don't figure it out, you and me are going to keep eating alone for the next twenty years."

"ARE you tired?" Garrett asked. He was lying on his bed as he spoke with Theresa on the phone.

"Yeah. I got in just a little while ago. It was a long weekend."

"Did it turn out as well as you thought it would?"

"I hope so. There's no way to tell just yet, but I did meet a lot of people who could eventually help me out with my column."

"It's a good thing you went, then."

"Good and bad. Most of the time I wished I'd gone to visit you instead."

There was a short pause.

"Garrett?"

"Yeah."

"Are you still mad at me?"

"No," he said quietly. "Sad maybe, but not mad."

"Because I wasn't there this weekend?"

"No. Because you're not here most weekends."

She spoke softly. "I just want you to know that I'm sorry about *this* weekend."

"I know."

"Can I make it up to you?"

"What did you have in mind?"

"Well, can you come up here to visit after Thanksgiving?"

"I suppose so."

"Good, because I'm going to plan a special weekend just for the two of us."

WHEN HE ARRIVED IN BOSTON two weeks later, Theresa met him at the airport. She had told him to wear something dressy, and he walked off the plane wearing a blazer.

"Wow," she'd said simply. "You look great."

They went straight from the airport to dinner. She'd made reservations at the most elegant restaurant in town. They had a leisurely, wonderful meal, and afterward Theresa took Garrett to *Les Misérables,* which was currently showing in Boston.

It was late by the time they got to Theresa's apartment, and to Garrett the following day seemed just as rushed. Theresa took him to her office and showed him around, and they visited the Boston art museum in the afternoon. That evening they met Deanna and Brian for dinner in Anthony's, a restaurant on the top floor of the Prudential Building that offered wonderful views of the entire city.

Garrett had never seen anything like it.

Their table was near a window. Deanna and Brian both rose from their seats to greet them, and Theresa made the introductions.

"It's good to meet you, Garrett," Deanna said. "I'm sorry I forced Theresa to come with me to that conference. I hope you haven't been too hard on her."

"It's okay," he said, nodding stiffly.

"I'm glad. Because looking back, I think it was worth it."

Garrett looked at her curiously. Theresa leaned in and asked, "What do you mean, Deanna?"

Deanna's eyes sparkled. "I got some good news yesterday. I talked to Dan Mandel, the head of Media Information Inc., and it turns out he was very impressed with you. He liked the way you handled yourself. And best of all . . ." Deanna paused dramatically, doing her best to stifle a smile.

"Yes?"

"He's going to pick up your column in all his papers, starting in January."

"You're kidding," Theresa cried. She put her hand to her mouth to stifle a scream, but it was still loud enough that the people at the nearby tables turned their heads.

Deanna shook her head. "No. He wants to talk to you again on Tuesday. I've got a conference call set up for ten o'clock."

"I can't believe it." Theresa leaned in and impulsively hugged Deanna, excitement animating her face.

Brian nudged Garrett with his elbow. "Great news, huh?"

It took a moment for Garrett to answer.

"Yeah . . . great."

DEANNA and Theresa chatted nonstop throughout the rest of evening. Garrett was quiet, not knowing quite what to add. As if sensing his discomfort, Brian leaned over to Garrett.

"So how long are you staying?"

"Until tomorrow night."

Brian nodded. "It's tough not seeing each other much, isn't it?"

"Sometimes."

"I can imagine. I know Theresa gets down about it now and then."

Across the table Theresa smiled at Garrett. "What are you two talking about over there?" she asked cheerfully.

"This and that," Brian said.

Garrett nodded briefly without answering, and Theresa watched as he adjusted himself in his seat. It was obvious he felt uncomfortable—though she wasn't sure why—and she found herself puzzling over it.

"YOU were kind of quiet tonight," Theresa said.

They were back in her apartment, sitting on the couch with the radio playing softly in the background.

"I guess I didn't have much to say."

"Did you have a good time talking to Brian?"

"Yeah. He's easy to get along with." Garrett paused. "But I'm not very good in groups, especially when I'm sort of outside the loop. I just . . ." He stopped.

"What?"

He shook his head. "Nothing."

"No—what were you going to say?"

After a moment he answered, choosing his words carefully. "I was just going to say that this whole weekend has been strange for me. The show, expensive dinners, going out with your friends . . ." He shrugged. "It's not me. None of this is anything I'd normally do."

"That's why I planned the weekend like I did. I wanted to introduce you to something different."

"I didn't come up here to do something different. I came up here to spend some quiet time with you. We haven't even had a chance to talk yet, and I'm leaving tomorrow."

"That's not true. We were alone at dinner last night and again at the museum today. We've had plenty of time to talk."

"You know what I mean."

"No, I don't. What did you want to do? Just sit around in the apartment?"

He didn't answer for a moment. Then he rose from the couch, walked across the room, and turned off the radio.

"There's something important I've wanted to say since I came up here," he said.

"What is it?"

Turning around and gathering his courage, he took a deep breath. "It's been really hard this past month not seeing you, and right now I'm not sure if I want to keep going on like this."

Her breath caught for a second.

Seeing her expression, he moved toward her. "It's not what you're thinking," he said quickly. "It's not that I don't want to see you anymore. I want to see you all the time." When he reached the couch, he knelt in front of her. Theresa looked at him, surprised. He took her hand in his.

"I want you to move to Wilmington."

Though she'd known this was coming sometime, she hadn't expected it so soon and certainly not like this.

Garrett went on. "I know it's a big step, but if you move down, we won't have these long periods apart anymore. We could see each other every day." He reached up, caressing her cheek. "I want to walk the beach with you. I want to go sailing with you. I want you to be there when I get home from the shop. I want it to feel like we've known each other all our lives."

The words were coming quickly, and the more he talked, the more her head began to spin. It almost sounded to her as if Garrett were trying to re-create his relationship with Catherine.

"Wait a minute," she finally said, cutting him off. "I can't just pick up and leave. I mean, Kevin's in school. He's happy here. This is his home. He's got his friends, his soccer."

"He can have all that in Wilmington. And didn't you see how well we got along?"

She let go of his hand, growing frustrated. "What about my column? You want me to give that up?"

"I don't want to give *us* up. There's a big difference."

"Then why can't you move to Boston?"

"And do what?"

"The same thing you do in Wilmington. Teach diving, go sailing, whatever. It's a lot easier for you to leave than it would be for me."

"I can't do that. Like I said, this"—he motioned around the room and toward the windows—"isn't me. I'd be lost up here."

Theresa stood and walked across the room, agitated. She ran her hand through her hair. "That isn't fair. It's like you've put a condition on it—'We can be together, but it's got to be my way.' You want me to give up everything I've worked for, but you're not willing to give up anything." Her eyes never left his.

Garrett rose and moved toward her. When he got close, she pulled back, raising her arms like a barrier.

"Look, Garrett, I don't want you to touch me right now, okay?"

He dropped his hands to his side. For a long moment neither of them said anything. Theresa crossed her arms and glanced away.

"Then I guess your answer is that you're not coming," he finally said.

She spoke carefully. "No. My answer is that we're going to have to talk this out."

"So you can try to convince me that I'm wrong?"

His comment didn't deserve a response. Shaking her head, she walked to the dining-room table, picked up her purse, and started toward the front door.

"You're running out?"

She opened the door, holding it as she spoke. "No, Garrett, I'm not running out. I just need a few minutes alone so I can think. And I don't appreciate you talking to me like that. You've just asked me to change my entire life, and I'm taking a few minutes to think about it."

She left the apartment. Garrett stared at the door for a couple of seconds, waiting to see if she would come back. When she didn't, he paced around the apartment. He glanced in the kitchen, then Kevin's room, and kept moving. When he reached her bedroom, he paused for a moment before entering. After walking over to her bed, he sat down, put his head into his hands, and wondered what to do next. Somehow he didn't think there was anything he could say when she got back that wouldn't lead to another argument.

He thought for a moment before finally deciding to write her a letter, outlining his thoughts. Writing always made him think more clearly.

He glanced toward her bedside table. Her phone was there, but he didn't see either a pen or pad. He opened the drawer, rifled through it, and found a ballpoint near the front. He continued shuffling—looking for some paper—through magazines, a couple of paperback books, some empty jewelry boxes, when something familiar caught his eye.

A sailing ship.

It was on a piece of paper, wedged into a slim Day-Timer. He reached for it, assuming it was one of the letters he'd written to her over the last couple of months, then suddenly froze.

How could that be? The stationery had been a gift from Catherine, and he used it only when he wrote to her. His letters to Theresa had been written on different paper.

He found himself holding his breath. He quickly made room in the drawer, removed the Day-Timer, and gently lifted out not one but three pieces of the stationery. Still confused, he blinked hard before glancing at the first page, and there, in his scrawl, were the words "My Dearest Catherine."

Oh, my God. He turned to the second page, a photocopy. "My Darling Catherine . . ."

The next letter. "Dear Catherine . . ."

"What is this?" he muttered, unable to believe what he was seeing. "It can't be." He looked over the pages again just to make sure.

But it was true. They were his letters, the letters to Catherine that he had dropped from *Happenstance* and never expected to see again.

He barely heard the front door open and then close.

Theresa called out, "Garrett, I'm back." She paused, and he could hear her walking through the apartment. Then, "Where are you?"

He didn't answer.

Theresa stepped into the room and looked at him. His face was pale, his knuckles white as they gripped the pages he held.

"Are you okay?" she asked.

Looking up slowly, he glared at her.

Like a wave, everything hit her—the open drawer, the papers in his hand, the expression on his face—and she knew immediately what had happened.

"Garrett, I can explain," she said quickly, quietly.

"My letters," he whispered. He looked at her, a mixture of confusion and rage. "How did you get my letters?"

"I found one washed up at the beach and—"

He cut her off. "You found it?"

She nodded, trying to explain. "When I was at the Cape. I was jogging and I came across the bottle."

He glanced at the first page, the only original letter. It was the one he had written earlier that year. But the others . . .

"What about these?" he asked, holding up the copies.

Theresa answered softly. "They were sent to me."

"By whom?" Confused, he rose from the bed.

She took a step toward him, holding out her hand. "By other people who'd found them. One of the people read my column."

"You published my letter?" He sounded as if he'd just been hit in the stomach.

"I didn't know . . ." she began.

"You didn't know what?" he said loudly, the hurt evident in his tone. "That this wasn't something that I wanted the world to see?"

"It was washed up on the beach. You had to know someone would find it," she said quickly. "I didn't use your names."

"But you put it in the paper." Again he glanced at the letters, then looked back at her, as if he were seeing her for the first time. "You *lied* to me," he said.

"I didn't lie."

He wasn't listening. "You lied to me," he repeated, as if to himself. "And you came to find me. Why? So you could write another column. Is that what this is about?"

"No, it isn't like that at all."

"Then what was it?"

"After reading your letters, I . . . I wanted to meet you."

He didn't understand what she was saying. Remembering Catherine, he held the letters out in front of him. "These were mine—my feelings, my thoughts, my way of dealing with the loss of my wife. Mine, not yours."

"I didn't mean to hurt you."

His jaw muscles tensed. "You took my feelings for Catherine and tried to manipulate them into something *you* wanted. You thought that because I loved Catherine, I would love you, too, didn't you?"

She felt suddenly incapable of speech.

"You planned all this from the beginning, didn't you? The whole thing was set up."

He seemed dazed for a moment, and she reached out to him.

"Garrett, yes, I admit I wanted to meet you. The letters were so beautiful. But I didn't know where it would lead, I didn't plan on anything after that." She took his hand. "I love you, Garrett. You've got to believe me."

When she finished speaking, he pulled his hand free and moved away.

"What kind of person are you? You got caught up in some weird fantasy—"

"Stop it, Garrett!" she cried angrily, tears welling up in her eyes.

His voice breaking, he held the letters out again. "You think you understand what Catherine and I had together, but you don't. No matter how many letters you read, no matter how well you know me, you'll never understand. What she and I had was *real.* It was real, and she was real."

Then, stiffening, he said something that hurt her worse than anything he'd said so far. "We've never even come close to what Catherine and I had."

He didn't wait for a response. Instead he walked past her, toward his suitcase. Angrily throwing everything inside, he zipped it quickly. For a moment she thought to stop him, but his comment had left her reeling.

He picked up the bag. "These," he said, holding the letters, "are mine, and I'm taking them with me." Without another word he turned around and strode through the living room and out the door.

Chapter Eight

GARRETT caught a cab to the airport, but no flights were available, and he ended up staying in the terminal the rest of the night, still angry and unable to sleep. For hours he wandered past shops that had long since closed for the evening, stopping only occasionally to look through the barricades that kept nighttime travelers at bay.

The following morning he caught the first flight he could and made it home a little after eleven and then went straight to his room. As he lay on his bed, however, the events of the evening before kept running through his head, keeping him awake. In the end, he gave up. He showered and dressed, then sat on his bed again. Staring at the photograph of Catherine, he eventually picked it up and carried it with him into the living room. On the coffee table he found the letters where he'd left them. With her picture in front of him he read the letters slowly, almost reverently, sensing Catherine's presence filling the room.

"Hey, I thought you'd forgotten about our date," he said as he watched Catherine walking down the dock with a grocery bag.

Smiling, she took his hand as she stepped on board. "I didn't forget. I just had a little detour on the way. I went to see the doctor."

He took the bag from her and set it off to one side. "Are you okay? I know you haven't been feeling well."

"I'm okay," she said. "But I don't think I'm up for a sail tonight."

"Something is wrong, isn't it?"

Catherine smiled again as she leaned over and pulled a small package out of one of the bags. Garrett watched as she began to open it.

"Close your eyes," she said, "and I'll tell you all about it."

Still a little unsure, Garrett nonetheless did as she asked and heard as tissue paper was unwrapped. "Okay, you can open them now."

Catherine was holding up baby clothes in front of her.

"What's this?" he asked, not understanding.

Her face was buoyant. "I'm pregnant," she said excitedly.

"Pregnant?"

"Uh-huh. I'm officially eight weeks along."

"Eight weeks?"

Hesitating from the shock, Garrett took the baby clothes and held them delicately in his hand, then finally leaned forward and gave Catherine a hug. "I can't believe it."

"It's true."

A broad smile crossed his lips as the realization finally began to sink in. "You're pregnant."

Catherine closed her eyes and whispered in his ear, "And you're going to be a father."

Garrett's thoughts were interrupted by the squeaking of the door. His father peeked his head into the room.

"I saw your truck out front," he said. "I didn't expect you back here until this evening." When Garrett didn't respond, his father walked in and spotted Catherine's picture on the table. "You okay, son?" he asked cautiously.

They sat in the living room while Garrett explained the situation from the beginning—the dreams he'd been having over the years, the messages he'd been sending by bottle, finally moving on to the argument he and Theresa had had the night before. When he finished, his father took the letters from Garrett's hand.

"It must have been quite a shock," he said, glancing at the pages. "But don't you think you were a little rough on her?"

Garrett tiredly shook his head. "She knew everything about me. She set the whole thing up."

"No, she didn't," he said gently. "She may have come down to meet you, but she didn't make you fall in love with her. You did that on your own."

Garrett looked away before finally returning his gaze to the picture on the table. "But don't you think it was wrong of her to hide it from me?"

Jeb sighed. "She may not have told you about the letters, and granted, maybe she should have. But that's not why you're angry now. You're angry because she made you realize something that you didn't want to admit."

Garrett looked at his father without responding. Then, rising from the couch, he went to the kitchen, suddenly feeling the urge to escape the conversation. In the refrigerator he found a pitcher of sweet tea and poured himself a glass. Opening the freezer, he pulled out the metal tray to crack out a couple of cubes. In a sudden spurt of frustration he pulled the lever too hard, and ice cubes flew over the counter and onto the floor.

As Garrett muttered and cursed in the kitchen, Jeb walked to the sliding glass door. Opening it, he watched as cold December winds from the Atlantic made the waves crash violently, the sounds echoing through the house. Jeb contemplated the ocean, watching it churn and roll until he heard a knock at the door.

He turned, wondering who it could be. Strangely, he realized that in all of his visits here no one had ever dropped by before.

In the kitchen Garrett apparently hadn't heard the knock. Jeb went to answer it. "Coming," he called out.

When the front door swung open, wind gusted through the living room, scattering the letters to the floor. Jeb, however, didn't notice. All his attention was focused on the visitor on the porch.

Standing before him was a dark-haired young woman he'd never seen before. He paused in the doorway, knowing exactly who she was. He moved aside to make room for her.

"C'mon in," he said quietly.

As she entered, closing the door behind her, the wind abruptly died. She glanced at Jeb, uncomfortable.

"You must be Theresa," Jeb said. "I've heard a lot about you."

She crossed her arms, hesitating. "I know I'm not expected . . ."

"It's okay," Jeb encouraged.

"Is he here?"

Jeb nodded his head in the direction of the kitchen. "Yeah, he's here. He's getting something to drink."

"How is he?"

Jeb shrugged and gave her a slow, wry smile. "You'll have to talk to him."

Theresa nodded, suddenly wondering whether coming down was a good idea. She glanced around the room and immediately spied the letters spread around the floor and, over Jeb's shoulder, Catherine's photograph.

Normally the photo was in his room, and for some reason, now that it was in plain view, she couldn't take her eyes off it. She was staring at it when Garrett reentered the living room.

"Dad, what happened in here—"

He froze. Theresa faced him uncertainly. For a long moment neither of them said anything. Then Theresa took a deep breath.

"Hello, Garrett," she said.

Garrett said nothing. Jeb picked up his keys from the table. "You two have a lot to talk about, so I'll get out of here."

He went to the front door, glancing sidelong at Theresa. "It was nice meeting you," he murmured. He raised his eyebrows and shrugged slightly, as if to wish her luck. In a moment he was outside.

"Why are you here?" Garrett asked evenly, once they were alone.

"I wanted to see you again," she said quietly.

"Why?"

She didn't answer. Instead after a moment's hesitation she walked toward him, her eyes never leaving his. Once she was close, she put her finger to his lips and shook her head to stop him from speaking. "Shh," she whispered, "no questions, just for now. Please."

Instead she wrapped her arms around him. Reluctantly he drew his arms around her, and she rested her head against him. She kissed his neck and pulled him closer. Her mouth moved tentatively to his cheek, then to his lips. Without conscious thought he began to respond. His hands traveled up her back, molding her against him.

In the living room, with the roar of the ocean echoing through the house, they held each other tightly. Finally Theresa pulled back, reaching for his hand. Taking it in hers, she led him to the bedroom.

LATER that afternoon Garrett woke up alone. Noticing that Theresa's clothes were gone as well, he grabbed his jeans and shirt. Still buttoning his shirt as he left his bedroom, he quickly searched the house for her.

He found her in the kitchen, seated at the table. On the table in front of her he saw a cup of coffee, nearly empty. The coffeepot was already in the sink.

Theresa glanced over her shoulder at him. "Come sit with me," she said. "There's a lot I've got to tell you."

Garrett sat down at the table.

Without looking at him, she reached into her lap and removed the letters, laying them on the table. Apparently, she'd gathered them up while he slept.

"I found the bottle when I was jogging last summer," she began, her voice steady but distant. "After reading the letter, I started to cry. It was just so beautiful. I guess I related to the things you wrote because I felt so alone, too."

She looked at him. "That morning, I showed it to Deanna. Publishing it was her idea. I didn't want to at first. I thought it was too personal, but she didn't see the harm in it. She thought it would be a nice thing for people to read. So I relented."

She sighed. "After I got back to Boston, I got a call from someone who'd read the column. She sent me the second letter, one that she'd found a few years ago."

She paused. "Have you ever heard of *Yankee* magazine?"

"No."

"It's a New England regional magazine. That's where I found the third letter."

Garrett looked at her in surprise. "It was published there?"

"Yes, it was. I had three letters, Garrett, and every one of them touched me the same way the first one had. So with Deanna's help I found out who you were, and I came down to meet you."

She smiled sadly. "I didn't come down here to fall in love with you or to write a column. I came down to see who you were. That was all. But then we talked, and if you remember, you asked me to go sailing. If you hadn't, I probably would have gone home that day."

Theresa reached over and placed her hand over his. "But you know what? We had a good time that night, and I realized I wanted to see you again. Not because of the letters, but because of how you treated me. And everything seemed to grow naturally from there."

He sat quietly for a moment, looking at the letters. "Why didn't you tell me about them?" he asked.

"There were times when I wanted to, but I guess I convinced myself that it didn't matter how we met. The only thing that mattered was how well we got along." She paused. "Besides, I didn't think you'd understand. I didn't want to lose you."

"If you'd told me earlier, I would have understood."

She watched him carefully as he answered. "Would you, Garrett? Would you *really* have understood?"

Garrett knew it to be a moment of truth. When he didn't respond, Theresa shook her head and glanced away. She dabbed at the corner of her eye, clearly fighting tears, determined not to break down.

"When you first told me about Catherine, I saw the way you looked. It was obvious that you still loved her. And last night, despite your anger, I saw the same look again. Even after all the time we've spent together, you're still not over her. And then . . . the things you said . . ." She took a deep, uneven breath. "You weren't angry simply because I found the letters; you were angry because you felt I threatened what you and Catherine shared—and still do."

Again she reached over and touched his hand. "You are who you are, Garrett. You're a man who loves deeply, but you're also a man who loves forever. No matter how much you love me, I don't think it's in you to ever forget Catherine, and I can't live my life wondering whether I measure up to her."

"We can work on it," he began hoarsely. "I mean, I can work on it. I know it can be different—"

Theresa cut him off with a brief squeeze of his hand.

"I know you believe that, and part of me wants to believe it, too. If you put your arms around me now and begged me to stay, I'm sure I would. And we'd go on again like we have been, both believing everything is okay. But it wouldn't be, don't you see?" She stopped. "Garrett, I can't compete with her. And as much as I want it to go on, I can't let it, because *you* won't let it."

"But I love you."

She smiled gently. Letting go of his hand, she reached up and softly caressed his cheek. "I love you, too, Garrett. But sometimes love isn't enough."

Garrett was quiet when she finished, his face pale. In the long silence between them Theresa began to cry.

"I can't stay, Garrett. As much as we both want me to, I can't."

The words hit hard. Garrett's head suddenly felt woozy. "No . . ." he said brokenly.

Theresa stood, knowing she had to leave before she lost her nerve. Outside, a light, misty rain began to fall. "I have to go."

She slipped her purse over her shoulder and started for the front door. For a moment Garrett was too stunned to move.

Finally, in a daze, he rose from his seat and followed her out the door. The rain was falling steadily now. Her rental car was parked in the driveway. Garrett watched as she opened the car door, unable to think of anything to say.

In the driver's seat she fumbled with the keys for a moment, then put them in the ignition. She forced a weak smile as she shut the door. Despite the rain, she rolled down the window to see him more clearly. Turning the key, she felt the engine crank to life.

"I'll miss you Garrett," she said beneath her breath, uncertain if he could even hear her. She slid the transmission into reverse.

Garrett stood, frozen. "Please," he said raggedly, "don't leave."

She didn't answer. Knowing she would start to cry again if she stayed any longer, she rolled up the window and began to back out of the drive. Garrett took a step toward the car and put his hand on the hood as it started to move, his fingers gliding along the wet surface as it slowly backed into the street.

He felt his last chance slipping away. "Theresa," he shouted, "wait!"

With the rain coming down steadily, she didn't hear him. The car was already past the house. Garrett jogged to the end of the drive.

"Theresa!" he shouted again. He was in the middle of the road now, running behind the car, his feet splashing through the puddles that had already begun to form. The brake lights blinked for a second, then steadied as the car came to a halt. Garrett knew she was watching him in the rearview mirror, watching him close the distance. There's still a chance . . .

The brake lights suddenly flicked off, and the car started forward again, picking up speed, accelerating more quickly this time. Garrett kept running behind the car, chasing it as it made its way down the street. The rain was coming down in sheets, storm drops, soaking through his shirt and making it difficult for him to see.

Finally he slowed to a jog, then stopped. While the rain came down around him, he stood in the middle of the road, watching as her car moved farther into the distance and vanished from sight.

She was gone.

A few moments later a car honked its horn behind him, and he felt his heart surge. He turned quickly and wiped the rain from his eyes, almost expecting to see her face behind the windshield, but immediately saw he was mistaken. Garrett moved to the side of the road to let the car pass, and as he felt the man's curious stare upon him, he suddenly realized he'd never felt so alone.

Chapter Nine

WINTER arrived early the following year. Sitting on the beach near the spot where she'd first discovered the bottle, Theresa noted that the cold ocean breezes had grown stronger since she'd arrived this morning. Ominous gray clouds rolled overhead, and the waves were starting to rise and crash with greater frequency. She knew the storm was getting close.

She'd been out here most of the day, reliving their relationship up until the day they'd said good-bye. For months she'd been haunted by Garrett's expression as he stood in the driveway, the reflection of him in her rearview mirror chasing her car as she drove away. Leaving him then had been the hardest thing she'd ever done.

Finally she stood. In silence she started walking along the shore, imagining him walking beside her as she looked toward the horizon. She paused, mesmerized by the churning and rolling of the water, and when at last she turned her head, she realized his image had left her as well. She stood there for a long time, trying to bring him back, but when his image didn't return, she knew it was time to go.

Her thoughts went back to the days after their last good-bye. *We spend so much time making up for things we failed to say*, she mused.

If only, she began for the thousandth time. Images of those days flashed behind her eyes like a slide show she was powerless to stop.

If only . . .

AFTER arriving back in Boston, Theresa had picked up Kevin from a friend's house on the way home from the airport. When they got home, she surprised him by asking him to sit with her for a while instead of doing his homework. As he rested against her quietly on the couch, he occasionally sent her an anxious glance, but she merely stroked his hair and smiled at him abstractedly, as if she were somewhere far away.

On Monday she had a long lunch with Deanna and told her everything that had happened. She tried to sound strong. "It's for the best," she said resolutely when she finished. "I'm okay with this."

Deanna gazed at her searchingly, her eyes full of compassion. But she said nothing, only nodding at Theresa's brave claims.

For the next few days Theresa did her best to avoid thinking about Garrett. Working on her column was comforting. The hectic atmosphere in the newsroom helped as well, and because the conference call with Dan Mandel had turned out to be everything Deanna promised it would, Theresa approached her work with renewed enthusiasm. In the evenings, however, after Kevin went to bed and she was alone, she found it difficult to keep Garrett's image at bay.

That weekend she reluctantly told Kevin that she and Garrett wouldn't be seeing each other anymore.

"Mom, did Garrett do something that made you mad?"

"No," she answered softly. "It just wasn't meant to be."

The following week she was working at her computer when the phone rang.

"Is this Theresa?"

"Yes, it is," she answered, not recognizing the voice.

"This is Jeb Blake, Garrett's father. I know this is going to sound strange, but I'd like to talk to you."

"Oh, hi," she stammered. "Um . . . I've got a few minutes now."

He paused. "I'd like to talk to you in person if it's possible. It's not something I'd be comfortable with over the phone."

"Can I ask what it's about?"

"It's about Garrett," he said quietly. "I know it's asking a lot, but do you think you could fly down here? I wouldn't ask if it weren't important."

Finally agreeing to go, Theresa left work and went to Kevin's school. After picking him up early, she dropped him off with a friend, then went to the airport and caught the next flight to Wilmington. She went directly to Garrett's house, where Jeb was waiting for her.

"I'm glad you could come," Jeb said as soon as she'd arrived.

"What going on?" she asked.

Jeb looked older than she remembered. Leading her to the kitchen table, he pulled out a chair so she could sit with him.

"From what I could gather from talking to different people," he said quietly, "Garrett took *Happenstance* out later than usual. . . ."

IT WAS simply something he had to do. Garrett knew the dark, heavy clouds on the horizon presaged a coming storm. They seemed far enough away, however, to give him the time he needed. Besides, he was only going out a few miles. Even if the storm did hit, he would be close enough to make it back to port.

For three years he'd taken the same route whenever he went out, driven by instinct and memories of Catherine. It had been her idea to sail directly east that night, the first night *Happenstance* was ready. In her imagination they were sailing to Europe, a place she'd always wanted to go. She wanted to see the châteaus of the Loire Valley, the Parthenon, the Scottish Highlands—all the places she'd read about.

Of course, they never made it to Europe.

The night they first took *Happenstance* out, however, Catherine's dream was still alive. She stood on the bow, looking far into the distance, and it was that vision of her he always remembered: her hair billowing in the wind, her expression radiant and hopeful.

Less than a year later, while pregnant with their child, Catherine died in the hospital with Garrett at her side.

Later, when the dreams began, he didn't know what to do. In a fit of desperation one morning he tried to find relief by putting his feelings into words. He carried the finished letter with him when he went sailing later that day, and reading it again suddenly gave him an idea. The Gulf Stream, which flowed northward up the coast of the United States, turned east once it reached the cooler waters of the Atlantic. With a little luck a bottle could drift to Europe and wash up on the foreign soil she had always wanted to visit. His decision made, he sealed the letter in a bottle and threw it overboard. It became a pattern he would never break.

Since then he'd written sixteen more letters—seventeen if you counted the one he had with him now. As he stood at the wheel, gliding the boat directly eastward, he absently touched the bottle nestled in his coat pocket.

After writing this letter to Catherine, he had written a second one as well. That one he'd already taken care of. Because of the second letter, though, he knew he had to send Catherine's letter today. Storms were lined up across the Atlantic, moving slowly westward in a march toward the Eastern Seaboard. From the reports on television, it didn't look as if he'd be able to get out again for at least a week, and that was too long to wait. He'd already be gone by then.

The choppy seas continued to rise, the swells breaking higher, the troughs bottoming out a little lower. The sails were beginning to strain in the heavy winds. Garrett evaluated his position. The water was not quite deep enough here. The Gulf Stream—a summer phenomenon—was gone, and the only chance the bottle had of making it across the ocean was if it was far enough out to sea when it was dropped. The storm might otherwise wash it ashore within a few days. Of all the letters he'd written to her, he wanted this one to make it to Europe most of all. It would be the last one he'd ever send.

Happenstance began to bob as she moved farther out to sea. He held the wheel with both hands, keeping her as steady as he could. When the winds shifted and picked up—signaling the front of the storm—he began to tack, moving diagonally across the swells despite the hazards.

Overhead the clouds continued to thicken, rolling and twisting into new shapes. Light rain began to fall. "Just a few more minutes," he muttered. He needed just a few more minutes. To keep his balance, he spread his legs farther apart. The wheel was steady, but the swells were rocking the boat like an unsteady cradle.

He grasped the wheel with one hand as he reached into his jacket and removed the bottle. He pressed on the cork to make sure it was wedged in tightly, then held up the bottle in the waning light. He could see the letter inside, rolled tightly.

Staring at it, he felt a sense of completion, as if a long journey had finally come to an end. "Thank you," he whispered, his voice barely audible above the crashing of the waves.

He threw the bottle as far as he could. It was done.

Now, to turn the boat around.

At that moment two bolts of lightning split the sky simultaneously. The storm seemed to be gaining speed and strength, expanding like a balloon, coming directly toward him.

He used the loops to steady the wheel while he returned to the stern. Losing precious minutes, he fought furiously to maintain control of the boom. The ropes burned in his hands, ripping through his gloves. He finally succeeded in shifting the sails, and the boat leaned hard as it caught the wind. As he made his way back, another gust blew a cold blast from a different direction.

He switched on the radio just in time to hear a small-craft advisory being issued. Quickly he turned up the volume. "Repeat . . . dangerous winds forming . . . heavy rain expected."

He leaned into the wheel with a growing sense of urgency.

Nothing happened.

He realized suddenly that the rising swells were lifting the stern out of the water, not allowing the rudder to respond. The boat seemed frozen in the wrong direction, teetering precariously.

"Come on . . . catch," he whispered, the first tendrils of panic unfurling in his gut. This was taking too long. The sky was growing blacker by the minute, and the rain began to blow sideways in dense, impenetrable sheets.

A minute later the rudder finally caught, and the boat began to turn . . . slowly . . . slowly. The boat was still leaning too far to its side. . . .

With growing horror he watched the ocean rise around him to form a roaring, giant swell that was headed straight for him.

He braced himself as water crashed over the exposed hull, sending up white plumes. *Happenstance* leaned even farther and Garrett's legs buckled, but his grip on the wheel was solid. He scrambled to his feet again just as another swell hit the boat.

Water flooded onto the deck. For almost a minute it poured in with the force of a raging river. Freezing rain blew sideways, blinding him. *Happenstance,* instead of correcting, began to tilt, the sails heavy with rainwater. Garrett lost his balance again, the angle of the boat defying his efforts to get up. If another swell hit . . .

Garrett never saw it coming.

Like an executioner's swing, the wave smashed against the boat with terrible finality, forcing *Happenstance* onto her side, the mast and sails crashing into the water. She was lost. Garrett clung to the wheel, knowing if he let go, he'd be swept out to sea.

Happenstance began taking on water rapidly.

He had to get to the emergency kit, which included a raft—it was his only chance. Garrett inched his way toward the cabin door, holding on to anything he could, fighting the blinding rain, fighting for his life.

Lightning again and thunder, almost simultaneously.

He finally reached the hatch and gripped the handle. When it cracked open, he realized he'd made a terrible mistake. The ocean rushed in, quickly obscuring the interior of the cabin. Garrett immediately saw that the kit, normally secured in a bin on the wall, was already underwater. There was nothing to prevent the boat from being swallowed up by the ocean.

Happenstance began to sink quickly. In seconds half the hull was submerged. His mind suddenly clicked. Life jackets . . .

They were located under the seats near the stern.

He looked. They were still above water.

Struggling furiously, he reached for the side railings, the only handholds still above water. By the time he grabbed them, the water was up to his chest and his legs were kicking in the ocean.

Three fourths of the boat was underwater now.

He placed hand over hand, straining against the weight of the waves and his own leaden muscles. The ocean reached his neck, and the futility of the situation hit him at last.

He wasn't going to make it.

The water was up to his chin when he finally stopped trying. Looking upward, his body exhausted, he still refused to believe that it would end this way.

He let go of the side rail and began to swim away from the boat. His coat and shoes dragged heavily in the water. He treaded water, rising with the swells as he watched *Happenstance* slip beneath the ocean. Then, with cold and exhaustion beginning to numb his senses, he turned and began the slow, impossible swim to shore.

THERESA sat with Jeb at the table. Talking in fits and starts, he had taken a long time to tell her what he knew.

Later Theresa would recall that as she listened to his story, it was not with a sense of fear as much as with one of curiosity. Garrett was an expert sailor, an even better swimmer. He was too careful, too vital to be bested by something like this. If anyone could make it, it would be he.

She reached across the table to Jeb, confused. "I don't understand. Why did he take the boat out if he knew there was a storm coming?"

"I don't know," he said quietly. He couldn't meet her eyes.

He was ashen, his eyes downcast as if hiding something. Absently Theresa looked around the kitchen. Everything was tidy, as if it had been cleaned moments before she arrived. Through the open bedroom door she saw Garrett's comforter spread neatly across the bed. Oddly, two large floral arrangements had been placed atop it.

"I don't understand. He's all right, isn't he?"

"Theresa," Jeb finally said with tears forming in his eyes, "they found him yesterday morning."

"Is he in the hospital?"

"No," he said quietly.

"Then where is he?" she asked, refusing to acknowledge what she somehow knew.

Jeb didn't answer. He bowed his head so she wouldn't see his tears, but she could hear his choking gasps.

"Theresa . . ." he said, trailing off.

"Where is he?" she demanded, leaping to her feet in a surge of frantic adrenaline. She heard the chair clatter to the floor behind her as if from a very great distance.

Jeb stared up at her. "They found his body yesterday morning."

She felt her chest constrict as if she were suffocating.

"He's gone, Theresa."

THEY buried him next to Catherine in a small cemetery near his home. Jeb and Theresa stood together at the graveside service. It was a simple ceremony, and though it began to rain just as the minister finished speaking, the crowd lingered long after it was over.

A reception was held at Garrett's house. One by one people came through—friends from high school, former diving students, employees from the shop—all offering their condolences and sharing memories. When the last few filed out, leaving Jeb and Theresa alone, Jeb pulled a box from the closet and asked her to sit with him while they looked through it together.

In the box were hundreds of photographs. Over the next few hours she watched Garrett's childhood and adolescence unfold—all the missing pieces of his life that she had only imagined: high school and college graduations, the restored *Happenstance,* Garrett in front of the shop prior to its opening.

Later that evening, as they sorted through the last few pictures, she saw the Garrett she'd fallen in love with. One shot in particular caught her eye, and she held it for a long time. Jeb explained that it had been taken on Memorial Day, a few weeks before the bottle had washed up at the Cape. In it Garrett stood on his deck, looking much the same as he had the first time she'd come to his house.

When she was finally able to put the picture down, Jeb gently took it from her.

The following morning he handed her an envelope. Opening it, she saw that he'd given the photo back to her, along with a number of others. With them were the three letters that had first enabled Theresa and Garrett to come together.

"I think he would want you to have these."

Too choked up to respond, she nodded a silent thank-you.

THERESA couldn't remember much about her first few days back in Boston, and in retrospect she knew she didn't really want to. She did recall that Deanna was waiting for her at Logan Airport when her plane touched down. After taking one look at her, Deanna immediately called her husband, instructing him to bring some clothes to Theresa's because she planned to stay with her for a few days. Theresa spent most of the time in bed, not even bothering to get up when Kevin came home from school.

"Is my mom ever going to be okay?" he asked.

"She just needs a little time, Kevin," Deanna answered. "I know it's hard for you, too, but it's going to be okay."

Theresa's only other recollection about that week was her relentless need to understand how this could have happened. Before she left Wilmington, she made Jeb promise to call her if he learned anything else about the day Garrett had gone out on *Happenstance.* In a curious twist of reason she believed that knowing the details—the *why*—would somehow lessen her grief.

Of course, deep down she knew that would never happen. Jeb didn't call with an explanation that week, nor did the answer come to her in a moment of contemplation. No, the answer eventually came from a place she would never have predicted.

ON THE beach at Cape Cod one year later Theresa reflected without bitterness on the turn of events that had led her to this place.

Ready at last, she reached in her bag. After removing the object she had brought with her, she stared at it, reliving the hour in which her answer had finally come.

After Deanna had left, Theresa had tried to reestablish a routine of sorts. In her confusion over the last week she'd simply piled the mail that accumulated in the corner of the dining room. After dinner one night, while Kevin was at the movies, Theresa absently began to sort through the pile.

There were a few dozen letters, three magazines, and a package wrapped in plain brown paper without a return address. There were two FRAGILE stickers—one near the address and the other on the opposite side of the box—and another sticker that said HANDLE WITH CARE. Curious, she decided to open it first.

It was then that she saw the postmark from Wilmington, North Carolina, dated from two weeks before. Quickly she scanned the address scrawled on the front. It was Garrett's handwriting.

"No . . ." She set the package down, her stomach suddenly tight.

She found a pair of scissors in the drawer and shakily began to cut the tape, pulling at the paper carefully as she did so. She already knew what she'd find inside. After lifting out the object and checking the rest of the package to make sure nothing was still inside, she loosened the surrounding bubble wrap.

The bottle was corked, and the rolled-up letter inside stood on its end. After removing the cork, she tipped it upside down, and the letter spilled out easily. Like the letter she'd found only a few months before, it was wrapped in yarn. She unrolled it carefully.

In the top right corner was a picture of an old ship, sails billowing in the wind.

> Dear Theresa,
>
> Can you forgive me?
>
> In a world that I seldom understand, there are winds of destiny that blow when we least expect them. Sometimes they gust with the fury of a hurricane, sometimes they barely fan one's cheek. But the winds cannot be denied, bringing as they often

do a future that is impossible to ignore. You, my darling, are the wind that I did not anticipate, the wind that has gusted more strongly than I ever imagined possible. You are my destiny.

I was wrong, so wrong to ignore what was obvious, and I beg your forgiveness. Like a cautious traveler, I tried to protect myself from the wind and lost my soul instead. I was a fool to ignore my destiny, but even fools have feelings, and I've come to realize that you are the most important thing I have in this world.

I've made more mistakes in the past few months than some make in a lifetime. I was wrong to have acted as I did when I found the letters, just as I was wrong to hide the truth about what I was going through with respect to my past. But most of all I was wrong to deny what was obvious in my heart: that I can't go on without you.

It is my deepest wish that you give me one more chance. As you might have guessed, I'm hoping that this bottle will work its magic, as it did once before, and somehow bring us back together.

For the first few days after you left, I wanted to believe that I could go on as I always had. But I couldn't. Every time I watched the sun go down, I thought of you and the wonderful times we had. I knew in my heart that my life would never be the same again. I wanted you back more than I imagined possible, yet whenever I conjured you up, I kept hearing your words in our last conversation. No matter how much I loved you, I knew it wasn't going to be possible unless we—both of us—were sure I would devote myself fully to the path that lay ahead. I continued to be troubled by these thoughts until late last night when the answer finally came to me.

In my dream I saw myself on the beach with Catherine, in the same spot I took you after our lunch at Hank's. It was bright in the sun, the rays reflecting brilliantly off the sand. We walked alongside each other, and she listened intently as I told her about you, about us, about the wonderful times we shared. After some hesitation I admitted that I loved you but that I felt guilty about it. She said nothing right away but simply kept walking until she finally turned to me and asked, "Why?"

"Because of you."

Upon hearing my answer, she smiled at me with patient amusement, the way she used to before she died. "Oh, Garrett," she said as she gently touched my face, "who do you think it was that brought the bottle to her?"

Theresa stopped reading.

Who do you think it was that brought the bottle to her?

Leaning back in her chair, she closed her eyes, trying to hold back the tears. "Garrett," she murmured, "Garrett . . ."

Outside her window she could hear the sounds of cars passing by. Slowly she began reading again.

When I woke, I felt empty and alone. The dream made me ache inside because of what I had done to us, and I began to cry. When I pulled myself together, I wrote two letters—the one you're holding in your hand right now, and one to Catherine, in which I finally said my good-bye. Today I'm taking *Happenstance* out to send it to her, as I have with all the others. It will be my last letter. Catherine in her own way has told me to go on, and I have chosen to listen. Not only to her words but also to the leanings of my heart that led me back to you.

Oh, Theresa, I am sorry, so very sorry, that I ever hurt you. I am coming to Boston next week with the hope that you find a way to forgive me.

Theresa, I love you and always will. I am tired of being alone. I see children crying and laughing as they play in the sand, and I realize I want to have children with you. I want to watch Kevin as he grows into a man. I will move to Boston if you ask, because I cannot go on this way. I am sick and sad without you. As I sit here in the kitchen, I am praying that you will let me come back to you, this time forever.

Garrett

It was dusk now, and the gray sky was turning dark quickly. Though she'd read the letter a thousand times, it still aroused the same feelings she'd had when she first read it. For months those feelings had stalked her every waking moment.

Sitting on the beach, she rolled up the letter again, carefully wrapped the yarn around it, and returned it to the bottle. When she got home, she would put it back on her bureau, where she always kept it. At night, when the glow of streetlights slanted through her room, the bottle gleamed in the darkness and was the last thing she saw before going to sleep.

Next she reached for the pictures Jeb had given her. After she returned to Boston, she'd sifted through them one by one. When her hands began to tremble, she had put them in her drawer and never looked at them again.

But now she thumbed through them, finding the one that had been taken on the back deck. Holding it in front of her, she remembered everything about him—the way he looked and moved, his easy smile, the wrinkles at the corners of his eyes.

Since the funeral she'd kept in sporadic contact with Jeb. She had explained to him what she had discovered about why Garrett had taken *Happenstance* out that day, and they both ended up weeping on the phone. As the months rolled on, however, they were eventually able to mention his name without tears.

It was a phone call from Jeb three weeks ago that had led her back to Cape Cod. When she listened to his gentle voice quietly suggesting that it was time to move on, the walls she'd built finally began to collapse. She cried for most of the night, but the following morning she knew what she had to do.

Now, as she stood on the beach, she wondered if anyone could see her. She glanced from side to side, but it was deserted. Only the ocean appeared to be moving, and she was drawn to its fury. She watched it for a long time, thinking of Garrett.

She loved him. She would always love him. She'd known it from the moment she saw him on the docks, and she knew it now. Neither the passage of time nor his death could change the way she felt.

She closed her eyes, whispering to him as she did so. "I miss you, Garrett Blake," she said softly.

The first few raindrops were beginning to fall by the time she uncorked the simple clear bottle she was holding so tightly. She removed the letter she had written to him yesterday, the letter she had come to send. After unrolling it, she began reading.

My Darling,

One year has passed since I sat with your father in the kitchen. It is late at night, and though the words are coming hard to me, I can't escape the feeling that it's time that I finally answer your question.

Of course I forgive you. I forgive you now, and I forgave you the moment I read your letter. In my heart I had no other choice. Leaving you once was hard enough; to have done it a second time would have been impossible. I loved you too much to have let you go again. Though I'm still grieving over what might have been, I find myself thankful that you came into my life for even a short time. In the beginning I'd assumed that we were somehow brought together to help you through your time of grief. Yet now, one year later, I've come to believe that it was the other way around.

Ironically, I am in the same position you were the first time we met. I am struggling with the ghost of someone I loved and lost. Sometimes my grief is overwhelming, and even though I understand that we will never see each other again, there is a part of me that wants to hold on to you forever. It would be easy for me to do that because loving someone else might diminish my memories of you. Yet this is the paradox: Even though I miss you greatly, it's because of you that I don't dread the future. Because you were able to fall in love with me, you have taught me that it's possible to move forward in life, no matter how terrible your grief.

Right now I don't think I'm ready, but I am hopeful that there will come a day when my sadness is replaced by something beautiful. Because of you I have the strength to go on.

You will always be with me. When I listen to the ocean, it will be your whispers. When a cool breeze caresses my cheek, it will be your spirit passing by.

This is not a good-bye, my darling; this is a thank-you. Thank you for coming into my life and giving me joy. Thank you for loving me and receiving my love in return. Thank you for the memories I will cherish forever. But most of all thank you for showing me that there will come a time when I can eventually let you go.

I love you,
T.

After reading the letter for the last time, Theresa rolled it up and sealed it in the bottle. She turned it over a few times, knowing that her journey had come full circle. Finally, when she knew she could wait no longer, she threw it out as far as she could.

It was then that a strong wind picked up and the fog began to part. Theresa stood in silence and stared at the bottle as it floated out to sea. And even though she knew it was impossible, she imagined that it would never drift ashore. It would travel the world forever, drifting by faraway places she herself would never see.

When the bottle vanished from sight a few minutes later, she started back to the car. Walking in silence in the rain, Theresa smiled softly. She didn't know when or where or if it would ever turn up, but it didn't really matter. Somehow she knew that Garrett would get the message.

NICHOLAS SPARKS

JERRY BAUER

Like the hero of *Message in a Bottle,* Nicholas Sparks is a writer of love letters. When he was courting his future wife, Catherine, he wrote to her twice a day. And, he says, it was worth the effort: "I got a great woman."

Time has not taken the edge off the couple's romance. Candlelight dinners and roses are still in the picture, and when Nick sold his romantic novel *The Notebook* for a million dollars, the first thing he did was buy Catherine a new wedding ring and ask her to marry him all over again.

The couple and their two small sons, Miles and Ryan, live in a rural corner of South Carolina.

"A dazzling thriller."

—New York *Post*

THE Cobra EVENT

RICHARD PRESTON

It's deadlier than the Ebola virus, more devastating than a nuclear bomb. And it's in the wrong hands.

The Cobra virus.

Ready or not, here it comes.

PART ONE: Trial

New York City, Late 1990s

KATE Moran was an only child. She was seventeen years old and lived with her parents in a loft apartment on the top floor of a handsome old building to the west of Union Square, just on the edge of Greenwich Village. One Wednesday morning in late April, Kate was slow getting up. She had woken in the middle of the night in a sweat, but it went away and she fell back asleep, into bad dreams that she could not remember. She came awake with a fresh cold.

"Kate!" It was Nanette, the housekeeper, calling from the kitchen. "Katie."

"Okay." She blew her nose and went into the bathroom. She brushed her teeth, then went back into the bedroom and dressed in a flowered dress she had found in a flea market.

Kate had wavy russet hair, which she wore medium length. Her eyes were grayish blue or bluish gray, depending on the light and her mood, or so she liked to think—complicated eyes. Her face was changing fast. She could almost see the bones of the woman emerging. She thought about this as she brushed her hair, pushing it back so that the two platinum earrings in her left ear were visible.

Kate's mother called her the Packrat, because she accumulated things. The worktable in the corner of her room was littered with old cigar boxes, metal containers, purses, puzzles—things that opened and closed. There was an old dollhouse she had found in a junk shop and had been taking apart, cannibalizing it for a project. She reached into it and pulled out a glass prism. She stuffed the prism into her knapsack. It would become part of the box she was constructing in Mr. Talides's art room at the Mater School, a private girls school on the Upper East Side.

She threw her knapsack over her shoulder and went out into the kitchen. Her parents had already left for work. Her father was a partner in an investment house, her mother an attorney.

In the kitchen Nanette had poured orange juice and toasted a bagel. But Kate wasn't hungry. She sneezed. Nanette handed her a paper towel. "Do you want to stay home?"

"Uh-uh." Kate was already out the door.

It was a glorious morning. She hurried along Fifteenth Street to Union Square, heading for the subway entrance. She threaded through the stalls of the farmers' market that filled up the northern and western sides of the square, and at the subway kiosk she ran down the stairs and caught the uptown Lexington Avenue express.

The Mater School was only a few blocks from the Eighty-sixth Street subway station. Kate was running a little late, and by the time she got there, the younger girls had gone inside, although some of the upper-school girls were hanging around on the steps.

"Kates, I have to tell you something." It was her friend Jennifer Ramosa. They walked in together, with Jennifer talking about something that Kate didn't follow. Kate felt strange, as if a feather had brushed across her face. For a moment she had a feeling of vertigo, and she dropped her knapsack. There was a sound of breaking glass. Kate shook her head, and it seemed to clear.

"What's going on, Kates?" Jennifer asked.

"Nothing. I'm fine." Kate picked up her knapsack. It slushed and rattled. "Something broke. Darn, I broke my prism." She headed into class, annoyed with herself.

AT ABOUT ten o'clock in the morning Kate went to the nurse's office and got some Tylenol. It didn't help her cold, which was getting worse. It was a real sinus cold. Her mouth hurt; it felt bumpy, and it stung. She was debating whether or not to go home. She decided to go to art class and leave after that.

The art teacher, Peter Talides, was a balding middle-aged painter, likable and disorganized. Kate settled at a table near the window, where her assembled box was taking shape. It was an ambitious construction, a kind of house made of pieces of dollhouses and all kinds of found objects. Kate tried to work on it but couldn't remember what she had planned to do. "I want to go home," she said aloud.

The students looked at her. She started to stand up, when suddenly she felt really dizzy. "Oh, no," she said. She sat down heavily on her work stool.

"What's the matter, Kates?" Jennifer asked.

There was a crash. Kate had slid off the stool and landed on the floor. Peter Talides came hurrying over. "Are you all right?"

"I'm sick," Kate said in a thick voice. She began to tremble. She was sitting on the floor with her legs out straight.

Talides bent over her. "We need to get you to the nurse."

She didn't answer. Her teeth were chattering, and her face was flushed. Peter Talides was frightened. Kate's nose was running. Her eyes flicked over his face without seeming to see him.

"Someone tell the nurse," he said. "Go on! Go!"

Kate said, "I think I'm going to throw up."

"Can you stand up?"

"No. Yes."

He helped her to her feet. "Jennifer, please take Kate to the bathroom, will you?"

The girl helped Kate out of the room and into the bathroom, while Peter Talides waited in the hallway.

Kate stood in front of the sink, hanging on to it. There was a mirror over the sink. For a moment she couldn't bring herself to look. Then she opened her mouth. The inside was dotted with black blisters. She screamed and crumpled to her knees.

Peter Talides ran into the bathroom. He found Kate sitting on the floor, looking at him with glassy eyes. She said in a thick voice, "I don't know what to do." Her expression went blank. The left side of her face rippled in a series of twitches that moved in a wave. Suddenly she uttered a fierce, guttural cry. She toppled backward. Her knees straightened out, and her body seized and froze in a clonic jerk. Her head hit the tiled floor with a crack. Her arms and legs began to jerk rhythmically.

"My God!" Talides cried. He tried to hold her arms still.

Her legs lashed out, kicking Talides backward. She was very strong. Then her body began to scissor back and forth. Her teeth clicked together repeatedly. Her mouth was working, and her lips moved and rippled. Her eyes were half open. Talides thought Kate was trying to say something, but no language came out.

Then her teeth sank into her lower lip, and blood ran down her chin. She bit her lip again, hard, with ferocity, and she made a groaning animal sound.

"She's biting herself," Talides yelled. "Help!"

Jennifer was next to him, weeping, crying for help, too. The bathroom door was open, and students were looking in, stunned with fright. Most were crying. Several of them had run to call 911.

Kate began to writhe. It was a type of writhing associated with damage to the base of the brain—the midbrain, the knot of structures at the top of the spinal cord. Her spine began to bend backward, and her body arched into the air until only the back of her head and her heels were touching the floor. Her body formed the shape of a C. Her nose began to bleed, staining Talides's shirt. She drew a rasping breath, inhaling blood. Cracking sounds came from her spine.

The nosebleed died down, then stopped. Kate's spine relaxed, and she sank to the floor.

Peter Talides was on top of her, his face to her face, crying, "Kate! Kate! Hang on!" He had taken a CPR class with the Red Cross years earlier, but he couldn't remember what to do.

Deep in her mind, Kate came awake. She heard Mr. Talides's voice begging her to hang on. There was an absolute peace, no feeling of pain. It was not possible to hang on. She fell away.

PART TWO: Forbidden Zone

Johnston Atoll, 1969

ONE evening late in July, a thousand miles southwest of Hawaii, the waters of the Pacific Ocean had calmed to a liquefaction of blue. A moderate swell rocked the deck of a fishing boat, and the boat's radio masts and weather sensors swung gently. The sun had descended to a handbreadth above the horizon. Mare's-tail clouds fingered in veils across the sky, but you could see the moon, a gibbous moon, as pale as a spirit. Somewhere on that sphere the Americans had been walking.

Captain Gennadi Yevlikov held his binoculars on the moon, wondering which of its dark areas was the Sea of Tranquility, but he couldn't remember. Then he focused on the horizon toward the north. He could not see Johnston Atoll, but he knew it was there and that the Americans were there, too. All around Yevlikov on the deck of the fishing boat, Ministry of Health scientists hurried to put out petri dishes and to set up their bubblers and glassware. Fishing nets, unused and in perfect condition, hung from winches above them.

A sailor standing near the bow shouted, pointing in the direction of the atoll. Yevlikov looked through his binoculars and saw a tiny brown dot on the horizon, above the water. It was not moving. For a moment he thought the dot must be a seabird. Then he saw the wings. They were greenish brown.

It was an American Phantom jet with Marine Corps coloration. The reason it seemed not to be moving was that it was heading straight for the fishing boat. It gave no sound, which meant it was traveling at supersonic speed. Yevlikov saw a pop-flash around the tail: The pilot had just fired his afterburner. The Phantom, already traveling close to Mach 1, was still accelerating toward the boat. It came lower, skimming the surface of the sea. They saw a V-shaped shock wave tearing up the water behind the Phantom. There was total silence.

"Down!" Yevlikov shouted.

With a thudding of bodies the crew and the scientists hurled themselves to the deck. They stabbed their fingers into their ears and opened their mouths wide. They all did this except for one scientist from the Ministry of Health, a thin man wearing spectacles. He stood by an assembly of laboratory glassware, his eyes fixed on the incoming Phantom like a man before a firing squad.

The Phantom passed ten feet above the Russian trawler, flicking by in silence. An instant later the sonic boom blew over the Russians like a bomb. Yevlikov felt his body bounce on the deck. Every window and port, every gauge, most of the petri dishes and laboratory glassware exploded. The air was filled with falling glass and the roar of the departing Phantom. Two more sonic booms passed over the boat—echoes of the Phantom's passage.

The Ministry of Health scientist stood in a heap of glass. His eyeglasses had cracked. He touched one finger to his ear, and his finger came away with blood on it—his eardrum had ruptured. They took him below, and Yevlikov set a course for the east, moving his trawler along the edge of the forbidden zone. "Try to find some petri dishes that aren't broken," he said to the scientists.

SEVENTY miles north of Yevlikov's boat, Lieutenant Commander Mark Littleberry, M.D., stood with his colleagues on the beach at Johnston Atoll. The sun had touched the horizon. The mare's tails of clouds feathered slowly, ice crystals moving in the upper air. The inversion had occurred. The winds had smoothed. The moon was rising. Conditions were perfect for a laydown.

"I feel sorry for those guys on the tugboats," one of the scientists remarked.

"I feel even sorrier for the monkeys," another scientist said.

Stationed at intervals downwind were tugboats pulling barges full of monkeys. Here on the beach each person was holding a gas mask in case the wind shifted unexpectedly.

"The men will be all right," Littleberry said. A tall, handsome African American with a crewcut and gold-rimmed spectacles, Littleberry was a medical officer for the Johnston Atoll field trials, and he was regarded as brilliant by the other scientists in the program. He had a degree from Harvard and a medical degree from Tulane. He had made valuable contributions toward explaining the ways in which the weapons they were testing entered the lungs, and he was bringing in crucial data from monkey dissections. But Littleberry was becoming unhappy with his success. He had begun to ask himself what exactly he was doing.

"Here it comes," someone said.

All heads turned to the left. They saw a Marine Corps Phantom flying about two hundred meters above the water, traveling just under the speed of sound, heading west toward the setting sun. It carried no stores underwing except for a small, strange-looking pod. They watched. In the evening light they saw it—something bleeding into the air from the pod. What was coming out of the pod was a living weapon in the form of a dry powder.

It was a whitish haze that almost instantly dissipated and became invisible. The particles were very small, between one micron and five microns across, the ideal size for a weaponized bioparticle. One or two such particles trapped in the lung can cause a fatal infection that kills in three days. You can't smell these particles; you can't see them; you don't know they are there until you start to get sick. Not even rain can wash them out of the sky—they don't get caught by raindrops. Rain actually improves the effectiveness of a bioweapon in the air, because rain clouds block sunlight. Bio-aerosols don't do well in sunlight. It destroys their genetic material and kills them.

The jet shrank and seemed to vanish into the disk of the sun, leaving a departing rumble. It was doing a biological laydown across the Pacific Ocean. The laydown line was fifty miles long.

"Beautiful," someone said. "Incredible."

The talk among the watchers grew technical.

"What's the dissemination rate?"

"One gram per meter."

"A gram per meter! That's nothing." The jet was spraying only one kilogram of hot agent per kilometer of flight.

"If it was anthrax," said one scientist, "they'd have to shovel it from a dump truck to have any effect on the monkeys."

"There's only about eighty kilos of agent in that pod." Less than two hundred pounds.

"Yow. And he's laying it for fifty miles."

"What's the agent?"

"It's the Utah cocktail. You didn't hear me say that." The identity of the material was classified.

"That's Utah he's laying down? Man, a fifty-mile laydown could create what? Two thousand square miles of hot zone?"

"If the stuff works. It won't work."

"Ask the doctor here what he thinks."

"I think it's going to work," Mark Littleberry said.

He went off by himself and walked along the beach. He was thinking about the monkeys, thinking about who he was, thinking about leaving the program.

But Littleberry had work to do, people to worry about. He stayed up all that night, maintaining radio contact with the navy crews on board the tugboats that were pulling the monkey barges.

The monkeys were rhesus monkeys, housed in metal cages. Some of the cages sat on the decks; some of them were in closed rooms in the holds. The scientists were interested in knowing if closing oneself in a room might provide some protection against a biological weapon drifting in the open air.

Littleberry stayed by a radio set in the command center on the island. "Tugboat Charlie, come in. This is Littleberry. How are you guys doing? Y'all hanging in there?"

Fifty miles downwind, at the far end of the test zone, a tugboat captain was standing at the wheel of his boat. He was wearing a rubber space suit with an army gas mask equipped with special HEPA filters. HEPA stands for high-efficiency particulate air. A

HEPA filter will trap a virus or a bacterial particle before it can get into the lungs.

"We're dying of the heat here," the captain said. "The heat's gonna kill us before the bugs do."

"Copy, I hear you. Wind direction is south-southwest, holding at eight knots. They're going to call you in as soon as possible."

On the tugboat's deck two army technicians in space suits were tending the bubbler and the blood clock. The bubbler was sucking air through a glass tank full of oil. The oil would collect particles from the air. The blood clock was a rotating dish that held a circular slab of blood agar. Agar is a jelly on which bacteria grow easily. Blood agar has blood mixed into it and has a dark red color. Biological weapons often grow better in the presence of blood. Later the blood clock would show the rise and fall of hot agent in the air.

Downwind, the Russian trawler moved along the edge of the forbidden zone. Most of the glassware had been broken, but a few petri dishes full of blood jelly sat in racks, open to the air. Captain Yevlikov steered on, wearing his green rubber suit, looking through the eyeholes and sweating like a man in a mine.

THE activity around Johnston Atoll in 1969 was officially a "joint naval exercise," but that was a cover for the fact that what was going on were hot field trials for the strategic uses of biological weapons over large areas.

The wave of bioparticles—the bio-aerosol—moved all night. It passed the monkey barges one by one, and later it passed over the Russian trawler. At four o'clock in the morning the order came to bring the last barge home. All the monkeys had breathed the particles by then.

The monkeys were placed in cages in the monkey labs on Johnston Atoll. During the next three days Littleberry and the other scientists saw the effects of the Utah cocktail. Half the monkeys became sick and died. They coughed and coughed until their lungs burned up. The other half remained healthy. The infected monkeys always died—there was no such thing as a mild case of Utah. As to whether a primate became infected or not, it seemed to be random chance. This is typical of biological weapons. It is essentially impossible to exterminate a population with a biological weapon. On the other hand, it is quite easy to crash a population, reducing it by half or more in a few days.

Captain Yevlikov and his crew survived, all but the shocked man from the Ministry of Health, who hadn't been wearing a mask; his lungs shriveled, and they buried him at sea. The Utah grew in little spots and colonies on the Soviet petri dishes. The scientists froze some samples and carried them back to Vladivostok. Captain Gennadi Yevlikov was given a medal for bravery.

The rising sun over the Pacific Ocean on the morning following the test began to neutralize the Utah, killing its genetic material. Eventually it biodegraded, and no trace of it remained in the sea or in the air. All that was left was knowledge.

INVISIBLE HISTORY (I.)

The White House, November 25, 1969

PRESIDENT Richard Nixon's prepared statement was very brief, and he took no questions from the press. Sticking to the text, he said that the United States was renouncing the first use of chemical weapons. Then he went on to what was clearly the more important subject to him: biological weapons. "Second, biological warfare, which is commonly called *germ* warfare—" He shook the word germ with Nixonian emphasis, as if he shuddered to his jowls at the thought of germs. "*Germ* warfare: this has massive, unpredictable, and potentially uncontrollable consequences. It may produce global epidemics and profoundly affect the health of future generations."

He said that, after consulting with experts, he had decided that the United States would renounce the use of any form of biological weapons and he was ordering the disposal of the existing weapons.

The next day, in an analysis of "What Nixon Gave Up," *The New York Times* noted that the President was repudiating only "a few horrible and probably unusable weapons in the American arsenal to gain possible advantages of security for the nation and prestige for himself." According to "informed sources," the chemical weapons given up by Nixon were expensive and unreliable. As for biological weapons, "experts" said that the United States would have been unable to use them. "In the first place, the germs and toxins have never been tested; it is not clear what effect they would have on enemy forces or population."

Of course, the experts had it wrong. Either that or they lied. Nevertheless, their position prevailed. The idea that bioweapons were never fully tested or are unusable is a myth that persists to this day. The existence of the Johnston Atoll field trials was not reported publicly and is unknown to most civilian scientists.

The trials, which went on steadily from 1964 to 1969, were successful far beyond the expectations of even the scientists involved. The results were clear: Biological weapons can be used to destroy an army or a city or a nation.

The reasons for Richard Nixon's decision to end the American biological-weapons program were complicated. His intelligence people were telling him that the Russians were getting ready to embark on a crash biological program, and he hoped to encourage them not to do it. The Vietnam War protests were going on. Not only did the protesters not want chemical or biological weapons used on anyone by their government, they also did not want them stored near where they lived, or transported across the country. The success of the Pacific trials was also a factor in Nixon's decision, for the trials had surprised everyone. The problem with bioweapons was not that they didn't work; it was that they worked too well.

The meaning of the Pacific trials was not lost on the leader of the Soviet Union, Leonid Brezhnev, or on his advisers. Brezhnev was reportedly furious at his scientific people for having fallen behind the Americans. The Soviets believed that Nixon was lying, that he never really canceled the American bioweapons program. So Brezhnev did exactly what Nixon was trying to head off: He ordered an acceleration of the Soviet bioweapons program.

In 1972 the United States signed the Convention on the Prohibition of the Development, Production, and Stockpiling of Bacteriological (Biological) and Toxin Weapons and on Their Destruction, commonly known as the Biological Weapons Convention. Soviet diplomats helped to write the treaty, and the Soviet Union became one of three so-called depository states for the treaty; the other two were the United States and Great Britain. By making themselves depository states, the three nations offered themselves as an example to be followed. It was believed that the resources of the intelligence community and the vigilance of the scientific community would serve to sound the alarm about any violations of the treaty.

But there was no way to verify whether violations were taking place, and the truth is that much progress was made in the development of bioweapons in various places around the world. This was not noticed for a long time. It was an invisible history.

PART THREE: Diagnosis

Atlanta, Georgia, Wednesday, April 22, 199_

THE weather in Atlanta had turned sunny and hot. At the headquarters of the Centers for Disease Control and Prevention, which is located northeast of the city center, the late April air was filled with a drifting scent of loblolly pines.

At the middle of the CDC complex is building 6, an old brick monolith, almost without windows. It was once an animal-holding facility that stored populations of mice, rabbits, and monkeys used for medical research. The CDC grew and became so short of space that the animals were moved and the animal rooms converted to offices. They are the least desirable offices at the CDC, and therefore they are occupied by the youngest people, many of whom are in the CDC's Epidemic Intelligence Service—the EIS. About seventy health professionals enroll in the EIS every year. During a two-year fellowship they investigate disease outbreaks in the United States and the world. The EIS is a training program for people who want a career in public health.

On the third floor of building 6, inside a windowless former monkey room, Alice Austen, M.D., a twenty-nine-year-old EIS officer, was on phone duty, listening to people talk about their diseases. "I got something bad," a man was saying to her. "And I know where I got it. From a pizza. It was a ham and onion. My girlfriend got the disease, too."

"What do you think you have?" she asked.

"I don't want to, like, get too specific. Let's just say I got a VD." The man described how he had been eating a pizza at a local restaurant with his girlfriend when he'd found himself chewing on a stained bandage. He was convinced it had given them certain symptoms that he was reluctant to describe.

"You could not get a sexually transmitted disease from eating a bandage," Austen said. "It would have been sterilized by heat in the oven. You should go to an emergency room and get an exam, and your girlfriend, too."

The man wanted to talk, but finally she managed to get him off the phone.

Austen was a slender woman of medium height, with wavy auburn hair and a fine-boned face. The daughter of a retired chief of police from Ashland, New Hampshire, she was a medical pathologist by training—her specialty was death. Her eyes were gray-blue and thoughtful. Her hands were slender but very strong. She wore no rings, and her fingernails were cut short so as not to pierce surgical gloves. It was Wednesday, uniform day at the CDC, and Austen was wearing a Public Health Service uniform—pants and a short-sleeved khaki shirt, with the gold oak leaf of a lieutenant commander on the right shoulder. It looked like a navy uniform. The U.S. Public Health Service is an unarmed branch of the U.S. military.

Like many pathologists, Alice Austen was a loner by temperament, independent-minded, curious about how things worked.

An older man walked into Austen's office and sat down at an empty desk. His name was Walter Mellis. He was a public-health doctor in his late fifties, and he had worked at the CDC for most of his career. "I'm looking for someone to observe an autopsy," he said. "You're the only EIS officer trained in pathology."

"I'm pretty busy writing up my last outbreak," she said.

"I had a call from Lex Nathanson, the medical examiner of New York," he went on, seeming to ignore her. "They've had two cases of something unusual. He asked me if we had anyone to help him out. Quietly."

"Why don't they use the city health department?"

"I don't know why." He looked a little annoyed. "I know Lex Nathanson from way back, so he called me."

Walter Mellis had a potbelly, gray frizzy hair, and a mustache. He refused to wear his Public Health Service uniform on Wednesdays, and today he had on a shirt the color of mud, with frayed cuffs. "This could be something good," he said. "You never know."

"Is this case part of your project?" she asked.

"The Stealth Virus Project? Yes, it is. My idea is that there may be unknown viruses out there. They don't cause obvious outbreaks. They sneak around. They're not very contagious, so they just hit one person here and one person there. Lex Nathanson knows about the Stealth Virus Project, and I've asked him to keep an eye out for anything like this."

She noticed that Walter Mellis was wearing a beeper on his belt. She wondered why. "Are you telling me everything?"

Mellis put his hand up. He sighed. He was accustomed to people ducking his project. It didn't seem to be going anywhere. "Look," he said, "if you don't want to do this, I'll call Lex and tell him we don't have anyone available right now. He'll understand."

"No. I'll go."

ALICE Austen drove her Volkswagen Jetta back to her rented condominium in Decatur, a few miles from the CDC. She changed into a blue silk-and-wool skirt and a silk blouse and put some extra clothing into a travel bag. A big chunk of the bag was taken up by her leather boots, encased in a white plastic garbage bag closed with a twist tie. The boots were Mighty-Tuff work boots, the kind construction workers wear, with steel toes and nonskid soles. They were her autopsy boots. She put her laptop computer into her briefcase, along with a cellular phone and a green cloth-covered Epidemic Intelligence Service notebook—an epi notebook, they called it. The notebook was for keeping records of the investigation. She packed a small digital electronic camera, which stored photographs on memory cards. The memory cards could be plugged into her laptop, and she could review the images on the screen. Finally, into her travel bag she placed a leather folder containing her autopsy knives. If they asked her to participate in the autopsy, she wanted to be ready with her own knives.

West of Babylon, Iraq, Thursday, April 23

APRIL in Iraq is normally dry and blue, but a cool front had moved down from the north, bringing an overcast sky. The United Nations Special Commission Biological Weapons Inspection Team Number 247—UNSCOM 247—was traveling along a narrow highway at the edge of the desert to the west of the Euphrates River. The convoy consisted of a dozen white four-wheel-drive vehicles. On their doors UN was stenciled in large black letters.

The convoy arrived at a crossroads and slowed to a crawl. All the vehicles' turn signals went on at the same time, blinking to the right. Vehicle by vehicle the UNSCOM 247 convoy turned to the northeast. Its destination was the Habbaniyah Air Base, where a U.N. transport aircraft waited to fly the inspectors out of the country.

A white Nissan Pathfinder 4 X 4 in the middle of the convoy had its right-turn signal on, like the others. Then suddenly, with a whirl of tires, the Nissan broke out of line. It swung left onto a ribbon of cracked tar and departed at high speed into the desert.

A hard voice broke over the radio: "Snap inspection!" It was the voice of Commander Mark Littleberry, M.D., U.S. Navy (Retired).

Littleberry was now in his sixties. He was a tough-looking man, but his age showed in the gold-rimmed half-glasses perched on his nose and in the silver at his temples. Littleberry worked as a paid consultant to various U.S. government agencies. He had top security clearances. Through his navy connections he had been appointed an UNSCOM biological-weapons inspector. Now he was sitting in the passenger seat of the breakaway Nissan, a military map of Iraq draped across his knees.

The Iraqi minders, or escorts, had been traveling behind the UNSCOM convoy in a rattletrap column of vehicles—beat-up Toyota pickups, smoking Renaults, Chevrolets without hubcaps, and a black Mercedes-Benz sedan. Most of the vehicles had been seized in Kuwait by Iraq during the Gulf war. Some had been cannibalized from junk parts, and these had body panels of different colors.

Mark Littleberry's words "snap inspection" created confusion among the Iraqi minders. Their vehicles came to a grinding halt, and they started yelling into handheld radios, reporting the breakaway to their superiors in Baghdad.

In a snap inspection, weapons inspectors suddenly change their itinerary and go somewhere without giving advance notice. But this time there was a problem—Littleberry did not have permission from the chief inspector, a French biologist named Pascal Arriet. This was a rogue snap.

Suddenly four Iraqi vehicles detached from the column and took off after the Nissan, which had picked up considerable speed. The Nissan hit sand drifts that covered the road in places, flinging out boiling yellow-brown puffs of dust. The Nissan seemed to leap out through the dust, at times nearly becoming airborne.

"Damn it, Hopkins. We're going to roll over," Mark Littleberry said to the man driving, Supervisory Special Agent William Hopkins, Jr., of the Federal Bureau of Investigation.

Will Hopkins was a rangy man in his early thirties. He had brown hair, a square face, and a seven-day beard. He wore baggy khaki trousers, a white shirt, and Teva sandals with green socks. The plastic pocket protector in his shirt pocket was jammed with pens and pencils and bits of junk. The belt that held up his trousers was a length of nylon webbing, from which hung a Leatherman Super Tool, a combination pliers and screwdriver and knife and various other tools. The Leatherman identified Hopkins as a tech agent. Anything secret, especially if it's high-tech, is guaranteed to break down, and a tech agent never goes anywhere without a Leatherman tool. Hopkins had earned a Ph.D. in molecular biology from the California Institute of Technology, where he had become adept with the machines and gadgets that are used in biology. He was a Caltech gadgeteer. His current job title was Manager of Scientific Operations—Biology, Hazardous Materials Response Unit, Quantico.

The Nissan hit a dip in the road. Two black metal Halliburton suitcases on the back seat bounced into the air.

"Are we going to wear any safety gear?" Hopkins asked.

Littleberry turned around and reached into the back seat, next to the suitcases, and pulled out a full-face biohazard mask equipped with purple HEPA filters. He gave it to Hopkins to clip onto his belt. "We're not interested in the whole building," Littleberry said. "There is a door I want to have a peek at. The folks at the National Security Agency have some information about that door."

Hopkins didn't ask what they were looking for, but he assumed it was bacteria or a virus. A bacteriological weapon is grown in a fermenter tank, and it gives off a yeasty smell, somewhat like beer, or sometimes a meaty smell. Virus weapons are produced in a bioreactor, a machine that amplifies a virus into more virus.

A bioreactor is a small tank containing a warm liquid bath that is saturated with living cells. When the cells are infected with a virus that is replicating, they leak virus particles, and the bioreactor becomes charged with them. A virus particle is a tiny nugget of protein that surrounds a core of genetic material, the ribbonlike strands of DNA or RNA that direct the activities of life. Viruses take over a cell and direct the cell's own machinery to make more virus particles. A virus keeps a cell alive until the cell is full of copies of virus particles, and then the cell explodes and releases hundreds or even thousands of copies of the virus.

A wide variety of viruses are made into weapons. Hopkins understood that there were many possibilities as to what they might find in the building where they were headed. Keeping track of what virus strains the Iraqis were working with in their laboratories was exceedingly difficult. Some of the possibilities included VEE and EEE (brain viruses), Crimean-Congo hemorrhagic fever, Ebola, Marburg, Machupo, Rift Valley fever, Lassa, Junin, Sabia, enterovirus 17, camelpox, monkeypox, and smallpox. And there was always the possibility that you would run into a virus that no one had thought could be used as a weapon. You could also run into a virus that you had never heard of before.

THE Nissan approached a windowless metal building about forty feet tall. It looked like a warehouse. Silvery vent pipes stuck up from the roof. The structure was surrounded by a barbed wire fence, and there was a gate and a very strong-looking guard post. Hopkins began to slow down.

"Don't," Littleberry said sharply. "Come up to the perimeter like you are not prepared to stop."

Hopkins floored the gas. Suddenly, up ahead, there were flashes of light at the guard post—the guards had opened fire in their direction. Hopkins gasped and ducked sideways on the seat. The Nissan slid down the road, out of control.

Littleberry stared straight ahead into the gunfire, holding the steering wheel for Hopkins. "Get your face out of my lap. They aren't going to pop a U.N. vehicle."

Hopkins took the wheel again. The car was going very fast.

"The brakes, Will," Littleberry said.

Hopkins jammed on the brakes. The Nissan spun backward and slid into the gate, punching out both taillights. The gate broke open. An instant later the Iraqi chase cars came screeching in behind the Nissan in a great cloud of dust. A rear door of the Mercedes opened, and a thin young man wearing jeans and a polo shirt stepped out. "Wow, you are really scaring us, Mark," he said. His name was Dr. Azri Fehdak. A molecular biologist educated in California, he was believed to be one of the top scientists in Iraq's bioweapons program.

"It's a snap inspection," Littleberry said.

"But there is nothing here," Azri Fehdak said. "This is the Al Ghar Agricultural Facility."

A door to the building stood open. Inside, the inspectors could see ultramodern stainless steel biological-production equipment. A woman wearing a white lab coat came scurrying out the door. "What is this?" she demanded sharply. She wore designer glasses, and her wavy brown hair was tied back in a loose roll.

"United Nations weapons-inspection team, ma'am," Will Hopkins said. "We're on a snap inspection. Who are you?"

"I am Dr. Mariana Vestof. I am the consulting engineer. We have already been inspected here."

"We're just doing a quick follow-up," Littleberry said. "What are you making here currently?"

"These are virus vaccines," she said, waving her arm.

"Oh, good, okay. What kind exactly?"

"Our work is medical," she said.

"Let's go," Littleberry said. He reached into the car, grabbed one of the black metal suitcases, and took off, running for the building.

"What about our biohazard suits?" Hopkins called after him.

"Never mind," Littleberry yelled back. "Come on, move it, Will." Littleberry wanted to get what he was after before the minders went berserk and shot someone.

Hopkins grabbed his suitcase and the shortwave radio and ran after Littleberry, the biohazard face mask dangling on his belt. A crowd of people followed them into the stainless steel jungle.

The building was lit with fluorescent lights. The floor was a kind of pebbled terrazzo. All around were stainless steel tanks and tangles of pipes and hoses. The tanks were bioreactors, and they were on wheels. The equipment in the Iraqi plant was portable. The entire plant could be moved. Dozens of workers were tending the equipment. They were wearing surgical masks and white coats and latex rubber gloves. When they saw the inspectors, they drew back and stood around in groups, staring.

Littleberry hurried toward one of the larger bioreactors. He snapped on a pair of surgical gloves. Hopkins also put on a pair.

"Has this equipment been tagged?" Littleberry asked Dr. Vestof.

"Yes, of course." She showed him the U.N. tags. UNSCOM was attempting to tag all biological-production equipment in Iraq so that the equipment could be traced.

As Littleberry studied a tag, he could feel a warmth coming out of the tanks, a warmth of body heat. "Nice equipment you have here," he said to Dr. Vestof.

She stood very primly, her feet close together. Her calm was in marked contrast to the agitation of the Iraqi minders.

"We'll just take a couple of samples, and we'll be out of here," Littleberry said. He opened his suitcase and pulled out a wooden stick about four inches long with an absorbent pad on the end, like an oversized Q-Tip. He popped open the flip-top lid of a plastic test tube that was half filled with sterile water. He dunked the soft tip of the swab stick into the tube to wet it and then rubbed the tip on a valve on one of the warm bioreactors, trying to pick up dirt. Then he jammed the swab back into the test tube, snapped off the wooden stick, and closed the flip-top lid. He handed the tube to Hopkins. "That's Al Ghar large tank sample number one," he said.

With a laundry pen Hopkins labeled the tube.

In a low voice Littleberry said to him, "Stay close."

Littleberry moved fast. He was heading deeper into the building, quickly, purposefully. He wasn't taking many samples, but he seemed to know his way around.

"Who built this plant?" Hopkins asked Dr. Vestof.

"BioArk. A respected concern."

"Is that a French company?" Hopkins asked.

"We are headquartered near Geneva."

"I see. But you personally—are you French?" Hopkins asked.

"I am from Geneva."

"So you are a Swiss citizen, Dr. Vestof, is that correct?"

"What are you? The police? I am born in St. Petersburg. I live in Geneva."

Littleberry had almost gotten away during this exchange. His figure was nearly lost among the tanks and pipes. He stopped at a metal door with no markings on it.

"Don't go in there," Mariana Vestof called.

Littleberry pulled open the door.

Everything happened fast. Beyond Littleberry, Hopkins saw a hallway lined with stainless steel shower stalls—the kind used for decontaminating biohazard suits and equipment. It looked like a level 3 staging room, an entry chamber leading to a level 4 biocontainment zone. "Mark, don't," he said.

Littleberry ignored him. He unclipped his mask from his belt and fitted it over his head, and suddenly he had gone into the staging room.

"Stop," Dr. Mariana Vestof said. "This is not permitted."

The far door of the staging room had a circular handle on it, like the handle on a pressure door in a submarine. Littleberry reached the door and spun the handle. There was a sucking sound of rubber seals giving way. The door opened to reveal a narrow set of rooms, jammed with equipment, and two men wearing green biohazard space suits. It was a level 4 hot zone.

"United Nations!" Littleberry yelled. He hurled himself toward the hot zone, a swab stick held in front of him. Just as he started to cross the threshold into the zone, there was a rumbling roar, the sound of a diesel engine revving up. A crack of gray desert sky opened up over Littleberry's head. The hot lab was inside a truck. It was a mobile hot zone, and it was pulling away from the building.

Littleberry slipped and fell to the ground. Hopkins, who had been following, saw him go down. He ran for the newly opened space in the wall, dragging his suitcase. The truck was moving away, and a rear door was swinging. Hopkins jumped to the ground and dropped the suitcase near Littleberry. He fitted his mask over his face and vaulted into the moving truck just as a gloved hand was pulling the door shut.

He found himself standing amid gleaming equipment and dim lights. There was a clap of rubber seals coming together. One of the men had shut the back door of the truck. Hopkins was inside a level 4 virus-weapons lab wearing only a mask.

Hopkins had to get a sample fast. From his pocket protector he removed a swab stick. He ripped the wrapper off and looked around for something to swab. At the far end of the hot zone was a small cylindrical glass vessel about two feet high. It had a stainless steel top that looked like a hat. The hat had steel and plastic tubes coming out of it. He recognized it as a virus bioreactor. Inside was a translucent core shaped like an hourglass. The reactor was full of a reddish pink liquid that looked like watery blood. The core would be producing some kind of virus.

The bioreactor was too far away to reach. But next to him stood a safety cabinet, a piece of equipment designed for handling infective materials. Inside the cabinet he saw trays full of clear hexagons—six-sided flat crystals, like coins. He touched the swab to a crystal just as one of the men grabbed his arms.

The other man wagged his finger at Hopkins and said in Russian, *"Ne trogaite."* He suddenly reached up with one hand and tore off Hopkins's mask and with his other hand hit Hopkins in the stomach. The air flew out of Hopkins's lungs with a whoosh. He doubled over and threw himself against the rear doors of the truck, one hand flailing for the handle, the other curled around the swab stick to protect it. There was a thunk and a burst of sunlight, and Hopkins was flying through the open air, landing in the dirt. The doors of the truck slammed shut, and it roared off down the road.

New York City, Thursday, April 23

ALICE Austen was not staying in a hotel. The CDC travel allowance was ninety dollars a day for accommodations in New York City. You can't get much in the way of a hotel room in the city for ninety dollars, so she was renting a room in a bed-and-breakfast apartment in Kips Bay, on East Thirty-third Street, a '70s-era development surrounded by gardens and nestled up against a huge complex of hospitals. Her hostess was a widow named Gerda Heilig, who rented out a room looking toward the New York University Medical Center and the East River.

Austen finished a cup of coffee and a sweet roll in Gerda's kitchen. She put her Mighty-Tuff autopsy boots and her pack of autopsy knives into a knapsack and went out.

Heading downtown, she walked past the complex of hospitals and research institutes. At the corner of First Avenue and Thirtieth Street she climbed the steps of a gray building, which was the Office of the Chief Medical Examiner of New York City. The front door was locked, and she pushed the buzzer.

A tall, somewhat overweight man in his sixties let her in. He had curly white hair at the temples and was going bald on top. He was dressed in a green surgical scrub suit. "I'm Lex Nathanson," he said. "Welcome to the OCME, the ugliest building in New York."

The marble walls of the lobby had a peculiar brownish, mottled, streaky color. It reminded her of a cancerous liver. On the liverish wall ran a motto in Latin, in metal letters:

TAQUEANT COLLOQUIA EFFUGIAT RISUS HIC LOCUS
EST UBI MORS GAUDET SUCCURRERE VITAE

"How's your Latin, Dr. Austen?" Nathanson said.

"Hmm, let's see. . . . 'Speech quiets the place where Death is happy'? That can't be right."

He smiled. "It means 'Let conversation cease, let the smile flee, for this is the place where Death delights to help Life.' "

" 'Where Death delights to help Life,' " she murmured as she followed Nathanson into his office, a big uncluttered room located near the front door.

A man stood up to greet her. "Glenn Dudley," he said. "Deputy chief medical examiner." He shook Austen's hand. Dr. Dudley had a massive grip and a tight mouth. He was a handsome, muscular man of about fifty. He had black hair and a square face, and he wore square metal-framed eyeglasses.

Austen opened her green epi notebook and wrote Nathanson's and Dudley's names on the first page.

"Are you a forensic pathologist?" Glenn Dudley asked.

"No. I'm a medical pathologist," she said. "But I have worked on forensic autopsies."

"Are you board certified?" Dudley asked.

"Not yet."

Dudley turned to Nathanson and said in a flinty voice, "They don't even send us a certified pathologist."

"I'll be taking my boards next year."

Nathanson said, "Well, as I imagine Dr. Mellis told you, we've had two very unusual deaths: a girl who died yesterday and a similar incident seven days ago—an unidentified homeless man known locally as Harmonica Man. He was about sixty years old, and he used to ride the subway playing a harmonica. I live on the East Side, and I actually remember seeing him riding the Lexington Avenue local. He died at the Times Square subway station."

"It was a spectacular death," Dudley said. "The guy seized in the middle of a crowd. He was screaming and biting. He was DOA at Bellevue. He was with a friend of his, another homeless guy named"—he flipped through the case folder—"named Lem. No last name given. When I did the autopsy, I found that this Harmonica Man had brain swelling and brain damage, with hemorrhage in the midbrain. It could be a poison, a toxin. But nothing came up with the toxicology."

"What got my attention," Nathanson said, "was the form of the seizure—that curvature of the spine. It's known as an *arc de cercle* seizure. It's a fake seizure. A real seizure doesn't make the spine curve. But the two decedents weren't faking. They were dying. This second case has gotten into the news media, and we're under some pressure to come up with answers."

"So you called the CDC, Lex, and you listened to Walt Mellis with his theories. He's a nut," Dudley said.

Nathanson shrugged and flashed a smile at Austen. "You're not a nut, are you, Doctor?"

"I hope not," she said.

Dudley stood up suddenly. "Let's get going." He picked up a

manila file folder that had been sitting on an empty chair. "We can talk in the morgue."

THE morgue was in the first basement level, next to the receiving garage. A mortuary van had just pulled in, and a couple of morgue attendants were unloading a body covered with a sheet of blue paper. They transferred the body to a mortuary gurney known as a pan, which is a sort of metal trough on wheels.

Nathanson approached a man in a green scrub suit. "We're ready, Ben," he said. "Let me introduce you to our CDC investigator. This is Dr. Alice Austen. And this is Ben Kly. He'll be the attendant." Kly, an Asian American of medium height, smiled and shook Austen's hand. Then he led the way through a pair of swinging doors and into the morgue, where they were enveloped by a thick smell, sour and penetrating—a smell as old as the world.

"There's the ladies' room," Nathanson said, pointing to a door off the morgue. "You can change in there."

In the rest room Austen found a shelf holding fresh surgical scrub suits. She changed into the scrubs, then put on her Mighty-Tuff boots.

She found Nathanson, Dudley, and Kly in a nearby room where the biosafety equipment was stored. Here they put on disposable surgical gowns, which went on over their scrub suits. Over the surgical gowns they tied heavy plastic waterproof aprons. They put surgical covers on their shoes, surgical caps on their heads.

Glenn Dudley pulled a disposable mask down over his nose and mouth. The mask had a blue button in the center. His voice came out of the mask. "Hey, Dr. Austen, where's your space suit? I thought you guys from the CDC have to work in space suits."

"I've never worn one," she said.

They put on plastic safety glasses to prevent blood or fluid from splashing into their eyes. Glenn Dudley didn't need safety glasses, since he was already wearing eyeglasses. They put on rubber surgical gloves. Then Dudley fitted a glove made of stainless steel chain mail over his left hand. The chain-mail glove indicated that he was going to be the prosector—the leader of the autopsy, the person who does the cutting and so is vulnerable to an accidental knife cut. Most such cuts occur on the pathologist's nondominant hand, which in most people is the left hand.

They put on yellow rubber dishwashing gloves over their surgical gloves. Dudley drew a rubber glove over his metal glove.

"The decedent is in one oh two," Ben Kly said.

The morgue was ring shaped, with a central rectangular core where bodies were stored inside crypts. You circled around the core to gain access to a particular crypt. The walls were made of bricks painted a pale green. The crypt doors were made of stainless steel.

They followed Kly through the morgue as he wheeled an empty pan to crypt number 102. Inside, lying on a tray, was a white body pouch. A human form gave it shape.

Kly took the shoulders, grasping them through the pouch, while Dudley took the feet. In one expert motion they transferred the body to the pan. Kly wheeled the gurney through a pair of doors into the autopsy room. "Welcome to the Pit," he said.

The autopsy room was seventy feet long, with eight stainless steel autopsy tables lined up in a row. Pathologists were working at four of the tables, where bodies were laid out. The Pit was a gray zone, a place neither definitely hot nor definitely safe. An ultraviolet light on the wall shed rays into the room that were supposed to kill airborne pathogens—viruses and bacteria. On the floor, air-filtering machines hummed, cleaning the air of infective particles that might get into the pathologists' lungs.

Ben Kly halted the pan next to an autopsy table and set the brake. He unzipped the white bag.

The eyes of the girl inside were closed, the lids puffy. She had had a bloody nose. Someone, probably a busy nurse, had attempted to wash her face, but the washing had not been thorough. The girl's hair was russet. With a start Austen saw that it was the same color as her own hair. There were two rings in the girl's left ear.

"Her name is Catherine Moran," Nathanson said. "They called her Kate."

Ben Kly unzipped the pouch completely. The dead girl was wearing a short hospital gown, as if for modesty.

Dudley opened the investigator's report. " 'Case number 98-M-12698,' " he read. "She collapsed in a school classroom." He glanced over the report. "Mater School, on Seventy-ninth Street. She became extremely ill yesterday about ten thirty in the morning. She was biting herself, chewing her lips. Grand mal seizures, heavy nosebleed, sudden unexplained death. Superficially, the case looks like Harmonica Man. She was DOA at New York Hospital. It made the news last night."

"A homeless man and a young woman from a well-to-do background," Nathanson remarked. "There's no obvious connection."

"Drugs," Dudley said. "Someone could have given her a hot load."

Nathanson explained, "A lethal dose, Dr. Austen. A hot load. Dealers do it when they want to get rid of a customer."

Dudley and Kly lifted the girl out of the pouch and transferred her to the autopsy table. They removed the gown.

The appearance of Kate's body disturbed Austen. The girl looked very much like her. She could be my younger sister, Austen thought. She reached out and took the left hand of the girl in her gloved hand. The fingernails were delicate.

Nathanson suddenly said, "Dr. Austen, I'd like you to be the prosector for this one. You can do the autopsy."

"But I came here to observe."

"I think your insights could be interesting," Nathanson said. "Ben, she'll need a chain-mail glove. You'll use your own knife, I assume."

She nodded.

Kly got her a chain-mail glove. She put it on her left hand and replaced the yellow rubber glove, then opened her pack and removed her steel prosector's knife.

"Glenn will help you with the forensics, and he'll sign the documents," Nathanson said.

Nathanson left to make his rounds in the Pit, stopping at each of the autopsy tables and chatting with the pathologists, having a look at each of the day's cases. As she watched him walk away, Austen felt that he had been sizing her up from the moment they met. From the beginning he had been thinking of turning the autopsy over to her, but he had held off making the decision until the last possible moment. She watched him out of the corner of her eye.

Dudley said to Austen in a low voice, "I never saw the point of Lex's calling the CDC. It was something he wanted to do, not me. You will follow my direction. Is that clear?"

"Yes."

"The last thing we need around here is a CDC trainee who's carrying on her education in public."

Ben Kly pretended not to hear a word of this. He took a rubber hose and rinsed the girl's body gently with water. Dudley called over a photographer, who took a few pictures of Kate Moran. Then Austen and Dudley together did an external examination. In the bright fluorescent light they looked at the skin.

An experienced morgue attendant can help find things. Ben Kly pointed to the girl's nose. "Lot of mucus there."

"You're right," Austen said. "It looks like she had a cold."

"She *has* a cold," Kly commented.

"What?" Alice said, looking at him.

"You know how a cold survives in a dead body?" Kly said. "I've caught colds from bodies. Cadaver colds are the worst. I think that the cold gets mean sitting in that body, saying, 'This guy is dead. Get me out of here.' "

Austen opened the girl's mouth and looked closely. The inside was shining with dark blood blisters. Next she gripped the eyelids delicately with small forceps and rolled them back one at a time. The inside of each eyelid was peppered with small red dots. The irises were blue-gray, with a ring of yellowish shiny pigment—a pupillary ring with flamelike offshoots. It had a metallic sheen, like the wing of a butterfly, making the pupil look as if it had caught fire. "These eyes seem unusual, Dr. Dudley. What do you think?"

Dudley bent over to look. "The conjunctiva's inflamed."

"But she has pupillary rings in the iris. Like some kind of crystalline or metallic deposit. I wonder if she could have copper poisoning."

"No way," he said, looking at her. "Rings from copper poisoning, Dr. Austen, would appear on the outside rim of the iris. This is on the inside of the iris, near the pupil. It's normal eye color."

Austen decided to look inside the girl's nose. "Do you have an exam light?"

Kly handed her a light. Austen pointed it into Kate's nostril. "Wow," she said. "There's a blistering process."

"Let me look." Dudley took the light. "Yeah. What is that?"

"She has similar blisters in her mouth. This looks like an infectious-disease process, I think."

"Yeah. Or a poison of some kind," Dudley said.

Austen took a scalpel and began to cut.

"Ephphatha," Ben Kly said softly.

"What was that?" Austen said, glancing at him.

"*Ephphatha.* It's a good-luck word. It's what Jesus said when he threw a demon out of a deaf-and-dumb man. He stuck his finger into the guy's ear and he put a dab of his spit on the guy's tongue. Then he said, *'Ephphatha.'* It means 'Be opened.' And the demon came out."

"You read the Bible too much," Dudley remarked.

"I don't read it enough," Kly answered.

Alice Austen examined the girl's heart and lungs. The lungs were heavy and dark—Kate had inhaled blood from her nosebleed. The heart was normal. Austen dropped tissue samples into a large glass jar full of formalin preservative. The jar would be sent to the OCME histology lab, where slices of the tissue would be prepared for viewing through a microscope. Austen also prepared a separate toxicology container with no preservative in it. The OCME's toxicology lab would test the samples in this container for toxins and drugs.

Now Austen examined the remaining organs one by one. They seemed healthy and normal. She turned her attention to the kidneys, sectioning one with her knife. She saw delicate golden-yellow streaks in the center. This was abnormal. The kidney should be a dark reddish brown color. So often in an autopsy, color carries meaning. A golden kidney was unusual. "Look at this, Dr. Dudley."

"That yellow tissue is dead," Dudley said. "Those are uric-acid infarcts. That tissue was killed by deposits of uric-acid crystals."

"She seems healthy. Why is there a lot of uric acid in her blood?"

"Maybe it's not uric acid. It could be a toxin. That would cause the blistering in the kid's mouth."

She caught Ben Kly's eye. "Cranial contents," she said.

It is the task of the morgue attendant to open the skull. Using a Stryker saw, Kly cut through the skull base. Then he lifted off the top of the skull and exposed the dura mater, a gray, leathery membrane that covers the brain.

Austen continued from that point. She took up blunt scissors and carefully cut the dura mater away. The folds of the brain came into view. The brain was swollen. It had an eerie, abnormal, pearlescent color, a color neither pathologist had ever seen in brain tissue before.

"Whoa," Dudley said.

Austen's heart thudded in her chest. This is a destroyed brain, she thought. She felt a mixture of fear and excitement.

"Flattened folds," Dudley said.

The folds of the human brain are ordinarily sharply grooved. The folds of this brain were flattened, as if pressed against the inside of the skull.

Austen touched the brain. It was very very soft. How to remove it? Working entirely by sense of touch, she found the optic nerves and cut them. The brain loosened.

The removal of a person's brain seemed to Austen more of a violation of the person's dignity and privacy than any other procedure in the autopsy, because the brain is the most personal part of the body, the only body part that studies itself. Alice Austen believed in the sacredness of human life. One very important way to honor life is to try to find out how it ended.

With a quick slice of the scalpel she cut the spinal cord, and the brain fell into her hands. It was huge, abnormally heavy, and so jellylike it threatened to fall apart. She placed it in the scale pan. "Oh, wow. Sixteen hundred and twenty-five grams," she said.

She turned the brain over. Its underside was speckled with tiny red spots. Yet there had been no general bleeding. When a person gets measles, the skin erupts with red spots. The brain, when infected with a virus, also can become spotty.

Austen began trying to make a diagnosis, but she was missing something. What was it? She moved around the table to reposition herself. In doing so, she brushed against the calvarium—the top of the skull—lying on the table. It was in the way, so she picked it up to move it, and it slipped from her already slippery fingers. It hit the the table, sending a fine spray of blood into the air.

"Damn!" Dudley said, drawing back.

There were tiny spots of blood on his eyeglasses.

"I'm sorry. I'm very sorry." A wave of nervousness swept over her, and her stomach clenched. "Did you get any in your eyes?"

"No, fortunately. That's why we wear eye protection." He had a cold look on his face.

There was nothing to do but keep going. Looking at the brain, she saw the effects of brain swelling. The brain is encased in a hard skull, and when it swells, through injury or infection, it has nowhere to go. The swelling brain pushes downward on the top of the brain stem, especially on the midbrain, which contains nerve branches that control basic functions, such as breathing and heartbeat. If you crush the midbrain, breathing ceases and the heart stops.

As the brain crushes itself, the body tries to drive blood into the brain at all costs. The blood pressure shoots sky-high. This is a shock response known as the Cushing reflex. The sudden spike in blood pressure can trigger hemorrhages, sudden bleeds anywhere in the body. That, Austen thought, was the cause of the girl's bloody nose.

"This could be a virus infection of the brain," Austen said. "It triggered a Cushing reflex, with a bleed from the nasopharynx."

Dudley looked at her. "Fine. We have an unknown brain virus that caused a nosebleed. Is that what you're trying to tell me?"

"This scares me. I've never seen anything like it. I want to section this brain," she said.

"Go ahead," Dudley said.

Inside the girl's midbrain and pons medulla Austen found what she was looking for—small weeping hemorrhages. "Something destroyed her central nervous system," she said.

"HOW did it go?" Lex Nathanson asked Austen half an hour later.

"It was bad," she said. She had changed into her street clothes.

They were in Nathanson's office. He opened a drawer of his desk, took out a cigar, then held up a second. "You want one?"

Austen grinned. "No, thanks."

Nathanson found his cutter, notched the end of the cigar, then lit it. "I'm afraid I am not an example to young people. Not only are these cigars a vice, but I have too much abdominal fat. When they autopsy me, they will find a rat's nest of problems." He drew on the cigar. A soft and mellow smoke suffused the room. "Tell me what you found."

Austen described the blood blistering, the damage to the kidneys, the pupillary rings in the irises of the eyes, the fatal brain swelling. "The brain was devastated," she said. "The total effect was . . . well . . . frightening. It made me think of a virus infection involving the central nervous system."

"We don't have the capability to test for a virus here."

"You don't have a lab for that?"

"No. We send biosamples over to the city health department's lab. They test for bacteria. They don't test for viruses."

"We can do it," Austen said. "May I send samples to the CDC?"

"Sure. Give them to Walt Mellis with my regards." He gave her a sharp look. "How are you getting along with Glenn Dudley?"

Austen answered carefully. "He's straightforward in his views."

"Boy, you're quite a diplomat." Nathanson drew on his cigar.

"Glenn's being a pain in the neck. He's having a bad time in his personal life. His wife recently left him. She took the children with her. He had been having an affair with a younger woman. But Glenn is a valued member of my staff."

"Of course."

"Do you want to continue with this investigation?"

"Yes, I do."

He smiled broadly. "All right, whaddaya need?"

"Well, I'd like to look at all your recent case files."

"Sure. What else?"

"I'll need a telephone. Also a map of New York City."

There was a pause while he smoked his cigar. "That's all?"

"Epi work is pretty simple," she said. She looked out the window and saw that it had begun to rain. "I forgot to bring a raincoat."

"I'll get you a slicker. And you'll need an office, won't you?"

"I guess so."

THEY gave Austen a tiny office on the third floor. Its one window looked out on the blank wall of a parking garage. Someone brought her a bright yellow rain slicker. Across the back in black letters it said OFFICE OF CHIEF MEDICAL EXAMINER.

She taped a map of New York City to the wall and marked an X at the location of the Mater School on Seventy-ninth Street, where Kate Moran had died. She marked another X on Times Square, where Harmonica Man had collapsed. The marks showed the location of death but not where the victims had been exposed, if indeed they had been exposed to anything.

If this was an outbreak of an infectious disease or a rash of poisonings, Harmonica Man was the first identified case. He was therefore what was known as the index case. Kate Moran, who died less than a week later, was the second case. There was no obvious connection between the two.

KATE Moran's tissues were being processed in the OCME histology lab, and they would not be ready for viewing for about a day. In the meantime Austen called a technician for samples of Harmonica Man's tissues, giving him the case number.

"Those slides have been checked out by Dr. Dudley," the technician said. So she went to Glenn Dudley's office.

She found him sitting at a table staring into a microscope. The instrument had two sets of binocular eyepieces, which allowed two people to look at a specimen at the same time.

"What do you want?" Dudley said without looking up.

"I wanted to take a look at the tissues of the first case."

He grunted and kept staring into his microscope. Austen sat down and looked into the other set of eyepieces. She saw a field of cells from Harmonica Man's brain.

"It's from the underside of the temporal lobe," Dudley said. "The area of the hippocampus. It seems damaged."

Letting her gaze relax, she saw neurons, the threadlike nerve cells that send signals in the brain. A bulge in the middle of each thread contains the cell's nucleus, where the cell's genetic material—its DNA—is stored. Austen did not like the way these brain-cell nuclei looked.

"The nuclei are abnormal," she said. "Would you zoom in, please?" The scene jumped. The nuclei were bigger. Then she saw something she had never seen before. There were objects in the cell nucleus—things. "What is this, Dr. Dudley?"

He grunted. He didn't have any answers either.

The objects were glittery angular crystals that had a mathematical shape. They were bulging with many facets, like soccer balls. They were far too large to be virus particles, which are invisible in a regular microscope. The light broke apart in the crystals and seemed to shimmer.

"It's weird," Dudley said, sounding unsure of himself. "This must be some kind of chemical compound. There's some new drug hitting the street."

"Maybe these crystals are lumps of virus in a crystallized form."

"Lumps! Lumps of virus. Don't be an idiot," Dudley snapped. And he continued to stare into the microscope in silence.

IT WAS STILL RAINING OUTSIDE the window of Alice Austen's office at the OCME. She put on the yellow raincoat, shouldered her knapsack, and took a taxi to Union Square.

A television van from Fox Channel 5 was double-parked on the street in front of Kate Moran's building. As Austen rang the buzzer, a woman reporter spotted her yellow raincoat. "You're from the medical examiner's office? What happened to Kate Moran? Can you tell us anything?"

"I'm sorry, but you'll have to talk to the chief medical examiner," Austen said. The buzzer sounded, and she slipped inside.

The girl's parents, Jim and Eunice Moran, sat holding hands on a couch in the living room of their top-floor loft apartment. A large black-and-white portrait photograph of Eunice Moran leaned against the wall across from the couch. In the photograph she looked thoughtful and elegant in a soft white turtleneck sweater. In real life she was haggard, her eyes red from crying.

Austen knew that people in the throes of grief can react unpredictably to an epidemiologist asking questions, and she very gently identified herself. Conversation was difficult. At times Jim and Eunice Moran lost their ability to speak. They knew there had been an autopsy; in a case of sudden unexpected death an autopsy is required by law. Austen chose not to tell them that she had performed it.

"Your daughter's body was released to the funeral home an hour ago," she said. "Because of the risk of possible infection, the city has ordered a cremation. The funeral home was instructed to take universal biohazard precautions."

"What do you mean biohazard precautions?" Eunice Moran said. Her voice sounded like breaking glass.

"I'm sorry. Your daughter may have had a contagious disease."

"What kind of disease?" Mr. Moran asked.

"We don't know. I'm here to ask you some questions about what your daughter did and where she went during the past days and perhaps weeks, while your memory is fresh. We want to find out if she was exposed to something."

Mrs. Moran held her husband's hand tighter. Finally she said,

"We'll try to help." She nodded toward a chair. "Please sit down."

Austen sat on the edge of the chair. "Can you think of anything Kate did lately that might have exposed her to something infective or toxic? Did she travel in a foreign country?"

"No," Mrs. Moran said.

"Was she taking any strong or potentially toxic medications?"

"No," Mrs. Moran said.

Austen asked them to carefully review Kate's movements over the past two weeks. The parents were vague. Kate's life had been quiet. She had friends, but she wasn't a heavy socializer.

"Do you know if she used drugs?"

"Absolutely not," Mr. Moran said.

"Did she go anywhere unusual recently?"

"The only thing I can think of is her project for Mr. Talides, her art teacher," Mrs. Moran answered. "It's a construction thing, and Kate was going around buying things in SoHo and at the Sixth Avenue flea market. Mr. Talides was—" Mrs. Moran's voice cracked. "I'm sorry. He tried to save her."

"Do you know, did he attempt CPR?"

"He had forgotten what to do. That's—that's what he told me when he called. He was very upset."

Austen made a note to interview the teacher. He might have been exposed. "Do you mind if I look in Kate's room? Sometimes looking can be helpful. Also, would you mind if I took some photographs?" Austen removed her electronic camera from her knapsack.

The Morans nodded somewhat reluctantly.

She went into a hallway. Down the hall was a door standing half open. It led to Kate's bedroom.

It was a beautiful room, illuminated by a skylight and filled with the clutter of a teenager's life. There was an unmade bed, a poster of Vermeer's painting of a young woman playing the clavichord. In the closet she found baggy jeans, tight silk tops, a short leather jacket. Kate must have been hip and somewhat arty. There was an old bureau, a maple box containing odd bits of junk jewelry. There was a desk with a computer, and a table piled with bric-a-brac.

There were joke dolls, a row of flutes and pennywhistles lined up next to each other, made of wood, plastic, reed, and steel. In the center of the table stood a dollhouse. This had to be Kate's art table. There were small antique boxes, a can that said TWININGS EARL GREY TEA, plastic containers of all shapes and colors, delicate boxes made of wood. Everything was well organized.

Kate had had quirky taste and an unusual sense of color and shape. Austen switched on her electronic camera and began to take photographs of the room. The light from the skylight gave everything a cool radiance.

Austen opened a box. Inside was a mechanical toy beetle. It stared at her with sad green jeweled eyes. In another box was a miniature metal car. Austen began photographing everything. There was a box full of bird feathers and one made of wood with a polygon painted on it. She tried to open it, but it had a puzzle catch she couldn't figure out, so she took a picture of it. She photographed a chunk of green malachite. An amethyst geode. An old skeleton key in a padlock. The dollhouse, which Kate seemed to be taking apart. Austen took a picture of the dollhouse, then the whole room. She jotted a few notes in her green epi notebook.

AUSTEN next followed the route that Kate had taken every morning to school. She walked to Union Square, then took the subway to the Upper East Side, trying to get a feel for Kate's world.

The Mater School was in a quiet, wealthy neighborhood, among town houses. Austen arrived there at three in the afternoon. The headmistress, Sister Anne Threader, led her to the art room. Only three students were there, sitting around, doing nothing. They had been crying.

"Where is Mr. Talides?" Sister Anne asked them.

"He went home," one of the students said. "He was feeling bad."

Austen faced the students. "Did Mr. Talides get close to Kate when she was ill?"

One of the girls nodded. Austen turned to the headmistress. "Do you have his phone number?"

It was late afternoon on Thursday now, still the first day of Austen's investigation, and rush hour was beginning. It was about thirty hours since Kate Moran had died. If Talides had been infected, he would probably still be in the incubation period, and he might well be showing no signs of illness. Austen did not think that an infectious agent would cause any but the most subtle sign of illness during thirty hours or so. But she wanted to have a look at Talides and to keep track of him.

She got on the train headed for Queens. Twenty minutes later she stepped off the train at the elevated station at Grand Avenue. A set of dilapidated iron stairs debouched into a bustling neighborhood of small markets, hair parlors, and Greek restaurants. The name Talides—she realized this must be a Greek neighborhood.

She walked a few blocks, turning up a side street. Peter Talides lived in half of a small duplex. She rang the front doorbell. Talides opened the door immediately. He was a pudgy man with a kindly, sad face. His living room was also his studio. There were canvases stretched on frames, and paintings piled up against the wall.

"I apologize for the mess," he said. "Please sit down."

She sat in a threadbare easy chair. He sat on a swiveling stool. He seemed on the edge of tears.

"I'm very sorry about what happened," she said.

Peter Talides thanked her for her concern. "My life is the school and my painting. I live alone. I have no illusions about my talent. But"—he pulled out a handkerchief and wiped his nose—"I try to make a small difference with the kids."

"Can you describe what you did to try to save Kate?"

"I—I tried to remember how to give rescue breaths. I couldn't remember. . . . I'm sorry, this is very difficult for me."

"Did you put your mouth to her mouth?"

"Very briefly, yes."

"Was there blood?"

"She had a bloody nose."

"Did any of the blood get on you?"

His voice trembled. "I had to throw away my shirt."

“Could I look at your face more closely?”

He sat on the stool, uncomfortable and embarrassed. She looked at him carefully. “Do you have a cold?” she asked.

“Yes. Runny nose, stopped-up sinuses.”

Austen took a deep breath. “I’m concerned.”

“About me? I feel okay.”

“I can’t give you an exam—I’m not a clinician. I’d like you to go to a hospital emergency room with me. We’ll get a medical team to work you up.”

He looked startled. “I don’t want to go. I feel okay.”

“If you don’t mind, may I just look at your eyes?”

She reached into her knapsack, felt around, and found a penlight. She removed it, switched it on, and pointed the beam first into one pupil, then into the other. The color of the irises seemed normal. Talides had deep brown eyes. She watched the responses of his pupils to the beam of light. She thought she saw a delayed response, which might be an indication of brain damage.

This is ridiculous. I’m overreacting, she told herself. There’s no clear evidence that Kate had an infective disease. There’s been no human-to-human transmission.

She said, “If your cold changes in any way, please call me.” She gave him her cellular-phone number and the number at her Kips Bay bed-and-breakfast. “Call me anytime, day or night.”

On her way back to the subway station she wondered if she had done the right thing. As a lieutenant commander in the U.S. Public Health Service, Alice Austen had the legal power to order a person into quarantine. Even so, officers with the CDC virtually never invoke this power. It is CDC policy for field medical officers to refrain from doing anything that might create a climate of fear in the public.

BACK at Kips Bay that night, Austen felt ravenously hungry. She found a Thai take-out restaurant and brought cartons of food back to her room, where she sat at the desk and ate noodles and lemon-grass chicken with the Boy Scout knife and fork she’d thought to bring with her from home. Then she telephoned Walter Mellis on her cellular phone. She did not want Mrs. Heilig, her hostess, to overhear the conversation.

"So what's up?" Mellis said.

"Walt, this thing has me scared. It could be an unknown virus that destroys the brain." She put her hand to her forehead. It was covered with sweat. "I think we may have done a hot autopsy this morning without strong biosafety containment."

"Good Lord!" He hadn't expected anything like this.

"The city health department's lab is testing for bacteria. But it can't test for viruses."

"Look, if this is serious, we need to get samples here to the CDC."

"That's what I wanted to arrange with you."

"I'll take care of it through Lex. How soon can you return?"

"I don't know. I still have some street work to do."

"All right," he said.

Afterward she took a long shower, collapsed into bed, and pulled the blankets up to her chin. For a long time she could not fall asleep. She thought, This can't be as bad as it seems. I haven't shown any connection between these two cases. The Moran girl's death may not have anything to do with Harmonica Man.

Outside, on the avenue, the traffic moved like blood swishing through an artery.

Al Ghar, Iraq, Thursday, April 23

MARK Littleberry was standing over Hopkins in the cloud of dust left by the truck containing the portable lab. He was holding a plastic sample tube. Without a word to Hopkins he grabbed the swab out of Hopkins's hand and jammed it into the tube. "Truck sample number one." Littleberry put the tube in his shirt pocket.

Hopkins stood up, brushing dust off.

The minders arrived and crowded around. They seemed almost hysterical.

"What was in that truck?" Littleberry demanded.

"I shall inquire," Dr. Fehdak said.

Littleberry let loose a stream of unprintable language.

This was nothing, Dr. Mariana Vestof said. It was a routine delivery of a vaccine.

"I shall try to get information on this," Dr. Fehdak said.

"Why did one of the men in the trucks speak Russian to me?" Hopkins asked.

"You must be mistaken," Dr. Fehdak said.

Hopkins and Littleberry looked at each other. "The inspectors need a rest room," Littleberry suddenly shouted. "According to Security Council agreements, inspectors are to be accorded private use of rest rooms whenever they ask for them."

Hopkins and Littleberry were led back into the building. When they arrived at the door of the rest room, some of the minders started to snicker. "I think it's a ladies' room," Littleberry said. They went in and locked the door after themselves.

The ladies' room was gleaming and antiseptic, set with green and white tiles.

"This situation is gonna blow sky-high," Littleberry said. "I didn't expect to find a truck. We have to do this fast."

Hopkins stripped off his rubber gloves and put on a clean pair. Then he placed his Halliburton case on a sink. He crouched down until he was looking at a small optical lens near the handle of the Halliburton. He brought his right eye close to the lens. The system recognized the pattern of blood vessels in his retina as that of "Hopkins, William, Jr., Reachdeep." Any attempt to open the case without the eye-key would initiate the self-destruct process.

The locks slid open, and he lifted the lid. Meanwhile, Littleberry placed his Halliburton case on a sink and opened it. The two Halliburtons contained biosensors used by the U.S. Navy for sensing and analyzing biological weapons.

"I'm gonna do a handheld Boink," Littleberry said. From the suitcase he lifted out an electronic device about the size of a paperback book. It was a biosensor. People called it a Boink because it let off a chiming sound if it detected a biological weapon. The Boink had a screen, some buttons, and a sample port—a little hole. The device could test for the presence of twenty-five different known biological weapons.

From his pocket Littleberry took out the tube that contained the truck sample. Using a disposable plastic pipette, he extracted some liquid and dropped it into the sample port in the Boink. He was hoping to hear a chiming tone. There was silence.

"Damn," he said. He was staring at the readout screen. "No reading. I've got a blank screen here."

"All right, Commander, should I run Felix?"

"Yeah. Quick."

One of the minders, an intelligence official named Hussein Al-Sawiri, was pounding on the door. "Is somebody ill in there?"

"It's just taking a little time," Hopkins replied. He took the truck-sample tube over to his Halliburton case, which held a device called Felix, a black box the size of a big-city telephone book. It was a biosensor device known as a gene scanner. It was controlled by a laptop computer, and it could read the genetic code of an organism. Hopkins lifted the laptop from the Halliburton and placed it on a window ledge. Working quickly, he ran a data cable back to the Felix and started the computer. The computer screen glowed. Hopkins hammered in his password. "Come on, come on," he said.

Using a pipette, he dropped a bit of liquid from the sample tube into Felix's sample port. He tapped the keys of the laptop.

More pounding on the door. "Open up!" Hussein Al-Sawiri shouted.

Hopkins gestured wildly to Littleberry. "We've gotta start beaming up," he hissed.

From his suitcase Littleberry removed a black notebook-size panel. It was a special satellite transmitting antenna. He plugged it into the laptop while Hopkins tapped the keys.

"We're getting sequences," Hopkins said. Running cascades of letters appeared on Felix's screen, combinations of A, T, C, and G—sequences of raw genetic code from a life-form in the sample.

"Beaming it up, Scotty," Hopkins said.

Felix was beaming chunks of DNA code into the sky through the transmitter panel. Overhead, a communications satellite operated by the U.S. National Security Agency was picking up the genetic code of the organism, whatever it was.

"I think we're going to get some matches here," Hopkins said.

Felix was matching the DNA sequences with sequences stored in its memory, trying to identify the organism. Names of tentative virus matches began to appear on the screen of the laptop:

Goldfish virus group
Porcine reproductive virus
Hepatitis D woodchuck
Humpty Doo virus

"Humpty Doo virus? What is this?" Hopkins whispered. Then the screen went blank—Felix had crashed.

"What happened?" Littleberry whispered.

"I think it's giving me gobbledygook."

The pounding on the door became very insistent.

Will Hopkins reached down to his belt and pulled the Leatherman tool out of its case. He opened it to alligator pliers and a screwdriver. From his pocket protector he pulled out a Mini Maglite flashlight. He hunched over Felix and lifted off the top of the box. Inside was a mass of tiny threadlike tubes and wires. He started pulling out wires.

"Will—" Littleberry said.

"The system isn't going to work perfectly every time."

"Put that suitcase together. We've got to radio for help."

Hopkins held up a metal object the size of a peanut. "That's a pump. I think it's malfunctioning."

"Enough. Shut the case."

"Mark, that was a bioreactor in the truck, and there were some crystals. That's what I took the swab from."

"What do you mean crystals?"

"Well, they were kind of flat, sitting in trays, clear—"

"That sounds like some kind of viral glass. Those bastards are making viral glass."

OUTSIDE THE AL GHAR facility, the UNSCOM convoy had arrived. The vehicles were lined up on the access road to the plant. In the lead vehicle Dr. Pascal Arriet, the chief inspector, was talking on two radios at the same time. The Iraqi guards had closed the gate. They were pointing their guns at the UNSCOM convoy. "These people have disobeyed my direct orders," Arriet said into the radios.

It turned into a standoff. The Iraqi security people wanted to break down the door and place the two U.N. inspectors under arrest. What held them back was the Iraqi government's desire not to annoy the U.N. any more than it already had. The day dragged on into evening. The UNSCOM convoy of vehicles remained sitting on the road outside the plant. The rules did not allow them to leave without Hopkins and Littleberry, and the Iraqis were determined not to let the inspectors go. They announced that all samples and all equipment belonging to the inspectors must be forfeited to Iraq.

"QUIT fooling with your machine," Littleberry said to Hopkins. "You need to get some sleep." Littleberry was lying on the floor of the bathroom with his head on his Halliburton suitcase for a pillow, and every muscle in his back ached.

Hopkins sat cross-legged with his back against the wall. Felix was spread out in pieces across the floor in front of him. Hopkins held the flashlight in his teeth. "I'm convinced the problem is in this pump," he said.

Littleberry could not fall asleep. Late into the night, as the Iraqi security agents continued to pound on the door at odd intervals, he stared at the ceiling and thought of his wife. "This is the last time I am ever going to stick my head in a weapons plant," he muttered.

A few hours later, early in the morning, Littleberry was talking on the shortwave radio. "We've got a deal shaping up, Will." The terms had been worked out by teams of negotiators. The two American inspectors would be allowed to leave, but they would be stripped of their U.N. status. They would have to surrender all their biological samples and equipment—namely the suitcases—to Iraq.

Littleberry and Hopkins agreed to the conditions of the deal, and by sunrise a helicopter had been dispatched from Kuwait City to pick them up. The disgraced inspectors emerged from the bathroom and were marched outdoors at gunpoint. They handed over both Halliburton cases and all their swabs and samples.

The guards patted down the two inspectors thoroughly. Eventually they were satisfied that the Americans no longer possessed any sample material. The guards opened the gate. Littleberry and Hopkins walked through and climbed into the waiting helicopter.

Then they were in the air, leaving Al Ghar.

On the ground, Hussein Al-Sawiri and Dr. Azri Fehdak carried the two Halliburton suitcases into the building, from where the cases would be retrieved by Iraqi intelligence. Fehdak was holding Felix. Something was wrong. He placed the palm of his hand on the case. "Ah!" he said, jerking his hand away. He put the case on the floor. "It's hot."

"Ay!" Al-Sawiri dropped his case to the floor.

Smoke began to boil out of both cases. As the two Iraqis watched, the cases melted, and catalytic heaters destroyed them.

INVISIBLE HISTORY (II.)

Near Baghdad, Iraq

DURING the 1991 Gulf war Iraq is said to have come close to using anthrax on its enemies. Anthrax is a bacterium, a single-celled organism that feeds on meat. Weaponized anthrax is made of anthrax spores, which are dried into a powder or made into a brown liquid concentrate. No one, except the Iraqi government, knows what particular weapons-production strain of anthrax Iraq possessed at the time of the Gulf war. It is believed to have been the Vollum strain. The U.S. Army used Vollum anthrax for its offensive warheads before the United States ended its biological-weapons program in 1969.

After Iraq's defeat by the coalition forces in the Gulf war, teams from the U.N. Special Commission inspected a biological-production plant called Al Hakam. Iraqi scientists told the U.N. that this plant was making "natural" pesticides. The UNSCOM experts believed the Iraqis. But one member of the team, an American, was mighty impressed. He said, "They've got a helluva good biological-weapons plant here at Al Hakam. How can I prove it? I've just got a feeling, that's all."

In 1995 one of the heads of Iraq's biological-weapons program, Hussein Kamel, defected and ended up in Jordan. Fearing that Kamel was telling everything about their bioweapons program, and in an effort to placate the U.N. Security Council, Iraqi officials suddenly disclosed that Al Hakam was, in fact, an anthrax-weapons plant. In June 1996, after a year of bureaucratic hesitation, the U.N. finally blew up Al Hakam with dynamite. The many tons of anthrax the plant produced have never been found. Unlike many bioweapons, anthrax can be stored indefinitely.

There was another revelation, this one more unpleasant. In the wave of panic following Kamel's defection, Iraq also confessed that a French-built animal-vaccine plant called Al Manal had been turned into a weapons facility dedicated to toxins and virus weapons. Al Manal is a modern level 3 biocontainment virology complex situated in the southern outskirts of Baghdad. Until 1990 this plant was apparently used for making vaccines for protecting animals from foot-and-mouth disease, and it had a staff of civilian scientists. In the fall of 1990, however, when the Gulf war was imminent, a military staff suddenly took over the operation. The plant was converted to a bioweapons facility, and in a short time it was pumping out large quantities of botulinum toxin, or bot tox, as military people call it. Bot tox is one of the most powerful toxins known. An amount of bot tox the size of the dot over this *i* would be enough to easily kill ten people.

Bot tox is a nerve agent. Iraq confessed to having made approximately nine thousand cubic yards of weapons-grade bot tox at Al Manal. In theory it was more than enough bioweapon to kill every person on earth a thousand times over.

Iraqi scientists had no problems making the toxin. They had

obtained their strain of botulism through the mail from the American Type Culture Collection, a nonprofit organization in Rockville, Maryland, that supplies microorganisms to industry and science. The seed strain cost Iraq thirty-five dollars.

Al Manal has become the responsibility of the U.N. As of this writing, the plant is standing, but much of its equipment has been destroyed. The buildings and infrastructure, including the bomb-hardened level 3 biocontainment zones, have not been destroyed. The decision-making process in the U.N. is so flawed that an admitted virus and toxin weapons biocontainment facility can't be dismantled. The Al Manal bioweapons plant could go hot in a matter of days. In the meantime not a single drop of bot tox made there has been found.

New York City, Friday, April 24

ALICE Austen began calling the hospitals in the New York City area one by one. At each she spoke to an ER doctor. "Have you had any emergency cases recently where the patient was in violent terminal seizure?" she asked. "These patients may have discoloration of the iris of the eye. There may be strong muscular rigidity. The spine bends backward in the shape of a C."

After hours on the phone she had come up with nothing. It was looking like a dead end. Then she had a breakthrough.

"Yes, I think I've seen this," said Tom d'Angelo, an emergency-room physician at the St. George Hospital on Staten Island.

"Can you describe it?"

"A woman named Penelope Zecker. She died here in the ER on Tuesday."

"Who was the attending?" Austen asked.

"I was. I signed the death certificate. Apparently she had been having dizzy spells. Her mother called 911. Penny was living with her mother. She was having a seizure. The EMT got her here. She had a cardiopulmonary arrest, and we couldn't resuscitate. With her history of hypertension we figured she must be having an intracranial bleed or an infarct. I think it was a brain bleed. Her pupils were blown—dilated and fixed. She was cooked."

"Did you do a brain scan?"

"No. We couldn't get her stabilized. She had this dramatic agonal seizure. Her spine bent all the way back and froze. I've never seen anything like it. Her faced twisted up. She started biting the air and bit down on her tongue."

"Was there an autopsy?"

"At a for-profit hospital? Who's going to pay for it?"

"What did you put on the death certificate?"

"Cerebral vascular accident." There was a pause. "You think this is something infectious?"

"I'm not sure. What's the mother's address and phone number?"

WITH a pencil Austen marked another X on her map, this one at the St. George Hospital on Staten Island. Now there were three points of death:

1. Times Square. April 16. Harmonica Man. The index case.
2. St. George Hospital. April 21. Penelope Zecker.
3. East Seventy-ninth Street. April 22. Kate Moran.

Austen was sure this was an outbreak. She stared at the map, pondering what to do.

There was a knock on the door. It was Ben Kly. "How are you doing, Dr. Austen? I thought I'd check in on you. You don't look too good."

"I'm okay."

"Do you think this thing is real?"

"I know it's real. Can you help me with something? Do you know your way around the city?"

"Pretty well. I used to drive a mortuary van."

"The first case was a homeless man called Harmonica Man. They don't know where he lived, but he had a friend with him when he died, a man named Lem. The report says that Lem lives under East Houston Street, in the subway. Can you take me there?"

He shrugged. "I'll ask the chief."

"Please don't. He may say no. If you would just take me there."

"We're going to get a transit cop to go with us. Okay?"

KLY and Austen stopped for hot pastrami sandwiches and coffee at a delicatessen on East Houston Street, on the edge of the Lower East Side. Austen had not eaten all day, and she was practically fainting with hunger.

When she and Kly were finished, they went out onto Houston Street and walked westward. The afternoon was getting along, and traffic was heavy. On the way Kly used Austen's cell phone to call the Transit Police. He led Austen into a subway-station entrance at the corner of Second Avenue. They waited, and eventually a transit officer showed up.

The station platform was a hundred and fifty yards long, and there were no more than three or four other people standing there. It was not a busy station.

"We're following Houston Street," Kly remarked as they walked. "We're going east." At the end of the platform they came to a metal curtain wall that went from floor to ceiling. Kly said that they were facing the East River. "The tracks turn south from here," he explained. "We're not going that way. There's an abandoned tunnel that keeps going east." Kly turned to the transit officer. "How far's it go?"

The officer was a chunky man with a mustache. "A ways," he said.

There was a small swinging gate at the end of the platform. They each had a flashlight, and now they switched them on and went through the gate and down a set of steps to the tracks. They walked along the track bed. On their left was a metal wall. Kly swung his light over it until he found what he was looking for—a hole in the metal. They bent over and went through. On the other side was a set of abandoned tracks heading east. The rails were rusty, and the crossties were covered with scattered newspapers and trash. They walked on, casting their lights around. A train rumbled nearby, filling the tunnels with a roar. The tracks and the ground were covered with black dust.

"Don't kick up that stuff," Kly said.

"What is it?" Austen asked.

"It's steel dust off the rails. It builds up in these unused tunnels."

They played their flashlights around. The walls were decorated with graffiti. "Lem?" Kly shouted. "Hey, Lem!" His voice echoed down the tunnel. "Anybody home?" No answer.

They moved slowly back and forth, shining their lights into grim-looking spaces. At one of the openings in the wall they noticed the sound of buzzing flies. This surprised Austen. She didn't expect to find flies underground.

He was lying on an aluminum-and-plastic folding lawn chair. His back was arched, his body wrenched backward into the shape of a crescent moon. Gases of decay had built up inside the body, swelling it.

After donning protective masks and gloves, Austen and Kly made a brief examination of the dead man. Then Austen stood up and looked around the tunnel, shining her light into corners. Lem and Harmonica Man had been friends according to the report. Friends and neighbors?

The transit officer was talking on his handheld radio, reporting the body.

Austen found a steel door a distance down the tunnel. Kly came over and pulled it open. Behind the door was a cramped space full of electrical cables. Most of the cables ran along a shelf above the ground. "They sleep up on the shelf," Kly remarked. "It's warmer."

Austen stood on a cinder block and looked. There were several empty vodka bottles on the ledge and a black garbage bag. She felt the bag with her gloved hands and pulled it down.

She opened the bag. It contained a black hooded sweatshirt, balled up in a lump, and two Hohner harmonicas.

THE Transit Police brought Lem's body out in a bag, working with city mortuary drivers. Austen left instructions for them to be especially careful about taking universal biohazard precautions with the body, and she asked that it be placed in a double pouch. She then called Nathanson at his office.

"You can do the autopsy tomorrow," he said.

"I'd like to do it right now."

"It's Friday. It's rush hour," Nathanson said, sighing, but he asked Glenn Dudley to stay while Austen did the autopsy. She was not authorized to sign the death certificate.

Annoyed, Dudley hurried the body into the X-ray room and took dental X rays. Later, in the Pit, as he inked the fingertips and rolled a set on a fingerprint pad, Austen noticed that Dudley's hands were trembling. She wondered if he had a drinking problem.

Staten Island, Saturday Morning, April 25

THE next morning Alice Austen took the ferry to Staten Island. From the ferry terminal she found her way to a yellow Victorian house on Bay Street. A sign on the ground floor said ISLAND ANTIQUES. Austen pushed the entryway buzzer.

Long pause. "Who is it?"

"Dr. Austen. We spoke on the phone." The lock was released, and she climbed a flight of stairs to another door on a landing.

"Walk in," a voice croaked. Austen opened the door.

Sitting in a recliner was a wrinkled woman about eighty years old. She was wearing a bathrobe and slippers. Her ankles were thick with edema. "I can't walk good. You have to come over here."

It was Mrs. Helen Zecker, the mother of the deceased Penny.

"I'm working with the city of New York," Austen said. "We are trying to find out what happened to your daughter."

There was a long pause. Mrs. Zecker looked at Austen with terrified eyes. "It got my Penny."

"What did?"

"The monster thing I kept tellin' the doctors about. It got my Penny. It'll get me next." She began to cry.

Austen sat down on a chair next to Mrs. Zecker. "May I ask you some questions?" she said. "I'm interested in Penny's activities in the time before she died. Can you help me?"

"It got her. That's all I know. It got her."

"Let's try to figure out what it is that got her."

"All these things happening, and they never tell us anything."

Austen touched Mrs. Zecker's hand. "Can you remember? Did Penny go anywhere, do anything unusual?"

"I don't know. I don't know."

"Where did she buy the things for the shop?" Austen asked.

"All over. I don't know. She always paid the taxes. Once, she went to Atlantic City. That was a bus tour."

"Do you mind if I look at the shop?"

"I can't go with you."

"That's all right."

Mrs. Zecker pulled a handle on the side of her recliner. The back came forward, and Austen helped her up. Mrs. Zecker shuffled across the room and picked up a coffee cup from a bookshelf. She tipped it over, and a key fell out.

Austen went down the stairs and let herself in through the front door of Island Antiques. She switched on a light. The walls were lemon-yellow, and there was dingy lace trimming around a plate-glass window. It was really a thrift shop. There was a rack of musty women's dresses, and a metal desk with the dried remains of a sandwich. Next to it was a glass ashtray full of cigarette butts. Penny Zecker had been a heavy smoker. There was a caned rocking chair selling for seventy-five dollars, which seemed high, and a scuffed chest made of stained pine, selling for forty-five. Austen opened the chest. Inside was a stack of *National Geographics*.

This was looking good. Something in this room was a clue. Penny Zecker was a pack rat, like Kate Moran. There was a similarity in their behavior. And they were now dead.

Austen went through the room carefully, taking photographs with her electronic camera. There were boxes of kitchen tools. Children's toys made of plastic, a chrome samovar, a lobster buoy.

Something was nagging at her. She opened the desk drawer and pulled out a folder marked PROFITS. In it was a list, handwritten on lined paper. The list was Penny's way of keeping track of her costs and profits as she bought and sold junk. Austen scanned the sheet quickly: "4/18—chair—$59 cost $5." It looked as if Penny had bought a chair for five dollars and sold it to someone for fifty-nine dollars. Penny Zecker had been no fool. She had been keeping herself and her mother alive with her business.

4/18—6 Ave. flea—black dress—woman—$32 cost $0 found garbg.
4/19—6 Ave. flea—box (joke)—$6 traded for postcards
4/19—jewel pin (green)—$22 bot $5

She photographed the page.

Austen said good-bye to Mrs. Zecker and promised to let her know if anything further was learned about her daughter's death.

Manhattan, Saturday

BACK in her borrowed office, Alice Austen opened her laptop. By now she had three memory cards full of images taken with the electronic camera. She slid the cards into the computer one by one, reviewing the photographs on the computer screen. Two of the four cases had been people who collected things, namely Kate Moran and Penny Zecker. What about Harmonica Man? He had been a collector, too. He had collected money in his cup, money that had passed through many hands. She didn't know about Lem.

Hitting keys on her computer, she brought up the images of Kate Moran's art collection. There was a geode of crystals. She hit a key and zoomed in on the image. She couldn't see anything. Rocks didn't carry diseases. She zoomed in on the image of the box that held the little green-eyed beetle. No. The image of the dollhouse. Anything unusual in it? No. She zoomed in on images of the boxes Kate had collected. A wooden box. What was inside it?

Next she called up the images of Penny Zecker's ledger and studied the pages. Something caught her eye:

4/18—6 Ave. flea—black dress—woman—$32 cost $0 found garbg.

Sixth Avenue. Kate's mother had said that Kate bought things at flea markets, and Austen was pretty sure she had mentioned Sixth Avenue. Her eye went down the ledger:

4/19—6 Ave. flea—box (joke)—$6 traded for postcards

Kate had liked boxes. Austen felt a chill. She reviewed the photographs of Kate's bedroom again on the screen of her laptop.

Then she found it. A little wooden box. It was small, rectangular, nondescript. Except for one thing: It had a shape painted on the side. The shape was a polygon, an angular, crystalline shape. She had seen it before.

She blew the image up until it was a maze of pixels. She stared at the painted design on the box. Where have I seen this?

It was the shape of the crystals she had seen inside Harmonica Man's brain. The diagnosis clicked, like a mechanism locking into place. She thought, Kate bought that box from Penny Zecker at a flea market. It's sitting in Kate's bedroom now.

BRAIN viruses can act fast, taking a person from apparent good health to a fatal coma in a matter of hours. Viral agents that grow in the central nervous system spread along nerve cells. You can go to bed healthy and never wake up. By the next morning the agent has amplified itself along the fibers of the central nervous system.

The brain virus had spent the night amplifying in Peter Talides. His mental state was not good. It was Saturday morning—not a school morning—but he got himself dressed for school, walked to the elevated train station, and took a train, as usual, to Manhattan, heading for the Mater School.

At the Fifty-ninth Street station, he got off the train and walked down a flight of stairs to the mezzanine. The mezzanine is covered with colored mosaics. Peter Talides should have headed for the door that leads to the uptown train, but he didn't. The mosaics disoriented him. He passed through a doorway and went down a set of stairs to the downtown side. A train came along. He stepped aboard and was carried away from the Mater School. His nose was running profusely.

The train carried him southward through Manhattan. It dived under the East River and emerged in Brooklyn. At the Borough Hall station in downtown Brooklyn, he seemed to realize he was lost. He got off the train. He sat on a bench and put his head between his knees. His midbrain was dying. He groaned. Eventually a transit officer named James Lindle touched Talides on the shoulder.

Talides uttered a sharp cry. It was a startle seizure, triggered by an intrusion into his world. He fell off the bench to the platform. He curled up on his side and straightened out, his body rigid.

A few people gathered around him. "Stand back, please. Don't touch him," Officer Lindle said. He called on his radio for an emergency medical squad.

Talides was near the yellow line at the edge of the platform. Suddenly he twisted and rolled off the platform, dropping down to the tracks. He landed in pools of water in the track bed. At that moment the station filled with the rumble of an approaching train.

"Aw, no," Officer Lindle shouted. He ran along the platform, waving at the train. "Stop!"

People were shouting at the man on the tracks, "Get up!" Talides seemed to hear the people calling to him. His eyes were half open. He rolled over onto his belly and began to crawl across the tracks, away from help, toward the third rail—the power rail. The train motorman saw the man crawling on the tracks and dumped his air brakes on full emergency stop.

Down on the tracks, a tremor shook Talides, and he flopped over. His clothing was soaked with water. His body fell against the electrified third rail. There was a sizzling flash, and his body snapped rigid, made rock-hard by ten thousand amps of electricity.

THE Morans' housekeeper, Nanette, answered the door. She said that Mr. and Mrs. Moran were staying with relatives.

"There may be something dangerous in Kate's room. Has anyone been inside?" Austen asked.

No one had been. Kate's parents couldn't bear to go into the room.

Austen had studied the photographs, and she had almost every object in Kate's bedroom in her mind's eye. She sat down at the worktable. There in front of her was the box with the angular crystal painted on it. She reached toward it, stopped. She opened her knapsack, pulled out latex gloves and a safety mask, and put them on. She also put on a pair of protective eyeglasses.

Now, very delicately, she picked up the box. It was about three inches square and was made of very hard, dense wood. It was a puzzle. There was a sliding mechanism somewhere that would open it. One of the sides was loose. That might be the mechanism.

Should I try to open this? she wondered. Four people are dead, maybe because of this thing. I may already be exposed anyway.

She slid her fingers over the box, feeling carefully. There was a click. The box opened, and something snapped out. She dropped the box with a yelp, and it clattered onto the table.

The head and neck of a small wooden snake had popped out. It was like a jack-in-the-box. The snake had struck at her fingers and missed. It was a hooded cobra, and its hood was flared open in the attack stance. It had a red marking painted across the back of its hood. Its eyes were bright yellow dots, with slit irises. Its tongue was red and forked and stuck out. The snake was attached to a spring mechanism. When you closed the lid and locked the puzzle, the spring was cocked. When you pulled on the correct facet, the spring tripped and the snake leaped out and struck at your finger. It was a children's toy.

Something else had come out of the box. She could just see it in the light of the skylight. It was grayish dust. Holding her mask tightly down over her face, she picked up the box with her gloved hand and looked inside. Nothing there except the mechanism and a bit of dust. The thing was a dust-dispersion device. Not very efficient. Just enough to put a little dust into the air near the person who opened the box.

"Oh, my God," she said. "It's a bomb. It's a biological bomb."

She turned the box over, rotating it only slightly so as not to cause any dust to fall out. Glued to the bottom was a tiny slip of paper with some words printed on it. She held the box up to the light and read:

Human Trial #2, April 12
ARCHIMEDES FECIT

She put the box down and looked around the room. The Twinings tea can would do. She stuffed a wad of Kleenex from a pack on Kate's bedside table into the can and then gently placed the snake bomb in the nest of Kleenex. She snapped down the can's lid tight. As soon as possible she would have to transfer the can to a biohazard container.

She looked around the room. She noticed a steam radiator. Good. Forced-air heating ducts might carry the room's air all over the building. She noticed an air-conditioning vent on the ceiling. She would have to make sure the Morans didn't turn on the air-conditioning.

Austen locked Kate's door from the inside, then went out. The door clicked behind her. She removed her mask and gloves but didn't know what to do with them. Finally she just put them into a pocket of her knapsack. She found Nanette and warned her not to let anyone go into Kate's room. "I found something in there that may be extremely dangerous. I've locked the door. Please keep it locked until the authorities arrive. And whatever you do, don't turn on the air-conditioning."

AUSTEN went out to the street and got a taxi to the medical examiner's office. There, in her office, beside her desk she had left the bag of Harmonica Man's possessions. She put on a clean pair of surgical gloves and a clean mask. Then she opened the garbage bag and pulled out the black sweatshirt. There was a lump in the front pocket. She reached in and pulled out a small box, nearly identical to the one from Kate's room. There was another tiny piece of paper glued to the bottom. This paper contained a very small drawing of some kind of jar, with a dumbbell or an hourglass inside. Under the picture was written, in very small print:

Human Trial #1, April 12
ARCHIMEDES FECIT

The boxes reeked of a plan and a precise mind. Austen sealed the two cobra boxes in several biohazard bags and did the same with Harmonica Man's clothing and her own knapsack. Then she took a taxi to Dr. Nathanson's apartment in the East Fifties. Nathanson's wife answered the bell. "Oh, yes, you're the doctor from the CDC," she said. "Come in."

Nathanson had a small office in the apartment. The desk was piled with papers and works of philosophy and medicine. The room smelled of cigars. He shut the door.

Austen said, "I've found the source, the cause of death. It's a human being. This isn't a natural outbreak. This is the work of a killer."

There was a long pause. "What makes you think so?"

"I have found two biological dispersion devices—bombs—Dr. Nathanson. I found one in Harmonica Man's clothing, the other in Kate Moran's bedroom. Penny Zecker was a junk dealer. She sold the device to Kate. Zecker's notebook indicates somebody traded the box for some postcards. That somebody is a murderer." She placed her laptop on Nathanson's desk and turned it on. "Look."

The chief medical examiner bent over to stare at the photograph she'd taken of the Zecker-Moran box.

"This is the device that infected Penny Zecker. She sold it to Kate Moran." Austen held up one of the biohazard bags. "This is the other device. I think someone may have given it to Harmonica Man in the subway. These boxes release a small amount of dust into the air when the lid pops open. I think the dust is a dried biological agent. It may be crystallized virus particles. I'm not sure."

Nathanson said nothing. Suddenly he seemed like an old man.

"We've been exposed," Austen said. "So have Glenn Dudley and Ben Kly. Everyone present at the Moran autopsy."

"Oh, no! They're doing the teacher now."

"What?"

"The art teacher—Peter Talides. He was killed on the subway tracks. Glenn's in the autopsy room now with Kly."

Nathanson called the OCME. He reached a morgue attendant and asked him to get Dudley on the phone. Soon the man came back, saying that Dr. Dudley was busy and would call later.

GLENN Dudley and Ben Kly were alone in the Pit when Austen arrived there, out of breath. She stopped at the door and cried out to them, "Wait! The body is infected with a hot agent."

Kly took a step backward.

"It's very dangerous, Dr. Dudley," Austen said.

"Then get yourself suited up before you come in here," he replied. He looked up at her. His nose was running, the discharge overflowing his breathing mask.

"Ben!" she said, backing away.

Kly had been holding a jar full of formalin. He looked at Dudley, and the jar dropped from his hands and crashed on the floor. The sound of the breaking glass seemed to upset Dudley. A twitch rippled across his face. He grunted and opened his mouth. Then he raised his prosector's knife and turned toward Austen, looking at her with shining, alert eyes.

The blade was of honed carbon steel, more than two feet long. It was slick with infective blood. Austen moved backward. Very slowly she raised her hands to protect her neck and face. "Dr. Dudley, please put the knife down. Please," she said.

Dudley moved toward her. She screamed and jumped back, and the knife passed under her arm.

"Over here!" Kly said.

Dudley turned.

"Go," Kly hissed to her. Dudley moved toward Kly, who backed up, keeping his eyes on Dudley's face, talking to him. "Calm down, Doctor. Put the knife down. Let's pray together, Doctor."

Dudley backed him into a corner. "Let's not pray," he said as he swung the knife with all his strength across Kly's neck. Almost beheaded, Kly went down.

Dudley looked around calmly, his lips moving, his teeth chewing. Suddenly his neck arched. His back curved and swayed. The writhing had begun.

Austen ran out of the room, shouting.

PART FOUR: Decision

Manhattan, Saturday Afternoon, April 25

THE Jacob K. Javits Federal Building at 26 Federal Plaza in lower Manhattan sits along Broadway, with a view of the Brooklyn Bridge. The offices inside include the New York field office of the Federal Bureau of Investigation.

Alice Austen and the chief medical examiner of New York City entered the command center on the twenty-sixth floor. The room was full of desks arranged in concentric half circles, facing a bank of video display screens. A stocky man in his forties came over to them. He had curly brown hair and dark intelligent eyes.

"Hello, Lex," he said, and he shook Austen's hand. "I'm Frank Masaccio. Glad to meet you, Doctor. We'll talk in my office."

Masaccio was the head of the New York field office and an assistant director of the FBI. When they got to his office three floors above, he said, "All right, run this by me again."

Nathanson's voice was shaky. "My deputy is dead, infected with something in the autopsy room. Before he died, he killed our best morgue attendant."

Austen placed her laptop on a coffee table. "Something seems to be causing people to attack themselves or others. We've had six deaths, and it looks like someone is planting the agent in a premeditated way."

Masaccio put up one hand. "Hold on. The first question I'm asking, Is this FBI jurisdiction? I want to do a dial-up with Walter Mellis at the CDC."

Within two minutes Masaccio had Mellis on the speakerphone. "Dr. Mellis? Frank Masaccio here. I'm the director of the New York field office of the FBI. Sorry to bother you on a Saturday, but we have a problem."

"Walt? It's Alice Austen."

"Alice! What's going on?"

There was some confusion for a moment about who knew whom, but Walter Mellis quickly explained Austen's role to Masaccio.

"Dr. Mellis," Masaccio said, "your researcher seems to have uncovered something."

"Wait. What's Walt's involvement?" Austen asked.

"He's a consultant to a special forensic unit of the FBI called Reachdeep," Masaccio said. "It deals with nuclear, chemical, and biological terrorism." He explained that Reachdeep was a classified operation and that he would obtain security clearance for her.

Austen turned to Nathanson. "Were you in on this?"

Nathanson was embarrassed. "Walt has involved me a bit. He asked me to watch for unusual cases. This one seemed unusual."

Austen was annoyed about being left out of the loop, but she tried to calm herself down. She described to Masaccio in greater detail what she had found.

"Why did Dr. Dudley become so violent?" Masaccio asked. "That high school kid didn't."

"The infectious agent damages the primitive parts of the brain and seems to exaggerate underlying aggression," Austen answered. "Kate Moran was a peaceful person. Glenn Dudley was—"

"Very unhappy," Nathanson filled in.

"So what is the bug?" Masaccio asked.

"Unknown," Austen said.

"All right," Masaccio said. "What we have is an apparent series of homicides using an unknown biological agent. That's FBI jurisdiction. Can the CDC identify this thing for us?"

"It could be difficult," Mellis answered on the speakerphone.

"How long?"

"Weeks to months."

Masaccio stared at the speakerphone. "We have hours to days to deal with this." He turned. "So tell me what you think the virus is, Dr. Austen."

"I don't know what it is. We're not even sure it's a virus."

There was a silence, and then Masaccio said, "I have the impression there's a lot on your mind you're not telling me, Dr. Austen. Good cops work their hunches. Tell me your hunches."

"It's a virus," she said. "It spreads like the common cold—by contact with tiny droplets of mucus floating in the air or touching the eyelids or by contact with infective blood. It can be dried into a powder, and it can get into the air, so it may also be infective through the lungs. It's neuroinvasive. That means it travels along the nerve fibers and invades the central nervous system. It replicates in the brain and kills in about two days. The virus makes crystals in brain cells. The crystals form in the cell's nucleus. It damages the brain stem, the areas that control emotion and violence and feeding. The virus causes people to attack themselves or others and eat their own flesh. It is not . . . natural."

"This is wild speculation," Mellis said.

"I'm thinking about the Unsub, " Masaccio said, using Bureau jargon for "unknown subject"—the unknown perpetrator of the crime. "Is this a group or a loner?" Nobody knew.

"Dr. Austen, I have to ask. Are you personally contagious?"

"Please don't take me off this case."

Masaccio grunted, "Hmm." He stood up and crossed to the window, which looked north, toward midtown and the Empire State Building. "Self-cannibalism spreading through New York like the common cold."

"I have to inform the director of the CDC," Mellis said.

Frank Masaccio hung up, then turned toward Nathanson and Austen. "I'm taking this to our National Security Division. The head of the NSD is a guy named Steven Wyzinski." He punched up a string of numbers. Wyzinski returned the call immediately, and they spoke quietly for a minute or two.

"Steve wants to do a SIOC calldown," Masaccio said.

"What's that?" Austen asked.

"It's a meeting of experts and federal people at FBI headquarters. SIOC"—he pronounced it Sy-ock—"stands for Strategic Information Operations Center. It's the FBI's command center in Washington. You'll go. Lex and I are going to stay in New York and get the ball rolling locally. I'm going to line up a joint task force with the police department, the fire department . . ."

Austen watched him. What she saw was a very bright man working out the opening moves of a chess defense. The problem was that the unknown opponent was in control of the game.

ARCHIMEDES of Syracuse, the great mathematician and weaponeer who died in 212 B.C., designed glass lenses or mirrors that focused sunlight on enemy ships and set them on fire. He also understood the principle of the lever and fulcrum—the idea that one can place a lever on a fulcrum and use it to move a giant mass. "Give me only a place to stand, and I can move the world," Archimedes said.

His modern-day successor liked to ride the subway. Archimedes could ride for hours, looking at people from behind his metal-framed eyeglasses, a faint smile on his face. He was a prematurely balding man of medium height. Usually he wore a tan cotton shirt, loose natural-fiber trousers, and sneakers. He had friendly feelings toward most people, and it made him feel bad that some of them would have to go.

The subway was the bloodstream of the city, with connections that ran everywhere. Archimedes liked connections. He stood on a platform at Grand Central Terminal and thought of the tracks that go out of Grand Central into the world. People were always talking about viruses from the rain forest that would find their way to modern cities and infect the inhabitants. But it works the other way around, too, he thought. Diseases that emerge from New York City can spread out and reach the humans who live in the rain forest. There are more connections to the rest of the world from New York City than from any other city on earth. Something can explode from here to go everywhere on the planet.

Archimedes walked west a few blocks to the New York Public Library, circled around it, and sat down on a bench in Bryant Park, among lawns and trees and, of course, people. Too many of them. He sat on a bench and watched them pass, the temporary biological creatures who would vanish in the reach of deep time. They are not going to understand my optimism and my hope, he thought. But I think we can be saved. I hold the lever in my hands.

En route to Washington, D.C., Sunday, April 26

BEFORE dawn Alice Austen was flown by helicopter to Teterboro Airport in New Jersey, where she boarded a twin-engine turboprop owned by the FBI. She was the only passenger. "If there's anything you need, Dr. Austen, please ask," the pilot said over the loudspeaker when they were airborne.

"I'd like a telephone," she said.

The copilot walked back and handed her a headset. She put it on and called her father in New Hampshire. She woke him up. "It's five o'clock, Allie," he said. "Where've you been? I was calling all over Atlanta. Nobody knew where you were."

"Sorry, Dad. I'm on a field investigation."

"I thought so. Where are you?"

"I can't say. It's kind of an emergency."

Her father lived in a small house in the woods. Her mother had died three years earlier. She thought about how excited her father, a retired cop, would be if he knew she was calling him from an FBI aircraft headed for Washington. "Dad, I just wanted to say how much I admire you," she said.

"You wake me up for this?" He chuckled.

"I may not have a chance to call you for a while."

"Hey, I'm going fishing, as long as you got me up."

"What are you going for, Dad?"

"Landlocked salmon. They're still hitting."

"Yeah. Get some."

"Keep in touch, sweetie."

"Good-bye, Dad. I love you." She sat back in the seat and closed her eyes. That wasn't a perfect good-bye, she thought. If I end up like Kate Moran.

She got up and went to the washroom and looked at her eyes in the mirror. She saw no color change. *I hope I'm right about this. If I'm wrong, I've just pulled the biggest fire-alarm handle in the world.*

WILL Hopkins and Mark Littleberry landed at Andrews Air Force Base at dawn on Sunday morning. Littleberry was due to go out to Bethesda, Maryland, to the Naval Medical Research Institute, where he would be debriefed about the attempt to obtain a sample of an Iraqi biological weapon. Hopkins had to go to the FBI Academy in Quantico. They had both been fired by the U.N. and caused a diplomatic incident. There was going to be a lot of explaining to do.

Littleberry called his wife, Annie, to let her know he was safe. He told her he expected to be back in Boston within a few days. "Get your bathing suit out, honey," he said. "We're heading for Florida."

Hopkins and Littleberry went in search of a shuttle bus into Washington. They were just arriving at the curb when Hopkins's SkyPager beeped. The number on the beeper was not familiar, but he plucked a cell phone from his pocket and dialed the number back. He identified himself and listened for a minute. "SIOC? . . . What? . . . Oh, man. When is she coming in? . . . I'm supposed to wait for her?"

Suddenly Littleberry looked down and frowned. The beeper in his bag had gone off.

"It's a calldown," Hopkins said to him.

They were waiting on the tarmac at Andrews when Alice Austen stepped off the FBI plane. Hopkins introduced himself. "Hi. Supervisory Special Agent William Hopkins, Jr. I'm the guy in the Bureau who is assigned to handle bioterror events. This is Dr. Mark Littleberry, a consultant to the FBI on biological terrorism. We will accompany you to the meeting."

THE Strategic Information Operations Center was a windowless radio-secure chamber at FBI headquarters on Pennsylvania Avenue. The interior was divided into sections visible to one another through glass panels. A tall silver-haired man in a suit came out to meet them. He was Steven Wyzinski, head of the FBI's National Security Division. "You're William Hopkins? Everyone cleared?"

"These people are basically sort of my group," Hopkins said.

He introduced Austen to a number of officials, but she had trouble remembering their names.

"We'll be going up on the bird in twenty-five minutes," Wyzinski said, glancing at a clock on the wall. "Please give us all the information you have, Dr. Austen."

She described the situation. They fired questions at her left and right, wanting to make absolutely sure the event was real before calling in the rest of the government.

"Satellite transmission in four minutes," someone announced.

The group filed into the videoconference situation room and sat down at a table, where a sound technician wired them with clip-on microphones. There were large video screens positioned on the walls, and several speakerphones were on the table. Steven Wyzinski cleared his throat nervously. One by one the video screens filled with faces. Voices came on the speakerphones. The room filled with power; you could feel it in the air.

"Welcome to SIOC," Wyzinski said. "This is a threat-assessment meeting for the Cobra Event. The FBI customarily gives a name to major crime investigations, and this one will be designated Cobra. You will understand the meaning of the term shortly."

Austen felt herself trembling ever so slightly, and she hoped it didn't show. Hopkins was sitting next to her.

On two video screens were the faces of Walter Mellis and the director of the CDC, Helen Lane. Mellis was wearing the full-dress white uniform of the U.S. Public Health Service. They were at CDC headquarters in Atlanta.

Frank Masaccio's face appeared on another screen.

"Is the White House coming on-line?" Wyzinski asked.

"White House on now," said a technician in the background.

A large viewing screen set in a commanding position showed a rumpled middle-aged man in a pink polo shirt. "Jack Hertog here. I'm with the National Security Council."

Steven Wyzinski turned the floor over to Austen. She stood up and took a breath. She said, "It's a very frightening situation. Six disease-related deaths have occurred in a short time." Her photographs flashed on the screens. She read the words printed on the cobra boxes. She said, "The words *Archimedes fecit* are Latin for 'Made by Archimedes.' The date on each of the boxes could be the date that Archimedes prepared them. The expression 'human trial' probably refers to human medical experimentation."

There followed a great deal of discussion about the motives of Archimedes. The Cobra Event did not seem like classic terrorism, in which a group acts with an agenda. Or if there was an agenda, it didn't seem obvious at this point.

"Are we sure we're dealing with a biological agent?" asked a colonel from USAMRIID. Based at Fort Detrick, Maryland, USAMRIID is the United States Army Medical Research Institute of Infectious Diseases, the army's principal biodefense lab.

"I am fairly sure we are," Austen said. She told them she suspected it was a virus.

"If so," the army colonel said, "then it's a level four hot agent. But there's been no identification, right?"

"Correct," Austen said.

"So how can you assess a threat if you don't know what the agent is?"

"Good point," Wyzinski said. "Dr. Littleberry?"

Littleberry leaned forward. The cameras followed him. "There are a lot of unknowns here," he said, "but we do know that the lethal-dose response in a population under biological attack can be enormous. A couple of pounds of dry hot agent released in the air in New York City—you might get ten thousand deaths. The top range would be two, maybe three million deaths."

"Your top range seems exaggerated," said Jack Hertog.

"I sure hope it's exaggerated, son," Littleberry said.

Hertog looked annoyed. People didn't call members of the White House inner staff "son."

Hopkins had been sitting there, wondering when to speak. He was still wearing clothes that needed laundering in the worst way. "It looks like we could have a very serious situation," he finally said. "I think—"

"Who are you again?" Hertog asked.

"Supervisory Special Agent William Hopkins, Jr. I'm a forensic molecular biologist, head of scientific operations for the biology group at the Hazardous Materials Response Unit in Quantico. I think we are seeing a biological terrorist going through a testing phase. Bioterrorists like to test their stuff. That's the meaning of the phrase 'human trial.' It happened with the Aum Shinrikyo sect in Japan before they let off nerve gas in the Tokyo subway in 1995. They tested anthrax two or three times, and they couldn't get it to work, so they switched to nerve gas. What's happening in New York could be the testing phase for a huge release of a biological weapon."

"This is just speculation," Hertog said.

"But we can use forensics to stop it," Hopkins went on. "Normal forensic science uncovers evidence after a crime has been committed. Here, with Reachdeep, we can use forensics to stop a terrorist event before it happens."

"The unit that doesn't exist," Hertog said.

Hopkins pulled a swab out of his pocket protector. "This is the heart of Reachdeep," he said. "This little swab. The evidence is mainly biological. All terrorist weapons contain forensic signatures that lead you back to the perpetrator. We can analyze the infective agent, and it will lead us back to its creator."

"This sounds off the wall," Hertog said.

Hopkins waved his swab around as he talked. "The idea behind

Reachdeep is universal forensics. You take the crime apart. You explore it with the limits of your intellect. Exploring a big crime is like exploring a universe. It's what astronomers do when they look at the sky with telescopes. You begin to translate the language, and the structure of the crime and the identity of the perpetrator are slowly revealed, like the structure of a universe."

"For heaven's sake, Hopkins." It was Steven Wyzinski. He was embarrassed.

Hopkins put the swab back in his pocket and sat down abruptly. His face was red. He looked sideways at Austen, and then he looked down. Austen began to feel sorry for him. "We need to be invisible," he went on. "The perpetrator may accelerate the killing if he or they know we're closing in. We need to do a secret field deployment of a Reachdeep lab."

The army colonel from Fort Detrick said, "Wait a minute. You can't isolate a hot agent using a portable field laboratory. You need a full-scale biosafety level four facility to do that."

"We're in the middle of an unfolding criminal event," Hopkins replied. "We don't have time to fly evidence down to Fort Detrick. We can move the crime lab to the evidence. I propose we set up a ring of investigative power around a Reachdeep lab. What I mean is, we'll have a core science lab with a forensic team. Around that we'll have a task force of agents and police officers. The science team will generate leads, but we'll need hundreds of investigators to run out the leads."

Jack Hertog of the White House broke in. "This is over the top. You're asking for a lot of money and for what? Another flight 800 media circus that ends up in a hopeless mystery?"

"Hey!" Masaccio ripped in. "My people gave their heart and soul—"

"Shut up, Frank. The FBI forensic lab doesn't exactly have a stellar track record. You people spent twelve years looking for the Unabomber, and in the end, his brother turned him in. Now you want to act out a sci-fi movie in New York."

Hopkins looked around the room, seeking support. Mark Littleberry stood up slowly. "I think I have something to add here that may put things into perspective. We've never had a situation in this country on any large scale where a population is threatened with a biological weapon. But we learned a lot about how these weapons work during tests in the Pacific in the late 1960s."

"Excuse me." It was Jack Hertog. "I don't think a discussion of those tests is germane here."

Littleberry stared at him. "I don't know if it's germane, but you'd damned well better take it seriously. With a biological weapon you can make people die like flies. In a matter of days the city's hospitals would run out of beds and supplies. If the agent was contagious in human-to-human transmission, then the first people to die would be the medical caregivers and the first responders. Doctors, nurses, firemen, police—they'd disappear."

There was silence in the room. Even Jack Hertog seemed affected by the weight of what Littleberry had said. It was Steven Wyzinski who finally spoke up. Though there may be doubt about the scale of the threat, he said, there seemed to be no choice but to start a major investigation. He thought the best chance was with Will Hopkins's Reachdeep team.

Everyone agreed more or less, even Hertog. "We can't take a chance of a big blowup in a place like New York," he said.

It was Masaccio who came up with the idea that set the operation in motion. "I've got a place for you Reachdeep guys," he said to Hopkins. "Governors Island. It's in the middle of New York Bay, right off Wall Street. It's federal property. Very secure. No media."

"Okay," Hertog broke in. "Hopkins, you put your science squad on the island. As for USAMRIID and the CDC, I want you to work in parallel. Both of you are national labs. Both of you will get samples to analyze. If the FBI thing goes down the toilet, both labs will be there to analyze the disease."

"Sir"—it was the colonel from USAMRIID—"there has to be some kind of biocontainment field hospital on the island. You do not—repeat, do not—want any human cases infected with an unknown biological weapon to be put into any New York City–area hospitals. That is just incredibly risky. The army has TAML units that can be palletized and flown in by Black Hawk helicopters."

"I'm sorry," Hertog said. "I don't know what a TAML is."

"That's a theater army medical lab. It's a biocontainment hospital in a box. It's rated biosafety level three plus. You hang it under a helicopter, and you can fly it anywhere."

"Good."

"One little item," Frank Masaccio broke in. "Dr. Austen opened the Cobra case. Here at the Bureau we'd call her the case agent. I want her sworn in as a deputy U.S. marshal with full law-enforcement powers. Somebody from Justice get her sworn, okay?"

"Thank you, everyone," Wyzinski said. "The first Cobra meeting is closed." The screens on the walls went dead one by one.

PART FIVE: Reachdeep

Quantico, Virginia, Sunday, April 26

IMMEDIATELY after the SIOC meeting Austen and Hopkins took a Bureau car to the FBI Academy in Quantico, an hour's drive south of Washington. Mark Littleberry set out in another car for the Naval Medical Research Institute in Bethesda, Maryland, to pick up some extra biosensor equipment.

Hopkins talked on his cell phone most of the way down to Quantico. He was "wickering together a team," as he put it. He and Austen barely had a word to say to each other. At one point he looked over and saw that she was asleep. Her hair had fallen off her face, a face that seemed delicate and tired to him, and he noticed faint circles under her closed eyes.

At Quantico, Hopkins drove through a checkpoint and parked in front of the FBI Academy, a group of pale brick buildings joined by glassed-in walkways. Here the Bureau trains new agents and maintains a number of its units, including Hopkins's Hazardous Materials Response Unit.

"We're here, Dr. Austen," he said. His voice woke her up.

Austen was given a guest room, where she changed into operations clothing—cargo pants and a blue shirt. She ended up with Hopkins at a large gray building known as the Engineering Research Facility, or ERF, the FBI's supersecret electronic-equipment facility. In the lobby Hopkins collected a plastic badge for Austen, indicating she had a national security clearance.

"The ERF is divided into security pods," Hopkins explained. "We're kind of new. We're still looking for a pod to call our own."

They entered pod D, a vast indoor chamber five stories high. The chamber was illuminated with bright lights on the ceiling, and the walls were shiny with aluminum foil and copper mesh. The floor was crowded with piles of equipment in boxes.

"Is this Reachdeep?" Austen asked. "It's huge."

"Oh, no. Most of this is other FBI stuff. We just have a little corner of pod D." Hopkins led her into an area walled off by boxes where people were working furiously.

"Will! Hey, Will's here." A man came over to greet them. He was about fifty, very fit, with huge shoulders. He was Special Agent Oscar Wirtz, the tactical operations officer for Reachdeep. He shook Austen's hand with an unmerciful grip.

Austen met the other people Hopkins had selected for the operation. Most of the selecting had happened over the telephone while she had been asleep in the car.

The team's imaging specialist and microbiologist was a pleasant woman in her late twenties named Suzanne Tanaka. She was not an FBI agent; until recently she had been working for the U.S. Navy. "Suzanne was bugging us to hire her," Hopkins explained, "so we finally stole her away from the navy."

"Should I bring the mice, Will?" she asked.

"Sure, bring a few. Not too many," he said.

Austen said to her, "Do you know how to work an electron microscope? Because we need to look at tissue samples right away."

"Sure," she said. "That's my specialty."

Hopkins looked at his watch. "Where's Jimmy Lesdiu, our materials genius?"

"Right here." An extremely tall man stood up. Special Agent James Lesdiu was a forensic-materials analyst. He analyzed hair and fibers, surfaces, and chemicals.

In a corner of the staging area a half-dozen men and women were sorting their biohazard space suits and body armor. They were all special agents with the FBI's Hostage Rescue Team, or HRT. Oscar Wirtz introduced Austen to them. "They're going to handle the operations side of this mission," Wirtz said. The space suits were jet-black, apparently for use in night operations, and the agents were known in the FBI as ninjas. "The idea," Wirtz went on, "is that you scientists are the evidence gatherers. If a terrorist weapon goes off, you have to go into a hot zone to gather evidence. But you may need ninjas around to keep you out of harm's way."

Just then Mark Littleberry entered pod D, accompanied by two FBI agents carrying Halliburton suitcases. He'd picked up two Felix machines and three Boink sensors in Bethesda.

The Reachdeep team had been working for an hour or so, taking inventory of firearms, ammunition, lights, and special breathing equipment. Now Oscar Wirtz and his people were moving the stuff out to a truck for delivery to the helicopter landing field. Meantime, a U.S. marshal swore in both Austen and Littleberry. They were now deputy U.S. marshals.

Governors Island, Sunday

GOVERNORS Island sits in the East River, not far from Brooklyn. Before the American Revolution the mile-long island was where the British Colonial governors of New York lived. More recently the island had been owned by the U.S. Coast Guard. But then the coast guard moved its operations, leaving the place dotted with abandoned buildings.

As the Reachdeep helicopters touched down onto the landing

zone late that afternoon, Frank Masaccio was waiting to greet the team. "Isn't this a great place?" he said, shaking their hands. "Now it's yours. Don't let the New York office down."

Seagulls were wheeling overhead, and the smell of salt water came off the bay. On the water's edge at the western side of the island, facing lower Manhattan and the Statue of Liberty, was the old coast-guard hospital. There was already activity going on there—soldiers were hurrying up and down the front steps carrying equipment and supplies. The idea was to bring the place up to standard as a biocontainment army field hospital.

Littleberry and Hopkins explored the old brick building from top to bottom. Littleberry, the team biohazard officer, found a group of rooms near the back of the building that he liked—a warren of interconnecting chambers. This area would be the Reach-deep lab, the biocontainment core.

The rooms were empty except for a few tables and chairs. There was a large adjacent conference area. It looked out through a line of windows across the bay to lower Manhattan and the Statue of Liberty. Outside the conference room there was an observation deck with a metal railing around it. A large investigation requires regular team meetings; this is standard practice. At least once a day all managers of an investigative group meet and share the evidence, trade ideas, and discuss leads that need to be run out.

"This is a good setup, Will," Littleberry said.

"It beats Iraq," said Hopkins.

WORKING with Hopkins, Mark Littleberry planned the layout of the biocontainment core. The goal was to contain infective evidence so that it could be studied safely in a biosafety level 3 zone—what they called the evidence core.

The evidence core was hot. It consisted of three connected rooms. The first room was the materials room, for holding and analyzing the basic physical evidence. The second room was the biology room, for growing cultures and looking at samples of tissue in regular optical microscopes. The third room, the imaging room, was for the electron microscope and equipment associated with it.

There was a glass window looking from the core into the conference room. The core rooms were accessible through a decontamination chamber, where team members would put on and take off their protective biohazard gear and decontaminate it.

The team's living quarters were situated in an empty coast-guard dormitory next to the hospital. "We're going to run this forensic investigation around the clock," Hopkins told the team. "When you need to sleep, let people know where you are, and try to keep a sleep session to four hours or less."

"Aye, aye, Captain Ahab," Special Agent Jimmy Lesdiu said.

The evidence core would be kept at biosafety level 3 plus, under negative air pressure. This was so that infective particles would not leak out of the rooms through cracks. Littleberry and Hopkins pounded a hole in one of the exterior walls of the core and attached a flexible plastic air duct to the hole. They ran the duct into a portable HEPA filter unit. This was essentially a vacuum cleaner that sucked contaminated air out of the core and filtered it before discharging it harmlessly out a window through a second plastic duct.

Hopkins and Littleberry finished setting up the air-handling system by nine o'clock in the evening, four hours after the helicopter had touched down on Governors Island.

The news media had not noticed the increased activity on the island. The coast guard had used the place for years as a staging area for rescue operations, and the Brooklyn neighborhoods closest to the island were accustomed to helicopters coming and going. People did not focus on the fact that the coast guard was no longer there and that the helicopters were from the FBI and the U.S. Army.

"I THINK we're ready to go hot," Hopkins said.

The team members put on surgical scrub suits and filed into the staging room for the core. They put on disposable Tyvek biohazard suits, rubber boots, and double surgical gloves.

Hopkins slung a nylon belt around his suit and hung his Leatherman pocket tool on that. They put on soft, flexible breathing helmets known as Racal hoods—transparent plastic bubbles with a filtered air supply. Battery-powered blowers drove filtered air into the helmets and kept them under positive pressure, so that infective bioparticles did not sneak in. The batteries for the blowers could last eight hours.

Littleberry pushed open the door, and the team members went into the core, deploying for their tasks.

Hopkins removed the two cobra boxes from a biohazard tube. Once the boxes were out in the air, the core had officially gone hot. He put the boxes on the table and wrote COBRA on a couple of evidence tags. Then he dated the tags and wrote down the laboratory control number. The sample numbers were 1 and 2.

"I've been thinking about something, Will," Littleberry said. "Whoever made those boxes used a lab setup much like this one. Somewhere in this city there's another lab, another core. And it's running hot, like this one."

Manhattan, Sunday

ARCHIMEDES lived in a two-bedroom apartment on the third floor. He kept the shades drawn at all times. The shades were lined with metal foil to block the sunlight, because sunlight might destroy his virus cultures. He was eating lunch now in the kitchen—a frozen vegetarian burrito. He did not eat meat. He knew he was a parasite on the plant kingdom. We all have to eat, he told himself. The problem is that too many humans have to eat.

He stood up and opened a door that led to a hallway. The hallway was his biosafety level 2 staging area, where he kept a plastic tub full of water and laundry bleach. That was for washing contaminated objects. There were also some boxes holding biosafety equipment he had ordered through the mail. He'd had the equipment sent to a mail service in New Jersey, where he picked it up in his car.

He pulled on a disposable Tyvek suit, double latex rubber gloves, a head covering, surgical booties, and a full-face respirator mask. Then he opened the door to level 3. He entered the bedroom and shut the door behind him.

His weapons lab was a comfortable working environment. There were some old Formica tables he had bought at a flea market. It was the flea market where he had traded the box to the woman who had tried to cheat him. He had enlisted her in the human experimental trials. Afterward he had scanned the newspapers and watched the television news, but nothing about her was mentioned. Also in his lab there was a bioreactor, his virus-drying trays, and the insectary. He had installed an air-filter system—a little fan set in a window. It had a HEPA filter. It pulled air out of the level 3 laboratory, passed it through filters, and discharged it outdoors, clean and safe. Air was drawn into the lab through a vent in another window.

The insectary, which sat on a table, was a collection of clear plastic boxes filled with moths. He kept the insectary for philosophic reasons. He didn't really need it, but it was fun. He pulled open the lid of a box and inspected the green caterpillars inside. He dropped in some lettuce.

The natural strain of his brainpox virus lived in moths and butterflies. The moth caterpillars crawled around in the boxes eating leaves. They became infected with the insect strain of his brainpox virus, not the human strain; human brainpox wouldn't grow in insects. The moth caterpillars became listless, but they kept eating. Then suddenly the meltdown occurred. It happened in an explosive final wave of virus replication. In less than two hours each caterpillar was transformed into mostly virus. This transformational speed and power of a virus never failed to impress him. The virus could keep its host alive—still hungry, still feeding—even while it converted the host's body almost entirely to virus crystals. The human strain of the virus could transform the human brain into a bag of virus crystals and make the human eat and eat and eat.

The human species is hungrier than a hungry insect. With its monstrous, out-of-control appetite, it is ruining the earth, Archimedes told himself. When a species overruns its natural habitat, it devours its available resources. It becomes weakened, vulnerable to infectious outbreaks. A sudden emergence of a deadly pathogen, an infectious killer, reduces the species back to a sustainable level. These mass dyings happen all the time in nature. Gypsy moth caterpillars sometimes overrun forests, eating the leaves off the trees. As the population of caterpillars grows, they use up their food supply. Then all kinds of viruses break out among them. Sooner or later some virus crashes the population, and for years afterward the trees are relatively free of caterpillars. Viruses play an important role in nature: They keep populations in check.

Natural thinning events are positive, Archimedes believed. In the year 1348 or thereabouts, the black death, caused by an infective airborne bacterial organism called *Yersinia pestis,* wiped out at least a third of the population of Europe. It was a good thing. The survivors prospered. They inherited more land and more property. A great economic boom followed, culminating in the Renaissance.

Now consider the AIDS virus. People talk about the depletion of the population because of AIDS, saying what a disaster it is, yet in the next breath they talk about how the environment is being damaged by overpopulation. The fact is that AIDS has not done its work well enough. Hence the need for a new disease.

Brainpox was beautiful. It transformed the human brain into a virus bioreactor, melting the brain in the same way the natural form of the virus melted insects.

The brain bioreactor went hot, and it filled up with virus particles until it melted down inside the skull. The reactor began leaking fluids and generally running out of control, causing biting and thrashing and hemorrhaging, spreading the virus around to other hosts in an effective way. Of course, brainpox caused human suffering, but it was over soon. None of this lingering, as with AIDS. And brainpox wouldn't harm any other life-forms on the planet, because brainpox infected only the human species.

Archimedes imagined brainpox turning New York City into a hot bioreactor. From New York, brainpox would amplify itself outward along invisible lines, following airline routes, spanning the globe. It would rocket to London and Tokyo. It would fly to Lagos, Nigeria, and it would amplify through Calcutta. The cities would go hot for a while. But it would not be the end of the human species, not in the least. It would merely remove one out of every two or three persons. He didn't know exactly. A biological weapon never exterminates a population. It merely thins. The greater the thinning, the healthier the effect on the species that has been thinned.

He checked on the bioreactor in his lab. It was running smoothly, making concentrated brainpox virus. The output liquid, saturated with virus particles, ran through a flexible tube to a jar on the floor. As the liquid settled, a white sludge formed on the bottom of the jar. That sludge was mostly virus. It was unbelievable how one little bioreactor could make so much virus.

Near the bioreactor stood the drying trays. Archimedes mixed the virus sludge with a special kind of glass in liquid form. It was rather like making candy. He poured the molten glass into the trays, where it hardened into coin-size hexagons of viral glass. He had bought the viral-glass mix through the mail. It was great stuff.

With his double-gloved fingertips he gently picked up a glass hexagon. He enjoyed holding viral glass in his fingers. He could see the rainbow colors of his virus.

He was interrupted by a squeal. He heard voices and then a crash. He put the crystal back in the tray. Those kids again. He pulled back the shade an inch and looked down. His laboratory overlooked an empty lot surrounded by a chain-link fence. People in the neighborhood had planted a garden there. He himself had planted alfalfa for his insects. The neighbors had also put in a swing set, a slide, and a small metal merry-go-round. Now the larger boys were standing on the merry-go-round, pushing it, shouting. They were making it go too fast, and it was squealing again. One of them hurled a rock at a brown-and-white stray cat. The cat twisted and screeched when the rock hit it. Then it ran through a hole in the fence and escaped.

It made him angry, but there was nothing he could do. For the moment he was stuck in level 3.

Governors Island, Sunday

A CITY morgue truck was backed in behind the coast-guard hospital. Inside the truck was a bank of refrigerated crypts. There was also a mortuary gurney on wheels—a pan. The bodies of Peter Talides, Glenn Dudley, and Ben Kly were triple-bagged in white body pouches that were plastered with biohazard symbols.

With the truck came Dr. Lex Nathanson. For any autopsies that fell under the jurisdiction of New York City's chief medical examiner, Nathanson would be present at the autopsy. He would also sign the death certificate and seal the evidence.

Nathanson and Austen suited up in a hospital storage room. They wore chain-mail gloves on both hands. Climbing into the truck, they started with Glenn Dudley. Leaving the body in the biohazard pouches, they lifted it out of a crypt and transferred it to the gurney. Nathanson unzipped Dudley's three body pouches but did not remove the body. This was going to be a minimal autopsy in a biohazard shroud. Dudley's blood and fluids would collect inside the shroud and would not flow anywhere else.

The two pathologists worked carefully. Nathanson did not remove any of Dudley's organs. He and Austen examined them in place. They took triple sets of biosamples—one for the CDC, one for USAMRIID, and one for Reachdeep.

"I splashed a drop of blood in Dudley's eyes," Austen said suddenly. "It was my fault."

"Put that out of your mind forever," Nathanson said.

What she could not put out of her mind was her last sight of Ben Kly alive. Kly had given her a chance to escape, and he had done it knowing it might well cost him his life. He was a city-morgue attendant, one of the anonymous handlers of the dead, yet she saw him as a man of perfect courage. He left a wife and a small child. Austen felt the unworthiness of a survivor.

When they finished collecting samples, the two pathologists exited the morgue truck and went into the autopsy decontamination room, where they sprayed their suits down with bleach, then disposed of them in biohazard bags. Nathanson returned to the OCME by helicopter, and Austen carried a box of tissue-sample jars into the Reachdeep lab area. She entered the level 2 decontamination vestibule, where she put on a black biohazard suit, rubber boots, double rubber gloves, and a Racal hood. Then she pushed through a door into the evidence core.

Austen gave the samples to Suzanne Tanaka, who took them into the biology room for culturing. If Tanaka could get the virus to grow, then it could be studied more easily. Austen went with her.

Tanaka made a water preparation of Glenn Dudley's brain tissue and injected it into several white laboratory mice, which were kept in clear plastic boxes. "This is our mouse biodetector system," she explained to Austen. Mice are used in virus labs somewhat like canaries in a coal mine. Scientists inject them with a virus. If the mice get sick, they are autopsied and their tissue is examined through a microscope. "We'll see if they get sick," Tanaka said.

Next she prepared samples for the electron microscope. She put tiny bits of Dudley's brain tissue into small test tubes and filled them with fast-drying plastic resin. She did the same with the dust from the Zecker-Moran box. The resin would penetrate the samples and harden them.

After all the samples became fixed in a hard plastic resin, Tanaka cut slices from the resin blocks, then went into the imaging room, where she placed the slices on copper sample screens.

"Let's look at the Cobra dust first," she told Austen. She dropped a copper-screen sample into a sample holder, then slid the holder into the electron microscope and locked it into place. She threw some switches and adjusted a dial. A screen glowed.

On the screen the two women saw an image of the dust particles from the cobra box. "This is weird," Tanaka said. The particles were crystals with slightly rounded sides, rather like soccer balls. She saw something inside a crystal and zoomed in on the image. "Look, Alice. Look at that."

Inside the crystals dark rods of material were scattered about, forming bundles in places. Tanaka pointed to a bundle. "I'd bet those are the virus particles themselves. You've got virus particles embedded in crystals."

Tanaka put another sample in the electron microscope. "We're looking inside one of Dr. Dudley's brain cells," she said. Some of the crystals inside the cells were cracking open and seemed to be releasing particles into the cell's cytoplasm—the cell's interior. The particles resembled rods or batons.

"Dr. Dudley's brain cells are a mess," she said to Austen in a low voice. "This is as bad as Ebola."

"Do you know what it is?" Austen asked. She suddenly felt dizzy, as if she were falling.

"There is a type of virus that makes crystals like this," Tanaka said. "It lives in butterflies and moths." She went over to a military transport box sitting in a corner of the imaging room and pulled out a textbook. She opened the volume and flipped through the pages until she came to a section on insect viruses. "There," she said. She pointed to a photograph that showed images of crystals.

"This is nuclear polyhedrosis virus," Tanaka said. "Let's call it NPV. You know, like HIV? This virus scares the daylights out of me. The crystals are like protective shells around the virus. This thing is an engineered weapon, Alice."

Tanaka returned to the microscope and began snapping photographs with the electronic camera that was attached to it. Image by image huge crystals appeared on a video screen.

"We have to tell Will," Tanaka said.

HOPKINS, dressed in surgical scrubs but not a space suit, had set up a work area on a table in the conference room. He would try to "see" the DNA of the virus using his two Felix machines. In this way he hoped to get a rapid identification of the virus.

Hopkins had a sample of Cobra dust in a small plastic test tube. The dust had been sterilized with chemicals and mixed with a few drops of water. It contained a quantity of DNA from the virus. He put a droplet of the water into a sampling port in one of the Felix machines. Nothing came up on the screen—Felix was having problems. Hopkins had to resist a temptation to bang Felix with his hand, the way you'd bang a television that isn't working.

Just then Austen and Tanaka came in. "Take a look at this," Tanaka said. She laid the photographs in front of Hopkins. "These particles are from Glenn Dudley's brain."

"Midbrain. The part of the brain that controls primitive behavior, such as chewing," Austen added.

"Look at the crystals, Will," Tanaka said. "See that blocky shape? This looks like the nuclear polyhedrosis virus, which lives in butterflies. It isn't supposed to live in people."

Hopkins stood up slowly, a look of wonder on his face. "It lives in people now," he said. "A butterfly virus. Suzanne, you're the best." He slapped her on the back.

She looked very pleased.

"All right!" Hopkins said. "What are we gonna do? Do we tell Frank Masaccio we've got a *butterfly* virus? He'll think we've gone lunatic. We need a gene fingerprint." Since many viruses look alike in a photoscope but are genetically very different, Hopkins would use Felix to prove this thing was a butterfly virus.

Using a micropipette, he put a sample of DNA into Felix. Austen found herself watching his hands as he worked. They were muscular, but they were gentle and precise in their motions. He tapped the computer keys, and letters of text began to appear:

TTGGACAAACAAGCACAAATGGCTATCATTATAGTCAAGTACAA
AGAATTAAAATCGAGAGAAAACGCGTTCTTGTAAATGCCTGCAC
GAGGTTTTAACACTTTGCCGCCTTTGTACTTGACCGTTTGATTG
GCGGGTCCCAAATTGATGGCATCTTTAGGTATGTTTTTTAGAGG
TATC

This was genetic code from somewhere in the DNA of the Cobra virus.

Molecules of DNA resemble a spiral ladder. The rungs of the ladder are known as the nucleotide bases. There are four types of bases, and they are denoted by the letters A, T, C, and G, which stand for the nucleic acids adenine, thymine, cytosine, and guanine. Human DNA consists of about three billion bases. That's enough information to fill three *Encyclopaedia Britannicas*. All of this information is crammed into every cell in the human body. A small virus, such as the virus for the common cold, has only about seven thousand bases of DNA. Hopkins guessed that the Cobra was complicated and would probably contain around fifty thousand to two hundred thousand bases of DNA.

Sometimes, using a computer program, as few as a dozen bases of DNA code are enough to match unknown code with known code. If you can make a match, you can identify the organism.

As strings of letters marched across the computer screen, Hopkins hoped that he would soon have a better idea of what kind of virus Cobra was. He ran Netscape on one of the Felix laptops. His computer then socketed into the World Wide Web. In a few seconds he arrived at a Web site known as GenBank, which has a huge database of genetic sequences. Hopkins clicked a button on the screen. The GenBank computer looked at the code and began matching it to known genetic codes. Soon an answer came back:

Autographa californica nuclear polyh . . . 900 4.3e-67 1

"Looks like we've got a rough identification," Hopkins said.

Cobra virus was similar to an NPV strain that lived in *Autographa californica,* a small brown-and-white moth that lives in North America. The caterpillar of the moth is a crop pest—a green inchworm known as the alfalfa looper. The virus invades the moth caterpillar and kills it. Cobra was based on a moth virus, but it had been altered.

NPV is a common virus used in biotech labs all over the world. It is available to anyone, and Hopkins's heart sank as he thought about this. The virus was going to be devilishly hard to trace back to its source. Furthermore, the genes of NPV can be changed easily without harming the virus. Many viruses are sensitive—if you change their genes, they stop working. But NPV is a tough, flexible virus. It can be given foreign genes that change its behavior as an infectious agent. Hopkins knew that buried somewhere in the code of the

Cobra virus he would find engineered genes—genes that had been put there, enabling the virus to replicate in human tissue.

Cobra was a recombinant virus, or a chimera. In Greek mythology the chimera was a monster with a lion's head, a goat's body, and a dragon's tail. "The chimera," Hopkins whispered, "was a tough monster to kill."

IN THE core, Special Agent James Lesdiu, the team's forensic-materials analyst, was running an analysis of the physical materials used in constructing the two boxes. When Austen came into the materials room, she found him sitting at a table holding a magnifying glass in one hand and a pair of tweezers in the other. He was dressed in an FBI biohazard suit, and he looked extremely uncomfortable. His Racal hood was beaded with sweat on the inside.

Lesdiu put his tweezers down. As Austen had discovered, the cobra boxes had bits of paper glued to them, on which were written the name Archimedes and the date. The bits of paper were glued to each box with a clear, flexible glue. With a razor blade Lesdiu cut away a tiny shred of the glue from Harmonica Man's box. Looking at it through the magnifying glass, he found black, powdery dirt embedded in the glue. "I'm going to nail this dirt," he said.

Using a solvent, he dissolved a bit of the glue in a small test tube and swirled the particles. A blackish-brownish haze hung in the liquid. Now he had to separate the particles. He rooted in one of the supply boxes and found a magnet. He held the magnet against the test tube. Black dust drifted toward the magnet. "It's a ferromagnetic material. It's iron or steel," he said. The brown haze did not move under the magnet. It was probably an organic material or rock or concrete dust. But having separated the dirt into two components—a black dust and a brown haze—Lesdiu had reached the end of what was possible with a Reachdeep portable operation. The sample of dust had to go to the FBI metallurgists in Washington, who would continue the analysis.

Into the test tube of dust he dropped a strong disinfectant to sterilize the contents, just in case it contained any live Cobra virus particles. A few minutes later a helicopter took off for Washington bearing the test tube. The team would have to wait several hours for the FBI metallurgists to tell them exactly what the black dust was.

LATE in the evening Will Hopkins had a breakthrough when the GenBank computer matched a genetic sequence from the screen of one of the Felixes to human rhinovirus. Hopkins jumped to his feet and ran to the window that looked out from the core to the conference room. He pounded on the glass. "Hey, everyone! Cobra's got a piece of the common cold in it!"

Using Felix, Hopkins continued picking the genes apart. He couldn't believe it. It took his breath away. *Impossible.* Cobra was partly a common cold. He couldn't figure how it had been mixed with a butterfly virus. It made no sense to him. Somehow the creators of Cobra had managed to make a sticky molecule of some kind on the virus particle that enabled it to grab on to the mucous membranes of the body, especially in the area of the mouth and nose.

"The victims look like they have a cold when they first get sick," Austen noted.

"This virus probably attaches itself to the eyelids—cold viruses do that—or to the membranes in the nose," Hopkins said. "That would explain the design of the cobra box—it blows virus in your face. I just wonder if it's engineered to get into the lungs, too."

"But how does it move to the brain?"

"It likes nerves," he said. "The optic nerves and the olfactory nerves in the nose are hard-wired straight into the brain. Cobra hits a mucous membrane and zooms for the brain. It's the ultimate head cold."

Governors Island, Monday Morning, April 27

SUZANNE Tanaka stayed up most of the night, working alone in the core. Most of the team had gone off to get some sleep. But she was too keyed up and decided to look at the mice again. It would be too soon to see any symptoms, but you never knew.

She bent over the clear plastic boxes. The mice, which are active at night, were moving around, as expected. They seemed fine except for one male mouse. He seemed wobbly. She looked at him more closely. He was chewing on a wooden nibble block. Chewing and chewing. But chewing is rodent behavior. She looked at the clock on the table. She had injected the mice with Glenn Dudley's brain material the night before, and now it was the early hours of the morning. That was too little time for a mouse, even with its fast metabolism, to be showing clinical signs of infection by Cobra. Nevertheless, the mouse's chewing behavior bothered her. She did not want to make any mistakes; she had begged Will Hopkins to put her in the group. She decided finally to take blood samples from all the mice. Maybe the blood would show signs of infection, maybe not.

She got some disposable syringes and pulled a leather glove over the surgical glove of her left hand. Then she opened a box and removed the first mouse, holding it in her left hand. The mouse struggled. She placed the needle under the mouse's skin and withdrew a few drops of blood. The mouse was struggling wildly. He's as afraid as I am, she thought. Just then the mouse flipped out of her left hand and landed across her right, which was covered only with a latex rubber glove. For an instant the mouse bit through the latex and hung on with its teeth before letting go. Tanaka gasped and juggled the mouse back into its box.

It was just a nip. For a moment she didn't think the animal had drawn blood. Then she saw it—two red dots on her right index finger. Was there any virus in the mouse's bloodstream? She had heard stories of people pricking their fingers in the army hot labs. If it was a hot agent, incurable, you had between ten and twenty seconds to remove the finger. Otherwise the agent would move down your finger and enter your main blood system, and it could go anywhere. You had a twenty-second window of opportunity to save your life by cutting off your finger.

She dashed over to a cargo box, found a scalpel, and slammed her hand down on the box. She held the scalpel with her left hand, poised to slash it down on her finger.

And didn't do it. Couldn't. This is crazy, she told herself. I don't want to lose my finger. And then the twenty seconds had passed, and the choice was no longer hers to make. She put the scalpel down. Sweat poured from her face. Her Racal hood fogged up, and Tanaka realized she was weeping. Stop this, she told herself. We don't even know if the virus can live in mice. I'll be all right. I will not tell anyone. Because they'll take me off the investigation.

ALICE Austen returned to the Reachdeep unit shortly after the sun came up. She found Suzanne Tanaka sitting in the conference room drinking coffee. Tanaka looked exhausted.

"You need to get some sleep, Suzanne," Austen said to her.

"I wish I could."

Hopkins was talking on the telephone to John Letersky of the navy's Biological Defense Research Program in Bethesda. "What I need, John, are some antibody probes for insect nuclear virus. We want to do quick environmental sampling for the presence of Cobra." A handheld biosensor device requires special antibody compounds known as probes in order to register the presence of a given hot agent. The probes are molecules that lock on to proteins in the hot agent. They change color as they lock on, and the biosensor device reads the color change.

"I hear you, Will. Let me start calling around."

Hopkins hung up. "I need some breakfast," he said to Austen. "What about you? Hey, Suzanne! Breakfast?"

"I'm not hungry. I'll eat later."

Manhattan, Monday

AUSTEN and Hopkins caught a helicopter to the East Thirty-fourth Street heliport. A few minutes later they were sitting in a coffee shop on First Avenue. "A four-star breakfast if you add in the airfare," Hopkins remarked.

Austen took a sip of coffee. She said, "How did you end up in Reachdeep, doing this?"

He shrugged. "My father was in the Bureau."

"Is he retired now?"

"No. He's dead."

"I'm sorry," she said.

"He was a field agent in Los Angeles. He and a partner went to talk with an informant, and they walked into a murder in progress. One of the subjects panicked and opened fire through the door when they knocked. My father was hit in the eye. I was thirteen. I grew up hating the Bureau, but I guess at some point I realized I was a cop, like my father."

"You're not a cop."

"I'm a type of cop, and I'm scared this investigation isn't going to work." He looked at the table and played with a spoon.

"I don't think we've diagnosed the disease yet," she said. "The self-cannibalism—we can't explain that."

The waitress brought a plate of fried eggs with bacon for Hopkins and fruit and an English muffin for Austen. "We do have a diagnosis, Alice," Hopkins said. "It's Cobra."

"No, we don't. Will, you're looking at the genetic code. I'm looking at the effect of the virus on people. We don't understand Cobra as a disease process." She thought, So many details. If you could fit them together, the pattern would emerge. "Will," she said, "how about the dust that James Lesdiu found? I'm wondering if it's steel dust from the subway."

"Steel dust? What's that?" Hopkins asked. He loaded egg and bacon into his mouth. Traffic went past outside the window.

"Ben Kly showed it to me. It's all over the subway tunnels. Two homeless men have died of Cobra, and they lived in a subway tunnel. I wonder if Archimedes lives in the subway."

"Impossible," Hopkins said. "You can't do lab work in the subway. A virus lab has to be spotlessly clean."

"If he had any steel dust on his fingertips, he might have spread some of it into the glue when he was making the box."

"All the dust shows is that Archimedes took the subway the day he made the box. Big deal."

"Maybe he's been exploring the subway to look for the best place to do a big release," she said.

ARCHIMEDES slept late by his own standards and was out of bed by seven in the morning. First he went into the staging area and suited up in a Tyvek suit. Then he entered level 3. He checked on the bioreactor. It was running smoothly. He checked on the viral glass. It had hardened nicely during the night. With double-gloved fingertips he picked out a hexagon, a sliver of brainpox viral glass, and loaded it into a widemouthed plastic flask. The flask would fit into his pocket. He screwed a black cap on the flask and tightened it. He dipped the flask in a pan full of bleach and water to sterilize the outside. The inside was hot in a biological sense. The hexagon contained perhaps a quadrillion virus particles.

He went down the stairs and out into the street. He walked for a while. It was a cool morning, with a high overcast and almost motionless air, the right kind of weather for a biological release.

He ended up in Greenwich Village, where he stopped for breakfast at a café. He took out the flask and put it on the table. It looked harmless, only a bottle wrapped in a plastic bag.

He mulled over his possibilities. The question was not just the power of the hot agent, but how it was to be dispersed. The boxes were okay for the phase I human trials, and it was clear they worked. The proof was the low-key warnings about the boxes now being broadcast on TV. It was time to move on to phase II—increasing the dosage and the number of people tested.

He reached into the pocket of his windbreaker, which was draped on the back of his chair, and pulled out a copy of a scientific report. He unfolded it and began to read "A Study of the Vulnerability of Subway Passengers in New York City to Covert Action with Biological Agents, Department of the Army, Fort Detrick, Maryland." It had been published in 1968, and he was reading it for about the hundredth time.

The study described how army researchers had filled glass lightbulbs with a powdered bacterial-spore preparation. The bacterial agent was *Bacillus globigii,* an organism that normally doesn't cause disease in humans. The researchers had dropped the lightbulbs full of spores at various locations on the tracks of the New York subway. The lightbulbs had shattered, and the spores had flown up into the air in puffs of gray dust. Subway trains whooshing through the tunnels carried the spores for miles. Within days the spores were disseminated throughout New York City.

"More coffee?" the waiter asked.

"No, thank you. Too much coffee makes me jittery."

Archimedes left the waiter a generous tip. Out on the sidewalk he headed eastward along a treelined street. He had conceived a strategy: He would not plan ahead. Then they couldn't predict his moves. He had a pane of viral glass in his pocket. By the end of the day it would be out in the world. In his apartment he had an additional eight hundred and ninety-one panes of viral glass. They would go into the world, too. Most of them all at once.

Walking home, he looked for a place to let the hexagon crystal go. As he turned south, heading for Houston Street, he had an idea. It might be taking a chance to do it so close to home, but this might bring more peace to his laboratory.

He arrived at the children's park next to his building. It was deserted. Good. He sat on the merry-go-round. It creaked under his weight. Then, using his gloved hand, he unscrewed the cap of the flask. He tipped the flask, and the piece of viral glass slid out onto the merry-go-round.

They will be back. They will jump on the merry-go-round, and they will yell and throw rocks at the cats, and meanwhile, their feet will be pounding the crystal to dust. *Shake the dust from your feet, children. You are a burden to the earth.*

HECTOR Ramirez, five years of age, went over to the merry-go-round. His mama sat on a bench talking with another lady. He climbed up on the merry-go-round and stood there for a moment. Then he saw it. He thought it might be candy and picked it up. It had colors in it, like a rainbow. He put it in his mouth. It seemed to turn rubbery and melt real fast in his mouth, but it didn't taste like candy. "Ew!" he said. He spit it out.

The cold symptoms came on in a matter of hours.

Governors Island

TWO helicopters lifted off from the heliport in lower Manhattan and crossed the East River. They passed over the coast-guard hospital and touched down in the middle of Governors Island. Five minutes later Frank Masaccio appeared with a group of men and women—FBI agents and New York Police Department investigators. They were the managers of his Cobra task force. They had arrived for the daily briefing.

There weren't enough chairs to go around. People sat on the floor. Masaccio brought the meeting to order. "You start, Hopkins."

Hopkins stood in front of the Felix devices and summarized the state of the Reachdeep investigation. The Cobra agent, he said, was a chimera, a recombinant virus that was a mixture of an insect virus and the common cold. Mixing the two viruses had produced a monster. "But that's not all that's going on in this virus," he said. "We're going to find more engineered DNA wetware in this virus. I'm sure of it."

Alice Austen and Suzanne Tanaka then gave their findings.

"My number one question is this," Frank Masaccio said to the Reachdeep team. "Are you any closer to the perpetrator?"

"It's hard to say," Hopkins answered.

"That answer sucks, Hopkins. I want this Archimedes. I want him yesterday." Masaccio summarized what had been happening outside Reachdeep. State and city health officials had been quietly informed of the situation. He also mentioned that his office had done "a tiny little news release" to the media.

"What?" Hopkins blurted.

"We had to warn people about the boxes, Will. We're saying it's a poison. We're not giving out that it's a germ weapon. But we can't keep a lid on this thing forever."

"I need an art historian," Hopkins said.

"What?"

"An art historian, Frank. Someone who can look at the boxes and tell us where they came from."

WITHIN the hour a helicopter landed on Governors Island carrying Herschel Alquivir, a professor of folk art from New York University. He was a slender man, middle-aged, with a passion for carved wooden objects.

Hopkins helped Alquivir put on an FBI biohazard suit, then led him to the core, where the professor examined the boxes. "They're children's toys," he said. "I think they were made in East Africa. Cobras don't live in East Africa. They live in Egypt, India, and other parts of southern Asia. But the king cobra is known, of course, to many people around the world. And there is a large Indian population in East Africa. I'd say the place of manufacture might be near the coast of the Indian Ocean, where the Indian influence is strongest."

That night two FBI agents from the New York office departed for Nairobi, Kenya.

New York and Washington, D.C., Tuesday, April 28

ARCHIMEDES was walking through the concourse of Penn Station with a flask containing one hexagon of viral glass tucked in his pocket. He looked at the Amtrak departures on the display board. A Metroliner train was leaving in ten minutes for Washington, D.C. He paid cash for a round-trip ticket.

IN THE Metro Center station of the Washington Metro at midday, a man was sitting on one of the benches along the wall of the station platform. A train came along. The man took a deep breath and stood up. As he was walking toward the train, he threw something along the platform casually, as if he were discarding a bit of trash, and he stepped onto the train. The shiny bit of trash broke into pieces and was quickly trodden underfoot by passing crowds. No one noticed that the man was wearing a flesh-colored latex rubber glove on his right hand or that he was holding his breath when he got on the train.

THE face of an FBI metallurgist appeared on a screen in the Reachdeep unit on Governors Island. "This dust you sent us is a type of medium-carbon steel. The annealed structure of the particles would indicate they formed through a pressure process such as the hot-rolling process."

"Railroad track," Austen said to Hopkins.

"We also found a grain of something that looks like pollen."

"Pollen? What kind?"

"We're trying to find out right now."

FBI agent Chuck Klurt consulted Dr. Edgar Adlington, a pollen expert at the Smithsonian Institution in Washington. Dr. Adlington was hunched over his desk in a windowless room that smelled of dried leaves. He was examining a flower under a magnifying lamp. Special Agent Klurt placed some microscope photographs of a single grain of pollen in front of Dr. Adlington. "We have a little problem. Can you tell me what this is?"

"Well, it is a pollen grain."

"Any idea what it came from, Dr. Adlington?"

Adlington studied the photographs. "This grain may come from one of several families of the Caprifoliaceae or certain of the Celastraceae, but if I had to say, I would place it in the family Oleaceae."

"Mmmm."

"Yes. And I would venture to say we are looking at *Forsythia intermedia* 'Spectabilis.' " He handed the photographs back to Klurt.

"So what is it?" the agent asked.

"I told you, it's forsythia, a flowering shrub."

Forsythia blooms in many places around New York City in the spring. Knowing that the pollen came from forsythia could not help pin down the location of the Unsub.

Nairobi, Wednesday, April 29

SPECIAL Agent Almon Johnston was a tall African American who had lived in Kenya for a year before he'd joined the FBI, having been posted there as a sales manager for an American company, so he knew his way around. Link Peters worked in the foreign counterintelligence division of the Bureau. He had never been to Africa until now.

They were joined by an officer from the Kenya National Police, Inspector Joshua Kipkel, who suggested they begin their search for cobra boxes by looking in some of the better shops on Tom Mboya Street and Standard Street in downtown Nairobi. They drove down the streets, stopping at the shops and showing the shopkeepers photographs of the boxes. All of the shopkeepers said they had seen such boxes, but they were out of stock.

Next Inspector Kipkel suggested they try the City Market.

The Nairobi City Market resembled an aircraft hangar. Inside, the two men were immediately surrounded by a knot of shopkeepers waving goods. When Johnston showed them photographs of the cobra boxes, the shopkeepers were certain they had seen such boxes. They were certain they could get more for the Americans. Meanwhile, would Johnston and Peters like to buy anything else? A beaded belt perhaps or a set of napkin rings? A carved mask?

For two hours the agents explored the City Market, stopping at all the shops, showing the photographs. No one could produce a box of the right type.

Inspector Kipkel said there was one more possibility—they should try outdoors, behind the building. They went out through a back door to a dusty open lot jammed with booths of people selling trinkets, people who couldn't afford the rent inside.

Kipkel made the break. Spotting an old lady with some small carvings, he went over to her. The boxes looked familiar. "Gentlemen, come over here."

On a plank table the old woman displayed a number of small

boxes that were not unlike the cobra boxes, except hers were made of gray soapstone, not wood. Johnston showed her photographs of the cobra boxes. "I know these things," she told him.

"Where do they come from?" Johnston asked her.

"Voi."

"What?"

"This is a town with many wood-carvers," Inspector Kipkel said. "Do you know who in Voi makes these boxes?" he asked her.

She hesitated. Johnston removed a wad of paper shillings from his pocket and handed her the banknotes. They were worth a few dollars.

Tucking the money away, she said, "Moses Ngona. He was my cousin. He passed away last year."

"Do you have any more of Mr. Ngona's boxes?"

She looked hard at him and said nothing. He handed her more banknotes. She reached down to a shelf beside her knees and pulled out a roll of old newspaper. She unrolled it and placed one wooden box on the plank.

Fiddling with the catch, Johnston opened it. A snake popped out. A king cobra. "Do you remember selling any of your cousin's boxes to any tourists?" he asked.

"Not many tourists here," she said. "There was a lady and a man from England. There was a man from America."

"Can you describe the American?"

"He was small. He had no hairs on his head. He was a little *mzungu*." *Mzungu* means white man, and it also means ghost. She smiled. "I give him two of my cousin's box. He give me twenty dollars!" Twenty dollars had made her month.

"When did this happen?"

"Oh, last year."

ALMON Johnston telephoned Masaccio and explained what they'd found. "A man paid the lady twenty dollars. That's way too high a price. And that's why the lady remembers. She's at police headquarters now. They're getting an artist to do a composite sketch. Link and I could start cross-checking the visa records. The problem is, about fifty thousand male Americans were issued visas to Kenya during the time period. It'll take forever to go through them."

"It's kind of a stretch, guys, but do it," said Masaccio.

That afternoon a fax machine in the Reachdeep unit extruded a composite drawing of a man's face. He wore glasses. He had a narrow nose and puffy cheeks. He was nearly bald, and he looked to be in his thirties or forties. Hopkins taped the drawing to the wall, where all the team members could see it.

Governors Island, Wednesday

IN THE biology room of the evidence core, Suzanne Tanaka inspected her mice. One animal seemed more active than the others and began grooming itself for long periods of time, but the periods of grooming activity were interspersed with periods of what looked like paralysis, when the mouse wouldn't move. Then it attacked itself. It gnawed at its front paws and pulled out some of its hair, especially in the belly. But the animal did not die.

With Austen watching, Tanaka killed the mouse and dissected it. Wearing triple gloves and full biohazard gear, she opened the mouse with a scalpel and obtained a sample of its brain. She prepped the brain material and scanned it in the electron microscope. Some of the brain cells contained Cobra crystals, but the brain tissue seemed less damaged than with humans infected with Cobra. The virus seemed to produce a nonfatal infection in a mouse.

"When did you see the first signs of illness in this mouse?" Austen asked. Tanaka didn't answer. "Suzanne?"

Suzanne looked up. Her lips were trembling. A drop of clear liquid fell from her nose.

"Suzanne!"

THE army medical management unit placed the first team casualty, technician Suzanne Tanaka, in a biocontainment hospital room on the second floor. They set up an access vestibule, where nurses and doctors could change into protective clothing before they entered. They started Tanaka immediately on an IV drip of ribavirin, a drug known to slow down the replication of some viruses. They told her not to worry. Yet with all their technology they were as helpless as doctors had been in the Middle Ages in the face of the black death.

They set up monitoring machines in her room and started her on Dilantin, an antiseizure medication. When she tried to bite her wrists and fingers, they restrained her arms with nylon straps tied to the bed frame. She was not incoherent, and she was deeply apprehensive of the future. "Will you stay with me, Alice?" she said in a thick voice.

Austen stayed with her as much as possible.

Tanaka said that she didn't feel very sick, just very "coldy." She did not know why she wanted to do "that thing." She could not find a word for wanting to destroy herself with her teeth.

HOPKINS continued to use the Felix machine to decode the genetic material in Cobra. All day Wednesday he ran samples of blood, tissue, and dust through Felix, pulling up genetic sequences from Cobra and trying to identify them. Gradually the structure of the organism's genes became clearer, yet parts of it mystified him. Cobra was a recombinant virus that had been engineered with skill and subtlety.

"It's a world-class weapon," Hopkins said to Littleberry and Austen late that afternoon. "It didn't come out of somebody's garage." Hopkins was staring at the screen. "Uh-oh. Look at this," he said. He had just fed a piece of code into GenBank. This is what had come up on the screen:

Variola major virus (strain Bangladesh-1975)

"Wow! Variola major! That's smallpox," Hopkins said. "Cobra's part smallpox."

Littleberry stared at the screen. He brought his fist down on the table. "Damn it!" he said. He turned and walked away.

INVISIBLE HISTORY (III.)

Manhattan, Wednesday Night

WITHIN the U.S. government, security matters are compartmentalized. Information from one agency flows to another through top managers. The flow is controlled by bureaucrats and intelligence people. This means that parts of the federal government don't know what other parts are doing. Files are routinely destroyed; people retire and die. The federal government does not know parts of its own history. The knowledge remains hidden in pockets.

In times of emergency, however, someone in one branch of the government may suddenly need information from someone in a different branch. Then these people have to sit down in a room together and trade sensitive information. This is secret oral history. It is not supposed to happen. It happens all the time.

On Wednesday night Littleberry telephoned Frank Masaccio and told him there was an area of knowledge that he, Masaccio, needed to become aware of, under conditions of security. Shortly afterward the two men entered the FBI command center in the Federal Building. Masaccio stopped before a steel door. It was the door to a secure room. He touched a combination keypad. As the two men settled into chairs around a small table, the door clicked shut.

"We've found a lethal smallpox gene in the Cobra virus," Littleberry said.

"Yeah?" The news didn't mean much to Masaccio.

"Hopkins calls it the rocketing gene. It makes a protein that rockets the virus particles around the infected cell. It destroys brain cells while it shoots the virus everywhere. That's why these people die so fast, Frank. The virus is rocketing through their brains."

Littleberry felt tired in his bones. Finding a piece of smallpox in the Cobra virus was like . . . dying. "It's strange, Frank. I'm proud of what I did as a scientist. But I'm sorrier than ever for what I did as a human being. How do you reconcile that?"

"You don't," Masaccio said.

"We tested strategic biosystems in the Pacific Ocean in the late '60s," Littleberry said. "We tested *everything* at Johnston Atoll—the lethal stuff, all the means of deployment. We learned what works. At the time President Nixon killed the program in late 1969, I was agonizing whether I should leave it. It was a decision I should have made for myself."

Following the program's cancellation, Littleberry decided that he had to do something to make up for his work with weapons. He applied to switch his officer's commission into the Public Health Service. He went to work for the Centers for Disease Control, where he took part in the war on smallpox. In the early 1960s a handful of doctors at the CDC had had an important idea: They would eradicate a virus from the planet. They chose the smallpox virus, variola, as the most likely candidate for total extinction, because it lives only in people. It doesn't hide in the rain forest in some animal, where you can't eradicate it.

"The last human case of smallpox occurred in Somalia in October 1977," Littleberry said. "Since then smallpox has never made another natural appearance anywhere on earth. We wiped it out. By 'we' I mean thousands of public-health doctors all over the world—doctors in India, doctors in Nigeria and China, doctors in Bangladesh with no shoes. Local people. Today, I'm afraid, you have to wonder just how successful the smallpox campaign really was."

What Littleberry had in mind was the surprise that history and nature came up with. It was the biotechnology revolution.

Cobra, Littleberry explained to Masaccio, was the direct result of the biotechnology revolution, which began in 1973, when scientists succeeded in putting working foreign genes into the bacterium *E. coli,* a microorganism that lives in the human gut. The genes they transplanted gave *E. coli* resistance to some antibiotics. The organisms with their new features—their resistance to antibiotics—were not dangerous. They could easily be wiped out by other antibiotics. The experiment was perfectly safe.

It was one of the historic experiments in twentieth-century science. Diseases would be cured in new ways, and great insights into the nature of living systems would follow. However, almost immediately scientists worried that moving genes from one microorganism to another could cause outbreaks of new infectious diseases or environmental disasters. The concern was very great: Recombinant organisms were frightening to think about. In 1975 scientists came up with guidelines to prevent accidents.

As it turned out, the concerns of Western scientists about the hazards of genetic engineering provided a blueprint for what was to become the Soviet bioweapons program. The Soviets established an ostensibly civilian biotechnology research organization called Biopreparat. Participating scientists sometimes called it simply the Concern. Its main business was the creation of biological weapons.

A complex of research institutes was set up in Siberia to develop advanced virus weapons. The centerpiece of the complex was the Institute of Molecular Biology at Koltsovo, twenty miles east of the city of Novosibirsk. The cover story was that the institute was dedicated to making medicines. But in 1991 a U.S. inspection team learned that the facility had bioreactor tanks for growing smallpox virus.

Masaccio sat in silence as he took in the context in which the Cobra Event was being played out.

"A lot of countries are into biological weapons now," Littleberry said. "Syria has a top-notch biological-weapons program. Syria is also believed to be a sponsor of terrorism. You would know more about that than I do, Frank. If Syria's got a program, you can wonder if Israel has gone seriously into black biology. Iran is heavily into biological weapons. They are also testing cruise missiles. China has massive biological-weapons facilities out in the Sinkiang desert. Sooner or later there is going to be a very serious biological accident. And I think it will be global, not just one city."

Littleberry went on to say that he sometimes wondered if there had already been major incidents. "The Gulf war syndrome," he said, "is almost certainly caused by exposure to chemical weapons. But we have not ruled out the possibility that it's some kind of biological weapon. You never know."

"What about Cobra? Did it escape from somewhere, Mark?"

"I doubt it. Someone stole it from a lab is my guess."

"And Russia? What's going on there now?"

"That's real touchy stuff. Real ugly. Real sensitive."

Littleberry explained that the staff at the Koltsovo Institute of Molecular Biology had numbered four thousand in 1991. By 1997, after economic troubles had hit Russia, the staff had shrunk to about two thousand. "So," he said, "two thousand scientists and staff members from Koltsovo no longer work there. Some of them are missing. Some have left Russia. Some are working for bio-weapons programs in other countries, probably in Iran and Syria, possibly in Iraq and perhaps in Asian countries. What strains they took with them and where they are now are questions that bedevil intelligence agencies.

"Today Biopreparat is broke and is trying to make money any way it can. It is very difficult to find a knowledgeable expert who believes that Russia has given up developing offensive biological weapons. The program is probably smaller in scope, but it is believed to continue at secret locations.

"Biopreparat was a Humpty-Dumpty," Littleberry continued. "It broke into pieces when the Soviet Union fell. The Biopreparat that's visible today makes face cream and vodka. But there may be other invisible pieces floating around. Dangerous fragments. Maybe Biopreparat has an evil child. Maybe the evil child has no connection to Russia anymore."

"So you think an evil child has put together the Cobra virus?" Masaccio said incredulously. "You think it's the Russians?"

Littleberry smiled. "Not exactly, Frank. This Cobra virus is so beautiful and so new that it has to be American engineering. But the smallpox in it—that's ancient and old and smells like Russia. I think Cobra has two makers. One is American and one is Russian. They've gotten together somehow, and there's money involved. I think Cobra does come from an evil child. And I think the evil child is an American company that is operating somewhere near New York City."

PART SIX: The Operation

Manhattan, Thursday, April 30

ALICE Austen was with Colonel Ernesto Aguilar, chief of the TAML unit, and two army nurses in an army medevac helicopter that had just lifted off from the Thirty-fourth Street heliport. It was carrying a five-year-old boy named Hector Ramirez, who lived on Avenue B. Hector was conscious, lying strapped on a gurney and covered with blankets. His lips, behind a clear oxygen mask, were bloody and torn. He stared at the ceiling of the chopper, and his brown eyes had a tawny gold center.

"Watch him. He's seizing," Dr. Aguilar said.

Hector Ramirez turned diagonally under the straps, and his head lashed back and forth. He began biting his lips behind the oxygen mask. An army nurse, Captain Dorothy Each, yanked it off with her gloved hands and held his head. It was impossible to control the boy's jaws, which continued to work as the helicopter descended to Governors Island. Austen, also wearing gloves, grabbed the boy's wrists. She was impressed with how strong a five-year-old could be.

Captain Each transferred her grip to the boy's jaw, holding it tightly in both hands to keep him from biting. Suddenly the boy arched his back. His teeth flashed, and he bit down hard on Captain Each's left hand. His teeth tore the rubber glove.

"Oh!" the nurse said. She pulled away momentarily, but then she was back over the boy, holding his head and jaw. Austen saw how her hand bled. Nobody said anything about it. Everyone understood that she would be placed in biocontainment quarantine.

THE boy's mother, Ana Ramirez; the boy's aunt, Carla Salazar; and his ten-year-old sister, Ana Julia, were admitted as patients in the medical management unit, where they were attended around the clock. The boy's mother exhibited symptoms of the common cold. She was deeply afraid and almost hysterical about her child.

The doctors had set up a biocontainment intensive care unit in the north wing of the coast-guard hospital. Hector Ramirez was placed there, along with Suzanne Tanaka.

The nursing staff had tied soft cords of gauze around his wrists and ankles and across his chest. They'd done their best to immobilize his head, but his mouth was uncontrollable. His eyes were half open, the pupils darting. "Mama!" he said. "Mama!"

Austen approached the boy and touched his forehead. Through her glove she could feel his facial muscles tightening and twitching.

WILL Hopkins entered the intensive care unit. He was dressed in a protective suit. The antibody probes had arrived from the navy, and Hopkins had programmed them into a Boink biosensor. "I've got a handheld unit that'll detect Cobra, I think."

The staff had taken samples of the boy's blood. Hopkins mixed a few drops in a tube containing salt water, then put a drop of the bloody water into the sample port of the device. It gave off a chiming sound. "Cobra," Hopkins said, looking at the screen.

Suzanne Tanaka was now suffering agonies in a bed on the other side of the unit. Hopkins tested her blood, and the answer was obvious. "I'm sorry," he said.

She could not answer, and it was not clear that she even heard.

Hopkins went down the hall to see Captain Dorothy Each. She had been placed in a biocontainment room. She was sitting in a chair reading a book, a bandage over the cut on her hand. Hopkins tested her blood. There was no sign of Cobra. "Looks good, but it's really too early to tell," he said to her.

"Thanks, anyway," Captain Each said to him.

AUSTEN continued to watch Hector Ramirez. She felt she was on the verge of understanding something important. The pattern was emerging, and then it slipped.

A doctor walked in with test results. Hector's white-cell count was too high. "His uric acid's high also," the doctor said.

"It's probably the result of his seizures," Dr. Aguilar said. People having muscle breakdown have high uric-acid counts.

Austen was remembering something. She ran the images of Kate Moran's autopsy through her mind. She remembered the golden-yellow streaks in the girl's kidneys. That was damage by uric acid. Something moved in Austen's mind. It was like a bird fluttering its wings. "Could you please loosen the boy's straps?" Austen asked. "I want to see how he moves his legs."

The medical staff hesitated but did as she asked.

With the straps loosened, the boy assumed a peculiar posture. One arm was bent toward his mouth, and the opposite leg was bent. The other leg was straight. It was a diagonal thrashing of the body, his legs crossing in an abrupt scissoring motion. The posture indicated damage to the midbrain. The diagnosis clicked.

"They eat themselves. They're children," Austen said with sudden clarity. "Lash . . . Lesch . . . What is it called, Dr. Aguilar?"

"Oh, no," Aguilar whispered. Suddenly he had seen it, too.

"High uric acid," she said.

"Yeah. This kid looks like he has Lesch-Nyhan syndrome."

LESCH-NYHAN syndrome is an extremely rare disease. It occurs once in a million births, and it occurs naturally only in boys. It is caused by a genetic mutation on the X chromosome, which is the chromosome every child inherits from his or her mother. Lesch-Nyhan boys lack an enzyme that breaks down a metabolic waste product, and the end result is a huge excess of uric acid in the bloodstream. That enzyme is called HPRT.

A boy with Lesch-Nyhan syndrome seems normal as a baby, except the parents notice what they sometimes describe as orange sand in the diaper. These are crystals of uric acid being passed from the kidneys. By the baby's first birthday there is something definitely wrong. The boy becomes spastic. He does not learn how to crawl or walk. His limbs become stiff. The body tends to assume the characteristic "fencing" posture of Lesch-Nyhan syndrome—one arm bent, the opposite leg bent. As the boy's teeth come in, he begins biting his lips and fingers. The action is uncontrollable.

Often doctors have trouble making a diagnosis. The boy may not be retarded. He may have normal intelligence, but it's hard to tell. He can't speak well, although his eyes are bright and alert. As he grows older and stronger, he attacks the people he loves, lashing out with his arms and legs, biting at them, and using obscenities. It is clear he is capable of love, and he forms strong attachments to his caregivers even while he is attacking them.

The pain of self-injury is excruciating for these children. They know what they are doing but can't stop. When they feel an episode coming on, they beg to be restrained. A Lesch-Nyhan boy may survive to young adulthood, but at some point he will die of kidney failure or self-injury.

FRANK Masaccio flew to Governors Island with the senior managers of his joint task force. They arrived at the conference room as Austen was giving a presentation to the Reachdeep team. She was telling the group how the Cobra virus appears to trigger a kind of Lesch-Nyhan disease in both men and women.

Masaccio was listening to this. Listening and staring at the fax on the wall that showed the face of an American tourist who might or might not be the Unsub, the unknown subject. Masaccio was trying to see how to use the new information to move the investigation forward. Now he turned to his senior people. "I see where we can go. We need to look at every biotech company that's doing research into this disease. We get their lists of employees. We see if any of them was issued a visa to Kenya. If we get a match, we've got Archimedes."

HECTOR Ramirez died late that afternoon. By that time the investigation had moved into financial territory. The New York field office's joint task force on Cobra studied recent Securities and Exchange Commission filings by companies in the biotechnology industry. They found nothing there. Agents telephoned the headquarters of the Food and Drug Administration in Maryland and asked for information on any new drug-research applications involving Lesch-Nyhan syndrome.

In a matter of hours investigators had determined that there were only two companies in the United States currently doing FDA-reviewed research into Lesch-Nyhan syndrome. One was a publicly held company in Santa Clara, California. The other was a privately held company in Greenfield, New Jersey. It was called Bio-Vek, Inc. Bio-Vek had recently submitted a filing with the FDA for permission to start phase I clinical trials of a bioengineered treatment for Lesch-Nyhan syndrome. Bio-Vek had just fifteen full-time employees.

"This feels right," Frank Masaccio said. "This Bio-Vek is where we want to look."

Greenfield, New Jersey, Friday, May 1

BIO-VEK, Inc., was located in a suburban business park. As the investigative team cruised past in a pair of unmarked FBI cars, Mark Littleberry pointed to some tall silver pipes coming out of the roof. "Vent stacks," he said. "Looks like they're venting a biocontainment lab. Level two or level three."

The two FBI cars parked in a back lot, out of view. Hopkins, Austen, and Littleberry got out. Littleberry was carrying a small Halliburton case, containing a Boink biosensor and a swab kit.

The Reachdeep team walked casually up to the entrance. Masaccio had decided to use some of the Reachdeep people for this part of the investigation, since they would know the questions to ask.

Leading the way inside, Hopkins told the receptionist that the group was from the FBI and was there to see Dr. Orris Heyert, the company's president.

"Was he expecting you?" the woman said.

"No, but this is important," Hopkins said.

She called Dr. Heyert on her telephone. In a moment he came through a door into the lobby, a puzzled expression on his face. He was a handsome man in his forties. He had dark hair, a smooth haircut. The sleeves of his shirt were rolled up, and there were many cheap pens in his pocket. He had the start-up–company look.

In his office—small and cluttered, with pictures of his wife and children on the shelves—they got down to business.

"I realize this is unexpected," Hopkins said, "but we need your help in an investigation."

"My company is not the subject of this investigation, I hope?"

"No. We are searching for an unknown suspect who has been making terrorist threats involving an infective biological agent. We have reason to think that he's knowledgeable about Lesch-Nyhan syndrome. We need your expertise and advice."

"This is very strange," Heyert said.

"Why?" Hopkins said. He looked calmly at Heyert. Time passed. More time passed. Heyert clearly expected Hopkins to say something more, but Hopkins did not. He just watched Heyert.

Finally Heyert answered, "Well, it just seems strange."

"Have you fired any employees lately? We're wondering if a disgruntled former employee might be making these threats."

"Nobody has left in a while. Our employees are very loyal."

"Can you describe the research your company is doing?"

"We are trying to find a cure for Lesch-Nyhan syndrome," Dr. Heyert said. "We are using gene therapy. This involves putting new genes directly into cells. We use viruses to put the genes into the cells. These viruses are called vectors. If you infect tissue with a vector virus, it will add genes or alter the genes."

"What kind of virus are you using?" Hopkins asked.

"Several, but principally the nuclear polyhedrosis virus."

"Oh," Hopkins said. "Doesn't that virus live in insects?"

"Normally, yes."

"Can you tell me, Dr. Heyert, what strain you are using?"

"*Autographa californica,* modified to enter human brain cells."

"I'm curious, Dr. Heyert," Hopkins said. "Could this virus be engineered so that it not only enters the brain but replicates there? Could it then spread from person to person?"

Heyert laughed in a way that seemed to Austen rather forced. "Good grief, no."

"There have been indications that the suspect plans to injure people with this insect virus."

There was another long pause. "This is way off base," Heyert said. "Statements like that are frankly offensive to me. I am a physician. What we are trying to do here is alleviate suffering. Have you ever seen a Lesch-Nyhan child?"

Orris Heyert led the investigators into a laboratory in a back wing of the building. As they were passing through the lab, Littleberry whispered to Hopkins, "Those vent stacks we saw on the roof—they're coming from somewhere near here. There's a level three unit around here, but we haven't seen it yet."

They went around a corner and entered a small waiting room. There were a few chairs and a door that said CLINIC. "We have a patient in the observation room with his mother," Heyert said. "His name is Bobby Wiggner."

Heyert brought Austen and Hopkins into the room. Littleberry chose to stay outside.

Bobby Wiggner was a young man. On his chin appeared the faintest beginnings of a beard. He lay in a wheelchair in a half-straightened posture. His back was sharply curved, his body rigid. A rubber strap across his chest held him in place. His mother sat on a chair facing him, reading to him from a book. His legs were crossed—scissored and rigid. He had no lips. From his wheelchair dangled an array of Rubatex straps. His hands were not tied down.

Austen and Hopkins introduced themselves. "Wha uh uh wah?" Bobby said. What do you want? He obviously had trouble speaking.

"We just wanted to see you and to say hello," Austen said.

"How are you feeling today?" Hopkins said.

"Uh guh tub uh." Pretty good today.

His body went into a writhing motion, the back arching. Suddenly his arm lashed out, aiming for Austen's face. She jerked her head back. Bobby Wiggner moaned, "Sorry. Sorry."

"It's okay."

"He needs his restraints," his mother said.

Quickly, with deft movements, Mrs. Wiggner and Dr. Heyert tightened the Rubatex straps around the young man, fastening his wrists to the chair.

"This is a vertically divided mind," Dr. Heyert said. "The brain stem has been deranged and wants to attack the things it loves. The higher cortex—the conscious, thinking part of the mind—hates this but can't control it."

Bobby looked at Austen and said something she did not understand.

"I'm sorry. Could you say that again?" she said.

"My son is asking if you are a *Star Trek* fan," the mother remarked. "He always asks people that."

Hopkins sat down on a chair next to Bobby. "I am," he said.

"Wee, too," Bobby said.

Hopkins listened. He found he could understand the words. Soon they were deep in conversation about their favorite episodes.

Austen watched Hopkins. He was leaning forward, and she could see the muscles of his back and shoulders through the jacket. She thought, He's very gentle. Abruptly she realized she had stopped seeing him in a purely professional way. But this was not the moment for that kind of thing, and she put it out of her mind.

IN THE waiting room, Mark Littleberry asked an employee the way to the men's room, then went off in that direction. Carrying the Halliburton case, he hurried down a hallway toward the center of the building. He found an unmarked door. On the far side was a short corridor leading to another door marked with the numeral 2. He opened it. Now he was in a corridor even shorter than the first one. There were some white Tyvek coveralls on a shelf and some full-face respirator masks hanging on a wall. At the end of this corridor was yet another door. This one had a window in it, with a biohazard sign on the window and the numeral 3.

He looked through the window at a small room. On a table in the center sat a bioreactor. The unit was marked with the name of a manufacturer—Biozan. He reached up for one of the masks and put it on. Then he opened the door.

The Biozan reactor was running. From the upper lid of the unit came tangles of flexible tubing. A pinkish red liquid was draining out of the Biozan into a glass collection jar, which sat on the floor. The cells in the reactor were sick and were pouring out virus particles into the liquid, and then the virus-saturated liquid was running out of the Biozan.

Littleberry opened the Halliburton and pulled out a sterile swab. He stripped off the wrapping and jammed the swab into the exit port of the Biozan. He held a Boink biosensor unit in his hands. He stuck the swab into the sample port of the Boink.

It chimed. The screen read COBRA.

He jammed the swab into a sample tube and dropped it into the Halliburton. He had seen enough. Time to get out of here. He opened the door, went out, and hung the mask back on the wall. Then he headed out through the vestibule.

As he emerged into the main hallway, he encountered a woman. Their eyes met. It was Dr. Mariana Vestof, whom he had seen just a week earlier, during his UNSCOM inspection of the Al Ghar site in Iraq. He blurted out, "I was looking for a men's room."

Time hung suspended. Then she smiled. "Still inspecting toilets, Dr. Littleberry?"

"Still making vaccines, Dr. Vestof?"

At that moment Hopkins and Austen appeared, coming down the hall, followed by Heyert. The sight of Hopkins seemed to paralyze Dr. Vestof for a few seconds. Hopkins reacted not at all.

"I will attend to some business," Dr. Vestof said, turning away.

Hopkins looked at his watch. "Well, thank you, Dr. Heyert. You've been very helpful."

Once outside, Hopkins, Austen, and Littleberry dived into the waiting FBI car. Hopkins was on his cell phone immediately with Frank Masaccio. He asked for perimeter surveillance to be thrown around the Bio-Vek building. "Mark says it's a weapons facility. He took a sample from a bioreactor, and it came up positive for

Cobra." He explained who Dr. Vestof was. "I saw her last week in Iraq. She's Russian-born, lives in Geneva. Bio-Vek may be connected to BioArk, the company that Vestof said she works for."

"Welcome to the global village," Littleberry said.

AT BIO-VEK, Dr. Heyert, Dr. Vestof, and two other managers sat in the conference room. Heyert was speaking. "I want production stopped immediately. I want those rooms nuked with bleach. We will restart the production line with our nonweaponized virus. Destroy all weaponized product, including the master seed cultures. Erase all data pertaining to the project from the computers."

"If they search, I assume they'll find nothing," Dr. Vestof said.

"The problem is Tom Cope," Heyert said. "He's done something. I don't know what, but they are looking for him. He was a sick man—Cope. I knew it at the time. When we fired him, that number four Biozan went with him. He stole it. He must have taken a master seed culture of the weapon."

Dr. Vestof held Dr. Heyert in a hard gaze. "That is incredible. The Concern will be appalled."

Sweat was pouring from Heyert. "This isn't my fault."

"You are the manager of this division," she replied coolly.

"Where is Cope now?" Heyert asked his managers.

No one had any idea.

Dr. Vestof decided to fly out that night. The American subsidiary was about to blow up, and she didn't want to be anywhere near the United States when that happened.

THAT night on Governors Island, Special Agent Oscar Wirtz readied his people for an operation. His squad consisted of six agents from the Hostage Rescue Team who were trained in chemical, nuclear, and biological hot operations. It was clear that a freeze-and-seize raid would be made on Bio-Vek, but it was not clear when. Masaccio wanted to wait to see if more evidence would develop, and he also hoped that the surveillance of the company might lead directly to the Unsub.

The rule of thumb the FBI uses for a freeze-and-seize raid is for the evidence team to outnumber the employees at the site. One agent is assigned to each employee. The employee is ordered to move away from any company equipment and then to freeze. The entire company can become federal evidence. Masaccio thought the raid on Bio-Vek could be accomplished with about forty agents, including the Reachdeep operations squad. He gave Hopkins the job of getting a search warrant.

At one o'clock in the morning, agents watching the Bio-Vek building observed Heyert putting paper into a shredding machine.

"That's it. They're destroying evidence. Freeze them," Masaccio shouted. He was sitting in the command center of the Federal Building in New York City. Helicopters took off from Governors Island. Bureau cars converged on Bio-Vek.

Alice Austen did not go on the raid. She stayed with Suzanne Tanaka, sitting by her bedside, wearing a protective suit. She was with her when Tanaka died.

FBI agents found Heyert in his office talking on the telephone. They served him with a search warrant and informed him that all of Bio-Vek, Inc., was being confiscated as federal evidence. They did not place him under arrest. They asked him if he would mind waiting voluntarily in his office until Hopkins could speak with him. Heyert agreed to wait. He did not want to seem to be fleeing.

Wearing a space suit, Littleberry led Hopkins and Wirtz, both also in protective suits, straight to the bioreactor room. The bioreactor was shut down, and the room stank of bleach. They took out swabs and collected samples. Hopkins ran the samples through a handheld Boink. It chimed and chimed. The effort to clean the room had failed completely. The bleach had killed the virus but could not destroy all the DNA of the dead virus particles.

They went back to the office, where agents waited with Dr. Heyert. Hopkins sat down facing Heyert, with Littleberry next to him. They removed their face masks. Hopkins said, "I want to offer you an opportunity to make the right decision, Dr. Heyert. We have found evidence that you are making biological weapons here. Your company has been seized, and you are under investigation. I believe you will be arrested in violation of Section 175 of Title 18 of the United States Criminal Code. That's the biological-weapons section. Conviction can result in life imprisonment. If the crime is connected to a terrorist act, then it is a capital crime, and the death penalty can be imposed."

Heyert stared at him.

"We can't do a plea bargain with you," Hopkins continued. "But if you cooperate with us, we can recommend leniency to the sentencing judge."

"I haven't committed any crime. If there was anything wrong, it was an accident."

"We took samples from your bioreactor yesterday, when you were running hot, Dr. Heyert. We found a virus. It's a nasty mixture of an insect virus, smallpox, and the common cold. It seems to alter a gene in the human body, creating Lesch-Nyhan syndrome in normal people. It is a lethal weapon."

"This is a lie."

"The evidence will be introduced at your trial. You could be charged as an accessory to terrorism."

Heyert was deeply frightened now. "There have been deaths?"

"You tell me," Hopkins said.

Something began to fracture inside Heyert. "It isn't my fault."

Littleberry, who had been staring at Heyert with a fierce expression, yelled, "Then whose fault is it?"

"We don't control things," Heyert said. "We are controlled by BioArk, the Concern. BioArk is our silent general partner. I'm an employee. I am only a middle manager."

"There's a terrorist threatening New York. Who is he?" asked Hopkins.

Heyert almost shuddered. "His name is Tom Cope. He's a good scientist. We hired him to do research on the virus. It wasn't able to replicate in human tissue very well. He fixed it."

"Why did you want the virus to replicate in human tissue?"

There followed a long pause. Heyert seemed on the edge of tears. "I have a family," he said. "I am afraid for them."

"Why?"

"BioArk. I am afraid. These people are . . . without pity."

"We can't make any promises," Hopkins said. "But if you help us and agree to testify, there is a Witness Protection Program."

"I'm more afraid of BioArk than I am of you." The words tumbled out. Heyert couldn't stop now. "BioArk is a biotechnology company. Part of its business—only part of it—is black research into weapons. They also make medicines. They were paying me and my staff well, but if we talked, we would be killed. They located a subsidiary here because this is . . . well . . . this is America, where the most talented people in biotechnology are. They set up Bio-Vek to do weapons research in focused areas. One of them was the development of NPV as a weapon. I—I hired Tom Cope to figure out how to get NPV to infect humans. There is very big money in this, Mr. Hopkins."

"What about the patients, the kids with Lesch-Nyhan?"

"I am a doctor. I do want to help them. It's just that there's no money. It's a rare disease."

"Cope—did he develop the virus?"

"No. Others at BioArk had mostly developed it already. Tom merely sharpened the edge of the weapon. I fired him because he was unreliable and seemed . . . really odd, kind of scary."

"How much virus did he steal?" Hopkins asked.

"I don't know. . . . He stole a Biozan."

"A bioreactor?" Littleberry said.

"Yes." Heyert was trembling.

"We need to see your records on Cope," Hopkins said.

Thomas Cope was the Unsub no longer. The employee file contained his company photo ID. He was of medium height, with hair thinning on top but not completely gone. He was thirty-eight years old, and he wore metal-framed eyeglasses.

Hopkins telephoned the information on Cope to Frank Masaccio, who put his task force to work on it. They ran a credit check on

Cope. This is one of the easiest and best ways to locate someone. They found out that he had been using a Visa card under his own name to order laboratory equipment, which was shipped to a mail drop at a shopping center in East Brunswick, New Jersey.

Hopkins was now standing in the parking lot of Bio-Vek, talking on his cell phone to Masaccio. Masaccio said, "We're going to have Cope in a day or two, maybe in hours. Hold on a minute, Will. I have to take a call."

Just then Hopkins's beeper went off. He checked it. It was the contact number for SIOC in Washington.

When Masaccio came back on the line, he sounded like a different man. "We've got a problem in Washington," he said.

Governors Island, Saturday, May 2

THE second Cobra Event SIOC meeting began thirty minutes later. It was ten in the morning when Hopkins and Littleberry landed on Governors Island. They went straight to the conference room in the Reachdeep unit, where Austen was already in a videoconference with Washington. Masaccio was sitting beside her.

From his office at the FBI's National Security Division, Steven Wyzinski had given the order—with White House approval—to deploy disaster medical groups in Washington. Overnight there had been eleven deaths in the capital from what looked like Cobra.

"The news media is starting to go berserk," said Jack Hertog of the National Security Council. "They're saying it may be food poisoning. They're also saying it may be deliberate. What if we've just been bombed with a chemical weapon?"

The CDC's Walter Mellis was in the SIOC room with him. "We've got a team in place, and we're looking at the epidemiology now," he said. "I have a preliminary result."

"What is it?" Hertog asked brusquely, turning to Mellis.

"All the cases seem to have been commuters on the Washington Metro. There was a release of hot agent in the subway."

"Damn," Hertog cried. "What's the casualty projection?"

"We've seen only eleven cases so far, which tells us that this was a small release," Mellis said.

"A warning," Hopkins said.

Mellis turned aside and listened. Someone was speaking to him. Then he said, "We have confirmation that the agent in Washington is, in fact, Cobra virus."

Jack Hertog laid down the White House line. He said, "I am here to tell you that the President of the United States will hold a news conference later today. He is going to explain to the American people what is happening. It seems that the Reachdeep operation has failed totally."

"We have the Unsub's name," Hopkins said. Silence fell over the SIOC team. "His name, we believe, is Thomas Cope. He is a former employee of Bio-Vek, Inc., a biotech company in New Jersey."

Cope's face appeared on screens in Washington.

"Is he under arrest?" Hertog asked.

"Not yet," Frank Masaccio said.

"That's not good enough," Hertog said. "Where is he?"

Masaccio explained about Cope's mail drop in New Jersey. "He recently placed an order for breathing filters from a company in California. The shipment went by Federal Express, marked for Saturday delivery. It's due in today. We've got nearly a hundred agents waiting to nail him when he comes to get that package. I'm confident we'll have him soon."

"Cut the bull," Hertog shouted. "People are dying here. This is not Podunk. This is *Washington.* People who run the world live here. You marshmallows with your test tubes have left us open to a real mess. I want some straight FBI work here, coordinated with anybody else who knows how to get results. I want those Reachdeep jerks off this case, and I want your top guys, Frank, your pros, taking this one down fast."

AUSTEN and Hopkins sat facing each other in the conference room outside the Reachdeep core. They had had nothing to do for hours except talk about the case. Mark Littleberry was out on the deck outside the conference room, staring across the water at the city. He'd been there for a long time.

"I'm worried that Masaccio's going down a blind alley," Hopkins said. "What if Cope doesn't pick up his mail? He could be anywhere."

Austen doodled with a pencil on her map of the city. "You know, I've been thinking. The cases in New York fall in one part of the city. Look." She showed him on the map. She pointed to lower Manhattan, toward the eastern side. Her finger moved over Union Square, where Kate Moran had lived; over East Houston Street, where Harmonica Man and Lem had lived; over the Lower East Side, where Hector Ramirez lived, and then to the Sixth Avenue flea market on Twenty-sixth Street, where Penny Zecker and Kate Moran had met. "When you have a cluster of illnesses, you go out and find the threads that link them," she said. "Cope is the thread."

"You can't check that out. We're grounded." Hertog had made it clear that Reachdeep was restricted to Governors Island and to doing lab work only.

Nagged by the possibilities, Austen went to the hospital wing, where the army medical management unit was situated. She put on a protective suit and headed for the rooms where the family of Hector Ramirez was quarantined. Hector's young mother, Ana, was now in critical condition and was not expected to live.

Austen visited Carla Salazar, Ana's older sister. Carla had shown no sign of Cobra infection, but she had been kept in quarantine. She was frightened and distraught over the condition of her sister and the death of her sister's little boy.

Austen sat down next to her. "Do you feel okay?"

"I am okay now. But what about later?" She began to cry.

"I want to show you a picture, Mrs. Salazar." Austen handed her a color photocopy of Cope's face.

Carla Salazar studied the image for a moment. "Maybe I have seen this man," she said. "Is this who murdered my sister's son?"

"It is possible. Who is he?"

"I'm trying to think. I seen him a couple times, I think. I'm not sure. I think he's the guy that yelled at some of the boys one time. He was real mad. It was something about a cat."

HOPKINS telephoned Masaccio. "Frank, listen. We have a possible identification. One of the Ramirez boy's relatives thinks she remembers Cope in the neighborhood."

"How strong is she about it?"

"Weak. But this could be real."

"Will, look, I know it's tough being shut out of the investigation, but there's nothing I can do about it. You're not a street agent. You're a scientist. We're set up and going to take Cope. My guess is it's going to happen any minute now."

"He could do a lot while you're waiting around here."

"The guy's modus has not been to try to destroy a city. He had his chance, and he didn't take out Washington."

"He has been in the testing phase," Hopkins said. "What if he's finished with his tests?"

"All right, I'll send someone to run your lead for you. When I get someone available."

"LET'S do the important elements again," Hopkins told Austen.

They had been trying to find a pattern, but nothing was coming. She listed the details she thought had meaning. "We have Hector's aunt, who thinks she saw Cope. That would be around Avenue B. We have Harmonica Man living nearby on Houston Street. We have the black dust in the glue—it's subway dust."

"And there was a pollen grain in the dust, remember? Forsythia."

"We need to go to that part of the city and look in the subway tunnels again," she said.

Hopkins slammed his hand on the wall. He knew they were supposed to be off the case. He looked around, then picked up his gun and holster, which had been sitting next to a Felix. He took a Saber radio—his last voice contact with the federal government. He picked up a handheld biosensor, programmed to detect Cobra. He also took a color Xerox of Tom Cope's photograph. The mild bespectacled face stared at nothing. Hopkins folded the paper and put it into his pocket.

Mark Littleberry came in from the deck. "Where are you going?"

"Stay here," Hopkins said, "and do the explaining if anyone asks where we've gone."

Austen and Hopkins walked out the front door of the hospital and down the long steps. The hospital was quiet now, the army doctors gathered in the biocontainment suite. Austen and Hopkins passed down an avenue of plane trees and arrived at a pier, where a police launch was tied up, manned by two cops. They were listening to a news-radio station that was carrying sketchy reports of some kind of outbreak of disease in Washington.

"Can you guys give us a lift?" Hopkins asked.

As far as the cops knew, Reachdeep team members still had a priority for anything they wanted, and the two policemen were happy to oblige.

After Austen and Hopkins had left, Littleberry walked out onto the deck again. The west winds of the past few days had shifted, then almost died, and the air had gone soft and mild. An air inversion had fallen over the city, trapping dust and particles, holding them suspended. The sun was going down and the moon was rising, and he was reminded of what he'd seen almost thirty years earlier on Johnston Atoll in the South Pacific. He had not heard the television and radio broadcasts, but he knew that news of the attack on Washington was beginning to fill the airwaves. The breaking news and the atmospheric conditions would force Thomas Cope to act. "He'll do it tonight," Littleberry whispered.

Manhattan, Saturday Night

THE early human trials were finished. A large glass tube with metal ends sat on the lab bench in Archimedes's level 3 biocontainment zone. He had just finished filling the tube with hexagons of viral glass about the size of quarters. He was wearing a white Tyvek suit with double gloves and a full-face respirator.

He went to his supply of BX 104 biological detonator, or bio-det, a military low explosive used in biological bomb cores as a dispersant. One kilogram of viral glass, shattered and dispersed in a fine cloud, would plume out nicely in the city.

He tucked a lump of bio-det into the tube, pushed it in with his thumb, then added a blasting-cap detonator. For a timer he used a microchip clock and a nine-volt battery.

He could set the timer for any length countdown. Three hours was enough time for him to get out of the city. Of course, it might be two days before the city truly realized that it was sick. In the meantime he would stay in Washington, where he would observe the situation while considering his next move.

He repeated the arming process with a second large glass tube. Now he had two mother bombs, which he would put in two different places. That was a fail-safe.

Next he armed two smaller weapons, his bio-det grenades. Filling two plastic lab jars with a mixture of viral glass and pieces of broken bottle glass, he added half a pound of explosive to each grenade. Anyone hit by them would have a skinful of broken real glass mixed with virus. The grenades operated on a simple push-button timer.

He carried the bombs out of level 3 into the staging area, where he sprayed his external suit with bleach and then stepped out of it. He washed the bombs in bleach to sterilize their outside surfaces, then placed them in a black leather doctor's bag. My little joke, he thought. I'm the greatest public-health doctor.

Now he went into his bedroom. From his bureau drawer he took out a 10-mm Colt Delta Elite semiautomatic handgun. It had a laser-beam sight, which threw a spot of red light on the target, making the gun extremely accurate. Now he was ready to defend himself as he moved into the bloodstream of the city.

AUSTEN and Hopkins boarded a Lexington Avenue train bound uptown. Austen, reading her subway map, led them off at the Bleecker Street stop. They walked east toward the Bowery and over to Second Avenue, where they entered the station for the F train on East Houston Street. This led to the tunnel where the homeless victims had lived.

They walked to the eastern end of the platform and down the steps to the tracks, where they picked their way through piles of debris, edging around steel columns that were almost hairy with black steel dust. They went through the hole in the metal wall to the unused tracks, the stub-end tunnel, which extended under Houston Street.

When they arrived at Lem's place, Hopkins took out his Mini Maglite, and they looked around. There did not seem to be any way in and out of there except through the subway station.

They retraced their steps and went back up to the street. They walked slowly along Houston Street, watching the faces, studying people. Hopkins pulled the piece of paper from his pocket and looked again at the face of Archimedes. It was early Saturday evening, and the streets were crowded with people going to restaurants or movies.

They kept moving, heading uptown into the East Village. They looked left and right, staring into people's faces. "This is hopeless," Hopkins said. "There are nine million people in this city."

They searched the East Village in a back-and-forth pattern, walking along numbered streets, turning up avenues. Hopkins felt an odd pang of envy watching the kids hanging out, talking about nothing in particular. He glanced over at Austen and realized he was thinking of her in something other than professional terms.

Eventually Hopkins and Austen found themselves in the less fashionable part of the East Village, close to Avenues C and D. They passed a fence that opened into a vacant lot where children's play equipment was scattered among raised beds of flowers. The little park extended between two buildings. Hopkins wandered in and sat down on a merry-go-round. Austen sat next to him.

"They're going to nail us to the wall for doing this," he said. He scraped his feet in the dirt. A stray cat walked past. It was a dirty brown-and-white cat. Hopkins planted his feet on the ground and pushed, causing the merry-go-round to turn. It gave off a creak. He pushed harder, and he and Austen turned around.

"Cut it out. It's bothering me," she said.

Slowly they came to a halt. Austen found herself facing a row of bushes. They had yellow horn-shaped flowers, now shriveled and fading with the coming of May. "Will, that's forsythia." She raised her eyes. The back of a brick building rose beyond the flower bed. On the third floor the windows were covered with white shades, and there was a small high-tech fan whirring in one of them. They sat on the merry-go-round, stunned.

"Oh, my," Hopkins said. "Oh, my." He stood up slowly. "Don't stare. Walk casually."

They walked out of the park and looked at the front of the building. It was a small turn-of-the-century apartment building faced with yellowish brick, with a heavy cornice running along the top. They went up the steps and looked at the names on the buzzer. None of them was "Cope." The button for apartment 3 said "Vir."

They crossed the street and stood in a doorway, facing the building. "*Vir* means 'man' in Latin," Austen commented.

The front door of the building suddenly opened.

TOM Cope was carrying his black leather doctor's bag. He saw them as he was going out the front door—a woman and a man standing across the street staring at him. He turned around and went back into the hallway. *Am I imagining things?*

HOPKINS saw the door open, and he locked eyes with a modest-looking man wearing eyeglasses, with hair going thin and a face that was burned into his mind. He switched his Saber radio to the emergency channel and got an FBI dispatcher. "It's Special Agent Will Hopkins. Get me Frank Masaccio. This is urgent."

Then, "Frank, we're in the East Village, near Houston Street." He looked around, gave the address. "We've got Cope! He seems to be going under the alias Vir. V-i-r. I need backup. He may have a bomb. I'm standing in a doorway here with Dr. Austen."

"Hopkins, number one, you're fired. Number two, I'm sending you everything I've got."

TOM Cope raced up the stairs to his apartment. He bolted the door and sat down on a couch in the living room. *They were staring at me as if they knew. They just looked federal. They cannot possibly be the FBI. There's no way they can have found me. But why were they staring at me like that?*

He stood up and went over to a shaded window. He pulled back the shade an inch or so and looked out onto the street. They were now sitting in a doorway across the street. They seemed to be talking.

He returned to the couch. This is crazy, he thought. I'm going crazy. Get ahold of yourself. You're being paranoid.

The timers in the bombs were running. He should disarm them. To do that, he had to go back into level 3.

Minutes later, inside the hot lab, all suited up, he opened the bombs, removed the timers, and disconnected the wires.

A CABLE television repair van pulled up at the corner of Avenue C. The driver looked at Hopkins and nodded slightly. Hopkins and Austen walked to the corner, the back of the van opened, and they climbed inside.

The van double-parked on a quiet street two blocks from Cope's apartment. Suddenly a furniture-delivery truck appeared and parked in front of the television van. Hopkins and Austen got out and climbed into the back of the furniture truck. Mark Littleberry, Special Agent Oscar Wirtz, and a number of Wirtz's ninjas—the Reachdeep tactical operations squad—were inside. There were boxes of biohazard gear in the truck. For the moment the furniture truck was a staging-and-supply area for a biohazard operation.

"Are we going into action?" Austen said.

"Not you, Dr. Austen," Wirtz said to her.

Hopkins was listening to Masaccio on his Saber radio.

"The lady below him is a shut-in with diabetes and a heart condition," Masaccio was saying. "We can't disturb her. We can't get into the apartment above him without risking discovery. The good news is that the building on one side of him shares a common wall with his building. We're going to get as close to him as we can, Will. Tell your guy Wirtz to get ready to move fast in a very hot mess."

The sun had set. It was eight thirty in the evening.

ANOTHER truck pulled up near Tom Cope's building. It was a Con Edison repair truck. Three Con Edison employees in hard hats—one was a woman—entered the building next to his. When they got to the third floor, they knocked on an apartment door. A man answered. It turned out he was a columnist for a rap-music magazine. The Con Edison woman held up her FBI credentials. "My name is Caroline Landau. I'm an agent with the Federal Bureau of Investigation." She explained that there was a killer next door. "We think he has a bomb. We're appealing to you for help."

"I can't believe this," the journalist said.

"Sir, you are in great danger," Landau said. "We all are."

He went downstairs with one of the "Con Edison" people, and the truck carried him away. He spent the night at a hotel, courtesy of the FBI.

Floor by floor the FBI evacuated the building next to Cope's. In the journalist's apartment Caroline Landau set up her remote sensing gear, working with a group of tech agents. With a silent drilling machine they cut through a layer of Sheetrock on the wall. Under it was insulation. They pulled it out. Next they came to a brick wall. On the other side was Cope's apartment.

Landau set out an array of contact microphones on the wall. You could listen on headphones and hear everything happening in Cope's apartment in stereo sound.

The furniture truck occupied by the Reachdeep team swung around the block and parked on the sidewalk near Cope's building. Under cover of darkness the operational ninjas unloaded a series of duffel bags and brought them into the building next to Cope's.

Special Agent Landau and her crew set up two thermal-imaging cameras on tripods. The cameras could see in infrared light, which is heat. They could see warmth through walls. Landau wired the thermal-imaging cameras to display screens. A thermal image of Tom Cope's apartment appeared on the screens. Now they could see Cope walking around. He was in the living room, holding a tubelike object in his hands. He seemed calm.

They saw a large, warm cylinder in another room, and they thought it might be a bioreactor. To get a better look, the tech agents silently drilled a cone-shaped hole in the bricks. Then they slid a cone-shaped optical assembly into the hole. The point of the cone was a fish-eye lens as small as a pencil point. Everything else in the assembly was behind the wall. If Cope had looked directly at the lens, he might have thought it was a speck of dirt.

"We're a fly on his wall," Caroline Landau remarked.

The optical cone was connected to an electronic-imaging system. On a flat screen appeared a fish-eye view of Tom Cope's laboratory. But they could not see Cope. He remained outside the laboratory, visible in the thermal imagers as a ghostly orange figure sitting on the couch or moving restlessly around the living room, mostly keeping the long tubelike object in his hands, as if he couldn't let go of it. A fuzzy shape rested on a table in front of the couch. Hopkins and Austen thought it was the bag he'd been carrying when they'd seen him. Then he opened it—it *was* the bag—and he seemed to play with another long tube and a couple of smaller objects, and then he pulled out something recognizable.

"He has a gun," Caroline Landau said. "Could be a .45. Oo-ee."

Cope placed the gun on the table and lay back on the couch not ten feet from a massive FBI surveillance and SWAT group, with no apparent inkling of the weight of agonized law enforcement that pressed up against his living-room wall. They were fascinated with the large cylinder that he held in his hands—it had to be a biological bomb.

COPE sat on the couch. Were they watching him? Or was he imagining this? He was so nervous, he was trembling. He went into the bathroom and looked into the mirror. His eyes had a strange color. Was that a golden ring around the pupils? His nose was running. His upper lip was glistening wet.

AT THE FBI command center in the Federal Building, Frank Masaccio and his people monitored the situation and stayed in touch with Washington. Masaccio had command: He would call the moves. He was not going to burst in on Tom Cope, not if the man had a bomb. That was far too dangerous. He was going to wait until Cope came out of the building, then swoop down on him and make the arrest.

Snipers with Remington .308 rifles were standing by on the rooftops. Masaccio instructed the snipers not to shoot without orders. If there were indications that Cope was going to detonate a bomb inside his apartment, then the Reachdeep people had orders to move through the wall and stop him. The goal was the same as always—not necessarily to kill Cope, but first and foremost to render him harmless.

Wirtz put in a call to Quantico for a master breacher to prepare the way into Cope's apartment.

The man, whose name was Wilmot Hughes, arrived at ten o'clock. He inspected the brick wall, tapping it lightly. "Fortunately, this is trivial," he remarked. He began laying plastic explosive charges in a pattern over the bricks and gave instructions to the Reachdeep team to stand flat against the wall when the charges went off.

Wirtz and the Reachdeep ninjas began putting on biohazard suits and body armor.

Littleberry said, "I'm going in. I want to see his lab."

"You're too senior for this kind of action," Hopkins told him.

"You can't deny me." He turned to Austen. "You comin' too?"

"Sure am, Doctor," she said to Littleberry.

"Hey," Hopkins said. He gave orders for the doctors to stay behind, but he thought he was fighting a losing battle to keep them out of it altogether.

Austen and Littleberry pulled on black Racal biohazard suits, and

Wirtz made them wear body armor. They had lightweight radio headsets. Wirtz told Hopkins to stay well back. "You and the doctors come in after we've secured the place."

"I'll be climbing over your back, Oscar," Hopkins said. He buckled a pouch to his waist, which he filled with certain essentials: swabs, his pocket protector full of pens and other junk, his Mini Maglite flashlight, and a Boink biosensor. He strapped on his SIG-Sauer 9-mm semiautomatic. He ran his radio headset wire down to a transceiver at his waist.

IT WAS now three o'clock in the morning. Cope had not been able to sleep. He was indecisive. Part of the reason was that he was no longer completely him. The transformation was occurring rapidly now. Crystals were forming in his brain stem.

Austen had been watching Cope on the screens of the thermal-imaging cameras. He seemed to be making involuntary gestures, and he was talking to himself. "I'm not sick. Not sick."

"Listen, Will, I think he's infected," Austen said.

They studied his body movements, but Austen couldn't be sure. Then Cope seemed to make up his mind. "Option two," he said.

"What was that?" Hopkins said.

"He's losing it," Littleberry said.

The blurry thermal image showed Cope bent over the object in his hands. They heard a sound. It was the sound of the metal endpiece being unscrewed from the glass bomb tube. He fiddled with something. They heard a dry, cracking sound—the sound of wires being pulled through a packed mass of viral hexagons in the tube. He was rearming the bomb.

Hopkins stood and put his hand up. "Wirtz, he may blow something. Get ready!"

Everyone put on Racal hoods. They zipped up their suits and started their air filters running.

If the building goes hot with that bomb, Hopkins thought, it could kill all of us, space suits or not. The air near bioground zero would be so thick with virus, it might overwhelm the suit's protection.

Wirtz and the ninjas positioned themselves against the wall, on either side of the charges. They were carrying flash grenades and assault weapons. The breacher readied his controls.

As Hopkins stared at the thermal image, Cope placed the armed bomb inside the doctor's bag, then walked into the corridor that led to the laboratory. He did not put on a protective suit. He opened the door of the lab. Now, in the fish-eye lens, they saw him clearly for the first time. He stood by the door, looking across the room toward the bioreactor, and suddenly he picked up a glass beaker and hurled it. The bioreactor, made largely of glass, exploded. The contents flooded across the floor in a running meltdown of amplified Cobra virus.

"It's gone hot," Hopkins yelled.

"Go!" Masaccio responded.

Everyone pressed flat against the wall. The breacher detonated the charges, and an oval hole opened up. Wirtz and the ninjas poured through it. Flash grenades exploded into brilliant light, momentarily blinding the thermal cameras, and the screens went white.

Then the screens came back to normal. Hopkins watched Cope's thermal image as Wirtz and his people moved through the apartment.

"Wirtz, he's in the kitchen," Hopkins shouted. Suddenly he saw the form of Tom Cope curl up in a ball and, unbelievably, drop out of sight. "He's going down," Hopkins yelled.

MANY old buildings in New York City have dumbwaiter shafts that are no longer used. The dumbwaiter was Cope's planned escape route. Carrying his doctor's bag, he had curled up on the dumbwaiter platform. He let the ropes go, and the platform went down fast. He came to a halt with a bang in the basement, inside a closet. He flung himself out the door. No one around. He raced through a heating tunnel and came to a small opening in the brickwork, covered with a sheet of plywood. He tore the plywood off. There was his crawl space, his escapeway. He went through it, scraping his knees on broken concrete. Ahead he heard the rumble of a subway train.

In the apartment, Oscar Wirtz and some of his team headed for the kitchen, where they found the dumbwaiter shaft. Seconds later Hopkins entered the room, carrying a spray tank full of Envirochem, a powerful antibiological liquid. Austen followed behind him, and Littleberry after that. They headed for the bioreactor room, where Hopkins sprayed Envirochem all over the walls, floor, and ceiling. On his radio he heard Wirtz calling to him. He headed for the kitchen, Austen and Littleberry behind him. "He's gone down a shaft," Wirtz was saying. "We're heading after him."

They followed Wirtz down the stairs to the basement. It didn't take long to find the crawl space and the sheet of plywood lying on the floor. Wirtz noticed a spot of blood on the floor. Hopkins swabbed the blood and jammed the swab into his Boink. The biosensor chimed. "Cobra," he said.

"Scientists, back off," Wirtz said. "Operations people in first." He vaulted up into the crawl space. One by one his people followed, squirming on their hands and knees, pushing their weapons ahead of them. They barely fit. They had no flashlights; this was an unforeseen development.

Wirtz, the first in line, came to the end of the crawl space. It dropped down into a low, narrow passage running at right angles.

"What's happening down there?" Frank Masaccio asked from the command post, where he was listening to the audio feed.

A rumbling sound was being picked up by Wirtz's mike. "That's a subway train you're hearing," Wirtz said. "We're near the subway. I'm behind some kind of wall here."

Cope had gone into the subway, and he was carrying a biological bomb or bombs.

"Maybe we can biocontain him," Hopkins said into his headset.

"What do you mean?" Masaccio asked.

"The subway tunnels are a natural biocontainment area. If he blows a bomb in there, maybe we can seal the tunnels off and stop the trains. We'd rather have him down there than up in the open air. Let's try to trap him in the tunnels. Frank, you need to shut down the air-circulation fans in the subway."

Masaccio went into a flurry of shouting and orders. He called the Transit Authority Operations Control Center on West Fourteenth Street. The system operators began stopping the trains and turning off all the air blowers and fans.

FBI agents and New York City police officers were to seal off all subway entrances in the neighborhood and then go down into the subway to find Tom Cope. Almost none of these law-enforcement people were equipped with biohazard masks or protective clothing. If Cope's bomb went off, many of them would die.

Manhattan, Early Sunday Morning, May 3

THE Reachdeep team came to a door at the far end of the Houston Street subway stub-end tunnel. This was Cope's escape route. The route went past the place where Harmonica Man and Lem had lived. They had died because they had seen Cope using the door.

Oscar Wirtz led the way, then came the five ninjas, and then, bringing up the rear, came Hopkins, Austen, and Littleberry. Faintly they heard Masaccio's voice on their headsets: "What are you doing? Report."

"I can't hear you, Frank. You're breaking up," Hopkins said. "We're coming into the Second Avenue station. You've got to seal it off."

COPE had come out onto the Second Avenue platform a few minutes ahead of his pursuers. Should he wait for a train? At three in the morning he might have to wait a long time.

Don't wait. Keep moving.

He now knew that he had probably been infected, but he could still move. Perhaps he had developed some kind of resistance to the virus.

He climbed down the stairs at the end of the platform and got onto the tracks, following the route of the F train toward the center of Manhattan. He noticed something that he did not like—the tunnels were silent. The power was off in the rails. Then he heard a sound behind him. He looked back. People in black space suits were moving across the platform of the Second Avenue station. He broke into a run, his feet splashing through puddles, stumbling on the ties. *They don't have me yet.* He felt a cool determination sweep over him. *Have courage. You will be remembered as a man of vision and heroic will.*

Heading westward through the main subway tunnel, he saw that he was approaching another subway station—the Broadway-Lafayette stop. He had explored this tunnel before as part of his research looking for places to do a biological release. Now he was looking for a side tunnel he remembered, a little-used cutoff that doubled back. He could circle around his pursuers if he could just remember where it was. Then he saw it—a single-track tunnel breaking to his left. It headed south and east, toward the Lower East Side.

AT THAT moment Frank Masaccio was learning about the side tunnel from a subway-system operator in the control center on Fourteenth Street. Earlier he had sent an FBI team into the Broadway-Lafayette subway station, and that team was now moving east toward the Reachdeep team, which was moving west. They would trap Cope between the two stations.

"There's that BJ 1 tunnel," a system operator was saying to Masaccio. "If you're trying to trap the guy and he finds it, that tunnel will be his only way out."

"Where's it lead?" Masaccio asked.

The BJ 1 tunnel led south and east to a station at the corner of Delancey and Essex streets. Masaccio ordered a police or FBI team—whichever was closest—to deploy there fast.

Meanwhile, the Reachdeep team entered the BJ 1 tunnel. It was curving, poorly lit, and black with steel dust. As they went deeper into it, their radio contact with the FBI command center vanished. The team was on its own.

TOM Cope moved cautiously through the BJ 1 tunnel, carrying the black bag with its Cobra virus–dispersal bombs. The Delta Elite handgun was also in his bag. The tunnel passed underneath the Bowery, then headed downtown beneath the Sara Delano Roosevelt Parkway, a strip of greenery and playgrounds. It was three twenty on a Sunday morning, and when police cars and FBI cars suddenly began pouring into the neighborhood and police teams began running down into subway entrances, there were not too many people around to notice. Since reporters listen to the police radio, television news trucks soon headed for the Lower East Side, tracking reports of a possible terrorist incident. The Cobra Event had been kept a secret, but the moment Cope slipped away and the operation turned into a chase, it started to blow in the media.

The tunnel led Cope deeper underground, under the old heart of the Lower East Side—under Eldridge Street, Allen Street, Orchard Street. Then it headed due east under Delancey Street.

Cope knew where he was going. He'd explored these tunnels and had memorized a variety of escape routes. He was heading for the Williamsburg Bridge, which rises from Delancey Street, connecting Manhattan with Brooklyn. One of his legs hurt, and it was slowing him down. He had cut his knee while scrambling out of his building.

The tunnel began to rise. He saw lights ahead. It was the platform of the Essex–Delancey Street subway station at the foot of the Williamsburg Bridge. The platform was deserted. Cope hurried along the tracks. He heard the sound of running footsteps, voices shouting, and he turned around and retreated back into the tunnel. They were searching the platform. Any moment they would come into the tunnel looking for him. What to do?

I should do it here. Set it off. He hesitated. But the issue wasn't so simple. He wasn't absolutely certain he was infected with the virus. It is hard to choose to die. It is easier to choose to be alive. As long as you have life left in you, there might be a way out.

He heard the rustling sound of the space suits, the pounding of their rubber boots. They were coming fast.

He crept along the wall and entered a dark area, some abandoned rooms, where he found old air-blowing equipment and broken machinery. A refrigerator. For a moment he thought he could climb inside. It had been painted black—weird. But it was too small. He got down on his knees and curled up against the wall.

THE Essex Street station contains a large abandoned area that was once a trolley-car station. The police officers, having swept the platforms, prepared to move into the trolley area. At that moment the Reachdeep team arrived at the platform. The ninjas conferred with some of the police officers. Cope seemed to have vanished.

"He could have gone onto the bridge," a policeman said, "or he's in that trolley area."

"You guys stay back. You don't have protective gear," Wirtz told the police officers. The FBI people borrowed the officers' flashlights and began to sweep through the trolley area. Hopkins, Austen, and Littleberry remained where they were, standing on the subway tracks near the BJ 1 tunnel. In their suits, with their soft, clear helmets, it was difficult to pick up sounds, but Hopkins thought he heard something at his back. He spun around and found himself facing a group of abandoned rooms. He saw a black refrigerator. The sound seemed to have come from behind it.

Hopkins drew his gun. He circled around the refrigerator. Nothing there. But he noticed blood. He opened his pouch and pulled out his Boink and a swab. He swabbed the blood and stuck it into the sampling port of the Boink. The device chimed. On the screen it said COBRA.

Hopkins spoke quietly into his headset. "Hopkins here. Breaker. Emergency. We're on him." Silence. "Frank! Frank, come in," he hissed. "Anybody hear me? We're tracking Cope." While he was talking, Hopkins turned to Austen and Littleberry. "Lie down on the floor, please." He moved forward, inching around some machines. "Dr. Cope! Dr. Cope! Please surrender."

There was nobody there. But on the far side of the machines he found an open doorway leading to an unlit area heaped with trash. Homeless people had been living there. Hopkins crept along the wall in semidarkness. He came to an opening in the wall. It was a low tunnel, about three feet high, full of electrical cables.

Hopkins debated what to do. He could hear snatches of talk on his headset. "Frank! Wirtz!" he called. No dice. Should he go into the tunnel? He had his Mini Maglite flashlight. He switched it on and shone the light down the tunnel. He yelled over his shoulder, "Mark! Alice! Go back and find Wirtz. There's a tunnel."

He bent over and entered the tunnel, shining his minilight along the electrical cables. He moved quickly now, hunched over, wondering if at any moment a shock wave from the bomb's going off would ram down the tunnel.

Hopkins had gone an unknown distance when he realized he was being followed. He stopped. It was Austen directly behind him. He turned to face her. "You don't have a gun. You don't have a light."

"Get going," she answered. "Or give me your light."

"Where's Mark?"

"He went back to find Wirtz."

Without another word Hopkins surged forward, annoyed with Austen but most of all angry with himself. He felt responsible for having let Cope get away. *If a lot of people die . . . Don't think about that. Stay on Cope. Find him.*

Hopkins and Austen moved through the tunnel until they came to a crossing point—a choice of three tunnels to take. Which way to go? Hopkins got down on his knees and searched for blood with his minilight. There was no blood. He noticed a puddle of water on the floor of the right-hand fork. The puddle had been recently splashed. Cope had gone this way.

Now the tunnel narrowed into a crawl space. Hopkins got down on his hands and knees and began to crawl forward on his belly. He talked with Austen on his radio headset. "Dr. Austen, will you stop now, please? You're going to get yourself hurt." She did not reply.

They came to a steel plate blocking the way. It was a small access hatch. Hopkins pushed on it, and it opened with a drawn-out creak. The sound bounced away into deep echoes, and then silence. A vast black space loomed beyond the hatch. Hopkins shone his minilight around the space. It was an enormous underground tunnel with a line of concrete columns marching down its middle. Twisted and bent pieces of steel reinforcement bar stuck out of the walls like black thorns. The hatch opened out of a wall about ten feet above the floor of the tunnel.

COPE had a flashlight, but he didn't want to use it, because he thought it might give him away. At intervals he flicked it on and off, but mostly he moved through the tunnel with his hand on the wall, going by sense of touch.

When he had arrived at the hatch, he had lowered himself into the big tunnel, holding the bag, trying to protect it. He landed hard on the concrete floor, and an ominous cracking sound came from the bag. One of the glass tubes had cracked. Best to leave it here.

He checked to make sure the timer was running; then he placed the glass cylinder in a shadowy corner by a column. It contained some four hundred and thirty-five hexagons of viral glass, along with the biological detonator. Flicking his light on and off, he moved up the tunnel, his bag still containing one large bomb, the grenades, and the gun. He had no idea where he was.

In fact, he was in a length of tunnel intended for the never completed Second Avenue subway line.

HOPKINS leaned out of the hatch door. What he saw looked like a subway tunnel, but there were no train tracks; the floor was smooth concrete. Hopkins swung himself out of the hatch, hung on the lip, and let go. He landed on his feet. Austen dropped down next to him. He said, "I'm giving you a direct order to freeze. I am the chief executive—"

She brushed past him.

The unfinished subway tunnel ran from north to south under Chinatown. As they proceeded along it, Hopkins played his light around, holding his gun at the ready. There seemed to be no exits. Hopkins tried his radio again. "Frank? Wirtz? Are you there?" There was no radio reception in the tunnel. They came to a set of metal stairs leading up to an open doorway. Had Cope gone up the stairs, or had he continued to follow the tunnel?

They went on along the tunnel until it ended at a blank concrete wall. Cope must have gone up the stairs. They hurried back.

Hopkins climbed the stairs and found himself in an empty room. It led to a number of doorways.

IN THE command center, Frank Masaccio was beginning to understand the situation. Wirtz and Littleberry had reported that the team had become separated. It appeared that Cope was still in the subway, still underground. He had apparently disappeared into an electrical service tunnel. Hopkins and Austen had followed him. After a delay Wirtz and the ninjas had also entered the service tunnel. As soon as they went in, they dropped out of radio contact.

"Where's Littleberry?" Masaccio said to an agent on the radio.

"Dr. Littleberry has gone into the tunnel with Wirtz."

"What? My whole damned Reachdeep team has gone down a rathole," Masaccio shouted. "Go in there and find them."

Masaccio got on the telephone with engineers from Con Edison and with the subway-system operators. They told him about the unfinished Second Avenue subway line. The best access was a hatchway at the foot of the Manhattan Bridge in Chinatown.

HOPKINS had to decide which of the doorways to choose. He tried to think the way Cope would. Cope would be heading for the street, into the open air. Hopkins tried all the doors, and behind one he found a steel ladder leading upward. He climbed it, with Austen following him. They reached another room. There was a dark, open doorway on the far side. He heard a sound coming through the doorway—a metallic clink. A light blinked on and off.

He dived for the ground, dragging Austen down with him, and turned off his flashlight. He heard a sharp clattering sound. He moved across the floor, gun ready, light off, afraid of dying and afraid that Austen might die, too. He arrived at the open, black doorway. He could hear Austen behind him. He was so angry at her that he wanted to scream. He couldn't bear the thought of something happening to her.

He lay behind the edge of the door for cover and briefly flicked on his light into the space where the sounds had come from. The light revealed a deep chamber. The floor was twenty feet below the level of the doorway. There was nobody there. But on the floor of the chamber lay a flashlight. It was off. Cope had dropped his flashlight—that was the source of the clattering sound.

On the inner walls of the chamber there were small openings—vent tunnels, reachable by ladders that ran vertically up the walls. Cope had obviously been climbing one of the ladders moments before. That was the metallic sound they'd heard. He must have gone into one of the vent holes. Which one? There were six.

Hopkins started down a ladder, gun in hand. He was going to climb each ladder, looking into all the vent tunnels one by one. What else could he do, except give up? But if Cope got away . . . Hopkins reached the bottom of the chamber and stood looking up the ladders at the vent holes. He realized he was a vulnerable target, and he began to think that he had just done something stupid.

He was moving to pick up Cope's flashlight when Austen's voice over the radio burst in his ears. "Will, heads up!" At the same moment a plastic object flew past him. It bounced at his feet, rolled a short distance, and came to a stop under a ladder. A red light was blinking on it—grenade. He heard Austen screaming.

He picked up the grenade and threw it into one of the vent openings. That wasn't good enough. He still had to get out of there. The explosion was going to come out of the vent hole.

He leaped for a ladder and raced up it, dropping his gun in the process. He was heading for cover in another vent hole. He reached the opening and hurled himself inside.

There was a yellow-red flash and a boom. A thudding shock wave rolled down the tunnel and tugged at his biohazard suit. This was followed by a crunching, creaking sound, and a piece of concrete fell off the roof of the tunnel, trapping him. He was left wedged face first into a small vent tunnel. There was a whining, pinging sound in his ears, like a jet engine.

"Alice?" he called. There was no answer.

He assumed that the grenade had had virus material in it—Cobra crystals. He wondered if his suit had been breached. It was almost totally dark, but not completely. Where was the light coming from? He realized he was lying on his Mini Maglite. He got a hand under his chest and pulled the flashlight out.

WHEN the grenade had exploded in the vent hole, Alice Austen was back behind the doorway. She saw the light from the explosion, but the flash died instantly, and now she was lying in total darkness. "Will? Will, are you there?" she called on her headset. Nothing. No answer. She did not want Hopkins to be in trouble. She really did not want him to be in trouble.

"Will," she screamed. "Please talk to me. Will! Will!" Nothing.

Then she thought, I'm making a lot of noise. If Cope is around here, he'll hear me. She would climb down into the chamber to help him if she could. She felt around in the darkness and grasped the ladder that went down into the chamber. It came away in her hand—the blast had broken it. There was no way to get down there.

Now what? She could either stay where she was, lying on the floor waiting for help to arrive, or she could try to get back to the main tunnel. Soon there would be people and lights in that tunnel. That was where she wanted to go.

She stood up in pitch-darkness. Trying to remember which way she had come, she retraced their route, waving her hands back and forth in the blackness in front of her. She reached a ladder. *Yes, we climbed up this ladder to get here.* She called softly on her radio again. "Will? Are you all right? Please answer me, Will. Can you hear me?" She inched down the ladder, working by sense of touch. Now she was standing in a room. Which way to go?

She was feeling her way along the wall when her hand came into contact with some fabric. Then she felt an arm. It was Cope. He had been waiting against the wall.

He fired his gun twice. The muzzle flashes illuminated the two of them, frozen in the light like nocturnal creatures caught in the flash of a naturalist's camera. Both shots missed her by inches. She dived across the room, howling with terror, and leaped through a doorway. Suddenly she was tumbling and falling. She fell down the metal stairs into the main tunnel, gasping with pain, weeping with terror. Everything hurt. She wondered if she had broken any bones. She stood up. She had to get away from here.

It was pitch-dark again. She moved off to one side, then crouched by what felt like a wall. She waited, absolutely still, trying to avoid the slightest rustle of her suit, but she could not do anything about the hum of the Racal blowers, which provided the suit's fresh-air supply. A great deal of time seemed to pass. Her muscles became stiff and sore.

Suddenly she noticed a tiny light, a red spot on the wall. It moved and jumped like a red firefly. She couldn't tell where it came from, but it was seeking her. It was a laser pointer. She almost screamed. She couldn't see Cope, but she realized he was standing in the doorway at the top of the stairs, aiming the laser out into the tunnel.

"I can hear your suit humming," he said calmly. "I'll find you." The red dot moved up the floor toward her. It touched her suit. She screamed and dived sideways. The gun roared—a flat deafening smack in the tunnel, with a bright flash.

She found an opening between two columns, rolled through it, picked herself up, and ran in total darkness. The red dot hopped around, looking for her. She stopped running and crouched low, ready to jump in any direction. His voice came out of the blackness. "I am not wearing a mask." The voice was about forty feet away, to her right. "I can hear you better than you can hear me."

On her radio headset she heard Hopkins say, "Hey, anyone there?" He's alive, she thought.

"Ah, your radio," Cope said.

She reached for her belt and ripped the headset out of the jack, then tried to keep herself still.

"The gun is loaded with hollow-point bullets. Each bullet has a viral glass bead in the tip." His feet clanked down the metal stairs. "You don't understand what I'm doing. I'm not trying to kill too many people. Just some of them."

In the FBI command center, Masaccio was talking with the subway-system operators. "You've got a lighting system in that tunnel complex? Well, turn on the damned lights!"

In the darkness she could almost feel the heft of the gun swinging toward her. She tensed, preparing to jump away. She sensed the fragility of her body, the delicacy of her mortal being.

Suddenly, with a humming sound, banks of fluorescent lights clicked on. Cope was holding the gun in a police stance. Fluid was running from his nose. His lips were bloody. He had started chewing. He fired. The bullet splashed on the concrete. She was running fast. The lights went out again.

In total darkness she ran at full speed. Suddenly everything exploded. She saw purple flashes, and she sprawled on the ground, certain she had been hit. She had tripped over a piece of concrete and was lying behind it. She stayed where she was, afraid to move.

Hopkins was lying on his stomach in a low horizontal passage. The tunnel was not meant to fit a human body, especially someone wearing a space suit with chest armor. The tunnel was about eighteen inches high and two and a half feet wide. Hopkins could not possibly turn around in it. His feet were blocked by a fallen chunk of concrete. He had to go forward. He was now feeling the first tremors of claustrophobia. If he stayed where he was, he might run out of breathable air. So he crawled forward, occasionally calling on his radio headset.

He was coming to a dead end. "Oh, no," he said. Now he would have to back up. But as he reached the end, his fingers felt a lip of some kind. He pushed his face over the lip and pointed his light into a shaft that seemed to be about twenty feet deep. It ended with a flat dead end. Just looking at it made him feel sick. What now?

He tried to back up. It was more difficult than pushing himself forward. Then it occurred to him that the vertical shaft, which joined the horizontal shaft at a right angle, might provide enough space in which to turn around. He squirmed and twisted and fought against the confinement. His face suspended over the hole, he tried working his shoulders this way and that. The problem was the armor vest. "It's a mathematical problem with no solution," he muttered. Then a terrible thing happened.

He slipped. He fell headfirst down the hole—a plunge of twenty feet. He whumped to a halt facedown in the bottom of the hole with a sudden wedging jerk. He was jammed vertically in the shaft, his arms at his sides. He had lost his minilight. He was upside down face first in a dead-end hole, with no light and no air. There was no way he could back out.

The roaring in his ears was the sound of his own voice begging for mercy. The panic shook him like a series of electric shocks. He was screaming uncontrollably, howling from claustrophobic terror. He took a deep breath, held it, then let all the breath out of his lungs. He tried to hold his breath again, wanting to make himself pass out. If he could pass out, then this would be ended. But he could not, which meant there was enough air in here to keep him alive.

For a week.

Don't think about that. I've got to relax. If I'm going to die, I've got to come to some kind of peace. Think of something. Think of California. Think of the best beach in California.

He tried to imagine himself lying on his back on the warm sand at Laguna, as he had done in his Caltech days, tried to remember the whush-haaa of the surf, the smell of the salt air, the sun falling into the Pacific Ocean. *So many lost opportunities. . . . You geek, if you get out of this alive, you really should ask Austen out. Strike a blow for geekdom. The air really is depleted here; it's making me slightly demented.*

He realized something was pressed against his cheek. It felt like . . . the Mini Maglite. He got one hand around it and twisted it, and it came on.

Light. This was progress. He moved his neck left and right. He saw bare concrete a few inches from his eyes. His face was flushed and sweating, engorged with blood from hanging upside down.

That was when he got a shock. There was something dark behind his head. An opening! Twisting his head as far around as possible, he saw a tight passage that went off into darkness. Wedging his flashlight around, he managed to get a view into the tunnel. Then he got another shock.

He saw a large glass tube standing upright on the floor of the tunnel at the foot of a ladder. It was Cope's biological bomb, with enough viral glass to render areas of New York City and downwind lethally hot. He would have to disarm it. It must have a timer of some kind.

This was going to be difficult. He managed to slowly rotate his body. He was still hanging upside down, but now he was facing the bomb. By wrenching his shoulders, he got one hand through the opening. He reached out for the tube. It was too far away—three feet from his fingertips.

Three feet might as well be three light-years.

He got one hand up to the pouch at his waist and unzipped it. The pocket protector fell out, scattering things. He said to himself, Think. A wise man can build gadgets in hell.

He tapped his fingers around the stuff that had fallen from his pocket protector, taking inventory and speaking out loud. "Mechanical pencil. Box of pencil leads. Fisher Space Pen, writes in zero gravity. Swab. Two more swabs. Length of duct tape wrapped around a pencil stub. Ticket stubs from a Redskins game. Half an Oreo cookie."

Nobody but a fool goes into a federal counterterrorism operation without duct tape. "To build a sticky probe," he said out loud. With his head twisted to see what he was doing, and working with one hand only, he pulled a strip of tape from the pencil stub and began taping objects together. He debated trying to remove his glove for better coordination but decided against it—too much virus around.

He taped the mechanical pencil to the Fisher Space Pen and the pencil stub end to end, making a kind of extended stick. Then he stripped the swabs from their wrapping and taped them together end to end. Next he taped the swabs to the pencil-and-pen stick. What he had now was a long probe. The flexible end of the probe consisted of the three medical swabs. Using extra strips of tape, he firmly attached a small ball of tape to the soft tip of the first swab.

Such sticky-ended probes are used to remove nuts and washers that have gotten loose inside tangles of high-tech equipment. He gripped the probe with his Leatherman pliers and reached out toward the bomb. It wasn't long enough by about five inches. "Damn, damn!" he said. *Think*. "Your flashlight," he blurted. Now he taped his Mini Maglite to the probe and then held that in the Leatherman pliers. He reached out. The tape ball touched the bomb. He let it sit for a moment to allow the adhesive to bind to the glass. Then he pulled it toward him. The cylinder shifted and toppled over.

It thudded on the concrete, and the glass broke, dumping out hexagons of virus. They skittered here and there, gleaming like fire opal in the beam of the Mini Maglite.

"Excellent," he said. The warhead material had spilled out, giving him access to the detonator. He could see a chunk of explosive in the center of the pile of virus. There was a blasting cap stuck in it, and what looked like a microchip timer. Boy, this was crude. But then, you didn't have to be a rocket scientist to make a virus bomb, as long as you had the virus material.

Then Hopkins saw movement. It was a rat approaching the viral glass, apparently intent on eating it. "Get away, stupid rat." The rat looked at him, unafraid.

He found the piece of Oreo cookie and pushed it toward the rat. "Eat that." The rat took it and waddled away.

Now to disarm the explosive. Hopkins touched the sticky end of the probe to the timer, and it stuck. Good. He dragged the probe toward him, and slowly the timer came along, pulling the blasting cap and the chunk of detonator with it. He got the timer in his hand. He turned it over and looked at the numbers.

They were running. Currently they said "00.00.02."

"Yaaaaahhh!" he yelled, and he pulled the blasting cap out of the explosive and flung the cap away.

Whank! The cap had gone off somewhere down the tunnel. I wonder if it killed the rat, he thought.

There was still a heap of viral glass lying near him. But it was underground. It could be dealt with.

Now I have to get my living body out of here.

He shifted his hips, jamming himself tighter in the shaft, twisting and trying to crunch his body down. He got his head into the tunnel full of hexagons of viral glass. He took a deep breath and let it out, his Racal blowers still humming, still protecting him, he hoped, and got himself a little farther around the corner. By exhaling and pushing, he could slide along on his back.

"Yes!" He propelled himself on his back out of the vent hole, and he stood up, his feet in viral glass. He checked his suit with the minilight. There didn't seem to be any holes or tears.

There was a ladder. Cope had climbed down it and left the bomb there. There was also a tunnel leading off horizontally.

Just then he heard gunfire—two shots, coming down the tunnel. It was a low tunnel. He hurried along it, hunched over, and came to a sheet of plywood across the tunnel. He pushed on it, and it fell away into a large, dark, open space. "Anybody there?" he said. He shone his light around and caught a glimpse of columns, a figure moving. "Alice?" A red light appeared on his chest. What was this? Then he heard Austen scream, "No!"

There was a roar in his ears and something slammed into his chest, driving him backward. It came to him that he had been shot and was dying.

AUSTEN had heard Hopkins say "Anybody there?" as she was lying in darkness. At the same moment she saw the gleam of his flashlight. He was waving it around, trying to determine where he was, and she saw Cope, bent, writhing slowly, taking aim at the light. The laser touched Hopkins.

When Cope fired into Hopkins, she heard a smacking oof! The minilight flew away, throwing its beam around crazily. Cope fired again and again, using the laser to aim.

Shrieking, she got to her feet, raced across the space, and fell on Cope, knocking him off balance. She tore at him. She had a glimpse of Cobra-infected eyes glittering in the light of the minilight. Then she had his gun, and she aimed it.

There was a clunking sound, and the tunnel lights came on.

Cope trembled. An arm lashed out at her, while the other bent suddenly, and his neck arched and lashed around—Lesch-Nyhan writhing. In the fluorescent light he looked shrunken, pathetic.

"You killed him," she whispered. She stood up slowly, keeping the Colt aimed at those eyes. The red spot trembled on his forehead. Her finger tightened.

"Don't . . . Alice."

She spun around. Hopkins was standing behind her. There were two bullet pocks in his armor vest. The other shots had missed him. He was holding what looked like a bunch of junk taped together. "Arrest . . . " he choked. The bullets had knocked the wind out of him. He doubled over, looking at her.

To Cope she said, "You're under arrest."

Hopkins tried to straighten up and coughed. "Need to . . . charge—"

"I'm a public-health officer," she said to Cope. "You are charged with murder."

Cope's eyes widened. His lips drew back, and his face rippled as he was gripped by a seizure.

THERE was a growing chatter of voices on their radio headsets and a rush of people running up the subway tunnel. It was Oscar Wirtz with the operations group. Simultaneously a SWAT team of New York City police officers was moving down through the street hatch by the Manhattan Bridge. As the groups converged on the scene, they saw what had happened. The suspect was having some kind of seizure. Hopkins told them the tunnel might be biologically hot. "Where's Mark?" he asked.

"He was behind us, Will," Wirtz said.

Just then they heard Littleberry. He was coming up the tunnel toward them. They heard him shout, "Down! Get down! He left one back—" A flash ended his words.

They saw the blast wave come up the tunnel. The wave came from the bomb Cope had left beside a column near the hatchway. No one had noticed it except Littleberry.

The blast wave took the form of a meniscus, a thin, curved, bubble of powdered viral glass. It passed over them and was gone. For an instant it showed them the face of the Cobra virus in fully weaponized form. It filled the tunnel with a gray haze that was alive and aching to find blood.

Hopkins went down on his knees. Austen knelt beside him. She saw the tears falling inside his faceplate.

"Everyone out!" Oscar Wirtz was screaming. "We've gone hot!"

THEY made their exit through the steel hatch at the foot of the Manhattan Bridge, into a maelstrom of emergency lights. The area was awash in halogen lights, the air full of the deafening flutter of a half-dozen helicopters.

The Cobra Event had not been lost on New York City residents. Early morning groups of onlookers were being pushed back by police officers. In the east over Brooklyn a red thread of a cloud suggested that dawn was coming. There was no traffic on the Manhattan Bridge, which had been blocked off, and most of the subway lines in lower Manhattan were out of service.

At the command center in the Federal Building and at SIOC in Washington, a feeling was spreading that the situation was still dicey but might possibly be manageable. Fragmentary reports were coming in—a bomb had gone off, an attempt would be made to keep the dust from the bomb contained in the tunnel. The reports were confused, sometimes contradictory, but some things were beginning to emerge. Frank Masaccio listened to his headset. He said, "He's what? . . . The subject is under arrest? Are you sure? Who made the arrest?" He suddenly leaped to his feet. "Austen made the arrest? Are you kidding me?"

THOMAS Cope was brought up by some of the Reachdeep ninjas. He was placed on a gurney and loaded into an ambulance that screamed to the Wall Street heliport. A medevac helicopter lofted him to Governors Island, where he died four hours later.

IN THE classified after-action report, experts agreed that New York City had been very lucky. Fire trucks had poured chemicals and water into the tunnels all day, and the air vents were piled with batting soaked with chemicals. Meanwhile, HEPA filter trucks—essentially vacuum cleaners on wheels—had drawn air out of the tunnel system and passed it through large filters before the air was discharged into the city.

In the end, fourteen citizens contracted Cobra virus infections, for, inevitably, some particles escaped the chemicals and filters and ultimately found a human lung. Five emergency workers also came down with Cobra virus infection. They were mainly fire department people who, in the chaos, had not had time to put on breathing masks. All were given anticonvulsants and the experimental anti-smallpox drug cidofovir, but the treatments had no effect. Another victim was Captain Dorothy Each, who had been bitten by Hector Ramirez. She died on Governors Island.

The overall toll of infections in the Cobra Event stood at thirty-two cases, including Thomas Cope. Ben Kly did not count as a Cobra case, because he had not been infected, although he died as a result of the Cobra infection of Glenn Dudley. Mark Littleberry counted simply as a man lost in action.

Manhattan, Wednesday, May 6

AUSTEN and Hopkins were put in a quarantine unit at New York University Medical Center, where they remained in level 3 biocontainment for four days. They had done their work and needed some peace. Frank Masaccio would not allow them to be held on the island. He felt that they had been through enough and should not have to be kept near people dying of Cobra.

Hopkins called Annie Littleberry in Boston. He told the widow of Mark Littleberry that in recent weeks her husband had made important contributions to the safety of people everywhere. He had helped develop evidence for the existence of a biological-weapons program in Iraq, and he had helped break open a case of a corporation involved in criminal activity in the United States. "Big prosecutions are going to occur as a result of Mark's work. One or more multinational biotechnology companies based in Switzerland and Russia are likely to end up with their top executives under warrant for arrest in the United States," he said. "It's going to be a nightmare for the diplomats. I know Mark would be proud, Mrs. Littleberry. He always enjoyed creating extra work for the diplomats."

"I'M GOING nuts in here," Hopkins said to Austen on the afternoon of the fourth day.

They were dressed in bathrobes and hospital pajamas, and they had been pacing in opposite directions across a small recreational room on the twentieth floor of the hospital. They felt fine. They were the equivalent of the lucky monkeys in the Johnston Atoll tests, the survivors, who might have received one or two particles in the lungs but had remained healthy. It seemed hard to believe that both of them had had no exposure to the Cobra virus, especially Austen. Probably they had received an exposure. On the other hand, perhaps the protective suits had worked.

They had spent the past four days talking on the telephone, it seemed, to every senior official in the U.S. government. For the moment the news media knew little of the details of the operation. Frank Masaccio's people had described Austen and Hopkins as nameless "federal agents" who had "arrested the suspect Thomas Cope." No mention was made of Reachdeep. As far as the public knew, the Cobra Event had been one more brutal act of terrorism, resulting in somewhat more than two dozen fatalities. Few people understood just how grave the situation had been. Austen and Hopkins were grateful for Masaccio's efforts to protect their privacy.

In meetings they had had with each other, neither of them had mentioned a subject that had become increasingly obvious to both of them.

The telephone rang. Hopkins picked it up. "Supervisory Special Agent Hopkins speaking." He had a stiff way of answering telephones. Austen wondered if it was his Bureau training. "Yes, Frank, she's here. I don't think she wants to speak with you right now."

She said, "For the third time, tell him no."

"But he's serious. He says you could rise fast."

"I'm going back to work for Walter Mellis. That's it."

"It's final, Frank. She's going to stay at the CDC." He hung up and walked over to the window. He sighed. "I knew from the moment they put us in here that we weren't going to get sick. It's a law of the universe. When they put you in quarantine, it guarantees your health." He looked at his watch. "They're letting us out at five. What are you going to do anyway?"

"I don't know," she said.

He turned and faced her. "Do you like sushi?"

"Yes, I love sushi."

"So do I. There's this incredible sushi place downtown. What do you say we ditch everybody and go eat some sushi?"

That seemed like a fine idea.

The Host

TOWARD the middle of summer a three-year-old boy living on the Lower East Side developed Cobra brain virus infection and died at Bellevue Hospital. Alice Austen flew up from Atlanta and interviewed the boy's family. She discovered that three days before his death the boy had been bitten on the foot by a rat while he slept.

Then, in early September, a homeless man died in Elmhurst Hospital in Queens of what later turned out to be Cobra infection. He had been living in a subway tunnel in Jackson Heights. The Jackson Heights tunnels connect to the east side of Manhattan through a tunnel under the East River. Possibly, infected rats had migrated through the tunnel from Manhattan.

Investigators from the Centers for Disease Control captured dozens of rats and tested their blood for Cobra. One tested positive.

The rat seemed to have pulled out much of its fur in the belly area. The rat had survived a Cobra infection and had become a carrier. CDC investigators tested more rats from other areas of the city and found that Cobra had entered the rat population, where it could survive without killing its host. Cobra and the rat had made an adjustment with each other.

Suzanne Tanaka had first uncovered evidence that Cobra can survive in rodents when one of her mice became infected but didn't die and when it passed the virus to her, she inadvertently showed that transmission of Cobra can go from rodent to human. Viruses jump from one species to another all the time, and some researchers believe they have a tendency to fill ecological niches—habitats for disease. Cobra seemed to have found a niche in the rat population.

Like all viruses, Cobra had no mind or consciousness, although in a biological sense Cobra was intelligent. It was an opportunist, and it knew how to wait. The rat was a good place to hide for an indefinite time, since humans would never exterminate the rat. In its new host Cobra would cycle through generations of replication, perhaps changing, taking on new forms and strains, awaiting a chance to make another move, a wider breakthrough.

AFTERWORD

The Reality Behind the Cobra Event

THE characters and story developed in this book are fictional, but the historical background is real, the government structures are real, and the science is real or based on what is possible. My sources included eyewitnesses who have seen a variety of biological-weapons installations in different countries, and people who have developed and tested such bioweapons.

The transparent substance I call viral glass is an actual material. I have chosen not to give its technical name or describe it too precisely. I have deliberately distorted and blurred key aspects of the bioweapons-making process so as not to publish a deployable recipe.

The biosensor technology that I call Felix does not presently exist but is in development. Biosensor research is often classified, so I have made educated guesses as to what may be possible. What I call the handheld Boink biosensors actually exist in prototype form. They have been partly developed by the U.S. Navy.

The natural strain of the virus in this book is real, and engineered strains of it have been developed. The virus has great peaceful potential because it is so versatile. Its versatility also makes it a potential weapon. The knowledge is public; the techniques are commonplace. The dark apple hangs on the tree.

For many years the scientific community told itself and the public that biological weapons were not much of a problem. But now many scientists believe that they are a serious threat that has not been reckoned with. Even so, some experts are reluctant to talk too freely about such weapons, for fear that the information could spark bioterrorism.

I say that problems that aren't moved into the light of public discussion become less manageable as time goes by. Public awareness can help shape a constructive response from governments and scientists far more effectively than the lone warnings of a few experts.

Genetic engineering is a process, like metallurgy. Steel can be used for plowshares or swords. What is dangerous is human intent. To think that the power of the genetic code is not being bent toward weapons is to ignore the growing body of evidence, the lessons of history, and the reality of human nature. As Thucydides, the Greek historian, pointed out, hope is an expensive commodity. It makes better sense to be prepared.

RICHARD PRESTON

RICHARD PRESTON

JERRY BAUER

"I've been in love with science from childhood," says Richard Preston, whose earlier best seller, *The Hot Zone,* was a nonfiction account of an outbreak of Ebola virus. The author, however, never actually studied science. "I'm a highly trained journalist," he explains. "I know how to conduct detailed interviews. I'll often go back and interview a scientist five or ten times until I understand exactly what he's talking about."

Preston, who lives what he describes as "a solidly middle-class existence" in New Jersey with his wife and three children, is thinking about writing "another work of fiction based on a lot of fact." His proposed heroine? Dr. Alice Austen.

Sooner
or Later
Elizabeth
Adler

Evil has a way of catching up
with the nicest people,
but so does love. . . .
Sooner or later.

Prologue

1971

THE cushiony leather seats in the back of the white Bentley convertible were Eleanor Parrish Duveen's favorite color. Red. They were also extremely hot. It was early afternoon, but as she was only five years old, she wasn't much good at telling the time.

Ellie's father was sitting next to her mother, who was driving. His arm was flung lazily across the back of her seat, and he was singing "Onward Christian Soldiers." He threw back his head, belting out the verses while her mother laughed gaily at his antics. Occasionally he turned and winked at Ellie, escalating the volume for her benefit and making her mother laugh even harder as she negotiated the dangerous bends leading down the mountain.

The hot California sun beat down on Ellie's red curls. It was so hot she thought it would shrivel her brains. She retrieved her straw hat from the floor and crammed it on her head, pulling it over her eyes. A yawn took her by surprise, and she slithered farther down in the hot red leather seat.

She and her parents had just lunched at the old staging post, hidden in a valley of the Los Padres mountains. It was a place Ellie loved, where fake cowboys barbecued steaks and quail and corn, and sang songs and strummed guitars. Her father sang along, waving his beer glass aloft in time to the music. Then her mother got up and danced, swirling her long, gauzy skirts and clapping her hands over her head like a Spanish Gypsy girl. Ellie was fascinated by her mother's stomping little feet encased in expensive white lizard cowboy boots. She thought she was a wonderful dancer.

Sometimes Ellie overheard people's comments about her parents. "Mad," said those who didn't know them. Those who did know smiled and called them eccentric, rich hippies. They said if there was a great party anywhere in the world, her parents would be there.

"Why not?" Romany Parrish Duveen would reply when asked why she felt the need to fly six or seven thousand miles across the world for one night's entertainment. "Life is meant to be fun" was Rory Duveen's motto, and one he lived by.

Today's lunch had been long and Ellie had eaten too much. The sun beat down on her as she half dozed. Somewhere in the background she could hear her mother laughing, and she thought it was the most delightful sound in the world. When her mother laughed, everything was all right with Ellie's world.

"Oops!" she heard her mother exclaim when the big Bentley wobbled skittishly as it took the curve.

Ellie half opened her eyes. She peered over the edge of the car, over the edge of the road at the jagged rocks in the ravine below. Her mother straightened the wheel, the big convertible rolled smoothly on, and Ellie contentedly closed her eyes again.

"Onward, Christian so-o-o-o-ldiers, Marching as to war, With the cross of Jesus going on before. . . ."

Her father's strong voice and her mother's laughter bounced from the mountain peaks, echoing around the valleys. Then "Oops," her mother said again as the Bentley did another little shimmy.

Her father was still singing when the big car suddenly flung itself into a violent spin.

"Oops," her mother yelled once more, laughing as she tried to straighten out. She was still laughing when the car hurtled over the edge, bouncing from the rocks, deep into the canyon. Because wasn't life all a joke? And maybe death too?

Chapter One

Present Day

THE Hudson Sanitarium was built into a stretch of rocky land overlooking the river in upstate New York. Dark green ivy climbed the walls and circled the barred windows, where, in springtime, starlings and sparrows made their nests.

Those patients who understood what their surroundings were like did not feel quite as happy as the sparrows. Besides the barred windows, there were locked doors, security alarms, and armed guards. The nurses were chosen for their stature and strength, as well as their ability to distribute medication and keep control. The Hudson was a private maximum-security facility for violent patients, committed there by families fearing for their own safety.

The man in room 27 was considered lucky by the other patients. His room was on a corner and had two windows. Both were barred, but they let in light and a glimpse of the trees. He was also remarkably well dressed. He wore smart button-down shirts and chinos in summer and cords and neat sweaters in winter, and he had a seemingly inexhaustible supply of cigarettes and special foods sent in. It was also rumored that he paid a guard to keep him supplied with secret bottles of vodka.

Patrick Buckland Duveen did not agree with the other patients' assessment of his luck. It was not lucky to be incarcerated, and his "privileges" were not due to his wealth. They were to appease the conscience of the woman who'd had him committed to this place, locked in like a "crazy animal," as she had called him in her stern, unafraid voice.

The fact that she was not afraid of him was one of the reasons he had felt compelled to kill her. Too bad he'd not succeeded.

"You should go to jail," she had stormed at him while her guards held him down, his face pressed into the rich, soft carpet at her feet. "But I will not allow you to disgrace our name."

She had told the police she would not press charges against him, but since he was a danger to the public, she intended to have him committed. At her command three eminent doctors signed the documents that had put him away in this place.

In Buck Duveen's book, decent clothing and the occasional bottle of vodka did not make up for a lifetime of missed pleasures. He missed the bars, the booze, and the women. And he missed *power.* He had spent twenty years without it, and he craved it as a child craves candy.

One cloudy, blustery morning in early April he was marched from his room to the office of Hal Morrow, the chief administrator.

Morrow was sitting behind a large teak desk piled with papers. He took Duveen in quietly for a few moments, noticing how fit he looked. He was a tall, well-set-up fellow of . . . Morrow checked his papers: Duveen was forty-two now. He had a fine head of copper-red hair, dark eyes, and a lean-jawed, handsome face. He also had the wiry physique and strong hands of a peasant.

Morrow glanced at the file again. Those same hands had been used to attempt to strangle the woman who had put him in here, as well as, it was suspected, two other women, both prostitutes. No evidence had ever been found to link him definitively with those last two cases, and he had never been prosecuted for them.

Buck Duveen was a psychopath: attractive, charming, unemotional, ruthless. And clever. New guards at the Hudson facility always said you couldn't meet a nicer guy: pleasant, soft-spoken, intelligent. But just when you were lulled into thinking he was okay and began wondering what he was doing in here, he'd surprise you.

Once, he'd almost succeeded in strangling a guard. It took three men just to get him off, and even when they'd knocked him unconscious, they still had to pry his fingers from the guard's neck. He was strong as an ox and crazy as a loon, they said.

Now Buck Duveen watched Morrow, his eyes hooded, face impassive. He knew he was smarter than Morrow. And cleverer than the psychiatrist whom he saw on a weekly basis, twisting the man's smug scientific brain around by feeding him what he would like to hear: about erotic dreams, fantasies, visions. He would watch him, scribbling his notes, nodding his head approvingly, and Buck would be laughing inside because he knew he'd fooled him.

But he wasn't clever enough to escape, though he'd tried a couple of times, and it gnawed at his innards like a cancer. He needed to take his revenge on Charlotte Parrish, the old woman who had put him here. He wanted everything she had, everything that should belong to him. He brooded over it night after night.

One day he would get her. But then there would still be another obstacle. He didn't know what had happened to the child, Ellie Parrish Duveen, only that she must be a grown woman now. Alone in his cell he had conjured up her red-haired image thousands of times, imagining what he would do with her when he got her.

HAL Morrow studied the papers in front of him, considering what he was about to do. The Hudson Sanitarium was a private institution. The inmates' expenses were paid by their relatives, and when those fees could no longer be paid, he had no choice.

He looked up, met the man's eyes. He said, "Duveen, you will be leaving here today. You're a free man."

Duveen's head shot up, his usually dead eyes glittered like polished dark stones in a beam of weak sunlight. "And about time too," he snarled.

"We have been informed by the attorneys in charge of your case that no further money is available to keep you here. However, there is the sum of three hundred and twenty-five dollars left in your account with us. This will be given to you in cash, along with your Social Security card and other personal documents. Your possessions have been packed, and you will be driven to the nearest rail station."

Duveen stared at the ceiling, waiting for him to finish. Three hundred bucks, he thought. A hundred and fifty for each decade he had spent in this place. Fifteen dollars a year . . .

"That is all." Morrow dismissed him. "I wish you good luck in your new life, Duveen."

He did not reply, and as Morrow watched him go, he hoped he was doing the right thing.

ELLIE Parrish Duveen backed the taxicab-yellow Jeep Wrangler out of the garage of the tiny Santa Monica house she called home. Like the Jeep, her house was old and decrepit. Since the last big earthquake none of the walls quite met at the corners, and the bedroom floor trembled when she walked across it, but the house did have a view of the ocean, and it was cheap.

Main Street was at a standstill, and she fretted behind the wheel. As usual, she was running late. Keeping an eye on the traffic, and without the benefit of a mirror, she dusted powder onto her freckled nose, swept black mascara onto her lashes, and added a slick of deep mocha lipstick. Years of being late had made her an expert at the quick traffic-light fix-up. She put the car into gear as the traffic moved off again.

Ellie was twenty-nine years old. She had her mother's misty blue-gray eyes and curly red hair, which she wore long and flowing, except when she was at the café she owned. Then she skewered it beneath a black baseball cap that had ELLIE'S PLACE inscribed on it in green silk.

The café had been open for just over a year, and she worked hard. She did the ordering, kept the accounts, and helped serve the food. She also cooked up a storm whenever the chef quit, which he did every few weeks, as well as baked her own bread and her famous *tarte Tatin,* the specialty of the house. Plus she cleaned the place when the crew failed to show. She was practically a one-man band and she loved it.

Ellie's Place was ticking over, not making a fortune yet, but enough to keep a roof over her head and to stay open. She was, she reminded herself determinedly, doing all right.

Snagging the only free parking spot, she jumped out, shoved a quarter into the meter, and stopped for a minute to look at the café. It was cheerful, painted forest green, with lace café curtains. *Ellie's Place* was written in gold script on the window. An old-fashioned bell tinkled musically as she opened the door.

Inside, it looked like an old Parisian bistro, with smudgy mirrors on the walls, a sprinkling of fresh sawdust on the floor, inexpensive cane chairs, and crisp white tablecloths.

It was a Monday, her day off, but there were still things to be done. She checked the tiny kitchen. Opening the refrigerator, she removed the stacked boxes containing leftover food from the previous night, plus the rosemary-olive bread she'd baked. Laden, she staggered back to the car, tripped over her feet, and lost her backless brown shoe. "Shoot," she muttered. Balancing precariously on one leg, the boxes shifting and sliding, she felt around for the shoe with her bare foot.

"You look like a stork without wings," Maya Morris said as she pulled her red Pathfinder into the curb and leaned out the window, laughing.

Maya was Ellie's best friend and her co-helper at the café. "You might help instead of laughing," Ellie said, pointing to her bare toe.

"Or maybe a ballet dancer." Maya climbed from the car. She was a blond goddess, a knockout, with a helmet of golden hair, whiskey-brown eyes fringed with long dark lashes, and a voluptuous, tightly toned body. She was on her way to yoga class and had on a black leotard and sneakers and not much else, and she was stopping traffic. She slid the shoe onto Ellie's foot. "Anyhow, where are you going?"

"To see Miss Lottie."

Maya nodded; now she knew why, instead of her usual jeans, Ellie was wearing the ice-blue flowered skirt and a deeper blue skinny-knit top. And her mother's pearls—the ones taken from her throat after the automobile accident that had killed her.

Maya dropped a kiss on Ellie's cheek. "Give her my love."

Ellie locked up, then climbed back into the Jeep and headed north on Highway 101. As she drove, Ellie worried about her grandmother. Miss Lottie lived in a run-down old mansion in

Montecito with just a housekeeper to help her. She was well into her eighties, and her mind wandered. She could lose decades between one thought and the next, but then she would recall in perfect detail the time she had bought a hat in Paris in 1939. There were moments, though, when Ellie suspected she simply chose to be vague, when there was something she just didn't want to discuss.

"Old age has its advantages, my dear," Miss Lottie had said smugly when Ellie exasperatedly accused her of faking. "I brought you up properly after your poor mother died. You've flown the nest; I have no more responsibilities. Now I'm without a care in the world."

Ellie only wished it were true. Meanwhile, the traffic was bad, and she was going to be late. Again.

LOTTIE Parrish's "cottage" stood on twenty prime acres of land ten minutes south of Santa Barbara, in the affluent little resort township of Montecito. Tropical-hued bougainvillea sprawled in abundance along Coast Village Road, which was lined with little boutiques and restaurants, and tourists. But for all the activity down in the "town," life up on Hot Springs Road might not have changed since the '30s, when the grand Italianate mansion had been built by Charlotte Parrish's father.

Waldo Stamford, a Boston Yankee, had fallen in love with the tiny, flower-bedecked coastal community. He'd built his house of imported cream limestone, with a columned arcade, tall French windows leading onto shady patios, fountained courtyards and gardens. He'd called the house Journey's End. Each of the twelve bedroom suites had its own bath and sitting room, and each had been fitted out with European antiques and priceless rugs, gold faucets shaped like dolphins, and the very best Irish linen sheets.

Waldo and his young daughter, Lottie, had entertained lavishly, filling the house with flamboyant movie stars, as well as "proper" people, meaning California's tycoons and gentry. But now Miss Lottie, as she was always known affectionately, never entertained.

Miss Lottie was still in her room, supposedly getting dressed for Ellie's visit, but instead, she was sitting at the antique Venetian desk.

An old green celluloid visor that her father used to wear for his poker games shaded her eyes, and she was busy at her personal computer, answering her E-mail. She typed:

> Dear Al,
>
> Thank you for your message. I'm sorry to hear of your problem with your paramour. I think you should marry her at once. Settle down, have children. This is what life is for. Believe me, I know.

She'd bought the computer when her old lawyer died. She just couldn't get along with Michael Majors, the new fellow who'd taken his place, and she'd decided to manage her money herself. A nice, very clever young computer expert had come in for a week to teach her how it all worked, and to her surprise she loved it. She had her own Internet address and corresponded with any number of strangers, some of whom seemed to have become friends.

She also moved her investments around on a daily basis. Sometimes she won; more often she lost. Too often, it had turned out.

A few weeks ago the lawyer and accountants had told her that there was no money left. They'd come to see her, carrying bulky files and ledgers, and she had sat, bewildered, while they went over everything point by point, expense after expense. Miss Lottie had no choice but to approve the termination of what they called "the unnecessary expenses." That meant the charities dearest to her heart, old friends who'd fallen on hard times to whom she gave money, retired servants whose medical expenses she helped with. She'd sighed regretfully and agreed it could not go on.

"You have to think of yourself, Miss Lottie," the lawyer admonished sternly. "You'll need whatever money we can salvage. You're just not a rich woman anymore."

But no matter what the accountants had said, somehow Miss Lottie didn't think life at Journey's End would change much. After all, it hadn't changed in sixty years. It was still elegant, still beautiful, still home.

Sighing for the past, she picked up her cane and went to get dressed. Half an hour later she was waiting for Ellie on the marble-paved terrace, sitting in a high-backed rattan chair that was probably almost as ancient as she was, with Bruno, her beloved old golden Labrador, dozing beside her.

Taking a sip of the cool lemonade brought to her by Maria, her dear friend and housekeeper, Miss Lottie reminded herself to count her blessings: The sun was warm, the sky a clear blue. Bruno was sprawled by her chair. And Ellie was coming to visit.

ELLIE had been shocked when the lawyer told her of the destruction Miss Lottie's stock market gambling had brought. He'd explained what he'd done, and said there would be just enough to keep her grandmother in comfortable, if not lavish, style. Then he'd asked if Ellie could persuade her to sell the property.

"A run-down mansion won't bring much on today's market, but the prime twenty acres in Montecito certainly will."

But Ellie would have none of it. Miss Lottie had lived at Journey's End for more than sixty years, and that's where she would stay, even if Ellie had to work double hours to keep her there. Miss Lottie and Maria had looked after her when she was a child; now it was her turn.

The tall oak doors stood welcomingly open, and she shook her head worriedly as she strode into the flagstoned great hall, thinking how unaware her grandmother and Maria were of present-day dangers. Open doors invited robbers—or worse. But the two women never gave it a thought.

Maria appeared, wiping her hands on a tea cloth. "Late again, Ellie."

"Anybody would think I made a habit of it." She swung Maria into her arms, whirling her around. "Oooh, Maria. I've missed you. And you smell so good, of vanilla and sweetness."

"That's just my soul you can smell, the goodness of it." Maria's face was pink with pleasure. "Anyhow, it's just some cookies I baked. I thought you might enjoy them."

"You spoil me. And you know I'm just a brat."

"Somebody's got to spoil you. You look tired, Ellie."

"I know. And don't tell me—I'll bet I'm untidy as well."

Smoothing her windswept hair, Ellie bent to pet the dog as he lumbered to his feet, doing his best to gambol toward her. "Sweet old boy, lovely dog. Who loves you, mmmm?"

"There you are," Miss Lottie called to her from the terrace.

"Sorry I'm late, Miss Lottie. It's the traffic. But now I'm here, let's hit the Biltmore. I'm famished."

"It's a good thing I still remember where the Biltmore is." Miss Lottie put on a wide-brimmed straw hat trimmed with pink roses. "And I also remember exactly where I got this hat. In Paris, in 1939. Long before your time," she added. "I bought it at Madame Pepita's on the Faubourg Saint-Honoré. Fifty-five dollars it cost. And that was a small fortune then, I can assure you."

"See, Miss Lottie. You can remember when you want to." Ellie helped her into the custom-built 1972 white Cadillac, whose only outings these days were to the Biltmore and back.

The Caddy purred smoothly down the drive, cushioned as a baby carriage, and Ellie said, "The manager is expecting us. No doubt they'll roll out the red carpet for you."

"Nonsense, Ellie. They see us every Monday. Besides, they understand a lady doesn't like a fuss."

Secretly, though, Miss Lottie enjoyed the attention. After all, she'd been dining at the Biltmore for more than half a century now. And maybe later she would persuade Ellie to sleep over. Then it would be just like old times.

IN MANHATTAN, Buck Duveen checked into a cheap hotel near Times Square. He went out and bought himself a steak dinner and found a bar where they stocked reasonably good bourbon. He bought a bottle.

Tanked up, he found himself a hooker and took her into a dark alley. He felt a surge of power. It was a feeling he had not experienced in a long time. While he was doing it, he put his hands around her slender neck and began to squeeze. He had no worries about anyone coming into the alley and seeing him, because he was in control. He was invincible.

She gagged, fought back, so he punched her senseless. When he had finished, he let go of her and she slid to the ground. He took a switchblade from his pocket and carefully etched a deep cross into her forehead. Temple to temple, scalp to nose. It was something he liked to do, his personal mark. Hefting her easily in his strong arms, he flung her into a Dumpster, took the bottle of bourbon from his pocket, and poured it over her.

He straightened his clothing, took out a cigarette, lit it, and tossed the lit match into the Dumpster. Whistling "Dixie" under his breath, as he always did when he felt elated, he strolled back down the alley. He felt like a new man. He felt glorious again.

As he turned the corner, he heard the whoosh of flames. He smiled. He'd always enjoyed fire.

This was only a warm-up, but he thought it wasn't bad for his first day's work in twenty years.

HOMICIDE detective Dan Cassidy was at his desk in the squad room of Manhattan's Midtown South Precinct fiddling with the computer. There was no need; his notes were as complete as he was ever going to make them. Shutting the machine down, he turned his attention to his files. They were all in order. He opened the desk drawers and closed them again. They were empty.

Pushing back his chair, he sipped his fifth cup of coffee of the evening and wondered anxiously if he was doing the right thing. Didn't they always say you couldn't go home again? He shrugged off the misgivings. It was too late now.

Dan was dark-haired and blue-eyed, like his Irish ancestors, and built tall and rangy like his mother's family. He'd grown up in Santa Barbara, a typical outdoorsy Californian—a champion swimmer and an avid surfer and fisherman. He was a lean, hard-bodied thirty-nine-year-old, attractive, and with an ex-wife in L.A.

They'd married young, when Dan was still in college. The breakup came a couple of years later, and he'd wanted to put as much distance between himself and the past as possible. He'd needed a new direction, so he'd gone to New York and become a cop. He'd never regretted it. He cared about his job and cared about the victims. "Dan's only failing is that he can't set the whole world to rights all by himself," the chief had complained, but he was smiling when he said it.

Two years ago Dan had been badly wounded, shot in the chest while arresting a murder suspect. Only quick action by his partner and friend, Detective Pete Piatowsky, had saved him.

He'd been lucky this time, but the injury left him with a stiffness in the right arm and shoulder that hampered his speed when drawing a weapon. The police medical board had assigned him to permanent administrative duties.

Life behind a desk did not appeal, and that's why, tomorrow, Dan was on a flight back to California, where he'd bought a small winery not far from the town where he grew up. He told himself he'd had enough of murder and mayhem to last him several lifetimes. He wanted to get back to the simpler life the countryside offered. Horses, dogs, chickens—small-town living.

He'd never actually visited the property, though when he first saw the ad, he'd remembered the area from when he was a kid. And he wasn't a complete greenhorn. He'd earned college tuition working at a vineyard. He'd done everything from toiling in the fields to harvesting grapes, to working in the bottling plant. He'd experienced all the problems—like the sudden frost that could wipe out a crop overnight if you didn't get out there fast and mist down the vines. He'd seen grapes shriveled by disease. And most of all, he'd learned how dependent a winemaker was on the weather. Good vines plus good weather equaled a good crop. It was a simple equation. He only hoped he could make it work.

The sunshiny photos of Running Horse Ranch had shown a rolling landscape scattered with scrub oak, shady eucalyptus, and bare-looking rows of vines. There was a little wooden house, complete with a wraparound porch, a red barn that housed the winery, and Spanish adobe-style stables set around a picturesque courtyard.

It looked so good he had fallen instantly in love with it. Besides, it was cheap. With his savings and his disability pension he could just about swing it. And now he was hoping, uneasily, that it was really as great as it looked in the pictures.

Heaving a sigh, he wandered back into the squad room just as the call came in about the burned-up body in the alleyway off Times Square. His adrenaline rose as he headed for the door. "What the hell, I'll ride with you one last time," he told Piatowsky.

"You're never going to make it in the sticks," Piatowsky said. "You can't even get yourself outta here and into the saloon for your own farewell party. I'm bettin' you're back in three months."

Dan was tall, but Piatowsky was a blond giant. He was forty-two years old, wore his thinning blond hair combed carefully across his high forehead. His blue eyes had a deceptively mild expression. Dan knew him to be sharp as a razor, a good detective as well as a good friend. And Piatowsky had saved his life. He owed him.

THE sickening stench of charred flesh hit them as soon as they stepped out of the car. Death on the streets was never pretty, and this one was gruesome. The flames had not eliminated the cross etched deeply into the woman's forehead, exposing her skull.

The medical examiner was leaning over the stinking Dumpster, doing what he had to do.

"I'd bet it wasn't the knife that killed her," the M.E. said finally. "It was strangulation. Mutilation came after death, and the fire was probably an attempt to destroy the evidence."

To the disgust of the two detectives the fire department had washed away any possible clues with the fierce water hoses.

"Whoever he is, he's a sicko," Piatowsky said wearily to Dan. "Anyhow, why did he have to carve a cross on her forehead after she's dead?"

"It's his signature, an ego thing. My guess is he's done it before. You might check records, see what nut has just finished a prison sentence and hit the streets again."

"Thanks a lot, buddy, but why don't you take your smart-guy FBI profiling outta here and go to your own farewell party." He shook Dan's hand, slapping his shoulder affectionately. "Wish I could get there, but as usual, I'm stuck with the body."

Dan hated to leave. Friends like Piatowsky didn't cross your path often in life. Straightening his shoulders, he walked into the crowds and the anonymous night.

Chapter Two

DAN backed his brand-new white Explorer into a tight spot on Main Street. The California sun blazed down, bronzed people in shorts and T-shirts whizzed by him on Rollerblades or simply took it easy at sidewalk cafés, and his parking meter still had half an hour left on it. It was early April, and he'd seen the weather back east on TV: They'd just had another two inches of snow. Feeling that life wasn't too bad after all, Dan strolled into a café called Ellie's Place.

The red-haired young woman behind the coffee machine gave him a dazzling smile of welcome that seemed to spread from one pretty diamond-studded ear to the other.

"Be right with you," she called. "The coffee machine's acting up again, though, so if it's caffeine you're after, you might want to try Starbucks. It's on the next block."

"Juice is fine. It's eggs I really want, scrambled."

"Okay." She wrote the order and headed toward the kitchen.

Cute, he thought, as she came back with a basket of fresh bread and set it in front of him. Her eyes were the pale bluish-gray of opals, her nose was freckled, and her red hair was bunched through a black baseball cap in a long, curly ponytail. It was odd, but he felt he'd seen her somewhere before.

"Out here on vacation?" She arranged the table mat and cutlery. Her voice was deep and soft as melted chocolate.

"How do you know I don't live here?"

"It's that East Coast pallor. It's a dead giveaway. A couple of days at the beach, and you'll be fine."

"How come you're so pale, then?"

"That's my grandmother's doing. She always made me wear a hat when I was a kid, never let me sunbathe. And you know what? She was right. I thank her every time I look in the mirror. No lines, no sunspots. I'm a lucky woman."

Ellie smiled at him, then walked back to the kitchen and returned a few minutes later with a plate of eggs, which she set in front of him. Back behind the counter, she cast him a speculative glance.

Cute, she thought, if you could call a guy that rugged "cute." Deep blue eyes that looked as though they had seen it all, thick dark hair, hawkish nose, and blue-stubbled jaw. Lean, broad-shouldered, muscular.

She shrugged regretfully. She didn't have time for men. A career girl was what she was now, determined to make her way in the world. Ellie's Place was only her first venture. One day she would be the owner of a Michelin-starred restaurant. Besides, she had her grandmother to take care of. She definitely didn't need a man to complicate her life.

The cute guy finished his eggs, then came over to pay his check. "Thanks," he said with a smile. "I enjoyed it."

"Enjoy your vacation," she called as he strode to the door.

He stood on the sidewalk, hands in his pockets, taking in the street scene before getting into the white Explorer. Ellie thought he surely had a great walk, confident, sexy.

Then she put the thought determinedly from her mind.

DAN drove up the coast, savoring the scenery. Running Horse Ranch lay just to the north of Santa Barbara in an area of gently rolling green hills that in summer would be scorched by the sun to the color of crusty French bread. He drove past other wineries, admiring their orderly rows of vines, already bursting into leaf, and the attractive winetasting facilities set in manicured gardens.

Running Horse Ranch was not quite like that. He got out of the car and stared at the slopes of shriveled vines, then picked up a handful of earth, let it trickle through his fingers. It was dust-bowl dry. Squaring his shoulders, he climbed back into the car and bounced over the ruts to the top of the hill to inspect his new home.

The little New England–style farmhouse hadn't seen a coat of paint in a decade. A sagging porch ran around it, and every window was cracked. The steps creaked ominously as he walked across and unlocked the door. Years of dust covered the few bits of broken furniture. Ominous trails of droppings led to holes in the baseboards.

Pete Piatowsky's words echoed in his head. "You're buying a pig in a poke, man," he'd warned. Was he ever right.

Wondering which he would have to tackle first, the vines or the house, Dan went out to look at the winery. The big red barn housed tall steel fermenting vats, the crushing machinery, and stacks of moldy-looking oak barrels. In the bottling plant in the adjoining shed everything was covered in a thick coat of dust.

Gloomily he walked through the graceful arched gates into the stables courtyard. There was an old tiled fountain in the center of the courtyard, and scarlet petunias and purple bougainvillea tumbled picturesquely from clay pots. It looked exactly the way it had in the photograph when he'd lost his heart to it—a perfect rustic idyll.

To Dan's surprise the stables weren't too bad. Sure, the paint was blistered and peeling, but the roof looked fine, and the six stalls were in good condition. Cheering up, he decided first thing, he would buy a couple of horses. He hadn't ridden since he was a kid, but they would make the place feel more like home.

There was a satisfied smile on his face as he circled the reedy pond at the back of the house and strolled around the porch. He saw exactly where to place his chair for that sundown drink and began to think maybe it wasn't such a pig in a poke after all. Suddenly he couldn't wait to tackle it.

He thought regretfully of the attractive young woman at the café.

There would be no room for romance in his life for a long, long time. Not with all this work to be done.

WHEN the big locomotive pulled out of Penn Station, Buck Duveen felt as excited as a child leaving on vacation. He was on his way to L.A. at last. The only thing bothering him about going back to California was his mother. Over a couple of drinks in the bar car he had plenty of time to brood over her and their life together.

In the small town near Santa Cruz, where they had lived in a pin-neat yellow Victorian house with white gingerbread trim, Buck had been a mama's boy. Delia Duveen never let him out of her sight. It was always, Buck come here, Buck do this, Buck do that. He was not allowed to play with other kids after school, because he had to do his homework and practice his piano. And then there were the chores. Saturdays he got to mow the lawn and wash her immaculately kept, old Plymouth. And on Sundays she drove him to church.

He sat quietly beside her, in his dark blue blazer and starched blue shirt, with his short-cropped red hair combed flat, his striped tie neatly knotted. Plump Delia wore pastel dresses in summer and a nice tailored gray suit in winter, and she always wore a hat. Nothing frivolous, just a plain straw with a ribbon or a dark felt with a feather.

Evenings, Delia and Buck sat opposite each other in the small, overfurnished dining room, beneath the blaze of a mock-crystal chandelier, sipping plain water because she disapproved of soda pop and, anyhow, never allowed soda bottles on the table.

Buck Duveen hated his home, hated his life. And from a young age he loathed his mother with an overpowering force that made him itch to kill her. But to Delia Duveen and the neighbors he was the perfect son. "Wish my boys were like him," the neighboring mothers said to each other when their own kids were wreaking havoc.

Buck had never really known his father, Rory Duveen. His mother had divorced him when Buck was three years old. She'd implied that she had no time for what went on in the bedroom. In her mind, sex was a word with a capital S. S for sin. S for sickening.

S for shame. So Rory had left. He'd given Delia everything he had—the house and all his money—in settlement. He wanted nothing to do with her or her child.

The only thing Buck remembered about his father was his singing in church. There was a particular hymn that was his father's favorite, because it was the kind you sang loud and strong: *Onward, Christian soldiers, Marching as to war, With the cross of Jesus going on before. . . .*

Buck could hear Rory's voice in his head, see that cross he sang about. Somehow it made him feel like a god, crusading for his rights. To him the cross was a symbol of his power and masculinity. The sign belonged to him and to his father.

Buck thought he would escape from Delia when he went away to college, down the coast at U.C., Santa Barbara. By then he was a clever young man, tall, strongly built, with copper-red hair and deep-set dark eyes that shifted slyly away when he spoke to you. Still, he was attractive and he got himself a date the first week. She wasn't available for a second date, though, and told her friends he was creepy. Same thing happened with another girl, then another. So he paid a hooker. It was over in seconds. Then he beat her up, took back his money, and kicked her out of his car. Hookers were easy; he was the one in control.

Delia kept him short of money, and he was working two jobs to pay his way through college. He felt demeaned by his poverty and by the shabby old wreck of a car he drove. He wanted Delia's money, and he wanted to be rid of her.

One night, after a bottle of vodka, he saw the light. A voice in his head told him all he had to do was remove his mother from his life. He made his plans carefully, going over them again and again. He even did a test run one night, driving from the campus at Santa Barbara and sneaking up to the house.

The night of the killing, everything went according to plan. She never heard him come in, never spoke, never screamed. Only her puzzled eyes, bugging from her head, had fixed on his, while his strong hands squeezed the life out of her. Submitting to an overwhelming compulsion, he carved the sign of the cross into her forehead. He looked at it, pleased. It was his signature.

Before he left, he jimmied the back door, ransacked the place, took the money from her purse so the cops would think she'd been robbed. The next morning he drove back again and "found" the mutilated body. He called the cops, distraught, his voice choked with sobs. The evidence of a fight was all around: a table tipped over, vases smashed, her purse flung to the ground.

Buck was never a suspect. He was always a good kid, people said sympathetically, a bit of a loner, but he surely looked after his mom.

He inherited the house and the bank accounts. He bought a Porsche convertible, a Rolex, and some smart clothes.

He'd found killing easy after that. No need for much planning, the way he'd had to with Delia. Random killings without motive, by a stranger in a strange place, were almost impossible to solve.

He'd had the formula down pretty good until the old woman had him locked up. Now her turn had come to join the elite, he thought, as he stared out the train window into the dark night. She was as good as his. And this time he meant to really enjoy it.

DAN exited the freeway and halted at the stop sign at the turn to Olive Mill Road in Montecito. The Explorer's engine idled perfectly as he waited for the oncoming traffic to slow. Glancing in the rearview mirror, he observed uneasily the yellow Jeep coming up too fast behind him. He couldn't believe the driver would just keep on going, until, with a squeal of brakes, she rear-ended him.

Blood boiling, he leaped from the car. "What are you, blind?" he yelled. "Or just crazy?"

"No, I am not," Ellie yelled back hotly, climbing from the Jeep. "And you might at least be civilized about this."

"Civilized? Lady, I've had this vehicle exactly five days. You want me to be *civilized?*" He stared angrily at the dent in the back of the Explorer, then turned and glared at her. Her red hair whipped around her face in the breeze. He said, surprised, "Oh. It's you."

Ellie suddenly recognized him. It was the blue-eyed macho man.

"And it's you," she said coldly. "And if you don't behave in a civilized fashion, I'll call the police."

He grinned at her, a mocking little smile. "Lady, I *am* the police. Homicide. Manhattan." Then he remembered. "Delete that. I *was* the police. Now I'm just Dan Citizen who's mad because his new car has been smacked up. Can you blame me?"

"Of course not." Ellie looked disconsolately at the Explorer. "My hair blew across my face just for that second. I usually tie it back when I'm driving. It was all my fault." She fished her bag from the car and took out a card. "Here's my registration and insurance."

Dan looked at the name: Ellie Parrish Duveen. It had a familiar ring to it. "Don't I know you from somewhere?"

"The café. You came in for eggs, no coffee."

"But I know your name. I lived around here when I was a kid."

Ellie inspected him warily for a minute. Of course, how could she forget? He'd been the heartthrob of the beach.

"We called you Danny Boy. I think I even had a crush on you. All the girls did, even though you were an older man."

"I was eighteen, and you must have been about eight or nine. I think I taught you to surf."

"But I seem to remember your Irish eyes were always smiling then. What happened to make you so angry at the world?"

He shook his head at the female way she'd just managed to twist things around. "No man's eyes, Irish or otherwise, smile when his brand-new vehicle has just been severely dented." He began busily writing down his new address for her and the name of his insurance company. "Business is business."

"Tell me about it." She sighed dramatically. Then she read his address. "Running Horse Ranch," she remarked, surprised. "It's been on the market for years. Don't tell me you bought it?"

"Yup. Why?" He was beginning to suspect he knew the answer.

She hesitated, avoiding his eyes. He obviously hadn't heard about the jinx. "Oh, no reason. It's really pretty around there." She glanced at the traffic circling them. "We'd better get going. It was nice to meet you again, Dan Cassidy. Good luck with the winery.

Maybe I'll be able to buy some wine from you before too long."

"I'll take you up on that," he promised as she got back into the Jeep. As he drove off, he eyed her through the rearview mirror. Cute was definitely the wrong word. If she hadn't wrecked his new Explorer, he would have called her beautiful. He sighed regretfully, then put her out of his mind and drove to the cottage he was renting at the beach until he got his property in shape.

It wasn't until later, sitting alone on the deck of his beach house, enjoying the view of the ocean, that he remembered who she was. One of the megarich Parrishes. Lottie Parrish had been one of the society leaders in the area. He seemed to remember talk of a butler and uniformed housemaids and a French chef. He wondered why Ellie Parrish Duveen was driving a beat-up old Jeep Wrangler.

THE next evening he was again out on his deck overlooking the ocean. He'd put in a long, hard day walking his property, all forty dried-out acres of it. He'd advertised for a winemaker and spoken to a building contractor about fixing up the house.

He poured a glass of wine and stared moodily at the opalescent sky. The color reminded him of Ellie Parrish Duveen's eyes. Taking her card out of his shirt pocket, he dialed her number.

"Ellie's," she said. "Can I help you?"

The soft voice made him smile with pleasure. "I just thought I'd let you know the Explorer isn't as bad as it first looked."

"I'm glad to hear it, Danny Boy." There was laughter in her voice. "And so, I'm sure, will my insurance company."

"I was just wondering . . ."

"What?"

He heard the background music and clatter of dishes. "Can you tell me why, though Montecito is on the edge of the Pacific, the sun sets over the mountains and not the ocean?"

"That's because the coastline faces south at that point, and the Santa Ynez Mountains run east to west. Confusing, I know, for newcomers, but a fact of nature. Anyhow, you can't fool me. You already know that. What are you doing watching the sunset over the ocean? I thought you were inland, at Running Horse Ranch?"

"Unfortunately, the ranch house needs a bit of work before it can be termed habitable except by rats and gophers. That's why I'm in a rented cottage on Padaro Lane, watching sunsets, all alone. . . ."

"And lonely."

Dan said, "You've got it. And that brings me to my other question. I know you're a busy workingwoman, but even you must get a night off? I thought it might be a good opportunity to check out the competition. Say, dinner at Chinois?"

Ellie laughed at the idea. "Danny Boy, I'm no competition for them. I'm just a speck in L.A.'s ocean of little cafés." Then she gave her stock reply that she gave any guy who asked her out these days. "Look, I'm sorry. I just don't have any free time right now." She glared at Maya, who was eavesdropping. "Thanks, anyway."

"Sure," Dan said. "Anyway, it was nice to meet you. Again."

"Good-bye." She sounded edgy as she put down the phone.

Maya stood, arms folded, chin belligerently sticking out. "Did I miss something? Or was someone asking you out on a date?"

Ellie nodded. "He was."

"And?" Maya held up a protesting hand; she already knew the answer. "No, don't tell me. You said you were too busy. Woman, you can't go on like this. There's real life out there."

Ellie grinned. "I simply told him I was too busy right now," she said. "And if you paid a little more attention to the customers instead of eavesdropping on my conversations, you'd notice that table three is waiting for menus."

Maya glared at her, then flounced off in a huff.

MAYA Morris had been Ellie's best friend since college. She had arrived in Phoenix from the East Coast, a Manhattan Jewish girl—blond, beautiful, with a fast mouth. And Ellie had arrived from the West Coast, all tumbling red hair and long legs, perfect manners, and a wild look of newfound freedom that spelled trouble. The two of them recognized each other instantly. They were soul mates.

In a couple of weeks they'd found themselves an apartment off-campus and began throwing parties. After a month the landlord threw them out.

Undaunted, they found another place, a house where the noise would be less noticeable. Then Ellie, high on freedom, traded in her Pathfinder for a Harley. Metallic scarlet, flashy with polished chrome. Maya, ever fashionable, tuned right in. "We'll need proper outfits."

"Right."

Maya climbed on the back, and they shot downtown to the bike shop. An hour later they emerged, sleek as panthers in tight black leather pants, boots, and sinister black-and-silver helmets.

"Perfect" was Maya's comment.

They soon became known as the Arizona State Hogettes, famous for their speed and their general outrageousness.

Until the boom came down. The dean threatened expulsion, and Miss Lottie and Mr. Morris showed up, furious.

"I've come to take you home, Ellie," Miss Lottie had said coldly. "Mr. Morris agrees with me that there's no point in you girls staying at college if you're not going to learn anything."

"But Gran . . ."

"You're forgetting your manners. Ellie, say hello to Mr. Morris."

Ellie shook hands, smiling uncertainly at Maya's father. "There's nothing for it but to apologize to both of you," she said humbly. "I didn't mean to upset you. I'm sorry, truly I am."

She meant every word of it. Maya could tell.

Then they all went out to lunch, and Miss Lottie and Michael Morris decided on a three-month probationary period, with mandatory good grades. The girls shouldered their responsibilities. They went to classes, worked nights in the library, got those decent marks, and, finally, graduated.

Since then they'd both fallen in and out of love several times, but only one affair was serious. Ellie met Steve Cohen in New York City at a party in SoHo. He was tall and lean, and an intellectual. Overnight Ellie changed from a sexy dresser to black turtlenecks, long black skirts, and Doc Martens.

Maya knew Steve wasn't worth it. But she went along with it, hanging out with the SoHo crowd, while Ellie went to culinary school and she attended creative writing classes at Columbia.

Ellie always said it was the New York winter that killed her plans to marry Steve. Or maybe he was always too busy pursuing a new career as an art dealer. Either way the winter storms kept them apart, and so did his new, upwardly mobile social life. Ellie was wounded, but typically, she took it on the chin. Brokenhearted, she went off to Paris to gain culinary experience instead.

When she returned to California, Maya soon followed. The two of them rented an apartment in Venice Beach while they looked around at the men and the job opportunities and decided how to play out their lives.

Maya wasn't at all sure she'd found the answer yet, but Ellie certainly had. She knew what she wanted: her own café.

It had taken her over a year of sheer, teeth-gritted hard work to pull it together, and that was on a shoestring. But together it was at last. And Ellie was not about to let it fail, even if she worked all hours that God sent. And that, Maya thought, was where the problem lay.

IT WAS one in the morning before Ellie got home. Her back and feet ached, and there were ripples of tension in her neck.

Kicking off her shoes, she thought wistfully of Dan Cassidy's invitation. Dinner out? The idea was laughable. *She* was the one who organized and served dinners. *She* ate hers in the café kitchen, not in smart restaurants.

Besides, she was afraid of getting involved. Too much was at stake. Everything she had and could borrow was invested in Ellie's Place, and that meant her whole life, her future.

She took a shower, pulled on an old T-shirt and a pair of white sweat socks, and sat in front of the mirror, patting cream into her face. Then she brushed her long hair, wishing it didn't curl and wondering how she might look with a straight bob.

Wandering to the window, she stared out at her tiny glimpse of ocean, which reflected the high-riding moon, and imagined a date with Dan Cassidy. Dressing up, a good restaurant. It didn't seem to fit somehow. Still, as she climbed wearily into bed, it wasn't a bad image to fall asleep with.

All the next day, while she was working, she couldn't get that image out of her mind. Finally, when it got to evening, she picked up the phone and called him.

"Hi," she said. "It's the surfer girl who rear-ended you."

She heard the smile in his voice. "You again."

"I was just thinking, the café is closed on Mondays. I usually drive up to see my grandmother. Why don't we have dinner? It doesn't have to be fancy. A barbecue on the beach would be fine."

Over the phone came the sound of barking. Ellie asked, astonished, "Was that a dog I just heard?"

"Meet my new friend, Pancho," Dan said. "I couldn't stand watching the sunset alone, so I visited the animal shelter."

"That bad, huh?" Ellie was smiling.

"That bad," he agreed.

"Around seven, then? I'll bring the fixings; you chill the wine."

He gave her the address. "I'm looking forward to it, Ellie."

"Me too. See you Monday." She kept her voice cool, but a little wellspring of excitement bubbled inside her like champagne.

MUCH later, after the café was closed, Ellie set up the tables for the next morning's breakfast, enjoying the temporary peace and quiet. The traffic had slowed on Main Street, and the few passersby never even glanced at the darkened café.

She poured a cup of coffee, then sat at a table by the window, gazing into the quiet night. Fog was rolling in, muting the streetlights, drifting, silent as smoke. She found it soothing after her hectic day.

Her conversation with Dan Cassidy floated through her mind, and she again wondered if he'd heard about the jinx on Running Horse yet. She'd hate to be the one to tell him, but no wine had been produced there in years, and they said it was a bad-luck place. She hoped for Dan's sake it wasn't true.

She thought of her mother and father: Romany and Rory. Wistfully she wondered if they would have approved of Dan. It was silly, she told herself, to still long for a mother and father to share things with. Even now, a grown woman, she missed them. Miss Lottie had been a wonderful companion: grandmother, mother, father, friend, and loyal supporter. She'd shown up for PTA meetings, cheered on the sidelines at softball games, sent her off to camp and written faithfully every day. She had even bailed her out when she was acting like an idiot that time at college. No one could have done it better.

But there was still something inside Ellie that yearned for the closeness she remembered in the big car, driving home with her parents. Just the three of them. The memory of that day still troubled her. She recalled every detail: the hot leather seat, her mother's white lizard boots, her father's last smile, and the wink he'd given her. At least, she told herself, she remembered everything, but often, in her dreams, she thought there was something else. Something important out there on the blackest edge of her dream. Just when she thought she'd got it, she would see herself sitting by the side of the road, alone and crying, with the blood running down her face. And silence all around her. The silence of death.

A shiver ran down her spine. She swallowed the hot coffee quickly and carried the empty cup into the kitchen. She didn't sleep well that night.

Chapter Three

BUCK thought L.A. was hot, meaning more than just the sun was shining. He was sitting at a café table on Sunset Plaza, taking in the crowded lunch scene. Things had changed in the couple of decades he'd been incarcerated, and he couldn't believe women like this existed outside of magazines. Tall blondes with long, swingy hair; lustrous dark-haired women with bold eyes and long, long legs. Now and then a girl smiled at him as she pushed her way through the crowded tables, and he smiled confidently back. With his new look he fit in.

It was more than the expensive beige chinos, the light linen shirt, the suede Gucci loafers, and the rented convertible parked in the lot behind the café. Now his red hair was a dark chestnut, courtesy of the smart hairdressing salon down the block. The new dark mustache suited his long, lean face, and the cool steel-framed sunglasses hid the heat in his eyes. He looked like a different man: rich, sleek, good-looking. He felt the power again. He could do whatever he wanted, have whichever woman he wanted. But right now his mind was fixed on business.

He was instinctively a man of the streets, and he knew how to find what he needed. He drove downtown and took a stroll. He hadn't gone more than a couple of blocks before he was accosted.

"Coke, mister?" a voice called from the darkened doorway.

Buck's eyes darted quickly to the man. He was black and big and menacing, but Buck was buzzing with power and had no fear of him. He had the open switchblade palmed, ready.

"What if I told you I was a cop?" He grinned as he said it, savoring the flash of alarm in the drug pusher's eyes.

The guy didn't breathe. "I . . . I didn't mean nothin', Officer. It's nothin'. . . . I'll just get going."

Suddenly the pusher reached for his gun. With the same speed and strength of the madman who had almost strangled his guard, Buck slashed the switchblade into his hand.

The man made no sound. He just stood there looking at his bloody hand and at the Glock 27 automatic lying in the dirt.

"You ain't no cop," he gasped. "Look, y'can have all I got. . . . It's yours, man. Just let me go, that's all."

Buck was enjoying it. "You give me the information I need. Maybe I'll give you your life." He pushed the tip of the knife against the man's ribs.

"You got it, man. Whatever you want."

"Identity cards, Social Security . . ."

"Alvarado Street, that's where you go. Twenty, maybe fifty bucks. Buy anything you want—green cards, driver's licenses."

Buck gave the knife another little push, and a red stain grew quickly around the point of the blade. For an instant he contemplated whether to finish the job, but killing men wasn't his thrill.

"Thanks," he said, "for everything."

Pocketing the Glock, which was a nice little bonus, he turned away. "Consider yourself lucky," he called over his shoulder.

Alvarado Street was bustling. Buck didn't even need to look for the sellers. They found him. Within a couple of hours he had acquired the name and life of one Edward Jensen, complete with Social Security card, driver's license, and the registration of a stolen and revamped BMW convertible.

He abandoned the rental car, which he would later report stolen, then drove the BMW to the Santa Monica branch of the First National Bank, where he opened a checking account and arranged for the remainder of the money he'd inherited when his mother died to be transferred from a bank in New York.

With his new luggage in the BMW's trunk, "Ed Jensen" drove up the coast. In Montecito he swept grandly up the driveway of the Four Seasons Biltmore, handed the car keys to a valet, checked into an ocean-view room, then strolled into the bar and bought himself a double bourbon to celebrate.

Excitement stirred in him. His plan was under way. At last.

IT WAS Monday afternoon, and as usual, Miss Lottie was waiting for Ellie. Today was Miss Lottie's birthday, and Maria had helped her choose the lilac floral dress with the matching little bolero jacket. She also had on her diamond rings and a scatter of old brooches and the Vacheron gold watch she'd bought in Switzerland on one of her grand tours of Europe in the '30s, just before the terrible war.

"Something's wrong with you," Maria had said to her this morning when she brought her breakfast in bed and Miss Lottie mentioned the war again. "You remember only the bad things."

"I do not," she'd replied indignantly, attacking her boiled egg with a silver spoon. "I remember good things too. I always know when Ellie's coming. And when Bruno needs to take his pills."

The old Labrador rested his big head on the coverlet, his eyes fixed on the silver toast racks. Miss Lottie slathered a piece of toast with imported French butter and held it out to him. Bruno dropped it, butter side down, onto the carpet—an antique Aubusson, pale green, covered with roses and lilies. He ate it, then licked at the butter stain.

Miss Lottie knew butter wasn't good for him and only made him fat, but she figured when you were as old as she and Bruno, a little fat didn't matter. Being happy did.

But now, sitting out on the terrace waiting for Ellie, she was thinking about Europe again. She'd been a young woman then and had thought life would always be carefree and happy. She never imagined that she would be forced to live through the tragedy of her daughter's death in a car accident. Only the fact that she'd had to raise her granddaughter had kept her from tumbling into despair.

Images of the young Ellie flickered through her mind. The laughing child with her father's flaming-red hair and large feet, and her mother's beautiful misty blue-gray eyes. Ellie, six years old in a pink tutu, tripping over those feet in a clumsy pirouette, but she knew Ellie had *felt* as beautiful as a ballerina and that was what mattered. And the school essay she had written, titled "My Parents," saying proudly that her grandmother was both her mother and her father and she was sure her grandmother was better than everybody else's put together. Then there had been the boyfriends and the house full of young people. It had given Miss Lottie a new lease on life just when she ought to have been considering slowing down.

She smiled, glad that not everything had been expunged from her faulty mind and she still had a few treasured memories to sustain her.

"Hi, Miss Lottie. Here I am."

As Ellie bounded up the steps to the terrace, Miss Lottie checked her watch. "And almost on time. Whatever happened?"

"Your birthday, that's what." She knelt on the marble tiles and put her arms around her grandmother. "Happy, happy, happy, darling Miss Lottie. So why are you wearing the eyeshade? Uh-uh, don't tell me you've been at the computer again, shifting stocks around and losing your shirt."

"Nothing so vulgar, dear. I just like to play with the Internet."

"You've been surfing the Internet?" Ellie's jaw dropped. "How on earth did you learn to do that?"

"The young man showed me. I found it quite easy, and it's so amusing, making new friends, chatting to them. It's more amusing than the television programs. All violence and sex."

"Miss Lottie, you should wash your mouth out with soap at once. That word has never passed your lips before."

"Don't be ridiculous, Ellie. Of course I know all about sex." Miss Lottie grasped her silver-topped cane for support as she got slowly to her feet. "And as ladies together, you can feel free to tell me all about your sex life. Experience counts, you know."

Ellie felt herself blushing. "Miss Lottie, I don't have one."

"At your age you *should* have. You can tell me why you don't, over tea."

Ramming the green visor over her eyes, she strode through the drawing room into the hall. "Bye, Maria," she called. "See you later."

AT THE Biltmore, Buck gave the valet his ticket and waited under the awning for his car. An old white Cadillac circled into the drive, and the valet rushed to open its door, forgetting all about him. The manager appeared, and the reception staff thronged around.

Must be a politician, Buck thought. Or a movie star.

The manager was helping an old woman out of the car, smiling, shaking her hand. Leaning on her stick, she walked toward Buck.

And time seemed to stop. The blood froze in his veins.

Fate had delivered his victim to him on a plate. He closed his eyes, his strong fingers flexing; he could almost feel her buttery flesh bruising under his grip.

"Excuse me, but are you all right?"

He opened his eyes and looked at the most beautiful woman he had ever seen. She was very tall, gracefully elegant in a sunshine-yellow dress.

"Do you need help?" she persisted.

"No, no, it's okay. I'm all right. Thank you."

"Good afternoon, then." Her long red hair swung prettily around her shoulders as she walked away, and Buck knew he was looking at Ellie Parrish Duveen.

His heart was doing double time.

"Your car, sir." The valet had the BMW's door open, waiting.

Buck shook his head, unable to speak. Turning away, he walked slowly back into the hotel and sank onto a couch. He hadn't been prepared for this.

When his pulse slowed sufficiently, he followed Ellie into the high-ceilinged room overlooking the ocean. Tables were set with pink linen. Tea was being served. Waitresses hovered near Lottie Parrish's table, and the old lady sat there, regal as a queen.

Taking the table next to theirs, he ordered tea, then pretended to read a newspaper, watching and listening.

"Hot scones with Devonshire cream and strawberry jam. And Earl Grey. No tea bags, mind you. Tea simply doesn't taste the same out of bits of paper."

Buck had heard her voice in his dreams for what seemed like a thousand years. And she had not even recognized him. He wondered whether it was because of his successful new image: the dark hair instead of the red, the mustache, the dark glasses. Or whether old age had simply blotted him from her memory.

"Ellie, what do you have to say? Why is there no man in your life? A lovely girl like you?"

Ellie sighed. This was obviously one subject her grandmother was not going to forget. "I told you, I'm too busy, Gran, and it's likely to continue that way until I make enough to open a second café." She laughed, just thinking about it. "And then it'll probably get worse."

Miss Lottie wished passionately that her granddaughter didn't have to work so hard. "I was thinking," she said, carefully selecting a scone, "perhaps we should sell Journey's End."

Buck dropped the newspaper. *Had the Parrishes come down in the world? What had happened to all that money?*

"We've been over this before, and there's no chance," Ellie replied serenely. "You can't sell the house."

"I don't see why not. I could always go and live in one of those condos somewhere. And you could open as many restaurants as you like. You might even find time to get married, give me some great-grandchildren." Miss Lottie smiled teasingly at her.

"Well, this should please you. I have a date tonight."

Miss Lottie's blue eyes brightened. "So? Tell me about him. Do I know his family?"

"Probably not, but he's a local boy. He taught me to surf when I was eight years old."

"A *surfer?*"

Ellie laughed. "He's not a surfer now. He was a homicide detective in Manhattan. Now he's bought a winery out here."

"A homicide cop?" Miss Lottie shuddered. "Ellie, dear, are you sure you're moving in the right circles? However did you meet him?"

Ellie licked the cream from the top of her scone. Buck was fascinated by every move she made, the tilt of her head, her rich glossy red hair; he could almost feel the smoothness of her bare golden arm under his predatory fingers.

Ellie said, "I smacked up his brand-new car, right here on Olive Mill Road. I'm surprised he even spoke to me after that."

Miss Lottie shook her head, bewildered. "Young people meet in such strange ways these days."

She glanced up, surprised, as the manager hurried toward her. Behind him walked the pastry chef, bearing a frosted cake with a single lit candle. The wait staff gathered around and sang "Happy Birthday." Then Miss Lottie blew out her candle and everyone applauded. After that the manager produced a bottle of champagne.

Buck fought back the overwhelming urge to leap at her there and then. Trembling, he summoned a waiter and ordered a double bourbon. He gulped it down quickly, never taking his eyes off the two women.

He could see his father, *their* father, in Ellie's face. He saw himself as he had been two decades ago, when he was young, like her.

Vital. Alive. Before they locked him away. Could it be that, making him feel this new emotion? Or was it the luminous quality of her skin, the rich tumble of hair, those remarkable eyes? His plans were thrown into chaos. The old woman must die. But sooner or later Ellie Parrish Duveen would be his.

When they finally got up to leave, Miss Lottie's gaze lingered on Buck as she passed by. There was a puzzled little frown between her eyes as Ellie took her arm and led her from the room.

IT'S SPRING, Dan thought gloomily, the time men's minds were supposed to "lightly turn to thoughts of love." But his thoughts were on what he was going to do to salvage the winery.

That morning he'd bought a big nine-year-old bay mare named Honey, and now he rode her out over his forty acres. Stopping at the top of a slope, he looked around for Pancho, but the lazy hound was nowhere in sight, and he guessed the dog had slunk back to the stables. Dan slid from the horse and stood drinking in the silence.

A hawk hovered in the clear blue sky, and a couple of rabbits bounced along a furrow, their quick movements a dead giveaway to the hawk poised above. Maybe life on the ranch wasn't so different from life on the streets after all. Predators and victims, sudden violent death on a fine afternoon. He was missing the action, though.

The cell phone rang, and he fished it from his back pocket.

"So? How's Farmer Dan?"

He grinned. "Are you into telepathy or what, Piatowsky? I was just thinking about you."

"Answer the question, Cassidy. How's it goin'?"

"Fine, fine. For a pig in a poke. I'm standing here, in the glorious California sunshine, admiring my withered vines. But it's beautiful. And have I got a horse for you." Dan glanced at the big bay mare pawing the ground nearby.

"The closest I ever got to a horse is a Harley," Piatowsky said. "But listen, Angela's taking the kids to visit her mom in Maine the end of the month, so I thought maybe I'd get out there, give you a hand with the plowing and whatever."

"Sure," Dan said. "I'll probably have the house fixed up by then."

"The house needs fixing also?" Piatowsky's voice cracked with laughter. "I'm buying a new sign for your ranch. A flying pig with dollar signs all over it."

"Thanks, friend. I miss you too."

"I'll call, let y'know when to expect me."

"You're gonna love it. Give my best to Angela."

The phone clicked off, and Dan shook his head, smiling. He looked at the beautiful curve of the hillside silhouetted against the blue sky and listened to the silence. He wouldn't swap it for New York for a million bucks.

He admired his new bay mare. She was whinnying and tossing her head, flicking her tail restlessly. He swung himself onto her back and said, "Okay, okay, Honey, let's get going."

She threw her head up again and did a little dance, testing him. Gripping her firmly, he said, "Let's get this straight. I'm the boss, you're the horse. I ride, you obey. Got it?" The mare rolled her eyes, but she trotted obediently back toward the stables.

Dan breathed a sigh of relief. He couldn't have stood it if he'd bought another dud. First the crumbling house and vineyard; then Pancho, who stole food like the veteran street dog he used to be; and then the mare, with a mind of her own, ready to throw him the minute he relaxed. Plus he'd advertised for a manager last week and so far hadn't had a single response. He figured he wasn't doing so good as Farmer Dan. Not good at all.

At the stables he removed the saddle and bridle, gave the mare water and oats, then went to check the pretty Appaloosa in the next stall. He'd bought this one for her looks. Dapple-gray with a creamy mane and tail.

"How're y'doin', Paradise?" She came to snuffle his hand, and he took a carrot from his pocket. The horse crunched it noisily. "Sweet girl," he said. "Unlike your wild new sister out there."

He walked back out and was wondering what chore to tackle next when Pancho suddenly leaped to his feet, barking madly at a man galloping into the stable yard on an old palomino.

A bottle of whiskey poked from the man's jacket pocket. His denims were full of holes, and he wore a greasy red bandanna around his neck and scuffed leather cowboy boots with silver toe caps. A wide sombrero was clamped over his thick black curls, and a bushy Zapata mustache almost hid his beaming grin.

Dan pushed back his baseball cap, astonished, as the palomino pawed the air in a flashy finale. "You a circus act or what?"

"No, senor." The man leaped from the saddle and beamed again. "I am Carlos Ortega. Your new wine master. I have come to offer my valuable services to you." He swept off the sombrero with a flourish, and both he and the palomino bowed low.

Dan was laughing. He doubted Carlos Ortega knew a merlot from a sauvignon, but he liked him. "Come to my office and we'll talk."

Carlos quickly took a seat opposite Dan in the bare but clean little tack room that had become Dan's office. Placing the sombrero carefully across his knees, he stood the bottle of whiskey on the trestle table between them. "Senor Cassidy, I will not lie to you," he said, suddenly serious. "I am a good winemaker, maybe even great. I first came to California when I was a boy, to pick the walnuts, then the pistachios, then strawberries. When I was fifteen, I went north to Napa to pick grapes. I worked hard, I was intelligent, I was promoted from the field to work in the winery. I learned everything I could. I loved the winemaking. I loved the smell of it. First I worked at Mondavi, then for Beaulieu, and then, senor, this"—he tapped the whiskey bottle—"was my undoing. But I will not lie to you. My little problem is my own, and it will not affect my work."

Dan shook his head. "What makes you think, Senor Ortega, that I will take on an acknowledged drunk as my winemaker?"

Ortega leaned closer across the table. "Senor Cassidy, I do not think either of us has much choice. You need a winemaker. I need a job. You will not get another man of high caliber to come and work at Running Horse. It has a bad reputation; they say there's a jinx on it. But I know this land. The slopes are south facing; the soil is light. Good robust wines can come from this soil, senor, but to get them, you need an expert."

Looking levelly at Dan, he said, "I am not a greedy man. I do not demand high wages. All I need is a roof over my head. The little house near the gate will do fine. I can fix it up for me and my family. Later, when we are successful, then we shall renegotiate."

Dan threw back his head and laughed out loud. "It seems we're stuck with each other, Senor Ortega. It's a deal. Only no drinking on the job."

The Mexican pumped Dan's hand enthusiastically. "Senor, you will not regret it. I promise you." He stood up, pocketed his bottle, and swaggered to the door.

Whistling for the palomino, he leaped on its back and galloped out of the stable yard in a swirl of dust.

A short while later Carlos was back, driving an ancient pickup with a dusty-looking brown mongrel standing in the back and a plump young woman with long, shiny black hair sitting in the front, holding a baby on her lap.

Pancho ran at the brown dog, barking ferociously, and Dan hauled him back by the collar as Carlos said, "Senor, this is Florita, my wife. And this"—he swept the baby from her lap and held him proudly aloft—"is my son, Roberto Carlosito Ortega. An American citizen." He raised his hand to his heart in a solemn salute. "God bless America."

BUCK had driven slowly past the gates of Journey's End twice already. He pulled onto the soft shoulder opposite and was half hidden in the shadow of the eucalyptus trees. Lighting a cigarette, he stared at the elaborate iron gates. They were flanked by two enormous pink granite columns, topped with a pair of winged griffins. Guarding the rich woman's palace, he thought bitterly. And keeping out the rest of the world. Except him, of course. He would find his way in there.

Flinging the cigarette out the window, he started up the engine. "Happy birthday, Miss Lottie," he called mockingly as he slid past the gates. "Better make the most of it. Because it's your last."

The dark road spiraled down from the foothills, but he took the bends at top speed, not caring. *You are invincible,* the voice in his head told him triumphantly. *You are smarter, better, stronger.* Besides, he knew all about them now. He had asked the waitress when she'd brought him his check.

"Miss Lottie's a lovely lady," she'd said.

"A charming woman," Buck had agreed pleasantly. "They don't make them like that these days. A true lady."

The waitress smiled approvingly at him. "*And* she brought her granddaughter up the same way. Ellie's a real lady, too, even if she does run a café in Santa Monica."

Buck handed her a large tip. "And where would that be?"

"On Main Street. They say it's a nice little place."

Buck felt better. Now he had a new plan of action.

He shifted gear, and the BMW shot out onto the freeway, speeding south. He was in L.A. in less than an hour; then traffic slowed him down. He switched onto 405, then the Santa Monica Freeway, and exited at Fourth Street.

A patrol car sitting at the traffic light brought him to his senses. He couldn't afford to get a ticket. The new driver's license and registration looked good for everyday purposes, but he wasn't sure how well they'd stand up to police scrutiny.

He drove slowly down Main until he found it. Ellie's Place. A CLOSED sign hung over the door, and no lights were on.

Frustrated, he wondered where she lived. He would need to find out. The thought filled him with excitement. Buzzing with power, he drove back to Sunset Boulevard. He needed a woman.

Even on a Monday night the strip was lively. Keeping an eye out for cops, he cruised slowly, checking the roadside action. There were plenty of women, any shape or size you wanted. With Ellie in mind he chose a redhead. She was tall and wore a skimpy black skirt and top.

He rolled the window down and leaned across. "How much?"

She looked him up and down. "Depends what you want, mister."

"Get in," he said, deciding. "We'll negotiate on the way."

She slid into the passenger seat. "First, give me fifty."

He fished the money from his wallet, and she tucked the bill into the top of one of her black patent leather boots. “Make a left here, then another. It’s just an alley, but it’s quiet.”

He parked at the far end of the alley near the trash cans, then sat back while she took care of his needs. Then he slid his hands around her neck, and she jerked backward.

“What y’ doin’ . . .” Panicked, she dived for the door, but he still had her by the throat, and nothing would have pried him off. She choked and flailed around, clutching at his hands. Then she went limp, her eyes bulging.

Buck dragged her from the car and let her drop. He retrieved the fifty from her boot, then took out the switchblade, knelt over her, and etched the deep cross from temple to temple, scalp to nose. There was little blood because her heart was no longer pumping, but he wiped the knife fastidiously on her short skirt, then got back into the car and drove out of the alley. He was whistling “Dixie” happily under his breath as he headed back toward Montecito.

Chapter Four

ELLIE nosed the Jeep down the quiet lane, looking for Dan’s cottage. In the back were two grocery bags with the steaks, salad, cheese, fruit, French bread, and a chunk of Miss Lottie’s birthday cake. After the birthday luncheon at the Biltmore, she had changed from the yellow dress into narrow white jeans and a soft white shirt, tied at her waist. As always, she wore her mother’s pearls, and she’d taken the time to apply mascara and lipstick properly instead of at the traffic light, as she usually did.

She checked her watch: two minutes before the appointed hour. Being early might be a first in her life, and she wondered whether she was acting too eager. He was just an old childhood friend, she reminded herself, then corrected that. Well, almost a friend. At least she'd known him way back when.

Dan Cassidy had looked great at eighteen: abs like a washboard, zero body fat, deep-set Irish-blue eyes. She remembered being clasped against his tanned chest as he hauled her from the ocean after she'd been hit on the head by a surfboard, and her throwing up seawater all over him. Ellie hoped he didn't recall that little incident.

An old wooden board with PINES COTTAGE carved clumsily into it hung askew over a wooden gate. She parked the Jeep, hauled the grocery bags from the back, and walked toward the house. It was small and painted white with nautical-blue trim. There was a big old brass ship's bell by the door.

Shifting her packages to one arm, she tugged on the bell rope. A shaggy black-and-tan dog with skinny legs and a long, plumed tail leaped out as Dan flung open the door.

The mangy dog pranced on his hind legs, whining eagerly as he scented the steak. "No chance, Pancho," she said severely, "even if you are a beauty."

"You think the mutt's beautiful?" Dan looked astonished.

"I'm a pushover for waifs and strays."

"I hope you're not including me in that category."

Ellie laughed. "I thought it was the other way around." Following him into the kitchen, she began to unpack the bags as he poured her a glass of wine. "Iron Horse," he said, "a class-act winery. Taste it and tell me what you think."

She gazed, too innocently, into his eyes. "I think it's been a long time since I had dinner with a man." Then, laughing, she added, "Of course, I have dinner with dozens of men every night. But that doesn't count, if you know what I mean."

"I know." His eyes were still on hers. "It's nice. Especially because you're an old friend."

They stepped out onto the wooden deck, which looked out over the ocean. A flight of steps led down to the beach. As they leaned on the rail, drinking in the view, a soft wind blew the hair back from

Ellie's face. Noticing the scar on her forehead, Dan wondered, shocked, how she had gotten it. Then he said, "Want to take a walk before the sun sets?"

She had her sneakers off in a second and almost beat Pancho down the steps to the sand. Rolling up her pant legs, she took off down the beach, red hair flying.

He jogged after her, every muscle groaning with agony from his long horse ride that afternoon.

"Just look at the old man." She was kicking up her heels at the edge of the waves, enjoying her freedom. "Whatever happened to Dan, Dan, the surferman, with abs of steel and a butt to die for?"

He grinned. "You've got a pretty good memory. How about that time you threw up all over me?"

She groaned. "I was hoping you wouldn't remember."

"Total recall."

"Race you to the rocks," she challenged, taking off again.

He huffed after her, limping.

She circled back, hands on hips, regarding him critically. "Uh-uh," she groaned. "I knew it. It's whiplash and you're going to sue me."

He laughed. "Rear-ending my new car had absolutely nothing to do with it. It's just that I rode a horse today for the first time in years, and now I ache in places I didn't know I had."

She linked her arm companionably through his as they ambled back to the house. "So what made you do it?" she asked suddenly. "Give up the police?"

"A bullet had my name on it. I thought I was lucky it didn't kill me. Then they told me I'd be stuck in a desk job from then on."

Ellie nodded. She sniffed the salt air, enjoying the warmth of his bare arm against hers, the maleness of him.

He said, "So? What about you? I remember you were a pretty ritzy family. The mansion on top of the hill. Family retainers."

"Somehow the money ran out before it reached me."

"No regrets?"

"Are you kidding?" She laughed. "Of course I have regrets. The money would have made my own life a lot easier." Heaving a sigh, she added, "But you know, I probably would have done exactly what I'm doing now. So I guess that says something. Like, if you want it badly enough, you go for it, money or no money."

"Looks like we're in the same boat. Running Horse is a mess. It'll probably take years before I get it into shape."

Pancho streaked ahead of them, up the steps to the house, then darted past them again on his way back down. From the corner of his eye Dan caught the flash of red meat in his jaws. Dan groaned. "That darned dog has just run off with our dinner."

Ellie peered over the rail. Pancho was lying in the sand, demolishing the last of the filet mignon. "He chose his moment perfectly," she said, awed. "He's pretty smart."

Dan eyed him, exasperated. "I can't send him back. He thinks he's mine now. He's even started to sleep on my bed."

"You're a sucker, Dan Cassidy. You have to train them from day one; otherwise they peg you for a soft touch and you're a goner." She grinned as the dog rolled in the sand, waving all four paws in the air. "It's a good thing I brought bread and cheese. With a bottle of wine, who could ask for anything more?"

"I forgot to ask you," Ellie said in the kitchen, cutting the baguette into hunks. "Weren't you married?" The minute it was out of her mouth, she wished she hadn't said it. The wine must be loosening her tongue. "I take that question back," she added.

Dan leaned against the counter, arms folded. "I was," he said. "And as a friend, you have a right to ask. And no, I'm not married now. It was kid stuff—all romance, no reality."

She carried a basket of bread into the living room and set it on the coffee table. Dan brought the plate of cheeses, then filled their glasses and sat on the floor next to her. "Tell me about your father and your mother."

Ellie sipped the wine thoughtfully. There was so much to tell—and yet so little. So few years together for her to remember.

WHEN she was a child, it was her favorite bedtime story. "Tell me again about my mother and my father," she would ask, and Miss

Lottie would repeat it one more time, often with tears in her eyes that Ellie would brush away with her small finger.

"When my grandfather died," she told Dan, "Miss Lottie was left to bring up Romany alone. Romany lived up to her name. She was a wild gypsy of a young thing. Miss Lottie always assumed she would calm down, but when Romany was twenty-four, she ran off with Rory Duveen, penniless and a nobody. Plus he was fifteen years older and divorced. Romany had her own money, inherited from her grandfather, and the happy pair flitted around the world, partying and enjoying life. Because, as Rory always said, life is meant to be fun.

"A few years later Romany took time out to give birth to me, and then they were off again. Mostly they'd leave me with Miss Lottie. But sometimes, over her protests, they'd take me with them."

Ellie lifted her shoulders in a little shrug that somehow expressed her sadness. "And that's the way life was. Until the day their white Bentley convertible threw an unexpected snit and hurled them into a rocky canyon in the Los Padres mountains.

"It's so strange," she added with a frown. "I can see us on that mountain road. I can even remember them smiling at each other, my father singing . . . and then they were gone.

"I was tossed out onto the bushes at the side of the road. They found me there later. I had a big cut on my face, but that was all."

Dan saw her shiver. He closed the windows and put a match to the fire, then gave Ellie his sweater. It felt good, soft and masculine-scented, and she snuggled into it.

"I don't know why I'm telling you all this," she said, looking at him across the coffee table. "I've never really talked about it with anyone except Miss Lottie and Maya, but I have the feeling something is missing from that memory. It's on the edge of my mind." She sighed wistfully. "It just didn't seem possible that my vivid, life-loving parents could be gone. I felt so sure they were going to pop out from behind a tree, calling 'Surprise, surprise,' the way they used to when they came back from their travels."

Dan took her hand. "That was tough. You were so young."

Firelight bathed them in a soft reddish glow. From outside came the roar of the breakers, curving along the shoreline. Ellie felt suspended in time, as though she had stepped back and was seeing things that had happened that she had chosen not to remember.

"I learned all about violence that year," she said quietly. "First with my parents and then with my grandmother."

She hesitated. "I've never told anyone about this before. Miss Lottie asked me not to."

He took a sip of wine. "Do you want to tell me?"

It had been locked inside her for so long, Ellie knew it would be a relief to speak of it.

"It happened a few weeks after the accident. Miss Lottie always put me to bed herself, and then she would read me a story."

Ellie could see herself in her blue-and-white-gingham room, in the narrow French sleigh bed that had been her mother's when she was a child. As always, Miss Lottie had left the window open, because, she said, a child needed fresh air. But the branches of the juniper tree tapped scarily against the window, and Ellie couldn't sleep, so she did what she often did those days. She climbed from the high bed and ran to the top of the wide staircase. Clinging to the oak banisters, she walked slowly down the wide, shallow steps and through the hall. She knew Miss Lottie would be in the library.

Often, those nights, she would sneak in and just sit quietly, watching her grandmother while she opened her mail or wrote letters. Miss Lottie would pretend for a while not to see her; then she'd glance up and say, "Now be off with you, child. It's late. Come, I'll take you up myself and tuck you in again."

Only not that night. Voices came from the half-open door, and Ellie peeked in at the visitor. Unnoticed, she slipped into the room and took her usual seat on the oversize Chinese elmwood chair that Miss Lottie called the mandarin's chair. Its smoothly polished wood felt cold through her thin pajamas, and she shivered, watching the man and her grandmother, wondering what they were talking about.

Suddenly the man stood up. He was yelling at Miss Lottie in a hard, furious voice. Then he leaped at her, clasped his big hands around her throat. "I'll get you and I'll get what's mine."

Ellie clutched the chair arms in terror. "Gran," she cried.

The man turned and saw her. Their eyes met, and she shrank back, transfixed by the naked evil in his. She began to scream.

The door burst open. The menservants ran in, and behind them were the security guards. In an instant they had the man on the floor, his arms twisted behind his back, his face pressed into the carpet.

Ellie watched, numb with terror, as Miss Lottie walked slowly across the room and stood looking down at the man. She was pale, trembling, angry, but she was not afraid.

Then Maria came in. She grabbed Ellie and carried her off, still crying, still terrified, to her room.

Later Miss Lottie explained things to her. "It was just a crazy man," she said. "He's gone now, and I want you to forget you ever saw him. Promise me that you'll never speak of it to anyone."

"And until tonight," Ellie said to Dan, "I've kept that promise."

"Did you ever find out who he was?"

She shook her head. "I told you, we never spoke of it again."

He sighed. "That was quite a year for a five-year-old. All credit to your grandmother for getting you through it."

The log sputtered in the grate, and she yawned, exhausted. "I've talked half the night away," she said. "Thanks for listening." She reached for his hand. "Friends?" She smiled into his eyes.

"Friends." Her hand felt firm and cool in his. "And as a friend, I'm not about to let you drive home. You've drunk too much wine, talked yourself out, and you're about the tiredest woman I ever saw. The sheets are clean, and I guarantee the bed's all yours. Please be my guest."

Ellie shook her head. "Can't," she said, yawning. "Sorry. It must be the sea air." She slithered farther down in the comfortable sofa, her eyes half closed. "I have to get back," she mumbled. "I'm expecting deliveries at the café tomorrow at eight."

Dan grinned. She'd be asleep before she even knew it. He walked into the bedroom and came back with a blanket. As he had guessed, she was down for the count. He tucked the blanket around her, letting his hand rest lightly on her soft hair for a second.

HE WOKE HER EARLY with coffee and toast.

Ellie leaped to her feet, running her hands distractedly through her tangled hair. "What time is it?"

"Six. And take it easy, friend. There's time for coffee and a shower before you go."

She smiled at the word friend. Tilting her head to one side, she looked into his eyes. "Thanks, Danny Boy," she murmured.

All he said was, "You're welcome, ma'am." But he figured it might be tough staying just friends with Ellie Parrish Duveen.

AT ABOUT the time Ellie and Dan were having their early morning coffee, Buck was sprawled on a sofa in one of the Biltmore's luxurious terry-cloth bathrobes. Room service arrived, and he devoured the oatmeal-blueberry pancakes hungrily, then dressed, packed his things, and checked out. Too long a stay at the Biltmore would make him known to the management; people would observe him, get too friendly, ask questions. Besides, Journey's End might take a while to sell, and Buck Duveen wanted to conserve money.

Back in L.A., he rented a cheap studio apartment on a narrow little street just south of Sunset. He dumped his bags there, then drove west to Santa Monica.

It was early evening when he got to Ellie's Place. He got lucky. A car was pulling out of a parking spot directly opposite, and he slid the BMW in. He slipped two quarters into the parking meter, then got back into the car and sat watching the café.

It was only six o'clock, but already a couple of tables were occupied. A sexy-looking blonde was taking orders and bringing glasses of wine, but there was no sign of Ellie.

Half an hour passed. Then he saw her, loping breathlessly down the street, long red hair flying. She was clutching a large box and dodging passersby expertly. As he watched, she shoved through the café door and disappeared from sight.

"ABOUT time," Maya said, greeting her from behind the counter. "I thought you must be making that coffee machine."

"Sorry"—Ellie dropped the box onto the counter—"but I had to do something, or the customers will be deserting us for Starbucks. Anyway, this will do until the big machine is fixed."

She dashed into the back to check the chaos in the kitchen. Chan, the dark-eyed temperamental chef, was slamming woks and pots around, frowning, while Terry, his twenty-year-old assistant, prepped vegetables.

"I gotta get another job," Chan declared, scowling. "This kitchen is too small."

"Small is good, Chan." She wrapped a spotless white apron around her waist. "You don't have as far to walk. In a big kitchen your feet would be killing you." Capturing her hair into a ponytail, Ellie pulled on the baseball cap, then hurried out front to greet her customers.

Maya leaned against the door, blocking her way. "Not so fast, Ellie. First, tell me about last night."

"Last night?" Ellie shrugged, grinning. "Oh, it was nice."

"Has he asked you for another date?"

"Maya, this was not a date. We had a nice friendly dinner. Then I fell asleep, and he woke me this morning with coffee."

Maya's whiskey-brown eyes widened. "Wait just one minute, woman. Are you telling me you stayed over? On the first date?"

"We just talked, that's all. Or rather, I did the talking. He listened. And believe me, it's good to be listened to for a change instead of being lectured." Ellie pushed past her, checking tables and smiling greetings to a couple of regular customers.

Buck walked across the road just then and into Ellie's Place. He glanced around, looking for her, but then the beautiful blonde came toward him, menu in hand.

"Good evening." Maya smiled politely. "A table for two?"

He gave her a charming smile. "I'm afraid I'm alone tonight."

"Too bad. But you've come to the right place. Alone is not a problem here, and you'll enjoy the food." She showed him to a table by the window. "I'll just tell you tonight's specials; then I'll leave you to look at the menu."

Buck was polite, charming. He ordered a glass of red wine, the *soupe au pistou,* and shrimp and scallops Chan-style. He nibbled on the good bread, waiting and watching.

He was halfway through the glass of wine when Ellie emerged from the kitchen. She threw him a smile as she served the table nearby. Buck quickly drained his glass, then caught her eye. "Could I have another?" He held up the empty glass, smiling.

"Of course, sir. What were you drinking?" Her voice was sweet and soft as sugar.

"The red. I think she said it was the Ferme something. . . ." He looked vague. "Wait a minute," he said, pretending astonishment. "Weren't you at the Biltmore yesterday? In Montecito?"

She looked puzzled. "Yes, but . . ."

"You noticed I wasn't feeling well. You were kind enough to stop and ask if you could help me." He looked warmly at her. "A man doesn't forget an act of kindness like that."

Ellie's puzzled frown cleared. "Of course, I remember now. I'm glad to see you've recovered, anyhow."

"It was nothing. Just too much sun, I guess."

His smile was warm and friendly, and Ellie smiled back. "I'll get that wine for you right away, sir," she promised.

Elated, he watched her walk back to the kitchen. Humming "Dixie" under his breath, he waited for her to return, but instead, the blonde brought the wine. "Compliments of Ellie's, sir," she said. "Enjoy."

Buck did enjoy. The food was good, but the fact that he had a grandstand seat watching Ellie made it even better. He took his time over coffee, and the customers had thinned out when he finally got up and walked to the counter to pay his bill.

"I hope you enjoyed your meal, sir."

He held out the cash and Ellie took it from him. "It was very good. And so was the wine. You're very generous."

"We try to look after our guests at Ellie's Place."

"Thank you. And my name is Ed. Ed Jensen."

"Hope to see you again, Mr. Jensen." She gave him that big smile, and he waved a hand as he turned away. He was pleased. Contact had been established.

Back across the road again, he fed coins into the meter and got back into the car, waiting. At ten the sexy blond waitress left, calling good-byes over her shoulder. He saw Ellie turn the OPEN sign to CLOSED, then waited as she locked the door and strode rapidly down the street. Buck made a quick U-turn and cruised slowly behind her. After a couple of blocks she turned right, heading for a four-story car park. He pulled into the curb.

A few minutes later Ellie drove past in a bright yellow Jeep. He was right behind her as she took off down Main.

CARLOS Ortega was on his hands and knees, his face pressed to a single sticklike vine, inspecting it branch by branch.

"You see this, senor." He indicated a frail-looking twig. "These vines were budded, grafted onto the cabernet franc rootstock. Neglect and possibly bad weather spoiled them. The rootstock is good. If we baby them, love them, senor, they will revive."

"You mean I'm going to have to *love* my vines as well as give them all my money?" Dan asked. "It sounds exactly like a bad marriage."

"No, no, senor, it's not the same like loving a woman. These are your children. Is different." He got to his feet, wafting dust from his knees with his straw sombrero. "Is good news, Senor Dan. I'm already saving you money."

Dan was on his knees, staring at the vines. He could feel the warmth of the earth under his hands, smell its sweet, flat odor, see tiny tufts of reddish green growth that might almost be buds. A surge of pride went through him. This was his land; these were his vines, his buds. Ortega was right—they were like his kids.

"How much?" he asked, getting back to basics.

Carlos tugged thoughtfully on his mustache, considering. "Good cabernet budwood, maybe ten cents each one."

Dan brightened. That number didn't sound too drastic.

"For the whole hillside"—Carlos swung around, surveying the slope—"maybe thirty, forty thousand dollars."

Dan sighed resignedly. He might have known it. "I guess I'd better make an appointment with the bank manager again."

"First, senor, you call the Foundation Plant Material Service at U.C., Davis. If they no have the right cabernet, we go to Napa. I know exactly the vineyard. Later, closer to harvest, we go taste the grapes on the vine, and I shall know if it is the best. We shall produce a beautiful cabernet."

Dan hoped he was right. He looked at the gentle slope, imagining it filled with leafy vines, burdened with luscious ripe grapes, ready for harvest. Already a half-dozen Mexican workers were spread out down the hillside, backs bent as they chopped out the weeds and cleared clogged irrigation pipes. From the top of the hill he could hear the whine of a saw as the carpenter tackled the sagging boards on the porch, and he could see Florita hanging out the wash. His horses were in the stables, and in a few days he would be sleeping in his own bed. The place was almost beginning to feel like home.

BACK at the office the phone was ringing. He picked it up on the run. "Running Horse Winery."

"Almost sounds like it's real," Piatowsky said.

Dan could hear the grin in his voice. "It sure is. It just cost me another thirty thou for budwood, maybe forty. But Ortega says we'll have great cabernet."

"Whoever Ortega is, if he's talking you out of thirty thousand bucks for buds, he sounds like a terrific con artist."

"I'll tell my bank manager that. So when you coming out?"

"I just want you to run this little nugget of info through your California sun–addled brain before it atrophies. I caught something on the computer this morning. About a hooker murdered in an alley not too far from Sunset Boulevard. There was a cross carved into her forehead—temple to temple, scalp to nose."

Dan gave a low, surprised whistle. "It's the signature killer."

"And this one's in your neck of the woods, buddy. I contacted the LAPD and the FBI, gave them the info on the Times Square woman. It's the same fella, all right. He used the same knife, probably a switchblade. We're issuing warnings," Piatowsky said. "Much good it'll do the girls. Anyhow, I thought when I get out there, I'll check in with the LAPD, see what's doing."

"When do you get here?"

"In a couple of weeks. Around the fifteenth. That okay?"

"I'm ready and waiting."

"By the way, how are the women out there in sunshineland?"

"Dazzling," Dan said, thinking of Ellie. "Terrific, as a matter of fact. If you act civilized, I might let you meet one."

"If she likes her men civilized, what's she doing with you?"

"Get lost, Piatowsky." Laughing, Dan put down the receiver. He circled the fifteenth on the wall calendar and wondered about the signature killer. He'd have bet money on his being a just-released prisoner. One killing on the East Coast, one on the West. Could be a long-distance driver? Or just some bum who'd hopped a Greyhound to satisfy his Hollywood fantasies? Dan shrugged. Either way, it wasn't his problem now. He had budwood to worry about.

His hand lingered on the telephone. He could call Ellie, just to say, "Hi, friend, how are you doing today? Thanks for coming by. I loved having you sleep on my sofa."

He dialed her number. When she answered and heard his voice, she said, "I was just thinking about you."

"You were?"

"I wanted to call to say thank you. I enjoyed myself."

"Me too. Sorry about the steaks and Pancho."

She laughed. "That's okay. Next time—"

"About that next time." He jumped in quickly. "I know you're a busy woman, but what about next week? I thought maybe you'd like to take a look around the vineyard."

"I'd love that," and she sounded as though she really meant it. He was still thinking of her when he dialed U.C., Davis about the cabernet budwood.

BUCK kept watch on Ellie for a week. Following her at a discreet distance, he learned her routine. By now he knew her hours, where she went, who she saw, and what she did. He knew that she visited Miss Lottie every Monday and they had tea at the Biltmore. He knew she left the house at seven and didn't return until after midnight.

Now it was just dark as he parked opposite her house. He was smartly dressed. Anybody who saw him would think he was a prosperous businessman, but there was no one around to notice. Hurrying across the street, he pushed open the little white gate and strode the four paces up the brick path to the front door. It took seconds to jimmy the lock; then he was inside.

He leaned back against the door, buzzing with excitement. A lamp was lit in the tiny sitting room on his left. He took a seat on the sofa and looked calmly around as if he owned the place.

A pretty Venetian mirror hung over the pinewood mantel, adorned with a pair of old silver candlesticks and some photos. He got up to look at them, greedy for a glimpse of her, but none were of Ellie. Disappointed, he walked back across the entry hall into the dining room. A dozen gilt-framed paintings covered the walls, and an open archway led directly into the minute white kitchen.

A mug of cold tea stood on the kitchen counter with an imprint of Ellie's lipstick on the rim. Trembling, he pressed his own lips over it. A shiver of ecstasy throbbed deep in his gut.

Even before he reached the top of the creaking stairs, he could smell her scent. He stood in the bedroom doorway, his eyes closed, inhaling her. He was in paradise.

When he came to his senses, he went systematically through her closet. He noted that her clothes were size six, and her shoes an unexpectedly large ten. He wrote down the name of her perfume and her bath soap. He saw that her favorite color was blue, that there was Evian in her refrigerator, Fuji apples in a bowl. He went through every cupboard, every drawer. When he left an hour later, he knew all there was to know about Ellie Parrish Duveen.

BUCK put the car in the lot around the corner from Main. Then, stoked with power, he swaggered into Ellie's Place. The beautiful blonde greeted him again.

"Hi," he said. "It's Ed. Ed Jensen, remember?"

"Oh, sure. How are you, Ed? Good to see you back."

"Alone again, I'm afraid."

He smiled cockily at her, and warning signals flickered suddenly in Maya's head. There was something about him. Maybe it was the eyes: They didn't smile when his mouth did.

"Where's Ellie tonight?"

So that's it, Maya thought. He was interested in Ellie.

"Busy," she said briskly. "Can I get you something to drink, *sir?*" Placing the relationship back on a formal footing, she handed him the menu, then brought his glass of red wine.

In the kitchen, she said to Ellie, "Who is this Ed Jensen, anyway? He seems pretty darn friendly with you."

"Jensen?" Ellie lifted her eyes from the grill, where she was about to burn a fine piece of ahi tuna if she wasn't careful. Chan had quit again and she was in charge. "Oh, him. I've only seen him a couple times. I bumped into him at the Biltmore; then he came here."

"Yeah, well, he's here again and he's asking after you."

"I think he's from out of town." Ellie was busy with the fish. "I guess he's just lonesome."

"Oh, sure." Maya's voice had a skeptical edge. "And that's probably exactly what they said about your everyday axe murderer."

Buck ordered steak and *pommes frites.* After a good day's work he was in the mood for a hearty meal. He was disappointed when the blonde served him and Ellie did not appear, but contented himself with picturing her in her home, in her room, in her bed.

Lingering, he drank another couple of glasses of wine and was the last to leave the restaurant. Maya rang up his bill, then took his money briskly. Cash, she noted, not a credit card. Hmmm, this guy was leaving no traces.

"What's your name?" Buck was waiting for his change.

"It's Maya, *sir.*" Politely she handed him his change.

"Thank you, Maya. I enjoyed it." He gave her that sly smile again, but she refused to lift her eyes from the cash register.

"Good night, Mr. Jensen," she murmured.

"Good night, Maya. And the name is Ed."

He walked confidently to the door, then grinned back at her. Maya's cheeks burned. He'd known she would be looking at him.

Remembering his strangely cold eyes, she hurried to the door and locked it securely.

Chapter Five

THIS is it." Dan stared proudly at his rows of neatly cropped vines. "We're starting cabernet here, on the south slopes, and chardonnay on the other side of the hill. It was all I could afford, but I look at it this way: If I make a success of it, I got a bargain."

The bare sticks were trained like an army of little soldiers into perfect rows that curved over the hillside into infinity. "Impressive." Ellie threw him a mocking grin. "Not a grape in sight."

"Wait till next year. Then the word to use will be 'burgeoning.' "

She stared skeptically at the skinny, dead-looking branches. "Aren't we being a little optimistic here?"

Dan shook his head. "The fact is, Running Horse failed because they planted the wrong grapes for the soil."

Ellie smiled. There was something magical about the place, she thought. In the distance she could see the road curving around the bottom of the hill, and opposite, under a clump of oaks, black-and-white-spotted cattle were bunched together in the shade. The setting sun warmed her back, and a light wind tossed her hair around. Eyes closed, she listened to the special silence of the countryside: the soft moan of the wind sweeping over the hill, a whir of wings as a bird took flight, secret rustlings in the grass. She was entranced.

"This is how it must have been years ago," she whispered, her eyes still shut tight. "Before there was traffic and planes. Nothing but slopes of vines and silence for miles."

Dan heard it first: mariachi trumpets shrilling from a radio. A minute later a rusty pickup crested the hill. Dan and Ellie glanced at each other, laughing, as the driver pulled to a stop, jumped from the pickup, and strode toward them.

"Senorita." Doffing his sombrero, he took her hand and held it to his lips. "I am Carlos Ortega. It is a great pleasure to meet such a beautiful woman."

Ellie had to laugh. "Thank you, Senor Ortega. I've heard a lot about you."

"The senor will have told you I am the best winemaker in the county."

"I was just about to show Ellie the winery." Dan grabbed her hand and led her back to the Explorer. She turned and waved to Ortega. He bowed low, still smiling.

"You think that's a great act," Dan told her, grinning, "wait till you catch him on the palomino."

It was cool inside the red barn, and silent. Dan ran an appreciative hand over his sleek new barrels. "These are American oak, not French. It'll give a softer, more subtle oaky finish to the wine. Of course, there'll be no harvest this year, but one day visitors will flock here to try our wines."

As he showed her around the property, Ellie thought how much he seemed to love what he was doing. He was such a physical man, and she could tell he enjoyed the hard work; he loved getting his hands in the earth, back to his farming roots.

Later, as he led the way back to Montecito and she followed in the Jeep, she thought about the life Dan had chosen, far from the city's stresses and pleasures. Maybe there was something to it, but it wasn't for her. She was a city girl now.

They had dinner at Mollie's Trattoria on Coast Village Road.

Looking at Ellie across the candlelit table, with her long, curling red hair, Dan thought what a sunshiny person she was. Or was she? "I feel like we're old friends, but I know so little about you."

"I thought I'd told you everything." She took a sip of the Chianti he'd ordered to go with the Italian food.

He leaned closer, across the table. "There's a big empty space between the kid on the beach and the woman sitting opposite me. What happened in those years? Where did you go to college? Who are your friends? Have you ever been in love?"

She eyed him warily. "That's a very personal question."

"Where you went to college is personal?" His pseudo-innocent expression made her laugh.

"I'll answer that one. Arizona State. That's where I met Maya, my dearest friend. It's also where we almost got ourselves thrown out."

Dan laughed when, over lobster ravioli, she told him the story of her college career; it was quite different from his own, more serious one as a married student with an impossible romance.

"Of course, I fell in love there once or twice. Though love doesn't even enter into our personal equation." Reaching across the table, she took his hand in hers, held it to her lips, and kissed it.

His blood pressure lifted a few notches. "Of course not," he agreed, though he didn't mean it. "I just don't get it," he added.

"Get what?" She spooned up the last of the sauce.

"What exactly makes you tick. I mean, why are you driven to devote all your energy to your café?"

Ellie sat back, considering the question. "It's like I have to prove something to myself," she said honestly, after a minute. "That I *can* do it, that I *can* succeed. That because I had a privileged upbringing, doesn't mean I can't make it on my own."

The young waiter took their plates, then returned with the tiramisu she'd ordered and two forks. "You still haven't told me about being in love," he said. "Seriously in love?"

She heaved a sigh, scooping up the delicious creamy dessert. "You don't quit, do you?"

"Not when it's a subject that interests me."

She grinned, thinking about Steve Cohen and how young she had been then, and how naïve. "I've only been seriously in love once," she admitted. "He ditched me and broke my heart," she added, then laughed. "But you know, it's a funny thing. Hearts seem to patch themselves right back up again if you let them."

A yawn surprised her. "It's all that fresh air," she apologized. "I'm a big-city girl. I'm not used to it anymore."

"You could always stay the night," he said, ever the optimist.

"Thanks, friend"—she squeezed his hand across the table—"but this time I really must get back. Thanks for showing me the ranch. I loved it." Ellie meant it too. Being with Dan Cassidy was as seamless as being with a friend she'd known all her life. Impulsively she put her hand to his face and drew him toward her, then kissed him on the lips. It was a light, friendly little kiss. Nothing important, she reassured herself. "Good night, Danny Boy."

Outside, she backed her Jeep too quickly out of the tight parking spot, and there was a crunch as it hit his Explorer.

Dan slapped a hand to his head. "Ellie! Not again!"

"Sorry." She poked her head out, inspecting the damage. "Oh well, what's a little dent between friends?"

Dan could hear her laughing as she took off.

BUCK reconnoitered his enemy's position, circling Hot Springs Road in the daylight hours until he was familiar with every twist and turn, every house, every horse trail. After dark he drove up Hot Springs Road, past Journey's End, and turned into a narrow riding trail, half hidden by trees that ran behind the property. He was wearing a black tracksuit, black Reebok Walkers, and black gloves, and carried his tools in a backpack. After parking, he walked along the trail until he came to a pair of tall, rusting iron gates. He shone a tiny flashlight up until he spotted the chain and the big padlock.

He'd anticipated just such a problem. Taking a small bolt-cutter from the backpack, he got to work. It took only seconds before the lock and chain dropped into the grass at his feet. The gates couldn't have been used in years, and the rusty hinges squealed as he pushed them open and slipped inside. He was in a copse of silver birch. He stood for a minute, letting his eyes adjust, getting his bearings.

He knew the house lay due east. Taking a compass from his

backpack, he threaded his way through the trees until he came to a long, low building. He skirted it cautiously. Coming to a window, he shone his flashlight inside. The thin beam of light showed a large, empty room, with old pot sinks and antiquated laundry machinery.

He followed an overgrown path leading toward the house, then adjusted his stopwatch, timing himself. So far it had taken him ten minutes. Another five, and the massive house loomed into view.

He stood looking at the prize that would soon be his, contemplating his final moment of revenge against Charlotte Parrish, who had made him suffer for more than twenty years.

Leaving the path, he walked silently through the gardens, past the empty pool and the tennis courts. He was calm, collected, his heart wasn't even pounding as he strolled along the terrace. Security lights illuminated the front of the house. There was a light on in the great hall, but the rest of the downstairs windows were dark. Lamplight also glowed behind four upstairs windows. Miss Lottie's, he assumed.

He was almost at the front door when he heard the key turning in the lock. With a lightning reaction he ran soundlessly back along the terrace and slipped behind the bushes outside the library window.

An old Labrador lumbered out onto the front terrace, followed by a small gray-haired woman in a plaid bathrobe and slippers. Buck trained his night-vision binoculars on her.

"All right, you old scrounger," he heard her say, "but this is our little secret. No telling Miss Lottie." She gave the dog a cookie, then patted its head affectionately. "There's no wonder you're fat," she added. The dog ate the cookie, then padded down the steps into the garden. The woman followed him, and then they were out of his view.

Buck looked speculatively at the light streaming from the open door. It was a golden opportunity: He could go in, kill his enemy, have done with it. But there were too many unknowns. He had to be certain. Besides, he wanted to take his time, enjoy it.

A few minutes later Maria walked back into the sights of his binoculars and up the steps. The dog lumbered stiffly after her. It stopped and looked directly at Buck. Then it barked loudly and began to trot toward him.

Buck froze. Now his heart was thundering.

"Bruno! Come here, you silly old boy," Maria called.

The dog turned its head. It looked at her, then back again at the bushes where Buck was hiding. It barked loudly.

"Bruno, come here at once." Maria was impatient. The dog looked uncertainly at the bushes for a second; then it turned obediently and followed Maria into the house.

Breathing a sigh of relief, Buck heard the heavy door slam.

He checked the stopwatch; now he knew approximately what time Maria took the dog out. An hour or so later the lights were turned off upstairs. Again he made a note of the time, then jogged back the way he had come.

When he reached the car, he checked his time again. Eighteen minutes to run the mile from the house to the car. It was way too long. He needed to get his time down to seven minutes or less.

Still, it wasn't bad for a first try. He would do it again, tomorrow night and the night after. Until he was ready.

Swinging left out onto the road, he drove quickly back to L.A.

IN THE kitchen at the café Ellie was in her element—cool, efficient, enjoying what she was doing. With swift, neat strokes of a cleaver she dismembered a chicken. She chopped shallots, then made a chiffonade of spinach, rolling it into a cigar shape and then finely slicing it. She did the same with fresh sorrel, then destalked watercress leaves and chervil. Throwing some butter into a cast-iron casserole, she added the shallots, the chicken, and salt and pepper, then put the lid on and let it cook slowly. Next she cooked the spinach over a high heat until it wilted, and threw in the rest of the herbs. She stirred it for a couple of minutes before adding it to the chicken with a small amount of cream beaten with an egg, then stirred again until the sauce thickened. Tasting it, she was pleased with the result. She had come across the recipe at a little farmhouse restaurant in Provence, and with its pretty green color and light summery taste, it was exactly the kind of thing she liked to serve.

She offered a piece of chicken to Maya. "What d'you think?"

Maya rolled her big brown eyes. "This is heaven."

Ellie beamed. She washed her hands and had just gone back to her marble board to prepare the pastry for the night's *tarte Tatin* when the phone rang. It was Dan.

"Hi, Ellie. I just wondered what you were up to."

"Oh, slaving away. You're calling to tell me the Explorer is totaled and it's all my fault."

"You're lucky, it's just a minor graze this time. I was thinking, I'm planning on being in L.A. later today on business. I thought I might come by and have dinner at your place."

Pleased, Ellie pushed back her hair with a floury hand. "You'll have the best table in the house, and this time dinner's on me."

"I guess you'll still be slaving?"

" 'Fraid so. The unsociable hours go along with the job. But I'll make time to have a glass of wine with you."

"Around nine, then, Ellie."

"I'll be waiting." She fairly sang the words, her face glowing.

Maya looked shrewdly at her. "You look happy."

Ellie laughed. "Who? Me?"

MAYA knew it was Dan the minute he walked in. He was wearing a simple white linen shirt and jeans. His eyes were a startlingly deep blue, and they had a kind of wise expression as he turned to look at her, as though he had seen it all.

"Let me guess," she said. "You're Dan Cassidy."

"Guilty." He grinned at her. "And you must be Maya."

"Welcome to Ellie's Place." She showed him to a table by the window and handed him a menu. "I'll tell Ellie you're here."

Dan looked around interestedly. The lighting was low and intimate, with little rose-shaded lamps on each table instead of candles, and a nice buzz of conversation and laughter came from the other tables. The place was three-quarters full. Not bad, he figured, for a Wednesday night.

As he studied the menu, he caught Ellie's delicate perfume, felt her lips on his cheek, and glanced up, smiling. She looked delicious in her white Ellie's Place T-shirt and black jeans, with her hair in a ponytail under the black baseball cap.

"Okay, Cassidy," she said, placing a bottle of wine on the table and taking the seat opposite him. "You're on my turf tonight."

Dan insisted Ellie choose a simple meal for him, because he was an uncomplicated man—white bean soup, rack of lamb, garlic mashed potatoes, and ratatouille. She served him herself.

It was ten thirty before the café quieted down and she finally got a break and could sit with him.

From across the room Maya thought they looked like a pair of lovers, alone at their window table in the rose-shaded light. It was all so romantic.

Outside on Main Street, Buck saw them too. He'd just been about to walk into the café, but now he stopped. He took a step back, staring angrily as they gazed into each other's eyes. *How dare she,* the voice in his head shouted angrily. *She's yours. You will have to kill him, too, if he doesn't get out of your way.*

LEANING her elbows on the table, Ellie watched as Dan picked up his fork and cut carefully into her famous *tarte Tatin.* If he hated the pastry, she would just die.

Dan closed his eyes as though he were allowing the taste to linger, then opened them.

"Go ahead," she said, "tell me you hate it. I can take it."

His blue eyes looked innocently into hers. "Was I supposed to say something?" He downed another mouthful.

She sat back in the chair. "Beast!" she hissed.

Dan grinned. "That was just to pay you back for what you said about my vines." He finished the tart, put his fork on the plate, and sighed with satisfaction. "I could eat that all night."

"Thanks. How about the rest of the meal?"

"Truly wonderful, Ellie. How about having some coffee with me?" He was pushing his luck, but she was weakening.

Ellie glanced around the almost empty café. "I'll do better than that. We'll have it at my place. I'll have Maya close up."

A few minutes later, as they walked out of the café, Maya thought they looked great together. And they looked even better when Dan slid his arm around Ellie's shoulders.

Resting her elbow on the counter, Maya sighed, happy that Ellie had finally found someone she cared about. Not that Ellie would ever admit it. It would take a miracle, or a catastrophe, before she'd do that.

"AND this," Ellie was saying to Dan, leaning from her bedroom window, "is why I really love this house."

Dan peered over the rooftops, down the hill at the distant gleam of silver. "Do I assume that's the ocean?"

"Of course," she said indignantly. "Listen, you can hear it."

He listened. "All I hear is traffic."

Ellie slammed the window shut and drew the curtains. "And I thought you were a romantic."

"If I were a romantic, I'd have brought you flowers," he said as he followed her out of the bedroom and down the creaking stairs.

"I'm perfectly capable of buying my own flowers, thanks."

Flouncing into the kitchen, she measured coffee into the filter, poured in water, then switched on the machine. She took a couple of mugs from the cupboard. "I don't even know whether you take sugar in your coffee."

"Obviously I know you better than you know me."

"That's the cop in you. You observe everything."

"I've observed the cracks in the walls. Are you sure this place isn't going to fall down around you one night?"

She shrugged. "Not until the next earthquake, I guess."

"Spoken like a true Californian."

"What can I tell you? I like it."

Dan liked it too. He liked the colors and the overstuffed sumptuousness of the furnishings. She had a talent for creating a welcoming atmosphere, he thought. Taking the tray from her, he carried the coffee into the sitting room.

Ellie switched on the CD player, lit the candles on the coffee table, dragged a cushion from the chair, and sat cross-legged on it. Pulling the band off her ponytail, she shook her hair free.

He watched, fascinated, as it rippled back over her shoulders, glossy as a roan pony's. Her skin was translucent in the candlelight, and her opal eyes reflected the flames. Looking at her, Dan couldn't think of anywhere else he would rather be.

"It's your turn now," Ellie said, handing him a mug. "I poured my heart out to you the other night. Now I want to hear about you."

"My life hasn't been as exciting as yours. In fact, it was pretty ordinary until I stopped the bullet. Dad was a firefighter. I loved it when I was a kid, the excitement of it, seeing him there at the firehouse with all the other guys. The day they let me climb on the fire engine was the biggest thrill of my young life. Of course, it didn't occur to me it was dangerous, not until I was seven and Dad ended up in the hospital with third-degree burns. Still, he survived and went on to become fire chief. We were so proud of him."

"We?" She raised her brows inquiringly.

"Mom and I. Mom taught third grade. She died four years ago, breast cancer. Dad was pretty shaken up. He'd just retired, which made it even harder, but somehow he dragged his life together. He died last year. With what I inherited, plus my own savings and disability pension, I was able to buy the vineyard." He spread his hands. "And that's about it. The story of my life."

She wasn't about to let him off so lightly. "So? Where did you go to college? Who are your friends? Have you ever been in love?" She gave him a teasing sideways glance, repeating his own questions to her. He threw back his head, laughing.

"College was the University of California, Santa Barbara. My closest friend is an NYPD homicide detective, name of Pete Piatowsky. And yes, I have been in love."

He was still laughing at her as he passed her his mug for a refill. She poured the coffee. "Tell me about your wife."

He took a sip of coffee. "We met in high school. Fran was the prettiest girl I'd ever seen. Small, blond, slender as a greyhound. Ah, we were so young. Nineteen when we married and both in college. Teenage love in a cramped, rented, furnished apartment."

He shrugged. "How could it last? In a way I found freedom, though. I ditched grad school and took off for New York, full of high ideals about working to protect the good and tracking down the bad."

"Did you ever fall in love again?" Her voice was low, sweet.

"I did, but never again like that. . . ."

He wanted to add "until now," but it was too soon.

She took his hand. "Thanks for telling me all that, Dan."

"You think you know me now?"

Her eyes were serious as they met his. "Somehow I think I've always known you," she replied quietly.

He didn't have to ask what she meant by that. He understood. "It's late." He got to his feet, thinking longingly of the many-pillowed white-canopied bed upstairs and Ellie in it. But it wasn't the moment, wasn't the time.

She walked with him into the hallway. Her scent enveloped him, and a strand of her soft hair encountered his lips as he brought his mouth down on hers. He held her lightly for a second as their lips clung. He opened his eyes first. "Beautiful," he said, looking at her. "I could never think of the right word to describe you, but now I know. It's beautiful."

He saw the color rise in her face at the compliment. A real old-fashioned blush, he thought. She never ceased to surprise him.

"Thank you." She pulled away from him and opened the door. "Good night, Danny Boy."

PARKED in the shadows across the street, Buck saw Dan lift his hand in farewell as he walked down the path, and Ellie's smile as she waved back. The clock on the dash said three fifteen. The pain of jealousy was like a stake in his heart. Tears were streaming down his face.

THE following afternoon a large bouquet was delivered to the café. Plump, creamy peonies, paper-white narcissi, and bronze lilies.

Ellie buried her nose in them. They were all scented, all beautiful. Opening the accompanying note, she read it, smiling:

> Thanks for the wonderful dinner and a spectacular *tarte Tatin*. Somehow the colors and scents of these flowers reminded me of you.

They would have pride of place on her night table, and she would call Dan later to thank him. She couldn't wait to see him again. Next Wednesday. Dinner at his place this time.

IT WAS chaotic at the café the following Wednesday, and Ellie never made it to the ranch for dinner. The following evening she was still thinking about Dan, and her heart wasn't in her work. Slamming dishes around tiredly, she thought maybe Chan had a point—the kitchen was too small. The new kid acting as dishwasher this week suddenly dropped a few plates, and she gritted her teeth, telling herself it didn't matter.

"What you need is a night off." Maya stacked plates on the wooden rack. "It's still early. Why don't you just close up tonight? Go see your fella. Or your grandmother or a movie. *Anything.*"

Ellie shook her head. "How can I just close without warning? What will my regular customers think?"

"We'll tell them to try again tomorrow, that's all."

Ellie looked doubtful, but Maya could tell she was thinking about it. "Well, that's settled," Maya said, shrugging on her jacket. "See you tomorrow, then."

"Wait, where are you going?" Ellie grabbed her arm. "What do you mean, *tomorrow?*"

"Didn't you hear? We're closed tonight." Maya's laughter drifted back into the kitchen as she strode out the door. "Get a life, Ellie," she yelled over her shoulder.

Oh well, Ellie said to herself, Maya was right. She could drive up and surprise Miss Lottie, but what she really wanted was to see Dan.

She made good time until she got to Camarillo, and then the mist began rolling over the valley, slowing her down. Fretting in the dawdling traffic, she dialed her grandmother's number on the car phone. There was no answer, and a few minutes later she tried again. Still no answer. Could Miss Lottie be ill? But surely Maria would have called to let her know.

Ellie's heart lurched. Dialing Dan's number, she sat, fingers tapping nervously against the steering wheel, listening to the phone ring, unanswered. She groaned. "Where is everybody this evening?"

DAN walked the still steaming mare back through the stable yard. He heard the phone ringing in the office but let it ring; the mare was more important right now. Throwing a blanket over her, he slapped her on the hindquarters and sent her trotting off into the stall. The phone was still ringing.

He shrugged out of his shirt, wiped the sweat off with it, then picked up the receiver. "Yeah. Running Horse Winery."

Ellie grinned, relieved. "This is no way to run a business. What if I were an important customer waiting to place an order for a hundred cases?"

"Then you'd be unlucky. We don't have ten cases, let alone a hundred. And what we do have, I plan on drinking all by myself."

"That bad, huh?"

"Worse." He tossed the shirt over a chair. "So? Where were you last night?"

"Let's just say I was unavoidably detained at the café. Listen," she went on. "I've taken the evening off. I'm on my way to see my grandmother. I thought perhaps we could meet later? Maybe I could make up for last night?"

"I've never seen Journey's End." Dan was hinting.

"Then this is my opportunity to give you the grand tour. You know how to get there?"

"Up Hot Springs Road and look for the gates with the griffins."

She laughed. "See you there, Danny Boy."

A few minutes later she dialed her grandmother's number again. The line was dead. Peering through the fog, she wished worriedly she could get there faster.

Chapter Six

THE night Buck had chosen to kill Lottie Parrish was a fortunate one weatherwise. It had been a hot day, and now the sea mist was rolling in, smothering the lower part of the town, swirling through the treetops, all the way up into the hills.

He swung the BMW onto the horse trail that circled the back of the property, bumping over the ruts until he was far enough from the road that the car would not to be seen. He wore his black tracksuit, with the drug pusher's Glock 27 automatic tucked into the waistband, a down-padded black ski jacket, a black ski mask, sneakers, and fine latex surgical gloves. The flashlight was in his pocket, and his friend the switchblade was sheathed to his calf.

The moon flickered intermittently through the mist, lighting his path to the old laundry. He jogged through the copse of silver birch, past the empty swimming pool and the overgrown tennis courts. He stood for a moment, looking around at the playground of the rich that soon would be his. Then he walked silently along the terrace.

He had two problems: The easier one was the housekeeper. The second was the dog. He'd considered a piece of poisoned meat but decided it would look premeditated; he wanted this to look like a random robbery gone wrong.

The kitchen door was unlocked. He slipped inside. A clock ticked into the silence. It was hot in his down ski jacket, and sweat trickled down his back.

In the hall a lamp glowed softly on a small table. He switched it off, easing the gun from his waistband. His sneakered feet made no noise on the thickly carpeted stairs.

The sound of running water came from a bathroom, and he guessed the housekeeper was taking a shower. He heard her singing and listened. Suddenly he wanted to laugh.

Warbling his favorite song, "Dixie," Maria dried herself in a big bath towel, then put on her nightdress and her plaid flannel bathrobe. She was thinking about the chocolate cake she'd made that afternoon. She was planning to go downstairs and fix some tea; then she and Miss Lottie would enjoy it together in front of the television set in Miss Lottie's sitting room. Humming her little song, she pushed her feet into her fluffy blue slippers, hung up the towel to dry, then brushed her hair and rolled it into a gray-speckled knot. Then she opened the bathroom door.

The light behind her gave Buck a perfect silhouette. He wasn't an expert with the Glock, but at this range he couldn't miss. The little flame spat from the barrel—one, two, three times.

Maria jolted backward. She clutched at the door, then said "Ohhh" softly and crumpled to the floor.

Buck nodded, satisfied. Target number one accounted for.

Along the hallway a sliver of light shone from Miss Lottie's door. Flexing his strong fingers, he glided toward it.

Miss Lottie had been answering her E-mail, and the computer was still switched on. Now she was brushing her hair, counting softly to a hundred, as she always did.

She glanced at her old watch. It was foolish, she knew, to look forward so much to a piece of Maria's double chocolate cake, but when one was older, life's small pleasures counted for so much more. Like Bruno's morning toast and butter. She ruffled his fur.

"Ah, my boy, I remember when you were just a pup," she said. "Roly-poly, all big paws and floppy ears, and with a foolish grin on your face. Ellie fell in love with you right away, and she was absolutely right."

The door handle squeaked and Bruno's ears pricked up. He struggled to his feet, back stiffened, staring at the door.

"Stop showing off, you silly boy," Miss Lottie said fondly. "It's only Maria." She turned her head, smiling.

The door swung slowly open. Bruno's mouth drew back in a snarl. Growling, he hurled himself forward. There was a sudden popping noise. Miss Lottie heard him whimper; then he turned and staggered slowly back. His trusting eyes were fixed on hers, life fading from them as he sank down at her feet.

His blood gushed over her slippers. Miss Lottie bent, stroked his soft fur lovingly with a trembling hand. Her heart was breaking.

Lifting her head, she looked into the eyes of the masked man standing in the doorway. There was a gun in his hand. Pointed at her. Anger flared in her eyes. "You shot my dog," she said, her voice cold as chipped ice. "There was no need for that. He was old and harmless. If you've come to rob me, the safe is in the wall in the dressing room, over there. It's never locked."

"I know."

His voice was low, almost a whisper. "Who are you?" She stared imperiously at him. "Only a coward would come into the house and frighten two old woman, kill a dog . . ."

The hand holding the gun wavered. She was meant to be afraid, terrified, begging for her life. Instead, she was telling him what to do, ordering him around. *Go get her,* the voice inside his head commanded. *Tell her what you intend to do. Make her grovel.*

"Put down that gun at once," Miss Lottie commanded. "Take what you want; then leave my house."

"I came for you, Miss Lottie." Buck laid the gun, obediently, on the lamp table.

Miss Lottie gripped her cane firmly as he took a step toward her. It was her only weapon and she intended to use it. She was an old woman and not afraid of dying, but she would go when her time came and not before.

Buck pulled off the ski mask. "Take a good look, Miss Lottie," he said mockingly. "It's been a long time."

Miss Lottie stared. Seconds ticked past. "Of course," she said at last. "I couldn't put my finger on it at the Biltmore. Now I know. It was the eyes. You can't change those, Buck Duveen."

"And you don't change either, Miss Lottie. Still playing the dowager queen. Only this time there are no faithful retainers to come running to save you." His face was in hers. "You had me put away for half my life while you and the girl lived in splendor."

"You were locked away because you are mad," she replied calmly. "Now I see it was a mistake, a kindness that went wrong. I should have let you go to jail. Let you be branded for what you are. *Murderer.*" She smashed the cane across his face.

Buck staggered back, half blinded with pain.

Miss Lottie knew there was no escape. She could not run, but she had to warn Ellie. She had only moments.

Her fingers trembled as she found the computer keyboard and began to type DUVEEEEEEE. Buck's powerful hands fastened around her throat, and her finger stuck on the E.

Her flesh was pliant under his fingers; he could feel it bruising, feel her fragile bones snapping. But her blue eyes never wavered from his. It was as if she was mocking him, saying, "See, even now, you can't win. I'm not afraid."

"Close your eyes," he howled. "Close your damn eyes."

But Miss Lottie did not close her eyes, even when she was dead.

Buck let her drop. Still trembling, he looked triumphantly down at her. He had dreamed so often of seeing her like this.

He dragged her into the dressing room, then took the pearls and the few rings and brooches from the open safe and stuffed them into the pockets of the ski jacket.

Then he knelt beside her and carved his sign into her forehead. He had won. Finally the prize would be his.

He opened the French window, swept aside the gauzy white curtains, and looked out at the land, his land soon. As if to help him, the mist rolled back, and pale moonlight showed on the gardens. *And on Ellie's yellow Jeep, parked in front.*

His sharp indrawn breath rattled in his throat. He hadn't heard her drive up; he couldn't let her find him here. But it was too late. He could already hear her calling for Maria, her footsteps on the stairs. He stepped quickly through the French window and out onto the balcony. The switchblade was ready in his hand.

"MARIA, HELLO," ELLIE CALLED. "It's me." She waited, expecting Bruno to come waddling down the stairs to greet her. "Maria?" she called again. Silence wrapped around her like a blanket, and goose bumps prickled up her arms.

"Nothing's happened," she reassured herself, taking the steps two at a time. "Gran, it's me. . . ." Flinging open the door, she rushed in and almost tripped over the dog. She took a step back, her shoes sticky with blood. Bruno's dead eyes stared back at her.

"Ohhhhh . . ." The breath caught in her throat. "Bruno," she whispered, shocked. "Oh, Bruno . . ." The hair at the back of her neck stood up as she looked warily around the room.

"Gran . . ." Her voice wavered. She took a hesitant step toward the dressing room, saw her grandmother's bare foot. Her eyes widened with shock. "Gran!" she screamed.

As she backed out of the dressing room, something caught her attention. She stared at the billowing curtains. Something out there caught the light, glittering. Suddenly the adrenaline of terror gave her feet wings, and she turned and fled.

BUCK sighed happily as he stepped back into the room, sheathing the knife. Tonight his beloved Ellie lived. If she had seen him, he would have been forced to kill her, and it wasn't time yet. He heard her running across the hall, the door being flung open, the engine as she started her car.

He glanced at the silver-framed photograph on the nightstand. Ellie's eyes gazed into his, her lips curved in that dazzling smile. A smile meant just for him. Sweeping the framed photo into his pocket, he hurried from the room.

He ran noiselessly back down the stairs, through the hall to the kitchen. The lock clicked shut as he closed the door behind him. Keeping to the shadows, he jogged back down the trail to his car.

Lottie Parrish was dead and he was a happy man.

THE Explorer cruised smoothly up Hot Springs Road, and Dan smiled as he swung between the massive pillars with the griffins.

Ellie was right. You couldn't miss them; they were big enough for Buckingham Palace. Too late, he saw the yellow Jeep coming at him. Slamming on the brakes, he threw the wheel to the right. The Jeep sideswiped him and, tires screeching, skidded into a tree.

Ellie jumped from the car, her eyes blinded with tears. He ran to her, grabbed her by the shoulders. She was screaming hysterically. "What's gotten into you, Ellie? Have you gone crazy? Ellie," he yelled. "Ellie, stop it."

Something penetrated her terror-fogged brain. Trembling, she looked at him.

"It's okay," he said gently. "It's only a car, even if it is a new one." He smiled encouragingly, but there was no answering smile.

"It's Miss Lottie . . . dead . . . murdered . . . the dog . . ." She gulped back the sobs that were choking her. "I saw her. I saw . . . Oh, God. Oh, my God . . ."

Dan pulled her close, holding her, remembering that the old ladies lived alone and were careless about security. Could she really have been murdered?

"I've got to go in there and take a look," he told her quietly. "I want you to stay in the car. Lock all the doors."

She shook her head, afraid to be left alone.

He put his arm around her as he walked her back up the road to his car. "Okay, but I don't want you to go in there again."

When they got back to the house, the front door stood open, just as she'd left it. She stood in the hall as he walked up the stairs.

Dan could smell violence even before he saw it. The dog was already stiff. The curtains billowed gently in the breeze from the open French window. He saw the pool of blood, the cane thrown to the ground. He walked into the dressing room, saw Miss Lottie's body, so pathetically small and frail. Her eyes were wide-open, and there was a cross carved into her forehead. *Temple to temple, scalp to nose.* He drew in a shocked breath.

He was too experienced a cop to touch anything or to try to move her. He checked the closet, the bathroom, the balcony.

From the top of the stairs he saw Ellie looking up at him.

"Which room is Maria's?" he asked. She pointed to the next room.

He found Maria's body just outside her bathroom door. She had been shot several times in the chest. There was a lot of blood, but there was no cross carved into her head.

WITH lights shining from every window, Journey's End looked the way it used to years ago, when Miss Lottie was throwing a "little soiree." Which had meant dinner for three hundred people, with champagne, women in gorgeous evening gowns, and handsome, suntanned men in black tie. Now, instead of sleek limousines, there were squad cars and ambulances parked out front.

Upstairs, Dan was telling Detective Jim Johannsen how he had found the bodies and that the cross etched on the face linked the crime with the hooker murdered in New York and the one last week in L.A.

"I'm trying to figure out the connection between a robbery with violence and the signature serial killing of prostitutes," he said worriedly. "It just doesn't make sense."

"It's an ugly scene," Johannsen agreed. The detective had worked in the L.A. Police Department for many years before transferring to Santa Barbara. He was a veteran of violence, but there was something infinitely pathetic about the killing of two old women and their dog. Still, he wasn't about to discuss the case with a civilian. And a witness.

He stood in front of Miss Lottie's computer, looking thoughtful. "What d'you make of this, Cassidy?"

Miss Lottie had been writing to a friend in England. The letter was chatty and charming and a bit vague.

And she had broken off in the middle of a sentence. Underneath, in caps, was the name Duveen, except it wasn't completed.

"Looks like her finger got stuck on the E," Johannsen said. "Why was she writing Ellie's name?"

Dan remembered Ellie's story about her grandmother. "Her mind wasn't what it used to be. She might have been thinking of her daughter, Romany, who died in an auto accident years ago."

They stared at the computer. "You dusting it for prints?" Dan asked. Johannsen threw him a skeptical look. Dan held his hands up, palms out. "Sorry, sorry. You're in charge."

"That's right." Johannsen's tone put Dan in his place. "What I'd like now is to speak to Miss Duveen."

Detective Johannsen had dealt with shocked relatives in sudden-death cases many times in his career, and it never became any easier. "I'm sorry, Miss Duveen. If you could, I'd like you to tell me exactly what happened when you got to the house." He waited, ballpoint poised over his notepad.

She didn't even have to pause to think about it; each moment was engraved on her heart. It took just a few minutes.

"Do you know of any person who wanted Miss Lottie dead?"

Dan knew instantly where his questioning was heading. Ellie was a suspect until the real killer was found.

"No. No one."

"Thank you. I know how hard this is for you."

Ellie's eyes followed him as he turned away. She wanted to tell him it wasn't difficult at all, that she remembered it perfectly, that she would never forget.

ZIPPED into a body bag, Miss Lottie was bundled onto a gurney, covered with a white sheet, and carried downstairs. Ellie's tearless eyes were fixed on the slight shape under the sheet as she followed that precious burden over to the waiting ambulance. Then the doors were shut, and the medics walked back into the house, first for Maria, then for the dog.

Ellie had been unable to cry for Miss Lottie or Maria, but now tears stung her eyes. "Bruno," she whispered. "Oh, Bruno . . ."

"I'm taking you home now." Dan's arm slid comfortingly around her shoulders, and she rested against him. It was an arm to be leaned against, a shoulder to cry on, a still beating heart that offered her love and compassion.

She looked back, bewildered, at Journey's End. "But this is home," she murmured.

Even as she said it, she knew it was no longer true.

DAN BROUGHT HER TO Running Horse Ranch. He offered her brandy, coffee, wine, hot tea. She declined everything but the tea, yet even that had failed to melt the icy numbness.

The big pine bed piled high with pillows looked soft, inviting, but she knew she wouldn't sleep, nor would she submit to a sedative. She needed to be awake, needed to keep her grandmother in her head, close to her. Awake, she was with Gran. Drugged and sleeping, she would be in a limbo of nothingness. Wandering to the window, she looked out. A gray, sunless dawn was already lightening the sky.

There was a scrabbling noise at the door; then Pancho's nose snuffled through the crack. Pushing it open, he bounced joyfully into the room, but instead of leaping all over her, as he usually did, he sat quietly, gazing up at her.

Ellie suddenly realized that she was smiling. It was amazing, she thought, how animals and children could bring you back to square one, to realizing that innocence still existed in the world.

Climbing into bed, she lay back in the nest of pillows Florita had arranged for her. The sheets were cool and smelled of lavender. Pancho leaped onto the end of the bed, turned around once or twice, then settled down, his head on his paws. Ellie closed her eyes and fell suddenly into a dark pit of blessed oblivion.

MAYA was up early that morning. She had a yoga class at eight thirty. Yawning and stretching, she switched on the TV.

> "L.A. Today. Here is your local news. A well-known Santa Barbara woman was found murdered in her home last night, along with her housekeeper and the family dog. Eighty-six-year-old Charlotte Parrish was found dead . . ."

Maya stood staring at the TV.

> ". . . along with Maria Novales, age seventy. The crime was discovered last night by Mrs. Parrish's granddaughter and only living relative, Ellie Parrish Duveen, and police are questioning her."

Maya's jaw dropped. Heart thumping, she leaped for the phone.

Ellie's home number didn't answer. Of course it wouldn't. She was up in Santa Barbara. But where? She dialed Dan's number.

"Is Ellie there?" Maya asked when Dan answered. "It's Maya Morris, Ellie's friend. I just heard the news on television. I'm so afraid for her."

"It's okay, Maya. She's here with me."

"Oh, thank heavens." She sagged with relief. "Is she all right? No, that's a foolish question. How can she be all right? I have to see her. I'm on my way right now. . . . Tell me what I can do for her."

"She's numb, Maya. It's going to be tough for her to get over it, seeing her grandmother like that."

Maya wiped tears away. "Oh, poor, dear Miss Lottie."

"Ellie could use a change of clothing, if you could bring that."

Dan gave her directions to the ranch, then said, "We're on our way to Santa Barbara now. The police want to talk to Ellie. We'll probably be back by the time you arrive."

"I'll get there as soon as I can."

JOHANNSEN took a sip of his coffee and cleared his throat. "Miss Duveen, I'd like you to go over again what your movements were last night. With exact times, if you can recall them."

They were in a bleak gray room at the Santa Barbara Police Department. Coffee steamed, untouched, on the table in front of them. Ellie slumped in the hard chair. "I was on Highway 101, driving to Montecito. I was near Camarillo and it was foggy. I called Gran to tell her I was coming by. There was no reply."

Wearily she went through her story. She would tell it a thousand times if she had to, if it would help them find the killer.

"And you arranged to meet Mr. Cassidy at the house?"

She nodded. "Yes. He'd never seen Journey's End. I said I would show him around."

"How long have you known Mr. Cassidy?"

She ran a hand through her hair. "Maybe . . . a few weeks."

Johannsen's voice lost its softness; it was firm, even harsh. "Miss

Duveen, it's my understanding that you are the sole remaining family member. That, in fact, you stand to inherit Mrs. Parrish's entire estate. Is that true?"

She nodded, puzzled at the tack the questioning was taking. "Yes, but—" She sat back, shocked. "You can't think I killed her."

"No one has suggested you did anything, Miss Duveen. It's just a line of questioning we have to pursue." Personally Johannsen thought it likely. Somehow the robbery scene didn't sit right. He had the impression there hadn't been much to steal. "I'd appreciate it, Miss Duveen, if you'd accompany us back to the house. We need you to check Miss Lottie's possessions and tell us, if you can, what's missing. It might be helpful in finding the killer."

"I'll do anything for that," Ellie agreed. "But I want Dan with me."

He could have lived without that one. "Sure, bring him along if it makes you feel better." He hadn't completely dismissed the idea of the pair of them as murderers.

ELLIE held Dan's hand tightly in the squad car as they raced along Cabrillo Boulevard. The palm trees ruffled in the breeze, and the sun sparkled on the blue sea. Everything looked the same, normal.

"You okay?" Dan asked as the car turned in between the massive griffin gateposts. She nodded. It wasn't easy, what she was going to do—going back to that room—but she'd do it.

A pair of uniformed officers guarded the gates, and there were more at the front door. Yellow crime-scene tape was still in place, and men hurried purposefully in and out of the house.

Johannsen ushered Ellie inside and led the way up the stairs.

I'm doing this for you, Gran, Ellie was thinking as she walked into that terrible room again. *I promise I'll help find who did this to you.* But it was so hard. The brownish stain on the rug was Gran's blood; she had lain here, lost her slipper there. This was where Bruno died.

"We found the door to the safe open, Miss Duveen." Johannsen was brisk, businesslike.

Ellie nodded. "Miss Lottie never locked it. She said she had nothing worth stealing."

"Can you tell us exactly what is missing?"

She peered inside the safe. "Her pearls. It was an eighteen-inch rope of twelve-millimeter South Sea pearls."

Johannsen's brows rose. "Worth a small fortune in themselves."

"I suppose so, but I don't think Miss Lottie ever considered their value. They were treasured for their memories more than their value."

Johannsen looked disbelieving. "What else?"

"Her diamond engagement ring. I've no idea what it's worth. Maybe her attorneys will know. A couple of smaller diamond rings and a sapphire. Some antique brooches. That's about it."

"Take a look around, Miss Duveen. Anything else missing?"

Averting her eyes from the bloodstains, Ellie looked around at the familiar objects that had formed part of her grandmother's life. The French ormolu clock with the three fat cherubs she had liked so much when she was a child. The crystal and silver knickknacks, the old photographs. Her eyes widened. "The photograph is gone."

Johannsen hurried forward. "What photograph?"

"It was of me, in a silver frame. Gran kept it by her bedside."

"Anything else, Miss Duveen?"

"No, nothing else." Weariness settled over her. She took one last, long look around, then turned and walked away. She knew she would never see that room again.

SHE was silent on the drive back to Running Horse, her head back, her eyes closed. The damaged Explorer grunted as Dan gunned up the crumbling blacktop lane that led through the vineyard to the house. Without opening her eyes, she said, "Sorry for smacking up your car. Again."

"That's okay." His mind was on the missing photo. There were more valuable things in the room, so why would a thief take Ellie's picture? Not just for the silver frame, he was sure of that.

In the house there were a dozen messages on the machine—from Ellie's friends, from the Parrish family lawyers and accountants, from Maria's relatives in Guadalajara.

The news had been on all the networks. Ellie sat on the sofa, looking helplessly at Dan. "I have to call Maria's family. And what about the funeral? What shall I do?"

"Why don't you let me take care of it all for you?"

"Would you?" She was so pathetically grateful. "You're my friend. I'd trust you with anything."

Dan put a match to the fire, then knelt, slipped off her shoes, and wrapped a blue horse blanket around her. Then, just as he called Florita to bring hot tea, a car squealed to a stop outside.

"Ellie, Ellie . . ." Maya raced up the steps, flung herself across the porch and through the door. She stood in the hall, clutching a bunch of summery flowers to her chest. "There you are." She ran past Dan and grabbed Ellie. "Oh, baby, I'm so sorry." Their tears mingled as they held each other, sobbing out their sorrow.

Dan took the flowers to the kitchen for Florita to find a vase. He told her they had another guest tonight. Then he went to the office and made a call to New York.

"WHAT'S up?" Piatowsky asked when he heard the serious tone in Dan's voice.

"A friend of mine's in trouble. Her grandmother was killed last night. I get the feeling the police suspect her of doing it."

"Yeah, I heard about it." Piatowsky hesitated. "How good a friend is she?"

"As good as it gets."

He knew Dan was talking romance here. He would need to tread carefully. Clearing his throat, he said, "Dan, I kinda wondered about that myself. I mean, she's the only living relative of a rich old lady who's been murdered. It's a logical thought."

"Not a chance," Dan said. "I'd arranged to meet her there. I was *there,* at the scene, immediately after she found them. This is one woman who really loved her grandmother—she'd been more like a mother to her. And the housekeeper was more than just that; she was family. Even the dog got it. The safe was robbed; he took her jewelry, turned the place over. And get this. The old lady was strangled. And he left a signature. The same cross as on the Times Square hooker."

Piatowsky was stunned. "But it was a robbery with violence. Our man wouldn't go for that. It's not his kick."

"Exactly. So do we have a copycat?"

Piatowsky shook his head. "Makes no sense to me."

"The robbery looked fake to me—like a setup, you know? To cover up something else." Piatowsky heard Dan sigh at the other end of the line. "I sure could use you out here."

"Okay, fella, don't sweat. I'll be there tomorrow."

As he rang off, Piatowsky thought regretfully about the fishing and the long, lazy evenings on the front porch, sipping cold beer and enjoying all that clean, fresh country air. Somehow he got the feeling this visit wasn't going to be quite like that.

Chapter Seven

LATER that evening Dan ran through the facts in his mind. The two different methods of killing made it possible there were two killers. But something about this murder also spoke of a meticulously planned ritual. Detective Johannsen, though, was on a different tack.

They were back in the bare little gray room at the police station, with Johannsen at one side of the table and Ellie and Dan at the other. Johannsen's partner, Detective Mullins, propped up the wall.

"You understand there's no pressure, Miss Duveen," Johannsen was saying. "This is just an informal discussion."

Dan's antennae pricked up. "Do I understand you are questioning Miss Duveen, and possibly myself, as suspects?"

Johannsen cleared his throat. "Not exactly . . ."

Dan said, "Then I suggest you Mirandize both Miss Duveen and myself and that we wait for her attorney to arrive." He was very glad he had called Miss Lottie's attorney from the ranch and that the man had agreed to meet them at the police station right away.

Johannsen sighed. He'd hoped to break her down a bit before getting to this point. He waved Mullins forward, and he proceeded to read them their rights.

Ellie's stunned eyes met Dan's. "I don't understand."

"It's all right," he said quietly. "We'll just wait for the lawyer."

"But I want to tell them everything." She leaned across the table, her hands clasped tightly together, looking at Johannsen. "I want you to find who killed my grandmother."

"That's all we're asking of you right now, Miss Duveen."

There was a knock on the door, and a female officer admitted Michael Majors, Miss Lottie's attorney. A small man in dark pinstripes and a pink shirt, Majors walked over to Ellie and patted her shoulder. "I can't tell you how distressed I am, how shocked. My deepest sympathy, Ellie. It is truly a terrible loss."

"Thank you. This is Dan Cassidy, my friend. And Detectives Johannsen and Mullins."

Majors shook hands. "Can I ask exactly why you're holding my client here?"

"We're not holding your client, Mr. Majors. We've merely brought her in for questioning," Johannsen replied mildly.

"Then I assume you've read her her rights."

He nodded. "I did. Miss Duveen volunteered to answer any question we choose to ask. In the hope of jogging her memory."

Majors looked uneasy. "Of course, if that's what she wishes . . ."

"I want to help," Ellie said. "I'll do anything I can."

"Well, that's settled." Johannsen smiled. "Now, tell me again, Miss Duveen, exactly the sequence of events last night."

She was reliving the hell: She saw herself calling her grandmother from the car, the swirling fog in the valley, her surprise that there was no reply. The silence that had sent goose bumps up her arms, her own voice as she called for Maria. Herself running up the stairs two at a time. Bruno's dead eyes staring up at her, his blood on the rug, on Miss Lottie's slippers . . .

Her grandmother, sprawled faceup in the dressing room, her tiny blue-veined feet, and her face . . . Oh, her face . . .

She saw herself backing out of the dressing room. The curtains billowing in from the French window . . .

"Someone was out there"—Ellie grabbed Johannsen's hand across the table—"on the balcony. I'm sure of it."

"Okay, so tell me, slowly, exactly what you saw."

She concentrated. "I heard something. The window had blown open, and the curtains were billowing in." She closed her eyes, searching for it, that flicker of something that had caught her attention. A glint of light in the darkness outside on the balcony. "It was the reflective patch on a sneaker," she said carefully. "You know, the kind runners wear." She nodded, triumphant. "That's what I saw."

"And what did you do then?"

"I . . . well, I don't know." She was floundering. "I remember running down the stairs, getting in my car . . . I was—"

"Miss Duveen was terrified, Detective." Dan's voice was harsh. "What else did you expect her to do?"

"And where were you, Mr. Cassidy, when all this was going on?" Johannsen eyed Dan's strong hands speculatively.

"I was on my way to Journey's End to pick up Ellie. We'd arranged to meet there." Dan's voice had a weary edge to it, but he was alert, on guard. "I'd just turned into the gates when I saw the Jeep coming at me, fast. I swung to the right, but it hit me. I saw Ellie get out. She was screaming."

"And what happened then?"

"We went back to the house. Ellie waited at the foot of the stairs while I went up and looked around. I found the scene exactly as you saw it yourself. I checked the bathroom, the closets, the balcony. I did the same in the housekeeper's room. Then I called the police."

"So there was no man in sneakers on the balcony?"

"No, sir. Not by the time I got there."

"And how long would you estimate that was, Miss Duveen?"

Ellie looked blankly at him. Time had had no meaning. "It was all a blur."

"I estimate a max of ten minutes." Dan was sharp, businesslike.

Majors stood. "If I were you, I'd be delighted with what Miss Duveen came up with, Detective. There was someone out on that balcony, wearing sneakers."

"And would you by any chance own a pair of sneakers like that, Mr. Cassidy?"

"Wrong tack, Johannsen," Dan said smoothly. "No, I don't."

Johannsen stood, hands in his pockets. "Miss Duveen, thank you for being so cooperative."

Ellie got to her feet. "I did see that, you know."

He nodded coolly. "I know."

She frowned, bewildered by his attitude.

"Come on." Dan had her by the arm.

Outside in the parking lot, Ellie gave a weary sigh. "I don't believe this. They think I murdered Miss Lottie."

"At the moment they don't have much to go on except motive," said the lawyer. "Unless something incriminating turns up in forensics or the autopsy, or they prove you owned the gun, they don't have a leg to stand on."

"It's a storm in a teacup." Dan put his arm around her. "Tomorrow we'll sort it all out."

He thanked heaven that Piatowsky was arriving tomorrow.

BUCK was restless. He had that itchy feeling again, the way he used to in the Hudson Sanitarium when he needed to break out, to do something. He needed to see Ellie, but Ellie was not around.

He was sitting in the car on the hill near her house, wondering where she could be, when two squad cars sped past him and turned into Ellie's street. A minute later a black Crown Victoria passed him and parked next to the others outside Ellie's house. A couple of plainclothes detectives got out and joined the four uniformed officers.

Buck lit up a Camel, got out of the car, and strolled casually along the street. To his surprise they didn't knock; they simply opened the door and walked in. They were searching her house.

Stamping out the cigarette, he walked quickly back to the car and drove down the hill onto Main Street. It was a Saturday, hot, a beach day. There were no parking spaces near the café, but he didn't need to stop; the CLOSED sign was visible on the glass door. *Where was she?*

His mind shifted to Dan Cassidy. He had the sudden gut feeling Ellie was with him, and rage filled the pit of his stomach. He needed to know who Cassidy was, where he lived. Spotting a liquor store, he made a quick turn into its parking lot, went inside, and bought three bottles of Jim Beam. Then he headed back toward Sunset Boulevard.

At his apartment, he kept the drapes permanently closed. He switched on a lamp and the TV, clicking until he found the local news. Prowling the perimeter of the small dark room, he slugged bourbon from the bottle, his eyes fixed on the TV screen.

The weatherman was telling what a glorious day it was going to be, if you discounted the air quality, of course, and just felt those wonderful warm rays. "Take care," the man said. "This is a factor-five burn day."

Buck tilted the bottle to his mouth again. Dammit! Why didn't they get on with the news, tell him what was happening with Ellie?

"IT LOOKS just like the photos." Piatowsky stood at the top of the hill, looking back at the immaculate rows of vines and the black-and-white cattle clustered under the shady oaks on the hill opposite. He swung around, taking in the house, while Dan hauled the bags from the Explorer. "I thought you said it was falling down?"

"It was. Where d'you think my money's gone?"

Piatowsky laughed. Cocking his head to one side, he listened to the birdsong and the soft sigh of the wind. He said, baffled, "Isn't it kinda quiet around here?"

"You'll get used to it. Life is better without traffic, believe me."

Piatowsky nodded. Still, he thought, for a guy living in sun-shineland, his friend looked tired. Dan's jaw glistened blue-black with stubble, and his hair looked as though he'd run his hands through it once too often. He seemed like a guy with a lot on his mind.

"So how're ya holdin' up?" he asked.

"You're not gonna believe this, but the local cops think maybe I did the job, along with Ellie."

"Why you?"

"I've been cast as the boyfriend, an ex-cop who knows how it's done. I had the strength to strangle the old lady while Ellie shot the housekeeper. And the dog."

"They found the weapon yet?"

Dan shook his head. "If they have, they're sure not telling me. It's an execution, Pete. I feel it in my bones." They had both seen enough execution-type slayings to know the pattern. "Maria was shot. Miss Lottie was strangled, even though he had the gun and could have shot her too. Why would he do that? Strangle her?"

"Kind of a vengeance thing?"

"That's what I thought. But Ellie doesn't know of anyone with a grudge against her grandmother. Though there was one incident she told me about, years ago. Some guy broke into the house and attacked her. Ellie was just a kid, but she saw it all."

"So what happened to the guy? He do time or what?"

"Ellie didn't know. Anyway, it all took place more than twenty years ago, so I'm not sure how relevant it might be."

"Old grudges never die, they just get more bitter."

Dan shrugged. "There's no one left who knows anything about it. But *I saw* the crime scene. I *know* what it felt like."

Piatowsky knew exactly that feeling—it was part instinct, part experience, part guess. Whatever, it raised the hackles and sent the mind questing further than the obvious.

Piatowsky spotted two figures in the distance. A couple of dogs were chasing after them, and faintly he heard their excited barks.

"Here's Ellie and Maya. And this is Pancho." The mutt flew toward Dan, covering the ground like a racehorse, yipping madly, with Ortega's dog bringing up the rear. They bounced up at him, then turned their lavish-tongued attentions to Piatowsky.

"Terrific, great." He patted them cautiously. "What kinda guard dogs are these?"

"They're country dogs. They come with the territory."

"Yeah, well, forgive me, but I'm not familiar with the breed. Though they sure aren't any prettier than city mutts." He glanced up as Ellie and Maya approached. "But the women are," he murmured. "Boy, Cassidy, you attract 'em in pairs now?"

Ellie was tall, slender, elegant in a pale, waiflike sort of way, with no makeup and her hair pulled tightly back in a knot at the nape of her neck. She was wearing white shorts and an Ellie's Place T-shirt. Maya, also unmade-up, looked fresh-faced as a schoolgirl, except for that body encased in a yellow Lycra tank top and shorts.

"Ellie, this is Pete Piatowsky, my old buddy from New York. Maya Morris, Pete." As they shook hands, Piatowsky knew why Cassidy was in love with Ellie. There was sorrow in her beautiful eyes but also strength. This woman was wounded, but not broken.

Ellie stared at him. Dan trusted Piatowsky, had said if anybody could help, he could. "I'm glad you came," she said quietly. "And I'm sorry if all this is interrupting your vacation."

"Don't worry, I'm the kinda guy who can never take a real vacation. I need to keep on my toes."

"Are you going to help Dan find out who did it?" Maya was nothing if not direct.

"I'll try, Miss Morris."

Her big whiskey-brown eyes fastened on him. Maya laughed, linking her arm in his. "Call me Maya."

"Pete," he said, dazzled, walking with her into the house.

Florita was waiting in the hall with the baby perched on her hip. "Senor, welcome. You like some hot coffee? Iced tea, maybe?"

Accompanied by three attentive women, Piatowsky wafted into the sitting room and sank onto the sofa. He figured life didn't get much better than this.

Dan saw there were two messages on the machine. The first was from Johannsen, saying that a warrant had been issued in Santa Monica to search Ellie's house.

He closed his eyes, stunned. They were really serious.

The second was just a long silence, then a cutoff. Wondering who it had been, Dan went to tell the others the bad news.

"They're searching my home?" Ellie felt a clutch of fear. "But why? They can't be serious. How could anybody think that . . ."

Maya plopped onto the sofa next to her. "It'll be all right," she said, sounding as though she didn't quite believe it would.

Piatowsky rearranged the thinning blond hair over his scalp, glancing at Dan. "It's just a logical move on their part," he told them. "A cop has to check out every angle, Ellie."

"What's really disturbing is the missing photo," Dan broke in. "It just doesn't fit with the rest of the robbery-with-violence scenario. Nor with a murder by a killer who left a signature. I keep asking myself exactly why the killer would take it. And I come up with only one answer. It has to be someone who knows Ellie."

"You mean I *know* the killer?" Her anxious eyes met Dan's.

He smiled reassuringly. "We're going to sort it all out, don't worry," he said. He hoped he was right.

BUCK took a slug from the second bottle of bourbon, feeling it fizz through his veins like rocket fuel, then stared at the TV screen, waiting for the next news bulletin. If the cops were searching Ellie's house, they must think she did it. He bellowed with laughter at the thought. How ironic, the doting granddaughter as the murderer.

Then there it was at last.

> "Police are still searching for the killer of Charlotte Parrish, society doyenne. We understand that her granddaughter was taken in for questioning but was not detained."

Buck set the bottle down on the table, suddenly sober. *His Ellie. They were questioning her. They might put her in prison; then he would never have her.*

He had to find her. He had to see Ellie.

DETECTIVES Johannsen and Mullins were sitting in the black, unmarked Crown Victoria, parked in the driveway at Journey's End. Gray clouds were sweeping across the mountains, and huge raindrops splattered suddenly across the windshield, blurring their view of the officers with German shepherd tracker dogs, who were combing the grounds for any clues the killer might have left.

The rain would take care of any scent the dogs might have found, plus erase any tracks, Johannsen thought gloomily. So far the guys had come up with zero.

The phone beeped. He picked it up. "Johannsen."

"Good morning, sir. This is Detective Pete Piatowsky, NYPD."

"What can I do for you, Detective?"

Piatowsky thought the man sounded weary. He knew that feeling. "I know my department has been in touch, sir, about the prostitute murdered near Times Square. The killing was very similar to the one you have here, in Montecito. Manual strangulation with mutilation."

"A very particular mutilation." Johannsen had spoken not only to the New York police department, but also with the LAPD and the FBI. Now everybody was getting in on his act.

"I'm in Santa Barbara now, Detective. I'd like to get together with you, discuss the similarities in the cases."

Johannsen sighed. "I can be back in my office at noon."

"I'll see you then, sir."

Piatowsky grinned at Dan as he dialed the New York precinct number. "Yeah, George, it's Piatowsky here. I'm on my way to see the detective in charge of the Montecito signature killing, see if it ties in with ours and the L.A. hooker. . . . Yep, I'll let you know what develops." He listened. "Yeah, you could call it a busman's holiday, but life's like that." He looked out the window at the clouds pressing on the hilltops. "And guess what? It's raining."

Dan could hear the guffaw of laughter on the other end of the line as Piatowsky put down the phone and said plaintively, "I thought it never rained in southern California."

"You've been listening to too much Beach Boys. We're meeting Johannsen, then?"

"*I'm* meeting Johannsen. *You* are a civilian, Cassidy. And also a suspect." The phone rang and Piatowsky picked it up. "Yeah," he said.

Dan waited for him to say who it was, but Piatowsky was pacing the floor, the phone tucked under his chin.

"Yeah," he said again. And, "No kidding. Okay, will do."

He put down the phone again and looked at Dan. "There's been another woman killed. In L.A. again. A hooker. Manual strangulation with mutilation. She was dumped in a canal in Venice Beach."

Piatowsky shrugged on the old black leather bomber jacket he hadn't seriously expected to have to wear in sunshineland. "Gotta go, fella. I've got an appointment with your destiny."

JOHANNSEN was leaning across his desk with his horn-rims perched on the end of his wide nose, studying the information on the new killing when Piatowsky was announced. He glanced up, assessing his visitor, the way he knew Piatowsky was also assessing him. He guessed Piatowsky had him pegged for a small-town cop and had cast himself in the role of the all-wise, all-knowing New York big-time detective. Well, he was wrong. Johannsen had been there, done that.

"Detective Piatowsky"—he waved to a chair opposite the desk—"have a seat. Coffee?"

"Thanks, but no." Piatowsky had already been through enough caffeine to jump-start a cadaver. He worked better that way, and besides, Florita's coffee was a whole lot better than police brew.

"I heard there's been another murder?"

Johannsen read from the sheet of paper in front of him. "A hooker, Caucasian, blond, five two, name of Rita Lampert. She worked the dives off Hollywood Boulevard. The body was found in a canal at five thirty this morning by a jogger. She'd been clubbed around the head, then strangled and her face disfigured."

"The same as Charlotte Parrish?"

He nodded. "But not the same as Maria Novales, the housekeeper. She was shot and she was not mutilated."

"You have a theory about that?"

Johannsen nodded again. "I think the mutilation of Mrs. Parrish was a deliberate attempt to throw us off the scent. He wanted us to believe it was the signature killer."

"You still working on the possibility that the granddaughter had something to do with it?"

"I am. Probably with the help of an accomplice. Though, I admit, we don't have any hard evidence as yet. A search of Miss Duveen's home revealed nothing. Forensics says that black fibers found at the crime scene were wool, possibly from a sweater or a ski mask. They're pursuing it further. The weapon used was a Glock 27 automatic pistol." He hesitated. There was one other piece of evidence that he was reluctant to talk about yet because it might prove his case. Or it might just shoot down his theory. He decided against telling the New York cop about it. He shrugged, spreading his hands, palms up. "That's about it."

"Thanks for your cooperation." Piatowsky stood.

"Why not leave me your number," Johannsen said, "so I can keep you informed. Are you staying in Santa Barbara?"

"Didn't I tell you?" Piatowsky smiled. "I'm at Running Horse Ranch with Dan Cassidy. He's an old buddy of mine. We were partners for five years."

Johannsen's smile had slipped from his face as though it had never been.

ELLIE was on the phone, attempting to pick up the pieces of her life and reconstruct it in a different framework. Michael Majors was telling her that apart from a generous bequest to Maria that was no longer relevant, she was the sole heir.

"I can't advise you strongly enough to put the house on the market right away," the lawyer said. "The land is valuable, and it should sell without too much trouble."

"I can't sell it. Not yet." It was too soon to let go of her past and the memories.

"I understand, but give it some thought, Ellie. And when you decide, I'll take care of it for you."

Ellie put down the phone, thinking that everyone was taking care of something for her. She had to get a grip.

Coming down the stairs, Maya saw Ellie standing by the phone, staring at it as though it were a strange, unknown object.

"What happened?" She crossed the hall. "You okay?"

"It was just Gran's attorney telling me I've inherited Journey's End and asking if I'd put it on the market right away."

"You can't do that yet," Maya said.

The telephone rang again and Ellie picked it up. "Running Horse Ranch." There was silence on the line, and she said again, "Hello, Running Horse." There was still no reply. Her eyes met Maya's as she slammed down the phone.

"Who was that?"

Ellie shivered. "I don't know."

It rang again and this time Maya grabbed it. "Who the hell is this?" she snapped. Her face turned pink. "Oh, excuse me. . . . Yes, she's here. Hold on please." She handed the phone to Ellie.

Ellie's heart sank as she recognized the voice of Detective Johannsen. He told her that the coroner had released the bodies of Miss Lottie and Maria for burial. "Thank you for letting me know," she said, then was surprised to hear him ask about her shoe size. "It's ten," she replied. "Quite large for a woman, I know. It's always been the bane of my life." She listened as he spoke again. Then she thanked him and put down the phone.

"The coroner has released Miss Lottie and Maria," she told Maya. "The funeral can go ahead for Thursday."

There was a quiet resignation in her voice, and impulsively Maya hugged her. "I'm sorry, baby, but it'll be better after it's over. Then Miss Lottie and Maria will be at peace."

Ellie knew she was right, and she wished she could feel comforted, or relieved, or pained. Anything. Because she still didn't feel a thing.

"What was that about shoes?" Maya asked.

"They found a print on the balcony. . . . Mud and blood . . . They say it was made by a Reebok Walker DMX."

"You mean he thought you were standing out there on the balcony after killing your grandmother? Hah." Maya expressed her contempt for the police in one short word. "Do they know what size?"

Ellie shrugged. "If they do, they're not telling me."

"It's all nonsense." Maya slung her black leather overnight bag over her shoulder. "I'm on my way, Ellie. I'll be back tomorrow to help with the arrangements."

"Whatever would I do without you?" Ellie asked.

"You're doing great, Ellie, just great. After the funeral you're going to feel much better. And then they'll find the killer, and the score will be settled. I promise you, that's what will happen."

Of course, Ellie told herself, that was what would happen. The police would find the killer and lock him up. Her life would go on and become "normal" again. After the funeral.

IT WAS the kind of day California gloried in—clear blue sky, warm breeze rippling the silken surface of the ocean. The mountains encircling the city were draped in the softest green velvet. Miss Lottie would have approved.

She and Maria were being buried on the same day, though in different countries. Dan had arranged to ship Maria's remains back to her family in Guadalajara, and Ellie had sent a check to pay for a High Mass and for a stone angel to guard Maria forever. Later, when the estate was probated, she would send the amount Miss Lottie had left Maria in her will to Maria's brothers and sisters.

Now, in the black limousine that was slowly following the hearse that carried her grandmother's coffin, Ellie's thoughts returned to the only other funeral she had attended. She remembered clearly sitting next to Miss Lottie in a big black car like this one, following her parents' coffins on their final journey.

Recalling how Miss Lottie had dressed her up in white organdy and shiny black patent Mary Janes, as though she were going to a party, today she had chosen the sleeveless white linen sheath that her grandmother had always liked to see her in. She'd borrowed a wide-brimmed black straw hat from Maya. Big dark glasses hid the sadness in her eyes. This afternoon she would share her sorrow with Miss Lottie's friends and acquaintances, but she would deal with her grief, and her guilt, alone.

Sitting beside her in the limo, Dan put his warm hand on hers. "You okay?" he asked.

She nodded, glad he was there for her. He looked handsome in a blue suit.

Sitting opposite, Maya smiled encouragingly. She was wearing a black silk dress, sleeveless and soft, that swung around her body like gossamer. Next to her, Piatowsky was neat in a dark jacket and tie.

Flanked by a motorcycle escort, the two funeral cars drove slowly down State Street, followed by a hundred others. Ellie thought how Miss Lottie would have enjoyed all the fuss as the procession turned up the cemetery driveway to the chapel.

She was almost relieved when her grandmother's coffin, covered in a blanket of scented white roses, was received by the Reverend Mr. Allan, who had known her grandmother for forty years. Finally Miss Lottie was among friends.

It seemed to Ellie as if the whole town had turned out. Everyone was there: the mayor, the council members, the socialites, and the celebrities, many of them as old as Miss Lottie.

"It's the passing of an era," someone said quietly. "This place will never be the same again."

Michael Majors and his wife were there, as were Miss Lottie's accountant and the bank manager. And Detective Johannsen.

In a dark suit and sober tie Johannsen was eyeing the mourners as they arrived. It was not unknown for a killer to attend the funeral of his victim. It was a kind of ghoulish triumph, he supposed. But there were no shady-looking characters lurking around today. Everyone was respectable and respectful. Still, he knew as well as any cop that most often a killer looked just like anybody else. Besides, in his view he was looking at the killers right now.

Johannsen couldn't get the memory of the computer message out of his mind: DUVEEEEEEE. The old lady had been trying to tell them something. Who else could it mean but Ellie?

BUCK'S gaze fastened on Ellie, graceful in a white linen sheath, her glossy red hair in a chignon under a big black hat. He knew it was risky to attend the funeral but felt compelled to do it. He was wary, though. He prided himself on being able to spot a cop at fifty paces. He had the men in dark suits, standing at the back, pegged for detectives the minute he'd slipped in among the mourners. He himself was impeccably turned out. His tie was correctly muted and his Gucci loafers gleamed. He looked exactly like the rich lawyers, bankers, and businessmen. He was one of them.

It burned his gut when he saw Dan Cassidy standing with Ellie at the graveside, though. *As though she belonged to him.*

He saw Cassidy grip Ellie's arm as the Reverend Mr. Allan intoned, "Dearly beloved, we are gathered here today to pay tribute to a great lady. . . ."

Then the congregation was singing. Buck knew every hymn by heart. After all, hadn't he attended church with his mother every Sunday? Until he'd decided he'd had enough, that is. Fixing a suitably sorrowful expression on his face, he listened to the minister recite the words of the Twenty-third Psalm.

He was careful not to go too far and pretend to wipe away a tear when the minister said the words he'd waited so long to hear: "Ashes to ashes, dust to dust . . ." But neither did he smile, which is what he wanted to do. He wanted to dance and shout hurrah. *There she goes. Good-bye, Miss Lottie. At last.*

ELLIE felt Dan's arm beneath hers, his strong shoulder ready for her to lean on. For a minute there was silence on the breezy bluff overlooking the ocean. There was only the peace of the rolling green lawns and the shade trees. Lifting her head high and straightening her back, as Miss Lottie had taught her, Ellie took Dan's arm and walked quickly away.

THE black limousine cruised slowly past Buck, taking Ellie from him again, but he didn't follow. There was no point. As long as she was with Cassidy at the ranch, there was nothing he could do. He would wait until his plan was complete.

ELLIE flung her black hat onto the bench in the hall as she strode wearily back into the house. Florita came running from the kitchen.

Grabbing her hands, Florita stared anxiously at Ellie. "All is well?"

"Thank you, Florita. All is well."

Florita suddenly flung her arms around Ellie and hugged her. "Is better for you now, senorita. You will see, is better it is over."

Ellie's eyes met Piatowsky's. "Did you see anyone who looked like a killer?"

"The only person I saw who looked suspicious was Johannsen, lurking around like a stage detective."

"He was only doing his job." Dan's voice was mild as he walked into the hall with Maya.

A little later the four of them were sitting around the supper table. Florita was setting out steaming dishes of *arroz con pollo* and freshly made corn tortillas. Florita's baby crawled after her, raising himself up the side of Ellie's chair.

"Ay, Carlosito, no." Florita swept him up.

But Ellie held out her arms. "Come here, Carlosito, and tell me what kind of a day you've had." He perched contentedly on her knee, twisting a lock of her long hair in his chubby fingers.

"Better than ours, I'll bet," she murmured, dropping a kiss onto his soft black curls.

"Well, at least that's over," Maya said. "Now you can get some rest, Ellie. Maybe you should take a little vacation? Somewhere tropical, with soft white sand and hot sunshine?"

The baby held out his arms for his mother, and as Ellie handed him over, Dan thought, enviously, that it made a pretty picture: Ellie, a baby, the family dinner table, home and hearth. Every cliché he could think of just fit right in.

"I have to get back to work." Ellie sounded brisk, businesslike, as though now that the funeral was over, she had snapped out of grief. But Maya knew her better.

"Then I'll come and stay with you, keep you company." Maya didn't want her to be alone.

"Thanks, but I've got to get on with things."

"Please stay." Dan's eyes were on hers. He spread his hands, palms up. *"Mi casa es su casa."*

"Gracias, señor." But Ellie knew she had to go back to her own life, her own world.

After supper they wandered out to the porch. "Care to take a walk?" Dan asked. It was almost dusk and a waning moon glimmered in the cobalt-blue sky. Taking his hand, Ellie walked with him down the steps and along the path leading behind the house to the pond.

"I'm going to miss this place," Ellie said as Dan slid his arm around her waist. She thought they fit together as snugly as if they had been made for each other.

"And I'm going to miss you. Are you sure you can't stay?"

It was so tempting just to be an old-fashioned woman, collapse into his arms, let him take care of her. But she reminded herself quickly that her goals were still in front of her. She needed work. "There's no point in taking it easy; it leaves too much time to think. Besides, I have to get away from Johannsen."

He wanted to tell her it would be difficult to get away from Johannsen, that when the detective wanted her, he would be down in Santa Monica in a heartbeat.

"I thought I learned everything there was to know about violence that year my parents died," she said. "Now I know I didn't. This is even worse."

"It's over now, Ellie. Let it go. Keep the good memories, and put Journey's End on the market."

She shook her head. "I can't. Not yet. It's as if Miss Lottie and Maria are still there, waiting for me to help them, to find their killer."

They were standing by the pond, listening to the frogs revving up to serenade the night. "Will you come and see me, Dan?"

Her face was uptilted to his. Lowering his lips to hers, he kissed her gently, sweetly. "I promise," he murmured.

Like a friend, Ellie thought, wrapping her arms around him. A dear, good friend.

ELLIE'S brand-new Cherokee was forest green, almost the same color as the paint at the café, with black interior and plenty of room for hauling stuff. It felt smooth, peppy, luxurious as she drove back to Santa Monica. Her old Jeep Wrangler had been a write-off, and she had wondered nervously if Johannsen would suspect her of spending what he considered to be her ill-gotten gains. But Dan had laughed off her fears.

Dan was very much on her mind. He'd tried so hard to help her come to terms with what had happened, and he'd protected her from Johannsen's endless questioning. She felt closer to him than ever. But as she turned up the hill leading to her house, she warned herself not to fall in love with him; it would mean trouble. There was a direct conflict in their aims in life: She was for city and success; he was for the country and serenity. They inhabited different worlds, and she wasn't ready to give up her ambitions yet. At least not until she had made a success of her life; then she might consider it. But by then, she suspected, it would be too late. She smiled wryly. Her timing had never been great.

Her little house looked just the same, as though nothing momentous and horrifying had happened since she'd left it just over a week ago. But as she turned the key and went in, it *felt* different.

Everything seemed to be in its place. In the kitchen the green mug from which she had drunk a cup of wild-berry tea was still in the sink. She opened the refrigerator. The carton of milk had gone off. Wrinkling her nose, she threw it down the disposal.

She heard a tapping noise and swung around, spooked. Relieved, she saw it was only a bird outside the window. Still, she thought uneasily, the house did feel different. Telling herself it was because the police had been in here searching through her things, she trailed despondently up the creaking stairs.

Sunlight streamed into her bedroom, and the air felt stale and hot. Flinging open the window, she peeled off her clothes and took a long shower, washed her hair, did all the usual things. Then why did the place seem so different? She sighed as she pulled on her work uniform of jeans and T-shirt. Everything *was* different. She was alone in the world now. Work was the only antidote for grief, and she had plenty of that in front of her.

She ran a comb through her wet hair, slung her big black bag over her shoulder, grabbed the car keys, and was on her way.

Main Street had that early summer feel: school not yet out but freedom on the horizon, hot sunshine, a glimpse of the glittering blue-and-silver ocean down the side streets, girls in pale summer dresses and sandals, the art galleries displaying colorful acrylics by local artists. This was her world. And it was a long way from Running Horse Ranch.

The café looked sad and abandoned with the chairs piled upside down on the tables, no flowers, no aromas of cooking. She phoned Chan, told him they would be opening again tomorrow, and asked him to come back to work. It was time for a change, she added. A summer menu.

"Let's make it a feast, Chan," she said. "A celebration."

"Sure," Chan said on the other end of the line, though he wasn't sure what they were celebrating.

Ellie knew, though. She was alive again, full of energy, raring to go. She wrote out her menu suggestions, then put on her apron, opened the big container of flour, and went to work. Soon she was up to her elbows in dough, getting ready for tomorrow.

When she left the café at around six, the tables were already set for morning, and the dough, covered with a clean, damp cloth, was left to rise. The menu had been worked out, lists made for the produce market, orders placed for supplies. She had organized Chan and his assistant, Terry, and the kid who did the washing up and stacked the dishes. Ellie was back in business.

There was a pleased smile on her face as she walked to the shop across the road to buy a sandwich for her supper. She wasn't used to having an evening to herself, alone. She would do something mindless—watch TV in bed, go to sleep early.

BUCK couldn't believe his luck. Sitting alone at a table by the window of the sandwich shop, he watched her as she stood, arms folded, waiting for her order. Like the spider and the fly, she had walked right into his trap.

He'd been watching Ellie's house, as usual. He hadn't recognized the new green Cherokee when it turned into her street, but then he saw her get out and carry her bags indoors. And of course, he'd followed her to the café. He'd seen the lights go on inside, caught a glimpse of her bustling around, setting up tables. Half an hour ago he'd gone into the sandwich shop and ordered coffee and a muffin.

Now he got up and walked toward her. "Ellie, I didn't expect to see you here." His face was suitably serious, no smile, just a hint of concern in his voice.

"Oh hi, Mr. Jensen." She was surprised. She hadn't expected to meet him there either.

Daringly he put his hand on her arm. "I'm so sorry. There is no way to console you for what you've gone through."

"Thank you. I appreciate it, Mr. Jensen. I'm trying to get back to work, get on with living. . . ." Her voice trailed off.

"I'm glad you'll be opening the café again. If I'm in the area, I'll stop by and have dinner."

Ellie's sandwich was ready. She took the box and smiled goodbye. "Sure, that'll be good," she said, edging past him.

When she looked back from the door, he was watching her. She hurried across the street to her car. He hadn't said a single wrong word, but there was just something about him. Maybe Maya was right and he really was a creep.

Back home, she stood at the kitchen counter, slowly chewing her sandwich. It was very good, but her mind wasn't on it. Sighing, she fixed herself a cup of wild-berry tea and carried it upstairs to the bedroom. She would get into her night things, put on her comfy old robe, watch TV. And wait for Dan to call.

FROM his position across the street Buck saw the upstairs lights go on, then Ellie as she opened the window and stood for a minute, looking out. She drew the curtains and disappeared from his sight. For now, he was content. His plan was set; everything was ready. All he needed was the right opportunity.

Chapter Eight

ELLIE was drowning in darkness, it was all around her, there was no light anywhere. Then a thin ribbon of scarlet appeared. It slid slowly toward her, widening, until it touched her skin. Now it was engulfing her in heat and redness, sticky . . .

Fighting back the bedcovers, Ellie shot upright. The faint light from the window showed her the reassuring shapes of her dresser, the fireplace, the nightstand. She was safe, at home.

Shuddering, she bent her head over her clasped knees. Tears stung her eyes. "Oh, Gran," she whispered, "I'm so sorry."

Two weeks had passed since she'd come home. In that time she had become a free woman, without the prospect of a murder trial and jail looming over her. The forensics people had identified the knife used to mutilate Miss Lottie as the same one used in the New York and L.A. murders. Johannsen had confirmed that the bruise prints on Miss Lottie's throat had been made by a man with large, very powerful hands. They did not match Dan's. And the man on the balcony wore size twelves. Ellie and Dan were no longer suspects. She knew she should have felt elated, but all she felt was exhausted. And the nights were the toughest of all.

It was always the same. She worked as many hours a day as she could, hoping to be weary enough to just crawl into bed and fall instantly asleep. The trouble was, the deep sleep lasted only a couple of hours; then, regular as clockwork, she woke at three a.m. with the same dream. She was drowning in blood.

Night after night, guilt washed over her. If only she had gotten to Journey's End earlier; if only she'd still lived at Journey's End instead of allowing two old ladies to stay there alone. If only . . .

Often she was tempted to pick up the phone and call Dan. Stubbornly she resisted. She was determined to manage on her own.

Still, though Ellie didn't want to admit it, the highlight of her day was when she was home in bed, anticipating his nightly call.

"Just checking on you," he'd say.

"I'm all right," she would reply, resisting adding, "*Now* I am. Now that I hear your voice."

Dan would tell her how busy he was, grafting chardonnay budwood and getting deeper in hock to the bank. He sounded cheerful about it, as though he were enjoying the whole process, and his enthusiasm made her wish she could share it with him. But the conflict was clear between them: She was city, he was country. She had long-term career plans, and so did he. She couldn't allow herself to fall in love with him. He was her good friend, and that's the way it would stay. Forever, she hoped.

WITH Ellie off the hook as a suspect, Piatowsky decided it was time to go home to his wife and kids. Dan drove him to the airport.

At the boarding gate Dan slapped him on the shoulder, then hugged him. "Thanks, buddy," he said.

"Anytime," Piatowsky said. "I'll bring the kids next time; they'll enjoy the horses."

Dan hadn't seen Ellie in a week, and he decided now was the time, before he went to Napa with Ortega. The vines at U.C., Davis had not met Ortega's high standards, and they were still searching for the perfect grape.

He began to dial her number on his cell phone, then changed his mind. He'd surprise her instead.

The day had been warm, but with nightfall the temperature dropped and the mist slunk in from the ocean, wreathing halos around the streetlights and rolling ghostly fingers along the boulevards. Because of the mist, the drive to Santa Monica took longer than Dan expected. It was nine thirty when he pulled the car into a spot opposite the café, directly behind a black BMW.

The street was quiet, but lights still glowed welcomingly from Ellie's Place. The old-fashioned bell tinkled sweetly. Only two tables were occupied, and there was no sign of Ellie or Maya.

He went to the back, pushed open the kitchen door, and stuck his head around it. Ellie was cleaning up the big stoves.

She hadn't heard him, and he watched her for a second. There was a look of sadness on her face and a weary slump to her shoulders. His heart ached for her as he called her name.

It was there instantly, the warm megawatt smile that lit up her whole face. "Hi there. This is a surprise."

"I hoped you were going to say 'an unexpected pleasure.' " He dropped a kiss on her smiling mouth.

"That too," she agreed. "You must be hungry. I'm cooking tonight. Just tell me what you'd like." Ellie was already taking out pots and pans. She enjoyed having him on her turf. It put her on her mettle.

"Scrambled eggs and a toasted bagel would be fine," he said.

She smiled at him. "I can't do the bagel, but I promise you some very good rosemary bread. Are you sure that's all you want?"

He couldn't think of anything better than eggs prepared by Ellie. "No, it's not all. I want you to join me for supper."

"I think I might be able to manage that," she said lightly. "Would you like a glass of wine?"

Ellie hadn't eaten, but now that Dan was here, she fixed eggs for them both, gave him the basket of bread to carry, then followed him into the café with the steaming plates.

"*Bon appétit, m'sieur,*" she murmured as she took a seat across from him.

"Good," Dan mumbled as he ate the eggs. "These are truly great." She smiled her thanks. "So tell me, Ellie, how are you really?"

She lifted her shoulders wearily. "It's tough to sleep. You know, that old three-in-the-morning guilt trip, the 'if onlys' . . ."

"Whatever you're thinking, it wasn't your fault."

"I guess not." She sounded uncertain. As the mist pressed at the café window, the specter of nightly loneliness crushed in on her again. "Want to come home and have coffee with me?"

He nodded. "Sure."

Jake was taking care of the other tables; the customers were just leaving, paying their checks. "I'll close up for you, Ellie," he called from the counter. "Take it easy for once, go home."

Beaming her thanks, she carried their plates into the kitchen.

Outside, the dense fog pressed up against their faces. Visibility was down to about ten yards. Definitely not good for driving.

Ellie had taken the Cherokee out of the lot earlier and parked half a block from the café. The black BMW was still parked in front of Dan's car, and he saw a man sitting in it, in the darkness. Wondering briefly what he was up to, he edged the Explorer out from behind the black car, waited for Ellie to catch up, then drove slowly down the silent, fog-bound road.

INSIDE Ellie's cozy little lamp-lit house, vanilla-scented candles flickered on the mantel, and soft string music played gently in the background. Ellie was pouring fragrant hot coffee. She put a mug on the low table in front of Dan. He was sitting next to her on the sofa, his head thrown back, listening to the music.

She studied the strong planes of his face, his muscular body. He was such a physical man, and she liked that about him. But even a strong man looked vulnerable, somehow, with his eyes closed, his face unguarded. She was pleased he was able to be that way with her—relaxed, easy.

Reaching out, she ran her fingers gently through his hair. Now that she had him here, she couldn't bear to let him go. "I was thinking," she said carefully, "you can't possibly drive home in this fog. It's way too dangerous."

There was something in her voice, a silkiness he's never heard before. Opening his eyes, he looked directly at her. "True." He nodded, his eyes fixed on her.

"Then it's my turn to offer hospitality. I have pillows, blankets; you'll be comfortable here on the sofa."

"True." He nodded again.

She stood. "I'll go get the blankets."

He caught her arm, pulled her down on the sofa again. "Stop running from me, Ellie."

She could feel the warmth of his hands on her shoulders. His mouth approached hers, and she felt herself relaxing in his arms.

Dan dropped gentle kisses across the sliding curve of her cheekbone, over her eyelids, on the tip of her nose where the freckles were close together. He found the upturned corner of her mouth.

"Delicious," he breathed. "Better than *tarte Tatin.*"

The kiss deepened; she felt as though the breath were being sucked from her body, leaving her soft, helpless.

"We really shouldn't," she murmured in between kisses, feeling his heart beating against hers. "After all, we're not involved. . . ."

"Mmmm, uh-uh . . . Certainly not involved."

Opening her eyes, she looked dreamily into his. She saw the question in his eyes, and he saw the answer in hers. They stood, and taking her hand in his, he guided her up the creaking stairs.

BUCK sat in the car, staring at the upstairs window. Tears streamed down his face. He didn't know a heart could contain this much pain. He started the car and drove like a madman through the dense fog, back to Sunset and the apartment. Bolting the door, he hurled himself around the room, flailing his fists against the walls, howling his despair.

His neighbor, a young guy watching a loud music video, lowered the sound for a second, listening. He shrugged, wondering what channel the horror movie was on, then turned up the sound again.

THE café was busy the night after that, and the next, which suited Ellie just fine. The more work she had to do, the less time she had to think, and maybe tonight she would sleep.

The dream still returned night after night, but somehow she coped with it better. Now when she woke trembling, she imagined Dan was with her, felt his strong masculine presence in her room.

Lack of sleep was taking its toll, though, and she didn't know what to do about it except to keep plowing on.

The doorbell announced new arrivals, and she gathered up her menus and went to greet them.

Watching her, Maya thought Ellie was doing okay, though she had the sense not to keep asking. After all, what was Ellie going to reply except, "Sure, I'm fine"?

Maya rubbed her aching jaw. Her wisdom tooth was acting up again, she was sure it was impacted, the pain was getting bad.

"If you don't want a face like a full moon, you'd better get yourself to the dentist," Ellie advised in passing.

"Dentists terrify me, all that whining machinery and needles."

"Okay, so be a coward and lose your looks."

Maya knew she was right. "I'll go tomorrow, first thing."

"Take the day off," Ellie said. "You'll need it. And I'll come around later with chicken soup and champagne, though, of course, you'll have to drink them both through a straw."

"Sadist."

It was close to midnight when the last couple left and Ellie finally latched the door and turned the sign to CLOSED. She looked at Maya, sprawled in a chair, holding her aching face in her hands. "Go home," she said. "You look terrible."

"Thanks, I appreciate that. But maybe I will go."

The phone was ringing as Ellie pushed Maya out the door and picked it up. "Ellie's Place."

"I thought I'd give you a call, see if you were still slaving."

Her heart lifted at the sound of Dan's voice. "Still slaving."

"I'm leaving for Napa tomorrow, early. Carlos and I are going to inspect a few vineyards, maybe buy some rootstock. I'll be back in a couple of days, though. I'll come down and visit you."

Ellie imagined him in her house and how his presence would change the dark mood. "I'd like that."

"Good. I'll call you from Napa. Take care, Ellie."

"You too, Dan." She almost said "Love you" as she rang off, but caught herself just in time.

Feeling better, she busied herself with the routine chores: putting the day's receipts in the safe, whisking cloths off tables, tidying the counter, and cleaning out the coffee machine. It was close to two o'clock, and the fog was rolling in again when she finally stepped out into the misty street. The four-story parking lot was shadowy and silent, and she found herself wishing nervously that she'd taken her car out earlier and put it on a meter near the café.

Her footsteps rang in the silence as she hurried into the elevator and pressed the button for three. It jolted to a stop, and she waited for the doors to open. Nothing happened. She glanced at the indicator. It was stuck between two and three.

She jiggled the button. The elevator still didn't move. Frantic, she pressed every button, sighing with relief when it finally jolted slowly upward again. Only this time it went past the third floor.

"Stupid thing," she muttered anxiously. When it stopped at four, she shot out and ran to the stairs. She heard a noise behind her. Footsteps. Fear rushed hotly up her spine, and she turned and fled down the stairs. She emerged breathless, frantically searching the bottom of her bag for her keys. *Where were they? Her car was all the way over on the other side. There wasn't enough time to get there.* The elevator door was open. She jumped in and pressed the button for the ground floor. She must get out of here, run, get help.

It stopped again, on two.

"Oh, God. This can't be happening." She slammed her fist on the button this time. Crouched against the scarred steel wall, all she could hear was the pounding of her own heart. She tried to remember the lessons she'd taken on how to protect herself in a mugging. "Don't panic," she told herself, taking a deep breath.

The elevator began to descend again. Breathing a shaky sigh of relief, she took an eager step forward as the doors slid open.

He was waiting for her, masked, his arms outspread, holding back the doors. The knife in his hand glinted icily under the white fluorescent light.

For a breathless second her eyes met his. Then she flung her purse at his feet. "Take it, please. Just take it."

"It's not your money I want, Ellie," he whispered.

And then his powerful arms gripped her.

Adrenaline and anger suddenly gave her a crazy strength. Twisting around, she slammed her elbows into his chest. His grip loosened, and she swung again, kicking.

He reached for her ponytail and yanked it back, dragged her to the floor. He kneeled over her, pinning her arms down. She stared up at him, frozen with terror, saw his fist coming at her, then a terrible pain. Her eyes rolled back in her head, and she was unconscious.

Winded, Buck scooped her up in his arms. He grabbed her purse, pressed the UP button, and exited on the fourth floor. The BMW was the only car there. He tossed her into the trunk, covered her with a blanket, and slammed down the lid.

In the driver's seat he pulled off the mask. Still breathing heavily, he drove down the ramp, out onto the empty street.

He was home free and Ellie was his.

AT FIVE thirty that evening Chan was in the kitchen rattling pots and pans around and grumbling to Terry. "So where is everybody today? Ellie's not here; Maya's not here. How am I supposed to manage this place on my own?" He slammed the cleaver angrily into a lamb shank he was preparing for braising.

Terry was used to Chan's tantrums. "Maya had her wisdom tooth out today. I guess Ellie's with her. She said something about chicken soup and champagne."

"They are drinking champagne while I run the place for them?" Chan snorted. "Who's gonna serve? That's what I want to know."

Terry removed the baked Idaho potatoes from the oven. "Jake's coming in for Maya."

"And who's coming in for Ellie?"

"She'll be here later, I guess."

Chan chopped his lamb shanks viciously. Suddenly he wiped a tear from his eye. "Poor Ellie," he muttered. "Such a tragedy—terrible, terrible. So I run the café for a night, so what?"

DAN and Carlos had dinner in a Napa Valley restaurant. It was seven before he got a chance to phone Ellie at the café, but she hadn't come in yet. He called again at ten, but she still hadn't been in, and she still hadn't called to say where she was. He asked for Maya's number, then dialed it, drumming his fingers impatiently.

"Hi, I can't speak to you right now," Maya's voice said on the answering machine. "Leave me a message at the tone."

Frustrated, Dan dialed Ellie's home number. She didn't answer.

At eleven he tried again, and again at midnight. Still no answer. Hands thrust into his pockets, he paced the carpet. Where was she?

A WHITE-HOT light flickered inside Ellie's head. She groaned. Pain throbbed behind her eyes. Slowly the light faded to a pallid, uneven gray as she swam back to consciousness.

She was lying on a soft bed, staring up at a wood-planked ceiling. The pillow beneath her head was white satin, the coverlet white lace, threaded with pink ribbon. There were fluffy white rugs on the floor, a dressing table with a flounced lace skirt and swags of pink ribbons, and a pair of white satin mules, trimmed with marabou, waiting by the side of the bed. She wondered if she had died and this were a motel in hell. Then she remembered.

Trembling, she swung her legs over the side of the bed and stood up. She was still dressed in her black jeans and white Ellie's Place T-shirt, but her boots and jacket were gone. She stared around. The room was paneled in dark wood, oppressive, like a coffin. She looked for a window. It was boarded up. She darted to the door. There was no handle. Panicked, she took in the room's details. No TV, no radio, no telephone. There was a bottle of Evian, a plastic glass, and a blue bowl with Fuji apples.

Sliding open the closet door, she stared at the collection of clothes: dresses, sweaters, jeans, shoes. She checked the labels. They were all her size. There was a bottle of Eau d'Issey on the dresser—her perfume. Bobbi Brown lipstick in nude—her color. Her favorite bath oil, her lotion, her powder . . .

He knew every intimate thing about her. He must have been in her home, gone through her personal things. He'd touched her life with his filthy hands.

Her knees buckled, and she sank onto a pink velvet boudoir chair as the realization overwhelmed her.

She seemed to sit in that hellish room, in the rose-shaded lamplight and brittle silence, for hours. Her head throbbed, and her ears buzzed with the strain of listening for him.

Then she heard the key in the lock, and her heart seemed to shrivel, then stop. The door creaked slowly open. Frozen, she stared at her abductor. He was still wearing the ski mask. He walked toward her, reached out, touched her arm. She shrank back, her flesh crawling, eyes wide with terror.

"I'm glad to see you're feeling better, Ellie," he said. "I apologize for having to hit you, but you left me no option."

His whispered voice triggered a memory somewhere in the caverns of Ellie's panicked mind, yet she couldn't place it.

"My dear Ellie," he went on silkily, "I've brought you to this lovely place because I want you to be happy. As you can see, I've thought of everything. But if there is anything else you need, tell me and it's yours."

She stared numbly up at him, and he added gently, "All I want is for you to be happy. Here, with me."

Stepping out the door, he returned with a room service cart, complete with white linen cloth and a white rose in a silver bud vase.

"Tortilla soup," he said, wafting off the silver dome covering the food. "Cold roast chicken with a green salad." He opened a bottle of wine and poured a little into the glass for her to taste. "Madame?" He stepped back with a courtly little bow. She said nothing, and he sighed as he walked out. He locked the door securely behind him.

The finality of the key turning in the lock chilled Ellie's blood.

She ran to the table, picked up the knife. It was sterling, from Christofle. The wine goblet was Baccarat, the plates Limoges. The food was exactly what she liked and so was the wine.

Hunger gnawed incongruously at her stomach. She had no idea of how much time had passed since she had eaten, but suddenly she was starving.

She took a piece of bread, held it to her mouth. *Maybe he was a poisoner? Or the food was drugged.* Dropping the bread, she backed away. She sank into the pink chair again.

She wondered if Maya had discovered she was missing. But then she remembered Maya had gone to the dentist; she wouldn't be at work for a couple of days. And Dan was in Napa with Carlos. Would Chan try to call her at home? She doubted it. Chan had been going out of his way not to upset her.

Tears fell from her eyes. *Nobody would even have missed her yet. Nobody was even looking for her. She was on her own.*

DAN was on the phone at six the next morning, then again at seven. "It's no good," he said to Carlos. "I have to get back."

Three hours later, when they'd returned to Running Horse Ranch, the red light was flickering on the answering machine in the office. Praying it was Ellie, Dan punched the PLAYBACK button.

"This is Chan from Ellie's Place. Do you know where she is? I cannot open the café again tonight by myself. I need to hear from her. Please call me."

Where could she have gone?

AN HOUR later Dan was driving down the Pacific Coast Highway to Santa Monica. He called Chan on the car phone.

"She's still not here," Chan said, sounding desperate. "Tonight we cope, but not tomorrow. Maybe tomorrow I quit."

"Don't quit," Dan said as he turned into Ellie's street. "She'll be there."

A couple of little kids were kicking a red ball around in the garden of the house next door. The street looked quiet, normal, an everyday scene. In a second he was pressing the bell, hammering his fist on the door. The silence was ominous. "Ellie," he yelled.

The kids next door stopped their playing and came over. "Nobody's there," a towheaded boy said.

"Have you seen Ellie today?"

"No, sir. She hasn't been around for a while."

"Thanks, guys," Dan said, already back in the car.

THE PHONE WAS RINGING. MAYA searched for it under the litter of Kleenex and magazines. She picked it up. "I'm in pain. Who is it?"

"Maya, it's Dan Cassidy."

She grinned. "Well, well, the rancher who managed to get Ellie off the straight and *very* narrow. I guess she's with you, waiting to apologize. She was meant to be here with chicken soup and champagne. Some friend, huh? Deserting me in my hour of need."

"Maya, no one has seen Ellie in two days. I was hoping she was with you."

"You're kidding. I haven't seen Ellie since the night before last. I left her at the café. Oh, Dan, where can she be?"

"Take it easy," he said. "She's okay, I'm sure of it. We'll find her. I'm on my way to the police now."

DETECTIVE Mike Farrell of the Santa Monica police was a humorless, methodical man with thinning hair and a waxy complexion that spoke of too many doughnuts and late nights.

"People go missing every day in California," he said, twisting a ballpoint pen endlessly through his stubby fingers.

Dan nodded. "But how many of them have had their grandmother murdered only weeks before?"

Farrell sat up straight, ballpoint poised over the work sheet. "She datin' anyone else? Someone you didn't know about?"

"No."

Farrell grinned. "That's what they all say." He pushed back his chair. "Did you ever think of this scenario? Maybe the grandmother's death has been too much for her? Maybe she's just cracked, walked away from it all?"

Dan thought about that steely core of self-reliance that fueled Ellie's ambitions, made her pick up her life and go back to work instead of languishing at Running Horse. "She's not a quitter."

Farrell nodded. "Then we'd better get out and look for her."

DAN felt like a rookie cop again, driving in Detective Farrell's unmarked black Ford through the clogged Santa Monica traffic. There were no kids playing outside Ellie's house this time, and the street was quiet. A squad car pulled in behind them as he and the detective got out and walked up the little brick path and pressed the bell. It rang with the same hollow sound as before.

Farrell had the search warrant in his pocket, and he motioned to the waiting officer to break the lock. Inside, the police fanned out on the ground floor as Dan ran up the creaking stairs.

Ellie's bed was made up, and her old pink robe was flung across the chair by the window. In the bathroom the towels hanging on the rail were dry and so were her toothbrush and the soap. Ellie had not been home recently.

THE CLOSED sign was up at Ellie's Place, and a squad car was parked outside, lights flashing. Maya, Chan, Terry, Jake, and the kid who did the dishes were sitting around a table with Farrell while a couple of officers stood by. A lamp shone on the green-checkered tablecloth. Dan listened while each told what he knew, which wasn't much.

"The café was very busy Friday night," Chan repeated one more time. "I cooked the last meal at eleven; then I left."

"I finished up a half hour later," Terry said. "Then I ate dinner in the kitchen, and I left after midnight."

The kid ran his hands nervously through his hair. "I finished the cleaning up. I left right after Maya did."

Farrell fixed his bland gaze on the kid. "Then you were the last person to see Ellie that night."

The kid swallowed hard, red in the face with panic. "I never thought of that. I don't know. I heard Ellie tell her to go home and then the doorbell chime as she left. Maybe somebody else came in."

"Where did you go when you left the café?"

"To Victor's. It's a club. I go there all the time."

"Then someone will have seen you there?"

"Sure, oh, sure . . ." He surely hoped so.

"Maya?" Farrell looked questioningly at Ellie's friend.

"I had a bad toothache that night," she explained. Her face was still swollen, and her eyes were red from crying. "Usually I stay to help Ellie tidy up." Maya threw her hands over her eyes. "Oh, God, I shouldn't have left her alone. I should have stayed with her."

"Do you know where Ellie usually parks her car?" Dan asked.

She lifted her head, looked blearily at him. "In the multistory lot, a couple of blocks away. Usually, if it gets too late, she gets the car out and puts it on a meter right here on the street. But she didn't that night. . . ."

THEY found the green Cherokee on the third floor, locked and empty, just the way Ellie had left it on Friday. Dan knew then that she was in serious trouble.

Farrell moved fast after that. In minutes there were cops all over the place, intercepting owners coming to collect their cars, questioning them about whether they used the lot regularly, whether they had been here on Friday night.

Disheartened, Dan left them to it. He checked into Loews Hotel in Santa Monica, then went to the bar and ordered a Scotch. The Lakers game was on, but he couldn't summon up any interest. His mind and heart were on Ellie as he went over the scenario again and again.

When the game finished, the news came on. Dan's stomach clenched as Ellie's face appeared on the screen. He drained his glass, then paid the check, went to his room, and got Piatowsky on the phone.

"So what's new?" It was a slow night at the precinct.

"Ellie's missing. I believe she's been abducted." Dan filled him in quickly on the details.

"You think it's the same guy?"

"Possibly."

"I'm getting the red-eye outta here. I'll be with you tomorrow, early." He hesitated. "Dan . . ."

"Yeah?"

"Just hang in there, Cassidy."

Dan put down the phone. His heart was falling into the pit of his stomach. He had to find Ellie.

It must have been morning when the man came again, because this time he brought breakfast. "There's juice, granola, low-fat milk, whole wheat toast, butter, and blueberry preserves. Fresh coffee is in the thermos jug." He looked at her. "Please enjoy it, Ellie," he said quietly. Then he left her alone again.

The smell of coffee and toast taunted her. She wanted it so badly, she could almost taste it. Getting up, she saw herself in the mirror. Her hair was a wild tangle, her jaw a swollen blur of purple-yellow bruises. She opened the bottle of Evian and took a long drink. She longed for a shower but didn't dare take her clothes off in case he came back. She brushed her teeth and dragged a comb through her hair. Then she lay on the bed, counting the minutes, trying to figure out what to do.

She was sitting in the pink chair when he returned with the room service cart and dinner. He removed the silver dome, then turned his masked face to her. "Chicken soup, Ellie," he said in that throaty whisper. "I thought you might find it soothing. Some French bread, a green salad. A little wine."

Her eyes followed him to the door. He did not turn around. "Who are you?" She was desperate, frantic. She had to know.

He turned, smiled at her behind the mask. "I'm your friend, Ellie," he said. Then he went out, locking the door again.

Drained, she sank back into the chair. She stared at the food displayed appetizingly in front of her. She was weak and starving, and no longer cared if it was poisoned. Her hand shook as she took a piece of bread. It stuck in her dry throat, choking her. She drank a little wine, forced down another piece of the bread. Then she went over to the bed and lay back, waiting to see if she was going to die.

Hours dragged by. Had she been here two days? Or three? Surely Maya must be missing her by now. Dan would be calling, and Chan couldn't run the restaurant on his own.

Angered at her own helplessness, she snatched up the Baccarat goblet and hurled it at the wall. It shattered loudly into a hundred pieces. She hurled the Limoges plates after it, then ran to the closet, grabbed the clothes, and flung them to the floor. Then, inspired by rage, she grabbed the bottle of red wine and emptied it over the white-satin-and-lace bed.

She stared, wild-eyed, at the spreading red stain. It was her dream come true, the blood seeping through the bed, engulfing her. She began to scream.

Buck came running. He looked at the broken dishes, the ruined bed, all the pretty things he had bought specially to please her. Flexing his strong fingers, he circled the bed toward her.

Ellie took a quick step back. Another step, and her back was against the wall. He was so close she was breathing his breath.

His hands were on her. "No." She was pinned against the wall, twisting her face away. "No, no, no . . ."

Behind him, she saw a crack of light; he had left the door open. The sudden glimpse of freedom gave her a crazy strength, and she slid down through his arms, grabbed his legs, and pulled. He crashed down next to her. Scrambling to her feet, she made a dash for the door. He caught her arm, dragged her back.

The beautiful Christofle silver fork sparkled in the lamplight. In a flash it was in her hand. She felt the soft, sinking sensation as the fork went into his flesh, heard his roar of pain. He staggered back, blood trickling from his eye socket. She ran.

He snarled, agonized. But even wounded, he was still fast. He grabbed her, slapped her hard across the face, but she didn't cry out. She just stood there, looking at him.

She was looking at him just the way her grandmother had. Loathing him, despising him. As though he were nothing.

He looked around for something to tie her up with. Jerking the lamp out of the wall socket, he bound her wrists behind her back with the wire. He stood looking at her for a minute, then breathing heavily, he slowly eased the mask over his bloody face.

For a long, horrified second she stared at him. "Ed Jensen," she whispered, unbelievingly. "But why?"

Without answering, he left the room. He was back in seconds with a length of cord. He tied her ankles, then cut away the electrical wire and retied her wrists behind her back with the cord.

He looked at her. "Oh, Ellie, Ellie, what a foolish woman you are." He sighed. Then he hefted her in his arms, carried her down the corridor into another room, and flung her onto a sofa.

Cautiously she turned her face to the light.

She was in a log cabin. Through a window she could see a mountain range and gray sky. Trees and silence. She was somewhere where nobody would ever find her. They wouldn't even find her body, because she was sure now, Ed Jensen was going to kill her.

He was dragging something, huffing as he carried it into the room. It was a large wooden crate. He came over, picked her up, carried her across, and dropped her into it.

Helpless, she folded up in the bottom like a broken doll, knees bent, arms twisted behind her. Lifting her head, she stared up at his bloodstained face. Then he fastened down the lid.

Ellie heard the hammer striking on the nails. Heard him walk across the floor. Then the slam of a heavy door. The click of the lock behind him. And then there was only darkness.

WHEN Dan met him at the airport, Piatowsky thought his friend looked like a man who hadn't slept in two nights—rumpled, with a blue-stubbled jaw, his hair standing on end.

"I'll bet the bastard knew her," Dan said after he went over the story with Piatowsky again. "He lay in wait for her, I know it."

"There had to be a motive. How about rejection? Are there any ex-boyfriends around?"

Dan maneuvered the Explorer through the busy airport traffic. "She never told me about any."

"How about obsession?"

"I guess it's possible, but she works all the time. Who's been around her enough to become obsessed with her?"

"Let's try revenge."

"You mean maybe someone had a grudge against her?"

"Yeah, like someone who works at the café."

"She and the chef fight all the time, but that's out in the open. The others like her, enjoy working there."

"So who would gain by Ellie's death?"

The word "death" sent a jolt down Dan's spine. "She owns nothing of great value except the house and the antiques."

"*And* twenty prime acres in one of the richest little communities in California. Worth quite a few million, I'll bet."

Dan remembered how Ellie had not been able to bring herself to part with the house. Now he wished with all his heart that she had put it on the market right away, let go of her memories, and gone on with her own life. "She told me she had no relatives, no cousins twice removed, no aunts and uncles in distant countries."

"So who would stand to benefit?" Piatowsky asked again.

"The Parrish accountants might know," Dan said. "They're not going to give away the family secrets to a rancher, but maybe they'll talk to a cop."

THE opulent offices of Makepeace and Thackray, accountants to Mrs. Lottie Parrish, were in a Century City skyscraper. The carpet was a muted gray, the desks weighty and expensive.

The sleek young receptionist was obviously not used to having a detective on the premises, nor was Mr. Harrison Thackray. He was in his fifties, tall, suntanned, unsmiling, with a mane of well-coifed silver hair. He shook their hands and invited them to sit. Dan let Piatowsky lead.

"I'm involved in the investigation into the disappearance of Ellie Parrish Duveen," Piatowsky said.

"Terrible, terrible." Thackray shook his head. "After what happened to Miss Lottie, this is just too much."

"Mr. Thackray, Ellie said that her grandmother supported various charities, and she'd been forced to give them up recently. We'd like to take a look at a list of those charities, if you don't mind." Thackray hesitated, and Piatowsky gave him his benign, little-boy smile. "Just checking, y'understand?"

Thackray pressed the intercom and told his secretary to bring the Parrish file. "I have a meeting in five minutes, gentlemen. You can use the boardroom while you look through the file."

The list was a long one, mostly women's names. Dan guessed they were old friends Miss Lottie had helped. There was also the children's ward at the local hospital, the animal shelter, and various other local charities. Tucked away near the bottom of the third page was a name that triggered a memory.

He glanced up. "You heard of the Hudson Sanitarium?"

"The maximum-security facility for psychos? What was Lottie Parrish doing involved with a place like that?"

"That's what I'd like to know." Dan shuffled through the papers until he found the right one. "She'd been paying the bills for someone in there for years. More than twenty, according to this."

He found the page, read on. He looked at Piatowsky. "Remember when we saw the dead hooker, I said check out what nut they'd let out of prison recently? Well, he didn't get out of prison. He got out of the Hudson Sanitarium because his fees weren't paid. And his name is Patrick Buckland Duveen."

Their eyes met, remembering the DUVEEEEEEE on Miss Lottie's computer screen. "Bingo!" said Piatowsky.

Chapter Nine

THE flickering neon sign just off Highway 101 caught Buck's eye: THE AVALON MOTEL. It was a low, shabby wooden building, and only one other car was parked out front. It was exactly what he needed.

He checked in the driver's mirror. His right eye was practically closed; there was blood on his sweatshirt. He tugged it over his head, revealing a black T-shirt underneath, then wiped the dried blood from his face, smoothed his hair, and put on his dark glasses. With the switchblade in his palm he walked into the minuscule office.

"Evenin'." The old man behind the counter dragged his gaze away from the TV. "Rates are twenty-nine dollars; checkout's at eleven."

"Fine." Buck handed over the cash.

The old man plucked a key from the wallboard behind him. "It's room twenty-three, on your left."

Buck parked in the slot outside room 23 and unlocked the flimsy door. The thin brown carpet was stained, and the room smelled of age and motel air freshener. It was a long way from the Biltmore. Flinging his keys onto the bed, Buck stripped off the rest of his clothes, then stood under the shower. The hot water felt sharp as needles on his wounded eye, but he barely noticed. He was thinking of Ellie, locked in the crate.

Anger sent his pulse racing again. He should have killed her then and there, but he couldn't. He needed to torture her; he needed revenge. He whimpered, distraught. Besides, he loved her.

After a while he stepped from the shower, got dressed again, and went out in search of a liquor store. Half an hour later he was lying on his bed, drinking Jim Beam from the bottle. The TV set was on, but he wasn't watching. He checked the time. Ellie had been locked in the crate almost five hours. He took another swig of the bourbon. He hoped she was enjoying it.

THERE was no light where she was, no sound, no air, no space to move. Claustrophobia was crushing her chest; her throat was tight with panic, her hair drenched with sweat.

She shifted a fraction of an inch, and the rope cut cruelly into her ankles. She was in a fetal position, knees under her chin, head bowed, arms twisted behind her back. The pain in her shoulders was excruciating, but at least it kept her from passing out. She needed to stay awake, stay alert, if she wanted to live.

Dan's strong image floated in front of her eyes. Longing for him made her weak: the warmth of him, the safety of his arms, the security of knowing he cared. Surely by now he must be looking for her.

But how would he ever find her in this godforsaken place? No one would ever find her. She might as well be dead.

AT THE HUDSON SANITARIUM, Hal Morrow was not surprised to get a call about Buck Duveen; he'd been half expecting it ever since he'd watched Duveen walk out the door a free man. Nevertheless, what he heard shocked him. "I didn't know about Charlotte Parrish's death," he told Dan, "but I've no doubt he did it."

"How was he related to the Parrishes?"

"Hold on a minute. All this happened more than twenty years ago. I have to bring myself up to date." Morrow shuffled through some papers. "Ah, now I have it. Buck is the son of Rory Duveen by a previous marriage. Later Rory married Charlotte Parrish's daughter, Romany."

Dan was shocked. "Buck is Ellie's half brother."

"Right," Morrow said. "I have the full story here. Apparently, he'd gone to Journey's End to claim his father's inheritance, but his father didn't have any money. That belonged to Romany, and she had spent it. There was nothing left.

"He went crazy and tried to kill Charlotte Parrish, but the child, Ellie, was in the room. Her screams brought the servants running. Mrs. Parrish refused to press charges against Buck. He had the same father as Ellie, and she refused to taint her granddaughter publicly. Instead, she had him committed. Clinically, the man is a psychopath, absolutely capable of the crimes you've described."

"Then why the hell did you let him out of there?"

Morrow sighed. "Believe me, I wish I hadn't. But this is a private facility; when the money wasn't paid, I had no choice. I also had no evidence that he'd committed any crime. The state facilities were not willing to take him; they're overcrowded as it is."

"He fell through the net."

Morrow nodded. "Exactly. But I do have a recent photograph of him; plus I can tell you he is a big man. Six three, weighs two-twenty, copper-red wavy hair. He has dark eyes and he's very strong."

Dan put down the phone and told Piatowsky what Morrow had said. "There's your motive," Dan concluded.

Piatowsky nodded. "With Miss Lottie and Ellie out of the way, Buck might legitimately claim the estate as the last of the Parrishes and Duveens." He began pacing the floor. "So why didn't he just kill her at the café? Or at the car park?"

Dan thought of Ellie's photograph, stolen from her dead grandmother's room. "Because he's in love," he said quietly. "He's obsessed with her. He must have stalked her, known her every move. Buck Duveen has *all* the motives: gain, revenge, passion, obsession. All we can hope is that he hasn't killed her. Yet."

ELLIE'S Place was closed, not because Chan had quit, but because with Ellie missing, none of them had the heart to go on.

Farrell had summoned the staff one more time, and they were sitting at a table passing Buck Duveen's photo around.

Chan, Terry, and the kid knew nothing—they rarely saw the customers—and Jake swore he would have remembered. "I always notice the faces," he added.

Maya studied the photograph intently, wishing with all her heart she could say, "Yes, I know him." But she didn't. "There was a guy kind of hanging around Ellie, but he didn't look like this."

Dan's ears pricked up. "What *did* he look like?"

"Very tall, good-looking, I suppose, in a strange sort of way. I mean, he had this pale skin . . . and dark hair, mustache. He usually wore dark glasses. I told Ellie I thought he was a creep, but she said he was just lonely."

Dan shoved the picture in front of her nose. "Put a mustache on this face, Maya. Put on the dark glasses, the dark hair."

Maya stared again at the photo. Then she nodded. "His name is Ed Jensen." She shuddered. "He had the coldest eyes." Thinking of Ellie in his clutches, she began to sob.

"YOU'VE gotta eat, gotta get some sleep." Piatowsky was sitting opposite Dan in the hotel bar. "At least take a shower. Buy yourself a clean shirt."

Dan slumped wearily in his chair. "I can't stand not doing anything. All I can think of is her. I hear her voice in my head." He stared bleakly in front of him.

"So? Where d'ya think he'd take her?" Piatowsky asked.

Dan frowned. "There has to be some special place, somewhere that meant something to him."

The cell phone rang and he answered quickly. It was Farrell.

"Just wanted to fill you in. We traced Duveen's mother. She was murdered when he was still in college. Strangled. There was a cross carved in her head. He inherited everything she had, around a hundred thousand after the sale of the house. He was never a suspect, and the case is still open."

BUCK woke from a deep, drunken sleep. His head felt stuffed with lead, and the sound of the TV grated like a steel file across his raw nerves. Slowly the newscaster's voice penetrated.

> "This is the face of the man suspected of abducting the heiress Ellie Parrish Duveen. He is six feet three, pale-complexioned, with red hair, possibly dyed darker. You are looking at an artist's concept of the way he looked when last seen."

Buck jolted upright. On the screen he saw his own face.

> "The suspect's name is Patrick Buckland Duveen, a.k.a. Ed Jensen, and he is also being sought in connection with the deaths of Charlotte Parrish and her housekeeper, Maria Novales. As well as the strangulation and mutilation deaths of three prostitutes. He is armed and dangerous. If you have seen this man, the police ask you to call the following number."

Buck leaped to his feet. He'd thought he'd beaten them all. He thought he'd won and the prize would be his.

Blood pounded in his ears, and he leaned against the wall, gasping. Pulling himself together, he flung on his clothes, stumbled to the car, and drove back up the mountain.

ELLIE was so tired, but she couldn't let herself fall asleep, because she was afraid she would never wake up. Never see the sky again, never feel the warmth of the sun, never kiss Dan Cassidy . . .

At the sound of wood splintering, Ellie lifted her eyes.

The lid was wrenched back, and light streamed in, blinding her. Panting, he dragged her from the crate. Her cramped muscles refused to unlock, and she fell to her knees. She couldn't move, couldn't see. She was helpless.

"The Lord is my shepherd; I shall not want. He maketh me to lie down in green pastures. . . ." Her brain wavered in and out of reality. She was a child again, and Miss Lottie was reading the beautiful psalm to her.

Buck stared at her kneeling on the floor, at her long tangle of red hair, at her once graceful body and her bloodied limbs where the rope had cut into her. His golden girl: dirty, wounded, beaten. The moment was perfect.

Dropping to his knees, he pushed her down. His strong fingers fastened around her throat, squeezing. Panting with excitement, he waited for her to scream, to excite his passion by begging.

But she was not frightened enough, not screaming, not begging for her life. It was no good.

The acrid smell of his stale sweat was in Ellie's nostrils as he picked her up and carried her across the room. Then they were outdoors, and she was inhaling cool fresh air. He flung her onto the cold leather seat in the back of the convertible.

The fresh air began to revive her. She was in an agony of pins and needles, but she was alive.

The convertible lurched from side to side as they swung down a steep mountain road. He was driving dangerously fast. Suddenly he swung the wheel all the way to the right. The car went into a spin, tires shrieking.

Ellie screamed. For the second time in her life she saw herself hurtling from a car, crashing down the mountainside.

The car stopped, its wheels quivering on the brink. Buck turned and looked at her. His dark eyes were malicious. "Recognize this place, Ellie?"

Just then the memory that had lain dormant in the back of Ellie's mind for more than twenty years was dormant no longer.

She had looked into those eyes when she was five years old and he was crouched over the hood of her father's white Bentley. She had asked him what he was doing, and he'd quickly slammed down the hood. He'd put his finger to his lips, smiling at her.

"Shhh, it's a secret," he had whispered. "You know how to keep a secret, don't you?"

"Of course I do," she'd retorted, upset. "I kept my Christmas presents secret, even though I was bursting to tell."

"Well, this is the same. Only now we both have to keep the secret. Promise."

"Promise," she had repeated reluctantly. She'd crossed her heart and said she hoped to die, and he had burst out laughing at some joke she didn't understand.

"Good-bye, then, Ellie."

She had turned and run down the hot sandy lane, back to her mother. And everything was all right in Ellie's world again.

Until a few hours later, when everything changed.

"You killed them," Ellie said now. "You fixed the brakes."

Buck nodded, smiling lazily. He had her now.

"Who are you?"

"You don't know? Then let me introduce myself. I'm Buck Duveen, your half brother."

Ellie's mind went blank with shock. She had known Rory had been married before, but she hadn't known he had a son.

"Rory was my father too. He had everything and I had nothing. With them out of the way, I'd inherit their fortune. And with you out of the way, I'd be the sole remaining heir. Unfortunately, I've had to wait more than twenty years to complete my task."

Ellie closed her eyes, unable to look at the cold evil in his. He had smiled at her just like that in the library that night when she had seen him trying that first time to kill her grandmother.

Buck's expression changed. He looked longingly at her. "But there's no need for you to die, Ellie. You know I love you. We could have such a wonderful life together."

She lifted her eyes. "Murderer." She spat the word at him.

His eyes glittered angrily; then he turned away, gazing across the ravine, his fists clenched, his face an expressionless mask. And Ellie knew she had signed her own death warrant.

She thought despairingly of Dan, whom she would never see again. "Dan," she said in her heart, "I know I never told you this, but I do love you. Oh, I hope you will know, Dan. Dan, my friend . . ."

Buck switched on the ignition, and Ellie opened her eyes for her last glimpse of blue sky, her last look at life.

Then the car swerved back onto the road, and they were heading, too fast, down the mountain again, skidding around the bends.

She was not dead, because Buck had another plan.

DAN looked at Piatowsky. "Let's walk."

It was cool and moonless, and Santa Monica's Third Street Mall was still crowded with young people. The two men walked to Ocean Avenue and strolled along the seafront, among the palm trees. Dan didn't even notice. In his mind he was running through everything he knew about Buck Duveen. Buck had wanted revenge; he'd wanted Journey's End. And he was just crazy enough . . .

"Let's go," he said abruptly.

Piatowsky stared wearily after him. "Where now?" he called.

"Journey's End"—Dan was running—"where it all began."

WHEN Buck reached the foothills, he stopped the car and got out. He dragged Ellie from the back seat, opened the trunk, flung her in, and slammed down the lid.

Claustrophobia hit her again. She closed her eyes tightly. She must get a grip. She must think.

He was speeding again, flinging her from side to side as he took the bends. She felt a sudden, sharp pain, blood trickling down her arm. She wondered hazily how badly she was hurt, then realized it no longer mattered. She was going to die anyway.

Anger rocketed through her. *I don't want to die. I refuse to die.*

She kicked her feet, angrily twisting them against the rope until her flesh was raw. Blood still oozed slowly down her arm, and she recalled the sharp edge that had inflicted the gash.

Shuffling around, she felt for it with her fingers. It was a spade. The spade with which he meant to bury her.

Sobbing, she pushed her bound hands back and forth over the sharp edge, not caring if she slashed her wrists. . . . Better to die that way than to feel his hands on her throat.

Suddenly the cord snapped. She slumped forward, tears of relief flowing down her face. Hunched over, she wriggled some more, grabbed the spade, and began to saw at the cord binding her ankles. Sweat dripped into her eyes. She could see nothing, only feel. The car kept swerving around the bends, making it difficult to keep the sharp edge on the cord. She chopped savagely at it, harder, harder, until at last she was free.

By now the air was thick. Each breath was a gasp. She knew she didn't have much time left.

She shifted around in the cramped space until she was kneeling, the spade gripped in both hands. *I'm not going to die, I'm not going to die. . . .* She repeated the mantra over and over, hoping that her strength would hold out.

THE Explorer ate up the miles, but Dan was aware of every minute ticking away. He had to find her. She trusted him.

Piatowsky glanced at him. "You really believe she's there?"

"I feel in my gut he'll return to the scene of his crime. Journey's End is what he really wants. I'll bet he's dreamed of it, all those years in Hudson." He shrugged wearily. "It's our only chance."

FINALLY Ellie felt the car roll to a stop. She heard the engine idling, smelled gas fumes, guessed they were at a stoplight. Maybe she could bang on the trunk with the spade, attract attention. But she could hear no other cars. Then they made a left turn and began to climb a hill. She lifted her head, alert. She knew every bend in that road. Now she knew where he was taking her.

The tires crunched on the gravel; then the car stopped. She heard him get out, heard the door slam, his footsteps coming closer. The trunk lid swung slowly up.

Screaming, she slammed the spade into his face. He was clutching his head, yelling with pain. She fell from the trunk, scrambled to her feet. He was coming at her, arms outstretched.

Oh, God, help me, please. She swung the spade again, it crunched sickeningly against his skull, and this time he dropped to the ground.

Fear gave her wings. She was running for her life. But she was weak, her muscles leaden from the hours in the cramped space.

"You are dead," he was screaming.

She veered off the drive, weaving her way through the trees, stumbling over exposed roots. She stopped, waited, listening for him. It was pitch-dark and she edged deeper into the copse. A fallen branch cracked loudly under her feet. She leaned against a tree, her heart thundering.

He grabbed her by the throat.

Ellie could feel the heat of his breath on her cheek, the cold steel of a knife at her neck. She closed her eyes, waiting . . .

"Walk," he commanded.

She stumbled in front of him to the house, stood trembling while he fumbled with the kitchen door. Then he pushed her inside and locked it behind them. There were no lights, but Ellie knew her old home so well, she could have walked through it blindfolded.

Buck hustled her in front of him into the library. He switched on a lamp, his dark eyes glittered icily as he looked at her.

"Kneel." He pointed to a place near the desk. She stared mutely at him. "Kneel, I said." He threw her to the floor, pressed her face into the beautiful red silk Turkish rug.

Now he had Ellie Parrish Duveen at his mercy. And she knew he had no mercy to give.

BUCK lifted his head at the sound of tires on the gravel. Panic clenched in his belly. He could kill her now, have done with it. But then his revenge would not be complete. They might catch him, and he would be a prisoner again.

They were hammering at the front door now, calling Ellie's name. Hefting her in his arms, he carried her upstairs to the grandmother's room, locked the door, and threw her onto the bed.

He tugged cans of lighter fluid from his pockets. He'd meant to use them to incinerate the car when he was done with it. Now he emptied them over the carpet, the furnishings. Then he lay next to her on the bed. She stared wide-eyed at him.

"I really loved you, Ellie," he said. Then he kissed her.

She lunged off the bed. He laughed as she crawled to the French window and tugged desperately at the catch. It was locked. Her fingers groped for the key. It wasn't there.

Trapped, she turned and saw him toss a match to the floor. Then, with a great whoosh, the room burst into flames.

DAN saw her, a dark shape against the hot red glow. He yelled, "Ellie, Ellie, break the window, jump." But Ellie couldn't hear him, couldn't see him, didn't even know he was there.

Piatowsky sped off in search of a ladder as Dan ran for the Explorer. He drove it back along the terrace and positioned it under the balcony. Then he climbed onto the roof of the vehicle. An old fig tree grew up the wall; it would give him a handhold if it could take his weight.

Grasping the thickest branch, he hauled himself up. It creaked ominously, and he leaped for the balcony rail, hanging by one hand, suspended in space. Sweat beaded his forehead; he could feel himself slipping.

BUCK was bursting with laughter. Through the smoke Ellie saw Buck's mad eyes lit red by the flames as he reached for her, dragging her back toward the bed. The smoke was choking her, searing her lungs. The whole world was going black. She was dying after all.

Suddenly the window exploded inward. Fueled by the oxygen, the room roared into an inferno. Ellie's brain was hazy, her eyes unfocused. For a minute she thought it was Dan standing there, with Piatowsky behind him.

Quick as a panther, Buck lunged for Dan's heart, but Piatowsky's gun was quicker than the knife. It spat once, twice. Buck jerked backward, like a puppet with the strings cut, then dropped to his knees. Ellie lay on the floor in front of him, and he watched as the flames licked at her long red hair. It was burning like a halo around her beautiful face. "Ellie," he whispered, smiling, "Ellie . . ."

Dan beat out the flames with his hand. He picked her up, put her over his shoulder. "Let's get out of here."

Piatowsky held the ladder steady as they climbed down. Then they eased Ellie down onto the cool grass. Dan didn't know if she was dead or alive. Piatowsky was already on the cell phone, calling for paramedics, the fire squad, the police.

A terrible howl split the night and they looked up.

Buck was crouched at the window. With a tremendous effort he hauled himself to his feet, his strong arms gripping the window frame. He looked like a great bird of prey, wings outstretched. The buzz of power was humming through him. He was alive as he had never been before, every part of him in an agony of pain. Flinging back his head, he howled.

He was still howling when he fell backward into the flames.

DAN had not budged from Ellie's hospital bedside all night. They had bandaged his burned hands and kept telling him to go home, that she'd had a strong sedative and would sleep for hours, but he'd refused to move.

Ellie's bruised face glowed yellow and purple, antiseptic gauze covered her singed arms, and they had cut off what was left of her beautiful long red hair. It wrenched his gut when he remembered how close it had been. He still didn't know what had happened during her abduction, and he sighed deeply, hoping it would not scar her soul forever. She had already been through so much.

ELLIE had never dreamed of such peace, such sweet silence, such a soft pillow. It smelled of hospitals. Fighting the drugs and the pain, she opened her eyes. Dan's face swam into view.

"Hello, friend." Even raspy, her voice was sweet as spun sugar.

Dan threw his hands up helplessly. "I'm afraid to touch you. And I want to kiss you so badly."

The big grin was the same. "Go ahead, friend."

He leaned across and brushed his lips lightly over hers. "Consider that a down payment," he said.

"A down payment? On what?"

"On future kisses and . . . Enough of this friend stuff. I need you, woman."

"Oh?" She couldn't resist teasing him. "For what?"

"Let me think." He ran a hand through his disheveled dark hair, frowning. "To run the tasting room at Running Horse. Maybe open a café there, a little French kind of place, sawdust on the floor, green-checkered tablecloths, great food . . ."

Ellie heaved an enormous sigh. "Dan Cassidy, any woman could do that. Where do I figure in all this?"

"Right in the middle," he said. "I can't live without you."

Her sigh was happy this time, but the sedative was kicking in again and her eyelids drooped. "Right in the middle of your life," she murmured. "Exactly where I want to be."

His lips brushed hers as she drifted contentedly back to sleep.

Dan was smiling as he watched over her. He knew that what had happened would have to be spoken of later, addressed, resolved. It would take a long time to recover from something as terrible as this, but with his help, and the peace and quiet of Running Horse Ranch, they would survive. His car might be a wreck, but his life was great. He had no regrets.

They were the winners.

ELIZABETH ADLER

© RICHARD OPEN

Asked about all the mouthwatering cuisine in *Sooner or Later,* Elizabeth Adler explained, "We're a food family." Both she and husband Richard, a retired attorney, love to cook. "He does Indian, I favor Italian: risottos, osso buco, and really first-rate salad dressings." Another link between the book and real life is daughter Anabelle, who studied architecture and then surprised Mom and Dad by opening a café on Main Street in Santa Monica!

Today the family is at home in southern California, where British-born Elizabeth delights in the sunshine. Once a month, though, she pays tribute to her Yorkshire roots with a traditional English Sunday lunch of roast beef, Yorkshire pudding, "and of course a good Santa Barbara pinot noir."

The volumes in this series are issued every two to three months. The typical volume contains four outstanding books in condensed form. None of the selections in any volume has appeared in *Reader's Digest* itself. Any reader may receive this service by writing The Reader's Digest Association, Inc., Pleasantville, N.Y. 10570 or by calling 800-234-9000.

Visit our Web site at http://www.readersdigest.com

ACKNOWLEDGMENTS

Pages 6–7: photograph copyright Wayne Cable, Cable Studios Chicago.
Pages 164–165: photo by Woody Woodworth/SuperStock.
Page 286–287: photo by Frances Roberts/NYT Permissions.
Pages 442–443: illustration by Greg Harlin.

The original editions of the books in this volume are published and copyrighted as follows:
The Street Lawyer, published at $27.95 by Doubleday, a division of
Bantam Doubleday Dell Publishing Group, Inc.

Message in a Bottle, published at $20.00 by Warner Books Inc.

The Cobra Event, published at $25.95 by Random House, Inc.

Sooner or Later, published at $22.95 by Delacorte Press, a division of
Bantam Doubleday Dell Publishing Group, Inc.